Necroscope

DEFILERS

BRIAN LUMLEY

A TOM DOHERTY ASSOCIATES BOOK
NEW YORK

NOTE: If you purchased this book without a cover you should be aware that this book is stolen property. It was reported as "unsold and destroyed" to the publisher, and neither the author nor the publisher has received any payment for this "stripped book."

This is a work of fiction. All the characters and events portrayed in this book are either products of the author's imagination or are used fictitiously.

NECROSCOPE DEFILERS

A Tor Book
Published by Tom Doherty Associates, LLC
175 Fifth Avenue
New York, NY 10010

www.tor.com

Tor® is a registered trademark of Tom Doherty Associates, LLC.

ISBN: 0-812-56673-4
Library of Congress Catalog Card Number: 00-023325

First edition: May 2000
First mass market edition: May 2001

Printed in the United States of America

0 9 8 7 6 5 4 3 2 1

For Barbara Ann
(or Varvara . . . with two rs)

Necroscope

DEFILERS

Necroscope: Invaders

(A Résumé)

HARRY KEOGH, THE FIRST NECROSCOPE, IS GONE, his essence splintered, dispersed, and shards of his metaphysical mind dispatched into the darker corners of the myriad Universes of Light. Thus, to all intents and purposes, he is dead.

Death: the cessation of life. The *absence* of life, and the End of Being. Or at least, the living have always deemed it so. But as the Necroscope above all others (except perhaps the dead themselves) was aware, death isn't like that. Mind goes on.

For how may any great poet, scientist, artist, or architect simply dissolve to nothing? His body may quit, but his spirit—his mind—will go on, and what he pursued in life he will continue to pursue in death.

Great paintings are planned, and landscapes scanned in the dead mind's eye, and never a brush applied to canvas. Magnificent cities rear, and ocean-spanning roadways circle the planet, but they are only the dreams of their dead architects. Songs as sweet and sweeter than anything devised by Solomon in his lifetime are known to the teeming dead, which can never be known to the living; for he sang the ones we know more than two thousand years ago, and time has improved him.

But here a seeming contradiction: if death is such an empty, silent place, how then all the singing, painting, building? *How* do the dead go on?

To questions such as this there was no answer until there was the Necroscope: a man who could look into the graves of men and into their dead minds. And through him—*only* through Harry Keogh—the dead were enabled. He taught them deadspeak, how to converse with one another, and joined them up across the world; he brought sons and daughters to long-lost mothers and fathers, reunited old friends, resolved old doubts and arguments and reinspired the brilliance of great minds guttering low. And without ever intending it—scarcely realizing what was happening—he became a lone candle flickering in the long night of the dead. And they basked in his warmth and loved him for it.

But as much as Harry Keogh gave the dead, just so much and more he received. From his mother, who in life had been a psychic medium, the germ of that metaphysical skill from which his greater abilities derived. From August Ferdinand Möbius, a long-dead mathematician and astronomer, knowledge and mastery of the Möbius Continuum, an undimensioned *place* (for want of a better description) parallel with all time and space. And from Faethor Ferenczy, the history of a vampire world and its undead inhabitants, some of which—much like Faethor himself—had from time to time found their way into our world. But it should be stated that this latter knowledge was obtained more out of the extinct vampire's longing for life than his love of the Necroscope . . .

And from that time on—from Harry's discovery of vampires in our world, to the time of his "death" in Starside—the Necroscope was dedicated to their destruction. For he knew that if the terrible Lords and Ladies of the Wamphyri weren't put down, then that they must surely enslave mankind.

But in the end—himself a vampire and fighting the Thing within him to his last breath—even Harry gave in, "died," and was no more. Oh, really . . . ?

But for every rule there has to be an exception, and Harry Keogh, Necroscope, was—he *is*—the exception to the rule of negative interaction between the Great Majority and the living. For in life he was the master of the Möbius Continuum, and used it to pursue vampires. So that now, in death . . . ?

* * *

Harry Keogh was not alone in his lifelong war against the Wamphyri. Recruited into E-Branch as a youth, he had the backing of that most secret of secret organizations almost to the end. And even when Harry was himself no longer entirely human, still Ben Trask, the Head of E-Branch, was his friend. It was Trask, the human lie detector, who saw the "truth" of Harry: that he would never turn on his own kind; but still, best to take no chances, and Trask had been tasked to hound him from Earth.

Nevertheless, when at last the Necroscope returned to Sunside/Starside, to fight his last great battle there, he went of his own accord and not because he was driven out.

And it was Ben Trask, too, along with many more members of E-Branch, who saw—who were *given* to see—Harry's passing on the night he died.

It was a vision, a hologram, a real yet unreal thing. They saw The End of Harry as if it were here and now when in fact it occurred in an alien world on the other side of spacetime.

Thirteen witnesses in all, in the ops room at E-Branch HQ; they all saw the same thing: that smoking, smouldering, hideous corpse, cruciform and crucified in midair, tumbling backwards, head over heels, free of the floor as on an invisible spit. And despite the crisped and blackened face, Ben Trask had known who it was, that this was Harry.

And for all that they encircled it, still the thing seemed to fall away from them, growing smaller, receding toward a nebulous origin—or destiny?—out of which ribbons of neon light reached like myriad writhing tentacles to welcome it.

The figure dwindled, shrank to a mote, and finally disappeared. But where it had been—

An explosion! A sunburst of golden fire, expanding hugely, silently, awesomely! So that the thirteen observers had gasped and ducked down; and despite that this thing was in their group mind, they instinctively turned away from the blinding intensity of its glare—*and* of what flew out of it.

All except Trask, who had shielded his eyes but continued to watch, because that was his nature and he must know the truth.

And the truth of it had been fantastic.

Those myriad golden splinters speeding outwards from the sunburst, angling this way and that, sentient, seeking, disappearing into as many unknown places. Those, what, pieces? *Of the Necroscope, Harry Keogh? All that remained of him, of what he'd been and what he'd meant? And as the last of them had zipped by Trask and vanished from view, so the writhing streamers of red, blue, and green ghost-light had likewise blinked out of existence . . .*

. . . Returning the ops room's illumination to normal. Then everyone had known that Harry was no more, that he had died in Starside in an alien vampire world. And only Ben Trask—Trask the human lie detector—recognized the "truth" of what he had seen, and knew that death, especially in the Necroscope's case, simply wasn't like that . . .

Time has passed, twenty-one years of time, during which a different Necroscope—but a true son of his Earth father—has come to manhood in that same alien world that claimed Harry. And no less than his father, Nathan Kiklu (called Keogh by his friends in our world) is a vampire hunter. But Nathan has his own problems and hunts his enemies in Sunside/Starside.

Between the Earth and Nathan's parallel vampire world are two "Gates." One is natural, the other came into being when an ill-conceived Soviet experiment backfired. The first Gate lies along the route of a subterranean river flowing through a cavern system under the foothills of the frowning *Carpatii Meridionali,* the Transylvanian Alps.

The second Gate lies in an artificial complex built in the late '70s and early '80s by the Soviets in the base of the Perchorsk ravine in the northern reaches of the *Uralski Khrebet*—Russia's Ural Mountains. While E-Branch has access to and control of the natural Gate, the Perchorsk Complex lies outside the Branch's sphere of influence. Closed down five years ago by the Russian premier, who diverted water from the Perchorsk dam into the mainly ruinous scientific complex to flood it, recently the artificial Gate has been reopened by the leader of a burgeoning military faction. This was done out of greed; the power-mad Russian general who ordered it had found out that Sunside/Starside is rich in gold; he and a platoon of soldiers went through into Starside in an attempt to fathom the extent of its riches.

Their expedition coincided with a vampire resurgence; the Russians were taken, and before the general was done away with, two Lords and a Lady of the Wamphyri extracted from him and the men in his command knowledge of our world.

Under constant guerilla attack by Nathan, the three Great Vampires, Wamphyri, decided to take their chances on Earth. Invaders (albeit secret invaders), they used the natural Gate to enter our world at E-Branch's Romanian "Refuge," a special hospice for traumatized orphans on the banks of the Danube at the junction of Romania, Bulgaria, and the former Yugoslavia.

Slaughtering the Refuge's personnel and inmates, the trio split up, dispersing themselves abroad in the world . . .

E-Branch alone knew of the vampire invasion. Zek Föener, the love of Ben Trask's life, had died in the massacre at the Romanian Refuge; but in her final moments the telepath contacted Trask to tell him what was happening. Thus Trask was "with her" when she died—at which moment, in his grief of griefs, he had vowed revenge!

But the rest of the world couldn't, mustn't be told. Else panic at the thought of an invisible, almost invincible plague loose among us would run riot. E-Branch's Minister Responsible must be told, however, and he gave the Branch carte blanche to track down and destroy the monsters out of Starside. Moreover, liaison with many of the world's great powers guaranteed their assistance, too, in the event that Trask's organization should need it. These were, of course, covert agreements; only the most tried and trusted leaders were privy to the facts, and then not to all the facts . . .

Some three years after the invasion, finally E-Branch "locators"—human-bloodhound trackers of men and monsters—picked up the "mindsmog" spoor of the Wamphyri in Western Australia's desolate Gibson Desert. But even as plans were made to counter the menace, so a timely quirk of synchronicity (not to mention the paradox of a once-familiar phenomenon) took place.

Jake Cutter, a young man with a dubious record, had been incarcerated in a top-security Turin prison for certain acts of vengeance which in fact amounted to murder. But murder only insofar as the law's legal definition. For Jake had taken revenge on a gang of drug-running thugs and rapists—affiliates of the Russian Mafia—who had brutalized and murdered a woman of his intimate acquaintance.

In answer to Jake's revenge serial killings, the leader of the gang—a mysterious Sicilian called Luigi Castellano—made arrangements to have Jake killed inside the prison. Learning of this, Jake had attempted to escape. But prison guards in Castellano's pay had opened fire on him as he scaled the prison wall. In which moment of extreme danger, there had come an astonishing intervention. At first, Jake had thought that he'd been shot; he had actually seen the bullet—or the track of a golden bullet, or the coruscation of its ricochet, or *something*—strike home into his forehead. And then he had fallen, but not to the hard-packed earth of the prison's exercise yard.

Instead, Jake had "fallen" into the Möbius Continuum—*and instantaneously more than five hundred miles through the Continuum*—to Harry's Room at E-Branch HQ in London! Harry's Room, which decades earlier had provided accommodation for the original Necroscope during his brief tenure as prospective Head of Branch, and which Branch espers had since maintained in pristine condition.

Simultaneous with Jake's appearance at E-Branch HQ, so the same espers—especially the locator David Chung—

sensed that something of the Necroscope had returned. Trask, however, remembering what Harry had become *before* he quit Earth for Starside, could scarcely help but wonder what facet of him had come home. And Trask was also given to wonder: when Harry Keogh died, had his vampire been purged, or had it purged him . . . ?

The three invaders from Starside are Lords Malinari and Szwart, and the female Vavara. Malinari "The Mind," a mentalist of phenomenal power; Lord Szwart, who is the very essence of darkness, a constantly mutating victim (and survivor) of his own metamorphic nature; and Vavara, whose hypnotic disguise is that of a beautiful woman when in fact she is a hag.

When these Great Vampires came into our world they brought four lieutenant servitors with them, one of whom, Korath Mindsthrall (whose name identified him as being "in thrall" to Malinari the Mind), was sacrificed as a means of gaining entry to the Romanian Refuge.

Thus when the vampire trio destroyed the Refuge, butchered its staff and inmates, and took new thralls before splitting up and venturing out into our world, Korath Mindsthrall's dead and broken body was left behind, pulped and drowned in a metal pipe in the shattered sump of the gutted Refuge. The true death for a vampire thrall whose ambitions were always above his station, or so Malinari had suspected.

For Korath had been his man for long and long, and a great deal of Malinari had rubbed off on his lieutenant. Too much for his own good . . .

Meanwhile in the Möbius Continuum, some faint echo—some fragment, residual memory, ghost, or intelligence—of the Necroscope Harry Keogh had become aware of scarlet life-threads where they crossed the blue threads of men. One such blue life-thread was Jake Cutter's, and because of its prevalence in some future conflict, the Harry revenant traced it back to its source . . . to Jake in the Turin prison, and indeed to the rigged jailbreak.

But the revenant had its limitations; spread throughout all the Universes of Light, Harry's presence—his ability to effect changes in the mundane world of men—was at best tenuous. Also, his nature and Jake's were opposites in so many ways, and yet very much of a kind in so many others. And here he was, the very man, Jake Cutter himself—as unknown to the spirit of the ex-Necroscope as Harry was to him—about to die under the hammer blows of brutal bullets. But down future-time streams Harry had seen Jake's blue thread crossed by scarlet vampire threads, and the once-Necroscope knew for a fact that, "what will be has been," or that it *would* be. Wherefore Jake's life couldn't possibly end here. But how to save it?

The answer came in a moment, but *without* Harry's instigation! A golden dart, one of his myriad familiars, striking home in Jake's head to enhance whatever there was of the metaphysical in a currently mundane mind. A dart of knowledge, yes, and a set of scrolling numbers—like a computer screen running amok, conjuring the Möbius Continuum—which in its turn bore Jake to Harry's Room, at E-Branch HQ in London . . .

Australia, and Trask took Jake along for the ride. For whatever Trask's misgivings—and he of all men should know the truth of things—the rest of his espers saw Jake as a possible answer, and perhaps the only answer, to their needs: a weapon as powerful as anything the Wamphyri could bring to bear. But first, of course, he must accept what had happened and come to terms with it, learn to utilize the great gifts that he *may* have received, which as yet remained undeveloped in him.

To which end and between times, when the Keogh revenant was able, it/he spent time with Jake; usually in Jake's subconscious mind, his dreams, when he was relaxed and more receptive of esoteric knowledge. But just like Ben Trask, the ex-Necroscope found Jake obstinate, cynical, and frequently infuriating. For Jake had his own agenda, a certain Sicilian criminal called Luigi Castellano, and until that had been dealt with, he knew he could never be his own man or anyone else's . . .

In the nighted, gurgling black sump of the ruined Romanian Refuge, Harry and Jake used deadspeak to talk to the sloughed-away Korath Mindsthrall where his polished bones clattered endlessly in the swirling water of a filtration conduit, and they learned the histories of Malinari, Szwart, and Vavara. And now the ex-Necroscope can only hope that in the waking world, Jake will remember what he learned in dreams.

But here a problem:

Despite Harry's warnings, Jake—of his own cognizance, his own free will—has agreed a pact with Korath, giving him limited access to his mind. For without the vampire he could never remember Harry's numbers, the formulae that conjure the Möbius Continuum. And without Jake, the dead but still dangerous—*very* dangerous—vampire can never stray from his watery grave.

Together, however, they have the incredible mobility of the Möbius Continuum. Moreover, Korath (once Mindsthrall) now knows hope where no hope existed. Enabled, he can now begin scheming toward a suddenly feasible future . . .

On Australia's South Pacific coast, Trask and his team of espers have tracked down and attacked Lord Nephran Malinari in his casino aerie in the Macpherson Range of mountains; his lieutenants and various vampirized victims have been killed, destroyed utterly, but the Great Vampire himself has escaped.

Jake Cutter played a major part in what measure of success E-Branch enjoyed; but aware of his compromised position—and alone in this knowledge, unable or unwilling to tell Trask and his espers about his "problem"—he can find little or no satisfaction in his newfound status within the organization.

All Jake wanted was to be rid of a strange, unwelcome

tenant: the ex-Necroscope, Harry, who had seemed intent on taking up partial (and perhaps even permanent?) residence in his head. But now that Harry has gone, a very different and far more devious intruder has taken his place. Now, too, Jake finds himself plagued by Harry's warning: "Alive or dead makes no great difference. *Never* let a vampire into your mind!"

As for Ben Trask: many of his concerns have been assuaged, but still there are questions that remain unanswered. Foremost among them: why Jake? Why has this problematic young man been chosen, apparently against his will, for work as important as this? Jake Cutter—spoiled as a child, unruly as a youth, and reckless as a man. Why him?

And not only the Head of E-Branch, but the ex-Necroscope, too (in his immundane, incorporeal fashion), has wondered why. For those myriad attendant golden darts, revenant of his once-being, are apart from Harry and given to act of their own accord. He is the advance guard and scout, but they are the soldiers, the army. Thus it was with Jake: the ex-Necroscope found his life-thread, and so found him, but the dart struck home of its own cognizance. Why? Why was Jake chosen?

Perhaps Harry should look to his own past for an answer, but in certain cases the past may be just as devious as the future. Even in a mind freed of bodily restraints there are bound to be blank spots, times and places that remain forever unremembered. And in the Necroscope's life entire years were lost like pages torn from a book.

Perhaps the answer lies there . . .

Part One
Images

1
Images of the Past

BEN TRASK AND HIS PEOPLE WERE HOME AGAIN, but there was little enough time for rest and recuperation. The world might well be described as a small planet, but it was still a big place; its evils were many, and England had always had its fair share.

Compared with what Trask and his principal espers—David Chung the locator, and Ian Goodly the precog—had encountered in Australia, the routine of E-Branch HQ seemed drab and almost boring. Almost. But here in the heart of London, in Trask's own even smaller world of gadgets and ghosts, he knew that he could never really get bored. For even when the ghosts were quiet, the gadgets would keep right on going, and vice versa, though often as not they were active at the same time.

Right now the gadgets—in the shape of the HQ's telephones, its ground-based and satellite communication systems, its computers, TVs, and video screens—were in ascendance, catching up on time lost when Trask, a handful of his espers and technicians, plus a couple of new people, had been out of touch by virtue of their work on the other side of the world. But the Head of E-Branch knew that the ghosts would come into their own soon enough. He knew it because he commanded them. Ghosts of a sort, anyway.

And for eight days now he had been steadily working his way through all the paperwork, sorting the priority jobs, detailing his workforce to whichever tasks best suited their various talents, and generally breaking up the logjam. It had to be done, because Trask knew that sooner or later he'd be on his way once again—that he, personally, would be on his way, for this was a personal thing now—out into a world threatened by the greatest of all possible evils.

An evil born in another world, with a name that was similarly alien and undisguisably evil . . . Wamphyri!

Despite that there was other work to be done, this was the name, and the thought, that was uppermost in Trask's mind where he sat at his desk, in his office at the end of the main corridor in E-Branch HQ, pen in hand but stilled for the moment, not scratching away at one or another of a hundred different documents and forms. Stilled, brought to an abrupt halt by this sudden thought—or perhaps not so sudden, because for some three years now it had never been far from his mind—that in a world where Zek was no more, in this monstrously, unbelievably depleted world, the Wamphyri were. *They* were here, and because of them, she was not.

And he was surprised to hear the rumble in his throat that was a growl trying to escape, surprised to see his hand turning white where it now gripped the pen like a dagger. The Wamphyri: Malinari, and Szwart, and Vavara, alive or undead in his world, the world where they had murdered Zek! And still her last words—her last thoughts, which she had sent winging to him—sighing in his memory, from which he could never hope to erase them and would never want to, but guessed he'd be the better man for it if he could:

Goodbye, Ben. I love you . . .

Then the blinding flash of white light that had woken him up that time three years ago—which he had hoped was only the glare of his bedside lamp, perhaps blinking into life where his arm had hit the cord as he threshed in his nightmare. Trask had hoped so, yes, but deep inside he'd known it wasn't so. For the truth and Ben Trask were soul mates. The truth was his talent, and sometimes his curse. Times such as *that* time.

That blinding flash of white light . . .

. . . Which wasn't white at all but green, and which wasn't blinding but merely blinking. One of the tiny lights on Trask's desk console, drawing him back to Earth, to the present, to the now. He unfroze, tripped a switch, spoke to the duty officer:

"What is it?" His voice was a harsh rasp.

"Sorry to interrupt you, boss," the answer came back; Paul Garvey's voice, even softer than usual. Garvey was a full-blown telepath, and despite Branch protocol—a mainly unspoken policy that espers would never use their talents on each other—still it was possible he'd inadvertently detected something of Trask's mood of introspection. "This one's for you. It's Premier Gustav Turchin, calling from—"

"Calcutta?" said Trask, cutting the other short. And casting a glance at the small occasional table where he'd deposited the morning newspapers, he frowned.

"Right," said Garvey. "He's calling from—"

"The German embassy," Trask nodded, understanding dawning. "The sly old bastard!"

After a pause, mystified, Garvey said, "Well, you seem to be way ahead of me! Anyway, it sounds urgent."

"Earth Year," Trask said, nodding to himself.

El Niño had let India off light this time around, but the world's rapidly changing weather patterns were only one of the Earth's problems. Pollution was another, and a big one; Turchin would be in Calcutta to lie his head off at the Earth Year Conference there, answering Russia's accusers in that respect. Not that he would want to, for just like Trask he knew the truth of it: that indeed the destitute Russian military was muddying the world's waters. But at least the conference—one of many Earth Year conferences—would free him from several far more weighty problems back home. It would also make him the spokesman of his people, helping with his image to boot.

In Brisbane Trask had worked out a deal with the premier: his help with Turchin's problems in return for certain important information; this could be it coming through right now. As for where it was coming from:

The morning newspapers carried the story. Last night Turchin had been insulted by Hans Bruchmeister, one of the German delegates. There and then he'd threatened to abandon the conference, fly home, and leave the rest of them to get on with it. But since Russia (along with the USA) was alleged to be one of the worst offenders, what would the conference amount to without a Russian representative? The other delegates had tried to cool things down, but Turchin had insisted:

"When I have received Herr Bruchmeister's apology—when I've stood face-to-face with him in the German Embassy here in Calcutta, bearding the lion in his own den, as it were—then and only then will I be encouraged to stay. For after all, I'm the Russian premier. And I must consider my reputation and the honor of my people . . ."

Of course, Herr Bruchmeister had been persuaded to apologise, with the result that Gustav Turchin was now in the German Embassy building in Calcutta. But:

Oh sure! thought Trask, reading between the lines, understanding the real meaning of the report. *Bearding the lion in his den, bollocks! Turchin engineered the whole thing in order to get a few minutes on a secure line and speak to me!*

Paul Garvey was waiting patiently, and Trask said, "Patch him through to my office, will you?"

"Just pick up your telephone," Garvey answered. "I've put him on scrambled, so there may be some static."

The intercom quit blinking, and one of Trask's telephones took over the job. He picked it up and said, "Trask?"

And an edgy voice on the other end said, "Ben? You appear to be busy. I told your man this was urgent."

"It's only been a minute," Trask answered.

"It felt like an hour!" the other grunted, and continued: "Look, I'm in the German embassy, and this is supposed to be a secure line—"

"And scrambled at my end," Trask told him.

"—But it's still risky. I like to keep my conversations as private as possible. So I'll be brief and probably a little cryptic."

"Wait!" said Trask, and tripped his intercom switch to the Duty Officer. "Paul, is John Grieve in? Good. Find him and tell him he's needed in my office right now." Then back to Turchin:

"Okay, go ahead, and I'll try to follow you."

"You . . . *and* your Mr. Grieve?" said the other.

"That's right," Trask answered. "You could say he's my interpreter." And to himself: *When the gadgets can't get it done, then it's time for the ghosts!*

"Your E-Branch always did have the pick of the crop," Turchin said knowingly, a touch of jealousy coming through.

And Trask told him, "Yes, but all natural-grown. It's well known that when you force a crop, the produce is usually inferior."

"We're blunt today," said the other, as a knock sounded on Trask's door.

"Blunt and highly pissed off!" Trask told him. And then to the door: "Come in."

"Ah!" said Turchin. "Mr. Grieve. And now we can get on. But tell me: what's pissing you off, Ben?"

"Admin," Trask told him. "Frustration. All the duties that won't let me get to my real duty. Too many small things getting in the way of the big things." And then he sighed. "I'm sorry I was rude. But still, this isn't a good day to try, er, bearding *me* in my den, I assure you!"

"And I am sorry I was so impatient," said Turchin. "Nerves are showing on both sides, it seems. As for bearding you,"—his voice lightened up a little—"you've obviously read this morning's papers. The *Times,* perhaps?"

Trask switched the phone to his desk speaker and said, "Yes. Your little tiff at the conference? You're getting good at that sort of subterfuge. But very well, now you can be as cryptic as you like." John Grieve had come in and was standing by the desk with a notepad.

Grieve was in his mid-to-late fifties and had been with E-Branch for half that time at least. Despite being extraordinarily talented, he had never been a field operative; Trask and previous Heads of Branch had found him too useful in the HQ, as duty officer or on standby, to send him into the far more dangerous world outside. In any case, he wasn't a particularly physical sort of person.

A little pudgy now, a lifetime smoker and short of breath, he was balding, grey, and prematurely aged. But he was also upright, smart as his physical condition would permit, polite and very British. With his head held high and stomach pulled in to the best of his ability, he might be an ex-Army officer or maybe a failed businessman—to the man in the street, anyway. But in fact he had always been E-Branch, and Trask relied upon him. Sometimes heavily.

In earlier times Grieve had two extrasensory talents, one of which had been "dodgy" (Branch parlance for an as yet undeveloped ESP ability) and the other quite remarkable and possibly unique. The first had been the gift of far-seeing (remote viewing), which had eventually ceased to work for him; his "crystal ball" had finally clouded over. But in any case this lost ability had probably been a facet of his greater talent, which was a different slant on telepathy. And with the loss of his "scrying," so his telepathic skill had increased proportionately.

The trouble with his far-seeing had been that he needed to know exactly where and what he was looking for—otherwise he could "see" nothing. His talent hadn't worked at random but required direction; it had to be "aimed" at a definite target.

And Grieve's special brand of telepathy—which at times like this was invaluable—was somewhat similar. For yet again he must aim his talent: he could read a person's mind only when they were face-to-face, when he was talking or listening to the target . . . even on the telephone! And so, like Trask, there was no way anyone could lie to John Grieve, not directly, and on occasions like this his skill made every kind of mechanical scrambler redundant. That in the main was why he could usually be found on duty at the HQ. For his was one ghost that worked hand in hand with many of the gadgets . . .

Trask had indicated to Grieve that he should stand beside him; he did so, and placed his notepad on the desk where Trask could see it. Then the Head of Branch spoke again to the Russian premier. "So what's up, Gustav?"

And Turchin answered, "Not long ago we talked about—oh, this and that, a few small problems, some of them mutual—but nothing hugely important. Perhaps you remember?"

"Indeed I do," said Trask, and Grieve quickly scribbled on his pad: *Big stuff!*

"You asked if I could locate someone for you," the Russian premier continued. "An old friend, who flits about the Mediterranean quite a bit?"

Luigi Castellano? And: "Ah, yes!" said Trask. "Old what's-his-name! Can't seem to find hide nor hair of him. But then, he always did keep a low profile."

"Oh, I don't know about that," Turchin appeared contradictory. "Marseilles, Genoa, Palermo . . . He keeps in touch with the old gang. And he also has a good many new friends in my neck of the woods, too, or so I'm told."

Grieve wrote:

Mob. Mafia. Russian Mafia.

"But I knew that much already!" said Trask. "What I really need to know is his whereabouts at any specific time, so that I can . . . well, contact him, you know? I mean, I owe him, and you know how I hate being in anyone's debt."

"One of your finer points, yes." Turchin chuckled. "But as I was about to say, I've been looking for him myself—and for pretty much the same reasons—all of the good things he's done for us, and never asks a rouble in return. Not that I have much to offer him anyway. But now that you've opened my eyes to him, well, I really do think we should be more appreciative."

Grieve scribbled furiously. *Turchin wants him, too. Drugs. L. C.'s making millions; he's helping to ruin both Russia's economy and the world's health! Turchin hadn't realized how bad the drugs trafficking situation was. Now that he has, he wants L. C. taken out.*

"Well, what do you suggest?" Trask said. "Are you going to take care of it? Will you make some sort of presentation . . . or should I see to it? If it's me, please remember that I'm still in the dark as to his whereabouts—the old gadfly!"

"Well, it's like this," said Turchin. "I've had one of our local people back home come and see me, someone who owes *me* for a change. In a week or so he'll introduce and recommend an intermediary to our mutual friend—perhaps as a new club member? Then we sit back and wait for a report—place, date, and time. I think that should do it."

"Hmmm," Trask mulled it over, giving John Grieve time to scrawl: *He's coerced someone in the Russian mob to introduce an undercover agent to Castellano. When his man has learned L. C.'s routines, he'll get back to us with a venue.*

And Turchin continued, "But I'm afraid the presentation is going to have to be of your own devising, and preferably on our friend's home ground. The greater shame is that what with these Earth Year conferences and what have you, I won't be available. I *can't* be involved personally, if you see what I mean . . ."

Whatever you decide to do with Castellano, it will have to be on L. C.'s or our territory. Turchin doesn't want any part of it.

"Yes, I understand," said Trask. "You want to keep it politically correct."

"Well, I do have a certain position to maintain . . ."

He's much higher profile than we are and would make a bigger target.

"And of course," Trask said, "you don't want to commit too many of your own resources." (Meaning the Opposition—Russia's own equivalent of E-Branch—of which Turchin was now the head man.)

"Simply can't," said the other. "There's so much going on. I mean on a higher plane, you know?"

Up in the Urals. Perchorsk.

And Trask thought, *He's committed his espers to getting me those details on the Perchorsk Complex and Gate.* While out loud he said:

"Ah, well, it can't be helped. But still, we've got things moving at least. I'm glad that's all sorted now."

"Oh, but we've a long way to go yet, Ben. I'll be in touch as soon as I've filled in some blank spots. But if I seem a bit vague I'm sure you'll understand."

He'll fax you some stuff. In Code. But nothing you'll have too much trouble with.

"Good!" said Trask. And tried to finish it off with: "Talk to you later . . ."

But the other wasn't ready to let him go. "Wait!" he said, and that edge—an edge of fear?—was back in his voice. "We had also talked about a little personal problem of mine? Well, time is pressing—I expect that very soon people will be looking for answers—and you mentioned some sort of solution that you might eventually have to hand? How are things going on that front?"

Perchorsk again? Russian military types? Putting some kind of squeeze on him? And—Necroscope? Grieve raised a surprised and querying eyebrow, looked at Trask.

Trask shrugged it off for the moment and said, "I'm working on it. Believe me, Gustav, you'll be the first to know. But until then . . . well, I still have a few very big problems of my own. Three of them, in fact."

"Ah, yes, of course! But you'll also recall we talked over the possibility of your retirement and a place in the sun?"

Political asylum. Defection. But his, not yours.

"Indeed I do."

"Well, keep it in mind," said the other. "I would like to be able to visit with you some time—that is, if you do decide it's time you settled down."

For you read I. He is talking about himself. If or when he makes a run for it, he wants to come to us.

"And of course you'd be welcome," said Trask.

"My time's up," said Turchin. "I have accepted—*ahem!*—Herr Bruchmeister's apology, and he has allowed me these couple of minutes in private, away from my, er, retinue—"

"Your cretinue!" Trask grinned, however wryly.

"—Precisely, to make this call."

"Let's not leave it so long next time," said Trask.

"Goodbye, Ben," said the premier. And the line went dead . . .

* * *

Trask looked up and John Grieve was still there. Their eyes met and Trask said, "Do you want me to explain? I mean, a better or more complete explanation than the one you have now?"

"Only if you're so inclined," Grieve answered. "But in any case I think I got the gist of it—except maybe that bit about a Necroscope. I mean, Turchin knows we have a Necroscope?"

Trask shrugged. "He's a pretty shrewd old fox. But anyway, don't go worrying your head about it. He's only guessing. And I *will* explain . . . but not just to you." He glanced at his watch. "1350. I'm giving a briefing in just ten minutes, so I'd better be on my way. Whistle the rest of them up, will you, John? Especially Liz Merrick and Jake Cutter. I want every available man in the ops room in ten minutes—espers and techs alike—and woe betide any absentee who doesn't have a watertight excuse."

After Grieve had left, Trask sat there for a moment feeling old. Hell, he *was* old now. Or getting there, anyway. The reason he felt it so much on this occasion was because he'd failed out there in Brisbane, Australia. He'd failed Zek—failed to kill the one who had killed her.

And so back to that again. It was eating at him like acid, and he couldn't afford to let it. Because that way the bastards would win. They would win and the world of men, or of mankind's domination, would die—or undie. There would still be men, but they would be slaves, thralls, and the women would be odalisques, chattel, cattle. And the blood would be the life, but not human life. And *everyone* would be food.

That was why Malinari and the other two were here, but how they hoped to achieve it—how they planned to bring it about, in a world with equal amounts of night and day—that was something else, as yet unfathomed. Or perhaps not, for out there in Australia there'd been clues. Which was one of the things Trask must talk about (he checked his watch again) in just five minutes' time.

He went to straighten his tie but wasn't wearing one. Too

damn hot, in this ongoing, never-ending, bloody El Niño summer. Talk about Australia. *Huh!*

Trask stood up, slid out from behind his desk and paced to the door, paused, shook his head in disgust and went back again. And picking up his notes from the pending tray, he thought:

Old and absentminded: me, Ben Trask, who once thought he'd be young forever. That was Zek. With Zek I could be young until I died. Or until she died. And she did.

But he knew what would make him young again: to see Malinari cut down, beheaded, burned to ashes. Malinari and the other two, and all of theirs that they'd corrupted. When they'd gone, then he'd be young again. For a little while, anyway.

But what the hell . . . this was E-Branch, and in the Branch you could get old pretty damn fast no matter what. *If* you lived long enough! And:

Damn it to hell! Trask got angry with himself, stamped his feet, shook a fist. *There's plenty of life in this old dog yet!* And telling himself that he felt a little better, he headed for the ops room. On the way out, he remembered to snatch his light summer jacket from the coatstand. . .

For some forty-odd years now, E-Branch HQ in the centre of London had occupied the same site. Ostensibly, and viewed casually from the outside, the place was a well established hotel within easy walking distance of Whitehall; down below, it was precisely that—an expensive hotel. Its top floor, however, was totally given over to a company of "international entrepreneurs," which was and had always been the sum total of a string of hotel managers' knowledge about it.

The seldom-seen occupants of that unknown upper region had their own elevator at the rear of the building; private stairs, also at the rear and entirely closed off from the hotel itself; even their own fire escape. Indeed they—"they" being the only identification one might reasonably apply in such circumstances—owned the top floor, and so fell entirely outside the hotel's sphere of control and operation. And while their private elevator gave them access to the hotel's restaurants and various facilities, the hotel's elevators stopped short of the top floor. Their indicator panels didn't even show that such a floor existed. So that just like floor thirteen in many another hotel, E-Branch simply wasn't there.

Except it was.

The ops and briefings room was at the opposite end of the main corridor from Trask's office. Walking down that corridor, he necessarily passed Harry's Room. An old name plate, looking a little tatty and spotted now, said just that:

HARRY'S ROOM

Trask paused and tried the doorknob. They had had knobs in those days, not handles. Now they didn't even have handles! You just blinked at an eye-level spot marked ID; if the door recognized you it would let you in. Trask had often wondered about that: how did dwarves manage? Did they have to jump up and down or were they given special rooms? And what about someone sporting a recent black or bloodshot eye?

But Harry's Room was undisturbed. It had remained the same ever since he'd stayed over here, when for a time he'd considered a position as Head of Branch. That had come to nothing and he'd moved on, but the impression he'd made had stayed. And no one had ever thought to change Harry's Room, not even in the slightest degree.

The door was locked; its key swung on a hook in the D.O.'s key-press; no one went into Harry's Room because . . . well, just because. Because it was a region out of time, and sometimes out of space. Because it was still *his* room . . .

And Trask moved on, but Harry stayed with him.

Harry.

Harry Keogh, Necroscope. The only man in the world—in this world, anyway—who could talk to dead people. And Trask shivered despite the unaccustomed warmth. The only man who had spoken to Zek in life who would have been *able* to speak to her even in . . . in . . .

But he must put that out of his mind. For now, out of the blue, there was another. And Trask didn't know if he liked the idea of Jake Cutter speaking to Zek. With Harry, there had been warmth, courtesy, humility, and understanding. But Jake Cutter . . . was Jake Cutter. And there was something about him—*still* something about him, despite that he'd made a bloody good show of it out in Australia—that Trask couldn't fathom.

Perhaps that was it: simply that he was unfathomable, to Ben Trask, anyway. For Trask's talent no longer worked on him; face-to-face with Jake, his built-in lie detector switched off. The man's mental shields were that strong and getting stronger. Why, he could be lying his head off and Trask wouldn't know it, not for sure! He'd probably suspect that something wasn't quite right, might even suspect his own talent, but had no way to determine the truth of it one way or the other.

It was much the same for many of Trask's espers. Ian Goodly had difficulty reading Jake's future; even Liz Merrick—who had something of a rapport with Jake—could get into his mind only when he was asleep and his shields were down. And that was yet another reason why Trask . . . why he didn't like him? Why he couldn't cotton to him? Because it was Trask himself, the boss, the faultless Head of E-Branch, who must break the Branch's unspoken moral code by using Liz to discover what was going on in there, in Jake's unruly head.

Unruly, yes, and Trask was sure that he still had his own agenda, that given the chance he'd go off and do his own thing, and maybe even get himself killed doing it. What, Luigi Castellano? A gang boss, drug-runner, torturer, and murderer with the Italian and French police—some of them, anyway—in his pay, and Mafia contacts deep in the heart of degenerate Russia? You couldn't be a one-man army against odds like that and get away with it. You needed backing. Backing such as E-Branch might be willing to supply, and even Gustav Turchin, if only Jake would back off and give them the chance. If only he'd accept that he now had responsibilities ranging far wider than the gratification of his own blood-lust. And:

Hah! Trask gave a derisive snort. Jake Cutter's blood-lust, indeed! But the fact was that Trask wanted Jake for himself, to use in satisfying *his* blood-lust, his craving for the blood and the lives of the Wamphyri.

At the end of the corridor, people were going into the ops room. "Two minutes," said John Grieve, catching up with Trask and passing him. And three of four more of them right behind him, making sure they'd be there before he got started. He paused at the doors to let them go by, looked back and saw that the corridor was now empty, and followed them in . . .

The ops room. Half of it given over to gadgets, mainly communications, like the eye-in-the-sky links that could zoom in on an ongoing battle in Ethiopia and show you a pretty decent (indecent?) picture of a soldier grinning as he pushed his bayonet up the anus of a crucified "rebel." Or the links to GCHQ, the listening station that could tap any insecure (and some "secure") telephone conversations anywhere in the world. Or the extraps, computers whose sole function was to extrapolate: to use as many as possible of the known conditions of today's world to try to determine and describe the world of tomorrow.

Pretty amazing stuff . . . until you realized what it really was, that *all* it was was a disassociated brain controlling nothing whatsoever. Using it, you could see and hear, but you could never taste, smell, or touch. And except on rare occasions you couldn't change anything either. Trask sometimes likened it to God—but not exactly, because God is omniscient, and the computer can know only what you tell it; even an extrap is only guessing—but he *likened* it to God because of his belief that He was *not* omnipotent. Having given men free will, how could He possibly control their actions? Even if He could, how could He apply himself to any single act? How could He select or correct or counter any single atrocity when a million more were happening simultaneously all over the world?

Answer: He couldn't . . . and in Trask's case, He hadn't.

Trask had thought a great deal about God since Zek's passing. He had tried to come to terms with Him, but as yet hadn't quite managed it. Instead he put his faith in the gadgets and the ghosts.

The ops room and its gadgets, which were usually attended by the "techs," the men who controlled them. But gadgets, like God (in Trask's eyes, at least), simply couldn't do everything. And much less than God, their eyes and ears couldn't be everywhere at once. Hence the ghosts.

For where it takes time to make a telephone or video call, telepathy is instantaneous. And where mechanical extraps could only "guess" at future events, precogs such as Ian Goodly occasionally "glimpsed" the future. And however diligently spies in the sky might search for chemical and nuclear pollutants in the world's continents and living oceans, locators like David Chung could actually sniff them out, like an X ray finding a cancer. In other words—and insofar as Trask's weirdly skilled agents really did touch, taste, and smell much of the otherwise invisible—they were in many ways superior to the machines, principally in that they didn't need programming . . . but there were times when they did need inspiring.

Electrical and mechanical clatter—the hum and buzz and stutter from the other side of the large room—fell to a minimum as Trask climbed four steps up to the podium, then turned to face a semicircular array of chairs in three ranks, so organized that no one's face was hidden behind anyone else's. And there they were: his ghosts, or the people who dealt with them, looking right back at him.

"No niceties," he told them then, his voice rasping like a file on glass. "No congratulations on work well done. I've been through all that; and it *was* well done, but it wasn't finished. So no 'Good afternoon, ladies and gentlemen,' because it isn't, even if you are. It's a *bad* afternoon—it's a *black* afternoon—ladies and gentlemen. Worse, it could even be one of the last afternoons, before a hellishly long night. And without wanting to seem too melodramatic, you may be the only ones standing between the twilight and the final darkness."

He looked at all the faces—blank, emotionless, waiting to receive emotion, inspiration. But where to find it? Why, in the truth of course, where Trask had always found it.

"You all know the problem," he told them. "But until we—our Australian team—went out there, no one knew, we couldn't be sure, that the problem knew us. Now we know. There are Wamphyri in our world, and they know that *we* know about them. Which makes it a very different ball game. Now we hunters have to be doubly careful and ensure that we don't end up the hunted."

It had happened before, some thirty-odd years ago, when an Earth-born vampire, Yulian Bodescu, blood-son of Thibor Ferenczy, had set himself against E-Branch to destroy it. Then, only Harry Keogh and his infant boy child, a Necroscope whose powers rivalled his father's, had been able to stop the impending destruction of E-Branch and the plague of vampires that would have ensued. But Trask didn't need to elaborate; his espers had read the files and knew the story almost but not quite as well as he did. But Trask had actually been there. And their faces weren't so much blank or emotionless as respectful—deeply respectful. For of all the great survivors who ever were, surely Ben Trask must rank among the greatest.

And now that he had started—now that he'd settled down a little and saw how well he commanded the attention of his audience—Trask began to recognize those oh-so-respectful faces. Why, he even began to discover likenesses to faces that were no longer there! But with all respect, the latter were real ghosts now who existed only in fond memory and imagination.

Such as Darcy Clarke. Darcy, the world's most nondescript man, and the one with the world's most effective, most beneficent—to Darcy—and reliable talent. For he had been a deflector, the very opposite of accident prone: a man with a guardian angel, who could stumble blindfolded through a minefield in snowshoes and come out the other side completely unscathed!

Darcy had been Head of Branch once over—until the thing that had got into Harry Keogh got into him, too, and robbed him of his guardian. Some might say it was Harry's fault, but Trask didn't think so. It was E-Branch, the job, this work that would get them all in the end. Darcy's face lingered on for a second in Trask's memory, then it was gone. Gone like Darcy himself.

But there were others, far too many others, ready to take its place; crowding in, they appeared to superimpose themselves on the new faces in the small crowd of people waiting for Trask to continue. And he couldn't help but remember them.

Sir Keenan Gormley, first Head of Branch. Trask saw him as he had been: sixtyish and starting to show his age; round shoulders on a once well-built but inevitably sagging body, supporting a short neck and the lofty dome of his head. His green eyes a little muddied but missing very little, and laughter lines in their corners that belied the weight of his duties; his greying, well-groomed hair receding just a little.

Apart from a minor heart problem common in men of his age, Sir Keenan had been good for a lot more years yet . . . *had* been, until he'd met up with Boris Dragosani and Max Batu, ESPionage agents for Russian's E-Branch. Dragosani had been a vampire and a necromancer, while Batu had been so deadly that he could kill with a glance. His "talent" had stopped Sir Keenan's heart!

But all of that had been many years ago, and with the collapse of Communism the former USSR had suffered such turmoil it was still in a state of flux and political disarray even today. And in any case Dragosani and Max Batu had long since paid with their lives—paid in full, and more than paid—for all their evil deeds; they were gone into far darker places than poor Sir Keenan. All thanks to Harry Keogh.

Gormley's face faded from the eye of Trask's memory, and in its place, in his audience, was the living face of John Grieve, a contemporary of Sir Keenan's from the old days, whose presence here had probably invoked the memory in the first place . . .

But that wasn't the end of these faces from the past; they came in seemingly endless procession. Faces such as that of the seer, Guy Roberts.

Cursing, irreverent, far-scrying, chain-smoking Guy, who'd been the team leader down in Devon that time, after Harry Keogh had warned E-Branch about Yulian Bodescu. Trask remembered that time well; he still had small white scars back and front, under his right collarbone, where he'd been skewered by a pitchfork's tine in the barn of Bodescu's country seat.

That had been one *hell* of a bad time for E-Branch. And hell was the only word that adequately described it. Bodescu, a fledgling vampire, had killed Guy Roberts (or rather he'd butchered him, battered his head to a pulp) as Roberts tried to protect Brenda Keogh and her baby son. But Guy hadn't been alone in paying the price of working for E-Branch.

Their names . . . they weren't quite legion, but that was how Trask thought of them. So many friends gone from the world forever. Peter Keen, Simon Gower, and young Harvey Newton: Bodescu had killed them all. And then there'd been Carl Quint, blown to bits in the Moldavian foothills at the site of an ancient evil. Their faces came and went, and the list went on.

Alec Kyle, another ex–Head of Branch: his brain drained of all knowledge by the Opposition's scientists in their HQ at the Chateau Bronnitsy. Kyle was quite literally dead—kept "alive" on their machines—until the incorporeal Necroscope had stepped in and inhabited the man's body, reanimating it. Trask remembered it well: there'd been those who had hinted that maybe Harry had taken advantage of the situation, but again Trask had denied it. It hadn't been Harry's fault; he'd been sucked in by the vacuum that was Kyle's vacant head, without which the world would have been in dire straits a long time ago.

And on and on. Sandra Markham, a neophyte telepath who had been the love of Harry's life during the time of the Janos Ferenczy affair. But Janos's metalism may even have been as great as Nephran Malinari's, and when he'd got into Sandra's mind . . . that had been the end of that. The end of Sandra, too. The Necroscope himself had put the vampirized woman out of her misery, which only increased his own. But the list didn't stop there . . .

The twice-dead Trevor Jordan, another telepath tangled in a vampire's web of mentalism. Jordan had put a gun to his own head and pulled the trigger—at the "behest" of Janos Ferenczy. The Necroscope had brought Jordan back from the dead (*God,* that such things were or had been possible!) only to have E-Branch kill him a second time, believing that Jordan, too, must be a vampire. For when a man has died he should stay dead. Unless, of course, he's undead.

And Ken Layard, a Branch locator who had located something best left undiscovered, whom certain of Harry Keogh's "friends" from beyond the grave had been obliged to deal with in the Zarandului Mountains of Romania.

And Zek Foener, whose lost but beloved face had firmed up on the neck and shoulders of Millie Cleary. They were so different, those two, and yet in Trask's affections alike in so many ways. Telepaths, for one thing, and loyal and true, for another. But Zek, poor Zek! Gone from him these three years and still unavenged: her eyes seemed to stare at him from Millie's ever innocent face.

And finally the Necroscope—Harry Keogh himself—lost in time, space, and the Möbius Continuum. Dead, but not in the way we understand death. Gone . . . but not quite. Harry, wearing the face of Alec Kyle as he had worn it in life and somehow made it his own.

But here lay a problem, because Harry's face simply floated on the eye of memory, drifting there and refusing to settle on anyone else's shoulders. And then, as Trask searched through those suddenly real faces looking back at him, he knew why Harry's face didn't fit. It was because no one in his audience, in that small crowd of faces, would ever be able to accommodate it. And the one face he was searching for was missing.

With that realization the poignancy of Trask's mood gradually turned to anger, a slow burn that began to twist his lips into a grimace—

—Until the door to the ops room quietly opened, and Jake Cutter and Liz Merrick stood there for a moment in the ominous, brooding silence and the knowledge that everyone's eyes were on them. Especially on Jake.

Trask was scarcely surprised to note, in those same frozen seconds, that Harry Keogh's phantom face fitted Jake to perfection. Which only served to make him more angry yet . . .

2
Of The Future

TRASK'S THOUGHTS, HIS REFLECTIONS, HAD taken a few seconds. But they had felt like hours, and he coughed to cover his lapse—also to choke back some of his anger. For this was perfectly (imperfectly?) typical of Jake: insubordinate, contrary, and dilatory to the last. And he had Liz warming to him all the way, so that Trask was bound to think:

If we can't change him, turn him, make him 100 percent ours, it won't only be the waste of one man—one esper and all his incredible potential—but he'll take Liz with him, too! And I'm still *not absolutely sure of him. He looked good out in Australia, but ever since then . . . what is it with Jake? I mean What the* hell *is it?*

Thoughts, that was all, but in this place, with people such as these, thoughts had weight no less than in the Möbius

Continuum. And Liz Merrick was a neophyte telepath. She couldn't send (unless it was to Jake, or to some other mentalist deliberately scanning her mind), but she was a damn good receiver. And despite E-Branch's code of not PSIing (or, as some might irreverently have it, "pissing") on each other, she may have inadvertently picked up what Trask was thinking. Certainly her expression was cold where it turned aside his own burning gaze. And before Trask could actually say anything:

"We were practicing," she blurted. And then, wryly: "Or at least we would have been, if I—"

"—She means *we,*" Jake cut in. "If *we* hadn't lost it. But we have. It's gone." He shrugged, apparently unconcerned.

"Temporarily gone, anyway," Liz came back. "We were giving it one last try and we . . . sort of lost track of time." She bit her lip, glanced at Jake accusingly and then away from him.

Trask looked at her and read disappointment, but not with him. She hadn't "eavesdropped," inadvertently or otherwise. Her coolness was frustration born of her failure, or more likely of Jake's. Then, looking at Jake . . . Trask didn't know *what* he was reading. Nothing, truth be told! And if this were a game of lie dice in some bar, Trask supposed he'd be buying the next round; Jake's shields were that good. *But if you're telling the truth, why mess with shields?* Or was this simply a by-product of Harry Keogh's dart, some sort of self-regulating or intuitive protective device? Well, that wasn't totally unanticipated; Trask was fairly certain that the original Necroscope had managed to dupe him once or twice, too.

But all that aside, their excuses weren't good enough.

"All skills wax and wane," Trask rasped. "No one's talent is in top gear all the time. But there's time for practice and there's time for briefings, updates, staying in touch, knowing what's going down. There's no use being in tip-top shape if you don't know what's happening around you; no point in my posting a daily routine and calling O-groups if people like you simply ignore such obviously unimportant, insignificant little items! So, since you've already managed to hold things up for several minutes now, do take your time but eventually find a couple of chairs . . . *and sit fucking down!"*

Trask generally considered the indiscriminate use of curse words indicative of the lack of an adequate or "decent" vocabulary; he wasn't much given to swearing. But, however rarely, even he was wont to slip up and curse under pressure or, like now, use bad language to signal his exasperation or displeasure. His espers recognized that fact and knew when to back off—most of them.

Liz's face reddened but Jake merely shrugged—by no means apologetically—and continued to look disinterested. Then they separated; she took a seat at the back, Jake in the front, dead centre. Trask quite deliberately waited, his gaze tracking them to their seats . . .

Jake Cutter was thirtyish, but his looks hinted of life on the fast track and loaned him an extra seven or eight years. As Trask had once heard the country and western singer Johnny Cash explain it a quarter-century ago on one of his tours of England, "It isn't the years but the mileage." So with Jake: he had certainly burned a lot of rubber, not to mention candles.

He was tall, maybe six-two, long-legged, and with long arms to match. His hair was a deep brown like his eyes, and his face was lean, hollow-cheeked. In profile he had an altogether angular face. He looked as if a good meal wouldn't hurt, but on the other hand the extra weight wouldn't sit right on him; it would only serve to slow him down. His lips were thin and even cruel, and when he smiled you could never be sure there was any humour in it. But that could have been his background; he hadn't had it easy, especially the last few years.

Jake's hair was long as a lion's mane at the back; he kept it swept back, braided into a pigtail. His jaw, like the rest of his face, was angular, lightly scarred on the left side, and his nose had been broken high on the bridge so that it slanted at a steep angle: *hawklike,* Trask thought. But despite his leanness, Jake's chest was deep under shoulders broad and square, and his sun-bronzed upper arms were corded with muscle. His jeans and T-shirt displayed his hard, fast body to its full advantage, and there was little or nothing of shyness, reticence, or uncertainty about him. If anything, Jake was *too* quick on the uptake, and arrogant with it.

Indeed, Trask thought, *he has everything I would have liked to have when I was his age!* Not jealousy, but simple frustration: that all of this could end up wasted. But not if Trask had anything to do with it.

As for Liz Merrick: well he wasn't about to let her go to waste, either! As a telepath, she was just too valuable. Out in Australia, despite the fact that her mentalism hadn't fully matured yet, she'd worked well, had seemed a natural. So that if or when her talent came more fully into its own . . . well, Trask just wanted to see it happen, that was all . . .

Liz had settled into her seat, looked a little less flustered now. She was a very good-looking girl—no, a woman, Trask corrected himself. She was maybe five-seven, willow-waisted, and her figure was film-star stuff. Her hair, as black as night, was cut in a boyish bob, and when she smiled, her whole face lit up. A pity she didn't do it more frequently, but working for E-Branch was a pretty serious occupation. *Damn, but she'd* used *to smile a lot, before Jake Cutter.* Trask looked at Cutter, sitting in the front row, just slumping there with his long legs stretched out in front as if he didn't have a care in the world. *The next Necroscope? Jake? Huh!*

Trask felt his temperature beginning to rise, got off Jake, and looked at Liz again:

Her green eyes, looking back at him from under that fringe of jet-black hair. A pert nose—the only way to describe it, really—that could very quickly tilt when she was annoyed. Her full mouth, with lips so naturally red they needed only a daily dab of moistening colour, sitting slightly aslant over a small, determined chin that was wont to set like a rock when her mind was made up.

Still very young, Liz was full of life and character, and the fact was that Trask found it a damn shame that she had ever got mixed up with this lot—with *his* lot, yes—in the first place. For unless she was very fortunate, or one of a kind, the job was bound to age her, he knew. But what the—? That was no way to be thinking! In fact she was the very *stuff* of E-Branch, and the Branch always came first.

Trask knew that it came first with Liz, too, knew that she fitted in here almost as if born to it, and wanted nothing more than to be a member of the team. Or at least, that was what she *had* wanted; her eager smile and readiness to join in had always said so. So, what had changed now? For as Trask had so recently observed, Liz wasn't much given to smiling. Not any longer.

It could be that he had put too much on her out in Australia, that she'd "grown up" too fast out there, seen too much and come too close, until she'd realized just how rough, dirty, and dangerous the work could get. Or it could be that her so-called rapport with Jake was breaking down, and that maybe a different kind of rapport was developing.

As for that kind: E-Branch could do without such complications. But the two of them—developing and working in unison—what a force for good they might make! *Would* make, if Ben Trask had his way . . .

"Right," he let his gaze rove over his audience and began again. "Now that we're all here, maybe we can get on. Those of you who weren't with us out in the Gibson Desert, and later in the Macpherson Mountains resort and Jethro Manchester's island, will by now have read up on the initial report. Well, as reports go it isn't a bad one, but it was very quickly prepared and obviously doesn't tell the entire story; that will come later and I won't waste time on it here. So this isn't so much a debrief as my opportunity to reiterate, to tell you what we've achieved and what we failed to achieve, what little we learned and a lot more that we can only 'guess' at—though usually our guesswork is closer to the mark than most.

"First what we did:

"With all credit to David Chung—for picking up the first whiff of mindsmog—we successfully located and destroyed Nephran Malinari's bolt-hole in the Gibson Desert. We also took out one of his lieutenants, the engineer Bruce Trennier, who Malinari had recruited at the Romanian Refuge. He had only had Trennier for three years, but he'd done a good job on him: that one was . . . nasty! There's no question in my mind that Trennier was well on his way to becoming Wamphyri! This time the credit goes to Liz Merrick; she challenged Trennier—called on him to draw, as it were—lured him from his hole, and faced him down. And we, the rest of the team, finished it off, *cut* him down, and *burned* the poor bastard to a black, smoking crisp!" Trask took a deep breath, grunted his satisfaction, and continued:

"We also took out his thralls, an entire nest of them well gone into vampirism. But as you are all well aware, there isn't any point of no return for victims of vampirism; even part-gone is way too far gone. So we did them a favour, for there was no hope for any of them.

"But Trennier and Malinari were linked telepathically. In the moments of Trennier's dying he contacted his master, which David Chung likewise picked up; a momentary contact, which nevertheless led us to Brisbane and the Macpherson Range, and also to a second bolt-hole.

"Malinari had taken control of Jethro Manchester's Xanadu, a holiday resort in the Macphersons. The place was an up-market aerie, somewhat removed from any manse that he'd ever inhabited in Starside! In fact, his seat was a luxurious bubble apartment over Xanadu's central 'Pleasure Dome' . . . would you believe, a casino? Now, if we were cynics—which I know we sometimes are, by virtue of our talents—that sort of thing might even give us pause about Las Vegas, right?"

Trask appeared to have lightened up a little; his audience appreciated it, and there were even one or two wry smiles, nodding heads. "But hey, let's not go into that!" he jokingly went on. "Lord knows that place has *always* had its bloodsuckers!"

(Some muted laughter now, from Trask's audience.)

But as they settled down again, the smile was gone from

his face as if it had never been there. He'd simply been setting them up. And now the punch line:

"Xanadu is in ruins, gutted like a fish!" Trask rasped, no slightest trace of humour in his sandpaper voice. "Gutted, yes, which wasn't down to us but to Malinari. *He* did it to *us,* or he tried to, and we were damned lucky he didn't pull it off!

"Likewise on Jethro Manchester's island: his thralls there knew we were coming, even though they weren't any too well prepared. But then again, maybe they hadn't *wanted* to be ready for us, for after all, they were just people, dupes, victims.

"So what I'm telling you is this: that Nephran Malinari—this bloody vampire, this Lord of the Wamphyri—that he *knows* about us! He probably got quite a lot from . . . from poor Zek, a little from Trennier, and God only knows how much from us—when we were out there in such close proximity to him. He's a telepath; no, more properly a mentalist, a fabulously talented creature with vast reserves of what we call ESP, and he's our deadliest enemy since . . . well, since the day we caused the vampire world to turn on its axis and destroyed Devetaki Skullguise and her brood in Starside. *That's* how dangerous he is.

"And he escaped, got clean away . . . where to, we don't yet know, though we have evidence that suggests he's no longer down under in Australia. But wherever he is, one thing seems certain: finding and dealing with Malinari isn't going to get any easier the next time around. . . .

"Okay, *he* got away. But his people—or those poor damned souls who were once people—they didn't. We can at least congratulate ourselves that we got that right. So we're now satisfied about as far as we can be that the Australian continent is free of contamination. Naturally we'd like to keep it that way, and to be absolutely sure I'll be detailing a locator, a couple of spotters, and maybe a telepath to go back out there and pick it up where we left off. There were clues we didn't get the opportunity to look into, and other stuff that still needs tracking down. So those of you who'll be involved: I'm sorry for the short notice, but time is of the essence. We can no longer afford to sit around doing nothing while three Great Vampires out of Starside are on the loose preparing God only knows what mayhem and madness for our world.

"Very well, we'll know who's going within the next twenty-four hours, and after that the lucky ones will have just enough time to pack before they're heading down under . . ."

Trask paused to glance at his notes, then nodded and said, "A moment ago I posed something of a question. And it's a question that has to be in everyone's mind. Just what are Malinari, Szwart, and Vavara up to in our world? Just what is it they're doing or planning to do? Well, we know what they're *not* doing. They're not recruiting, not taking thralls or making vampires; or if they are, it's a small, localized, and tightly controlled industry. What I mean is, they're not spreading it around. Not yet, anyway.

"But surely that's what they do. It's their way of life—*hah!* Ask any vampire and he'll tell you, that the blood *is* the life!" (Trask seemed galvanized now, his eyes blazing in a suddenly ravaged face.) "They 'live' by taking thralls, by leeching on the blood of their servitors and victims, and by spreading death and undeath. So, why hasn't the plague come among us? I know that time isn't of any real consequence to the Wamphyri, but they've had three years! By now the great nations should be at war . . . even with each other! Half the population armed with crossbows and wooden stakes, and the other half with eyes dripping sulphur, hiding in the dark, waiting for the night. Cheap silver crucifixes selling for twice the price of gold. Noonday bonfires in every town centre, and the sickening stench of burning vampire flesh. And by night, the ever-growing ranks of the thirsty ones, raping, ravaging, and making more, hunting for new souls to toss on *their* bonfires—the ones that burn in hell!"

Again Trask paused to let all that he'd said sink in, and in a far more controlled, regulated voice went on: "If I seemed to go a little over the top just then it was mainly to wake you up, spur you on, give you something of an incentive—not that you need one, I'm sure. But it's been three long years, people, and all that time I've sweated over information which you weren't privy to. And now . . . I think it's time you were. A burden shared, and all that . . .

"So what am I talking about? Well listen up, and I'll tell you.

"When we first learned that we'd been invaded, we knew that Malinari and the other two monsters came out of the sump at the Refuge with three senior thralls, presumably lieutenants, which probably meant one lieutenant each. When we went out to Romania we discovered that they'd also recruited three of our people—not espers, no, but Refuge staff, personnel—to take with them wherever they were going, perhaps as sustenance—*God!*—but more likely as guides in this new world. And definitely as converts, recruits, vampires.

"One of the three was Bruce Trennier, who we don't have to worry about anymore. But at the time, that made two Lords and a Lady of the Wamphyri, three lieutenants or Wamphyri aspirants, and three up-and-coming vampires who—depending on Starside's laws of *un*natural selection—might or might not make it into vampirism's upper echelon.

"And those were the figures we fed to our extrap computers, along with several conjectural rates of transmission—of vampirism, that is. We were actually expecting an epidemic; we *prepared* for one, in the expectation that we'd find principal targets at three centres of maximum infection, and that then we'd be able to hit back in a massive military raid followed by the world's longest cleanup period lasting maybe a hundred years! So we prepared, but we didn't tell everyone. And by everyone I mean most of you.

"We didn't tell you that the extraps had worked it all out in their mechanical minds and given us between a year and eighteen months, to a maximum of three years, until Armageddon; and that by then, as I've said, the remaining human half of the population would be at war with the vampire half and probably with each other.

"We didn't tell you because first of all our Minister Responsible had forbidden it; *you* are human after all, and many of you have wives and families, and while we may be E-Branch, we're just as prone to panic as anyone else in the face of the ultimate disaster. In short, we needed you here, not running off to take care of your kith and kin. And we also didn't tell you because that doomsday scenario I painted a minute or so ago was just one of a handful of scenarios, and as the old saying goes, 'Where there's life . . .'

"But mainly we—myself and one or two others who were in the know—mainly we stayed silent because right from the beginning we'd seen signs of some kind of strategic cover-up, I mean by the Wamphyri. What they'd done to the Refuge, they'd made it look like vandalism on the grand scale. Maybe the three missing members of staff had gone crazy, wrecked the place and murdered everyone else before running off? Maybe that's what they wanted us or the world to think. And in any case surely the *last* thing we would think—in a world that doesn't believe in vampires—was that we had been *invaded* by them! And remember, only six of those Refuge kids had actually been . . . depleted, and even then they showed no *external* signs of vampirism. Even if some Romanian doctor had got there before we torched the place, it would have seemed 'obvious' that the children had been suffering from some form of pernicious anaemia. But pernicious? That isn't the word for it. And those kids . . . my God, those poor kids!

"And here we see something of Malinari's evil intelligence at work. He left no one alive to tell the tale, no one to alert the world to what had really happened. But after . . . after *examining* Zek, surely he would know that we—that E-Branch—would be on to him anyway?

"Well, I believe Malinari knew precisely what our world and its peoples are all about. I believe he'd got it all from General Mikhail Suvorov and his expeditionary force long before he ever set out to come here, and then that he'd had it corroborated by poor Zek and Bruce Trennier at the Refuge. He knew first from Suvorov that the people of our world didn't believe in his kind, that vampires are considered a myth born of ignorance and ancient superstition. But while that is generally true, he also learned from Zek that certain people *do* have all or most of the facts, which of course would tend to make E-Branch and its espers his deadliest enemies.

"So now let's look at it from his point of view, if that's at all possible. If Malinari and the others commenced vampirising every human being with whom they came in contact, how long before we people who know the truth broke silence? And how long then before mankind in its entirety fought back—and with what terrible weapons?

"Malinari, Szwart, and Vavara, they were Wamphyri . . . they *are* Wamphyri! But they are only three. Three of them, and oh so many of us. And so much still to be learned about the Earth and its peoples, this very different world that they would conquer, with all its many diverse races.

"Zek, my Zek, was the real key. She was a powerful mentalist, a telepath who knew others with stranger powers still. She knew E-Branch, and she knew—or she had known—other vampires before Malinari. And I can't help but wonder: when he locked on to Zek, did he see Harry Keogh in her mind? Did he perhaps glimpse the Necroscope in her memories? Ah, but just think how *that* would have given him pause: to have fled from one such in Starside, only to discover that there were, or had been, another or others of a like kind here! And so he must play this world with extreme caution, in the knowledge that he might call down metaphysical powers at least as great and possibly greater than his own . . .

"All of this is entirely conjectural, guesswork of course, but our experience of events—and nonevents—has shown it to be near to the mark. Malinari and the others, they *have* kept low profiles while they prepare to do . . . whatever. And the extraps' eighteen months are past, and likewise the maximum three years to Armageddon . . . yet until we got that whiff of mindsmog it was as if nothing was happening. So what *has* been happening, and what have they been up to?

"Well, in Australia we found a number of clues. But first

the clear evidence, which hit us right between the eyes: Malinari, for one, hasn't been hiding himself away in a ruined castle in the Carpathians! Indeed, he was where we might least expect to find him. Which begs the question, what of the others, Vavara and Szwart? Are they, too, in residence in places where we wouldn't dream of finding them?

"Okay, I see what you're thinking: that this isn't so much what they are doing as where they are doing it. But there might yet be answers to both questions in what we found under Xanadu. We—and by that I mean Liz and Jake Cutter—found a midnight garden, a mushroom farm of sorts, a breeding place for vampires. And while the rest of us didn't see it, Jake formed the opinion that Malinari had 'planted' his lieutenant out of Starside down there to fester in the earth. That's not such a wild notion; he would probably have been the only one of The Mind's retinue who was 'matured' or rotten enough to produce spores. And again according to Jake and Liz, the cave where they found this monstrosity was full of that filthy spawn.

"Worse, our Gibson Desert liaison person—someone called Peter Miller, who for his own crazy reasons had run off on us—was also down there. He'd been vampirized and . . . and something had been done to him. He had metamorphosed; he'd been converted, reduced to a mass of nutrients for black, spore-producing, vampiric fungi. And all of that loathsome corruption in the earth, it was feeding off his juices. *Ugh!*" Trask's shudder was by no means faked.

"Anyway, Jake torched the place and everything in it . . .

"But the point is, Xanadu was a spawning ground, literally. What if Malinari had cropped all of those spores, released them into the casino's air-conditioning or ventilation system? What? Legionnaires' disease wouldn't have a look-in! Forget it! But in fact we can't forget it because I might just have it right. And Xanadu wasn't The Mind's only place in Australia.

"Anyway, that's a job for the next Australian team, so maybe they're not the lucky ones after all. Malinari's 'bolt-holes' may have been more than just places to escape to.

We've really no notion what may be hidden away, breeding and waiting out its time, down in that old mine in the Gibson Desert. So we'll have to open it up again. As for Jethro Manchester's Capricorn Group island: we burned what was on the surface, but who can say what may have been—and what might still be—underneath?

"Let's for the moment just suppose that these three Great Vampires were preparing to seed the world with spores. Okay, so we've delayed the scheme for one of them, but what of the other two? That's why now, after three years of nothing, there's this sudden urgency. Or rather, that is why I'm bringing the urgency home to you, for it's been with me *all* of that time! And if you don't believe me, well just take a look at my hair!" There was no humor this time, faked or for real, in Trask's tone.

"Oh, I know how hard you've all been working," he continued, "using every possible means to track these creatures down; we've put every spare moment into it, and we've frequently neglected other tasks to stay focussed on this one job. So when I say 'three years of nothing' it's not to belittle anyone but to point up my own frustration. But now it's more than just frustration, and a whole lot more than simple anxiety for the world at large. For now I'm also anxious—deadly afraid—for you, me, us.

"Why? Well, let's go back to square one:

"Malinari *knows* about us. He knows now for sure that we've been looking for him all this time, and that we're not going to stop. And if he's in contact with the others, they know it, too. But if you've read the files on the Yulian Bodescu business all of thirty-odd years ago—and if you haven't, I suggest you do it now—you'll know what that means. It may well be that from now on the Wamphyri won't be so happy just sitting around waiting for us to come looking for them, *but instead may come looking for us!*

"I'm just about finished. But starting right here and now, I want extra effort, people. I want daily think-tanks, and more time spent at your machines and in your minds. Put your gadgets to their full use, and likewise your ghost talents. We have to find Malinari again, and Vavara and Szwart, and we have to find them soon, before those extrap computers are shown to have been correct. For remember, our three years are up!

"And one last thing. I want extra vigilance from everyone. Not for me but for you. And especially in the dead of night . . ."

As the espers filed out into the corridor and on to their workplaces, and the techs went back to their viewscreens and computers, Trask stood in the doorway and stopped his joint Seconds-in-Command, Ian Goodly and David Chung, telling them, "Come and talk to me in my office."

And when they were there: "I've pretty much left you alone since we got back," he told them. "No duties, and no additional pressures. That's because of all our people you two have enough on your plates already. David, although I have two other locators—Bernie Fletcher being the better of the two—with all due respect, they can't hold a candle to you. And Ian, our other precogs are precogs in name only. Mainly hunchmen, they're good at making clever guesses, at seeing how things are going to add up. But since we have machines that can do that, their only advantage is they don't require programming. So as usual, you two are my main men. Our telepaths aren't in short supply; it seems to me Liz Merrick is coming along just fine, and that's despite this sudden 'setback' with Jake Cutter, which—"

"Which you're not buying?" Ian Goodly, tall and skeletally thin, and looking like nothing so much as an out-of-work undertaker, raised a thinly etched, questioning eyebrow.

Trask shook his head. "No, I'm not. Liz: I read her like a book—and I also read some of the looks she was giving Jake in the Ops room. She thinks he's been stalling, keeping her out of his mind. And as for Jake: well, I can't any longer read him at all! So it's like I suspected: he doesn't intend on making it easy for us. And hardest of all for Liz, for I think she's got something of a crush on him."

"A crush?" (Again Goodly's raised eyebrow, lifting higher yet.) "Now you're really showing your age! 'Fancies him,' would be more in tune with the times, I think. Or perhaps, 'she'd like to get into his pants?' Good grief!"

"Whatever," said Trask, shrugging.

"But he *is* going to stay with us," Goodly declared with a quiet certainty that Trask knew of old.

"You've seen that?"

"I see lots of Jake, in the future. No great detail, nothing definite, but he's there."

"With us, or getting in our way?"

"I can't say. Maybe both."

"Huh!" Trask grunted, and took a deep breath before going on: "Anyway, and as I was saying, you are the top men and it's up to you to motivate, activate, and galvanize the others while continuing to do your own things to the best of your abilities in the current circumstances. Meaning, I know it's not easy for you to work under duress. Your skills aren't like that. They're more or less free agents in their own right."

"Exactly," said Chung. "And where Jake Cutter's concerned, my talent has never been freer. Anything that once belonged to Harry Keogh—such as that old hairbrush—it just comes alive when Jake's in the vicinity. So he can kid us all he wants that he's 'lost it' or it's 'gone away,' but I know better. Whatever it is that he got from Harry, he's got it in spades!"

Trask looked at Chung—a Chinese "Cockney" in his late forties, slight in figure but awesome in his abilities as a scryer and locator—and nodded. "We're agreed on that . . . we saw it in action out in Australia . . . we'd all have been dead without it! But having something, and being willing to explore it or put it to good use—to our use, the world's use—are entirely different things . . .

"Anyway, enough of Jake for the moment. When we're through here I'll speak to him and Liz both, see if I can find out what he's playing at." Trask went behind his desk, sat down, and continued:

"Meanwhile, how are things going with you two? We've

been home more than a week now, gentlemen, and I haven't heard a peep out of you. David, what about the Wamphyri battle gauntlet that our Australian major found in underground Xanadu? It could only have belonged to Malinari, or maybe to the lieutenant Jake says he used as fertilizer. Anything on that? Anything at all?"

Chung shook his head. "Right now, nothing," he said. "Malinari seems to have gone to earth. Nothing strange in that. For three years he hid himself away and we didn't get a sniff. He's so in control he never shows a trace of mindsmog. And remember, it wasn't him who gave the show away in the first place; it was Trennier's nest in the Gibson Desert that let him down. Even in Xanadu, I had to be *that* close before I located him! If it wasn't for Jethro Manchester and those others out in the Capricorn Group, we still might not have found him. So it's my guess that if or when we get our break it will be his thralls that let him down, not Nephran Malinari himself. And the same thing goes for the others, too."

Trask tightened his lips, growled, "Well stay on it. We'll set up a separate maps room away from Ops, give you more space, lots of privacy. You can *sleep* in there if you have to, you and that gauntlet! But we have to get results . . ."

He turned to the precog. "Ian, how's the future looking?"

Goodly's expression was, as usual, mournful as he answered, "My problems are the same as always. The future is a hell of a devious thing. And the more I force it, the less it works. You know that old saying: more haste, less speed? Well, that's what it's like. Like when you're given a Chinese wood puzzle, a jumble of geometric shapes, which in the correct positions all fit perfectly into a square box. If you're allowed to work at it in your own time you can do it. But the moment there's a time restriction your fingers turn to thumbs, and bits of wood go skittering in all directions. *You* may not have been pressuring me, Ben, but *I* have. And the future doesn't much like it."

"You've seen nothing?" Trask was obviously disappointed.

But the precog was chewing his top lip as he answered, "I have seen . . . things. Glimpses, flashes, daydreams—call them what you will—but I'm reluctant to call them the future. I'm as prone to déjà vu feelings, dreaming, and paramnesia as anyone else, and that could be all these things are. They haven't been those very definite scenes that send me reeling, the ones that can't be anything else *but* the future, and usually a dangerous future. So naturally I'm reluctant to send anyone off on a wild goose chase. Not when we might need all of the manpower we've got . . . and not that I'd know where to send him anyway."

"You'd better explain," said Trask. "Just exactly what are these things that you've been seeing. Anything has to be better than nothing."

"Not necessarily," Goodly sighed. "But, if you insist:

"I've seen—I don't know—*shapes,* figures. Black-robed figures, drifting or floating. And I've seen something sinking, deeper and deeper into groaning abysses of water. I've seen . . . a warren of tunnels and burrows, like gigantic wormholes in the earth, all filled with loathsomeness . . . morbid mucus in a cosmic sinus. I've seen hooded eyes, watching, and a weird shadow approaching, getting closer every time I see it. . . ."

The precog fell silent. He gave a sharp, involuntary shudder and blinked eyes that had seemed momentarily blind or vacant, until they refocussed on Trask. And:

"That's it," he said. "That's what I've seen . . ."

But Trask had fallen under the spell of the other's words, so that he, too, had to give himself a shake before he could say, "And you call that nothing?"

"Nothing we can do anything with," the precog answered. "I mean, it has no application."

"But it's not nothing," said Trask. "It's something, and I want you to write it down. And from now on you and David—and you can pull in one of our telepaths, but not Liz—I want you working together. In a special map room, yes. And then if these things—especially these eyes, or this shadow—

if they come any closer, perhaps you'll see them that much more clearly."

"Come closer?" Goodly looked more gaunt than ever. "But if they really are the future, that's one thing that's guaranteed. You see, the future never stands still but comes closer all the time . . ."

When Trask was alone again he got on to the duty officer, asking him, "Paul, where's Lardis Lidesci? I didn't see him at my little pep talk."

"He's where you sent him a week ago, presumably," Paul Garvey answered. "Downstairs in the hotel with his wife. Or maybe they're outdoors in the park. They miss the wild. Lardis was sitting on the desk when I relieved the night duty officer this morning. He said he wants to get back to work—*any* work! Says he thinks he'll go mad doing nothing."

"What about the knock on the head that maniac Peter Miller gave him in Australia? And then the complication of that infection he picked up on our flight home?"

"The infection has just about cleared up. A shot or two of penicillin was all it took. Lardis is lucky it wasn't worse. We have infections here that they never even heard of in Sunside."

"True," Trask nodded. "But they've got one I know of that's a lot worse than all of ours put together! Anyway, send someone to find him will you? I never did find the time to ask him about that job in Greece. Also, while I'm waiting, could you tell Liz Merrick and Jake Cutter to come and see me? Thanks . . ."

When Liz knocked on his door just a minute or so later, she was on her own. "Where's Jake?" Trask asked her, as she took a seat.

She had been told to keep an eye on Jake. He had a room at the HQ, but he didn't know that Liz had the room adjacent, with access to his quarters from the back of her small office. Liz's orders were simple: she was to listen in on Jake's dreams. She should have been doing so ever since they got back from Australia, and reporting her findings back to Trask. It went against E-Branch's code, Trask knew, but on this occasion he felt compelled. It was that important to find out what—or who (Harry Keogh, presumably)—was going on in Jake's mind. So far, however, she hadn't reported a thing.

Similarly, during waking hours, she and Jake were supposed to be working together, improving their telepathic rapport, becoming a team. But again Trask remembered that look she'd given Jake in the Ops room, the one that said she was baffled and maybe a little hurt. By her inability to get through? Trask didn't think so. No, it was far more likely obstinacy on *his* part.

Damn the man! he thought, feeling his frustration bubble up again.

"He said he'd made arrangements to meet Lardis Lidesci and Lissa in the park," she answered. "Lardis had said he wanted to see the British Museum; Jake offered to give him a guided tour. Actually, I think Jake was only too happy to get away from the HQ for a few hours. I get the impression that he's been feeling out of things here. He can't seem to fit in."

"What?" Trask got to his feet in a fury. "He can't seem to fit in? Well that's because he doesn't damn well *try* to fit in! I mean, what's going on here, Liz? Everything seemed to be working just fine down under, and now this? Is he really such a petulant child? And don't tell me I'm wrong. And don't go covering for him—I saw that look you gave him in Ops. He's obstructing you, right?"

His anger wasn't unexpected, but he'd blown up so suddenly that she was nevertheless taken aback. "I . . . I mean, I . . ."

"Did you know I'd called the dogs off?" Trask thumped his desk. "Jake's wanted for murder in Italy and for questioning in France, yet I've had our contacts in Interpol pull the files on him, albeit temporarily. His mug should be scowling at you from the front page of just about every newspaper in Europe, yet the lid's on so tight he doesn't even rate a half-inch of column on page six of the *Daily Sport*. *That's* what I've done for him, and probably damaged my own reputation in the bargain! But for E-Branch, Jake Cutter couldn't stick his nose outside this building without being arrested, and he shows his gratitude by going sightseeing with Lardis and Lissa to the British Museum? I just don't believe this! Who in hell said he could leave the HQ anyway?"

Liz's mouth opened and closed but didn't say anything, and Trask sat back down again with a thump and glared at her across his desk. "Well?" he snarled.

And finally she found some words to say, and said them despite knowing they would probably set him off again. "He has things to work out . . . he has problems . . . something's got him worried . . . that's all I know." And she sat there biting her lip.

But Trask was much calmer now. Colder, too. "No, that isn't all you know," he said. "Because even if my talent doesn't work on Jake anymore, it still works on you. And don't accuse me of spying on you, because you know that I don't control this thing of mine, it just is. It's like any other sense. If you stick me with a pin I hurt, and if you lie to me I know—which in your case hurts just as much. You've changed just recently, Liz, and it isn't for the better. Okay, so this is what you would call a white lie, correct? But it's a lie just the same. And me, I'm only interested in the truth."

Trask sat back, took a deep breath, and finished off: "Now tell me, *please,* is he obstructing you?"

Liz bit her lip again and said, "Yes, I think so. I think I could read him easily if he'd let me. And I think—in fact I know—that I could send to him. Let's face it, I did it in Australia, and that was when he was three hundred miles away!"

"That was under duress," he nodded. "You were stressed out and it was your last chance for life: a telepathic shout, a psychic cry for help. But still, three hundred miles! And he heard you, he even 'came' to you. And then his subsequent jumps, into and out of Malinari's bubble dome in the last seconds before it blew itself to hell. And finally he took an entire monorail car full of us—the whole damn car!—through the Möbius Continuum to our safe house in Brisbane. And now . . . now you can't get through to him across a desk?"

"I know," she was biting her lip again. "And he can't remember the numbers."

"Numbers?" Just for a moment Trask failed to connect, but then he remembered. "Harry's formula? For the Continuum?"

Liz nodded. "In his dreams, that's all he does. It's like a repetitive nightmare, like watching a computer screen processing an endless display of figures, fractions, decimals, algebraic equations and obscure mathematical symbols, and all of it scrolling and mutating down the screen of Jake's mind while he searches for that one all-important formula. But he can never find it . . ."

"And that's all he dreams about?"

"No," Liz shook her head. "Sometimes he dreams about that Russian girl—her dead face looking at him through the window of a car as it sinks into night-black water—and sometimes he . . . sometimes he dreams about me."

Trask shrugged (he hoped not negligently). "He, er, 'fancies' you, right?"

"No," Liz said again, perhaps ruefully. "He rejects me, as if I'm some kind of intrusion. He rejects everything, and he'll continue to do so until he's solved his own problems."

"Castellano and the mob," Trask said sourly.

"That's one of them."

"And the others?"

"One other, I think. But I don't know what it is. But I *do* know he's frustrated, and it would help—"

"Who isn't frustrated?" Trask cut in, becoming heated once more. But having gone this far, Liz wasn't about to be stopped.

"—It would *help,* if he knew everything and had access to *all* the Keogh files, or better still if you personally told him all you know about his . . . well, his condition."

For a long moment Trask was silent, and then he said, "And is that it, the lot?"

"That's it." And this time it was the truth. Or ninety percent of the truth, anyway. As for the other ten percent: that could be very personal, especially since she was in his dreams.

And after a moment Trask sighed and said, "Liz, I'm really sorry I blew up on you. You're not Jake's keeper, after all. It isn't your fault that he has 'problems.' And in a way it isn't his fault either. But believe me, I'm doing what I can to solve his problems, and I just wish we could get some mutual cooperation going, that's all. It's that important."

"I know it is," she said, standing up.

"Okay," he nodded, "you can go. If you see him before I do, please let him know I want to speak to him."

"I will," she said, and at the door turned and looked back. And yet again she was biting her lip. "Ben . . . ?"

"Eh?" He looked at her. So what was this about: the other ten percent, perhaps?

"I . . . I'm not sure about this," she said. "But when he's asleep and I'm in his mind, I get this weird feeling that someone's watching. I feel—I don't know—hooded eyes, burning on me. A strange image that retreats when I reach toward it."

Hooded eyes? Again? Trask remembered what Goodly had said. But this had to be different, surely. "Harry Keogh?" He took a stab at it. More than a stab, really, for to him it seemed perfectly obvious: some revenant of the ex-Necroscope was in there with Jake. But:

"No," Liz said. "I don't think it's Harry. I mean, I never knew him, but those who did always talk about his warmth. Well, this one isn't warm. This one's cold. Very."

"Maybe it's the other side of Jake," said Trask. "The dark side. The side that's lusting after revenge."

She looked relieved. "You think that's possible?"

"I'm no psychologist," he answered, "but I do know we have different levels of consciousness, and even when we're awake we don't always say what we're thinking. *Huh!* And personally, well, I don't always think what I'm saying—which, incidentally, is about as close as you'll get to a real apology! So, maybe those eyes are one of Jake's other levels, sensing an intruder."

"You're probably right," she said. "Because that's usually when his shields go up and I get driven out."

"And now you're out of here, too," Trask told her, and actually managed to smile. "Because I'm busy. But stick to it, Liz, stick to it. And next time don't hold back. You could have told me this stuff without all the agony."

"Except there wasn't anything to tell," she answered. "Not of any real importance."

"Even little things could be important." He forced himself to smile again. "You'd be surprised."

But a moment later, as soon as the door closed behind her, the smile slipped from his face.

Someone else in Jake's mind? Someone other than Harry? The teeming dead, perhaps? The Great Majority? But if so, why would their eyes be hooded? Because Liz was an intruder, and only the Necroscope Jake Cutter could be trusted with the secrets of the dead? Huh! *If* he could be trusted. But right now Trask wouldn't trust him as far as he could throw him.

What was Jake hiding that he had to carry on with this deception, pretending he was just another empty vessel again?

It was baffling, a mystery within a mystery.

And Trask had more than enough of those already . . .

3
Of The Present

FIFTEEN HUNDRED HOURS IN LONDON, BUT 1,400 miles to the east it was five in the afternoon, and the small Greek island of Krassos in the Aegean was coming awake from its siesta to the blazing heat of an El Niño evening. The last time it had been this dry was following a previous El Niño, the summer of '98. Then fires had swept across the Greek mainland no less than in the Philippines, Mexico, Florida, and South Western Australia. And the Greeks, along with everyone else, had learned from the experience.

Now, in every village and on every beach, there were warning signs in four languages, and apart from the native Greek it seemed likely that all the others read as badly as the English:

NO FIRES!
NO BARBEKU! SMOKERS:
PLEASE EXTINGUISH CIGARETE
BEFORE YOU THROWING AWAY!

But everyone got the message, and it gave the sun-scorched English tourists something to chuckle over other than the translations in the taverna bills of fare.

On the other hand, there was an item in the Greek newspapers that no one was chuckling over . . . especially not the Greek Islands Tourist Board in Athens. A woman's body had been washed ashore near the village of Limari. It couldn't as yet be called a murder, because the circumstances of her death were a mystery and her identity was unknown. The way she'd been found (the condition of the body, which had been in the sea for a week to ten days) left no clues as to what had befallen her. But there were several anomalies that at least suggested foul play: namely the fact that most of her face was missing, which included her upper teeth and entire lower jawbone. She wasn't going to be identified by use of any dental records, that much was certain. Of course, she could have been hit in the water by some boat's propeller, but how did she *get* in the water? Swimming? What, in the nude? There were nude beaches in the islands, true, but not on Krassos. Nor was the rest of her body intact; her nipples were gone (probably nibbled by crabs or fishes), her eyes were eaten away, and her ears had been shorn off close to the skull—accidentally or deliberately was similarly conjectural. And strangest of all, no one had been reported missing.

Detective Inspector Manolis Papastamos, an expert on Greek island life, lore, and legend, had come over by ferry from Kavála in answer to a request for help by the island's constabulary, which consisted of one fat old sergeant and four mainly untried village policemen. This kind of investigation fell well outside their scope on an island that was less than sixty miles around, where tourism—the sun, the sand, and the clear blue sea—was the principal industry. But tourism had been suffering for more than fifteen years now, and at a time when the drachma was only very shaky this sort of thing made for extremely bad publicity.

The body had been in cold storage for twenty-four hours by the time Papastamos and Eleni Barbouris, a forensic pathologist who had come over with him from Kavála, got to see it where it lay under a crisp white sheet and a light dusting of frost in a commandeered ice-cream chest in the back room of a whitewashed, bare-necessities police post at Limari.

Manolis Papastamos was small and slender, yet gave the impression of great inner strength. All sinew, suntan, and shiny-black, wavy hair, he was very Greek with one noticeable exception: in addition to the fierce passions of his homeland, he was also quick off the mark in his thinking, reflexes, and movements. In short there was nothing dilatory about him, and his mind was inquiring to a fault. In his mid-fifties, Manolis looked dapper in his charcoal-grey lightweight suit, white open-necked shirt, and grey shoes. And despite the weathered-leather look that was beginning to line his face, he was still handsome in the classical Greek arrangement of his features: his straight nose, high brow, flat cheeks, and rounded, slightly cleft chin.

Twenty-odd years ago he had been full of fire and zest—also ouzo, and Metaxa!—but then something had happened that changed him, turned his life around. He was a lot more serious now, far more studious and thoughtful. But if his hard-bitten, down-to-earth police colleagues in Athens knew what he studied, and what Manolis researched almost to obsession in what little spare time his duties allowed him . . . well, they might find it peculiar, to say the least.

"We should get her out of there, onto a table," Eleni Barbouris told him, after removing the sheet. "She's not so cold I can't cut. In fact the cold should help keep down the odours. You see the swollen abdomen, all bloated from immersion? There will be gasses . . ."

He knew what she meant. As a boy in Phaestos on Crete, he had seen a dead dolphin washed up on the beach. A large animal, seven feet long by four wide (because it was so badly swollen), it had been too heavy to move. Local firemen wanted to burn it, but they had thought it must be full of salt water, which would only hinder the burning. Best to let the water out first.

But then, when one of the men pierced the dolphin's belly with the pick end of his fireman's axe—

The creature literally exploded! With a great hissing, farting and shuddering—a veritable vibration of dead, rubbery flesh—the thing had split open like an overripe melon, showering every onlooker, including the young Manolis and his village friends, with a geyser of rotten vileness! The awful stench had seemed to last for days, and his mother hadn't been able to wash it out of his clothes . . .

"You'll perform an autopsy?" he said, backing off a pace.

"You've seen plenty of them before, I'm sure," Eleni answered. "Or is it that people don't die in peculiar circumstances in Athens?"

"This one's been in the water," Manolis said, and wrinkled his nose. "Gasses? I can do without gasses."

Eleni was about his age, but time and the work hadn't been kind to her. Her hair was greying and she seemed to have shrivelled down into herself. She was a small, pale woman, but still very capable, Manolis was sure. Moreover, he suspected that she wasn't nearly as cold or callous as she liked to pretend.

"I have gauze masks," she said. "Soaked in eau de cologne, or maybe ouzo, they'll dilute the smell. But they won't keep it out. Not entirely." Turning her head on one side, she looked at him quizzically. "On the other hand, you don't have to watch at all if you don't want to. A queasy stomach, perhaps?" There was no hint of humour in her voice; no sympathy, either.

So maybe it wasn't pretence and Eleni Barbouris really was cold and callous! "I'll stay," he told her, nodding. "But first let's invite the local boys to help us get her out of there . . ."

After the village policemen had left—and they wasted very little time in leaving—Eleni got down to it. First an external examination of the body. There was nothing to be done about the corpse's head, but if the damage to the ears and lower face was the work of a propeller, there was scant sign of any abrasions to the rest of the body. The neck was scarred on the left, where something had gouged a groove half an inch wide and quarter of an inch deep in the puffy flesh between the missing ear and the collarbone; this *might* have been caused by the blade of a propeller, but Eleni seemed dubious. The throat, however, was choked behind the missing mandible, probably with weed, and the pathologist started there, cutting the windpipe to lay it open in twin flaps above the clavicle.

Within the incision, near the top of the oesophagus, there was a dark mass that formed a solid blockage. Eleni prodded the mass with a rubber-clad finger, finding it resilient and spongy to the touch. It wasn't weed, and it wasn't a part of the human body—not unless it was some sort of grossly enlarged tumour.

Intrigued, she cut through the pectoral muscles to halfway down the chest and used an electrical surgical saw to separate the upper sternum from the ribs and detach it. And finally, she cut through the rest of the upper oesophagus, revealing more of the blockage. But still she hadn't exposed all of it.

Manolis had been watching all of this while doing his best to ignore the smell of death and decay that kept getting stronger all the time. Now, through ouzo-drenched gauze and the reek of aniseed and rottenness, he mumbled, "What in hell . . . is that?"

Looking back at him over the grotesque, somehow intimidating shield of her mask, Eleni's grey eyes were wide and uncertain. But then she shrugged and answered, "We won't know, until we get it out."

The object, whatever it might turn out to be, completely blocked the dead woman's gullet. It was grey blue, and corrugated like a concertinaed worm or slug. As for its texture: "It seems firm enough . . . *uh!*" Eleni grunted, digging her fingers in to expand the gullet, "that I don't think it's going to break up under pressure. Maybe I can get it out in one piece without more butchery." And without further ado she dragged the thing free, holding it up for Manolis's inspection.

He had backed off more yet, which was as well. For as with the dolphin in Phaestos, so now with this poor dead woman.

It was as if the pathologist had shaken a bottle of champagne and loosened the cork. But what had been released was anything but fine wine. Gasses and pus and mucus foamed out of the neck cavity, and disturbed by internal convulsions, a stream of yellow shit and gooey cadaverine spurted from the opposite end. The corpse seemed to writhe and flutter as it settled down into itself.

Manolis choked, "Good God!" and turned away. And: "I'll be back when I've been good and . . . and . . ." But he couldn't finish it. Open his mouth again and he'd be sick right there, not that that would spoil the looks of the room.

But in the toilets, throwing up, at least he had the dubious satisfaction of hearing Eleni doing the same in the ladies' cubicle next door . . .

"That rarely happens," she told him fifteen minutes later, when he came out of the toilet. "One gets used to such things. Maybe it was the sight of your face that did it, its colour and awful grimacing. Perhaps I . . . came out in sympathy?" She was hosing down the white marble floor, flushing the mess out through the front room of the police post into the street and down a drain.

Outside, there was no sign of the village policemen in the sun-bleached street, just two nuns of some obscure order, wearing cowled cassocks that covered them head to toe. The pair had paused in their strolling to stare, but in another moment their pale hands fluttered into view as they covered their faces with handkerchiefs before turning and hurrying away.

Manolis couldn't blame them. Still very drawn and pale himself, he said, "This place is going to stink forever!"

"No, no," Eleni answered. "Powerful antiseptics will clear it in no time. It will smell just like a hospital, that's all."

The corpse was amazingly clean, Manolis thought. Eleni had done a very good job. Well, better she than he! "Will you continue with the postmortem?"

"I can see no point," she answered. "I shall take a sample of the stomach contents, though of course they will have rotted down, degraded. But don't concern yourself. There's no need for you to be present, really. In any case I won't be able to complete an analysis until I'm on the mainland. So, if I may make a suggestion: why don't you go and have a drink?"

"No," said Manolis, "but I'll take you for one later. Meanwhile, what have you done with the . . . that thing?" He couldn't help the shudder that had crept into his voice, but hoped she'd think it was a late reaction to what had happened.

Manolis had caught only a glimpse of the thing in Eleni's hand before the interruption (or eruption) of the dead woman's body, but there had been something about it. Something that reminded him of a time more than twenty years ago when he'd been out in the islands—Ródhos, that time—on a different case. Different entirely from any other he'd ever handled or been involved with. That was when a group of men—and one very special man, who could not be denied—had told him about just such organisms as he had seen dangling from the pathologist's hand. Or perhaps not, for he had never seen one himself and couldn't be sure.

"The sea cucumber?" Eleni Barbouris was denying his morbid suspicions even now. "Well, that didn't kill her, if that's what you're thinking. It's under the sheet there."

"Sea cucumber?" Manolis frowned, but at the same time felt a great wash of relief flooding over him.

"A holothurian," she answered. "A cousin to the sea slugs. They normally live in holes in the rocks. This one crawled into a different hole and died there. It might even have battened on her—I don't know that much about them—but if it did, its own gluttony killed it. It got fat and stuck in her gullet."

The sheet, defrosted now and limp, lay on a small occasional table in a corner of the room. Two paces took Manolis to it, but he paused a moment before turning back the sheet. The thing lay there, lifeless, some fourteen inches long, blunt and spatulate at one end, tapered at the other.

It was like a blind, cobra-headed leech, its body corrugated or segmented, with rows of erectile hooks lying flat along its back and sides. Rooted in nodules at the base of the tapering neck, a frill of sticky, dew-beaded strings like the byssus threads of mussels lay limply on the glass top of the table.

Manolis took a ballpoint out of his pocket and lifted the tail. Protruding from a short tubular organ—an anus, or perhaps an ovipositor—a greyish, flaccid spheroid the size of a marble was half visible. It oozed a few droplets of a silvery, glistening liquid that slimed the glass.

"And that?" Manolis looked at Eleni where she had followed him to the small table.

She answered him with a shrug. "Some kind of sea mouse? I really can't say. Something the holothurian ate but didn't have time to digest?"

"A sea mouse?" Manolis said. "First sea cucumbers, now sea mice?"

And again her shrug, but a trifle impatient now. "An annelid, Aphroditidae, iridescent and quite pretty when alive. When I was a child, I was interested in every aspect of biology. But now I've put aside my childish interests and I'm a pathologist, *not* a marine biologist! What is it with you, Manolis—and why are you sweating?"

"I . . . still don't feel too good," he told her, which was true enough.

She'd taken off her elastic surgical gloves and now began to reach out her naked hand towards the organism on the table. "As for this thing, it's dead and smells, and it should be—"

"It should be burned!" Manolis said, and with a lightning-fast movement arrested her hand. "Don't touch that thing. Don't you *ever* touch anything like it!"

"What?" she stared at him in shocked astonishment.

He put her gently aside and said, "I may be wrong, and if so I apologise in advance, but I really don't think this is any kind of holothurian. I'll see to it that it's incinerated immediately."

Eleni continued to stare at him, following his every movement as he wrapped the organism in the sheet. "Not a holothurian? So what on earth do you think it is? And if it's in any way connected with this case—a clue to foul play or some such—why do you intend to burn it? What, you'll destroy evidence?"

"Our descriptions, from what we've seen, will suffice," he told her. "But one thing is for sure: I won't be letting anyone cut into *this* to see what made it tick! Just be happy that it's stopped ticking, that's all."

"You talk as if it's a bomb!" she answered. "But—"

"No buts," said Manolis. "You've done a good job here. Now I suggest we go back to Krassos town to our hotel, freshen up a little, and then eat at one of the excellent tavernas. The meal and that drink I promised you will be on me."

"Well," she shook her head in utter bewilderment. "I suppose you're in charge here, and—"

"Yes, I am," he was pleased to agree. "And now let's find those policemen. I want this body kept on ice—but deep frozen this time, perhaps in Krassos town. I have friends in London who may want to see it."

Holding his small white bundle at arm's length, he ushered her out of that place, and as they went said, "As for your alleged sea slug: you're right about evidence, of course. So we'll photograph it first—and *then* I'll burn it!"

Manolis was driving a small Fiat hired from one of the island's many tourist-oriented outlets. At about 7 P.M., driving in the shade of pine-clad mountains, he passed a stone-walled, gauntly impressive monastery built on a false plateau where high cliffs fell sheer to the sea. Concentrating on his driving upon the winding, contour-clinging road, he took no special note of a larger, heavier private vehicle where it indicated its driver's intention to pull out of the otherwise empty monastery car park. But as he sped by, Eleni Barbouris did notice it.

"On a tiny island like this," she commented, "someone desires yet more privacy."

"Umm?"

"That expensive car back there—the black one, with dark, one-way windows? They can see out, whoever they are, but no one sees in."

"There are plenty of cars like that in Athens," the inspector answered. "But you're correct: rich people do seem to enjoy their privacy more than most. Ah, but then, they can afford to! As for those windows: they're far superior to dark glasses when it comes to keeping the sun out of your eyes."

"I suppose so," she said. "But here on the eastern side of

Krassos, in the shade of these mountains and the gloomy evening light, they seem so unnecessary."

But Manolis, a frown etching his face, was scarcely listening to her. Instead, it was something *he* had said that continued to resonate in his mind. So that suddenly he found himself muttering, "When . . . when it comes to keeping the sun out, yes."

"Personally, I don't see nearly enough of it," she said.

"*What . . ."?* Manolis barked, startling her.

"The sun," she said. "I said I don't see nearly enough—" But then, as she glanced sideways at him, she saw that his eyes were fixed not on her but on his rearview mirror.

"Why, whatever is—?" she started to say, craning her neck to look back. Just a few feet behind, the other car was bearing down on them like some great blind snarling beast!

Manolis couldn't hit the brakes because the black car was immediately behind him. He couldn't accelerate because the road ahead made a sharp right turn and disappeared from view. On the right, a wall of rock where the road had been cut from the mountainside. And on the left . . . a sheer drop of a hundred or more feet to jutting rocks and the tideless sea. And no safety barrier between.

When the big car's horn blared, Manolis was trying to negotiate the bend. Centrifugal force sent his Fiat sliding across double white lines into the oncoming lane. Gritting his teeth, hauling desperately on the steering wheel, he gasped his relief when he saw that the road ahead was empty. But it made no difference. His car was out of control and skidding. Which was when the heavier vehicle, its horn still blaring continuously, slammed into the Fiat from behind.

The collision served to slow the big car down, whiplashed Manolis and his passenger, and sent the smaller vehicle rocketing out into empty space. And all of it happening that fast, as accidents usually do, so that human reactions and even thoughts are almost impossible. Except this wasn't an accident. And:

Well, I suppose it's goodbye to all that! Manolis did manage to think, quite calmly and uselessly. *And I don't even know why, or maybe I do. And where's my safety belt! Oh, shit!*

Eleni had just started screaming when the car hit a jutting outcrop, sliced through a clump of stunted, cliff-clinging heather, and struck something far more solid that sent it hurtling outwards again, spinning end over end.

And glimpsed through a crazily whirling pinwheel of stone and sky, the rocky base of the cliffs, washed by a slow-surging ocean, came rushing to meet them . . .

In London it was 9 P.M. and almost cool. In all the hotels the air-conditioning systems were running at full blast, and people were in the streets and the bars in their shirt-sleeves, enjoying the Indian-summer atmosphere. But for others there was work to be done.

At E-Branch HQ the work hadn't stopped, Trask's espers did their various things, but theirs was work with a difference. As for Trask himself: he was just about through for the day, looking forward to a drink and a good night's sleep. He would sleep at the HQ, which had been his habit for almost three years now. But waiting—*still* waiting—to see Lardis Lidesci and Jake, he'd found plenty to occupy his time. For where news, theories, or any information in general about the invaders from Starside was concerned, Trask's office door was always open.

Last of several people to come and see him was Millicent Cleary. Millie was a telepath and competent computer operator; she was also a member of E-Branch's master think tank, Trask's current affairs adviser, and one of his favourite people—the kid sister he'd never had. But she wasn't a kid anymore; none of the gang from the "good old days" was. Like Trask himself, they'd been here too long and E-Branch had aged them.

Such were his thoughts . . . just a second or so before she looked at him in a certain way that he recognized of old. And:

"If that was your idea of a compliment," she told him, "I don't think much of it. The kid sister bit's okay—I *think*—

but I can do without all those wrinkles you just gave me!"

Trask tut-tutted. "Oh, my! Here's Millie Cleary spying on the boss's thoughts."

She shook her head. "Not spying, just worrying about you. And incidentally, Ben, *I* neither look nor feel as old as I am, but *you* really do. And you're looking older day by day. That's why I worry about you—big brother!"

And in fact she didn't look as old as her years, which in any case were a good deal shorter than his. Millie would be in her late forties but looked five years younger. A very attractive blonde, her hair was cut in a fringe low over her forehead, flowed down onto her shoulders, and framed her oval face while partly concealing her small, delicate ears. Her eyes were blue under pencil-slim, golden eyebrows, and her nose was small and straight. Millie's teeth were very white, just a little uneven in a slightly crooked, frequently pensive mouth. Five feet and six inches tall, amply curved and slim-waisted, she had always made Trask feel big and strong, and sometimes clumsy. He liked her a lot—indeed, a great deal—and as far as he was concerned she was one of the few who could get away with murder.

But conscious of her talent, and channelling his thoughts anew—and wondering why he felt the need to—Trask got down to business. "So what's up?"

"I think I may have something," she told him. "You remember when you got back from Australia, you asked me to find out what I could about Jethro Manchester's financial affairs? Knowing that Malinari had coerced Manchester into some kind of, er, partnership, you were hoping that maybe cash transfers and other transactions might help track Malinari down? Well, as it turns out—and while Manchester may have been a big-time philanthropist—he wasn't *entirely* the big softy people think he was. And he certainly wasn't soft-headed." She paused to order her thoughts, and continued:

"So being, as you have often called me, 'a devious female creature,' it had crossed my mind that such might be the case. Let's face it, one doesn't get to be a billionaire without one has just a few extra cards up one's sleeve, right? So, just an hour or so ago, I had John Grieve call Manchester's accountant in Brisbane. That's Andrew Heyt, of Haggard, Haggard and Heyt, and—"

"You had him call who at what time?" Trask cut in, frowning as he did a quick mental calculation. "At six in the morning—Heyt's time, that is?"

"Deliberately, yes," Millie told him. "People are usually off guard at that time in the morning; that's why police carry out their raids in the early hours."

"And you were carrying out a raid on Manchester's accountant?"

"Exactly. Working on a hunch, so to speak. Anyway, without identifying himself, John asked Heyt a few leading questions—like: what would be happening now, to Manchester's 'hidden' deposits in Switzerland and other countries? And before Heyt could blink the sleep out of his eyes, get his mercenary little brain in gear, and slam the phone down—"

"John had done his thing," Trask nodded.

"Namely," she continued, "he read in Heyt's mind the facts of the matter, that apart from Jethro Manchester's regular accounts and holdings—stocks and shares and the like in various businesses in Australia, UK, and the USA—he also has several numbered accounts in Zurich."

"John got the numbers?"

Millie looked at Trask in that wide-eyed way of hers, innocent and shrewd at the same time, and said, "John's good, but not that good! I mean, what do you want, miracles?"

"Yes," he answered drily. "I'll accept nothing less. Okay, go on. I'm hooked."

"No, he didn't get the numbers," she answered, "but he did get the name of the bank: a branch of the rather obscure Bürger Finanz Gruppe, or Citizens Finance Group. In fact it's the only branch we were able to find, and I think if we were to dig just a little deeper we might well discover that it's owned—or *was* owned—by Manchester himself! His own little piggy bank, as it were. Anyway, as you know, seven years ago most of the world's countries, or their governments, were signatory to a convention that opened up their banking systems to scrutiny. This was supposed to spell doom for the world's crooked, high-finance speculators, and write finis on the money-laundering activities of the organized crime syndicates. It was *supposed* to, but didn't, mainly because several major players wouldn't sign up to it."

"I remember," Trask nodded. "Russia, China, Italy, Greece, oh, and one or two South American countries, naturally."

"*And* Switzerland!" she told him. "For in case you've forgotten, some of the big Swiss banks are still fighting off Second World War Jewish claims on massive sums of money that the Nazis stole and stashed away. As for Italy: well, the Italians didn't at all fancy the idea of opening up their Mafia-riddled banking systems to scrutiny. And Greece didn't have any cash worth arguing over! The Chinese weren't interested; indeed, in light of China's alleged 'lack of crime'—the fact that under its then regime merely socializing with international criminals was punishable by long terms in their infamous 'correction facilities'—they felt insulted! And then there were those South American countries you mentioned, which for obvious reasons wanted nothing at all to do with it. As for poor old Ma Russia: well, financially speaking the Russians didn't know—and still haven't discovered—which way's up . . ."

She paused again, and Trask noticed she was looking a little pensive.

"Go on," he urged her.

She shrugged and went on, but mainly on the defensive now. "The trouble is," she started slowly, "that I've always been an eager beaver, you know? Sort of rushing in where angels fear to tread? And this time I may have sailed too close to the wind."

"You're certainly full of cliches," Trask's eyes had narrowed. "And perhaps just a little of the other stuff, too?"

"Oh, I wouldn't try to, er, 'shit' *you,* Ben Trask," Millie said. "No, not you."

"So get on with it."

"Well," she shrugged, "I suppose that I really should have got authority before I, er . . ."

"Before you what?"

"Er, before I spoke to the Bürger Finanz Gruppe bank," she told him, and paused yet again.

Trask sighed and said, "This is like pulling teeth! So who did you, 'er,' speak to at the bank?"

"Not me, exactly," she answered. "I mean *I* didn't speak to anyone—or thing—at the bank. But I got our tame tech, Jimmy Harvey, to do it for me . . ."

And now things came together.

First the time: an hour ago in UK it was nine at night in Zurich. The banks would be closed. And Millie had said she didn't speak to anyone—or *thing*—but that Jimmy Harvey had done it for her. Harvey, a tech, one of E-Branch's whiz-kid communications and covert surveillance experts. The answer was obvious.

"You got Jimmy to hack into the bank's computer?" Trask's question was more an accusation, and his stare was penetrating.

Still looking innocent, but not, Millie tried to shrug but her shoulders weren't working. "The work of five minutes," she said nervously. "Enough time to get in, get Manchester's file, download a few details—like all deposits and withdrawals for the last five years—and get out again."

"A criminal act," Trask told her bleakly. "But more especially so if it served no purpose except to get me in trouble!"

"But it did serve a purpose."

"What did you get?"

"We got that someone had transferred a large sum—namely three quarters of a million dollars US—from one of Manchester's accounts just twenty-four hours *after* he died."

"You're forgiven!" Trask said, suddenly excited. "If these were numbered, personal accounts, no one but Manchester himself—or a 'partner'—could touch them. And we had made sure that news of the 'tragic accident' at his retreat wouldn't break until after our Australian friends had sanitized the mess on that island. So even Haggard, Haggard and Heyt wouldn't have had any reason to be interested in those numbered accounts just twenty-four hours after Manchester died. And even if they had it's unlikely they'd have the authority to move large sums of his ill-gotten gains around . . . is it?"

"No, it isn't."

"So, I think you're probably right and this was Malinari's work. And—"

"But it didn't have to be," she cut in.

Trask's face fell. But then he looked at her suspiciously, frowningly, and said, "Go on."

"Well, it could have been a payment to one of Manchester's beneficiaries, I mean, one of the many charities he gave to."

"What, after he was dead?"

"A standing order, maybe?" she answered. "I mean, it could have been in the computer, waiting to automatically click in on a certain date."

Trask shook his head. "Millie," he said, "you're a devious female creature. What you just said wasn't a lie, but it wasn't the truth, either. It was a 'what if?' Now, I know you wouldn't pick me up just to drop me again, so for whatever reason you've got to be teasing me. Well, believe me this is neither the time nor the place. So without more ado, let's have the rest of it—or is this perhaps one of your stumbling blocks?"

"It could have been," she answered. "For you see, the transfer *was* made to a charity."

Trask's face fell further yet. "Say again?"

"To charity number nineteen, of nineteen numbered charities," she nodded.

"No name or names?"

"Er, no," Millie shook her head. "Not of the charity. Just numbers. It was the fifth semiannual payment to a charity that Manchester had been supporting for two years."

"So what's our interest in it?" Trask knew the punch line

was coming. He read it in her face: that indeed she'd got something. But what?

"I've got the big one!" Millie had read his mind, literally. "That's what I've got."

"Do I have to say please?" he said.

She shook her head again. "No, but there are still stumbling blocks. So what do you want first, the good news or the bad news?"

"The good," he said.

"The previous payments to charity number nineteen were all in the sum of a quarter million dollars, all of them authorized by telephone by Manchester using his PIN and various authentication codes. Ah, but *this* transfer tripled that amount, and of course it wasn't Manchester's PIN but his partner's. It's dated the day after Manchester died—and the *name* of the partner is on Jimmy Harvey's printout."

All of this time she had been clasping a roll of printout. Now she stepped around Trask's desk to stand beside him, leaned over him and opened up the roll, and weighted it top and bottom with desk bric-a-brac. Trask saw that it was page fifteen, torn from a far larger printout. But then his eyes skipped to a serial that had been highlighted in yellow.

The details of date, time, and amount, were all as Millie had reported them, but Trask scarcely noticed them beside the one item that seemed to leap at him from the paper: the name in the authorization column . . . Aristotle Milan! Malinari's pseudonym!

And as that hated name burned itself into his brain, Millie said: "It's the first time in two years that Malinari has given himself away like this. Other times when he's used Manchester's account, he's had Manchester himself authorize it. This time he had no choice because his 'partner' was dead."

Trask felt galvanized. In his excitement he had started to his feet. He stared at the printout, glared at it, unwilling to take his eyes off the paper in case it should disappear. It was the best lead yet . . . possibly as good as the one that had sent him out to Australia. But—

"The extra money," he said, frowning, "or maybe all of

it, is obviously for his use while he gets himself set up again. So why didn't he take more?"

"Maybe he doesn't think he needs more," she said. "Perhaps he didn't want to alarm the bank. I can't say. But don't forget the extraps: our three years are up—you said so yourself—and things could be coming to a head. Maybe money won't be important in the world that Malinari and the others are planning."

"But we trampled on at least a third of those plans out in Australia!" Trask protested.

She nodded. "So now maybe they're going to speed things up a little. For as you also pointed out during your pep talk, the Wamphyri know for sure now that we're after them . . ."

Feeling tired, Trask sat down again. His mind was finding it hard to take in everything that Millie was telling him; the picture wouldn't firm up until the last piece was in place and he could scan the whole thing. And so: "Okay, now you can tell me the bad news," he said, angling his head to look up at her.

"Another one of those stumbling blocks I mentioned," Millie said.

"Like what?"

"Well, like I said—the charity is just a number: number nineteen of nineteen charities. There has to be a separate file that details exactly who, what, and where this charity is, but Jimmy didn't have the time he would need to hack into any more files. Let's face it, there could be thousands of them!"

"He didn't have the time?" Trask was astonished. "What are we paying him for? He could *make* time!"

Millie was looking uncomfortable again. "No, you don't understand," she said. "The bank's computer was programmed with a whole bag of countermeasures. Jimmy worked wonders but he could override them for only so long before getting locked out." She shrugged helplessly. "So that even if you'd sanction it—"

"Which I would—which I *do*—almost anything!"

"—We can't get back in. Er, and that's not all."

"Their system has probably backtracked us down!" Trask

got there first. "And there'll almost certainly be an official protest. Which means tomorrow morning, bright and early, I'll have our Minister Responsible bleating at me on the blower!"

"And I know that when you get bleated at, we can expect to get it in the neck, too," she said.

"Hence all of the shilly-shallying," Trask growled at her, "when you could have come straight to the point and maybe saved us a little time."

"But I wanted you to see how clever I was," she said, "and appreciate me for it. Which might take some of the sting out of it when you get around to shouting at me."

"Do I do too much of that?" Trask asked her, and shook his head, promising, "No shouting. Why, if I were ten years younger I might even try to kiss you!"

"What's age got to do with it?" she said. "You're as young as you feel, or as someone can make you feel."

Trask knew a different version of that, which went: "You're as young as the one you're feeling," but he didn't say so. Suddenly he was very aware of Millie's perfume where she was standing close beside him.

But as if she'd read his mind—and perhaps she had—she went back around to the front of his desk and stood there looking at him in that way of hers. One of her ways, anyway.

"Er, you said stumbling blocks," Trask said, bringing his thoughts to order. "More than the ones you've mentioned, presumably. Okay, I can see one such: we don't know where the money went, which is where Malinari is. But we're talking about three quarters of a million dollars here. Surely we can trace it?"

"We tried," Millie told him. "That international convention I mentioned? No problem; any major signatory can gain entry to the database. With our security rating Jimmy simply accessed it, went in, and took a look."

"And?"

"Would you believe that on that date about that time there were more than twenty movements of that precise number of dollars left, right, and centre around the world? Well, there were, but not one was destined for charities real or contrived."

Trask understood what she was saying. "Manchester's money went to a nonsignatory country, which is to say Italy, Greece, China, Russia, or one of those South American places."

"Or Switzerland itself," she reminded him again.

By now Trask's mind had sorted itself out. He was thinking again, and doing an excellent job of it. "That makes for a hell of a lot of places where Malinari could be," he said. "The way I see it, this so-called charity can only be one of his friends from Starside. When they came into this world they split up. He ended up in Australia, but where did the others go? Well wherever, he now needs a safe haven and has fled to one of them. And why not, since he's been subsidizing that one—let's continue to call it a 'charity'—for the last two years. Okay, we know where he *hasn't* gone: to one of the signatory countries. So now let's see if we can eliminate some of the places where he *might* have gone."

"I'm with you," she answered.

Trask waved her to a chair and told her: "Millie, sit down for God's sake . . . or mine, at least! It's nine-thirty at night and you're still mobile. You're tiring me out, little sister."

"Funny," she said, seating herself and crossing her pretty legs, "but I thought I'd woken you up! Anyway, let's do some of this eliminating."

"You're way ahead of me, right?" he said. "Okay, go on."

"Well," she began, "for five years now—ever since Hong Kong's third big financial collapse—China has hidden herself away behind a bamboo curtain, convinced that the decadent, capitalist West is deliberately trying to destabilize her. And now they have this plague to contend with, a new bubonic strain running rampant through China and spreading west, which they haven't the resources to combat. Also, what with their current disinclination toward foreign types in their country, especially rich foreigners, but including diplomats and aid agencies, well they're not the most friendly of people. In short, there aren't too many Westerners retiring to

Beijing these days! And I don't think Malinari would go there either."

"Strike China," said Trask. "And probably Russia, too. Oh, Malinari's dollars would be welcome there, for sure, but I have it on good authority that *he* wouldn't be. Gustav Turchin is the new head of the Opposition, and I've already alerted him to the threat."

"Which leaves Italy, Greece, Switzerland, and South America," she said.

"Of which I fancy Switzerland," Trask nodded. "Or perhaps South America?" Concentration lined his face. "Switzerland has high mountains and it's cold. Quite appealing, I should think, to someone—or some*thing*—from Starside."

"Not necessarily," Millie answered. "I read your preliminary report on the Aussie job, and I was at your pep talk. You make a point of saying that Malinari was where we would least expect to find him. So why not the others? Personally, I would think that the most Switzerland has going for it is its neutrality, its autonomy, and the fact that it welcomes people with lots of money. But Greece and Italy aren't dismissive of high rollers either."

"This gets us nowhere fast," Trask stood up. "Or should I say somewhere slowly? Whichever, it's given me a headache. And it's way past drinkies time. Also, I haven't eaten yet. You?"

"I'm trying to watch my figure," she said. "But—"

"It looks fine to me," he told her uncharacteristically. So uncharacteristically that he could bite his tongue off.

"*—But,*" she continued, "if you insist?"

"I do."

Millie smiled and said, "Our first date!"

And as Trask put on a tie and shrugged into his jacket, he found himself wondering, *Just how long have I been going blind, anyway?*

For the "truth" of something had suddenly become astonishingly clear to him—which made him also wonder how long she'd been hiding it from him.

Three years, maybe? Long enough for him to recover? Millie was thoughtful that way. The only trouble was that Trask didn't think he'd recovered yet.

Not yet, no . . .

4
Of Strange Places, Survivals, and Superstitions

THE TERM "E-BRANCH" WASN'T KNOWN TO THE staff of the hotel downstairs; to them, the upper floor was the headquarters of a firm of multifaceted international entrepreneurs, whatever that was supposed to mean. But Trask and his upper echelon *were* known to them, especially to the head waiter of the excellent restaurant and carvery: the peculiar hours that the "upstairs people" were wont to work—and at which they occasionally dined—sometimes made for problems in the kitchen. Such as tonight. The hour was late and the kitchen had been busy all day.

Trask and Millie took a table in a spot favoured by Branch personnel: a slightly elevated alcove surrounded by small palms in half-barrels, and varnished pine trelliswork interwoven with imitation clematis and bougainvillaea. Sufficiently remote from the rest of the restaurant, it was considered safe to talk business here; but to be absolutely certain, Jimmy Harvey or one of the other techs would eat here now and then and check the place for bugs . . . the electrical variety. To date, they hadn't discovered any.

Seating his companion and then himself, Trask reached for a pitcher and poured water into two glasses. He would have preferred to get straight back to their conversation, but decided to wait until they had ordered. The short walk to the elevator and the ride down had provided an ideal opportunity to get the blood flowing to his brain again and process Millie's information; he felt more able to concentrate; his weariness, more mental than physical, was lifting moment by moment.

Which made him wonder out loud:

"That office of mine. I sometimes feel isolated in there. Is it my imagination, do you think, or has it got smaller over the years?"

"The whole world is smaller," Millie answered. "A touch of claustrophobia, maybe?"

Trask shook his head. "I've been down in the Perchorsk Complex under the Urals, the site of the Russian Gate. I *know* what claustrophobia is! If you ever get the chance to see that place—which I hope you never do—you'll see what I mean. No, it's not claustrophobia, nothing physical, anyway. Though certainly I *sense* things closing in on me . . . or on us." His sigh, involuntary though it was, gave a lot away.

"You're carrying a lot of weight," she said. "Stressed out, and no way to relieve the tension."

"You'd think that being an empath of a sort," he answered, "I'd be able to figure that out for myself."

"Knowing it is one thing," she told him. "But admitting it is something else. Once you admit it you can do something about fixing it. There are ways to let off steam, I'm told."

He looked at her—really looked at her—and said, "You were never married, were you, Millie?"

Now it was her turn to sigh. "That's one of the ways," she said. And: "No, I never was. But you've known me almost as long as I've known me, so you know that. *And* you know why."

He nodded and said, "These so-called 'talents' of ours, of course. It's the same for quite a few of us. Ian Goodly because he wouldn't want to know in advance how things would work out—between himself and a woman, I mean—and he certainly wouldn't want to know when harm was coming her way and there was nothing he could do to avoid it! The future, as he's frequently wont to remind us, is a devious place."

"And so are other people's minds," Millie said. "I've been out with men, dated men, and behind the smiles all they've been worried about is how much my meal and the wine was costing, and what they'd get back for their investment. I've bedded men—oh yes, a few—who were mainly concerned about the size of their own egos."

"Only their egos?"

And Millie shrugged. "That, too," she said. "It seems that male egos and you-know-whats go hand in hand, er, and no double entendre intended! Oh yes, I know: that if I *didn't* know things would be easier. But if I see a certain look in someone's eyes, or maybe detect a certain tone of voice, then I've just got to know what's going on in there. The temptation is irresistible. Any telepath who tells you different is a liar. We may not want to look, but we just can't help ourselves."

"I know," Trask told her ruefully. "I have problems of my own, remember?"

"That thing of yours must be a real killer," she said. "I mean, everybody has their little secrets. But the one you love really shouldn't have. So how do you avoid getting hurt when a special someone slips up and tells you a lie, even a white lie, or simply covers up for something he or she promised and forgot to do, or—"

"Or, or, or," said Trask. "Precisely. But I've learned to differentiate between innocent and deliberate deceit. There are degrees of truth, you know? But yes, I know what you mean. It's never easy."

"And yet you were married, and to a telepath at that."

Trask thought about that, and for the first time in a long time found himself able to talk about Zek. "She never lied," he said. "If she couldn't tell me the truth she said nothing."

"But she could read *your* mind."

Trask nodded. "Funnily enough, she never read anything she thought shouldn't be in there. That's what she told me, and I'm the one who would know it if she . . . if she didn't mean it."

"Neither have I," Millie said. "Read anything in your mind that shouldn't be there, I mean."

"Am I that innocent?"

"No, you're just straight. It's the other side of your talent, Ben. You give what you expect to get."

"Maybe it's just that I'm careful where telepaths are concerned," he said.

"And maybe you shouldn't be," Millie answered. "I'm a big girl. I could stand the occasional shock, I think."

Then the waiter came . . .

Everything was off except room-service fare; if Trask was anyone but Trask, they wouldn't get served at all. "A little ham, mustard, sliced tomatoes, lettuce, and some fresh white bread," he told the portly, fussy, pseudo-Italian waiter. "White wine for the lady and a large Wild Turkey for me, on the rocks. But do please remember, Mario: the ice is for cooling it down, not for diluting it."

"Of course, sir," and then they were on their own again.

"That Swiss bank has a list of these so-called charities," Trask said. "They know who, or at least where, that money went to. Of course they do because they sent it."

"But getting it out of them could take time," she said.

"Probably more time than we've got."

"Even if we told them Manchester's death was suspicious?"

"They'd freeze his accounts," Trask said. "Now that they know he's dead they've probably already done so, but even with the Minister Responsible on the case I can't see them giving in too easy. Why, they might even see it as their 'duty' to inform the charity that it's under investigation—especially since Mr. Milan is/was Manchester's 'bona fide' partner! And knowing that Jimmy Harvey has been into their files, they may even have done *that* already, too . . . or first thing in the morning, when their computer starts telling tales on us."

"And that's my fault," she said, looking downcast. "Fools rush in, and like that. So maybe you should speak to the Minister Responsible tonight?"

"That's not a should but a must," Trask said. "I'll do it

when we've eaten. Maybe he can pull some strings, do something we haven't thought of."

"It makes me wish I were a bank robber!" she said.

"Well, you've made a very good start to your new career!" Trask told her without a trace of humour. "Damn it all, but if we had Jake Cutter up and running we wouldn't *need* to break in. He could simply . . . well, *go* there, take Jimmy Harvey with him, be in and out like a couple of ghosts, and to hell with all the Bürger Finanz Gruppe's gadgets!"

She looked at him. "So that stuff I've been hearing about Jake—the stuff you left out of your initial report—is for real? He really did do his thing out there in Australia?"

"If he hadn't," Trask answered, "you'd be talking to yourself right now. And incidentally, since I hadn't planned on making it general knowledge until he had it down pat, until it was routine, where did you 'hear' about it anyway?" He already knew the answer to that one.

Millie nodded. "I am what I am," she said, and fell silent while their meal was delivered . . .

But while they ate:

"Something else you mentioned during your pep talk," Millie said. "That you were pretty sure Malinari had fled from Australia. I accept that because you say so—also because we know his 'charity' isn't in Australia—but what made you so sure?"

"We saw Malinari in Xanadu," Trask told her, "Manchester's casino resort in the mountains. But 'saw' is probably the wrong word for it: rather, we glimpsed him as he passed overhead. But you can't know what it's like, Millie, until you've seen it for yourself. A man shape, yes, but only roughly. A bat, an aerial manta, a pterosaur—any of those things, or all of them. It's a fearful concept in its own right: that the Wamphyri have such power over their flesh. They're metamorphs, shapechangers. And we're just men and women, merely human . . .

"Anyway, he 'spoke' to us. To me mainly, but since I'm not a telepath he really drove his message home, had to in order to get it through my thick skull. He spoke of us meeting again, in a different place, a different country. Myself, I only felt the threat, but Liz Merrick got a deal more. Malinari was there and he was gone—it was over in a flash—but Liz received various impressions. He would go to one of his former colleagues, Vavara or Szwart, and lair with her or him while starting afresh."

"You said 'various' impressions," Millie said. "Like what, for instance? What *else,* I mean?"

"Opposites," Trask answered. "Like light and dark: a burst of sunlight on the one hand, and midnight in a mineshaft on the other."

"In other words like Vavara and Szwart themselves," Millie said, and nodded. "Vavara the gleaming jewel, albeit evil, and Szwart the heart of darkness, the Lord of Night."

"Maybe," Trask shrugged. "But it was fast, as I told you, and Liz is still thinking it through, trying to remember exactly what she saw in that monster's mind before he shut her out."

"Hmmm!" said Millie, and: "I think perhaps I'm jealous. In all these years you never sent me—or took me—on *any* field assignments! So maybe this kid-sister status of mine isn't getting me very far."

No, but it is keeping you safe, Trask thought—and hoped she wasn't listening . . .

They had finished eating, were almost ready to leave, when Lardis Lidesci joined them at their table.

"Been looking for you," he grunted at Trask, and sat down. "They said you wanted to see me."

"If you'd been a little earlier you could have eaten with us," Trask told him. And then, remembering that he was supposed to be angry: "And anyway, where the hell have you been? No, let me guess . . . you've been out with Jake Cutter, right?"

"Jake's not bad company," Lardis answered, momentarily surprised by Trask's tone. But then he recovered and snapped, "*And* he doesn't shout at me! What's more, it seems to me he's as out of place here as I am! So what else can I tell you?"

Lardis was Szgany: a Sunsider, a Traveller, a Gypsy. These terms all meant much the same thing, but he was a Gypsy from an alien parallel dimension, the vampire world of Sunside/Starside—homeworld of the Wamphyri!

He was shortish, maybe five foot six or seven, barrel-bodied, and almost apelike in the length of his powerful arms. His lank black hair, beginning to grey, framed a leathery, weather-beaten face with a flattened nose that sat uncomfortably over a mouth that was missing too many teeth. As for the ones that remained: they were uneven and as stained as old ivory. But under shaggy eyebrows his dark-brown eyes glittered his mind's agility, denying the encroaching infirmities of his body.

Seeming to jingle when he walked—clearly a Gypsy, even in jeans, a modern shirt, and Western boots, and perhaps especially in the latter—still there was something about the Old Lidesci that commanded respect. Rightly so, for Lardis had been a leader of his people for a very long time; he would be again, when things were put right in Sunside. *If* things were put right in Sunside . . .

"Huh!" Trask grunted. "First Millie, and now you. It seems I've been shouting all day long!"

Lardis shrugged and said, "Don't apol—er, apolo—er . . ."

"Apologize," said Millie.

"That's right!" said Lardis, who still wasn't too comfortable with the language. "It's inact-, er, inac*tivity*—that's all. I feel it, too. But my being here isn't anyone's fault, so I've no right to be shouting either. Indeed, I should be grateful, if only for Lissa's sake. *Huh!*—but she frets, too! About what might or mightn't be happening in Sunside."

"But it's almost ten at night," Trask said. "And I've been wanting to talk to you all day."

"You should have let me know!" said the other. "You can't expect me to just wander round looking for something useful to do. I saw my name on one of your pieces of paper on the notice board; at least I've learned to read that much!

I thought someone was sure to tell me if it was important. I wasn't about to show my ignorance by asking. No one mentioned it, so I figured it didn't matter. As for where we've been: we were in the park, the British Museum, the cinema!"

"The cinema?" Trask shook his head in disbelief. "Watching a movie with Jake?" And angrily: "Then *he* should have told you—except he probably doesn't go much on reading orders either!"

"With Lissa and with Jake Cutter, aye," Lardis nodded his grizzly head. "Lissa and I, we've been here three of your years, Ben Trask, one hundred and fifty Sunside sunups, and never been to a cinema! Anyway, I enjoyed it. A classic, Jake says, that's doing the rounds again, whatever that means. Anyway, it's about a ship that sinks and drowns a lot of people. The story's true, but some of the people were imag-, er, imag-?"

"Imaginary?" Trask helped him out.

"Aye, that's it. The imaginary hero dies in the cold after saving his beloved. Now I ask you, what kind of a story is that, where after all his troubles the hero sinks into the cold, cold water? *Huh!* It made my Lissa cry!"

"Titanic," said Trask, wearily now.

"That's it!" said Lardis. And after a moment: "So, why did you want to see me? And what is it that's annoying you so?"

An innocent, Trask thought. *No, a barbarian. A larger than life roughneck illegal immigrant from a parallel dimension. And yet an innocent, too. For no blame attaches to Lardis Lidesci.*

While out loud:

"I had a meeting, a talk with everyone this afternoon," he answered. "Everyone except you, that is. Timings were posted. I had hoped you would be there, so that I could speak to you when I'd finished with the others. We haven't had time to talk about that Greek job I sent you on. And you're quite right—I should have ensured that you were told, or told you personally. But in any case I'm sure that if you had found anything suspicious you would have reported it by now."

"The Greek thing you sent me on?" Lardis said. "I think it was what you would call, er, routine? Anyway, wasn't it you who called me off it? You sent for me, brought me out to Australia. And I'm glad you did. I wouldn't have missed the action for the world—for *anyone's* world, that is! *Hah!* But Greece? Too damn hot for my liking. And those Travelling folk weren't much to my liking either." He frowned, and his bushy eyebrows tangled over his nose.

"It's time I heard all about it," Trask told him. "But not here. Mario is getting ready to shut up shop, so we'll go up to my office. I can offer you a glass of brandy to settle you down for the night. What do you say?"

"I say it's a deal," said Lardis, smacking his lips. "That stuff of yours has a lot more kick than anything we ever brewed on Sunside, that's for sure!"

When they stood up, neither man noticed that Millie Cleary was looking just a little disappointed. Her plans for the night—or at least her hopes—had just flown out the window.

But there was always tomorrow . . .

Lardis sprawled in a chair in Trask's office. Nursing his brandy in its bowl, he stretched his stumpy legs, sighed his pleasure, and said, "It's good stuff. I can't taste the little green plums, but there's something in there that bites!"

"Not plums," Trask shook his head. "Grapes . . . I think."

"You don't know?"

"There are plenty of things I don't know," Trask answered. "Your world's a lot simpler than mine. That is, there's a great deal less to know." Which in a way was true, and in others not. "Anyway, tell me about that Greek job."

The "Greek job" was something he had sent Lardis on mainly to give him something to do. The Old Lidesci had not been exaggerating about the inactivity; he was seriously missing the ebb and flow of life—and the ever-present threat of death, or undeath—on Sunside/Starside. Lardis knew that even with Nathan fighting the war there, still it must be a terrible war for Sunside's Szgany. For Necroscope that Nathan Kiklu was—messenger of the dead and master of the metaphysical Möbius Continuum—still one man couldn't be everywhere at once. The Wamphyri were raiding on Sunside again as of old, and Lardis felt guilty that he wasn't there to lead his people in the fighting, not even in an advisory capacity.

But Nathan had offered to bring him and Lissa to safety in Ben Trask's world, and Lissa would hear no argument against it. "Old man," she'd told Lardis, "this fighting is for the young ones. It's for them to learn the way. For if you do it for them again, now, then who among them will know how to do it when you are gone? Trial and error taught you—and an amount of skill, I'll grant you, and some luck—but your legs can't run so fast these days, and your lungs are like bellows with holes in them. So come with me and Nathan now, and no more swearing and stamping your feet, or I'm off to find a younger, more agreeable man in the world beyond the Gate."

Her threat had meant nothing; her love meant everything in the world—in *two* worlds—to Lardis. And he'd known that she was right. His fighting days were over and younger men must now shoulder that burden. And who better than the Necroscope Nathan Kiklu, called Keogh in this world? But at least here in Trask's world Lardis could continue his fight against the Wamphyri, and not only in an advisory capacity. He and his trusty machete had been of indispensable use out in Australia . . .

But before Australia, when Trask had sent Lardis out to the Greek mainland, it wasn't simply a wild-goose chase, a subterfuge to keep him employed. There had been legitimate reasons, too.

Ever since the covert "invasion" of the Wamphyri, E-Branch had been on the lookout for signs of vampire infestations. Millie Cleary—nicknamed "Current Affairs" by her esper colleagues, and sometimes "the Reference Library," because she had the ability to log all sorts of mundane, day-to-day minutiae in her extraordinary brain—had been the one to bring a certain item of interest to Trask's attention.

Commuting in to the HQ on the tube one morning (one of the few lines still operating after the system's almost total collapse following the Great Flood of 2007), Millie had chanced to pick up a discarded copy of one of the more sensationalist newspapers. This was scarcely Reuters-quality reporting—it wasn't the sort of thing that Trask's sources would bring automatically to his notice—but a page-four headline had caught Millie's eye:

Vampires!—Folklore or Fact?

Also, there had been a picture of a girl with silver coins stuck to her eyelids, being lowered into her grave in a coffin somewhere in Greece . . .

But the story had been oddly atypical in this kind of publication; not at all lurid or sensational (certainly not in Millie's eyes, with her E-Branch background and inside knowledge), but a straightforward steal or direct transcript from an original Greek newspaper report, done without recourse to this dubious rag's usually hysterical attempts at dramatization.

The story had been simple: a band of Gypsies had wandered down from Hungary on some pilgrimage or other, and one of their young womenfolk had taken sick. Diagnosed with anaemia, she had been hospitalized in Kavála—until her menfolk had taken her by force out of the hospital before leaving the area! Traced to a nearby village, Skotousa, which lay on their route north, the band were then discovered in the act of burying the girl, as in the picture. Since there was no evidence of foul play, the local police had been reluctant to interfere with the ceremony.

A day or so later, pathologists at the hospital in Kavála had decided that since the cause of death was suspected but not known for sure, the body must be examined, the death registered, and a certificate issued. The doctors were of course simply covering for themselves and their hospital.

But when the grave in Skotousa was opened . . . the girl was found with a grimace on her face, burns on her eyelids—and a stake through her heart! Someone (if not one of her own band of Travelling folk, someone else) had obviously seen her as a dire threat to the local community. A vampire, of course . . .

Trask hadn't been too much impressed. He knew from experience that old myths and practices die hard in the Mediterranean islands and the Balkans, and these people were after all Travelling folk, Gypsies, with ancestral memories that went back centuries. Also, and for various reasons (mainly financial), Gypsies weren't the only ones who "believed" in vampires. Filmmakers in Hollywood were soon to release three new vampire movies, including yet another *Dracula;* the so-called vampire fad in popular fiction was still filling more than its fair share of shelf space in the bookshops; the Downliners Sect, a cult London rock group resurgent from the late '70s, were at number three in the charts with a grotesquery titled "Somethin's Up That Should Be Down" . . . ad infinitum.

As for "Somethin's Up": Millie had even caught herself singing the words from time to time:

> *Hey, man, look what's walkin' round.*
> *Somethin's up that won't stay down.*
> *Somethin's up from the rotten ground.*
> *—Time we all got outta town.*
> *Outta town. Get outta town . . .*

"Thus for a world that in the main *doesn't* really believe in the vampire," Trask had responded, "we appear to be doing a damn good job of promoting the fiend!"

And, much like the Head of Branch, the Old Lidesci hadn't been too impressed with Millie's find either. "Travelling folk, you say?" he'd queried Trask when the subject was broached. "Do you mean like those original Travellers—Szgany from Sunside—that you once told me about? Those misbegotten, fleabitten Wamphyri supplicants, banished through the Starside Gate with their vampire masters two thousand years ago? Aye, it could be them—their descendants, that is. But then again, *most* of the Gypsies of your world are Szgany descendants, all of them with the true Traveller blood, that is. Not that there was much of good blood in any accursed supplicant tribe that I ever heard of—*huh!*"

"Which is why I want to send you out there," Trask had answered. "You and a locator, and a couple of minders to make sure no harm befalls. I need to know that this burial ritual is *just* a ritual, something that has come down the centuries. I mean, I know that in some of the Greek islands, the Balkans, and especially Romania, even today they bury people who die in suspicious circumstances with silver coins on their eyes . . . presumably to keep them closed! Just in case, you know? But this stake thing is something else. We *know* what that's all about. So who suspected this poor girl, and why? And was it just superstition, or what?"

And so it had been Lardis's task—because he was a Gypsy himself, and with any luck would be acceptable to the Hungarian band—to fly to Greece and find out.

And now, finally, the Old Lidesci told his story. . .

"We got into Kavála in the early evening, just as the sun was failing. There was myself, Bernie Fletcher, and that burly pair of likely lad minders you found for us" (Special Branch men on loan from Whitehall's Corridors of Power, courtesy of the Minister Responsible). "We took a taxi—a short drive of just a few miles—into Keramoti on the coast where we could eat and hire a car. Bernie got the car while the minders and I ate at a taverna on the seafront.

"But the sea, Ben, the sea! Even with the sun going down—no, *especially* with the sunset—I never saw such a sight in my entire life! That incredible blue, like some vast mirror of the sky, turning darker as night drew on. It made me realize what I was missing—tied down in London, I mean—to see that wonderful ocean all curved on its horizon. You must use me more; send me out into the world so that

I can see it all. Ah, the stories I'll take back with me to Sunside one day!

"Where was I? Ah yes: Kavála, and Keramoti.

"We didn't go to the local police. Bernie thought it would only complicate matters. We were, after all, only 'tourists' and chances were they wouldn't care for us interfering in their business. Worse, they might want to know what was our business! And anyway, Bernie wanted to show off his skills.

"He got out his maps on the table where we'd eaten, picked a route to Skotousa. And:

" 'I have a feeling that that's the way they went,' he said, 'from Kavála to Skotousa. So we'll take the same route, see if I can get the feel of them.'

"And we did. Me, I kept wanting to tell him he was driving on the wrong side of the road, but of course I was wrong. They drive on the right in Greece! I can't see why you people don't choose a system and stick to it! Likewise your languages. What, a hundred or more different tongues, with as many and more dialects? No wonder you've been plagued with so many wars, nation against nation. In Sunside we have just the one tongue: Szgany! No chance of errors in transla-, er, translation. And no roads at all, just leafy tracks through the cover of the woods.

"But I'll tell you something: that Greek tongue has a damn sight more in common with mine than yours does. Why, in no time at all I could understand almost everything they were saying!

"Skotousa was some seventy-five miles; by the time we were there the sun was down and the light was going fast. I'll never get over your sunsets . . . you can actually *see* it going, especially in Brisbane, Australia. Bang—and it's gone!

"Anyway, in Skotousa:

"Lodgings weren't difficult. We stayed at an inn, and that night went down into the bar. I had changed into Sunside clothing for comfort's sake, but it wasn't all that far removed from the way some of the locals were dressed. Farmers and such, they came in for their ouzo and Metaxa, or just to cool off from the day's work in all that terrible heat. They sat under those big, slow fans, played board games or watched television, and didn't seem to find me at all out of place—not at first—though the bartender did ask if I was Szgany.

" 'Aye, from a long time ago,' I told him, with a nod. But I didn't say from how far away! 'My people used to wander through these parts, or so I'm told,' I went on. 'But they sold me when I was just a boy.' This was a lie, of course, a story I'd heard from Millie Cleary, about your world's Travellers, which hadn't surprised me a jot! Old habits die hard, Ben. What, descendants of gutless supplicants out of Sunside? Hah! But their ancestors used to *give* their children away, to the Wamphyri!

" 'Sold you?' The bartender looked shocked.

" 'To English people, who could care for me better.'

" 'Ah, that explains your friends, these English,' he said, nodding towards Bernie and the others. 'So then, what were your parents? Romanian Gypsies, maybe? I've heard they've been selling their children for years!'

" 'That's what I'm here to find out,' I answered. 'I'm told my people used to wander this way in their caravans, about this time of year. I'm looking for my roots, you know?'

" 'Going back to the Gypsies, after what they did to you?'

" 'No, not going back to them,' I answered. 'I just want to know what they are like, how they live. Wouldn't you be curious if you were me? About where you sprang from, I mean?'

"And then he looked around, all sly like, and said, 'If I were you, I'd forget about them. We get the Szgany through here from time to time. Some strange folks pass through Skotousa . . .' "

" 'Recently?' I said.

" 'Recently,' he nodded. And then he leaned across the bar and said, 'Try across the border into Bulgaria, a place called Eleshnitsa.'

" 'You think they're there?' I questioned him. 'But how do you know?'

" 'They've been travelling these old routes for years,' he told me. 'And aye, they were here, but the law moved them on. A dubious lot, my friend, your Gypsy clan. Once across the border they were out of Greek jurisdiction, which I say is a very good thing. Leave well enough alone, eh? I certainly wouldn't want a Gypsy curse on me! Can't blame the police for letting them go.'

" 'So what had they done wrong?' I persisted. 'For the police to move them on, I mean.'

"Again he leaned across to me and quietly explained, 'They buried one of their own, a young girl, in the woods nearby. But some folks didn't think they'd made too good a job of it. Local superstitions—you understand?' At which he must have seen how intent I was. Straightening up, he gave himself a little shake, glanced all about the room, and said, 'But there, I've said too much already, so let's have done with all that.'

"And so I was forced to push my luck. Before he could move off and serve someone else, I grabbed his arm. 'Haven't I heard something about that?' I said. 'Didn't someone dig her up again, open up her grave, and put a stake through her heart, as if she were a monster or something—or one of your *vrykoulakas,* eh?' For I knew that was what the Greeks call the Vampire.

"And how he backed off then! Him and the entire inn or taverna or whatever with him, each and every man of them in there. For if they'd heard nothing else, they had certainly heard that one ugly word: *vrykoulakas!*

"So that was that. From then on no one talked to us, and the next morning we moved out. Still, I didn't find it too odd, and I still don't. For it's like you said, Ben: in places like that old myths and superstitions never die. What, with Romania and the primal Gate at Radujevac just a hundred and fifty or so miles away? And the Szgany wandering those roads for a thousand years or more? Oh, I could well understand the fey of the folks in Skotousa . . . I even understood them digging up that girl and putting a stake in her heart, perhaps because they remembered a time when such had been routine. *I* could understand it, aye . . .

"But Bernie Fletcher couldn't. He wanted to know what the local police had done about it . . . apart from letting the Travellers go, that is. So the next morning, before we crossed the border, he sought out old newspapers for the last few days and read up on it. It was a good idea of yours, Ben, to send Bernie out there with me. Him being a Graeco-, er, a Graecophile? Is that it? Being able to speak and read it and what all.

"And there it was in the newspapers:

"When the pathol-, er, the *doctor* from Kavála—when he'd looked at the girl's body, cut her open and what have you, he'd seen that she had been well dead before she'd been staked. Dead of this anaemia, that is. And since there's no crime in killing the dead, and since there was no proof against the Gypsies anyway, it had been thought as well to let them go on their way.

"Almost enough to see us on our way back home, too—*hah!* Now see—I've even begun to think of this place as 'home'! But no, we carried on to Eleshnitsa in Bulgaria. Incidentally, that was Bernie Fletcher's choice, too. Before I'd even mentioned it to him, why, he'd already fathomed it for himself! These men of yours, Ben Trask: their skills are strange and rare . . .

"The people in Eleshnitsa told us where we'd find the Gypsies: in woods to the north of the village. And do you know, it was almost as if I really was back home again, when I saw those ruts in the track through the trees. The hooves of horses can't be that much different from those of shads, I reckon; anyway, I knew for sure that caravan wheels had chewed those deep ruts in the good rich soil, and I felt it in my bones that we were that close. And we were.

"When we saw the smoke of their fires rising over a clearing in the trees, Bernie dropped me and our minders off. Expert in covert—er, in covert sur-, er, in watching without being seen, *damn* it!—that pair of likely lads just seemed to vanish into the greenery. Quiet as mice they were, so as never to disturb a bird in the trees, but I knew they'd be watching out for me. And so I went on alone, on foot into the Gypsy camp.

"The leaves were all brown on the trees from this terrible summer, but at least the camp was in shade. The smoke came from the chimney stacks atop their caravans; only a madman would set a fire in open woods with everything as dry as this! But some of the Szgany folk were about, and they saw my approach. Of course they did, for I wanted to be seen. I even jingled as I came on, all dappled under the wilted trees. And long before their first greetings rang out, they knew that I was Szgany, too. But they . . . didn't jingle!

"Well, not strange. Wamphyri supplicants—and their descendants, too, apparently—don't wear silver. Perhaps there's a lesson in that, Ben. If you see a Traveller in your world, in this world that is, and he doesn't wear silver, you can be sure he's the son of the sons of some scurvy supplicant servant of a Lord or Lady of the Wamphyri in olden Starside! Take bets on it, if you like, for I don't think you'd lose. And yet again we see how old habits die hard.

"But whatever their customs, they didn't seem to notice *my* silver, though it should be said we didn't shake hands or clasp forearms either. So perhaps they only use silver in their money, or when they place it on the eyes of their dead when they lower them into the ground . . .

"In any case I was Szgany; they didn't shy from me or seem to consider me an outsider; I asked to see their chief, and was taken to him in his varnished caravan. But he was old, that one, an old, old man. If you think I'm old, he could give me fifteen years at least!

"He was all dark-stained leather, a glint of gold tooth, a plain gold ring in the lobe of a hairy right ear, and more gold on his gnarly fingers.

"After he had looked me over, satisfied himself that I was Szgany, he gave a nod and my escort left us alone together. And then he asked me: 'Why do you come here? Is there something you would tell me? Are you a messenger? For I can sense that you're from far, far away.'

" 'I have no message,' I answered. 'I'm just a Traveller—

as you and your people are Travellers—but indeed I have come from far, far away. What is this message you're expecting?'

"He had seemed eager at first, expectant, but now withdrew a little into himself, and mumbled: 'No message. Ah, no message for old Vladi!'—only to brighten in a moment, and say, 'Then perhaps you are something of a message in yourself!'

" 'In what way?' I asked him.

"But he only cocked his head on one side and winked, saying: 'That's for me to know, and for you to answer.'

" 'Then question me by all means,' I shrugged, 'and if I'm able to answer, be sure I will.'

" *'Hmm!'* He nodded his wrinkled old head of white hair, as if he pondered on something, and fell silent awhile. But then he started up again and said, 'There are some strange, strange places in the world, don't you think?' His voice was a dry rustle, like dead leaves stirred by a breeze.

" 'A great many,' I answered. 'Vast deserts, mighty oceans, and mountains high as the sky. But I fancy that's not what you mean. In what way strange, old chief?'

"Of a sudden his rheumy old eyes cleared, and clasping my knee he said, 'What clan are you? What Traveller tribe? What's your name, eh?'

" 'I'm Lardis, a Lidesci,' I told him at once. And why not, for I'm proud of it.

" 'A Lidesci . . . eh?' He blinked at me then. 'Ah, a Lidesci, you say! *Huh!* I don't know it, never heard of it—or if I did I can't remember. Perhaps in the old days . . .'

" 'We were only a few, and it was a long time ago,' I told him. 'Now we're no more, except me. And when I see the Travelling Folk, I always stop and speak to them. For the old times, you know? It seems only right.'

" 'Aye, you're right,' he answered. 'But not many remember the old times. And fewer still the strange old places!'

" 'The places of which you spoke?'

"He tapped his veined, crooked old nose and nodded wisely. 'Places this beak of mine can smell! Places it takes me when an owl hoots just so, or the bats flit sideways in the face of the moon. Strange and timeless places, aye. Places the Szgany remember—*some* of the Szgany, a few of us, anyway—which we visit from time to time. Old places we have always visited, but sometimes a new place if it smells right to this old beak. *Huh!* But this time it let me down. So perhaps I'm past it, eh?'

"Well, he was infirm of body—and probably of mind, too—and it seemed to me he was rambling. And despite that his forebears were most likely a dubious lot, or perhaps because of it, I felt sorry for him. For a while at least, until he said:

" 'So then, Lardis of the Lidescis: well met, whoever you are. But your use of the old tongue is strange—even antique—which is why I thought you were my messenger, for whom I've waited an entire lifetime, as my father and my father's father before me. For I am Vladi Ferengi, and much like you, the last of my line.'

"He must have seen me start, for he said, 'Eh? Eh? Do you know us then, know of us?' And now his voice was sharp.

"Did I know of them? But in Sunside their name has been a curse-word since time immemorial! Ferenc, Ferenczy, Ferengi—in all its forms, an evil invocation! Why, they had been legendary even among their own kind, the Wamphyri! The mutant giant Fess Ferenc had been the last of them that I knew of, one of a handful who escaped alive from the battle at the Dweller's Garden. *Hah!* Did I know of them? And so these people were the descendants of some ancient line of Ferenc supplicants, eh? Oh, a long time ago, I'll grant you: two thousand years or more, and all of it long forgotten if not in its entirety. But still, it had given me pause . . .

"I quickly covered up. 'Ferenczy is a name that's not uncommon in Romania, which is where you're headed,' I said. 'Why, I think there may even be a Ferenczy or two in my own ancestry, which is why I was startled to hear you speak it.' The last was a damned lie, of course, but not the first; for as you yourself have told me, Ben, the Ferenczys are an ancient, honoured, established line in old Romania, as are many old family names out of Sunside.

"But Vladi had soured of our conversation; now he sat silently glooming on me, until my escort reappeared with bad news.

" 'There are strangers in the woods!' that one reported to his chief, the while looking me up and down, with suspicion in his narrow brown eyes.

" 'Ah!' said I. 'But they'll be my colleagues, who brought me here to see you. They're not Szgany, so I didn't bring them with me into your camp.'

" 'So they're friends of yours, are they?' My young escort hissed, gripping my elbow. 'Reporters? Newspaper men, perhaps?'

"And old Vladi, he looked at me and grunted: 'Eh? Eh?'

" 'No,' I shook my head. "They're English, visitors to this country. Didn't I tell you I came from afar?"

"Then my escort held me more tightly yet, saying, 'The men are waiting on your word, Vladi. First Maria goes down with the blood curse, then those newspaper people show up with their cameras and notebooks, and those so-called Sisters of Mercy, poking their noses in. What with that doctor from Kavála, and the police, we've had enough! Now I think we should bloody this one up a little, him and these English friends of his. I think they are spies and we should fling them in a thorn thicket for their trouble!'

"But Vladi shook his head and said, 'Spies? But what would they be spying on? We have nothing to hide! So let it be. There is trouble enough in our wake. And anyway, this Lardis has spoken to me in an ancient tongue that my grandfather knew, and he may be of our blood.' But having said his piece, then he turned to me.

" 'You,' he said. 'I've seen enough of you, Lardis Lidesci. I'll accept what you've said, but I can't accept that you came among us in a sly fashion. Go, and take your secretive friends with you. I don't want to see you again.'

"And so I went.

"Bernie had turned the car around. My minders met me

halfway, and I rather fancy that for all they were burly lads, they were glad to be out of there, too. The Szgany are fearsome in a fight and can hurl their knives with awesome accuracy. Aye, and we could feel Ferengi eyes on us all the way out of the woods.

"In Eleshnitsa, at noon, Bernie contacted the HQ as usual. There was a message ordering our return, along with your instructions for me to join you in Australia.

"And that's it. I've told it all . . ."

5
Of The Night

TRASK POURED ANOTHER BRANDY INTO LARDIS'S glass, and for a little while remained silent while he pondered over what he'd been told. Then he said, "I think that maybe I should have spoken to you sooner."

"Eh? Something in it, you mean?" Lardis seemed surprised.

"You sensed nothing out of the ordinary?" Trask, too, was puzzled. Why had Lardis found nothing suspicious in what he'd seen and heard? "But the way you told it, there was a definite air of mystery about these people."

"Aye, but there's that about all the Szgany!" Lardis protested. "Now listen:

"They had been through a lot. They'd had sickness in their company, and when it was time for them to move on, they'd taken this girl of theirs from a hospital by force and without permission. That was stupid—or more likely stubborn—of them, yes, I agree, but such is their nature. Then they'd aroused old superstitions in Skotousa by burying her with silver on her eyes, which is probably a custom of theirs, just as it is among various Szgany clans in Sunside. And from the time of their leaving Kavála, all of these newspaper people had been following after them, not to mention the police. Then that poor lass was dug up again; perhaps by the Skotousa villagers, I don't know, but someone saw fit to put a stake in her, for sure! And after her grave had been opened yet *again,* by that pathol-, er, that doctor from the hospital, I mean—and after he'd cut her open and what have you . . . well, can't you just *see* how upset these people must have been?"

"Yes, I can see all of that readily enough," Trask agreed. "That doesn't bother me too much—or it does, the entire sequence of events, and the events themselves: the girl's sickness, and what have you—it's *all* bothering me! But not specifically, not at this stage. I mean, I accept your explanation of the facts as we know them. Leukaemia, anaemia, various blood infections, they're all killers. And I believe that in certain Greek islands and certainly in Romania they still bury people who die that way with silver coins on their eyelids. I'm not disputing that old customs die hard, Lardis, or that what we've seen here isn't perfectly normal practice among the Szgany. But there are other things that you mentioned which complicate matters . . ."

"Such as?"

"This old chief, er, Vladi Ferengi?"

"Yes, what of him?"

Trask sat chin in hand, fingering his lip, staring across his desk at the Old Lidesci. "Some five and a half years ago," he eventually said, "we had another visitor from Sunside . . . a *human* visitor, that is. I'm talking about Nathan Keogh when he came through the Gate into Perchorsk—if not exactly 'of his own free will . . .' " He paused musingly.

"Of course he didn't," Lardis nodded. "He was *thrown* into the Starside Gate by his vampire brother, Nestor of the Wamphyri! Or rather, by Nestor's first lieutenant, Zahar. Later, in this world, Nathan learned the secrets of the Möbius Continuum and brought you, your people, and your weapons back to Sunside with him to help us fight Vormulac Unsleep and Devetaki Skullguise. *Huh!* But that's old news. What of it?"

"When Nathan escaped from Perchorsk," Trask continued,

as much to himself as to Lardis, "he was helped by a band of Travellers. Strangely—or even incredibly—they were journeying *that* far north despite that it was winter! And as for what this Vladi hinted to you about these 'strange places . . .' "

"Yes?"

"Well, I never did have the entire story from Nathan—it wasn't considered relevant at the time—but if I remember correctly, he had much the same conversation with the chief of the band that helped him. Also, that chief's description as I recall it was identical to this Vladi's."

"His name, this chief?" Lardis was fascinated now.

"I never learned it," Trask shook his head. "But I do remember Nathan saying that these people were descendants of Wamphyri supplicants who must have come through the Gate with their masters millennia ago. Their name alone would have told us that much. He also said they believed that one day their masters . . . that they would return."

"And the strange places?"

"Well, it's pure speculation, of course," said Trask, "but couldn't the strange places be those regions to which these masters would return, or in which they were scheduled to reappear? For instance, the Gate under the Carpathians, upriver from the resurgence at Radujevac? They frequently had Szgany visitors in the neighbourhood of the Refuge. Then there's the old Moldavian Khorvaty; Faethor Ferenczy had a castle there, oh, fifteen hundred years ago. And Romania in the region of Halmagiu under the Zarandului Mountains, where Faethor held sway, and more recently his bloodson, Janos. We might even consider Perchorsk, which this Vladi might have sniffed out with that talented 'old beak' of his. It's by no means impossible, Lardis. Why, you yourself are fey in your Szgany fashion, and—"

"—And there'd be far more of the Wamphyri taint in their supplicant blood than in mine, that's for sure!" the other nodded.

"I'll give you odds that these are the same people," Trask said.

"Except I'm not taking you on!" said Lardis. "But . . . what does it all mean?"

"I don't know," Trask answered. "I'm not sure. But what I would like to know is this: where had these Szgany Ferengi been *before* that poor girl went down with her weird disorder, her so-called anaemia? And what was this Gypsy band doing in that part of Greece anyway?"

"To which I've no answers." Lardis shook his head.

"Nor have I, not yet," said Trask. "But if this Vladi Ferengi has the power to sniff out the strange places, as he calls them, the places where in olden times the Wamphyri came through from Starside, or where they then established themselves in our world . . . mightn't he also sense their presence in the here and now?"

"I begin to see what you're getting at," Lardis growled.

"And didn't he say that this time his old beak had let him down, suggesting that he and his people had been—I don't know—on some kind of mission, maybe searching for something?"

"For something or someone," said Lardis. "Aye, someone . . . though I think you're right and I, too, prefer some*thing*! Something . . . which had perhaps only recently arrived here?"

"Exactly!" Trask nodded.

"Huh!" Lardis grunted. And: "Am I blind, then? Why haven't I made this connection?"

"You didn't have all the facts," Trask told him. "And anyway, two heads are better than one." He sat up straighter. "And four or five heads are better yet. We have a think tank tomorrow. Good, for now I can give them something to think about. But right now—" He paused to stifle a yawn.

And Lardis said, "You're tired, Ben, and so am I. I fancy it's partly this good brandy's fault."

"No," Trask shook his head. "Maybe that's what does it for you, but for me it's this job. I need a good night's sleep, let things work themselves out in my head while my body rests. It's too late tonight to do anything more anyway. I feel the *need* to work at it, of course, but can't see us achieving anything more right now than we'll get through in a single hour tomorrow morning."

"I'll be on my way, then," said Lardis, easing himself upright in a creaking of old bones. But:

"Wait!" Trask stopped him, frowning.

"Oh?"

"There's something else in what you told me, which doesn't seem to fit in anywhere."

"You'll have to remind me."

"Something about Sisters of Mercy? Your escort listed them among his concerns when he was trying to have Vladi punish you. So who were they? Nuns? But who would complain about nuns 'poking their noses in'? I mean, poking their noses into what?"

"I didn't have time to question further," said Lardis ruefully. "For as I explained, I was ushered out of there in a bit of a hurry!"

Trask gave a shrug. "Well, not to concern yourself. Greece has a great many monasteries and such. If the Gypsies were seen as poor itinerants, these Sisters of Mercy might have made themselves available for . . . I don't know, whatever reason. To help them over their grief, perhaps?"

"Perhaps," said Lardis. "But all of the Szgany I ever knew were solitary people in that respect. Any grieving there was to be done, they did it alone. Aye, for in Sunside in the old days—and perhaps right now, for all I know—that was as often as not the only way . . ."

After Lardis had left, Trask pondered things for a few minutes more, until he remembered that he had to call the Minister Responsible. By then it was well after eleven.

Ah, well, he thought, reaching for the phone. *Why should I be the only one who works late?*

But in fact Trask wasn't the only one who was working late.

In her temporary secret accommodation adjacent to Jake Cutter's quarters, Liz Merrick had fallen asleep while waiting for him to return from his unauthorized outing with Lardis and Lissa Lidesci. It had been the sound of him slamming his door, and then his preparations for sleep—his occasional muttering and his toilet flushing, the liquid *hiss* of his shower, and finally the low hum of his fan—that had brought her awake just forty-five minutes ago. Of course *she* couldn't have a fan, in case he heard it. And if *she* needed the toilet—which she had, but had to wait until he was bumping around in his bed before using the "back door" and tiptoeing through E-Branch HQ's night corridors to the ladies'—well, that was just too bad.

But in fact these things weren't Liz's main concerns. She only got angry over these lesser details to cover for her impotence in the larger scheme of things: namely, the fact that she had to sneak around like this in the first place, and especially that she had to sneak around in Jake's mind.

Impotent, yes, because she couldn't do anything about it; she knew that Ben Trask was right and this was all-important—that Jake himself was all-important, and not only to the Branch and its work and the world in general. He was very important to Liz, too, and if he caught her spying on him like this (again), well, that wouldn't much help her case either!

By the time she'd returned from the toilet to what she had come to think of as her hidy-hole, Jake was on the verge of sleep. And when Liz extended her first, tentative probe in his direction, she received vague, swirling impressions that she at once recognized of old:

A dreamy wandering—indeed, a mental somnambulism—his mind's subconscious searching for a direction in which it might take itself . . . undecipherable anxieties . . . a nervous shifting of mental patterns . . . the lure of an incredible swirl of numbers, equations, caculi—a veritable wall *of numbers, enclosing Jake and shutting him in, yet hovering just beyond his reach—like some elusive, sentient cyclone.*

All of these things, and something else. The very weirdest of weird sensations: that he wasn't alone in there . . .

Well, and he wasn't alone, not any longer. But was it Liz herself, an echo of her intrusion reflecting from Jake's mainly relaxed shields, or was it something else? Was it perhaps something that the Necroscope, Harry Keogh, had left in Jake's mind to watch over him? But if so, why did he seem to shy from it?

Liz's questions were inward-directed, of course, but they were also intense, and as a telepath she should have known better. Thoughts are thoughts, and telepathy is telepathy. A sensitive person, whether a mentalist or not, may sometimes detect the uninvited interest of a talented Other (usually as a prickling at the back of the neck, a warning that someone is watching), and Jake Cutter was a lot more than merely sensitive.

His mental shields immediately strengthened—and Liz as quickly backed off! Fortunately she hadn't been detected, or if she had then her probe had been perceived much as a fly: an irritation momentarily sensed, brushed away, and otherwise ignored in the face of some other, more serious intrusion. Which caused her to wonder: if Jake's shields hadn't gone up on her account, then on whose?

And as on several occasions before Liz shuddered uncontrollably at the thought of what Jake was, and of what he could do, albeit subconsciously. For the *moment* subconsciously, anyway.

But in any case it would be prudent to play safe, she supposed, and keep her mind to herself until she was sure Jake was asleep. The trouble with that was that Liz, too, was tired. And as she finally drifted back into sleep she missed the deadspeak conversation that took place in the room beyond her cell's thin walls.

Not that she would have heard it anyway, though she might have *sensed* something of it—might have detected the swing of Jake's emotions, made guesses at his denials or rejections, his heated assertiveness—but that would be all. For only the dead are fully receptive of deadspeak.

And only a Necroscope can hear them when they answer . . .

You are being obstinate. Moreover, you would shirk your duty to your commitment, our agreement, the pact we swore!

Korath, once Korath Mindsthrall, made guttural protest, his dead voice welling up from the darkness of Jake Cutter's sleeping mind.

And because Jake could no longer pretend to ignore him, as he did when awake, he answered, "Yes, I want out of it! Because your interpretation of our 'agreement'—this 'pact' you say we swore—in no way agrees with mine!"

I saved your life! Korath continued. *But for my intervention, you and your friends—especially your woman friend—were dead in Malinari's inferno in Xanadu. Except before being rendered to her fats, sweet Liz would have suffered even worse torments in The Mind's garden of metamorphosis. Have you forgotten the thing with the not-so-vacant eyes, which once was Demetrakis Mindsthrall? Demetrakis, of the drooling mouths and swollen penises? They were for seeing, those eyes, or at least for gauging distance and direction, and the mouths were for eating, for reducing sweet Liz to mulch for Malinari's mushrooms. What, and do you suppose the penises were for nothing? Well let me inform you that Demetrakis was once an extremely lusty man who made no less a lusty vampire! What little of him remained in Malinari's garden . . . ah, but you may believe it when I tell you that* that *would have known what to do with your sweet Liz!*

And then, when Jake made no answer:

Now hear me out, Korath went on. *You can't dispute that in your hour of greatest need I showed good faith. Since when, for payment, you've betrayed or thought to betray me at every turn. And you dare to inquire what is that for a pact?* Hah! *What, indeed! But surely I should be the one doing the asking!*

"I've asked no such thing," said Jake.

But you have thought it, implied it.

"Damn right!" the other exploded. "That 'pact' you devised was sheer hogwash! Nothing but a ploy to give you unlimited access to my mind. Harry Keogh was right when he warned me to have no truck with vampires, dead or alive. Would you like me to remind you of how it was supposed to be, this alleged arrangement or agreement of ours?"

By all means! said the other, trying to conceal his pleasure that at last Jake was engaging him in conversation, however belatedly. For ever since Xanadu, Jake had become more and more leery and stubborn; so that during the handful of nights passed between, Korath had made little or no progress with him. As for the days: in Jake's waking hours his shields—the same shields that kept Liz Merrick out—were firmly in place, and if Korath came too close Jake would think of the sun, picturing its glare and its searing, cleansing fire, which tended to hold the vampire at bay however temporarily.

He thought of it now . . . but it was night and he was dreaming, and in any case he must have this out with the dead Korath sooner or later, one way or the other.

That, too! said Korath, momentarily shrinking as he glimpsed the notion in Jake's mind, the sun's cosmic furnace, origin and staff of life to living things, but molten death to the undead. *And was that, too, part of our deal? No, I think not!*

"And was this?" Jake countered. "This constant badgering? *I* think not! Let me repeat what you said—your very words, Korath—which I remember well, if only because they were lies:

"Was it too much to ask, you wanted to know, that in return for your gift to me I should give you my companionship—albeit rarely, however infrequently—when little else intruded on my time? That was it. That was all. My company, someone to talk to. But rarely, infrequently, when I wasn't busy. Yet this last week you haven't been out of my mind . . . literally! And you've very nearly driven *me* out of it! Do you know what Ben Trask and his people would do to me if they knew about you? Well, I don't know either—but I've a damn good idea! Why, I wouldn't put it past him to put a gun to my head and blow it off! I don't think anyone would blame him for it, either."

But they don't know, Korath answered. *Nor will they, if you keep your nerve. Also—*

"—Let me finish!" Jake cut him short. "So for one thing,

you're placing me in jeopardy, and in so doing placing *yourself* in jeopardy, which has to be sheer stupidity on your part. Without me you're nothing, a handful of bones washed clean in a subterranean sump, you've said so yourself. So whatever harm comes to me comes to you, for when I'm gone you'll have no one at all to talk to, 'rarely' or 'infrequently' or ever!"

But I know that as well as you! Korath protested. *It is to preserve you—us, if you will—that I persevere when others would simply give up on you.*

"And as for your gift," Jake ignored that last, "what gift are you talking about? You've given me nothing!"

Your life, and the lives of your friends and a loved one?

Jake knew he'd have difficulty arguing that one. He didn't try but answered, "That's all part and parcel of the same thing. If I had died then you would have gone with me."

Not so, Korath gurgled in his mind. *For I am already dead. But yes, I do know what you are talking about. This gift you so desire—which I agree was part of our pact—is the place of the primal darkness, the nowhere place which exists between the places we know, the Möbius Continuum. Am I right?*

"That's it," said Jake with a deadspeak nod, "and you know it is. You promised to give me the numbers, Harry Keogh's formula, the means to ride his Möbius strip."

And have I not kept my promise? Korath seemed taken aback, even hurt. *Of what do you accuse me now? Not once, not twice, not three times but* four, *I have given you the keys to the Möbius Continuum! Without which you were dead. Deny it if you can.*

"I can't," said Jake. "Even if I were expert at these word games as you, still I wouldn't try to deny that one. But what's that for a gift, which I can't use unless you're tagging along? It's only half mine."

And is it my fault, too, that you've no head for numbers? Korath chuckled now, like gas bubbles bursting in a swamp, only to sober in the next moment. And: *But of course it is only half yours!* he snapped. *For without me you have no formula, and without you I have no mobility.* Hah! *And what little I have of that is borrowed!*

"But I need to be able to use the Continuum of my own free will," Jake protested, "without recourse to you."

Good! I agree! said Korath. *Your own free will. Yes, certainly, that's very important. Here then, the formula! I give it to you!*

And at once, immediately—so rapidly that Jake was taken completely by surprise—Möbius equations commenced mutating on the screen of his (or Korath's) mind. An ordered march of evolving calculi and ever-changing algebraic characters and symbols, it was as if the solution to a mathematical problem of enormous complexity were unravelling onto the monitor screen of some gigantic computer.

But Jake had been here before, half a dozen times and more, first with the Necroscope Harry Keogh and then with Korath. The weird progression of numbers was just as baffling to him now as it had been the first time; but instinctively—or intuitively, with Harry's intuition?—he knew where to freeze it, knew how to stop it at the one point that he remembered.

He did so . . . and the numbers flowed at once into a trembling outline and formed a Möbius door!

"That's it!" Jake breathed. "A door to the Continuum!"

Aye, said Korath, equally in awe of what they'd done, despite that they'd done it before. *Aye, that's it. And I, Korath, have given it to you. It was our pact, do you remember now? And with this great gift I have earned the right to—*

"To nothing!" said Jake, letting the door collapse in upon itself. "I know where to stop it, yes, but not how to start it! I can't possibly remember the entire sequence. No man could."

But men did! said Korath. *More than one. Möbius was first, then the Necroscope Harry Keogh. And on Starside, I saw Harry's son, called Nathan, perform just such wonders. I myself learned it from Harry when he tried to show you how; I used a skill passed down to me by Nephran Malinari's bite, by his awful essence, which runs in my blood. Unlike yourself, I* do *remember the sequence! But what good does it do when I can't use it? Incorporeal, I can't move without I move with you, as part of your mind. And I say again: am I to be blamed that you've no head for numbers?*

Plainly that wasn't Korath's fault, but still Jake's principal argument—that the gift of life, however great, wasn't the promised gift—remained unshakable.

"Very well," he said, "we're at an impasse. But don't you see that the more you pester me the more likely it is you'll be discovered? Now frankly, I don't wish you any harm. You're dead and I don't see how you can do me any great physical injury . . . *physical*, that is. Though I have to tell you that you're slowly driving me crazy! And not so slowly, either. But anyway, if you should be found out, still Trask and his people couldn't do *you* too much harm. What, like they'd kill you again? But me, I just don't know what they'd do about me."

What could they do? Korath seemed genuinely curious. *Is it really likely that they would kill you? I doubt it. Please remember, Jake, that I have been present in or quite close to your mind almost since you and Harry first came to talk to me in the shattered sump where I drowned and was melted away. I know that in fact Ben Trask* desires *that you should commune with the teeming dead! It is, as you yourself might put it, all part and parcel of being a Necroscope. Therefore, since it would seem to be a basic requirement—that you speak to dead people, I mean—how can Trask complain? For surely it must be obvious that I am now one with the Great Majority.*

"You're a vampire!" Jake answered. "And I've seen vampires in the flesh. I know what you were like *before* you died. And as for 'being one' with the Great Majority: you're forgetting that I've heard them whispering in their graves and know it couldn't be further from the truth! And then there's Trask; but I don't think I could ever express just how much he detests you and all your kind. Vampires? The Wamphyri? Trask lives to destroy them! Even before Malinari murdered Zek, *after* he murdered you, vampires were Trask's main obsession. He's lost too many friends to them. You'd like to know what he could do to me in order to rid me of you? Well, at least one unpleasant solution springs readily enough to mind."

Such as? And now Korath really was curious.

"Did you ever hear of prefrontal lobotomy?" Jake inquired. "No, I don't suppose you did. It's a medical term for something they used to do to 'relieve' cases of severe schizophrenia. But you have to agree it's kind of drastic, right? So tell me, what the hell are you if not a case of severe schizophrenia?!"

Since deadspeak, like more orthodox mental telepathy, frequently conveys far more than any merely "spoken" word, Korath had seen in Jake's mind something of the procedures involved in prefrontal lobotomy. Now, thoughtfully, he said, *My once-master Malinari the Mind, could do much the same thing.* (And Jake actually felt the monster shudder!) *Except he did it with his bare hands, his liquid fingers, his awesome mind! Ah, but what Malinari did "relieved" his victims of . . . why, everything! It was a cure for life itself.*

"But I don't need or want relieving," Jake told him. "Only of you. So we have to work something out and put a limit on it. And we have to redefine the terms of this so-called pact."

Its terms? A limit?

"A limit in time," said Jake. "For see, I don't want to be a Necroscope and never did. Three weeks ago, I didn't know what a Necroscope was. And still don't know all of it because they won't tell me. What, something that's so weird, so unnatural, I can't be told about it? That's not for me. So until I know what it's all about, I don't want any, thanks. Oh, sure, I would use the Möbius Continuum—*will* use it, to my own ends—but after that, I don't know, I haven't made up my mind yet. On the other hand, there's something that I've very *definitely* decided: that I won't be beholden to *you* forever and a day!"

A limit in time, then, said Korath. *Yes, we can talk about that, I think. As for terms, what did you have in mind . . .*

well, apart from myself, that is? (Again his phlegmy chuckle, a glutinous reverberation that echoed hollowly and humourlessly in the deadspeak aether.)

"First the time limit," said Jake when the echoes had subsided. "Our—*God*, our 'partnership'!—our deal, lasts only as long as it takes both of us to achieve our objectives. But just as soon as we have, and whether I've cracked Keogh's formula or not, you're to get out of my mind. But I appreciate your absolute loneliness, and for my part I promise that if or when I can I'll give you *some* of my spare time. Talking to you, about your life in a vampire world, could prove interesting after all."

If or when? Some *of your spare time? But without the Continuum you wouldn't be able to visit me anyway.*

"All the more reason to ensure that I get it," Jake answered. "Also that eventually I'm able to remember it. But in any case, surely you're wrong? The way I understand it I won't have to visit you; we'll be able to communicate at a distance—just about any distance—much as we're doing right now. But without you being on my back all the time."

Hmmm! Korath mused.

And Jake urged him: "Make up your mind, before I change mine. The way I figure it, I'm making a deal with the devil anyway." But:

Let's move on, said the other cagily. *For you talked about objectives, and I'm interested to know what yours might be.*

"You haven't plucked them right out of my mind, then?"

I may be on *your mind*, said Korath, *but I'm not exactly* in *it. You've denied me the access I initially requested—and for which we bargained—else we wouldn't be having this conversation.*

Jake was taken aback. "What? Did you expect even more than you've already got? Because if so, I'd better tell you here and now that it's more than I intend to give! You wanted access and you've got it. You can talk to me whenever you like—though so far you've only chosen to do it when I *don't* like!"

But that's hardly access to your mind, said the other. *Be-*

ing able to talk to you does not define complete *access to your mind. Your shields exclude me, blanketing more than three-quarters of everything you're thinking. My original suggestion, the way I remember it, was that I should be, well, much like a* part *of you, and—*

"A part of me?" Thoroughly alarmed now, Jake cut the other off. "Are you crazy? Once you were in, how could I get you out? I'm having a hard enough time of it as it is!"

Exactly! said the other. *And I, too, am finding it difficult; I'm having an extremely "hard time" of it, as you put it. But don't you see how easy it would be if we worked more truly as one? Maximum efficiency! You with your expert knowledge of your world—which is an entirely strange place to me—and me with my unique knowledge of Malinari, Vavara, and Szwart . . .* and *of course with my keys to the Möbius Continuum. Two minds working as one, Jake, to the benefit of both! What could be simpler or more, well, accommodating*?

Warning bells rang deep in Jake's subconscious mind. Even dreaming he knew this was a word game, and also that Korath was very good at it. All factual discussion and legitimate argument to the contrary, if the Wamphyri and their disciples were politicians, all of their political opponents would find themselves right out of their depth, swept away by sheer word-power alone!

And so, in order to gain a little breathing space, he was obliged to resort to the other's ploy and murmur, "Hmmm!"—as if thinking it over.

Well? said Korath. And:

"To quote you," Jake answered, "Let's move on. But before we do there's something that needs clearing up. I've never said that I'd accept you as 'part' of me—as part of my mind, that is—not even temporarily."

But—

"—But before we got sidetracked," Jake cut the other off yet again, "we were examining our objectives. And you wanted to know what mine might be."

Indeed, said Korath. *What is it that you seek to do?*

Other than what Ben Trask and his people would have you do, that is.

Again Jake was taken by surprise, this time not so much by the dead creature's skill at arguments and word games as by his more than hinted knowledge of Jake's pursuits outside E-Branch. And he couldn't help wondering just how *often* had Korath "eavesdropped" on him. "Oh?" he said. "So you're thinking I have ulterior motives, are you?"

Not necessarily ulterior, no. (The shake of an incorporeal head.) *But wasn't it you who said you would "use the Möbius Continuum to your own ends?" Yours as opposed to Ben Trask's, that is, and perhaps running contrary to his? Or have I in some way, er, misunderstood you . . . ?*

And so Jake told him about his vendetta with Luigi Castellano, finishing by saying, "I've killed three of them who were there that night, but two remain. Castellano himself; he's the drug-running bastard who ordered that . . . that . . . who ordered what took place. And one other who—"

Who was one of the performers, aye, said Korath. And then, as if changing the subject: *But did you know—and this is an exceedingly strange thing, Jake—that when you talk to me, as we argue our points and so forth, gradually getting to know one another, you are—how may I put it?—you're a* warm *one? For despite your harsh, often hurtful words and your brusque manner of expression, I can* feel *your warmth! It is the warmth of life, I fancy, which I only knew as a youth on Sunside, before Malinari destroyed my people, stole me away into Starside, and made me one of his. Which was so long ago that I had almost forgotten it. But you . . . you have rekindled old memories.*

Jake had been a little choked up with memories of his own, but now he put them aside. "Are you going soft on me?" he growled. "I don't think so. So what's all this: some kind of scheme to help me see how badly life, and undeath, have treated you?"

Ah, no, said the other, his deadspeak voice as deep as the Arctic ocean and as bitterly cold. *For I am what I am, and I've done what I've done. And the truth of it is, I've no regrets at all! Well, except that it all ended so badly for me—and that while my bones are rubbed away, whirling in a watery sump, Malinari lives and laughs*—and *that while we argue and fight I'll go forever unavenged! But . . . you didn't let me finish.*

"Go on, then," said Jake. "Finish."

I was saying that when we engage in normal or shall we say "trivial" conversation, you are warm and I can sense your humanity. But when you speak of these dire enemies of yours, you are cold in your heart. Even as cold as I am in my sump. It isn't a physical thing but something of the soul.

"And so you know about souls, right?" Jake somehow doubted it.

I know that whatever it was that made me human, Korath answered, *Malinari the Mind took it from me. And I know that when all I had left was undeath, he took that back, too, in exchange for the true death; and that therefore he is in my debt as much and more than Luigi Castellano is in yours.*

"We'll, then," said Jake. "It seems to me we've defined our objectives."

But mine was known from the start, Korath told him. *Didn't I say that all I wanted was to hit back at Malinari? Just think of the irony of it: that I can strike back at him from the very heart of darkness, from the watery grave to which he sent me!*

"But only through me," said Jake.

Through you, and Ben Trask, and E-Branch, aye.

"So, it's not only me you've recruited but E-Branch, too!" Jake's tone was accusing, but with very little of energy in it. Instead he felt weary of this entire episode, tired of talking, tired of listening. Mentally and physically exhausted.

Except they don't know it, Korath "chuckled," in his hideous fashion. *Nor will they ever, for when Malinari has paid the price—along with these enemies of yours, of course—then I shall get me gone from you. Though I trust you'll abide by your word and visit with me and my poor old polished bones from time to time? Eh?*

The idea was seductive. But so was everything about

Korath. His dark, deadspeak voice; his almost hypnotic manner of expression; his very presence. Suddenly Jake could feel the lure, the strength of the dead creature's aura—*and* of his argument. Without Korath, what chance *would* he have of bringing Luigi Castellano and his henchman to justice, however rough? And without Jake, what would Korath have but an eternity of loneliness—or however long it took for him to fade away?

What say you, Jake? said Korath. *Are we finally agreed? Do we have a deal*? And:

"What would it entail?" Jake wanted to know, the question slipping from his lips (or from his mind) almost of its own accord, as the peculiar lethargy continued to creep over him.

It must be, I think, a very simple matter, Korath answered, his voice the merest whisper now, a sibilant hiss, the brush of cobwebs against Jake's sleeping being. *A simple matter of will, you might say—of your own* free *will, that is. For I remember upon a time, my once-master Malinari told me, "The mind is like a manse with many rooms, where thoughts wander like ghosts. And I have the power to reach in and exorcise those ghosts, reading their lives and learning their secrets—and then driving them out!" Aye, that is what he said. And there's a great deal of my once-master in me. I, too, might enter into one of those rooms, one of* your *rooms, that is, and listen with my ear to the door, until you have need of me . . .*

Korath was very open now; he could afford to be, because he could sense that the hypnotic spell he was casting was working. And even if this initial experiment should fail, still its subject would remember little or nothing of what had gone on here from this time forward.

"What's that you say?" said Jake, flopping uneasily in his bed, adrift on the mesmeric cadence of Korath's voice and gradually falling more deeply asleep.

Isn't there room enough for both of us, Jake, the vampire's deadspeak voice went monotonously on, *in the innocent, ech-*

oing, oh-so-spacious manse of your mind? Only say the word, Jake, bid me enter, and I shall be one with you. Ahhhhhh!

"The word?" Jake drifted between levels of sleep, one natural and the other hypnotic. But he felt lured toward the latter because it was so calm, restful, devoid of conflict. Once there he might stop worrying, reasoning, thinking, and let himself be guided by the deep, dark voice of the Other. It would be easier that way, yes . . .

Not so much a word as an invitation, Korath answered. *Only open up your mind, Jake, and invite me in. Let down the shields which even now protect you—and from what? From me? Why, I am your one true friend in a world that fails to understand or appreciate you! What would you rather be: Ben Trask's puppet, his tool as I was Malinari's, or a Power in your own right? A Power in* our *right, Jake my friend?*

"Open up . . . lower my shields . . . invite him in . . . my one true friend . . ."

And are we so very different, you and I? (Korath's clotted gurgling, his insidious whispering continued.) *I think not. For I have seen you perform deeds which the Wamphyri themselves, in all their cruelty, might not have dreamed. But you* have *dreamed them, and I Korath feel privileged to have witnessed them.*

"The Wamphyri? . . . Cruelty? . . . Deeds?" Jake rolled in his bed, got tangled in his single blanket.

Your deeds, aye. The things you nightmare. Not so strange, really, that you should feel afraid in the night. Even the most monstrous of creatures nightmare! They dream of what frightened them before *they were monsters! Perhaps of what* made *them monsters, eh? And the ones who made you a monster? . . . Ah, but what you have done to them! And I wonder, Jake: does this Castellano nightmare, too? And who do you suppose features in* his *dreams? Little wonder he wants you dead.*

"Castellano . . . dreams . . . nightmares."

Only let me in, and we shall make his nightmares real,

you and I. And who knows what else we shall make? Ahhhhhh!

Jake was struggling now, fighting as a drowning man fights the water, even knowing there's no land in sight; but he struggled mainly with himself. Tossing and turning, sweating a cold, clammy sweat—with his single blanket wrapped about him like a damp, strangling shroud—he flailed his arms and didn't feel a thing when his fist struck against the thin wall.

But on the other side of that wall, Liz Merrick came starting awake. Now what in—?

The wall at her ear bounced again, and Liz at once reached out with a clumsily groping probe.

It was Jake . . . fighting . . . but fighting what? Something was in there with him, something tangible yet intangible. Something in his room, or in his mind . . . his dreams? Not yet fully awake herself, Liz couldn't tell. But she sensed Jake's dread, and his determination not to go under. More than that, she also sensed that the Thing he was fighting *knew* that she was there!

Surprised and angry, it recoiled from her telepathic probe, the probe that only Jake should be feeling, if he felt anything at all. There was no actual contact, no communication with this Thing, not for Liz; it was sensation pure and . . . not so simple. But without knowing how, Liz knew that the Thing she sensed was utterly inhuman.

It was slimy, sluglike, sentient. And it battened on Jake like a leech. Then it dawned on Liz that she wasn't reading the Thing itself, but only what Jake was reading of it: his fear of it, and the fact that his shields were going down before it! It couldn't be read, not by Liz, but only sensed—in the same way that it was sensing her—and then not by any of the five mundane senses, or even telepathy. But it was more than any nightmare, she was sure. Nightmares are personal things; they don't recognize or react to outsiders, and they certainly don't snarl at them but confine themselves to their victims!

There was a telephone in the corridor. Liz reached it in a

tangle of bedsheets and a fever of trembling. The duty officer. She had to call the D.O.

But damn it to hell, she couldn't remember the number! And just a few paces away Jake's door, behind which something terrible was happening or about to happen. And Liz the only one who could stop it.

When she had called on Jake for his help in that hellhole at Xanadu, he had come to her without reckoning the danger. Yet here she stood like a ghost in her sheet, trembling for him but unable to do anything about it for fear that she would give herself and Ben Trask and E-Branch away. And no physical danger in it at all, not to Liz, not that she knew of. Only to Jake—or to his mind.

Well then, to hell with E-Branch!

She clutched at her sheet, stumbled to Jake's door, began to hammer on it with her small fists—and only then thought to try the eye-level scanner. Her hidy-hole, before they walled it off, had been a rear annex to Jake's room. If the scanners were still linked, his might identify and accept Liz's corneal patterns in addition to Jake's own.

Tilting her head, she stared up at the ID spot and forced herself to stand still. A small light glowed into life, scanned her eye and "recognized" her. And the door clicked open. Almost falling inside, she tripped on her sheet and went sprawling towards Jake's bed.

And as the door closed behind her, Liz fell on him, grabbed his shoulders, shook him with all her strength.

"Jake!" she slapped his face. "Jake, wake up!"

His body and legs were wrapped tight in his blanket; only his arms and hands were free, and they at once grabbed hold of her as his terrified eyes blazed open. "Korath!" he said. *"Korath!"* In the gloom, Liz felt her hair grabbed in one hard hand as the other released her and balled itself into a fist.

She managed to get a hand up, groped above the bed's headboard, found the overhead light cord. And giving it a yank, she flooded the bed with light. But only just in time.

The look on Jake's face was vicious, a snarl, and the muscles of his arm were bunched, coiled-spring tight, on the point of driving his fist into her face. Even now she feared he might do it!

But no, he was awake.

"Liz?" Jake said, his voice a shudder at first, a breathless gasp, and then a sigh of relief. "Liz? But I thought that you were—?"

"No, it's only me," she said, and fell against his chest—and in the next moment realized that only his blanket separated their naked bodies.

"God!" He held her tightly for a second or so, then kicked his legs in an attempt to free himself from his blanket. "I was—I must have been—nightmaring?" And then he, too, realized that they were both naked. "But how—?"

"You . . . you called out to me," she lied. "I had been working late and stayed over. My room is close by. You were calling out to me . . . and my telepathy . . . I heard you. I'm a receiver, Jake. And whether you'll admit and accept it or not, we *do* seem to have this rapport. You woke me up."

"Well, thank God for this rapport!" he gasped. And now she saw that he was shaking.

"What was it, Jake? What was it that scared you so?"

He shook his head, sending droplets of cold sweat flying. And blinking his eyes, he looked anxiously all about his small room. But of course there was nothing and no one there—only Liz. Then, getting a grip of himself, he said, "It was a dream, or a nightmare. Or something."

She sat up, wrapped herself in her sheet again, told him, "You said a name. Korath. And that's a name we've heard before, Jake. You asked me to write it down for you, so that you'd remember it. That was just before we started our simultaneous assaults on Xanadu and Jethro Manchester's island. So now perhaps you'll tell me: Who is he? Who *is* this Korath, Jake?"

But he was fully awake now and in control of himself.

"Forget it," he said, shaking his head. "It's—I don't know—a recurrent thing, a nightmare, something I dream from time to time, that's all. It's not usually as bad as this, but tonight it was. It was getting kind of . . . well, kind of rough. So I'm really glad you came . . ." It was all lame stuff; he wasn't nearly as good a liar as Liz, but it was the best he could do.

And suddenly she felt for him, really felt for him. Whatever it was about Jake Cutter, Liz knew that she was involved. Just a few weeks ago he'd come into her life and was now a big part of it. And she'd been telling herself to hold him at bay; but not really, for he hadn't tried that hard, hadn't tried at all; or maybe she'd simply been fooling herself that she wasn't getting involved, and trying to fool him, too.

But damn it, she *was* involved! And suddenly she was saying it, admitting it in a way that must be unmistakable:

"Are you really glad I came, Jake? I mean, I don't have to go, not if you want me to stay . . ."

"No, it's okay," he said. "I don't think I'll be trying to sleep anymore anyway, not tonight. Maybe I'll read up a little more on the files that Trask has given me, and—" And then he paused, for like a fool he hadn't seen her meaning, until now.

Then she was in his arms, feeling his body—and his longing—trembling against her. But only for a moment, before she felt the change in him, too, the need turning to fear. But fear of what? Of loving, and perhaps of losing again?

Instinctively, she tried to probe him, to look inside, but his shields were there as ever. And now he was holding her away from him, at arm's length, while the look in his deep brown eyes expressed his torment, the fact that he was torn two ways.

"What is it, Jake?" she said.

His shields wavered a little and she saw . . .

. . . Longing, and denial of that longing. Need, and fear of that need. Not fear of Liz herself or of sex, nor even of failure. No, it was something else.

But when she went to probe deeper, Jake's shields firmed up again and she was out. And.

"I wish you wouldn't do that," he said.

"I couldn't help it," Liz answered. "Don't you know that I . . . that I feel for you, Jake?" She got up and went to the door. "But is that what it is? My telepathy? Are you afraid that I'll see too much? That I'll see what you're hiding?"

"No," he said. "Yes." And then, shaking his head, "I can't say, can't explain it. I mean, I'm not ready to explain it."

"Well, when you are," she said. "I'm not far away. And try not to nightmare, Jake. But if you do, well," she shrugged helplessly. "Just remember: I'm not far away."

When he nodded, she stepped back out into the corridor and let the door close quietly behind her . . .

When Liz had been gone awhile, Jake relaxed his shields completely and listened. He listened to the far, faint, barely discernible whispering of the dead in their graves, to the ebb and flow of the deadspeak ether, like the hush of wavelets on some ethereal shore, and to a distant humming and throbbing that was composed of the "real" sounds of the downstairs hotel, and outside the rumbling of the metropolis, and farther yet the wheels of the world turning.

Korath wasn't there, but Jake was sure he would come if he called out to him. The trouble was that he might also come without being called. That was the trouble, yes.

For Jake wanted to be sure that if or when he made love to Liz Merrick, he would be the only one doing it . . .

6
Of The Dark Places

THE HIGH MOUNTAIN ROAD WAS AS STILL AND quiet as the night air, with only the molten-silver, one-note call of Greek owls to disturb the gloom. To the south, out across the sea, a sprinkle of bobbing lights spoke of fishermen in their boats, intent on securing their catch of what few fish remained in the still beautiful but decimated Aegean, whose temperature was up three degrees on the norm for this time of year.

The moon rode low in the sky, casting the shadows of Mediterranean pines over the marble-chip gravel of an empty parking lot that fronted the arched entrance to a cliff-clinging monastery—the same monastery that, only a few hours earlier, Manolis Papastamos had passed in a hired Fiat on his way to disaster.

From the roadway (had anyone been standing there) the fortresslike building's silhouette against the jewel-strewn indigo of the vaulted sky was not unlike that of some ancient Crusader castle, its bell towers rearing up like horns on the head of a creature risen from the deep. Nor would this picture have been so very far from the truth.

Along the approach road from both directions, and in the car park itself, prominently posted signs told of certain restrictions. Apparently the sweet Sisters of Mercy who inhabited the high stone sanctuary considered this a time of solitude and abstinence, and as an order they were repenting the sins of the world. Daytime parking was allowed in the parking lot—for the taking of panoramic photographs from dizzy vantage points—but not at night. The sounds of revving engines and slamming doors, even the murmur of voices, might distract the nuns at their devotions. Tours of the inner gardens, courtyard, outer balconies, and the order's gift- and workshops, had been curtailed indefinitely, or "until such time as the world's dark forces were in retreat." Other, older notices, inviting visitors in—*"ladies, wearing headscarves, skirts . . . limbs covered down to and including knees. Men: no shorts or lettered T-shirts, please!"*—had been crossed through with thick black *X*'s, or pasted over with signs that read:

NO VISITORS—
NO TRADESMEN—
EXCEPT AS AUTHORIZED!

It made for a severely austere scene, where in certain of the tower windows even the interior lights seemed dim, burning with only a flickering candle's strength. This, too, wasn't so far from the truth; for the convent's mother superior of three years disdained electricity and had banned its use—except in the telephone, of which she had charge, and several other vital areas, such as washing, cleaning, and cooking, lacking which the monastery couldn't function.

Right now she was asleep. She had been out in the car earlier—on monastery "business"—and wished to recuperate. For being up and about in the hours of daylight, and even the evening hours, depleted her. "Daylight is a wickedness created for the seeing and saying and thinking of things that shouldn't be seen, said, or thought. Likewise electrical communications that might be used to spread silly rumors abroad in the world, and artificial lighting systems other than good fat candles. What? Wax? Ah, well then, let it be wax. But fat has a certain agreeable pungency . . ."

Also, she had probably been weakened by her own passions. Before her drive, her voice had been heard raised in angry complaint against "father" Maralini, a guest from Rome (or so she said), who had been at the monastery for a week and a half now, despite a rule of long-standing that banned all men from residence here. But various sisters had seen this "reverend" figure, and knew that his nature was not unlike that of the Lady of the sanctuary (*ahhh,* no, no—be careful!—of their "mother superior") herself . . .

Now, against all the rules that Vavara had introduced oh-so-gradually during the three years of her takeover, two of the sisters, stronger than the rest, were out in the cloisters that surrounded the courtyard, seated on a bench in the shade of the fig trees. The one was Sister Delia, from Southern Ireland, the other Sister Anna, from New York. And they were out there talking during what was or should have been their watch:

"We are doomed, of course," said Delia, once a pretty redhead, now shorn of her hair and gaunt in a hooded cassock. Her Irish brogue was a thick, guttural whisper; her altered voice was hoarse or coarse, as were those of all the sisters. "If we tried to escape, went venturing out from here, we'd be doomed. Even if *she* didn't find us, still we'd be without hope. Driven by . . . by our unnatural lusts and desires" (a small shudder) "and forced to take blood, the lives of others, we'd be hunted down and destroyed by men. Or sooner or later by the sun—"

"Or by the Son," said Anna, who was once a dreamy one and something of a poet, and seemed bent on remembering and trying to retrieve that time. "The Son of Him on High. We served them both, and Mary, too, do you remember? And now we serve another, who serves the devil! The sun or the Son, or the 'mother.' One of them will destroy us, for sure. Now say, Sister Delia: What does one call that? Poetic licence, or poetic justice?"

"One calls it no justice at all, at all," said the other. "And you'd best forget all that. We're bound for hell, you and I, and all the rest of us together. God has turned his back on us, which has come of us living unnatural lives, so it has. No, I'm not just talking about Vavara's kind of unnatural. I mean, did you never fancy a man? Maybe the lad who brings the honey? Oh, I've seen you look at him from time to time. I've seen you smile at him, too. Or I used to, when you dared to smile! *That* was natural. Natural to love and lust, and to have a man lying on our bellies now and then, or even to imagine one there. But the way we were, never! All covered up and cowed and afraid of our own bodies? And certainly not the way we are now, which is utterly beyond nature."

"You mustn't talk like that!" said the ex–New Yorker. "If she were to hear . . ."

"She's up in her tower," said Delia. "Up there behind her thick velvet curtains, where never the sun reaches. And do you know, I've thought of a way?"

"A way?" Anna's voice was a shivery croak.

"A way to be rid of this vampire bitch," said Delia, "and so to rid the world of her!"

"She'll hear you!" Anna began to shrill. "She'll hear you and punish us. She *always* hears!"

"*Shhh,* now," said Delia, clasping the other and putting a hand over her mouth. "Or she really will hear us! But think on it now: if we were to go up against her as a body—*huh!* or as an 'order'—and if we took her in her tower room at noon, and threw open her curtains to let the sun blaze in . . . what then?"

"We'd burn, too," said Anna logically.

"But not as hot or as fast as Vavara. And wouldn't it be worth it, since we'll be burning soon enough whether or no?"

But now Anna was sobbing bitterly to herself. "Are we so reduced then, that we've come to this? Have we no hope, except we resort to murder? And even if we could, would the other sisters follow our lead? Vavara took us last, because we held ourselves off from her lying beauty. But the others . . . they *dine* on each other!"

"*Huh!*" Delia grunted. "Don't tell me you think that's all they do. Haven't you heard them on the creep when she's asleep? Haven't you heard them laughing? They strap on wooden cocks, to imitate the men that she won't let them have! Are you a virgin, Anna? Before you took your vows, perhaps? I think not. I wasn't, you can be sure. There's precious few virgins of my age in Ireland! I caught a dose, do you know what that is? And when I was cured I came here, I was that ashamed. So I did without men for twelve long years, stuck to my vows, didn't even finger myself. And for what? So that this beautiful bitch can visit me in the night to bite on my breasts and fill me with her special brand of poison? Ah, but if only there was a cure for this . . . !"

"Do you think they'll come for me?" Anna gasped. "I mean, with their wooden . . . things?" She pressed down on her cassock, between her legs, as if to protect herself.

"You can be certain of it," said the other. "By which time you'll probably be ready for it. For don't you see, we're falling more deeply under her spell—and more deeply into evil—day by day, or night by night. As for myself, I'll be the last. I'd rather a wooden stake than a wooden cock. Oh, ha-ha-ha! For I've had the real thing!"

"No, no!" Anna clutched at her, glanced all about with

eyes that were very slightly feral. "You must be quiet now, or someone will be bound to hear us."

"Well, what of it?" said Delia. "The sooner the better, and let's be done with it. But still I tell you, it's her or us. Do you think she won't deal with us as she dealt with Sister Sara? She *knows* which ones of us resist her, so it's only a matter of time."

"Sister Sara?" Anna's hand flew to her mouth. "Is it true, then? I had heard whispers, but—"

"Oh, it's true," Delia cut her short. "What, are you that much of an innocent, then? Did you really suppose that Sara was locked up in her room all this time? Well listen, and I'll tell you the story as I have heard it:

"Sara was the strong one, the wise one. And she was first in the long list of those whom Vavara would seduce and convert. Alas, she thought it was love! She thought that our new 'mother superior' had fallen in love with her, and in spite of an initial repugnance she couldn't refuse her advances—but then, who among us *has* refused them? For when this bitch Vavara turns it on, blood turns to water, or to poison. And so Sara was turned. But it was love not lust betrayed her. And with a creature beautiful as Vavara, she thought it was heaven, not hell-sent.

"But of course, our mother superior, Eileen was the first to pay the price. She was old, frail, no match for Vavara. And when that one first came here—so beautiful, and so penitent of her sins, filled with the need to be one of us—how could old Eileen refuse her? There was no way of knowing, not then, that this Lady was anything other than she pretended; she kept tight rein on the blood-lusting thing within, and no one ever suspected until it was too late. Yes, of course old Eileen would take her in, and in her turn be taken in. But the bitch saw no need to recruit her. Frail as a wrinkled, late autumn leaf and all dried up, the mother superior was no great challenge.

"Three months to a day after Vavara came, Eileen was dead and buried here in the crypt. But is she there now? Ah, she is not! For where Vavara is concerned, even dead women have their uses. And old Eileen, she was from my country, so she was, and I know she was a saint . . . also that she died before her time, by Vavara's will. All the more reason to loathe this vampire.

"Anyway, Sara was next. Next to be recruited, changed forever. But when she saw how Vavara proceeded—when she knew she was only the first of a long process which must eventually consume the entire monastery—then Sara rebelled. Ah, and strong in love she was also strong in her hatred, her will to survive, to fight the evil come among us.

"Vavara locked her away—to 'repent,' or so she said, the clever bitch!—and meanwhile went on recruiting all the senior sisters. In no time at all they were hers. But can we think ill of them, even as they are now? No, for this creature is a hypnotist without peer. Anything and everything that was good in the sisters, Vavara switched it off as surely as she's switched off the lights, so she did, and everything that was bad, she switched it on. For in our minds we are all wicked, as you must know, Anna. It's why we're here, so it is . . ."

"But that's not true!" the other gasped. "Or perhaps it *is* true, now that our minds have been made to dwell on . . . on such wicked things. But please say it wasn't always so?"

Delia sighed, nodded, and said, "Yes, you're right, so you are. Most of our sisters were here because of their purity—as pure as the driven snow—and only a small handful, of which I was one, to improve themselves. Oh, yes, in me there was plenty of room for improvement. But no good to deny wickedness, Anna, or to pretend it doesn't exist. For if that were the case, then why would any of us ever have needed to be here at all, at all? And then there's Vavara, the living proof of wickedness itself. She has defiled us, and all good things are flown. That is why you shouldn't listen to some of the things I've told you, some of the things I've said. For when my head is clear I know it's only the filthy stuff in my blood—the evil that she has put there—that makes me think and talk that way."

"We weren't strong enough!" said Anna, wringing her

hands. "Like our Lord, we should have put this devil behind us . . ."

"Hah!" said Delia. "Listen to you—such silliness! Where do you suppose mere mortals might find such strength? In faith alone? I wish it were so, but flesh is flesh and iron is iron. And Vavara *is* iron! Only try telling her to get behind you . . . and oh, believe me, she will!"

As Delia paused for breath and to order her thoughts, Anna gave a small gasp and whispered, "Hush, now! Is that a light up there, in her room?"

They drew back under the leaves of the fig tree, peered up through its branches at the highest windows in the square tower where Vavara had her apartments. *Was* that a glimmer of light up there? Had the Lady lit a candle?

"Moonlight on glass," Delia hissed in a while. "That's all it is."

"You're sure?"

"Yes, I'm sure. You're letting the night and your imagination run away with you, that's all. And anyway, we have a right to be here. Indeed we've no right to be anywhere else, for it's our watch. *Hah!* To think we keep guard on this place—on this monster—as if it were her fortress instead of a sanctuary . . ."

"But it is. It *is* her fortress!" said Anna. "Her aerie."

"Yes," Delia nodded, "so it is." And after a moment: "Anyway, where was I?"

"Sara," the other whispered. "She was jealous."

"Eh?" said Delia, frowning her surprise, her yellow eyes blinking. "Why, yes, I suppose she was. And hell hath no fury, eh? But it's true, it's true! And Sara in a double hell: first poisoned by Vavara, and now betrayed by her.

"And so Sara set about to defy Vavara at every turn. She escaped from her room, tried to make a run from the monastery. But Vavara caught her and locked her up again. And for the benefit of the sisters not yet taken—for there were still one or two, including ourselves—it was put about that Sara was a mad woman bent on mutilating herself. Her illness was temporary; it would pass eventually, until which time she must stay confined, 'cared for' only by Vavara and those seniors among the sisters who were Vavara's slaves.

"And so she was kept in what amounted to solitary confinement for two more years, tormented and tortured by this vampire bitch Vavara, who had determined that Sara would *never* get out. Not alive, anyway.

"But she did get out, just nine days ago, or should I say nine nights? For like the rest of us, and more than some, Sara had given in to her poisoned blood and could no longer bear the sun on her flesh or in her eyes. So she made her last run, in the evening while Vavara was still in her bed, down the road to Skala Astris, from where she'd take a taxi into Krassos town to the police station there. She would telephone the headquarters of the order in Athens; she would see doctors and show them her . . . her *disfigurements,* and she would make charges against Vavara and bring her evil reign to an end.

"How do I know these things? Because I was on watch that night as a penance for looking at Vavara in a certain way. She thought she had glimpsed hatred in my eyes—which she had—and warned me that there were greater as well as lesser punishments. But her threats had only strengthened my resolve, so it had. So then—why didn't I go with poor Sara to Krassos town and substantiate her story? Because I thought she would fail. Having watched Vavara for long and long, I knew it could never be as easy as that. And if Sara failed, who would there be to avenge her and put right the wrongs done to her and to others—indeed to all of us—in this fane of evil? Ah, but who better than someone already here, in the dark heart of the place? Who better than myself?

"And so I looked the other way, wished Sara well, and let her go, despite that I thought her errand was doomed. But you know, she might have succeeded—she just *might*—except that was the night 'father' Maralini came. And he was coming up the road as she was going down it.

"When he appeared at the wicket door—in his hooded robe, with his voice out of darkness . . . and that swooning bundle in his arms, which moaned and drooled—I knew that Satan himself had come visiting. I felt it: an enormous vileness swelling out of the night. And I even said so! Falling back, and refusing to turn the key to let him in, I gasped, 'Is it Satan, come to see his children?'

"And his eyes flared red as he answered me though the bars. 'Shaitan? Ah no!' he said. 'But I almost met him once in a far cold land, and know him for a Power! I thank you for your compliment, sister, if that's what it was. But no, I'm not Shaitan—just an old friend of your mistress, Vavara, here on business. Now let me in, for I've come a long way.'

"He stood Sara on her feet, held her there with one long-fingered hand, and thrust the other through the wicket's bars. He caught my wrist, and oh . . . the shock of terror, the bitter chill that went through me then! Look!"

Delia showed her wrist, and Anna's night-seeing eyes were drawn to the long white burn of four fingers and a thumb. And: "Not Satan, no," said Delia, "but Maralini's evil is as great, I'm sure. While he held my wrist I felt . . . I felt my *thoughts* and memories going out of me into him. He was reading my inner being, and his red eyes flared again as he said, 'And so I was right: you are indeed one of Vavara's. Now, save yourself some trouble and let me in. Your mistress is expecting me.'

"How could I refuse him? When he held my wrist like that, my mind was his to command. But he had seen into my thoughts; he knew things from my past; he smiled as I turned the key and opened the wicket gate. Such a smile! So handsome! So wicked!

"When he stepped in and after he had lain Sara aside, he turned to me. As quick and as brazen as that, he unfastened my cassock and fondled my breasts where I stood frozen. And after a while he said, 'Ah, but I know why *you* are here! Never fear, Sister Delia, your wasted years are at an end . . .' " And while I stood near-fainting, he gathered up the hem of my gown."

Sister Anna's face was ghostly pale in wan-moon and

starlight. "And did he—?" she gasped, squeezing hard on her cassock between her legs. "Did he—?"

But Delia shook her head in mock sadness and said, "Oh, ye of little faith! Only *see* how you are taken! And you say you're worried about their wooden 'things'? Why, you are almost ready, Anna! Ready and willing, for anything. And so are we all. Which is why we must see to Vavara at our earliest opportunity, while yet we are able. And after Vavara, this so-called priest, Maralini."

"Yes, yes, you're probably right," Anna whispered hoarsely, with a voice that might just as easily be hoarse from lust as from fear. "But go on with your story. *Did* he take you?"

"He might have," Delia answered. "His hands were hot on my body, and yet they were cold. And how his red eyes drank me in. 'But if you only knew,' he said, 'how hungry I am.' And then he kissed my hard-tipped breasts."

"Ahhhh!" Anna gasped, and clutched Delia's arm.

"Right there and then," the other went on, "I expected to be taken. And I knew it would be quick and hot and hurtful, but his fluids would be cold inside me. I was open, waiting, wanton and wanting. But Vavara . . . was up and about!" And now the bitterness in Delia's voice was almost regretful. "A candle glowed into life in her high room, its flame flickering in the window, and the night was suddenly alive with her presence. She was up, and she knew that someone was here—but don't ask me how. They *sense* such things, these creatures. Perhaps they can sense each other. And would you believe that I actually found myself warning him? But it's so, so it is. 'She comes!' I told him. 'Vavara comes!'

" 'Indeed she does,' he answered in a whisper. 'And so shall we, together you and I. But some other time.'

"I put right my clothing, stood back from him, and barely in time. He took up Sara, whose cowl was back so that her face was visible. And oh, that poor ravaged face—that poor soul—if she yet had a soul!

"But her face! Do you remember, Anna, how pretty Sara had been? Why, she was even as pretty as you yourself. And now with her hair all shorn, most of it pulled out by the roots, and her lips cut away so perfectly, so precisely, to make her look like a fish, and her yellow eyes—like yours, like mine—and her ears . . . but oh, she had no ears!

"And Maralini gathering her up, saying, 'Ah, but see. Your mistress hasn't lost her tender, loving touch.'

"At which Vavara came out of the tower stairwell, floating across the courtyard to the door under the archway. And:

" *'Malin—!'* she said or started to say, as she jerked to a halt. She was plainly startled, even agitated. And despite that her voice was, as always, the very sweetest thing—in tone, I mean—still it was stinging and angry. But he had stopped her midway to say:

" 'Ah, no, neither Malin nor Malinari, but *Maralini*. Father Maralini, Vavaaaara!' His voice was a breath from hell.

" 'But we had our plans,' she said. 'We had a pact, that we would not come together until all was secured . . . and then only in order to set the boundaries of our territories. And didn't I ask you not to come here? This is the worst possible time, when I have problems of my own to deal with.'

" 'So it would seem,' this 'good father' answered Vavara's angry words with ones that were carefully measured. 'Indeed, I believe that I may have bumped into one of your problems on my way up the road.' And he showed her Sara, drooling in his arms.

" 'Your touch?' she said then. 'And did you see into her?'

" 'I saw,' he answered. 'Enough to know that without I put an end to her flight, you were in serious trouble. Which would mean, of course, that I was in trouble, too. And I've had more than enough of troubles just lately. But—' (and he turned to look pointedly at me) '—shouldn't we be talking in private?'

" 'We shouldn't be talking at all!' she answered him. 'You shouldn't be here. But since you are, and since it appears I'm in your debt—come with me.'

"Then Vavara turned to me, saying, 'You, Delia—take care of . . . of *this*.' She meant Sara. 'You know where she belongs. No need to lock the door—' And she glanced knowingly at Maralini, '—not any longer. Sara is safe now and will never try to run away again. She doesn't know how to . . .'

"And then, before Maralini could give Sara to me, Vavara took me by the shoulders and shook me. But ah!—her unnatural vampire strength! 'We shall speak later, you and I, Delia,' she hissed. 'About Sara—how she got out while *you* were on watch!'

"But since then until now, she never has mentioned it. So perhaps she's forgotten all about it, for there have been other things on her mind. For which I'm glad, so I am . . .

"Anyway, it was my watch for the rest of that long night. And don't ask me, Anna, for I still don't know why I didn't run away myself in the nine nights gone by since then. Or perhaps I do, for I fancy my fate would be no less monstrous than Sara's. Which is what keeps all of us here: fear of this vampire bitch, Vavara. And now of Maralini, too.

"Later that night I saw him. He was up and about, acquainting himself with the place, I thought. He came to me and asked about Sara: how was the poor creature? As he had last seen her, I told him: drooling, feverish, moaning in her cell in the west tower. And he nodded as if he truly cared, and said, 'Aye, your mistress has not been kind to her.' Then he went away—in the direction of the west tower.

"I was curious, and in a little while I was under the west tower, huddling on the high stone balcony where it projects out over the ocean. From there I could look up at the barred window of Sara's cell two levels up. And I remembered how she had been when I'd taken her there, how I had to carry her, and how she'd mumbled in her weird delirium:

" 'He came to me out of a mist,' she'd rambled to no one in particular. 'And I ran to him, begging for his help. I hoped he wouldn't notice my eyes—but then I noticed his! And when he held my head and looked at me, I felt him sucking at my mind, my thoughts! I still have some, but faint, so very faint. I can remember you, Delia, but all else is ghostly, fading, receding from me . . .

"Then, as I seated her on her cot, she looked at me oh-so-vacantly and asked, 'What is this place? Where am I?' And oh, I knew we were all possessed . . . !

"But there I was, on the high stone balcony. How long? Not long, I think, before I saw candles lit, and heard his unmistakable voice, that voice out of hell—the voice of Maralini. He was with her, but for what? And that voice: so deep, so low, so seductive. And then his snarl!

" 'What?' he cried out, so that I heard him quite clearly. 'You have ascended? You have a leech?' And then his laugh. 'But my pleasure with you is doubled and redoubled! I shall have you Sara, and then your creature both.'

"Then Sara's screech—a bone-chilling sound—the cry of a madwoman, oh yes! *Driven* mad, by terror and torture. But Sara, she'd always been a strong one, so she had, and never more than that night.

"Whatever was left of her—of Sara herself, of the sweet sister that we'd known—it fought back, fought off Maralini's advances. I heard her cot go crashing, saw shadows clash in the light from her candles, and heard again her shriek, which ended in such a rending, tearing sound that I fancied flesh was being torn. Sara's flesh. And as it later turned out, I was right.

"But then—

"Whether she was thrown or threw herself, with all the passionate strength that a madwoman can muster, we may never know. But her window, bars and all, burst outwards. And with her tattered gown fluttering about her like the wings of a broken bird—which she was, poor thing, which she was—Sara came plunging out and down!

"Out beyond the high stone balcony she flew—such was the force of her headlong dive—and dwindling down the face of the cliffs, her ragged figure fell towards the night-dark sea. Sara, poor Sara, was gone. And I admit that I considered it a mercy.

"The next morning, before the sun was up, Vavara sent for me. She asked no questions about the previous night—said nothing about Sara getting out, and so forth—but told me to go and put Sara's cell to rights. And then she said, 'Let there be a lesson in what you find, Delia. The lesson is this: it is not wise to resist me, but it is *very* wise to resist Maralini. Remember, while you are by no means beautiful, still you have much to lose. Consider yourself fortunate, Delia, that you are older and your looks are fading. For the gap between beauty and ugliness need not be any wider than the cutting edge of a knife, as you have seen. And between homely and hideous? Ah, but you have not seen the best—or the worst—of my works! Now go!'

"And in the chaos of Sara's cell, her strewn books, tapestries, blanket, and broken cot, I found her lower jaw, its flesh all torn, like a discarded piece of a slaughtered animal . . ."

Sister Anna sat shivering under the fig tree, and her sulphur eyes were wide in the gloom. "But now I'm more afraid than ever!" she said. "I thought I'd find strength in your strength, but instead I've found horror in your story. When our watch is over, I shall pray to God the whole day through."

"He can't help us, else He surely would," Delia shook her head. "And it's a blasphemy for such as us to even mention His name. No, He can't help us—but we can help ourselves. There are sharp cleavers in the kitchen, and we can shape stakes out of pieces of good pine among the bolts of firewood."

"It's all too horrid!" cried Anna, starting to her feet.

But Delia was suddenly alert. Rising, she hissed a warning and caught the other's elbow. "Quiet now, and keep to the shade. *Look!*" And her head tilted upwards.

Up there, seen through the moon-dappled leaves of the fig, the window of Vavara's high tower was lit by a pair of flickering candles. Between them, a dark, silent silhouette gazed out on the night through scarlet pinprick eyes!

Then the head of the silhouette slowly inclined downwards, and it was as if Vavara's fiery gaze saw right through the canopy of fig leaves and into Anna's and Delia's hearts—and perhaps into their minds. Huddled together, the sisters held tight to each other and looked away. They closed their eyes and held their breath . . . they even held their *thoughts,* as for a minute or two, perhaps three, they stood frozen in their terror.

But when next they dared to look up, Vavara was gone . . .

London is two cities—one seen and one unseen. The one that is and the other that used to be, now joined by darkness. The darkness that two thousand years of men have made with all of their building, their bridging or arching over, their tunnelling of watercourses and vaults and cellars and shelters, and their veritable labyrinths of transportation and communication networks. Thus underground London, while it is still a *part* of London, is a world apart, one that has been set apart by men.

It is a subterranean city of sprawling sewers that used to be canyons, sweet-water streams and flourishing rivers, of low ways and no-go-ways that once were highways and byways, and incomplete or abandoned human-life support systems that now support hordes of squealing rats, slithering eels, croaking frogs, utterly silent, etiolated fungi . . . and who knows what else?

And there are men down there, too. The flushers.

Ten million cisterns are flushed above, most of them many times a day, and far below the city's upper pavements the flushers are paid to flush what was flushed. That's their work; it's what they do; they are the city's troglodyte antibodies, scraping away at the metal, crumbling brick, and reinforced concrete walls within its serpentine veins, keeping its systems free and its juices running, unclogging the sclerosis of inner arteries, and dispersing their accumulated detritus. For if not, then the outer skin of the city would erupt in poisons, and the city itself die.

Such might be the poetic viewpoint, while from a flusher's point of view it's far simpler: he shovels shit.

Wallace Fovargue had been a flusher, would still be if his erstwhile ganger and colleagues would have him. But they wouldn't, and neither would the Ministry of Sanitation or its subsidiary ICLC, the Inner City of London Council. For Wally Fovargue had been blacklisted and would never again work in the dark and dripping bowels of subterranean London.

He would never *work* there, no. But being who he was—the way he was, and having been a flusher all his life—Wally was always going to *be* there. For he had nowhere else to go . . . and anyway, the sewers and underground byways suited him to perfection. For one thing (and with the exception of other flushers), there were no people in them. But the flushers didn't go where Wally went, and they certainly didn't live there.

Wally had tried the surface world. He didn't much like it; he loathed his weekly excursion up from the guts of the city to collect his unemployment benefit. For to the wannabe civil servants who paid it, he was just another scruffy bum. Or not *just* a bum, but a freak, too. A stumpy-legged, long-armed, hunchback freak. And occasionally, in the dingy, half-tiled corridor that looked like the entrance to a urinal, Wally would hear the whispers of the other down-and-outers, where they waited in a queue to approach the pay-out windows in a stuffy, broom-closet-size room with reinforced one-way glass surrounds:

"That's the freak," those whispers would go. "Can you wonder why *that* specimen's out of work? Jesus, like who's going to employ some kind of fuck who looks like that?" And Wally had no doubt that the emotionless, cold-eyed cashiers counting out the money and paying him—without ever touching him—thought the same thing. One of Mother Nature's little errors, our Wally. But on the other hand they'd never argued with him, never tried pushing him into some job he didn't want. Oh, yes—they, too, knew that he wasn't going to find a job, also that they weren't going to find one for him.

Only glance at them suddenly, catch them unawares, and the thought was right there, written in their cold eyes and pinched nostrils: *Who in his right mind is ever going to employ a sick-looking fuck like this?* The one good thing about it, they paid up and got him out of there just as quick as you like. He never had to explain why he hadn't been out looking for a job, or how come he continued to be "of no fixed abode."

The money wasn't much, but that was okay; Wally could live on it, barely. That was the beauty of not having a mortgage to pay off, of *not* having a roof over your head. But in fact Wally had hundreds over his, an entire city of them. Westminster, the Houses of Parliament, Bond Street, Mayfair, the Bank of England, the Ritz, even Buckingham Palace! Some pretty high-class residences up there. And some high-class arses perching on the crappers that watered Wally's underworld.

But Wally didn't waste time while he was up there. He was obliged to go there, for the money, but once he'd been paid—shortly after nine o'clock on Thursday mornings, for he always tried to be first in the queue—then he would get off to the nearest supermarket with his list. Food came first, of course, then a six-pack of beers (he didn't drink on Sundays), candles and batteries, one newspaper (he liked to keep up to date with current events), and his favourite magazines . . . girlie magazines, yes.

Wally dressed as best he could—which only served to add to the incongruity of his appearance. If he were tramplike, he would scarcely warrant a second glance. But reasonably attired, he was out of place and people looked at him as they would at a dressed-up orangutan. That was what he couldn't bear about the overworld: the fact that people stared, frequently laughed, and then looked away in embarrassment.

He was—or might be, according to Darwin at least—the product of "natural" selection. Wally's great-great-grandfather had been a flusher of sorts (or, as he would have been known in his time, a "tosher," one of an early breed of sewer scavengers who earned their livings from whatever they could salvage), and likewise his great-grandfather, his grandfather, and his father immediately before him. So perhaps all those accumulated generations and years of stooping, shovelling, and scraping had altered his genes to suit. For in aspect he *was* a troglodyte.

Wally was forty-three and balding; a slipped halo of hair hung down like a curtain to cover his big ears and the back of his pock-marked neck, and was cut in a ragged-fringe over bushy-black-eyebrows. His broad shoulders were powerfully muscled, as were his gangly arms and short, thick thighs. Reduced in height by his stumpy-legs and S-bend-spine, he was just three feet and nine inches tall, ideal for work in sewers that were often only three to four and a half feet in diameter.

Except he no longer worked there . . .

As to how that had come about, his dismissal: it had resulted from what the tribunal had been obliged to call an "accident," for Wally had been the only witness. As to what had happened:

A flusher he had been working with had been sucked into a vertical sump where he had drowned in excrement. But since this was the second accident of its sort in nine months (another man had been crushed by a cave-in of rotten bricks), and since both of the deceased were known to be practical jokers who from time to time had preyed on the hunchback . . .

. . . The other flushers had flatly refused to work with him. For whether in malice or in passing, they'd all had their "fun" with Wally in their time, but no way were they about to let him have his with them! And the flusher gangs weren't the only suspicious ones; there had been serious doubts in the minds of several officials sitting on the tribunal. But lacking evidence to the contrary Wally had got away with double murder. At least to the extent that he hadn't as yet paid for his crimes, except in the coin of the rough companionship he'd shared with the flushers. *Well fuck them!*

Wally wasn't a well man. He had twice suffered from spells of a mild form of hepatitis, and he suspected he might have contracted Weil's disease from rat urine. Well-read on the hazards of his lifestyle, he knew that the disease finds a hold in cuts and scratches, and eventually attacks the brain.

Certainly he'd found himself thinking some weird things recently—and not so recently, either.

It had started maybe three years back, when Wally had been a flusher proper. Then, as now, his hearing had been more acute than the rest of his "mates," also his sense of smell, and he'd begun to hear and smell all sorts of unusual things in subterranean London. Sounds from regions where there shouldn't have been anyone or -thing to make them, and whiffs that weren't ammonia, or choke- or fire-damp, or the putrid stench of sulphurated hydrogen. Weird whiffs, really . . . *like* death and decomposition, and yet like life, too, though just what kind of life was anybody's guess. But in any case the sounds and stenches had always come from places he couldn't reach, the unknown, abandoned or forgotten nether levels of an older underworld entirely. Places that Wally's coworkers weren't authorized to visit, and where they would never wish to venture anyway.

Also, he had thought on occasion to see movements, shadows where there shouldn't be any. Shadows weren't a rarity; light a candle and he'd have shadows that moved with the flicker of the flame. But in torchlight, and especially when the torch was stationary—seated on a table, perhaps, for reading, or over his bed, as he settled to sleep—then Wally's shadows should stay sharp and really weren't entitled to move at all. But sometimes . . . sometimes he thought they did.

And very strange shadows at that. Not small, scuttling rat shadows, but those of something much larger, even man-size, and swiftly flowing. Except of course, men don't flow . . .

Such were Wally's thoughts on the Thursday morning in question, as he carried his bag of provisions into a lane off Fleet Street, entered a walled back garden running to wilderness, and went down on all fours to vanish under a canopy of brambles and rank shrubbery. South flowed the Thames, and east lay the inner City of London itself. The River Fleet, a submerged watercourse that once ran on the surface, gurgled soundlessly, directly underfoot. And there, under a thin layer of dirt and parched leaves, Wally lifted the Victorian manhole cover that was only one of his many entranceways to the underworld.

Fastening his bag to his belt, Wally let himself down into darkness. His feet found the rungs and he descended, only pausing to pull the antique manhole cover back into place overhead. Then, squeezing himself tight to the wall to allow for his malformed back, he continued his descent.

Twenty feet or so vertical to the first level, then a veritable labyrinth of conduits and tunnels, and walkways like towpaths that marched alongside turbid rivers of slurry, seemingly endless low-ceilinged sewers, and echoing, mist-wreathed galleries of rusting, abandoned tracks . . . then further descents down shaky, flaking rungs that browned his palms with rust, and more galleries, waterways, sewers, and so on. Ninety minutes, in all, to get to the place that Wally called home. A very short distance as the crow flies—but crows were in short supply in Wallace Fovargue's domain—and the way confused and wandering, literally labyrinthine.

If Wally had been a ganger, a boss, there were *such* places he could have shown his flushers, places they wouldn't believe! But to get to them they'd need to be daring, brave, and imaginative beyond their mundane imaginations. For they had only ever seen this underworld as a workplace, while to Wally it was the entire world—*his* world. And in it, some sumptuous places.

Sump-tuous, yes! And Wally chuckled as he covered the last few yards of the last tunnel to his "residence."

The tunnel was an uncompleted (in fact barely begun) railway line, where short, small-gauge ties were still visible, indicating the use of manual bogies in the removal of debris. The tracks, however, had been taken out, possibly to be melted down for war materials. During the Second World War this place had been opened up for use as an air-raid shelter. The access shafts had later been filled in; but the sweating brick walls still boasted a few tattered recruitment posters that dated back to 1943 and '44, while others continued to warn against fifth-columnists.

Wally read them as the history of a time he'd never

known, but that his father had remembered vividly—until Weil's disease had taken him. "The sirens would make an 'ell of a noise," his father had told him. "Then the Old Folks'd bundle us up, me and yer auntie" (she was in a "home" somewhere now) "and 'urry on darn the unnergrarnd. Well, that was like an 'ome from 'ome ter me, wot wiv workin' darn there and wotnot . . ."

And it was like going home to Wally, too. In fact, the one and only home he had known for more than a year now, since his landlord gave him the boot for "frightening" the other tenants. Frightening them? Why, Wally had scarcely ever *looked* at them! Which had been enough, apparently.

But what the hell, there were no snivelling, tale-telling "tenants" down here. Just the rats and frogs, the eels and mosquitoes, and various small bat colonies. And no grubby landlord to pay, either. So as for the overworlders—*fuck 'em all!*

Wally climbed up onto what might have been intended for a platform if the underground line and station had ever seen completion. Now he was at the hub of a system of radiating tunnels, none of them going very far, one of which had still been fitted with indestructible army-style bunk beds when Wally first found the place. He'd kept one such bed intact, dismantling and stacking the others to make more room.

He had long since tapped into the nearest water main, had all the drinking and washing water he needed; the same with gas for cooking. No problem there. But he'd steered clear of electricity; it was available but he'd avoided it. He had this aversion to messing about with live wires, and anyway he'd heard a rumour that they could track unauthorized users. Also, his eyes were pretty well suited to weak light; a couple of candles or a dim, battery-powered torch beam was about all he needed. No T.V. no, but he was equipped with a windup radio. Its aerial was a half-mile of wire whose other end was tied to a lightning conductor in the steeple of an old church near Moorgate. One hell of a job that had proved, but well worth it. The reçeption was quite marvellous.

Fat for cooking? No problem. The restaurants in the inner

city poured away thousands of gallons every night. They weren't supposed to, but they did. A flusher's nightmare, that: scraping or shovelling tons of that slop off of the walls and out of the pipes, before it hardened into giant candles and blocked up the entire works. *Huh!* And they wondered why the rat population was swelling the way it was!

Wally knew where there was a regular chimney of the stuff. The rats could chew all they wanted on the rancid external layers, but deep inside it was still pretty clean. It was similar to cheese, Wally thought: it went hard or stale on the outside but stayed soft in its core. He had a long-handled sugar scoop that could gouge right into it. And it smelled quite wonderful, of just about everything they'd been cooking up there. Sausages and beans could take on all kinds of oriental flavours . . .

As for toilets: three minutes in just about any direction, or less than that if you weren't fussy. And Wally wasn't especially fussy. Temperature? Winter or summer up above, down here it was constant, always mild; two blankets sufficed.

So he was home safe and dry, and all that remained was to visit the harem, let his ladies know he was back, and complain to them about the miserable day he'd had "upstairs."

His ladies: an entire gallery of them on the walls of the tunnel adjoining his bedroom. He would have them in the bedroom itself, but that might prove too much of a distraction. There's a time for sleeping and a time for the other—hence the harem. And now it was time for the other.

Wally had been looking forward to this moment all morning, and now his excitement grew as he sat down at his table (an old folding card table) and took out his magazines. Way back in the past there had been a men's magazine called *Playboy*—the women had been beautiful, and the pictures soft-edged, warm and glowing, even "artistic" in a prurient sort of way. All of that was old hat these days, when art had given way to pure pornography. But the centrefold tradition still held true, if not to its origins.

Wally still kept a few of those old *Playboy* centrefolds pasted to the walls of his harem, but they were there for when the mood called for love, not lust. They were pictures of women he would have been able to love (*if* he'd been able and acceptable), not sluts with their legs gaping and their fingers holding themselves open for viewing! But the sad fact was that the majority of the glossily, lewdly pictured "ladies" in Wally's harem were of the latter variety. For love had passed him by without a second glance, and lust was all that was left.

Removing the staples from the magazines, Wally spread the centrefolds on his table and examined them in torch-and candlelight. Flecks of drool dampened the corners of his mouth as he stared at close range at what would in most women be their most private places. But in these pictures he could look at and *into* them. He could look at them, touch them with trembling fingers and a fevered imagination, but never get into them or even near them "in the flesh." But there was always the next best thing—which of necessity had ever been the way of it with Wally.

"A man's best friend," he told himself—hurrying with his paste pot, brush, his new lady-friends, and the throbbing penis with which they'd suddenly, spontaneously endowed him, through into his gallery, his harem—"is his good right wanking hand!" And with his torch jammed firmly in a gap where the mortar had fallen from between bricks in a gradually buckling wall, Wally quickly pasted up his new acquisitions.

Then, taking up his torch in his *left* hand, he began plying his fat, veined cock, aiming his torch first at one photograph, then the next, and slowly rotating to take in the entire gallery. This was what his ladies liked, he knew: that he shared his affections equally between them, showing no favoritism. But after he had turned full circle, returning to his "raw" recruits, then he made fast his torch in the wall again, so that it would hold steady as finally he brought himself to climax. Except that didn't happen. For suddenly . . .

. . . There in the corner of Wally's eye, a shadow where

no shadow should be. And while his torch held steady in its crack in the wall, still the shadow moved, flowed—and it was cast by something *behind* Wally, something that was gradually occluding the torch's beam.

And while he stood there frozen, still clutching his rapidly shrinking penis, so that grotesque shape—or shadow, or dark stain—flowed over the circle of light and plunged Wally's ladies, and Wally himself, into inky darkness. And behind him something awesome breathed, just inches from his straining ears!

On legs like rubber, Wally turned, looked, saw . . .

Limned in weak torchlight, a jet-black silhouette, a fantastic shape, stood close. Scarlet eyes blinked, observing him closely and at close range. Then a hand—or something resembling a hand—reached out to settle on Wally's shoulder. And as he gave a massive start:

"Ah, no!" said a low, dark voice like the gurgle of one of Wally's drains. "Have no fear, my son, not of me. For we are as one. I have watched you for long and long: how you degrade yourself, hiding in the dark places like a moth, a fly-the-light—even like a Starside trog, or indeed like myself—because you are ugly. But believe me, you are by no means the ugliest."

And the shape flowed to one side a little, until the edge of the beam of light fell more surely upon it. And turning its face right profile halfway into the light, it tilted its head inquiringly, opened wide its furnace eyes, and cracked its unbelievable jaws in such a smile that Wally—

—That Wally simply fainted dead away . . .

Part Two
Intimations

7
Putting It Together

BEN TRASK SLEPT LATE. AFTER WASHING, SHAVing, and dressing, he made a few quick notes and was leaving his room to go to breakfast in the hotel downstairs (coffee, two slices of toast, and a boiled egg, as usual) when his phone rang. It was the Minister Responsible; he'd come through the duty officer and was on scrambled.

"Mr. Trask," he began, "I've spoken to the director of the Bürger Finanz Gruppe bank and managed to extract you from your little pile of mess—again!"

"This early?" Trask glanced at his watch—not quite 9:30 A.M. in London—but of course Switzerland had started off the day an hour earlier.

"The early bird catches the worm, Mr. Trask. But really, I have to ask you to take a firmer hand with your people. I mean, I know the importance of what you're doing, but—"

"*But* . . . I don't think you do know," Trask cut in. "If you did you'd have better things to do than come fishing for apologies, especially when I haven't had breakfast yet. And when it comes to digging people out of the shit, how deep in it do you think you and the rest of the world would be if not for *my* people? Okay, so I had an 'eager beaver' who got ahead of herself. But it's also possible she's given us our best lead so far. So I've reprimanded her on the one hand, congratulated her on the other. Now then, do you approve? If you do, try unloading that chip off your shoulder. If you don't, I'm open to suggestions. You could always retire me, I suppose."

And after a brief silence: "Must you always take things so personally?" the Minister's voice was still very calm, but much colder now. "I mean, where your people are concerned,

Mr. Trask? Last night you were *almost* apologetic."

"Last night I was very tired," said Trask. "I'm talking about three years' worth of tired—which to you probably indicates three years of not much happening, three years of running around and much ado about nothing? Maybe you've got used to the notion that these creatures are here, and since they don't seem to be doing too much their threat no longer seems as great. But just because it was quiet for a while doesn't mean it's over—Australia proved that much. And yes, I do take things very personally where my people are concerned. It's something they call loyalty. You should try it some time. Who knows, it might even be infectious."

"Mr. Trask, now you're trying to insult me!"

"I see it the other way round," said Trask. "Were you out there in Australia with me, fighting these bloody vampire invaders of our world? Did you see people dying out there, blown to bits in booby traps? Was it you who—er, how did you put it?—'extracted me from that little pile of mess' when it appeared I was next on the death list? Hell, no, it wasn't you, it was my people. But you . . . you haven't even found the time to say that you're glad to see us all back in one piece. And now you expect me to grovel because you've 'extracted me from a little pile of mess'? Of course, I take it personally!"

Another brief silence, and then: "It's true that I haven't yet congratulated you on the Australian job," the Minister said. "Well now I do so. I'm only asking you to remember that just as you answer to me—or rather, as you are *supposed* to answer to me—so I must answer to others above me. But sometimes answers are hard to come by. As you know, I coordinate our security services, Mr. Trask, which means that I'm just as covert in my work as you are in yours. And as vulnerable. When breaches of international etiquette occur, and when my people are responsible—for you *are* my people—then I'm liable to get just as upset as you. Our jobs are equally onerous, I assure you."

Upset, Trask thought. *Merely upset! The phlegmatism of the upper class English gentleman!* But he had to smile, for he knew that what the Minister had said was very true. "Big fleas have little fleas upon their backs to bite 'em," he quoted, and was rewarded by the other's wry chuckle.

"I know the next line to that one," the Minister answered. " 'And little fleas have smaller fleas, and so ad infinitum.' "

"And it also works in reverse, right?" Trask nodded. "We little fleas have to be careful how we ride the bigger ones in case they take umbrage and scratch us off. Okay, so thanks for helping us out . . ." And after a moment: "Can I take it that the director of the Bürger Finanz Gruppe won't be informing a certain 'charity' about a certain breach of security—or 'etiquette,' if you insist?"

"You can indeed," the Minister said. "Also, if any further funding is to be released through that outlet, I'm assured that we'll be advised well in advance."

Trask jumped at that, making no attempt to hide his eagerness. "But will that help us? I mean, do we know where the outlet is? What town, city, country? I'd just love to be there if or when any more money is paid out. We could trace it right to our . . . well, let's for the moment call him 'our man.' Or better still, our target. One of our targets."

"No," the Minister answered. "All of the Swiss banks still play it very close to their chests—er, their treasure chests? It's the closest thing you'll ever get to a doctor/patient relationship. Complete confidentiality. But anyway, good luck with whatever it is you've tracked down."

"Tracking," Trask corrected him. "We're not there yet. And talking about not being there, my breakfast is waiting and I've a think tank in just an hour's time. Thanks for calling, if not for the slap on the wrist."

"Think nothing of it," said the other. "But do please keep those eager beavers of yours on a leash, won't you?" And before Trask could answer he put his phone down. As the Minister Responsible, he liked to have the last word.

Oh, I won't, Trask told himself, meaning he wouldn't think anything of it. Then, slightly ruffled on the one hand, pleased on the other, he left his E-Branch accommodation and went for a late breakfast . . .

* * *

Going into the think tank in a smaller room off Ops, Trask stopped Millicent Cleary and had a word with her in private. "I had to take a little flak from the man upstairs," he told her. "But at least he took the heat off us. I'll tell you about it later. Meanwhile, have you given any more thought as to where Malinari might be?"

Jimmy Harvey was squeezing by them where they stood inside the door. "I couldn't help but hear that," he said, keeping his voice down as he joined them.

"What part of it?" Trask looked him up and down. "And what in hell have you been doing to yourself? A rough night or something?"

Harvey cut a gnomish sort of figure. A short, compact man at five feet and four inches, he was the whiz-kid computer and communications expert who—along with Millie—had almost got Trask into trouble last night. In his mid-twenties, and prematurely bald, but with long red sideburns and bushy eyebrows that tried hard to make up for his baldness; grey, watery eyes; and a positive genius for electronics, he did in fact remind Trask of a clever, occasionally mischievous gnome. Right now, though, there were bags under his eyes, his face was lined and sagging, and his clothes looked like he'd slept in them.

Yawning behind his hand, Harvey answered Trask's question: "Last night, after Millie went off to talk to you, I sat around awhile in Ops—more than a while, actually. I didn't hit the sack until around three A.M. But I found stuff to do . . . I was just following orders, putting in some of the extra time you've been asking for. Anyway, before I called it a night I fed some stuff into the extraps. This morning I was back in Ops, and the machines have come up with some interesting ideas."

As Harvey finished speaking, Trask looked beyond him into the room. The other think-tank members were all assembled; they sat at a large, oblong table with notepads and pencils to hand. They were Ian Goodly, David Chung, Paul Garvey, and John Grieve, all of them longtime members of

E-Branch; the "upper echelon," as it were. The only one who was missing—who really should have been here—was Anna Marie English, but she was in Sunside. And Zek, of course, or Mrs. Trask, as they had all-too-briefly known her. But Zek wasn't anywhere anymore, or if she was, then it was a place way beyond anyone's ability to reach.

Beyond Trask's abilities, anyway . . .

Others, who weren't from the original cast, were Liz Merrick (who was here because of her connection with Jake Cutter), and Lardis Lidesci, chiefly because he was wont to jump in now and then with some pretty sharp, intuitive comments. Jimmy Harvey was a recent recruit; he was here to represent the techs.

"Let's join them," Trask said. "And we'll start with you, Jimmy." And then, as they seated themselves, Trask at the head of the table: "Good morning," he greeted the others, then went straight into it. "We're going to start off with Jimmy. He and Millie have been working, er, privately, on something with terrific potential. It would seem they've come up with the goods. We're not there yet, but we're certainly halfway. That's what we're here for—to finish what they've started. Thinking caps on, everyone, and let's hear what Jimmy has to say. Jimmy?"

The tired-looking Harvey took it from there. "Millie and I did a little, er, poaching last night—that's illicit fishing. Mr. Trask might want to enlarge on that later," he glanced apprehensively at Trask, then at Millie, and quickly went on, "—or maybe not. Anyway, we narrowed down Malinari's possible whereabouts to just a handful of countries, and later I fed them into one of the extraps together with some stuff we'd come across in Australia. By then it was late and I didn't wait around to find out what the computer would come up with. But this morning—"

"Wait!" said Trask. "We'll all be better off if we can see the whole picture. Just what was this stuff from Australia that you fed into the extrap?"

Harvey shrugged. "Well, for one there was the Bruce Trennier connection. He was an Aussie, or a New Zealander, which to me seemed close enough. And then there's the fact that the Australian tropics are just about as far as possible from where we would normally have expected to find Malinari. And, since I was putting Trennier's name in there, it seemed sensible to include the names of the others who were taken from the Refuge when the Wamphyri came through. So I also entered details from our files on Andre Corner and Denise Karalambos. And finally, I requested the odds on our short list of locations."

"Corner and Karalambos," Trask frowned, and Millie Cleary stepped in:

"Andre Corner was a Harley Street psychiatrist who specialized in kids and young adults," she said. "He'd long since made his pile and wanted to give something back. His teenage son had died of a massive drugs overdose. Corner's self-imposed penance—for letting his son down, I suppose—was to work at the Refuge as a volunteer, helping all those young Romanian people."

Trask nodded. "Yes, I remember now . . ." It should have been hard to forget, really, but he'd erased a lot of the details of that time from his mind. "And Denise Karalambos was—?"

"She was a paediatrician from Athens, another volunteer," Millie obliged.

Things were coming together now, and Trask—and probably everyone else—was beginning to see where this was going.

"How come these things—these names and details—weren't already in the computer?" Trask wanted to know.

"They were," Harvey answered. "But the extraps aren't programmed to play hunches. They only work with hard facts, and we hadn't been asking the right questions."

And David Chung, the locator, came in with: "That's right. Instead of describing Starside as their sort of habitation, and trying to predict where the Wamphyri would feel most at home in our world, we'd have been a lot better off trying to figure out where their new lieutenants were likely to take them!"

"So," Ian Goodly piped up. "Just exactly what did your extrap come up with, Jimmy?"

And Harvey said, "I'd supplied the computer with the countries that Millie and I had short-listed: Italy, Greece, Switzerland, and some South American countries. And I had also paired off Malinari and Trennier in Australia. The rest must have been easy. If I'd stuck around for another ten minutes, I might well have had the answer last night."

"Greece!" said Trask, thumping the table and making everyone jump. "That's where Malinari has gone, to one of his bloody colleagues—Szwart or Vavara, whichever—in Greece. He took Trennier, and let Trennier take *him* to Australia, where he then gained his foothold. And as for that poor woman Denise Karalambos, she would have made the perfect tour guide in Greece. But for which one of the other monsters, Vavara or Szwart?"

"Vavara," Lardis Lidesci growled at once. "And now it begins to make sense . . . or most of it . . . or I'm a bloody fool!"

"Okay," Trask said again. "Let's calm it down, keep it orderly, though I'll admit I'm just as excited as the next man, or woman. So then, Jimmy, what *did* the extrap come up with?"

"You were right first time," Harvey nodded. "Greece it is. A high probability factor. But the machine wasn't able to pair Miss Karalambos off with one of the Wamphyri, couldn't 'guess' which one of them is there . . ." He paused to glance at Lardis. "So what makes you think it's Vavara?" And suddenly Lardis was the focus of everyone's attention.

"Why, because Miss Karalambos *is* a miss!" the Old Lidesci answered. "Because she's female! And according to immem-, er, immemor-, er—according to old Sunside legends, Vavara always preferred the company of women. Oh, she would have *had* her men . . . er, for various reasons." (He lowered his head a little to peer briefly at Liz and Millie.) "To fight her battles for her and so on. But when it came to company, Vavara's court was one of women. And she could sway them as easily as she could men."

"The Lady Vavara!" Trask sighed. "Vavara and Malinari together. Our chance to take out two of these birds of prey with one stone."

"Not Lady, no," Lardis shook his head. "Not the *Lady* Vavara, just Vavara. She spurned the title Lady, because she more than any other female of the Wamphyri knew it for a great lie. If you're right and she is in Greece, I fancy we go up against the worst possible combination of vampire powers. Malinari and his mentalism, and Vavara with her hypnotism. And whatever you do, you must never underestimate Vavara because she is female. Remember if you will Wratha the Risen, Ursula Torspawn, Zindevar Cronesap, and the worst of them all, Devetaki Skullguise. *Huh!* For weren't they 'Ladies,' too?"

"Thanks for the reminder," said Trask. "But just a moment ago you called yourself a bloody fool. Why?"

"Because I was there, as well you know! I was actually out there, in Greece, before you called me to Australia. I spoke to Travellers, to that old chief, Vladi Ferengi. A damned Ferengi! That in itself should have told me that something wasn't right. *And* they had known infection—that girl of theirs, buried with silver coins on her eyes—but someone had seen fit to dig the poor lass up again and put a stake through her. Who else, do you suppose, but the one who had vampirized her in the first place? Who else but someone trying to cover her tracks, eh?"

"You're right," said Trask, "and it is all coming together. "But you can't blame yourself for failing to see what now seems so obvious. Being a Traveller, Szgany yourself, you were simply too close to the problem, that's all."

"And Vladi and his people, they were out there looking for one of their 'strange places,' one of the Gateways!" said Lardis.

Trask nodded. "Or for someone who'd recently come through just such a Gate. Old Vladi and that beak of his, he'd 'sniffed out' Vavara but couldn't find her because she wasn't the 'great Lord' he was looking for. He and his people didn't find Vavara, no, but it now looks more than likely that she found them!"

By now the other members of the think tank were looking at both Lardis and Trask together, and he realized that they weren't in on this. Quickly he explained what had happened to Lardis in Greece, then said, "And so we've got several leads we can work on—for a start, Vladi and the Ferengis. We need to know where they'd been immediately *before* that girl went down with—with whatever it was, for we're not as yet one hundred percent certain. Pretty sure, but not certain."

And Chung came in again with: "Damn! You want to know something? Of all the places we've looked at, me and the other locators, mainland Greece is the one we've skipped. It's too close to Romania, and beyond Romania the USSR as was. Romania has always had its mindsmog, clinging to its old places like . . . like some kind of mental radioactivity. But as for the genuine article, radioactivity itself: well, the Russians have been dumping their crap in the Black Sea for so long now that whenever I try scanning anything in that direction all I get is a headache! So even if I'd tried, no way I was going to pick up Vavara or anyone else in all that smog."

"But what if you were physically there?" Trask said. "What if you were in Greece itself? What then?"

"The closer the better," Chung answered. "Even a blind man knows when he's stepped in something nasty. Will you be putting a team together?"

And before Trask could answer, Millie Cleary came in with: "I'm the one who found him—Malinari, I mean. Isn't it time I was given some fieldwork?"

Now the team's attention switched to Millie, and Trask had to agree: "She's right. While their methods may have been a bit unorthodox—or perhaps I should say downright illegal—still Millie, along with her colleague in crime Mr. Jimmy Harvey, did find us our target. At least they pointed us in the right direction. But we haven't pinpointed Malinari yet." And he quickly covered his and Millie's conversation of the previous night.

Following which Millie came back in with, "So since we now know or strongly suspect that Malinari is with Vavara in Greece, that narrows down the number of banks that could have made payment to that charity, right? Is there any way to find out which Greek banks the Bürger Finanz Gruppe does business with?"

"Nice try," said Trask, "but I've only just got our Minister Responsible off my back in respect of your *last* investigations! But . . . you might just have something. I don't think we'd get anywhere from the Swiss end—complete confidentiality, and all that—so what we could use is some good Greek liaison. And I think I know just the man."

David Chung was pretty certain he knew who Trask was talking about. A good deal of time had passed since the Janos Ferenczy affair in Rhodes and the Greek islands, but someone who had been of invaluable assistance had stayed in touch ever since. A firm friend of E-Branch, the Greek policeman—now an Inspector of Police, in Athens—would be sure to offer them all the help they needed. Indeed, he would probably want to be in on it as a leading participant. To be sure he was on the right track, however, Chung queried:

"You mean Manolis Papastamos?"

And Trask nodded. "The same. As soon as we're out of here, I'll contact him and see what I can arrange."

"So how will we handle it?" John Grieve spoke up. "I mean, I know it's early days yet, but what's the plan to be? If we're sending a team out to Australia, and if we're to man the HQ and carry out our normal duties at the same time—good Lord! You know I can't believe I said 'normal' just then?—won't it leave us a bit thin on the ground? Malinari *and* Vavara, together? But this will have to be some kind of task force that we're talking about here! We're not going to take them easy, assuming that we can find them. And in Greece . . . well, even with this Greek fellow on our side we can't expect the same level of local support that we had down under."

Again Trask's nod. "It's early days, yes. But time, as they say, is of the essence. So you're right, and the sooner we formulate a plan—a skeleton we can flesh out later—the better. And talking about skeletons, the follow-up Australian team will have to be just that: a spotter, a telepath, and that about covers it. Our Aussie friends will supply the muscle, if such is required. As for a Greek task force: again you're right. We'll have to be out there in strength—well, as soon as we know for sure just exactly where we're going."

"We should start with Vladi Ferengi and his people," Lardis Lidesci growled. "For once we know where they have been—"

"—Then we'll know where we are going," Trask finished it for him. And then, glancing at David Chung: "Is Bernie Fletcher on duty?"

"We're *all* on duty!" Paul Garvey reminded him. "We have a couple of men on foreign embassy duties, but the rest of us are here at HQ. You asked us to put some time in, and we're putting it in."

"Then let's go down to Ops," said Trask, standing up. "And on the way, someone can get ahold of Bernie."

"Wait!" said Garvey, as his face twisted grotesquely for a second or so. Then: "No need to go looking for Bernie," he said, letting his features return to what everyone was used to. "I've already got him. He's on his way to Ops."

Paul Garvey was a telepath. When he used his powers, as he had just this moment, it wasn't a pretty sight. It required concentration; "It's all in the way you chew on your lip," Garvey himself had often explained it, though never humorously.

Tall, well built, and still athletically trim despite his fifty-six years, Garvey had been good-looking, too, before he'd gone up against one of Harry Keogh's most dangerous adversaries, the necromancer Johnny Found, and lost most of the left side of his face. That had been some twenty years ago. At the time, and on several occasions since, some of England's best surgeons had worked on Paul until he looked half-decent—but a real face is made of more than just so much flesh scavenged from other parts. His reconstructed features had been rebuilt from living tissue, true, but the muscles on the left didn't pull the same as those on the right, and even after all these years the nerves weren't connecting up too well. Paul could smile with the right side of his face but not the left, for which reason and even though the other espers were used to it, he normally avoided smiling altogether . . . and avoided all other facial expressions, too.

Bernie Fletcher was waiting in Ops when they got there. He was a burly five-foot-eight redhead, an intuitive locator whose talent made him an ideal target for spotters in that it worked both ways: he was a locator, but he could also be located. Telepathic members of the Branch—indeed all of Trask's espers—never had much trouble homing in on Bernie; his mental activity was like magnetic north to a lodestone, and the telepaths could even send simple instructions which usually arrived in Bernie's mind as compulsive "urges." He might occasionally recognize the author, and then he'd follow up the "suggestion" as a matter of course even if he didn't know what was going on. Such as now.

"What's up?" he said, his green eyes narrowing to a frown as Trask and the think tank arrived in Ops.

"You are," said Trask. "Up for promotion, if you can pull it off."

"Eh?" Bernie blinked owlishly. "What's going on, boss? Why am I here?" The others were pretty much *au fait* with what Trask was talking about, but Fletcher wasn't in on it as yet.

"Maps," said Trask, glancing at the big wall screen. "Maps of Greece. The most detailed maps we've got."

But David Chung said: "Sir?" Which drew Trask's attention. The locator was still wont to call Trask *sir* in front of lesser members.

"Yes?" Trask looked at him.

"You asked Ian and I to set up a special map room. We did, including a big screen. We'd be better off three doors down the corridor. Less hustle and bustle."

"Lead the way," said Trask.

As the door to Ops closed behind them, a handful of espers and techs working there looked at it, then at each other, shrugged and went back to work.

While just outside the door, Paul Garvey stepped out alongside Trask and said, "Ben, that skeleton staff you were talking about? Back here at HQ, I mean? I'd like to be part of it."

Trask knew what he meant. Garvey had taken the plunge just two years earlier and his younger wife was very pregnant. Moreover she was blind, which made them the ideal couple. Receptive of his telepathic skills, she had found a new life in Paul; she could "see" through his eyes, his talent. And with her, he needn't concern himself about his looks; he had found an outlet for years of trapped emotions.

"Don't worry about it," Trask told him, as Chung opened up the door to his and Ian Goodly's study room. "You're already on my list for rear-party duties. You, Bernie, John Grieve, and—" But Millie Cleary was there, right behind him, looking at Trask in that way of hers. And so, shrugging awkwardly, he finished, "—Oh, and one or two others. Maybe."

Bernie Fletcher had overheard their conversation. "What's that?" he turned to Trask as the others filed by into the room. "I'm staying back? Again? Why me?"

"You know why you," said Trask. "Malinari's a mentalist—a proven mentalist—of extraordinary power. At close range he could suck you in like a vacuum cleaner. Let's face it, Bernie, you stand out like a sore thumb in the metaphysical aether. You glow in the dark, man! Oh, I can use you to discover the whereabouts of such as these Gypsies, but I'm not going to risk you anywhere near Lord Nephran Malinari."

"You think I'd maybe let the team down?" Bernie's face had fallen and his expression was suddenly glum.

"Not you," Trask answered, "but your talent. I'm not going to be sending up any signal flares, you can be sure. But that's not my main concern—you are. We've dealt with such as Malinari before. If you're out of touch with the Janos

Ferenczy business, I suggest you read up on it ASAP—and then I'm betting you won't *want* to come with us!" He turned to Grieve.

"And John: as usual you'll be our anchorman here at HQ. Do you have any problems with that?"

The other shook his head. "Since I'm not much on hand-to-hand combat, flinging grenades, jumping out of helicopters and all such, I have no problems at all with that. The rest of you can go get yourselves killed." His way of saying "break a leg," in the theatrical tradition.

Trask grinned and said, "You're just an old stay-at-home, that's all."

"And me?" Millie caught at Trask's elbow. "Am I to stay at home, too?"

"We can talk about that when we're finished here," he told her. "But right now it's business." Which told Millie something at least: that she wasn't business but personal—which in turn served to produce a warm if mildly frustrated feeling in her.

The room was small, a remodelled hotel room, with an oval, glass-topped table standing central, two chairs, and a big rear window fitted with bars and blinds (currently open) that looked out on an impressive view of central London. But in the middle of the table, Malinari's fire-scorched battle gauntlet sat like a grotesque, eighteen-inch, grey-metal alien insect, and on one otherwise naked wall a four-by-five-foot flat-screen viewer was hanging from the picture rail. Beneath the viewscreen, set back from the wall, a swivel chair stood in front of the white plastic casing of a sophisticated computer console and keyboard.

Chung sat down in the swivel chair and switched on the computer. In a moment, as he tapped at the keys, the screen flickered into life and displayed a detailed map of mainland Greece, with Athens at the bottom and Sofia in Bulgaria at the top.

"Swing northeast," Bernie Fletcher instructed, "into Bulgaria." He now believed he knew what was going on, knew what he was looking for. It could only be that Trask and company were following up on his and Lardis's Greek expedition. "But if it's their trail you're interested in—Vladi Ferengi and his people—I have to warn you it's probably cold by now." And to Chung: "Now centre Eleshnitsa, which is where we last saw them."

Trask and the others stood aside, looked on as Chung centred the screen on Eleshnitsa in Bulgaria, and Bernie reached out a hand and forefinger to touch the printed name that identified the village, then the sixteenth-of-an-inch black dot that located the place on the big screen. He stood stock-still for a moment, his face lined with concentration, then shook his head. "Stone cold," he said. "It's been—what, two weeks? Closer to three? And the Travellers, they've moved on."

"Maybe you need a hand," said Trask. And to Lardis: "Give him a hand. I mean literally."

"Eh?" said the Old Lidesci.

"You're Szgany," said Trask. "A Gypsy, a Traveller, a lot closer to these people than we are. And what's more, you've actually met them. Also, you're fey, 'with a seer ancestor's blood in you'—you've said so often enough yourself. So give Bernie your hand. And David, you might like to get in on this, too. I want to know where these damned people are!"

"*Hah!* Damned is right," Lardis growled. "By their name, if by nothing else." And he grasped Fletcher's free hand; likewise David Chung, reaching out a hand and forming a link with Lardis. And now things started to happen.

Fletcher's face was suddenly drawn, his green eyes rapidly blinking. And: "*Whoah!*" he muttered. "Now *that* is strong!" And to Chung, without taking his eyes off the screen: "Are you okay, working that keyboard one-handed?"

But Chief Tech Jimmy Harvey had already taken over the keyboard as Chung slid aside to give him room. And now both locators and Lardis concentrated together on the map on the screen.

"Strong . . ." said Fletcher again. "Go north, skirt the old border with Yugoslavia, then cross the Danube into Romania. *Damn,* but this is good! We're getting warm." And suddenly: "Now stop . . . hold it right there!" His index finger was now resting on Teregova in Romania. And:

"Is that where they are?" Trask's eagerness, his urgency, was showing. "Just for a moment there you seemed to be heading straight for the Romanian Refuge—or what used to be the Refuge. Come to think of it, this wouldn't be a bad route for someone who was 'sniffing out the strange places.' The subterranean Gate under the Carpathians . . . and Faethor Ferenczy's old place in the Zarandului Mountains. The more we work on this, the more it comes together. And yes, I'm sure now that old Vladi and his people are part of this. They might not realize it, but they've been where we want to go, and they were somehow touched by what we've vowed to destroy."

"Left," said Fletcher. "I mean west . . . go west across the border into Hungary." His face was very pale now, his eyes sunken and wrinkled up until they were almost closed. And his hand and finger trembled where they contacted the screen. "By God, I believe we're almost there!"

"Makes sense," said Millie Cleary breathlessly. "Nationalistically, these people are Hungarians. Now that Vladi's search for the 'strange places' is over for the time being, he's heading home for a little R and R."

"Didn't know you were in the armed forces." Trask's voice was hushed.

"Wasn't," Millie answered. "But I had a boyfriend who was. Er, it was a long time ago . . ."

"Not *heading* home," Bernie shook his head, "but *gone* home! They're there, and so are we!" Everyone's gaze was now riveted to the screen, where the locator's hand literally vibrated on a wooded area near the town of Szentes.

And Lardis said, "Would you believe there was once a campsite in Sunside called Szente? It belonged to the Szgany Szente and their leader, Volpe—miserable old shad-thief that he was—and was hidden away in the forest southwest of Lidesci territory . . . that is, until the night the Wamphyri found it. Aye, and they found old Volpe, too, since when the Szgany Szente are no more. *Huh!* But just look at this map:

all those woods, lakes, and rivers. They make for excellent hunting, gathering, fishing. Oh yes, Vladi and his people, they've gone home all right!"

"How are we fixed with Hungary, diplomatically and so on?" Trask was on it in a flash.

"Couldn't be better," said Millie Cleary. "They joined the European Union just three years ago; they're using the old NATO standard weaponry, and our armed forces are training their junior officers at Sandhurst and the other academies; we kept them out of the fire financially when Russia and her once-satellites went down the tube, and so they owe the West a heck of a lot."

Trask nodded. "Good. Excellent! More work for the Minister Responsible: to speak to his Hungarian counterpart and have old Vladi Ferengi taken into, er, 'protective custody' in Szeged or maybe even Szentes, depending on local public opinion. Lardis, you and I shall fly out there together, talk to Vladi, find out where he'd been immediately prior to that poor girl going down with . . . well, with whatever. But I'm beginning to think we can be pretty sure what was wrong with her."

"I'm ready whenever you are," Lardis nodded. "Just say the word. And maybe this time we'll actually get somewhere!"

"Right," said Trask, "and now it's time to make a few manpower plans . . . but I'm leaving that and the other logistics to the techs." He tapped Jimmy Harvey on the shoulder where he sat at the computer keyboard. "Jimmy, we're talking hours, not days. A breakdown of all available manpower, travel arrangements, all the usual logistics, yes. An Australian skeleton crew, a backup or rear party here at the HQ, and the main task force . . . well, somewhere in Greece. They'll probably be based somewhere on the Mediterranean coast close to Kavála. But they'll be the last to get under way, which will be just as soon as Lardis and I finish up in Szentes. Then we'll join up with them in—" he offered a shrug, "—wherever . . ."

Trask looked from face to face. "Questions?"

There were none.

"Then think some up!" he said, "And find the answers—and *then* tell me about them!" He headed for the door but Jimmy Harvey stopped him, saying:

"Maybe I should speak to GCHQ, the listening station? They have access to Brit and US spysats. Maybe they can confirm that the Szgany have gone home, actually get them on-screen in those Hungarian woods."

"No," said Trask. "GCHQ will only want to know what we're doing, why we need this information, and I would much prefer to keep this to ourselves. So we'll simply take Bernie's, David's, and Lardis's word for it, and work on that." And at the door he turned and said:

"David, I'll have to speak to the Minister Responsible directly, I mean right now, so that he can fix things up for me in Hungary. Since I can't be in two places at once, do me a favour and see if you can contact Manolis Papastamos, will you? Thanks. And Millie, and Liz: I'll see you in my office in half an hour. Liz first. As for the rest of you: thanks, everyone. Well done. But it doesn't stop here—this is only the start. So now it's back to work, people, it's back to work . . ."

Trask had barely done talking to the Minister Responsible when Liz Merrick came knocking on his door. He'd wedged it open in the vain hope that some fresh air might come wafting through his office; wondered if in fact there was any fresh air left—anywhere! The air-conditioning? That was a laugh! The one system that hadn't been updated in this place; and thirty years ago, long before anyone had begun to take note of weird El Niño weather patterns, even then the air-conditioning at E-Branch HQ had been inadequate.

"Come in and . . . and droop!" Trask called out. "Better yet, come in and flog me with some twigs or something . . ."

"Excuse me?" Looking not quite as wilted as Trask, Liz sat down opposite his desk.

"Well, since it feels like I'm living in a sauna," he told her, "I may as well act like I am!" Then, serious once more:

"So what's going on? All morning you've been looking worried. Something I should know about? Something with Jake, maybe—again?"

Trask's halfhearted attempt at humour was already a thing of the past, forgotten. And Liz found herself thinking: *This is just business to him. No room for anything else. He isn't going to understand.*

She looked down at the floor for a moment, then looked at Trask—looked straight at him—and set her jaw. And determined, but nevertheless stumbling over her words, she said, "I don't think I . . . that is, I don't want to . . . I mean, I *won't* be spying on Jake anymore."

Trask raised an eyebrow, sighed, and said, "Oh? And that's supposed to upset me, is it?"

Liz bit her lip. "Not intentionally, no. But I—"

"Well it *does* upset me!" He snapped, cutting her off. "It upsets me a great deal, because I'm now looking at the ruin of not just one potentially excellent esper but two. However, and before I chase you to hell out of here, out of the Branch, and out of a job, you'd better tell me why you've come to this . . . this *stupid* decision! And if you tell me it's a matter of loyalty, then I'll have to ask you just where *are* your loyalties, Liz? And which is more important: your job, E-Branch, the security of the world—or bloody Jake Cutter?"

And now she was angry, too, which was all to the good, because that way she would tell the plain and simple truth . . . or the truth as she saw it. And Ben Trask and the truth had always been the best of friends.

"My spying on him is getting in the way of . . . of Jake and me, of our relationship," she said. "He knows what I'm doing—or if not knows, then he more than just suspects it—which is why we're at an impasse. He can't let me get too close for fear I'll learn—well, everything. Including those things everyone has that really *should* be private, the things that—that—"

"That rattle?" said Trask. "You mean like skeletons in our closets? Or is it something worse than that?"

"No. Maybe. I don't know. Yes." And she looked down at the floor again.

"But isn't that just exactly what we've been trying to discover?" Trask said logically. "Don't we want to help Jake, and so clear the way for him to start helping us? God, but he has—or he could have—the powers of a Necroscope! Think about it! What a weapon he would make! Think about what he's already achieved out in Australia. But if there's something very wrong in there, in the depths of his mind, and if he's—"

"If he's been got at?" she cut in. "If he's a plant, despite everything we've seen so far? But is that really feasible?"

Trask shrugged, shook his head, then nodded however reluctantly. "Yes, it's still possible. I don't want it to be—it's the last thing I want—but that's the way it is. We must never underestimate the Wamphyri: their capacity for evil, their lust for life or undeath, their tenacity. You weren't here, Liz, but we, the rest of us, we won't ever forget what happened to Harry Keogh. Harry had the will, the guts, the strength to fight it, yet *still* he lost the battle. But Jake—? That's why I can't let you quit—not just for E-Branch and all that we stand for, but for Jake, too—*and* for you, since you feel that way about him. Now think: if he's in danger, shouldn't you be doing something about it, or letting me do it? If he had cancer, wouldn't you want us to cure it, cut it out?"

Even saying these things, still Trask felt treacherous. It was his lie detector working in reverse, detecting *his* lie. Yes, he wanted to save Jake and keep him safe; for E-Branch, for the world, but least of all for Liz. Not until Jake had proved himself beyond all reasonable doubt, anyway. Yet still he went on:

"Whatever it is that's affecting him—and I can't believe it's ingratitude, stupidity, or just plain stubbornness—we've got to find and get rid of it. But if you have . . . *feelings* for him, well surely you can see that for yourself?" And before she could answer:

"Okay, so tell me what's brought this on. Oh, I know, it's been coming for some time, ever since we got back home.

But the last time we spoke I thought we'd cleared it all up, that there were no more barriers between us, except maybe ethical barriers that really have no meaning compared to what we're dealing with. As for myself: it's not easy, but I simply can't afford ethics, Liz. Not anymore, and certainly not now. And as for the Wamphyri: they don't *have* any ethics and never have had. So tell me, why have things changed? What happened that we're right back to square one? Something last night, maybe?" For he had seen it in her eyes: that haunted look, and the sleeplessness, of course.

And so she told him about it—most of it, as best she was able to remember—and he heard her out in silence, his talent sorting out the truths from the half-truths. But at least there were no blatant lies. Oh, the picture she painted was in Jake's favour, but the colours she used were all true to life. And she finished by saying, "So you see, Jake is just as scared of this thing as you—or as *we* are—which is why he was fighting it. It isn't something he's in league with but something he's doing battle with, constantly. It's draining him, and if I keep doing what I've been doing it will drain me, too . . ."

And finally Trask spoke. "On top of which, he continues to have his own agenda: this thing with Luigi Castellano."

"That too," she said. "Plus the fact that he's not *au fait* with the Branch and its systems; but how could he be, when he's only been with us a few weeks? And he *still* doesn't know all of the facts with regard to his . . . let's call it his condition. I mean the condition we know about, that something of Harry Keogh is in him, as opposed to this other thing."

"So it's that again," Trask grunted. "The things I didn't tell him yet, about Harry."

"Yes," she answered, "it's that again. With all due respect, it's like you're trying to have your cake and eat it. And he's the one who's paying for it. You asked him to work for us, to be a Necroscope, without letting him know what a full-blown Necroscope really is, without explaining his awesome potential, all the terrible things—the unthinkable things—he might be able to do. But far worse, you haven't told him about the dangers, about what happened to the original Necroscope."

Trask thought about it and sighed. "What if I tell him and he can't take it, turns us down flat, runs away from it?"

"That's a chance you have to take," Liz answered, "if only for your own sake. And you can stop kidding yourself about your alleged lack of 'ethics'—which is just another word for conscience. Do you really think you're the only one who recognizes the truth when you see it? Well, you're not."

"Never con a con man," said Trask wryly.

"Or a con woman," Liz nodded. "Or a telepath. I know an injured conscience when I bump into one."

First Millie and now you, he thought. *Is there no privacy anymore?* "So, now I'm the bad guy in all this?"

"No, I just think you're too close to it," she said. "What with Zek and all . . ." In that same moment she could have bitten her tongue off. But Trask ignored it and said:

"So instead of trying to 'cure' Jake I should simply trust him, right?"

"All the others seem to think so."

"You've spoken to them?"

"I don't have to. But I can tell you one thing: during our think-tank session, there were more than one or two minds wondering why Jake wasn't there."

And after a moment: "Listen," said Trask. "From what you told me just a few minutes ago, I could be forgiven for thinking that perhaps—just perhaps—Jake Cutter is carrying the seeds of a plague. He has the symptoms, not in his body but in his mind. Something's in there, certainly. And as you yourself have admitted, you don't think it's something that Harry Keogh has dropped off for Jake's safe-keeping. Now, if Jake is 'just' a man, albeit a man with a Necroscope's powers, however undeveloped, that's all to the good. We'll help him develop and use them—yes, to our benefit, and to his own, but mainly to the world's. But if he should prove to be more, or rather 'other,' than an ordinary man with extraordinary powers . . ."

And she saw the rest of it in his mind—*Jake Cutter, cut*

down, decapitated, burning! And she knew that Trask had wanted her to see it, that he'd deliberately focussed his concentration upon it.

"My God!" Her hand flew to her mouth.

"What's the problem?" Trask asked her—knowing full well what the problem was. That while it was easy for her to spy on him, it was much harder to do it to the one she was falling in love with. That was part of it; but it was also that the truth, the terrible, terrifying truth, had suddenly been brought home to her with as much force as he could muster.

"But it's Jake we're talking about!" she cried.

Trask nodded. "Yes, and it's the difference between Bruce Trennier, or Jethro Manchester and his family, and someone you love. But Liz, I would far rather cure than kill. Which is why I've been so cautious. If he—if *we*—are in danger, I don't want to perhaps accelerate this thing by telling him what happened to Harry and two of his sons, and what *might* be happening to him! I want to watch, hope and pray, and wait for indisputable proof one way or the other."

"But—"

"*But* there is one other way," he cut her off. "I can do as you ask and tell him—tell him the whole thing—and see how it affects him. Then, if he continues to fight it, if he fights all the harder, we'll know he's worth working on, worth saving. But if he gives in, submits . . . we'll know that, too. And then it'll be a case of watching him all that much more closely. And *you,* because of your relationship with him, will have to be the one doing the bulk of the watching. Which in turn means that if or when the time comes, *you* will be the one who has to turn him in to me, because there is no other way. So then, is it a deal? Are you up to it?"

She thought about it. "You'll tell him the whole thing if I'll keep on spying on him?"

"Not spying on him," Trask shook his head. "Watching him. As we'd watch over a feverish child's symptoms, hoping they'll disappear or that he'll be strong enough to throw them off."

"And that's your best offer?"

"In my position," he answered, "it's the *only* offer I can make. And believe me, it's more than I'd offer anyone else . . ."

At which moment there came an interruption.

From the corridor, the sudden hustle and bustle of hurried motion, running footsteps and raised voices. Millie had arrived and was out there waiting to speak to Trask as he'd required of her. But so had David Chung arrived, and Trask had rarely heard him sounding so agitated:

"Excuse me, Millie, but I've got to see him now. And I do mean now!"

"But . . . what is it?" said Millie, anxious as she appeared momentarily in the open doorway, squeezing herself to one side, flattening to the wall as Chung hurried by without pause.

And almost skidding to a halt before Trask's desk, barely glancing at Liz, the Chinaman blurted:

"Ben, it's Manolis. He was on a case, got hurt, can't say how bad. But he's hospitalized."

"Hurt?" Trask started to his feet, his mouth falling open. "Manolis, in hospital? Where?"

"That's just it," Chung answered grimly. "He's in Kavála, Greece, on the Mediterranean coast. And during his few moments of consciousness, before they had to sedate him, he was asking to speak to you! He wouldn't say what it was about, but by all acounts he did say that it was desperately important, and that you would understand. So, do you want to take a guess at it? A 'wild' stab in the dark?"

Trask closed his mouth, shook his head, and said, "Nothing wild about it! But I do want you to get everyone to drop everything and make sure they're all in the Ops Room in the next ten minutes—or better still make that five." And turning to Liz: "That includes you, and Jake Cutter, too, and no arguments. Better go find him, and do it now."

"Or?" she said.

"Or I'll take it you've turned me down. In which case you know where the elevator is situated."

But as she turned away and headed for the door, he called after her, "Well?"

"Well," she looked back. "I'm going to *find* him!"

And Trask breathed a silent sigh of relief. His last for a long time to come . . .

8
Jake's Agenda

LIZ DIDN'T FIND JAKE CUTTER, AND WHEN TRASK was through bringing everyone up to date and issuing face-to-face instructions, he only had to look at her expression to know the truth.

Then: "What?" he said disgustedly. "He's out on the town again? I don't believe it! And this is the man you were pleading for? But if this isn't deliberate aggravation I don't know what is!"

Liz could only shake her head despondently. "He was in his room first thing this morning; I could hear him moving about in there. That's all I know about it. But it's like I told you: he was feeling totally out of place here. We hadn't given him anything to do, and *you* hadn't told him everything he should know. I mean, it isn't as if he's the kind who can just wander about the place looking dumb!"

"No," Trask answered, "but he can certainly act it! As for not putting him in the picture: I was about to do so, this morning, right now. But now he's gone missing again, and anyway I no longer have the time."

David Chung, Ian Goodly, and Millie Cleary had hung back; the rest of the staff were hurriedly vacating the Ops Room, on their way to prepare for the specific roles they'd been handed: packing their bags for what would amount to an operational mass exodus, or rearranging their schedules as members of the skeletal rear party, whichever.

Now Chung stepped forward and said, "Look, I wouldn't normally go rummaging around in someone's private belongings without his permission, but since this is something of an emergency . . . well there's bound to be some personal stuff in Jake's room that I can use to locate him. We only need to change his door's access code to get me in there, and—"

"No need for that," said Liz. "I can get in. As far as the security codes go, his room and my place—the old annex at the rear—are still one room, and the optical scanner will accept me."

"Say no more," the locator said. "The eyes have it!" And however nervously, he grinned at his own wit for a moment, then sobered and said: "So what are we waiting for? Let's go."

"Wait!" said Trask. And to Chung: "I also want you to sort out the travel arrangements. So when you've sent someone out to find Jake and bring him in, then get on to our friends at Heathrow and Gatwick. I know it's short notice, but I want us to be out of here ASAP—today or tonight, if at all possible. At the very least I want the advance parties underway. Okay, so do whatever's necessary. As for myself: I'll be in my office speaking to the Man Upstairs, finding out what kind of help, if any, we can expect from the Greek authorities. Report to me there."

Then, as Liz and the locator hurried away, Trask turned to the precog, Ian Goodly. "Now what? Do you have problems, too?"

"I don't think so," Goodly answered. "But you have me down with Lardis, going to see Vladi Ferengi. Can I ask why?"

Trask nodded. "We'll be dealing with powerful mentalists, or with one such for sure—Nephran Malinari. Remember, just as soon as we found Bruce Trennier, Malinari knew we were warm and getting warmer. He *knew* that we were coming for him, and he was ready for us. So this time we're not going to be sending up any signal flares; I won't upset things by having too many wild talents appear in any one place at any one time, cluttering up the psychic aether, so to speak. If psychic talents have signatures, then by now he knows ours only too well. So we'll have to build up our presence gradually—and yet as quickly as possible, you understand—without having us all arrive on the scene en masse. That's why we need to get the advance teams away posthaste, and you and Lardis form one such team. Oh, and you can speak to Liz, too. Take her with you. She'll know it if Vladi strays from the truth. I had intended to team her up with Jake, but now . . . I'm not taking him. Not even if we find him. Jake's what used to be called a loose cannon, and I can't risk him going off like that and blowing us all to hell."

"I see," Goodly nodded. "So the main reason you're splitting us up is simply as a wise precaution."

Again Trask's nod. "But in any case I'll have you close to hand, just across the border in Hungary: maybe an hour's flight time? And as soon as you and Lardis are through talking to this old Gypsy, this Vladi Ferengi, then you can join up with me and David somewhere in Greece. I'll keep HQ up to date on our location at all times."

"That's good enough," said Goodly.

"Good," said Trask. "And meanwhile, how's the future looking?"

"Secretive," said the other. "All I see is movement—lots of it."

"Oh?" said Trask. "But that's not the future, that's right now!" And: "Will you be okay with Lardis?" He looked around but couldn't see the Old Lidesci. "Where is he, anyway?"

"He went off to get his things together," the precog answered. "Also to tell Lissa what's going on, I imagine. He looked a bit apprehensive—not about the job but about Lissa! I can see her giving him all sorts of hell—going off to fight vampires again, *hah!*" And Goodly smiled a rare, wry smile. "As for working with him: I know we'll get on fine. I haven't forgotten what we owe him. That time in Sunside, we were the strangers in a strange land then . . ."

"Look after him then," Trask said.

"You're joking," said the other. "With that machete of his, he'll be the one looking after me!" And as Goodly went off, finally it was Millie's turn.

"I'm staying back again," she said flatly. She didn't say it accusingly, but Trask knew she was accusing him anyway.

"Walk with me," he said. And on the way along the corridor to his office: "Millie, you're not a field operative—it isn't your scene. And anyway you're more importantly placed back here than in the thick of it somewhere . . . somewhere out there." And he waved a hand, indicating nowhere special but everywhere dangerous.

"Important to you in my work, you mean," she said. A statement, not a question.

And again Trask was quick to catch on. "Important in every way," he answered. "And quite indispensable. Look, it's as I've just explained to Ian: where Malinari is concerned, we're dealing with a mentalist who can get into our minds—and more especially *your* mind—as easily as that." He snapped his fingers. "And if you don't believe me, you should speak to Liz. You're a telepath, Millie, and vulnerable. It's simple as that."

"Yes," she answered. "I'm a very *experienced* telepath, however untried in the field, and my shields are a lot better than Liz Merrick's. But Liz is going and I'm staying, and that's not fair. Don't you think it's time we put this kid sister thing to rest? I deserve the chance to get out there and prove myself."

"Oh? And will you also chance getting yourself killed—or worse than killed—into the bargain?"

"A fate worse than death?" They were at his office door.

"Once upon a time there was no such thing," Trask answered. "Not really, except to the Victorians and such, hypocrites that they were. But now there is." He almost added, *You really don't know what it would do to me if any harm should come to you,* but somehow managed to hold it in.

Maybe she "heard" it anyway, for now she said, "What about me, if something should happen to you?"

And after a while he said, "Some people certainly know

how to pick their times, don't they? First Jake Cutter, and through Jake, Liz—and now you. But we don't have time for this, Millie. So please try to understand and don't give me any more problems than I've got right now."

As he entered his office she paused, held back, and turned away. And over her shoulder: "Ben, don't forget to kiss me goodbye before you leave. It might be your last chance . . ."

Trask clenched both fists, put them on top of his desk, and leaned on them. He opened his mouth to call Millie back . . . and didn't. Damn it all to hell, he couldn't! Because she had to be safer here. But what if she wasn't here when he got back?

This time she really had heard him, and she'd probably felt his pain, too. And, from the corridor, "Oh, don't worry, Ben. I shall be here," she called out, softly. "I suppose so, anyway." Followed by the rapid *tap-tap-tap* of her footsteps quickly receding . . .

Trask had been right, and there wasn't going to be any help from the Greek authorities. Greece was still having territorial disputes with an increasingly warlike neighbour, Turkey, and a lot of trouble was brewing with illegal immigrants flooding in from famine-stricken Albania. The mainland was full of unrest, which put the ball well and truly in Trask's court. This time, unlike the Australian job, E-Branch would be on its own.

Trask was jotting down a few notes when David Chung reported as ordered to his office. And once again the locator was excited.

"It's Jake," he said. "I found him easily enough, but you won't like where I found him. And we won't be bringing him in."

"Tell me the worst," said Trask.

"He's in Marseilles, France," said the other.

And now, for just a moment, Trask was excited, too. "Marseilles? He must have used the Möbius Continuum!"

"It's the only answer," Chung agreed.

But Trask's excitement quickly ebbed and he was scowling. "He lied to us about losing it. And he's using it to serve his own ends when he should be helping us."

"His own agenda," Chung nodded.

Trask stood up, came from behind his desk and began pacing the floor. "Do you realize what we lose if we lose Jake?"

"On the one hand a load of trouble," the locator answered. "And on the other, we could lose the war. The fact is that we—and not just us but the world—we all need a Necroscope. And if Jake hadn't been there to pull us out of the fire in Australia . . ." He let it trail off and shrugged. "Er, do you think maybe we could have handled it better?"

"Meaning *I* could have handled it better," said Trask. "You all seem to think so. You, Liz Merrick, and Ian Goodly—oh, and plenty of others, I'm sure. Maybe I'm too autocratic."

"The Branch has to have a boss," Chung answered. "You have this talent of yours, and what could be more important than the truth? So obviously you're the right man for the job. And it's also obvious that you see something in Jake Cutter—some kind of problem—that the rest of us haven't picked up on."

"Then why don't I know what it is?" Trask quit his pacing, threw up his hands. And before Chung could answer: "Never mind. Let it go for now. What's done is done. We'll just have to wait and see how it works out. So now tell me about those travel arrangements."

"The choice is yours," said Chung. "We can fly into Athens tonight if you like, a commercial flight out of Heathrow. Or we can charter a small plane, fly direct to Kavála. The only problem there is that Kavála's mainly a military airport—we could have a problem getting permission to land. Or, we can pick up a couple of cheap tickets on a late-season package-holiday flight leaving at eight-thirty tomorrow morning. That one goes to Kavála, gets in midday. The airport takes just a handful of tourist flights for the sake of the country's economy."

"So what's wrong with Athens, tonight?" Trask queried.

"Ah! I forgot to mention," the locator answered. "There's no connecting flight till midday tomorrow. And Athens and Kavála are quite some distance apart."

"Maybe it's as well," said Trask. "In fact it might serve our purpose *very* well to take one of these—these what—package holidays?" He frowned and shook his head. "Hard to remember when I last had a real holiday. It was with Zek, I think, when we went out to sell her place on Zante . . ." He stirred himself, gave himself a shake. "Anyway, how come there are spare seats? Haven't I been given to understand that these flights are like sardine cans?"

"In any normal year they would be," the other told him.

"Oh yes," Trask nodded. "I was forgetting. El Niño."

"That's right," Chung said. "People are running *away* from the sun! Also, there are a couple of plague spots in the Greek islands, mainly Cyprus, Crete, and Rhodes. These things and various political problems—all the unrest and what have you—it puts people off."

"I suppose it would! But plague? That new strain of bubonic out of China? I thought we had that licked?"

"We have," the locator agreed. "The richer countries, anyway. But the not-so-rich are having trouble paying for the medicine. We're helping out, but it takes time—the usual bureaucracy. Anyway, that really shouldn't concern us; those shots we got in Australia have given us all the immunity we can use. I'm still sore from mine!"

"Okay," Trask told him. "Get us tickets for tomorrow. Eight-thirty out of—?"

"Gatwick," Chung answered. "But tell me, what do you mean, it will serve our purpose well?"

And Trask said, "As tourists—common or garden holiday makers—we'll be about as unobtrusive as we can get. You see, I'm trying to play this by their rules, Wamphyri rules, I mean. Or the rules they used to play by, anyway. Anonymity is synonymous with longevity. Isn't that how it goes?"

"That's how it goes," said Chung.

"So we'll keep it anonymous," said Trask. "At least until

it gets close up and personal. Okay, so what about the rest of the travel arrangements?"

"Ian, Liz, and Lardis are all fixed up for tomorrow. They fly direct to Szeged. By noon tomorrow or maybe a little later, they'll be talking to Valdi Ferengi and we'll be with Manolis."

"No trouble with Liz?"

Chung shook his head. "I told her where Jake is. She seems resigned to it—the fact that he's always going to have these problems. At least until—"

"Until he deals with them, I know," said Trask. "So on the off chance that he *can* deal with them—without getting himself killed, that is—maybe it's all for the best . . ." And he began pacing the floor again.

"What is it, boss?" said Chung concernedly. "I mean, apart from all this?"

"Apart from all this? Nothing. Not that I can't put right, anyway. Which I will as soon as you're out of here."

And as Chung headed for the door: "David, will you take it from here, make sure things run smoothly for a couple of hours? I need a little time to sort something out."

"No problem," said Chung, closing the door behind him . . .

When Trask was alone he got straight on the telephone to Millie Cleary. "Millie, about that goodbye kiss you mentioned?" And he took a deep breath and held it a couple of seconds before blurting out the rest of it. "What would you say to taking it a step or two farther than that?"

"Come again?" (She sounded more than a little surprised.)

"I have the evening off," said Trask. "How about you?"

"My time's my own, remember?" she answered. "I don't have any bags to pack." Her words were loaded, as usual.

"And mine are always packed," he told her. "So I was sort of thinking, maybe we can find a quiet bar with a big overhead fan somewhere. Share a couple of long, cool drinks . . . ?"

"And dinner later, on you?"

"Following which, it'll be just about time for bed," Trask said, and again held his breath. For after all, it was possible he'd read this all wrong.

But he hadn't read it wrong. And while *he* wasn't the telepath, still he knew she was smiling one of those smiles of hers when she asked him, "Your place or mine?"

The previous night, after Liz had left Jake in his room:

He had tried reading a handful of E-Branch files that Trask had given him but wasn't able to concentrate; his mind kept returning to the nightmare that Liz had interrupted . . . God bless her! Or it *would* return if only he could remember what the damn thing had been about.

A fight? He'd definitely been fighting something, and something monstrous at that. But what? He remembered talking to Korath, remembered the vampire's word games, something of his arguments, and that they hadn't reached any firm decision on how to handle their mutual agendas—mutual in that they both planned murders, if murder was the right word for it and not simply the extermination of vermin—but apart from that, nothing.

Jake suspected that he had fallen even more deeply asleep, perhaps in the middle of their deadspeak conversation, and that the dead vampire had then left him to his dreams. Or rather, to his nightmare. Well, and weren't nightmares commonplace to Jake Cutter? They certainly were, and especially since his introduction to E-Branch. But usually he recognized their sources, knew where they'd sprung from and what they were about, and was able to turn his back on them until the next time. This one, however, was different and continued to bother him—probably because he *couldn't* remember its details.

No, not a one of them—except perhaps the fear. For after all, it wasn't too often he'd wake up in a cold sweat, fighting for his life (*or for more than "just" his life—for control of his life, maybe? But it wasn't too hard to guess where* that *notion had sprung from!*) against something he couldn't recall.

Also, there had been his seeming rejection of Liz. But the last thing he'd wanted to do was reject Liz! There, he'd admitted it, he was attracted to her. Hell, no, he was a whole hell-of-a-*lot* attracted to her, but wasn't about to make love to her while there was even the slightest chance that Korath was still lurking around in there—or should that be in here?—or that he might return.

Shit—Jake's mind had become a *place* now! It wasn't just his any longer, but some kind of communal meeting place for the dead! Some of them anyway. Harry Keogh, Zek Foener, Korath, and all those other whisperers in darkness who as yet wouldn't commit themselves to conversing with him because for some unspecified reason they feared him, but whose voices nevertheless went echoing through the caverns of his mind . . .

. . . Say what!? *They,* the teeming dead, were afraid of *him*? So what kind of infernal monster had Jake become that he instilled fear in the incorporeal minds of the Great Majority? And who in hell would want to be a Necroscope anyway?

Thus his mind was a jumble of questions and kaleidoscopic images, all of them wheeling against a vast backdrop of mysterious numbers and the esoteric symbols of the Möbius Continuum.

And that was the biggest distraction of all: the fact that while the numbers were all there, just waiting to be activated, he still didn't know how to do it; he couldn't as yet send them scrolling down the screen of his mind to the point of numerical "critical mass," where they would form a Möbius door.

In this world only Korath could do that, and the dead vampire was something Jake could well do without . . . couldn't he?

Half a dozen times and more he reached over to his bedside table, picked up one of Trask's files, then sat propped against his heaped pillows, with the file unopened, trying to bring his turbulent thoughts to order. But no, he was too worn down, too weary—*made* weary by the constant fear of

Korath's unwarranted and unwanted presence, and when he *was* present, by the vampire's interminable nagging—to be able to single out and concentrate on any one facet of his predicament.

So that by the time the files on his bed formed an untidy patchwork quilt, the twisted, twirling loop of images in Jake's mind had become as repetitive, as monotonously hypnotic, as the Möbius strip itself . . . so much so that as he slipped down into his bed, and into sleep, his shields also went down, collapsing around him into so much mental confetti.

By then, too, in the once-annex at the rear of Jake's room, Liz Merrick—herself physically and emotionally depleted—was already asleep and telepathically remote from him. And this was just as well, for she was about to miss another of Jake's nightmares; one taken from life this time, crystal clear in his perceptions and scarcely designed to endear him to her.

The source of this one, however, wouldn't be nearly so difficult to trace. For in it, Jake was simply reviewing in detail an episode of his own recent past. And of course the source was his memory.

And possibly his conscience, too . . .

Jake was back in that room again, that torture chamber of muted lighting, heavy drapes, and an atmosphere that reeked of terror. The scene of a multiple violation of a by-no-means innocent but nonetheless helpless girl, the Russian mob's drugs courier, Natasha Slepak. The woman he'd thought he was in love with. And of course, in his dream, he still was in love with her.

Seven people in that room. Jake was one, tied to a chair so positioned that he was obliged to watch—indeed *determined* to watch, so that he wouldn't forget, and when his time came would know how to deal with his tormentors; an eye for an eye, and all that—and Natasha, not bound but completely naked, and in any case helpless, barely conscious under the influence of whatever drugs they'd given her.

Drugs that made her compliant while yet keeping her aware, knowing what was happening to her but incapable of resistance. Which might be just as well, for these people ("people": a dubious description, that) would probably relish a measure of resistance, and they would definitely know how to deal with it. But no, they hadn't wanted to do any real physical harm—not at this point, and not in this room—because that was to come later. The ultimate harm, yes, to Jake and Natasha both.

Jake and Natasha, and five others in that room: the bastard who had orchestrated this thing, Luigi Castellano, and the four who played it out for him while he sat there in the shadows and watched. No, he didn't . . . partake. But is the man who orders an execution any less responsible than the one who fastens the wrist- and ankle-straps, or the one who fits the metallic dome to the shaven head, or the one who throws the switch?

Castellano had *ordered* this, and perhaps because he didn't take part in it—perhaps because he sat there, a hunched blot of a figure whose laughter was pitiless, watching from behind a cone of white light that fell upon Natasha's nakedness, witnessing what he had started and only he could stop, but wouldn't—Jake hated him all the more for it. Others did this man's dirty work, and this was among his dirtiest.

But while Castellano himself kept out of sight, the others were far less retiring. One after another they went at Natasha, while Jake—barely conscious that he did it, awash with shame, disgust, and horror—studied each man in his turn, memorizing and measuring him and his . . . his *preferences,* against a future reckoning. Oh, there was little enough hope of any such future, but given only half a chance . . .

. . . The threat froze in Jake's mind as something new began to shape. There was one among the four who simply couldn't wait his turn but shuffled forward, panting like a dog, to where Natasha was being moved around like a human doll by another of her assailants, a man who stood by the edge of the bed, hugging her thighs, grunting as he thrust himself into her with deliberate, measured strokes.

And having seen this before, knowing what was coming, Jake strained more yet, uselessly at the thin nylon cords that bound him as firmly to his chair as his memory bound him to his nightmare. For the impatient one was a beast, a veritable torpedo of a man, whose preference was to defile his victims—totally.

Squat, ugly, and filmed with the sweat of eager anticipation, his shoulders were broad, his hands huge and heavy at the end of apish arms, and his eyes small and piglike in a moonish face that was filled with unnatural lust. Yet for all his brutish appearance, he affected the trappings of sophistication, of civilization however coloured by his gangland background.

He wore patent-leather shoes; a silk or possibly sharkskin suit, and (since he scarcely seemed to have any neck at all) an open-necked silken shirt. And in a hand like a hammer, a cigarette-holder and cigarette, with smoke curling from its hot tip. Approaching Natasha, whose body continued to jerk and flop from the thrusting of the one who grunted, the apish man reached out his cigarette towards her face—

At which the dark shadow that was Castellano straightened up a little in its chair behind the lamp, and said: "Francesco, no! I can't let you mark her." (The rumbling power of Castellano's voice, like the purring of a big jungle cat . . . but ready in a moment to turn into a warning growl, a menacing snarl.)

And Francesco at once withdrew his hand, half-turned his bullet head, and said: "Mark her, Luigi? Me? No way!" Then he looked Jake straight in the eyes, and smiled like a shark. "I was only offering the little lady a smoke, that's all. A cool, sweet drag to ease that burning throat. Can't you see how she gulps and gasps?" And now he reversed the cigarette holder to place its tip between Natasha's loose lips. "Isn't that right, little lady? Isn't that exactly what you'd like? A sweet drag from Frankie's cigarette?"

The one between Natasha's legs was finished. He withdrew, backing out of Jake's line of sight into the shadows, and Jake heard him zip his fly. Natasha flopped where he'd left her, her legs bent at the knees, dangling over the edge of the bed. What little of spirit or strength she had left, she somehow concentrated now into a fierce jerk of her head, spitting out the cigarette-holder and cigarette to send them twirling from the cone of light into the shadows, with the glowing tip spiralling like a maddened firefly.

And Francesco hoisting her legs onto the bed, drawing her upper body to the edge, and flopping his semitumescent member in her face, saying, "Well, if you won't smoke that, let's see how you do with this!"

And Jake watching it all, choking on his rage (and, truth to tell, his fear; for it was quite obvious by now that neither he nor Natasha were going to walk away from this) as the brutal Frankie did his thing.

Even then it wasn't over, not until he'd finished urinating on her, when Castellano had to remind him: "I think that's enough, Francesco. And remember, you are the one who will have to clean her up. When they find Natasha, I want her to be full of river water. Not piss, and definitely not shit! *Our* shit—designer shit, dream crystals—yes, of course. But the human variety, no."

Then it was over—

—But Jake's *real* nightmare was only just beginning: the realization of what his experience that night had done to him, how it had turned him into a killer in his own right . . .

Payback time, the future he had scarcely dared hope for, which now was here. It was a rainy night in Turin, and Jake had followed his quarry—his third victim-to-be, the torpedo, Francesco Reggio himself—to a hotel on the Corso Alessandria.

In the interim Jake had changed. Now, as a bearded, limping, "older" man, in a broad-brimmed hat and shabby full-length raincoat, his disguise was immaculate. Only his eyes had stayed the same: cold, deep, and as pitiless as his hatred, which was why he kept them hidden under the drooping brim of his hat, behind the tinted lenses of an invalid's glasses.

Even if Francesco "Frankie" Reggio had noticed him

(which he probably had, since on several occasions Jake had found himself irresistibly, murderously drawn to him during the tortuous train journey along the Mediterranean coast route from Marseilles to Savona, then inland to Turin), still he would never have recognized him as the man he and Castellano's other thug confidants had drugged and dumped in a swollen river under the Alps in Provence.

But conversely, Jake didn't *ever* intend to forget Frankie. Not until there was nothing left of him to forget, anyway . . .

Four hours earlier, Frankie Reggio had taken a taxi from Turin's main rail station and booked into his hotel. The Hotel Novara was an old but decent three-star place, a leap upmarket from the no-star flophouse which Jake had booked into because it stood directly opposite the Novara across a busy road about half a mile from the city centre. The dilapidated looks of the flop hadn't much bothered him, however; close proximity to the target was of far greater concern than a couple of cockroaches in the cupboards. And in any case, he hadn't intended to spend too much time there.

Jake had been in a hurry. Wanting to get settled into his room before Frankie reached his, he had taken the first room he was shown on the second floor, and as soon as he was alone he'd opened his suitcase and taken out the briefcase that housed the components of his long-barrelled 7.62 sniper's rifle. Assembly could wait; he had only been interested in the telescope.

And he had been lucky—but it wasn't all luck. For Jake had tailed Frankie several times before when the sadistic torpedo was running errands for Castellano. On those occasions he'd kept his distance while watching and learning, and he knew that Frankie usually took rooms in front and two floors up. Likewise tonight. On the other side of the road when the lights had come on in a second-floor room, sure enough it had been Frankie Reggio.

Then Jake had put his own lights out to sit in the dark, watching the thug through a chink in his room's drab curtains. But while his eyes—and his hatred—were drawn constantly to Frankie, still Jake hadn't forgotten his purpose here. Undying hatred had brought him here, yes, but revenge was his business, and attention to detail was all-important.

An eye for an eye.

Natasha's eyes had been put out forever—not literally, no, but the light in them, certainly. And the life behind them had been extinguished entirely . . .

The Novara's road-facing rooms had railed balconies, accessible via large walk-through patio-styled windows. The distance between balconies was some four feet, which was important to the plan that had been hatching in Jake's mind. He'd always known *what* he wanted to do, but the *how* of it had been a problem. Now the how was working itself out, too.

As for the Novara's rooms:

Sweeping Frankie's room with his crosshaired telescope, Jake had seen all he needed to see before the thug looked out for a moment or two on the street, then closed his curtains to shut both the night and Jake out. That was okay; Jake had seen enough and liked what he'd seen; it suited his purpose to perfection.

Even better, he could still see the spot where the room's main lighting effect—a pair of typically Italian, latter day art nouveau globes, in the shape of huge lotus buds sprouting from a cluster of gold metal leaves—continued to glow through the curtains from its location on the wall opposite the large bed, directly over a small desk and telephone.

And as Frankie's shadow had moved around behind his drawn curtains, Jake had quickly assembled his rifle and attached the sniperscope . . . then waited. And after a few minutes the lights in the room opposite had gone out.

Jake could have shot Frankie dead in his room, of course, or he could have put a bullet through his heart as he came out of the hotel. It would have been so easy to line him up in his sights and squeeze the trigger . . . much too easy. For that way the torpedo wouldn't have felt it, or only for a split second. And he definitely wouldn't have known or cared who had done it to him, or why. But as with those other two bastards who Jake had taken out, so with Frankie: Jake *wanted* him to know! Wherefore it would have to be done the hard way.

Jake had watched his target leave the hotel and get into a taxi; and as the car had headed downtown on the noisy, near-gridlocked night road, he'd picked up his telephone and called the Novara. His Italian wasn't good by any means, but at least he could make himself understood.

"Can I speak to Mr. Reggio?" he said. "He called me just a few minutes ago from room, er—I think it's room, two, one—er—?" While it was a decent-looking place, the Novara wasn't large as hotels go; there couldn't be more than two dozen rooms to each floor.

"Room two-one-seven, sir, yes." (The switchboard operator had fallen for it.) "Just a moment, sir, and I'll connect you."

But of course Mr. Reggio hadn't been available . . . so would Jake care to leave a recorded message?

No, he wouldn't. (Yes he would. He'd be *leaving* a message, certainly, but not on any answering machine.)

Fifteen minutes later, after Jake had packed his briefcase with items from his suitcase—a pair of heavy, two-litre glass carboys, which he had wrapped carefully in hotel towels—and after he'd changed into a dark business suit, brushed his hair, and dispensed with his limp, he'd attracted little or no attention as he crossed the Novara's lobby to the desk. And glancing at the hotel's layout plan, it had taken him just a few nervous minutes to register.

He'd required a room on the second floor. Two-one-five, if it was vacant? It was a room that overlooked the road, correct? Yes, he had stayed here before some years ago; he'd enjoyed his stay and liked the room very much—thanks.

Jake had been relying on his luck, but it was holding. The desk clerk hadn't been doubling on switchboard duties; he wasn't the person Jake had spoken to on the telephone and so didn't recognize his voice. And yes, two-one-five was vacant.

Ten minutes later Jake had been inside his room, following which everything else fell easily into place.

Putting out the lights in two-one-five, Jake had gone out onto the balcony, climbed over the rail, and crossed to Frankie Reggio's side. His glass-cutter hadn't been required; the glass door slid open almost at a touch. Frankie didn't bother himself too much with security; no one in his right mind would dream of crossing him, and anyway he'd left nothing in the room that was worth the trouble.

He hadn't, of course, reckoned with Jake Cutter—or with revenge—or even with the devious mind of his own boss, Luigi Castellano. For of course neither Frankie nor Jake had known at the time that the torpedo was simply bait, the lure in the trap that Castellano had set for Jake.

Anyway, it was very possible that Jake *wasn't* in his right mind that night, and that even if he had known it wouldn't have deterred him. And to Jake's way of thinking what *he* had left in room two-one-seven just across the road—the surprise package *he* had left for Frankie, and the grim message it would serve to convey to his boss—well, that had been worth all the trouble in the world . . .

All of which had been some three hours ago. Since when Jake had sat at his window in the flop, patiently waiting for Frankie to return—but not for much longer. For Jake's nightmare was rapidly gaining pace now, its mainly monochrome scenes shifting on the screen of his mind just as fast as he could follow them.

The traffic on the road outside was down to a trickle. Not surprising since it was 1:30 A.M. But the horns were blaring as loudly as ever. For Italian drivers there was only ever one way to drive . . .

A taxi came up the rain-slick road. Pulling into the kerb, it stopped outside the Novara, and the wedge-shaped Frankie got out. Turning up his collar against the drizzle and putting his hands over his head, he made for the dry area under the hotel's entrance canopy, paused a moment to adjust his collar, vanished within . . .

Cold now, but burning inside, Jake lightly oiled, cleaned, and fed two oddly dissimilar bullets into his weapon's magazine. And easing the magazine into the rifle's housing, he placed the completed assembly on a table where its long barrel pointed out of the open window and across the road . . .

Frankie Reggio's lights came on in his room in the Novara. Or rather, *one* of the large lotus buds lit up, its glow clearly discernible even through the drawn curtains. An unmissable target . . .

Jake had already set up his telephone to call the Novara's switchboard; now he hit the instant redial and got the exchange. "Room two-one-seven," he told the operator. And as Frankie Reggio shrugged out of his coat, his telephone began to buzz . . .

Jake could picture Frankie grumbling about defective lightbulbs as he crossed the room to the phone . . . then ignored the phone, went to the windows and opened the curtains. Now he was in full view. And *now* he went back for the phone . . .

"Si?" (Like the grunt of a pig.)

"Speak English, Frankie," said Jake.

"Eh? English?"

"I know you can do it because I've heard you once before," Jake told him. "Don't you remember? That night at Luigi's place in Marseilles? Me tied to that chair? And the girl, Natasha? And you and your *fucking* thug pals doing . . . doing what you did?"

"You!" said Frankie, and Jake saw him give a sudden start, straighten up and glance nervously, jerkily all about his room, looking everywhere except up.

"Me, right," said Jake. "You remember my name?"

"Jake Cutter, sure," said Frankie, a little easier. "Luigi said it might be you who took out the others." He reached under his arm, took an ugly little gun from its holster there.

"The others . . . were a message," Jake said. "I was letting Luigi Castellano know that it would soon be his turn. Well, now I have another message for him. You can deliver it—you ugly, unnatural bastard!"

"Listen, you fucking stupid British *fuck!*" Frankie started to curse and rant.

And Jake *was* listening. But he was also cradling the telephone between his chin and right shoulder, taking up his rifle, aiming it and beginning to apply first pressure to the trigger. And then he cut in on Frankie's cursing to say. "Hey, thug! Now *you* fucking listen. You remember when you pissed on her? I felt every splash. I mean, I really *felt* it: every splash burning on me like acid."

"Huh!" Frankie grunted, grinned poisonously, and promised: "Well, don't worry. On you it *will* be acid!" But:

"You first," said Jake. And then he squeezed the trigger.

It was in the lotus-bulb light fixture—almost one and a half litres of a colourless, odourless acid. Jake had unscrewed one of the globes, taken the light bulb out, and three-quarters filled the globe before screwing it back in again.

The shot was silenced. Frankie heard a high-pitched spitting sound—like a cat's sneeze—as the bullet punched a hole in his window. But from directly overhead a secondary splintering of glass was clearly audible in the frozen fraction of time before acid and sculptured shards rained down on him.

Jake heard Frankie's yelp of shock, astonishment, then his first shrieks as he dropped the phone, staggered away from the wall towards the bed. He was drenched; his clothes were already beginning to smoke, his flesh, too. He capered, danced, started tearing his melting clothes off. But the telephone was melting, too, and Frankie's cries rapidly hissing into silence.

"Do it!" Jake muttered, relishing the moment and yet horrified by it, wanting to get it over and done with.

And Frankie did it.

On his bedside table, a pitcher of water. Except it wasn't water any longer but accelerant, and Jake's second bullet was a tracer designed to flare on impact.

Frankie tossed the accelerant over himself, poured it over his head and shoulders. And Jake again squeezed the trigger.

The tracer hit Frankie's window and cracked it, sending a pencil jet of searing, sulphurous fire leaping across the room

. . . towards Frankie. And the room at once blossomed into a ball of blistering white fire. In a split second it was an inferno, and at its heart the thug danced a while longer, then crumpled down into himself as the windows shattered and flames billowed outwards . . .

It was done. But Jake was done, too.

The Italian police caught him as he left the flop. They'd been out in the street watching Frankie, not Jake; keeping covert guard on the thug, as per Castellano's tip-off. One of them had spotted the flash of Jake's tracer where it penetrated Frankie's window, and then he had seen the blued-steel glint of Jake's rifle protruding into the night.

And that had been that . . .

Though Jake's nightmares usually brought him shuddering awake, on this occasion that wasn't the case. Familiar now with these recurrent reminders of his lapses into inhumanity—reconciled to the fact that they would probably continue until he tracked down and removed their cause, or was himself removed—he was becoming more and more inured to them. And in addition, he was fatigued to the core.

So this time he slept on . . .

Jake's fatigue, more mental than physical, also accounted for the fact that his shields were down—as they had been for the duration of his nightmare. And with the more pressing problems of the real world temporarily forgotten, held in abeyance while his dream-self relived the horrific events of the recent past (and while Jake's conscience tried in vain to accommodate them), he had been completely unaware of his audience.

But the dead vampire Korath had been with him throughout, and he had witnessed everything.

For having been driven out of Jake's mind by Liz Merrick at such a crucial juncture, as he had been about to enter into it more surely and perhaps permanently (or rather, having left it of his own free will, rather than let her discover his true nature) Korath had been eager to return at his earliest opportunity. Thus he had been "on hand" to leech on Jake's troubled mind and see for himself the extent of the Necroscope's obsession: just how far he would go—and indeed how far he had gone—to exact a fitting revenge.

So that now, suspecting that Jake would react badly to any further intrusion while his nightmare was still fresh in mind—not wanting to be associated with it in parallel, as something to be avoided and detested—Korath waited on the rim of Jake's subconsciousness and let him drift on awhile.

But when after an hour or so Jake's mind had settled down, when it wandered into more mundane dreams—but dreams where the continuously evolving formulae of Möbius space-time were always present, like a word on the tip of his tongue, or a solution on the perimeter of his mind, but a word or solution that refused to come—then Korath made his presence known:

Time we talked again, Necroscope.

Jake tossed in his bed, fighting for a moment against the intrusion of Korath's deadspeak thoughts, but after a while he succumbed to the inevitable. After all, he would have to speak to him eventually, if only to gain access to the Möbius Continuum. But even so Jake's deadspeak sigh was bitter when he said, "What, you again?"

Of course it's me again! said the other. *We have a way to go and things to do. Our agendas, remember?*

"I remember we were arguing, word-gaming, whatever," Jake answered. "But after that . . . I remember very little."

You were tired, Korath told him. *You slipped into a dream so vague that it took you from me . . . I could no longer reason with you while your mind wandered so. And so I left you to it. Nor would I intrude upon you now, for I see that you are still weary. But in a few short hours a new day will be dawning, and time is of the essence.*

"How far did we get?" Jake queried. "Did we make any progress at all?"

By the time we were done, I suppose *we were more or less in agreement,* Korath told him. *Our agendas were made specific, and as for mutual cooperation, we agreed upon a time limit—which is to say that when our enemies are no more, we each go our separate ways. Or you go yours while I . . . go nowhere. As for what we have yet to decide: it's the question of who goes first.*

"Who goes first?"

Which agenda takes precedence.

"Mine, of course," said Jake. "It must be mine, because I won't be able to concentrate on anything else until—"

—Until you've had your revenge, aye, Korath finished it for him. And then continued: *But now that I have witnessed the full range of your passions in that respect, I must agree that your agenda has a certain appeal. A definite . . . entertainment value? While on the other hand I feel I really should inquire: what use to pursue this Castellano, a mere man, Jake, if while you're thus engaged you lose your world to the Wamphyri? Which is why I put it to you that* my *agenda is far and away the more important, the more urgent, the more valid of the two.*

But now Jake was suddenly wary. He had picked up on something that Korath had let slip. "What's that? You've witnessed the full range of my passion . . . ?" And before the vampire could erect shields of his own, Jake saw what flashed across his incorporeal mind . . . and at once remembered his nightmare. "Damn you, Korath! You were there—you were spying on me!"

Because you were disturbed in your sleep! The other's lie was instinctive, instantaneous. *And because you were tormented by your dreams. There was this great anger in you, and madness, and even regret! In all the turmoil I felt myself* drawn *back to you, Jake, by this link that exists between us, forged from our need for each other. It was as if I heard you crying out, calling to me, and I answered your call. But when I got here—*

"If that were true you would have roused me up, brought me out of it," Jake cut him short. "Instead you let it continue—and you saw what I did to Frankie Reggio. . . .

I am what I am, Korath answered. *I am the sum of all that I once was. And even though I am reduced by that same amount, I remember* how *I was. And I* know *my strengths, and my weaknesses. Is it so strange that I desired to know the strength of the one who shall be my . . . my partner? My strong right hand in a great venture, our mutual revenge against them that wronged us?*

"You were seeing how I measured up?" Jake was dubious. "Is that what you're saying?" He shook his head. "No, I don't think so. I think you were simply spying on me."

My first thought was to rouse you up, Korath kept right on lying. *But when I saw what you were about, then I became caught up in it.*

"Caught up? You mean you enjoyed it?"

It fascinated me. I was fascinated by . . . a concept.

"What concept?"

An eye for an eye, said the other. *Aye!* And he chuckled in his obscene fashion. *Ah, for when you spoke to Frankie and told him how every splash had burned you like acid—why, you were describing his own fate! How splendidly ironic! Then I was convinced of our invincibility; I knew you wouldn't shrink from whatever has to be done. And yet, having said all that . . .*

As Korath paused Jake sensed an incorporeal frown, a half-formed shrug of indecision. "Well?" he prompted him.

I have only one small concern, said the vampire. *The fact that I sensed your regret. You did not like what you had done.*

"I should like it?" Jake answered. "But it was inhuman!"

As are the Wamphyri, said Korath. *And, from what I've seen in your mind, as is this Castellano. So then, why do you regret your actions? Is it some kind of weakness in you?*

"No," Jake denied it, "it's a strength. I regret what I've done because it brings me down to their level—and to yours."

Hmm! The other mused. *You have a low opinion of me.* And he pretended to ponder on that for a moment or so until, in a little while: *Still, let's not argue any further. And as a show of good faith—in order to breach this impasse—I shall let you have your way. We'll go after Luigi Castellano first.*

"Good," said Jake. "But understand, I still won't have you in my mind. Not as a permanent fixture."

Not permanent, but merely—

"Not any way," said Jake. "Nothing more than you have now. Which in any case is too much."

Hah! said Korath. *Is there no give and take with you? Must you always win?*

"Winning isn't the point," Jake shook his head. "The point is not to lose. Losers end up in subterranean sumps with all of their flesh sloughed off! And me, I'm very much alive. So we do things my way, or not at all. In which case I might try to enlist Harry Keogh's aid in getting rid of you for good."

At which Korath gave a snort of frustration, "threw up his hands," and said, *Very well, very* well! *So what comes next? How will we proceed? Where and when do we begin?*

"When I call for you, you come," Jake answered. "And when I say you're out, you're out. Then, when we've dealt with Castellano, we'll rejoin E-Branch and go after the Wamphyri."

So be it—we are agreed! Korath grunted. But in his dark and secret heart, he knew that the sooner he guided or cajoled the headstrong Jake back towards E-Branch the better. For when he'd said that time was of the essence, he had spoken no truer word; and while the future seemed to offer more than a glimmer of hope—more than just a slim chance that he would discover some form of continued existence, perhaps even a superior form of physical life, in Jake—still he wanted to be sure it was a chance in a world ruled by men, or by him, and not by Vavara, Szwart, and Malinari. *Definitely* not by Malinari!

And we begin—where? How will you find this Castellano?

"There are people I can speak to."

People?

"The dead," said Jake. "They're not really dead—or they are—but they're not finished. Their minds go on."

As I myself am witness, aye.

"So who would know more about Castellano than his victims?" Jake went on. "Or if not his victims as such, the ones who are dead because of him—which is more or less the same thing. I think I'll start with them."

But isn't that one of your problems? said Korath. *That the dead won't speak to you?*

"Because of you, yes," Jake offered a deadspeak nod. "But those who are bent on revenge, as I am bent on revenge, they'll speak to me. I'm the only one who can give them what they want. And I know that there's at least one among them who . . . who . . . well, I *know* that she will speak to me."

You'll go to her first, your dead lover?

"Last," Jake shook his head. "When I'm better acquainted with what I'm doing, the how of it, and when I'm able to—I don't know—find some courage I suppose. For after all, I let her down . . . *Then* I'll speak to Natasha. But before that there are others. In life they were scum: vicious murderers and drug-running rapist bastards. And in death? What have they got now? We can be sure the teeming dead won't have anything to do with them—just as they won't have anything to do with you! These people were Castellano's followers, his gang, but from what I saw of them they feared him. Now that they've nothing left to lose, I'm their one last chance to wreak some kind of revenge, their one opportunity to catch up. Paybacks are hell, Korath."

Oh, indeed they are! Korath answered. While hidden in his secret heart, he promised: *And believe me, Jake Cutter, yours shall be the worst of all possible hells—you obstinate fool!* But to Jake he only said:

So then, I'm ready. And I know that I shall enjoy working with you. Let it begin. But:

"After I've slept my fill," Jake answered. "I've got a lot of sleep to catch up on, Korath—and again that's mainly down to you. So now be on your way. But be warned: if I sense even the slightest tremor in the deadspeak aether—"

—Very well! I understand. I shall wait on your call.

"And you'll hear it," Jake told him. "Because frankly I'm wasting my time with Trask and E-Branch. I don't think they'll ever understand what's eating at me—they can't because they didn't experience it. I was so lost, so helpless—but now I'm not. Now it's my turn. So don't worry about a thing, I *will* be calling for you. Tomorrow, just as soon as I'm awake."

But tomorrow is another day, said Korath. *Day, as opposed to night; awake as opposed to dreaming. Can you be sure you'll remember, Jake, when you're awake?*

"I think so," Jake answered. "You see, I seem to be getting better at this. I mean *all* of this, and all of the time."

It was true, and the vampire wasn't sure he liked it. *Tomorrow, then,* said Korath thoughtfully. *So be it. And sleep well, Jake Cutter.*

And Jake felt the creature depart, slithering away into the darkness of his dreaming . . .

9
Vavara and Malinari

IN LONDON, BEN TRASK AND MILLICENT CLEARY dined out. While in a taverna on Skala Astris's ocean-facing promenade, on Krassos:

Malinari sipped from a delicate flute of chilled, dark red Mavro Daphne, and inquired of his companion, "How are you finding the Greek food, my dear?"

Vavara looked at him, at his sardonic smile, which came as close as possible to an entirely human smile, however dark, and tried not to grimace. She knew that the question was Malinari's grotesque idea of a joke—his attempt to lighten her mood and perhaps bring her out of herself, which was the reason they had ventured out from the monastery tonight in the first place, because of her depression and bad humour—but she wasn't going to give him the satisfaction of acknowledging that fact. For after all, Malinari was the principal source of her displeasure.

So instead of throwing back her head, laughing, and assuming the convivial mode he had doubtless hoped for, Vavara repaid him in equally sardonic coin, by glancing at him through half-shuttered eyes, and answering:

"When first I came here, before the simpering, pious fools in the monastery took me 'into their care,' as it were, I found the local food edible—well, barely so, but at least it stayed down. Since that was all there was, however, and not wanting to place myself in jeopardy by—shall we say, foraging?—plainly it had to suffice. My larder in Mazemanse was far better provisioned, of course, with wild honey, wolf hearts, Szgany livers, and all manner of sweetmeats. And as for the 'fare' on Sunside: even under duress from that creature Nathan and his friends the Lidescis, that was infinitely superior! Alas that Mazemanse was five hundred years ago, and that more recently I allowed you to talk me into coming here. As for my current tastes: this Greek roughage isn't so very different from the Szgany fodder that we once knew, I suppose. It sustains one for a while, but scarcely satisfies a more . . . what, *sophisticated* palate? The one thing I will say for it: it is better far than the frozen, desiccated flesh of dead thralls on which we subsisted during our Icelands ordeal."

She paused, glanced scathingly at the slender glass in his long-fingered hand, and went on: "As for the red wine—"

"Ah!" came a drunken cry from a table on the other side of the dining area, where a handful of German tourists were throwing back their wines, beers, ouzo chasers, and vinegary retsina as fast as they could pour it. "Ah! But this is the life, *nicht wahr!?"*

The speaker—he spoke half in English, for the benefit of the English tourists—was bald, fat, and red in the face. But as he spoke, stood up, and raised his glass, he toppled over backwards and went down with a crash, much to the entertainment of his companions. But not to Vavara's, who continued where she had been interrupted:

"—As for the wine: I disagree with that idiot entirely."

And now she smiled, albeit sneeringly, scornfully. "*Hah!*—this is the life, indeed! Well for him, perhaps, but not for me. For no matter how deep or red the wine, it simply *isn't* the life!"

"Ah, no," he agreed. "For only the blood is the life!" And then, twirling his glass so that it sparkled, he added, "But it does help to throw a pleasant light on gloomy things. Maybe you should try a little?"

Vavara pretended not to have heard him.

They conversed in Szgany, the language of their own world, but they were Wamphyri and their linguistic skill was astonishing. They had been on Earth for only three years but understood every language they heard spoken in the taverna. Greek had been easiest of all, for it was the closest to their own tongue. And as for Szgany: some of the tourists at nearby tables might well have overheard something of Vavara and Malinari's conversation, and they may have wondered in passing about the tongue, but the Greeks didn't give it a second thought. The world had become a very small place, and catering to foreigners a way of life . . .

It was late evening; the sea was dark as Malinari's wine; the bouzouki music from half a dozen different taverna sources mingled meaninglessly, but Malinari at least didn't mind. "Personally," he said, "I find this place oddly pleasing, strangely attractive. The music is soothing, and the odours from roasting meats—" he lifted his head to sniff at the night air, "—they remind me of Sunside hunts in the long ago. Yes, I think I like this island."

"Well I don't," said Vavara, and at once returned her gaze to the sea and watched the languid lights of a string of fishing vessels bobbing in the near distance, as the boats returned to harbour.

"You don't care for it?" said Malinari, and poured himself more wine from a bottle in a bucket of ice. "Good! Then when we set the boundaries, I shall call on you to remember what you've said tonight. And perhaps I'll make Krassos my headquarters."

"What?" Vavara raised an astonished eyebrow and glanced

at him again. "You truly *like* this place? You're not joking?"

He shrugged. "It's isolated, and the thoughts of its handful of people are simple thoughts. Oh, they have their passions the same as all men, but far removed from those of Earth's more sophisticated throngs. In my casino in the mountains of Australia, I was surrounded by these so-called 'sophisticates'. They were vain, greedy, and overly ambitious to a man. Civilized on the outside, yet seething within, their massed thoughts were a tumult: always thrusting, intruding, seeking to gain the upper hand. You can have them all! But when I am a Lord again—which I surely will be, commanding of my own vast territories, my own peoples—then let any thrall of mine think to advance himself beyond food in his belly, a woman in his bed, borders to patrol and beasts to tend . . . and he shall go to the provisioning!"

Vavara heard him out but her eyes were hooded, thoughtful as they studied his expression, his words. "And so it begins," she finally replied. "Or so it will begin. 'Borders to patrol,' you said, and 'beasts to tend.' You speak of the provisioning: of your aerie, of course, or in this world your mountain range, or your island, or perhaps an entire continent? Is that how it will be, Malinari, one hundred years or more from now? Borders and . . . and beasts? But surely you mean warrior creatures? And as for provisions—or the provisioning of which *you* spoke—well that could only be for war, obviously!"

Again his shrug, but now he spoke more guardedly. For this was after all Vavara's territory (for the time being, at least). "In a hundred years . . . who can say how things will be? Vavara, we are Wamphyri! And as for what I said of sophisticated men—of their vices and passions—well, we have them all in spades! It's what we are and we may not change it. Nor would I want to. Nor would you. But for now we're allies, and we'll have enemies enough without that we fight each other."

"In spades?" She frowned. "We have them in spades?"

"It's a term I learned in my casino in Xanadu. One of many things I learned as I watched men at the gaming tables losing their money to me. Ah, but there's far more than that to be won from these people. Even their world entire."

"Their world entire," she repeated him. "And again there's that in your voice which reveals what's on your mind."

He sipped at his wine and said, "Oh, and are you a mentalist now?"

"Bah!" Vavara answered, curling her lip a little. "No, for I shall leave the voyeurism to you. And don't try to change the subject. You have already foreseen a time when we'll be at each other's throats again. I can't say I like the idea. And anyway, you see too far ahead. Things could get difficult enough today, tomorrow, or next week, without that we go conquering worlds or counting our shad calves tonight, even as the first wolf howls to his brothers on high."

That last was an old Szgany expression, for to Vavara and Malinari—having slept the centuries away in the Icelands—the lost paradise of Sunside seemed as yesterday. Also, Vavara was wont to cling to the old ways far more than her guest was. But as for the wolves of which she spoke: Malinari knew her meaning only too well.

"Hardly the first wolf," he said with a scowl. "And by no means the last. Yes, I had problems in Xanadu. Even a disaster, but I was fortunate and saw it coming. What's more, I think we can be sure it will come here, too. After all, you haven't done your best to stave it off. That Gypsy girl you told me about—that was a serious mistake."

"Nor have *you* helped!" Vavara snapped back. "What of sweet Sara?"

"Sweet before you got to her, perhaps," said Malinari. "Do not forget that I saw your handiwork. But at least her body was firm. Oh, I would have had her, aye. Despite her disfigurements I would have had her blood and body both, for my sustenance and pleasure. But she fought me like a mad creature—such furious strength! It was her vampire, waking up in her; she was ascending! So don't blame me, Vavara. Indeed, you might perhaps thank me. For if Sara hadn't died that night, what then? Ah, but that could have been a real problem. And anyway, it was you who gave her to me, remember?"

"You hungered for blood after your long journey here," she answered. "I gave her to you for the blood, not the sex! I fail to see how any man could *want* sex, not from Sara, not after—"

"After what? After you had . . . *teased* her, in your special way? Because she had been too pretty, perhaps?" Malinari smiled his sardonic smile. "But her buttocks were still very firm, and her legs were long and shapely. And gazing into vacant eyes, as opposed to eyes filled with dread . . . that might have made for a very pleasant change. Each to his own tastes, eh?"

"And then you let her best you," Vavara went on. "And she threw herself down from that high window, into the night ocean. Why, for all I know you might have thrown her down yourself, in a furious rage when she fought back! So don't you try lecturing me on *my* mistakes, Nephran Malinari! *Hah!*" She tossed her head.

"But when she washed up on the strand like that," Malinari pressed, "after I had told you that Sara was Wamphyri and had a leech—?"

"Aye, that, too," Vavara answered grudgingly but far less angrily. "With Sara locked up in her cell all that time, I had failed to notice her condition. Plainly I had let things go too far with her. Well, and what of it? The sea took care of that, and I took care of the rest of it, the ones who came to examine her. But yes, you are right: we've both made serious errors. As for whose mistakes were most damaging to our cause: at least I have corrected mine. But as for yours . . ." She shook her head.

"They lost me my foothold in Australia, true," said Malinari, "along with all that I had bred there in accordance with our plan. A setback, Vavara, that's all, and I can start again. Or perhaps you've been so industrious on my behalf that I don't need to start again. Have you forgotten your promise—to show me what you've made here, under the place called Palataki?"

"No, I didn't forget," she answered. "And indeed I need to check that all's well up there."

"So let's stop all this quarrelling," he said placatingly. "We should finish up here and go. These people are getting far too boisterous, and we can do without involvement. The Germans are drunk, and those Greek lads at that table over there: it's obvious that they find you fascinating. But there again, what would Vavara be without her fascination, eh?"

Malinari was correct. Several members of the German party were well and truly intoxicated by this time; they were staggering between tables, determined to introduce themselves where they weren't wanted, annoying the mainland Greek, British, and other holidaymakers alike.

As for the young, local Greek men he had mentioned: three of them sat at a dimly lit bar inwards of the taverna, where they drank cheap, undiluted ouzo from a tall bottle. Just a little while ago the bottle had been full; now it was three-quarters empty, and their interest in Vavara had increased commensurate with what each of them had drunk.

Now, inspired by Malinari's comment, Vavara deliberately turned in that direction, smiled at the men, and brushed back her shining black hair with both hands. This action not only revealed her pale bare arms as they rose from under her shawl, but also lifted her seemingly perfect breasts. And the points of her apparently erect nipples stood out in sharp definition beneath the red silk blouse that she wore.

Gypsyish and wanton, and delighting in it—for a single frozen moment she looked unbearably delicious. So much so that Malinari himself felt his mouth go dry. But unlike the youths, he knew that it was only her allure.

For chameleon Vavara could be all things to all men—*and* women—and liked to practice her art. But she hadn't mastered it yet, not by any means, and rarely presented the same facade twice. Malinari had known her for most of his life, albeit that more than half of that life had been spent in stasis, but even he couldn't have described her. Not the true colour of her eyes (other than when she raged and they were uniformly red), or the angle of her jaw, or even the curve of her lips, except to say they were always tempting.

For it was all a sham, a guise, a hypnotic image that she projected to cover her true form. But while Vavara's physical appearance was a lie, Malinari knew the truth of her mind very well indeed. For that was where *his* talent came into play. And at times like this, in close proximity, Vavara's mind was such a cesspool that if it was a reflection of her true being, then she was a monstrous, wrinkled, sagging hag!

And perhaps she was, perhaps this was how she compensated for some other deficiency. For Malinari knew that she was lacking as a metamorph, a shape-shifter; he had never once seen her take to the air, except upon the back of a flyer. If Vavara had aged accordingly—her sluggish flesh unable to keep pace with the years—then mass hypnotism would be a perfect foil against the ravages of time. And of course the Wamphyri were ever vain, not least their females.

His thoughts returned to earth and he looked for the proprietor to call him over and pay the bill. A bottle of wine and two bloody chunks of red meat (which had scarcely been touched) were the total of their meal. The *logariasmo* should not be more than a few thousand drachmas.

As for the drunken members of the German party: they were arguing now over a spilled table that one of them had collided with, and an English tourist was complaining bitterly over the retsina stains on his white jacket. Not only the mood but also the music had changed. Instead of the melodious bouzoukis, the air was suddenly raucous with heavy metal and the nasal vocals of some neutered rock group.

Feeling the first lightning-flash stab of a headache coming on, Malinari winced and put aside his wine. He could sense curious thoughts aimed in his direction, or far more likely in Vavara's, but ignored them and withdrew into himself a little, so avoiding painful contact.

The young Greek men who had been so obviously enamoured of Vavara were already leaving. Starting up their motorcycles, and swinging their slim backsides into the saddles, they roared off along the seafront three abreast in a cloud of dust, with their studded-leather jackets gleaming in the night.

As they went, one of them looked back, lifted his arm and waved a farewell, or a salute, at Vavara. And she responded by smiling and inclining her head.

"You ought not to play up to them," Malinari told her as he paid the bill. "They're young and they've had too much to drink. To such as them, a nod is as good as a wink."

"Oh, let it be," she answered carelessly. "It amuses me to set them drooling, to know that they're wondering about me, and fantasizing in their dirty little minds."

"Oh? Can we afford to have them wondering about you, do you think?" he asked her as they left the taverna, stepped into the night, and walked along the Skala Astris promenade, between the open-fronted tavernas and the sea wall, among a last handful of late-season tourists making their way back to their accommodations. "What, and you the mistress—the, er, 'mother superior'—of a monastery?"

"But they don't know that," she laughed deep in her throat. "This is the first time that I've been out on a night like this. And on those rare occasions when I'm seen in the evening, up at the monastery, then of course I affect the drab trappings of my order, which are designed to hide one's person away from prying eyes. I find it very easy to emit an aura of holiness . . . or of unholiness. So don't concern yourself, those panting Greek pups only saw what I wanted them to see."

"Don't we all?" said Malinari.

Skala Astris was little more than a strip of half a dozen flimsy hotels backing the tavernas, which themselves backed the sea wall that sprawled a quarter mile to the west before giving way to the beach. Beyond the wall, chunks of white marble stuck up from the deep ocean, huge blocks of the stuff, each weighing many tons. Other than tourism, the main industry of Krassos lay in exporting quality marble; its by-product, faulty or inferior rubble from the quarries, was put to use in landfill, building, and the substructure of jetties and quays.

But in the long ago, before tourism as it was today, there

had been other industries. The Germans had been here for a long time, and not only as tourists.

On top of a steep dark hill maybe a half-mile to the east, remote by Krassos standards from any other village or building, the structure that local Greeks had named Palataki rose up like a gaunt, out-of-place (and certainly out of time) very *un*-Greek gothic mansion. Its name meant "little palace," and some years before the Second World War a German firm had built it there as the headquarters and offices of an exploratory mining concern.

For as well as small deposits of gold and silver, minerals had been discovered on Krassos that were important to Germany's future war effort. And the island's artisans—without knowing exactly why the Germans were here or why they'd bought the hill and the lands around, but in need of the work as always, and so not bothering to ask too many questions—had set to with German plans and built Palataki.

Then, when the work on the literally palatial building was finished, rough labour had been easy to find among the island's poorer classes, who had been pleased to accept work in the mine tunnels that would soon burrow through the loose soil and rocks of a wooded spur and promontory between Palataki and the Aegean. Spillage from the shafts had gone down into the sea via a bight east of the promontory, where dark red flinty mounds were still visible in a region of the coastline that had been irreparably damaged.

But the mining operation had failed; the minerals had been low-grade, and the work had ceased. And as war came the Germans had moved out, retaining ownership of Palataki and its grounds, mining rights in the promontory, and nothing else.

Then for sixty years the place had stood empty, gradually falling into ruins, and because of its gloomy, gothic aspect it had gained something of a bad reputation among the local communities. All of which served Vavara's purposes very well indeed.

Explaining these things to Malinari as they strolled along the promenade, which was quiet now as taverna lights dimmed one by one, Vavara said, "There you have it." Then she pointed east and said: "And there it stands—Palataki! I purchased it from its German owners with the money you sent from your casino. And do you know, it would make something of a grand aerie in itself if I were not satisfied with my fortress monastery. But while a monastery makes a very fine manse, Palataki—"

"—Has other uses, yes," Malinari finished it for her, his night-seeing eyes taking in what they could of the near-distant silhouette: its four storeys rising up from the hill, with high gables, towerlike cupolas, and great windows. "I find it truly appealing and very impressive," he said. "Probably much more so close up. But you have to admit, it's in conflict with the rest of this island. I fail to see what the Germans wanted with such a place—or perhaps not. Do you know anything of this world's history?"

"Not a lot," Vavara answered. "But then, knowing so little of our own history before our time, why should I concern myself with theirs?"

"To know your foe is to be able to anticipate him," Malinari answered. "And knowing his history is part of the strategy. I think that if the war had gone in their favour, these Germans would have come back and remained here, and Palataki would have been far more than a block of offices for some mining operation. Far more likely it would have been a bastion of the Third Reich in this region, their headquarters in these islands. Looking at it, at its gaunt and grandiose style, I can see everything that der Führer was or wanted to be. With his sigils of power—his great black swastikas on fields of blood—hanging from those windows, Palataki would be perfect! He was something of a man, you know, this Hitler."

"He had his good points, I suppose," Vavara shrugged.

"His good points?" Malinari smiled grimly. "If he had been Wamphyri . . . ah, but then there would be no room for us, eh?"

They had reached the harbour. Most of the boats were in now and tied up, and the dark water lapped sullenly, gurgling among the berths and moorings. Back along the sea wall, no one was to be seen, and the lights in a huddle of houses behind the hotels and tavernas, the original old fishing village of Skala Astris, were out. This late in the season, with only a few tourists to cater for, the "night life" was wont to die an abrupt death . . .

Vavara had left her limo in the care of her driver, a senior sister, about a quarter-mile out of the village in a partly concealed lay-by. Since a good many local Greeks knew that the vehicle belonged to the monastery, she deemed it prudent not to be seen getting into or out of it in any guise other than that of a nun—and especially not in the company of Malinari.

But now, as they made to walk inland toward the main coast road, there came a diversion: the glare of headlight beams and the roar of revving motorcycle engines.

"Oh, dear!" sighed Malinari drily. "Didn't I warn you not to play up to them? The island's bad boys are back." It was, of course, the three young men from the taverna.

"They seem full of high spirits!" Vavara played their game, clapping her hands as the three leaned back in their saddles to perform wheelies in the middle of the harbour concourse.

"High spirits?" said Malinari. "If you're speaking of ouzo, then I have to agree! But the tall one with the long black hair—the one who waved at you—his thoughts are dark indeed."

"Can you read them?" she said, as the three bikers skidded to a halt, got off their machines, and lifted them up onto their stands.

"I don't want to," said Malinari. "My head is still aching from their racket! But he fancies himself, that one. And that's not all he fancies."

"Hallo," the man in question grunted, as he walked casually towards the pair. With a cursory glance at Malinari, he came to a halt facing Vavara.

"Hallo!" She smilingly greeted him, until her smile turned

into a sneer. And then: "Hallo—and goodbye," she said. "Goodnight."

"Goodbye? Goodnight?" He answered her back in the English that she had employed, cocked his head a little on one side and smiled his version of a worldy smile. "But is not late. I think maybe I walking with you. I want . . . talking with you."

"Walking and talking?" said Malinari, stifling a yawn. "Is *that* what you want? Is that all? Very well then, so now hear me talking. Go away. Go now, at once, while you can *still* walk and talk."

"Go away?" The other scowled, his unruly eyebrows meeting in the middle. "*You* go away! Is my island. I am man of Krassos. You thee stranger here."

"Indeed I am a stranger," said Malinari. "Just how much of a stranger you'll never know."

Meanwhile the other two men had approached and stood grinning where they leaned against the sea wall. One of them made a point of cleaning his nails with an Italian switchblade.

"She not liking you," said the tall one, his looks growing darker by the moment. For taking Malinari's indifference—his lackadaisical attitude—as a sign of uncertainty or cowardice, he felt very sure of himself. "I see you doing thee argues, see her not doing the smiling. I see her shouting . . . at you! Now *I* shout at you!" He prodded Malinari's chest, as if expecting him to flinch and cower back.

Malinari didn't flinch but merely grinned a wicked, barely controlled grin which made the corners of his mouth twitch, and said: "Young man, you are a very rude, very stupid person." And where before Malinari had appeared merely tall, now he was *very* tall, very strong, and incredibly fast.

Without seeming to move, his hands were clasping the young Greek's temples. And for two or three long seconds—while the other stood there paralysed—the vampire Malinari fastened on his mind like a leech, sucking at his thoughts . . .

. . . Thoughts mainly of Vavara, naked, writhing, panting out her lust on a beach somewhere, with her legs wrapped

round him. And others of his home in Astris, not Skala *Astris on the coast, but its sister village in the mountains. And of his mother, and the road home uncoiling under the whirling wheels of his motorcycle, just as it did every night.*

Then of his work in the quarries, where he sawed out those mighty blocks of pure white marble. And then again back to sex: an English girl he'd seduced last summer, and a German girl the summer before that . . .

Thus Malinari familiarized himself with the man's mind, its signature, and knew that in future—within certain strictures of distance, and given an uncluttered psychic aether—he would always be able to find him again.

Quite the little seducer, this one, but ugly with it. There was nothing of romance in it, only lust; much like vampirism in its way, and this Greek might even make a useful thrall or lieutenant. But no, for where women were concerned he would always be untrustworthy . . .

Malinari released him. For a moment the man staggered, then recovered and tried to lash out with an arm that felt heavy as lead and a clenched fist made of rubber. Almost without effort, Malinari caught his arm, twisted it into an armlock and turned him about, grabbed his belt at the rear, and hoisted him up and over the sea wall, out into the water. Lucky for him that there were no sharp marble boulders this close to the harbour.

Then Malinari stepped to the man's bike, picked it up as if it were a toy, whirled and lobbed that into the water, too.

The other bikers were no longer leaning on the wall. They had come erect, their jaws hanging slack and their leather-clad frames as stiff as poles. They looked at each other and then at Malinari. They had seen his speed, his effortless strength; now they saw his fixed grin—not quite a rictus—inviting them to try their luck, and perhaps join their friend where he splashed about in the sea.

The one with the knife looked at it as if he didn't recognize it, folded its blade, and pocketed it. And without saying a word, the pair backed away, heading for a break in the sea wall where steps went down to the water. But:

"Ah, no!" said Malinari in their own tongue. "Your friend got himself in trouble, so let him get himself out. Best if you leave now, for if you don't, I shall deal with your machines the same way I dealt with his—and perhaps with you, too."

They didn't argue. And as they got astride their bikes: "I don't expect we'll be seeing you again tonight," said Malinari. "Or any night, for that matter . . ."

"Bravo!" said Vavara sneeringly when they were gone.

"Thank you," said Malinari. "Since I kept myself in check, I deserve every bit of your praise."

"I could have handled it myself," she answered.

"Now there's no need to," he told her.

"Huh! But they were only boys."

"And they are still boys. But far more importantly they're still alive, and there won't be any repercussions . . ."

By Greek standards, the coast road east of Skala Astris in the direction of Limari was a good one, with a metalled surface and very few potholes. But over the distance of one-third of a mile from the lay-by where Vavara had left her vehicle and driver to Palataki's neglected old service road, it was serpentine in its winding.

Vavara's driver—black-hooded, servile, and occasionally shivering, but never looking back at her passengers—drove at a carefully measured pace; the drainage ditches at the sides of the road were deep, and where it had been cut through spurs and steep slopes there were stretches where the cliffs on the right fell sheer to the sea.

As they rode, Malinari looked out of his window, down into one such abyss of air and ocean, and asked, "Would this, by any chance, be the place where you, er, gave our visitors a nudge?" It was the first time he had been out of the monastery, and all he knew of Krassos was what he had seen of it on the night of his arrival and tonight's excursion.

"No," Vavara shook her head. "For that would have been too close to Skala Astris. I chose a place remote from the island's villages, a spot midway between Palataki and the monastery. The tides around Krassos aren't much, the sea is deep in that location, and the coast very rugged. When I saw the car go over the rim, I knew that if anything of the wreckage should drift away, it would not be found for some days. Ah, but then again, I also 'knew' that there would be no survivors! Yet—"

"Yet there was one," Malinari nodded. "And a policeman, at that. Did you read the report in the newspapers? It seems we've been very fortunate."

"My reading skills are rudimentary," she answered, tossing her head. "I have nuns to read for me. Are you referring to the fact that the policeman, this Manolis Papastamos, has no memory of the event? Yes, we are probably fortunate that he was banged about. But on the other hand, it was very quick . . . I doubt that he would have realised what was happening. He was much too busy trying to keep his car on the road to have time to wonder about what was pushing it off! And in any case, even if he remembered anything about it, why should he believe it was something other than an accident? Lying broken in that hospital in Kavála, I am sure he has other things to worry about. Also, in Krassos town, which is where I bought this limo, there are several other cars just like it; when they can afford it, the Greeks are very vain and inclined to show off. Such transports are status symbols on an island as small as this. And anyway, in a world such as this one, a world of religious fools, who would ever think to accuse a nun or nuns?"

"Perhaps you're right," Malinari shrugged. "But still, you should never underestimate these people."

"You sound as if you speak from experience," she answered. "Your problems in Australia, no doubt."

"Exactly," said Malinari. "And in answer to your question: Who would accuse a nun? But who would have thought to search *me* out—a Lord of Vampires—in a casino, in a mountain resort in Australia? Yet they did."

"Still," Vavara said, "I'm not overly concerned about this man's survival. What, a simple policeman? What could *he* make of the leech? But as for the female, the pathologist—she had to die. We couldn't afford to let her report what must have seemed to her a very strange anomaly: a thing like a leech, a parasite in a human body, and in peculiar circumstances at that. Granted our situation would be somewhat more secure if both of them had died, but what's done is done, and the matter can't be improved. But tell me, what *is* all this nitpicking? Your way of diverting responsibility, perhaps? Do not think I have forgotten, Nephran Malinari, that but for your weird appetites I wouldn't have had this problem to deal with in the first place. Be satisfied with what I have achieved."

"You are argumentative tonight," said Malinari. "It wasn't my intention to be critical. I was merely stating facts. But if you insist on harping on *my* appetites, then I would remind you of your own. That Gypsy girl, for instance. You must have known that in taking her you placed yourself in jeopardy. And then to have let her escape . . . !"

For a moment Vavara was sullen, silent. But then she said: "As I have already admitted, that was an error. But the girl was beautiful—so fey, so innocent, and *so* Szgany—and after all, it wasn't as if I deliberately lured her. No, for she sought *me* out! She came to the monastery of her own free will. But once I had seen her . . . I couldn't turn her away.

"Her people, caravans and all, had come over on the great ferries from the mainland. They danced for the tourists in the tavernas, played on their drums, fiddles, and tambourines. They sold paper flowers and other nonsense knickknacks door-to-door in the villages, earning what few drachmas they could. She told me these things, when she brought her flowers to the monastery. But she was the loveliest flower of them all. For a day or two I actually thought that I loved her."

"A beautiful bloom, eh?" said Malinari. "And so you sipped her nectar." However wry and unsympathetic, his remark was only very slightly caustic. Each to his own.

But in any case Vavara wasn't offended. And with a negligent shrug she said, "I took a little, and I gave a little back. I thought she was enthralled—indeed she *was* enthralled, to a degree—but the call of her kinfolk was stronger. A few days more, she would have been mine forever . . . but it wasn't to be. I tell you, Malinari: Szgany blood out of Sunside ran strong in that one! And as for her escape: it wasn't so much an escape as that she simply walked away. Mazed—but in control of her own mind, her own will—she left me. Which I suppose was just as well; by which I mean that things would even out in the end. If she had stayed, the time would surely come when I would find her presence . . . offensive? And in leaving, she simply hastened her own end. So there you have it. And all said and done, I make no bones of it: she *was* a mistake, yes."

By now they had left the main road, turned right onto the old service road to Palataki, and were climbing the steep hill on a narrow, zigzagging track that could scarcely be called a road at all. Flanked on the inside by undergrowth and covered with slippery moss—with grasses, roots, and creepers thrusting up through its crumbling surface—it was as well that the limo's nun driver took it in first gear and with great caution. And as the dark silhouettes of Palataki's cupolas soared above, Malinari saw at once what it was that kept the locals away from the place.

The air was made luminous by fireflies; glowworms appeared to burn like discarded cigarette-ends in the shrubbery; despite that the summer had been a long one, and the first rains yet to fall, still there was a sense of dankness, of mouldy rottenness about the place. And where before Malinari had said Palataki the structure was "out of place" on Krassos, now he saw that its grounds—even the hill on which it stood—looked and felt exactly the same. It was a place apart.

"On an island of the sun, such as this one," Vavara smiled at him from the darkness of her corner seat—a flash of gleaming teeth that could so easily transform into a cave of knives—"this is one of the few places where I feel comfortable."

He knew what she meant and answered, "It definitely has a unique atmosphere. There's nothing like it on Starside, and yet I've never felt so close to home. Well, perhaps in Romania. But that is understandable."

"When I first saw it," said Vavara, "and found it deserted and for sale—and when I explored it, discovering its cellars and old mine shafts—then I knew I had to have it."

"But on the other hand," Malinari said, "if I were a young Greek lover, in search of a place in which to pursue my heart's desire in private, it would suit my needs ideally."

"Just so," said Vavara. "And indeed they used to come here now and then, some of the braver ones, anyway. But I long since took care of that. Come, and I'll show you what else I've taken care of . . ."

The car was up onto the level now, and its cowled, pallid driver got out to open gates in a tall perimeter fence of metal staves and rusting chicken wire. There was an ankle-deep ground mist which seemed to ooze—no, which *in fact* oozed—up from the earth itself. And Vavara nodded when Malinari looked at her, seeking confirmation of what he more than merely suspected.

"Oh, *yesss!*" she sighed, her eyes glowing red now. "Everything is ripening down there. A few more weeks at most."

Then the car moved forward again, and now Palataki loomed up out of the night.

Malinari's mentalist probes went out as the limo drew to a halt before huge doors banded with iron. "There is a presence!" he warned . . . before recognizing the telepathic signature. "Ah, yes!" he said then. "It's your man, er—?"

"Zarakis, aye," she answered. "My most worthy lieutenant, Zarakis Mocksthrall, out of olden Starside. He tends the place, and by simply being here keeps away unwanted visitors."

As they got out of the car—Vavara's driver, too—Malinari noticed that the nun was still shuddering. Indeed, she was barely able to stand without leaning on the vehicle.

"Madame?" said a deep voice from the shadowed archway that covered the door. And there stood Zarakis, tall as Malinari but feral-eyed as opposed to the Lord's red. For here at Palataki, the vampires and lieutenant alike could relax a little and let themselves appear as their perverse "nature" intended.

"Zarakis," Vavara spoke to his bowed head. "Be easy now. I am here with Lord Malinari, to inspect the cellars and tunnels. Is all well down there?"

"All is well," he answered.

"And are you hungry?"

"Your women bring me food daily," he told her. "For which I am grateful."

She shook her head impatiently. "No, you misunderstand me. I inquired of you, are you . . . *hungry*?"

"Always, madame!" Looking at her, his eyes had widened in anticipation, until they burned like sulphur in the night.

Pointing to the nun, Vavara said, "Then while we go below, feed yourself. And if you feel inclined, see to any other needs that might require attention. We shall be a little while."

Now Malinari understood the woman's fearful trembling, but he also appreciated Vavara's concern for her lieutenant's well-being.

Then, as Zarakis grunted his thanks, moving eagerly towards the nun: "Zarakis!" Vavara brought him to a halt and cautioned him: "Be warned. Don't take so much that you leave her weakened and fainting. For I, too, have need of her services. She drives this vehicle for me."

And with that she turned away and led Malinari in through the great doors . . .

The place was a maze of rooms, most of them huge. The doors all hung askew on rusted hinges, the staircases sagged dangerously, and all other fittings had long since been stripped and stolen; even the panelling from the walls. Some of the good floorboards had been taken up, while others had rotted through. Great holes gaped everywhere, and as Vavara stepped ahead she warned Malinari of places where the floor was most likely to give way under his weight.

"The upper levels are in even worse repair," she told him, "and the attic is fit only for bats. Ah, but down below . . . the cellars are carved from stone, while the mine tunnels remind me of nothing so much as the basement of my aerie in old Starside. And since there was nothing to break or steal, only the ravages of nature are apparent down there!"

And she led him down into darkness.

The lack of light meant nothing. Night-seeing, to them it was like daylight. But still after several steep descents down stone-hewn stairways and some negotiating of places where the ceiling had fallen in, Vavara lit a torch and took it from its bracket on the wall.

"See how it flares and the flame bends back?" she said.

"A current of air," Malinari nodded. "This shaft has more than one exit."

"In the bight above the sea," said Vavara. "It is my bolt-hole, my escape route, if such should ever be required. And in a cave above the water level, I keep a boat. While just around this bend—"

She led the way to a cavern, *and* to what it contained. . . .

"Who were they?" Malinari inquired after a while.

"But can't you tell? What, you and your much vaunted mentalism?"

"You know better than that," he told her. "I can only read minds where minds exist. But here . . . they no longer exist."

"The one was the Mother Superior in the monastery," Vavara answered him then. "The other was the woman I recruited in that place in Romania when first we arrived here. She served me well, taught me the Greek tongue, explained away the many things that I found difficult. But she never stopped sobbing; day or night, it seemed I could never escape from her whining and whimpering! And so I put her out of *my* misery. Hah!"

"Was that your only reason?" said Malinari. "For if memory serves, she was also a pretty little thing . . ." And:

"That, too!" Vavara tossed her head. "Anyway, here she is. And as for the Mother Superior: she's not so superior now, eh?"

While they had been standing there, a number of purplish grey tendrils of proto-flesh had come creeping across the dusty floor to investigate. Though there was very little of sentience in them, only residual vampire instinct, still Malinari thought he detected a vague query:

Perhaps this intrusion means something good to eat . . . ?

But as Vavara stamped her foot and shouted—and Malinari reached out his mental probes to whatever was left, *if* anything was left—so the tendrils wriggled back, fusing with the rest of Vavara's handiwork: an ankle-deep, morbidly mobile carpet of gelatinous metamorphic filth, spreading out in an uneven circle from a pair of slumped, sucked-dry figures that lay as if reclining against the wall. And protected within that living or undead circle, a bed of squat black mushrooms, their caps dully glistening from a covering of moisture as thick as sweat. And a heavy mist going up from the whole, clinging to the ceiling and seeping into every crack and crevice there.

And eventually: "It would seem you've done . . . very well!" said Malinari. "*Very* well indeed."

And Vavara allowed herself to take some small pride in his words. For she knew that they were true and that his admiration was genuine in every respect.

Likewise his jealousy: that she had what he no longer had, which had been taken from him and destroyed in Australia . . .

On their way back to the monastery, Malinari said, "Something I don't understand."

"Oh?"

"Sara—who, er, *fell* from that high window—had a leech. She was one of the first you took, of course, but still to have developed a leech in so short a time?"

"But she got my egg," said Vavara.

"Really?" said Malinari. "Another error, perhaps? I cannot see that she would be your first choice!"

Vavara merely smiled.

"Which leads to my next question," said Malinari. "Zarakis has been your man for long and long. He would have been ideally suited to the production of spore-bearing mushrooms. And indeed, with Sara dead he would be your *only* choice, for who else could produce such a crop?"

"Any leech-bearer," Vavara answered, "or any egg-daughter, or egg-son, for that matter. Or any lieutenant who had survived the years and risen through the ranks until he aspired. Such as your man Demetrakis, for instance."

"Exactly!" said Malinari. "Just so, and Demetrakis was the spawn for my crop in Xanadu. But as my eyes are witness Zarakis lives, and your egg was wasted on Sara. So how is it that—?"

"I wasted *one* egg on the girl Sara," said Vavara. "But the *first* of my eggs went to the Mother Superior."

"The first of—?" Malinari knew what it meant but couldn't quite accept the concept. Not in connection with Vavara.

"Perhaps I should exercise better control over my passions, eh?" she said. "It would seem that when my emotions get out of hand, then that . . ." Shrugging, she let it trail off. But Malinari understood her well enough.

"You?" he said. "A mother? A mother of vampires?"

"All of that, *and* a Mother Superior!" Vavara laughed.

"But . . . you were not depleted?" Malinari was stunned. For he knew the legend: that very occasionally, very rarely, a Lady of the Wamphyri would be a mother, a creature with not just one egg but a great many. And that when they issued forth, together in one vast spawning, the mother would be so exhausted that she would wither to a wrinkled, empty sack, thus suffering the true death. It was nature's way, the legend said, of prolonging Wamphyric life; a mother could only come into being in the time of some great bloodwar, when the species was at a very low ebb and required replenishing and the one spawning could make vampires of a hundred aspiring thralls.

Vavara knew the legend, too, and said, "That has to be the answer. Here in this world we are so few that our scarcity must have triggered this thing in me. But in my case I issue my eggs one by one as I will it. So don't expect *me* to deflate, wither, and die, Malinari! I am as firm as ever, and firmer than most."

So then, something new. And Malinari sat and pondered upon it all the way back to the monastery. Vavara, a mother of vampires, capable of bringing them into being at will. And not only vampires but full-blown Wamphyri! Hordes of Lords and Ladies in the making, their seeds germinating, burgeoning even now inside her body, within her bastard mutant leech!

And with his shields firmly in place:

But not if I can help it! What, this new world filled with egg-sons and -daughters of Vavara, all in thrall to her, Wamphyri from the very moment of their conversion? Would I have room to breathe? Would there be any room at all for anyone else?

He very much doubted it but made no comment . . . why should he give her ideas? And putting the notion aside—burying it in his secret mind—Malinari changed the subject to inquire: "Are you satisfied, Vavara, with what you've achieved here?"

"Mostly, yes," she answered. "When the spores are ripened, bursting free, then my nuns shall carry them out into the world. They come from all parts, these women, and the seeds of vampirism shall go back with them to their roots, *new* roots for a new and very different order. And until then the nuns fill my needs. I take from each of them in their turn, and every sip increases their dependency upon me. So you see, apart from my one mistake with that Gypsy girl, all was in order and went according to my plans. Well, until you came."

"What?" Malinari pretended to be affronted. "Will you hold it against me forever that I came to you for help? Now tell me, without the money I sent you, how would you have purchased even this car, let alone Palataki? All revenue—those monies earned from the religious industry of your nuns, their needlework, art, and other knickknacks for the tourists—was lost when you had to close the monastery down for fear of prying eyes. Without my money, Vavara, how much of what you've achieved would have been possible?"

"Jethro Manchester's money, do you mean?"

"Whoever's money," said Malinari. "But never forget, I was the one who found a way to send it."

"For which I am grateful," she said. "And I shall help you however I can. But understand, Malinari: what I have worked for is mine and mine alone—the monastery, my women, Palataki and the crop ripening in its cellars—everything. So if you truly desire to remain on friendly terms, make your plans, state your requirements, take what I can give, and begone from here."

Malinari turned away from her. "So much for five centuries of friendship."

"Most of which we spent entombed in the ice," she reminded him. "And that, too, was your fault as I recall!" Then, when he made no answer, she sighed and said, "Nephran, you said it yourself: you've suffered a setback. Well now overcome it. Begin again, and this time be sure to win through. But do it somewhere else. And if you're afraid that in the interim I shall speed ahead of you, don't be. This is a big world, and room for all of us . . . well, for a hundred years, at least."

"So," he said sourly. "You are telling me that out of all those many spores under Palataki, you will not let me imprint a few with *my* authority, my personality? You are telling me quite literally . . . that I must start again? On my own?"

"There you have it."

"And if you in your turn, in some unforeseen but perfectly feasible future, should suffer just such a setback—what then? Would you turn to me for help, Vavara—*again*? I hope not!"

"No such future looms," she answered.

"But upon a time, I was of a like opinion," said Malinari. "And look at my situation now. I can promise you that even now, in London, people plot against us. How they avoided my traps in Xanadu . . . I don't know, can't say, but I'm sure that they did. The echoes of their group-mind are faint and far-distant—perhaps they are even shielded, for their skills are extraordinary among common men—but as I sniffed them out once before, so I can sense them now. And I'll tell you something else: there was a rare *Power* among them, such as I haven't felt since . . . since . . ." But here he paused and let his warning lapse into silence.

"This E-Branch?" Vavara shrugged. "But I have my own plots to hatch, and tomorrow *my* 'special agents'—two of these nuns, who have served me well in the recent past—will fly to London and seek out Szwart. Together with him, they will find a way to put some small obstruction in this Trask's way. Did I sit still in Starside when enemies plotted against me? Never! Nor shall I do so in this world. But I personally shall not be involved."

"Good!" said Malinari however falsely and halfheartedly. "And so it would seem you have everything covered."

"Yes." Vavara smiled. "Irksome, isn't it?"

Then they were at the monastery, sweeping in through its broad, high gates. And a moment later, as they got out of the limo: "Now you will excuse me," said Vavara. "There are things I must attend to."

"I know," said Malinari. "For you barely touched your food in that taverna."

"Nor you yours," she answered. "But here in my own place—at least *I* won't go hungry. You see? There's nothing quite like a manse and provisions of your own, eh, Nephran?"

"You forbid me to take from your women?"

"Absolutely. One way or the other, Malinari, I intend that you shall move on. And all this talk of E-Branch: it only makes me that much more determined. It seems to me that *you* are their real target, not I, and I won't have you leading them to me . . ."

Alone in his room, Malinari prowled the boards awhile. But then, pausing at a window to cast his mentalist probes out across the darkened island, he stopped scowling. Out there, a mind that he recognized.

Malinari homed in on it: *On a certain young Greek, clad in iron-studded leather, where he trudged all the weary miles home . . . He pushed a heavy, waterlogged motorcycle alongside . . . And he was alone . . . his so-called friends had deserted him, ridden off to Krassos town in search of adventures of their own . . . He cursed his American, Western-styled boots; they looked good and were ideal for riding his bike, but they were lousy for walking . . . The way was mainly uphill, and oh,* how *he looked forward to the next downhill stretch!*

A pity, thought Malinari, that he would never reach it.

A pity? Well, not really.

Blowing in through the window, a warm thermal rose from the night ocean. Malinari quickly shed his clothes, got up onto the window ledge, leaned out into the abyss.

A cloud of tiny Mediterranean bats were on the wing around the monastery's towers. Inaudible to human ears, Malinari heard them well enough. Their sonar cries welcomed him to the night.

His eyes filled with blood, burning like lamps in his face as he wrought the change. And in the next moment a greater bat, or something with a similar shape, soared outwards on the air.

A man has his needs, after all. And if by chance it should bring problems Vavara's way—well, what of it? She had stated her case, made her bed, so now let her lie in it.

And sniffing the air, Malinari turned inland and glided to his target . . .

10

Kavála . . . Krassos . . . Szeged . . .

THE SUNTOURS PLANE CARRYING BEN TRASK AND David Chung had left Gatwick some forty-five minutes late, touching down just after 1:30 P.M. local time at Kavála. And if the pair had thought it was warm in London for this time of year, the furnace interior of the spartan Greek airport had changed their minds in double-quick time. London was cool by comparison.

After reporting dutifully to the Suntours representative, a tourist-harassed young woman using her millboard as a fan and trying desperately hard not to sweat, they'd excused themselves from the scheduled ferry trip from Keramoti to Krassos and told her they'd find their own way across and see her later at their accommodation on the island. Then—little knowing that indeed Krassos was to be their destination—they had taken a taxi to Kavála hospital.

The hospital stood halfway between the airport and the port of Keramoti on the Mediterranean coast, and much like the airport itself it had been designed to serve the military. The scenario was that in any future border dispute or shooting war with Serbia or Turkey, wounded Greeks would be casualty evacuated to Kavála.

The drive was of mercifully short duration—only a very few minutes—but the antique taxi's air-conditioning had long since given up the ghost, and even with the windows wound down it was still like sitting in a pressure cooker.

Then, at the hospital:

Though the Minister Responsible had cleared something of the way for them, still there was the ID check, the obligatory security telephone call, and the halfhearted salute from an MP wilting in his sentry box, before the striped barrier pole went up and they were allowed through the gates, past the guardroom, into the hospital's grounds.

Finally, after Trask had handed the taxi driver a fat wad of notes, asking him to wait until told otherwise, they entered the large, gaunt, nationalistically blue-and-white square block of a building, where a nurse waited at the desk in reception to escort them down a white-walled corridor on the ground floor to the room where Inspector Papastamos presumably lay abed.

Outside the room, a heavy-set man in civilian clothes was seated on a chair with his arms folded on his chest. His chair was balanced on its rear legs, tilted against the wall, and he kept pushing himself forward an inch with his head, and letting himself fall back again. Patently it was some kind of balancing game designed to keep his mind occupied, for his expression was one of total boredom.

But as Trask, Chung, and the nurse drew closer, suddenly the man snapped out of it, came to his feet, and faced them. It was at once obvious to Trask that this was a policeman. As the Head of E-branch he had frequent dealings with the police, and in his experience (and however cliched it might seem) they all "looked the same" to him. From Toulouse to Tangier to Timbuktu, no matter their nationality, Trask could spot one a mile away. But this one left nothing to chance: he swept aside his jacket and showed them his badge, saying, "English?"

The "greeting" was abrupt and even blunt, but it told its own story: that he had been expecting them.

"I'm Ben Trask, and this is David Chung," Trask told him. "We're here to see Inspector Manolis Papastamos."

The policeman, short in the legs but built like a battering ram, used a huge left hand to push his jacket even further back, displaying not only his badge but also the pistol grip of a gun in its underarm holster. And tilting his head a little on one side, he grunted, "I seeing your IDs—please?"

The nurse had just started to explain something in Greek, when from inside the room an anxious voice called out: "Trask? Ben Trask? Is that you out there? Thank God for that! Andreas will let you in . . . or perhaps he won't!"

In the next moment the door was snatched open from within, and Andreas, the blocky policeman, stepped aside. After that:

It had been a good many years, but despite Manolis Papastamos's bruises and bandages, Trask knew him immediately where he stood framed in the doorway.

Papastamos's shirt was loose and hanging open, and he was bandaged under the shirt around his ribs. His face was bruised on the left side from the cheekbone to the chin, and his left arm was in a sling to relieve the weight on his shoulder where his collarbone had been cracked. He looked decidedly older—and rightly so, Trask thought, considering all the years flown between—and he was definitely shaky. But he *was* Manolis.

Recognition was mutual. After searching Trask's face for a moment, then seeing Chung standing beside him, the Greek policeman said, "You two, and still thee same! Well, perhaps a little older, eh?" He went to hug Trask, changed his mind, and grimaced apologetically, explaining, "It is thee ribs. Some bruised, and some broken, and none of them up to thee hugging. Come in, come in!"

Inside the room, two more policemen were seated at a table with a deck of cards laid out in three hands. There was a small pile of money on the table; also a bottle of ouzo and some tiny shot glasses. And Trask was at once relieved.

"I see we're not the only ones who are still the same!" He pumped Papastamos's hand, but carefully. "The message I got . . . I thought you were in a very bad way!"

"I very nearly was," said the other. But his welcome smile at seeing old friends had turned to a grimace now. And: "Ben, I need to talk to you—tell you things—and right now, because we don't have thee time to lose."

"I know," Trask answered just as grimly. "I knew from the moment we got your call, even before your call, that there was, er, something of a problem here?"

"You mean thee special kind of problem?" Papastamos looked at his men, a quick glance, but they obviously didn't know what he was talking about.

"Exactly," said Trask. "The kind we knew once before."

Now it was Papastamos's turn to heave a sigh of relief. "So, perhaps I am not thee obsessive lunatic after all! But for this kind of talking we needing thee privacy, right? These men, they don't speak thee English too well, but we take no chances, eh?"

He spoke quickly, authoritatively to his men, detectives from his own division in Athens. And without a word they stood up and left the room.

"There, is better." Papastamos invited his visitors to sit, poured ouzo, then prowled the room while he talked. And without further ado he told them what had happened, all of it up to the point where his car had been pushed over the cliff.

"And you survived that?" Chung shook his head; he couldn't conceal his astonishment and wasn't thinking straight. But then he checked himself and said, "Yes, of course you did! But how?"

"My seat belt," said Manolis. "She wasn't fastened—thank God! I remember we hit somethings going down; once, twice . . . I don't know, can't say. But thee car, she spinning. Then my door is torn off and I falling through thee air. I thinking: Manolis, you are dead! Then . . . nothing else. Some men in a fishing boat near thee cliffs see thee car go down. They saving me from thee sea. But Eleni—she was gone. Thee water was very deep in that part . . ."

"And afterwards?" said Trask.

"Afterwards, I wake up in Krassos town in thee hospital. I am shook up: my ribs, collarbone, jaw, and all thee bruises. I go a little crazy, you know? Because I remember but I can't say anything. Not about *that,* what I suspecting! They move me here, this ward for thee men with thee shell shock. And that is good, because I want be off that Krassos! Then, when I start thinking straight again, I call you."

Trask nodded and said, "You'd guessed what you were dealing with, and you knew who to call first."

"Not first," Manolis shook his head. "*First* I calling thee office in Athens, to get these men down here pretty damn fast!"

"You thought *they*—wherever they are—might try coming after you," said Chung.

"Right. And that kind of thing . . . I didn't *want* it coming after me!" Manolis shuddered. "Not when I was weak, unprotected. But this place, this hospital," he nodded his head in approval, "she is secure, I think. And my men are good."

Which prompted Trask to ask: "How much do your men know of all this?" It was a very important question.

"Only that I have thee accident, and that I need help. But how to tell them? I mean, hey—if they knew what I thinking—how do I do thee explaining?"

"You don't," Trask shook his head. "No way! I'm sure these men of yours are very good men, but even if they believed you—*especially* if they believed you, believed in what you suspected—it could jeopardize the whole thing. And E-Branch has been on this case for a long time."

Then, as briefly and as quickly as possible, he gave Manolis a sketchy outline of what had been happening and E-Branch's role in things.

"So, this is all on you," said the other.

"We were hoping to put some of it on you, too," said David Chung. "But not like this."

"Hey, I am alive!" said Manolis. "Thee reason I put it out that I bad hurt is for throwing these things off my trail. Waiting for you here, I am near thee scene. So you want to put some of this on me? Yes! Good! Do it! I expecting it! We are working together before, so now we doing it again. You thinking I *wants* these damn things in Greece? In thee Greek islands? What? These vrykoulakas dog bastards!?" His English was deteriorating commensurate with his mounting anger.

"Calm down, Manolis," said Trask, "and think. While you're certainly alive, still you're not in the best possible shape. I mean, just look at you . . . You're pretty much banged about. And I'm sure you haven't forgotten how it was on Halki, Rhodes, and Kárpathos that time? With Janos Ferenczy and his creatures? You wouldn't want to slow us down, now would you?"

"I want do whatever I can!" the other declared. And:

"Very well," said Trask, and went on to tell him about the transfers of large sums of money from Jethro Manchester's Swiss accounts to a bank "somewhere" in Greece. He finished by saying, "Find that out for us, and you'll be doing us a big favour."

"And myself," Manolis nodded. "And Greece, and thee world! But I can do that from here, I think. So, will you wait?"

Trask shook his head. "No, we're moving on. But we'll have your number and we'll stay in touch, let you know where we are. That way you can always call us if you get anything."

"And when I feeling a little better? When I getting rid of these bandages, then maybe I—?"

"They know what you look like," Trask cut him short. "The creatures who did this to you." It was only an excuse, for *they* knew what Trask looked like, too (one of them did, anyway) but the Head of E-Branch didn't want Manolis to get hurt any worse than he was right now.

Manolis chewed his lip, then breathed deeply, and finally grunted his disappointment. "I . . . I feeling *useless!*" And in a typically Greek display of frustration, he threw up his hands.

"On the contrary," Trask told him. "With what you've told us, you've corroborated everything we suspected."

"Huh!" said Manolis. "Right." But he seemed doubtful.

"Is there anything else you want to tell us before we go?" Trask asked him.

"Tell you, no—show you, sure." And Manolis scattered the playing cards from the tabletop, unfolding a map of Krassos in their place. The map was one of those cheap and cheerful, none-too-accurate, homegrown efforts that display sites of historic and archaeological interest, as well as local hotels, tavernas, and allegedly golden sand beaches; in short, a guide to all the island's tourist traps.

"Would you believe," said Chung, "that Krassos is where we were supposed to be going?"

"Thee island?" Manolis stared at him, remembered his weird talent. "Are you, er, *locating* something? On Krassos?"

"Not yet," Chung answered ruefully. "Later, maybe."

"We're tourists," Trask explained.

"Ah! Your cover. But Krassos? You knew to go there?"

"A coincidence," Trask answered. "And anyway, by now we've missed the ferry."

"There will be another ferry in a few hours," Manolis told him, "before thee night. But Ben, this island—this Krassos—she is thee very dangerous place for men like you. For *any* men! You have thee backup?"

"Shortly," said Trask.

And Manolis nodded. "*Very* shortly, I hoping! But not thee Necroscope, eh? Not thee Harry Keogh. Ah, he was thee one! That man . . . we are thinking *we* are thee bravos, yes?" He stuck out his chest, then winced and relaxed his posture. "But thee Harry . . . next to that one we are all thee big cowards."

"He was much too brave for his own good," said Trask, "and in the end came too close. Without him we wouldn't have stood a chance, wouldn't have understood even the basic hows or whys of such things. We still owe him for that, and now we're using the knowledge he left us all over again."

"That time, we *all* came too close," said Manolis, unashamedly shivering. "But we were thee lucky ones." He nodded again, checked his pocket telephone, and scrawled the number on the map. And stabbing at the chart with his pen, he explained the layout of the island and its various features.

"Thee map, she is showing it all," he said. "But anyway, I giving you thee running commentary:

"Thee island, she is like thee apple with some bites taken out. Ninety, or maybe one hundred kilometres right round. Coast roads mainly, except where thee mountains come down to thee sea. Krassos is thee green island; thee forests are up in thee hills and mountains. In thee north, five or six skalas; I explaining thee term skala. Many of thee villages are twinned. By thee sea, thee village gets thee name Skala—Skala this, Skala that. But thee twin in thee mountain is thee main town. In thee old times thee fishermen live by thee sea, of course—hey, they live *off* thee sea! Invaders come, they move into thee heights. Then came thee olives and thee farming; now thee peoples live in all thee villages. So, Astris in mountains, *Skala* Astris on thee coast.

"In a deep bay in east of Krassos, here is Limari, a 'big' town of more than fifteen hundred peoples; big by island standards, you understand. That mutilated body—thee one with thee leech—was found in thee sea a few miles south of Limari. Here is thee monastery, between Limari and thee place where I forced off thee road. Thee big limo was waiting for me there. I didn't get thee number." He gave an apologetic shrug. "But hey—I was busy! And on this southern point, here is Skala Astris.

"Now we are on thee south coast heading west. Here is thee village Portos, and thee skalas Peskari and Sotira. And here—after thee bend in thee coast—is thee *big* town, Krassos town, thee capital. Then, heading north, more villages and skalas all along thee west coast.

"Most of thee coast roads are very good. But inland, up in thee mountains, not so good." Manolis shook a cautionary finger. "Four-wheel-drive vehicle, my friends, if you going up into thee mountains.

"As for what you looking for," he shrugged again, "I don't know. This *vrykoulakas* woman's place . . . there are a great many high places on Krassos. But thee island peoples will know everythings about thee foreign peoples who are owning properties. In thee tavernas, you can talk, ask questions, but carefully. Hey, who I speaking to, eh? Of course you ask carefully!" He laughed and slapped Trask on the shoulder . . .

And then it was time to go.

Chung folded Manolis's map and pocketed it. Then, tossing back the last dregs of ouzo in his glass, he held it out empty in front of him. Trask likewise finished off his drink, and all three men clinked glasses. "Here's to success," said Trask, and Chung echoed his toast.

"Me, too," said Manolis. "Er, I meaning success—yes!"

In the taxi, on the way to Keramoti, Chung said, "Well, what do you think?"

"About the task?" Trask dabbed sweat from his brow. "When the rest of the team join up with us, time enough then to think about it. Half a dozen heads—the kind of minds and technology that we command—will give us a much clearer picture than just yours and mine alone. We're here to do a preliminary survey and organize a base of operations, that's all."

"So that's the job," said Chung. "But what about Manolis?"

"Ah!" said Trask. "You're obviously thinking he let us off the hook too easily."

"You told him he couldn't come with us . . . and he accepted it just like that?" Chung shook his head. "He didn't even argue the point but sat still and simply let us walk out on him? Does that ring true to you? Well not to me! It isn't the man we know. So, what are the odds we'll be seeing him again—and I do mean very shortly?"

"I'm not taking bets," said Trask. "Put it this way: let's say I wasn't convinced by his acceptance. And in fact he *didn't* accept it, didn't agree one way or the other that he would stay out of it. He didn't say anything much but just played at being frustrated. That *was* an act . . . I know because I got an instant reaction from my talent. He was hiding something: his desire to come with us, probably. And the hell of it is we could use him, if only he wasn't so banged about."

"Talking about talents," said Chung, "actually, I'm beginning to feel pretty lonely. Just you and me, and what's waiting for us out there."

"Waiting for us?" said Trask. "I hope not!"

"You know what I mean," said the locator. "The future, and whatever it has in store for us. The as yet unfurled, immutable and oh-so-devious future. At least, that's how Ian Goodly might describe it."

"Devious, yes," Trask mused, nodding. "And immutable. What will be has been, eh?"

"We must hope," said Chung, "that it *continues* to be as it has been, that we'll win this one just like we won the others."

"Amen to that," Trask agreed wholeheartedly. "But tell me: what's all this got to do with feeling lonely?"

"I'm switched off," the locator reminded him. "My talent, I mean. This close—or as close as we think we are—I daren't use it. For in Malinari's case, what I can find might as easily find me! So I'll just hang on to what I've got until it's really needed. Which also means I'm no longer in contact with the rest of our people. Not like a telepath, no, but just being able to reach out and sense them there. It's something I've had for—well, it feels like forever—a sense of security, of being in good company, and I hadn't realized how much I'd miss it. But I do. Hence the loneliness."

"Then I suppose in that respect I'm lucky," said Trask. "I can't switch mine on and off; it's simply there. But it doesn't reach out and can't be detected. Not that I'm aware of, anyway. It doesn't connect me to anyone, unless he starts lying to me—doesn't 'disturb the psychic aether,' so to speak—so it isn't something that Malinari can latch on to."

"Exactly," said the other quietly. "But that only makes me feel that much more lonely. For the time being there's just the two of us, and I'm the one who might forget himself, start glowing in the dark. Why, for all we know I could be doing it right now: like a myriad mental pheromones radiating away from me, my own personal version of mindsmog! So I'll be very glad when the other members of the team show up."

Then they were into and passing through the port of Keramoti: spears of dazzling yellow light, and dark-shadow smudges, where they sped through narrow streets between dusty buildings. But suddenly the air wafting in through the taxi's open windows tasted salty, and as the vehicle emerged into full daylight and halted in a sun-bleached parking lot close to the deep-water harbour, the Aegean was there: a horizontal bar of scintillant, blinding blue, slashed through by the lolling masts of boats at their moorings, and draped with their sullen pennants.

Even here on the coast the heat was appalling. But beyond the parking lot on the landward side of the street, the canvas awnings and motionless umbrellas of a long string of shops and tavernas offered jet-black blotches of shade and the irresistible promise of cold drinks.

Leaving the taxi, Trask and Chung shrugged themselves out of their damp jackets and folded them over their arms. Lugging a single suitcase each—in addition to which Trask carried a fat briefcase containing several "gadgets," one of which was a world-ranging telephone and scrambler device—

they made their way toward the street's hot tarmac, and beyond it to the shade and liquid refreshments of the tavernas . . .

Meanwhile in Szeged in Hungary, at the local police HQ:

In a grubby, unwelcoming, second-storey room with barred windows, a solid oak table and a handful of wooden chairs, Liz Merrick, Ian Goodly, and Lardis Lidesci "interviewed" old Vladi Ferengi—and Vladi in his turn viewed them with such contempt that it bordered on loathing. Hunched in his chair like a wrinkled old spider, grinding his jaws on several gold teeth and a very few ivory fangs, and endlessly knotting and unknotting his purple-veined, rheumatic fists, he glared his fury at the three across the heavy table. But mainly at the Old Lidesci.

"You," he grunted at Lardis. "You came to me in the woods at Eleshnitsa, came 'in friendship,' *hah!*—'in search of your roots'—but you were only spying on me and mine. I should have let my men bloody you up a little and tumble you in the thorns, should never have allowed a stranger in my caravan in the first place. Ah, but with your use of the old tongue, you made a fool of me. Szgany, you? *Never!* And if you ever were, then no longer. You are a traitor to your own kind, Lardis of the Lidescis, and that's all you are. I have travelled through and lived in these parts for all my years, and never any trouble, yet now you have brought the police down on me. I am taken from my people like a common criminal, and for what? A handful of old wives' tales and fairy stories, malicious lies and rumours. And you expect me to talk to you? I have no respect for you, and I have nothing more to say to you . . ." He turned his face away.

Lardis nodded and answered, "Old king—I respect that you *are* the king of your people, but no more than that. As to why I offer you even this much respect: it's because I'm a king in my own right. Except I prefer to be known as a leader, but one who never led his people into slavery, which is what your ancestors did. And I agree: I should *not* have approached you in your camp—not without first ensuring that I'd covered my back, also my front, and my two sides, and my top and my bottom—because to do so in the old times, the time of your father's fathers, in a world you've long forgotten, would be to place myself in direst jeopardy. And you call *me* a traitor? Why, the very names Ferenc, Ferenczy, and Ferengi are still curse words among all true sons of the Szgany! You probably don't know it, old man, but you are sprung from a long line of supplicant dogs who called a monster master, and tried to assuage his lusts with the blood of anyone unlucky enough to stray into their territory. Worse still, they even sacrificed the innocent flesh of their own children!"

Lardis had taken his time, considered his words, and delivered them in an emotionless monotone, in the guttural Szgany of old Sunside, an all but forgotten form in this world. But Vladi had understood enough that it caused him to sit up and listen.

"Eh? What?" His face creased into a thousand wrinkles, and his rheumy eyes came glittering alive. "Lies and insults? From such as you? Ferenc? Aye, I know the name, from stories that my grandfather told me where we sat by the campfire, as his grandfather told them to him. The Ferenc was glorious! A magnificent *Boyar* of olden times, who led my forebears into this world from out of one of the strange places. Why, we even took his name—the Szgany Ferengi—and I have made it the work of a lifetime to wander far throughout this world in search of his messenger, or even his kin. For our legends have it that one day, one such will come among us. And so I've searched and waited for him, or a Lord just like him, destined to return to us from the strange places and raise us to our former glory. Such has been my sole . . . my sole pursuit for years without . . . years without—"

But here, licking his lips and shrinking back, as if fearing that he had said too much, Vladi came to a faltering halt.

"—Years without number, aye." Lardis nodded, taking it up where the old Gypsy had left off. "For long and long, Vladi—a lifetime wasted, as your father wasted his before you. For what did you find but a fiend who took one of yours and changed her? What did you find but the *wampir*, the bloodsucker of legend? Do not be mistaken: I know the bloody history of you and yours, my friend. Now look at me and tell me: can't you see and even hear it in me? My looks, and the dappled light of distant forests in my eyes? And my tongue, which is the old, the *original* Szgany language out of another world? Surely you, of all people, recognize the truth when you see it? What, Vladi Ferengi and that knowing old beak of his? Well then, and what does your beak smell here, in the shape of Lardis Lidesci?"

The precog Ian Goodly, who had spent some time—or as he would have it, too *much* time—in Sunside/Starside, understood much of what Lardis had said. Straightening up where he sat, he glanced sideways, warningly at his old friend but remained silent. He was concerned that Lardis shouldn't give too much away. On the other hand, while Goodly did not agree entirely with the Old Lidesci's approach, he acknowledged that he was speaking to one of his own kind, a fellow Traveller, and had to accept that he was probably best equipped for the job.

And as for Liz, understanding little of what she *heard* yet knowing most of what Lardis had said by reason of her telepathy: to her it was as if his words were hypnotic in their monotonous pacing. And likewise to Vladi Ferengi.

The old man's jaw had fallen open. Leaning forward in his chair, balancing himself with his spindly arms on the table, he stared at Lardis at first in disbelief. But the more he looked, the more obvious the truth became to him. And yes, his nostrils gaped wide as he sniffed out Lardis's origins; and yes, his old eyes opened wider as he began to accept that Lardis was what he said he was.

"I could smell it on you in my camp, near Eleshnitsa," the old Traveller said then, his voice trembling. "The smell of the source world, where all of the Szgany had their beginnings. But I had searched for so long, and always in vain, that I supposed I was mistaken. There is no water in the desert, only mirages. *You* were a mirage in the desert of my dreaming! Also, what were you but a man? Only a man and scarcely a prince, or the mighty boyar of my searching. Now you tell me you are a king—and not only that but a messenger out of time, too! Except your message is a hard one, Lardis of the Lidescis, and I don't think that I can bear it. Are you saying that my people are . . . that they're less than honourable?"

"And even less than that," said Lardis. "Or if not you and your people, then your ancient line—your ancestors—certainly."

"Then I won't accept it!" The fire flared again in Vladi's eyes, and he thumped the table with both fists, making it jump.

"Oh?" said Lardis, without flinching. "Is it so? And yet I sense that you've suspected it for long and long, and that I am only telling you what you've known deep in your heart for years without number. As for *my* origins—and therefore my authority in such matters—I can prove them. There's a word I would say to you, Vladi of the Szgany Ferengi."

"A word?" the other fumed and sputtered. "What word?"

"Wamphyyyri!" Lardis growled it like a wolf.

"Ahhhh!" Vladi sighed, drawing back again.

"And when you sat by your grandfather as he told his campfire stories, as his grandfather told them to him," Lardis went on relentlessly, "didn't he ever speak that word? And didn't he tell you its meaning?"

"He did! He did!" said the old man. "He told me that they—the Wamphyri—were our enemies in the old times, which was why the Ferenc brought us away from the old world into this one. Also, he told me that the Wamphyri were bloodsuckers, who could not live in the sunlight but came in the dead of night to steal our wives and children in the dark. And that forever and always such would be our lot: to give away our children to strangers."

"Which you are still doing to this very day," said Lardis grimly and unforgivingly. "in Romania, Bulgaria, and many other places, giving away and even selling your own children. Because it runs in your vile blood, Vladi, come down to you through all the forgotten centuries. For I tell you as a true witness, that in a far vampire world your ancestors, the Szgany Ferengi, were Wamphyri supplicants who gave of their blood to a vampire Lord! And that is precisely what *you* have done, in Kavála, in Greece. Now, I can't yet say if that was deliberate, a monstrous act of sacrifice, or an accident which came about because you happened to be in the wrong place at the wrong time. But whichever, that poor young girl you buried with silver on her eyes was a victim of your search and perhaps of what you found—*or of something that found you!*"

"But I . . . I . . ." Vladi stuttered.

"If you *are* innocent, however," Lardis went on, "then your legends have been distorted in the telling—distorted by time, perhaps, or perhaps by shame—by the shame of your supplicant ancestors."

"By shame?" Old Vladi sat limply, shrunken now. All of the fire had gone out of him. "What are you saying? That because my forebears did wrong in the past, they changed the history of my people to suit, to hide their sins? Is that what you're saying? But even if you're right, what wrong have *I* done?"

"You've done according to your blood," said Lardis. "Right or wrong is for you and you alone to say. As for myself, *I* say: purge yourself of all these old legends, these dreams, which in fact are nightmares. Tell me what I require to know, Vladi, and help me and my friends rid the world of a great horror."

"So then," said Vladi, shaking his head in a dazed manner, trying hard to sit up straighter in his chair, "you are not the Ferenc. No, obviously not, for you are only a man, and you deny him." He was babbling now, and it was as if all that Lardis had told him had flown over his head, or as if he'd heard only what he wanted to hear and would only answer accordingly. "Very well, then perhaps you *are* the messenger, or a messenger of sorts? Is that it? Did you come to tell me . . . to tell me that the Ferenc and his kind . . . that they are no more? Are you saying that . . . saying that my long search is ended? Is that why you are here?"

"Ferenczys?" said Lardis. "So far as I know—so far as I pray—they are no more. The last of them was in my time: Fess Ferenc, a grotesque monster in his aerie in Starside, in a vampire world beyond the Gates you call the strange places. But if by 'his kind' you mean the Wamphyri . . . oh, yes, they are still here, old Vladi. Some of them are here even now, in this world. But haven't I already said as much? That girl of yours: she was taken by one of the Wamphyri, a female, we think, who came here recently from the source world. I and others like me would seek them out, to destroy them. That's why I've come to see you. Not to accuse you in person but to ask your help. Only refuse it—" Lardis nodded grimly, "—*then* I'll accuse!"

"Destroy them? The Wamphyri, our olden enemies? Of course they must be destroyed! But—" Vladi was confused; he began to rock to and fro, and his old eyes seemed suddenly glazed. "What am I to make of all this? I have spent a lifetime, and I cannot . . . I do not . . . and what of the old legends? . . . They spoke of the old times, the history of my people. And now you would tell me . . . you would say that they are lies, all of them?"

Lardis nodded. "Some of them, at least."

"But the Ferenc . . . he was a great—"

"A great monster!" said Lardis. "Aye, for whichever Ferenc this 'mighty boyar' of yours was, he was nevertheless a Lord of Vampires, banished out of Sunside by his own kind, the Wamphyri. Which tells its own tale: that this so-called hero was banished for his sins by the greatest sinners of all time! *Hah!* So there you have it. Ferenc, Ferenczy, or Ferengi, they were all of the one blood, Vladi, and they were monsters all."

"But the legends! The legends handed down to us out of the old times—"

"The old times?" Lardis cut him short, and Liz got up and went round to Vladi's side of the table, putting her arm around his frail shoulders to support and steady him. "Let me tell you how it was in those old times," Lardis went on. "How it was and how it is even now in Sunside/Starside, beyond those Gates that you know as the strange places. Aye, and how it might *yet be* in this world, if we can't stop this cancer from spreading further. Hear me out, and then judge for yourself whether or not I speak truly or falsely."

And finally Vladi nodded. "Go on then, I'll hear you out."

Then, after a moment's thought, Lardis went on to tell the whole story, but as briefly as possible, painting word-pictures in the old Szgany tongue, and letting the Gypsy king's imagination (and perhaps ancestral memories) fill in the blank spaces.

Until at last, when Lardis was finished, and after several long seconds of silence:

"I . . . I think you must be mistaken," said Vladi, steadier in his voice now but still trembling in his limbs. "I *pray* that you are mistaken. But whether you are or you aren't, I cannot—*dare* not—tell my people what you have told me! What, that our proudest legend is only the shameful lie of cowardly forebears? No, never that! But I can and must put an end to my search. For if what you say is true, then on this occasion this old beak of mine led me in an entirely wrong direction, which brought about a monstrous thing. The girl, yes—'little Maria,' which is how I shall always remember her—she was related to me, as are all of the Szgany Ferengi. But oh, that lovely child . . . drained of her life force, dead and gone from us, and lodged in the earth. And all because . . . because I led my people astray!"

"But better dead, buried, and gone from all of us," Lardis spoke more quietly now, "than one of the undead in the aerie of some Lord or Lady of the Wamphyri. Well, at least you suspected that much, and were wise enough to put a stake through her."

"Eh? What's that?" the old Romany king stared hard at him. "Do you think we did that? No, no—it must have been the work of frightened villagers, but never me and mine! Yet now . . . now it would seem they were right to do such a terrible thing." And there were tears in old Vladi's eyes as he looked at Lardis and said, "But the Wamphyri? In this world? And one of them took my sweet little Maria? Is it so?"

"We're seeking them out," Lardis told him again, "even the one who did this thing, and others like her, to put them out of their misery and out of our sight forever."

Vladi breathed deep and sat up straighter. "Then I'll tell you how it was," he said, "—and where *It* is—but I cannot be exact for I don't know all the details. Maria, she told us very little. She was mazed, and she was—"

"—Undead," said Lardis, "aye."

And Liz, her arm around Vladi's slumped shoulders, came in with: "Whatever you can tell us will be of great assistance. We don't know a lot, and this . . . this *creature* has hidden herself away from us. But one thing seems certain, if we don't find her there'll be a great many more innocents lost to the cold earth. Either that or they'll be walking upon it, lusting for blood in the night!"

And Ian Goodly said, "It's your chance to redeem yourself, Vladi, you and all your people. What was done is done. The past is beyond reckoning now, but the future is still to come. While we still *have* a future, we all must do our best to protect it."

"There's not a lot to tell," said Vladi then. "I dreamed a dream of the strange places, and of one who came out of them to seek his people. We would come south for the winter, as always, despite that this year the winter is late. And this old beak of mine smelled the wind off the Greek islands; I seemed to detect a scent out of time; I *knew* that something very strange awaited us, and thought that perhaps this time . . . this time the legend would be answered.

"In Kavála we took a ferry to . . . to the island. We didn't pay a lot, but still the Greeks were glad of our custom in what had proved for them a very poor season. And so we brightened up our caravans and wandered the island's villages. The coins were slow in coming, but they came little by little. And of course I followed my nose.

"We camped for some few days on the outskirts of a village called Skala Astris, where a deep gorge shaded us from the sun. Maria Cilestu sold paper flowers. She went out one morning with a basket . . . and she didn't come back! But this was scarcely an unheard of situation. We had had the occasional runaway before: handsome young men—and pretty young girls, too—who perhaps received offers they couldn't refuse. For you know, it can be a hard life on the road, and I had always tried to understand the feelings and motives of any who wanted to break with it. But on an island such as that, so very small, how far could Maria run? Not far, be sure. Also, since we would be there a while longer, we knew she could always change her mind and come back to us.

"Maria had never known her father, and her mother had died some time ago. Personally, I wasn't too concerned over her; she had always proved capable at taking care of herself. Of course, some of the younger men worried about her, the ones who fancied her, you know. But there were none who could lay claim to her. And anyway, I was far more concerned about the island itself.

"For to this old beak of mine . . . I don't know . . . I can't say, but it had an odd *atmosphere,* that island. Well, of course it did—which was why I had taken my people there in the first place! But now that we were there . . .

"I had dreams—dreams about the campfire, more properly a bonfire! I would find myself standing beside this great fire in the night, waiting. And all my people there with me, but all in a huddle, shivering, clinging tight together. Don't ask me what it was about, for I hate to think. But they were ominous, those dreams, and they left me feeling ill.

"In the daylight hours, that weird atmosphere was scarcely any weaker, while at night . . . I wouldn't even *consider* letting my men light a fire! What, music and dancing? And the smell of roasting meats going up into the night air? Not on *that* island, no! From the Greek tavernas—aye, by all means—but not from any campfire of mine! And yet I couldn't say why . . ."

"But I can," said Lardis grimly. "You dreamed what was in your blood, Vladi: dreams out of time, a time when the fires of your forebears called the Wamphyri to the feast. A time such as I've spoken of, when they came in the night and sniffed out the camps of the Szgany in Sunside. And your shivering people? They huddled together because they knew the meaning of that bonfire. It was a *signal* fire, to light the way for the Ferenc, for this 'great boyar' of yours, calling him to the tithe—to his blood tribute!"

"But—"

"—But that was in your dreams," Lardis continued, "while in your waking hours you fretted over it and wouldn't allow the setting of *any* fires in your camp! So there's hope for you yet, old king. You know what's right and what's wrong—even if your ancestors didn't."

"Do you think so?" Vladi's eyes were pleading now.

But Lardis only nodded and said, "Get on with your story."

And after a moment's pause: "Nothing more to tell," Vladi shrugged apologetically. "My dreams got worse; instead of discovering the one for whom I had searched for so long, my no longer trustworthy old beak had led me into the presence of something bad, something evil. That was when I decided to break camp and return to the mainland. And as we left that place, I never once looked back.

"At the ferry, Maria was waiting. But she was changed. And the rest you know: that business at the mainland hospital, when she begged to be allowed to go with us, and we took her without permission . . . the newspaper men . . . the police . . . those sweet Sisters of Mercy . . . *bah!* My camp was like a busy crossroads in the middle of some vast and sprawling city! Well, not that bad, but bad enough.

"So that by the time I saw you, Lardis of the Lidescis, in the forest at Eleshnitsa, I'd had all I could take of outsiders. I mention that now by way . . . by way of an apology."

"No need," said Lardis, with a shake of his head. "I think that you've acquitted yourself, King Vladi."

"And now all that we need," said Liz, "is the name of that island."

"It was Krassos," said the other. "And if that's where you

are headed, then good luck to you. But as for myself—"

"—Your wandering days are over," said the precog. "I can see your future very clearly, old king. From here you'll return to your people in the forests, where you will spend a good many years yet before your time is up. As for the strange places—" he shook his head, "—they won't call to you any longer."

"I believe you," said Vladi. "And since I'm the last of my line, what little of my bad blood still remains in my people is so diluted that I know there can never be another old beak like mine. As for the Ferenc: I know the truth now. His ways are not ours, and I have been an old fool. Now I'll make sure he's forgotten, and that no man goes in search of him again."

"But don't you understand?" said Lardis, frowning. "Didn't I make myself clear when I told you that there is no Ferenc?"

At which the old man gazed at him steadily and for several long moments before answering, "I wish you were correct, Lardis Lidesci, but I fear that you are mistaken. There *is* just such a one. Perhaps the last of his kind, I can't say, but he is still there. Somewhere on the shores of the Middle Sea, in the cities of men, he's there. I didn't find him for all my wandering, no, it's true. But I fancy that's because he hasn't found himself."

"Hasn't found himself?" Lardis's frown deepened, furrowing his brow. "What can you mean?"

"Perhaps he's biding his time," said Vladi, "not yet ready to reveal himself. If so, then he'll be too late; I'm done with him now. And when I'm gone mine won't know him. No, for I'll do my best to dismantle at least one false legend before I die."

"Your vow?" said Lardis, realizing that whatever the Gypsy king believed, it could make little or no difference now. And:

"Aye," said Vladi. "My Szgany vow!"

11
London . . . Bagheria . . .
Castellano's Story . . .

LUIGI CASTELLANO'S VILLA, ON SICILY'S TYRrhennian coast in the district of Bagheria—one of his several Mediterranean villas, or, more properly, bases of operation—was a two-storey affair of numerous externally louvered windows (all of them closed), a walled balcony that enclosed the upper structure, and variously angled, steeply sloping roofs of fish-scale tiles in a dark red terra cotta. A gravel drive wound from ornate iron gates set in high stone walls, through an ancient olive grove of grotesquely twisted trees, to a dusty parking area in front of the villa.

Once the seat of an olive-oil empire, the place had always been sumptuously appointed—but never more so than now. During the more than thirty years since the deaths or disappearances of Castellano's "uncles" (at which time he'd bought the villa out of what was rumoured to have been an enormous inheritance), not one of the many "business associates," the handful of visitors, and even fewer guests who had entered the place past the cordon of armed "soldiers" on the gates and in the grounds, had failed to be impressed by Castellano's ever-expanding, magpie collection of objets d'art.

In one of the ground-floor rooms, a large, gloomy, heavily draped, yet fabulously rich room (in fact Castellano's study in this, his principal dwelling), the walls with their old masters and antique tapestries, the shelved alcoves with rank upon rank of gilded statuettes and ivory miniatures, the display-cabinets and -tables strewn with every conceivable kind of jewelled bric-a-brac—everything offered mute testimony to the obsession of a dedicated collector.

But on a more businesslike desk in that same room—a desk free of priceless "clutter"—the repetitive, softly insistent purr of a telephone had been sounding for several long seconds before Castellano's right-hand man, a lieutenant of very long standing, hurried in through an arched doorway to answer it.

At the same time, coming from his bedroom behind an iron-banded second door, Luigi Castellano himself queried, "Who the *hell* is it, and why did you let it go on ringing for so long?" He voiced his question in an angry, rumbling growl, but yet in an accent that affected a cultured tone. "Damn it all, Garzia! You've let it wake me up!"

Fastening the belt of his flame-red dressing gown, he came to a halt in the central area of the room and stood glaring at his lieutenant where he in turn stood by the desk.

Castellano was tall, slim, and forward-leaning . . . but at such an odd angle that he gave the impression of being about to reach out for something with his spindly arms and long-fingered hands. Judging by his looks, he would be aged somewhere between his mid-thirties and early forties, while in fact he was almost ninety. His shining, night-black hair was brushed back to cover the tips of long ears where they lay flat to his head; his nose was broad and flat in a face that was long and slender to match his frame. Yet with his dark, sunken eyes—which at a certain angle flared a luminous, almost feral yellow—and despite his pallor and the weirdly alien design of his form and features in general, still he was possessed of a strange attraction.

"I was in the grounds," Garzia answered reasonably. "I was reminding the men that we're expecting a visitor—our Russian contact—and warning them to treat him with respect . . . well, for now, at least." Having acquitted himself, he spoke into the telephone, inquiring, "Yes?" And, in the next moment, "It's for you, Luigi. Alfonso Lefranc, calling you from London."

"Alfonso?" Castellano grunted. "Huh! Not before time—and yet at the *wrong* time, too! Doesn't that idiot Lefranc know any better than to disturb me at this time of day?"

At the desk he seated himself in an armchair before accepting and speaking into the telephone. "Alfonso? I'd almost given up on you. This has to be very important, that you'd call me at this time of day. I take it you have what I wanted? But please, be very careful how you answer."

That last wasn't any kind of threat (although in different circumstances it might have been: if, for instance, Lefranc had *not* got what Castellano wanted), but simply a reminder: that in the technologically advanced twenty-first century, no man could ever be sure that his telephone conversations were 100 percent secure. And Luigi Castellano, as the head of a small but expanding international illicit drugs empire, just couldn't afford to take that kind of chance.

In London it was 2:45 P.M. Alfonso Lefranc was in a hooded booth on Victoria railway station. About five-foot-five, thin and shifty-eyed, with badly pockmarked features and a twitchily nervous disposition, he had a certain animal aura about him . . . that of a small, bad-tempered, and generally unpleasant rodent. A human rat, yes, or—if not for his awkward, seemingly uncoordinated movements—perhaps a weasel.

Some might say it went with his job—the dirty work that Lefranc had *used* to do for the Surete and Belgian drug squads—as a nark, and informer on the gangland activities of his former underworld friends; work at which he'd excelled—until they'd asked him to look into the affairs of one Luigi Castellano. But where a majority of the European law enforcers were straight, a handful were on the take, in Castellano's pocket, and he always paid well for inside information.

The informer had been informed upon, and word of Lefranc's snooping had found its way back to Castellano . . .

They had picked him up in Marseilles, which would have been the end of him if Castellano hadn't recognized his talent. What Alfonso Lefranc had done for the police he could now do for his new boss, Castellano himself.

The pay would be good—better by far than the piddling handouts he'd seen from any of his former "employers"—

and the side benefits would be even better: Life on the French and Italian Rivieras, in the casinos, and on the yachts. Quality clothing, the best booze, good food, and bad women. Castellano made him an offer he couldn't refuse: work for him and live the good life, or stop living, stop dead . . . period.

They had been on one of the mob's yachts at the time, and Lefranc had been shown what could happen to anyone who crossed the Sicilian dealer. The trip had taken the form of a party—a really wild ride with plenty of Bollinger in buckets of ice, designer drugs on silver trays, and young girls strewn like so much confetti all over the place—to celebrate a declaration of peace between Castellano and a notorious French competitor. Frenchie Fontaine had a couple of minders with him, as always, but the atmosphere on deck was so friendly that it wasn't long before the hard men succumbed to the wine and to a trio of sirens both, retiring with the latter to a stateroom.

Their wine was drugged; they never fully recovered; they had to be half-carried back on deck after all the other guests except Frenchie had been sent below. But Lefranc had been told to stay and watch as Castellano cut the throats of the minders and his men wrapped their bodies in lead weights before pushing them overboard. By that time Frenchie, restrained by the Sicilian's men, had been complaining fairly volubly; so they'd taken turns at coshing him in the mouth to shut him up.

And finally it had been time to say a fond farewell, when Castellano had thrown back a tarpaulin to display a heavy steel locker. Frenchie—all bloodied in his face and spitting teeth—hadn't looked as if he really believed it, but he'd believed it enough to start fighting again when Castellano's men went to cram him in the locker!

This time, apparently pissed at Frenchie's very determined efforts to stay alive, they'd worked on his elbows, knees, ribs and spine, literally immobilizing him until all he could do for the moment was writhe about on the deck like a crippled snake.

Then into the locker, his metal coffin; and all the while the drugs boss Luigi Castellano talking to Frenchie, explaining things to him even as he slammed the door shut (with two of his men standing on it to get it to *stay* shut) against the frenzied kicking and hammering and cursing from within. And the Sicilian tut-tutting to himself as he attached a padlock, before continuing to explain that this wasn't personal but business pure and simple; that there wasn't room enough for both men on the drugs scene, but that there was plenty of room for Frenchie—lots of it—at the bottom of the ocean maybe two hundred metres down, midway between Marseilles and Perpignan!

Then the splash as the locker landed flat on the dead calm sea, bobbing there a while and settling before slowly turning upright like a wetly lolling tombstone half out of the water, and gradually sinking as the sea found a way in. By then all the kicking, hammering and head-butting had quietened to a dull thumping—an invisible squirming and heaving, and a muted shrieking that was sensed or imagined rather than heard—that only served to set the locker bobbing to and fro, sinking that much faster as Frenchie's weight shifted with his spasms.

And standing at the rail in the shade of the deck's black- and gold-striped canopy where they rode at anchor—shielding his head from the Mediterranean sun under a broad-brimmed hat, and his eager eyes behind the dark glasses that had become his trademark whenever he went out in daylight—Luigi Castellano had adopted that familiar, avid, forwards-leaning stance, with his knuckles white and his hands like claws where they gripped the rail.

And there he'd stayed as the locker slid from view, until the last few bubbles had risen to the surface . . .

By then Castellano's men had been swabbing down the deck, and one of them—the torpedo Francesco "Frankie" Reggio—had even popped a champagne cork and was sluicing telltale crimson slop overboard with fifty-francs-a-flute bubbly. That was when their boss had straightened up, backing away from the rail, as a fickle current began to drift the yacht more surely into the sunlight.

And as if noticing Lefranc for the first time, Castellano had said: "So there you have it, Alfonso. It's as easy as that. I can use you, but I certainly wouldn't *miss* you if you turned me down. So you'll either work for me . . . or you won't. What's it to be?"

At which Lefranc had asked him how soon he could start . . .

"Well?" Castellano's growing impatience was clearly evident in his sharp tone of voice, which brought Lefranc back to earth—and to the present, the here and now—with a jolt. "Have you got something for me, or haven't you? You got me out of my bed, Alfonso, and I'm sure there must be a very good reason why I'm standing here in my dressing gown talking to a *fucking* idiot—other than that you like the sound of my voice, that is!"

"I've got something for you, yes!" the other gasped. "I've got it, but—you're not going to like it, Luigi. Not at all."

"Where are you?" Having noted the fear in his man's voice, the drugs boss sat up straighter. It could only be that Lefranc really was afraid to tell him something he didn't want to hear. But since that was his job he had no choice.

"I'm in London," Lefranc answered. "The railway station at Victoria, which has to be the next best thing to a secure line. No one's ever likely to eavesdrop a telephone conversation from a railway station! Like, you know, all those calls from guys to their women, telling them their train's been delayed so they'll be late getting in? I mean, who's going to give a shit? Anyway, I *always* call in from this kind of place: public telephones in airports and railway stations, and like that. But hey, you know I wouldn't take any chances, Luigi! Not with security. Not with *your* security!"

"And if you're being watched, followed?"

"But I'm not." And despite that his boss couldn't see him, Lefranc gave a nervous shake of his head. "And even if I was—even if some guy had an amplifier on me—what could he hear in a place like this?" To illustrate his point, he held the phone outside the shielding hood, where an intercity diesel was roaring and jetting gasses, making the air shimmer and the platform vibrate as the driver checked out his huge engines.

"Very well," said Castellano grudgingly, after the racket in his receiver had subsided. "So what is it you've found out? Do you know who those people were, what they were doing in Australia, and why Jake Cutter was with them?"

"Er, all of that stuff?" Lefranc answered apprehensively. "Well no—not everything, not really. But *other* stuff—hell, yes! And this is . . . I mean, it's something really *big,* Luigi! It's just that I'm trying to find the best place to start."

"How about starting at the beginning?" Castellano growled. "In Brisbane, maybe?"

"Right," said Lefranc. "Brisbane, sure—after you said I should follow them and find out about them. No problem—I was on the next plane out . . .

". . . I'd managed to get their names off their luggage tags at Brisbane airport, but I had to be careful because that Jake Cutter guy might have recognized me. And like—you know what I mean—me and you, we're the only ones left, right?"

Lefranc was talking about Cutter's vendetta, and the fact that of the five people who had been involved with the Russian girl that night, only he himself and his boss remained alive. But when Castellano made no reply, he continued with his story:

"Anyway, when I got into Heathrow, I asked at the Quantas desk about these people I was supposed to be meeting: this guy called Trask, a Chinese guy called Chung, and a girl called Liz Merrick. Naturally they told me these people had come in on the earlier flight, which of course I already knew. But when I said no way—that wasn't right—and after I'd made out like I was pissed about it, they showed me the printout from the Skyskip's passenger list. Their names were there, of course, and I took a good long look and committed this Chung's address to memory. It was easy. Then all I had to do was explain to the people on the desk that I'd obviously made a bad mistake, apologize, and get the hell out of there . . .

"Pretty smart, eh?"

"Get on with it," said Castellano.

"Anyway," Lefranc quickly went on, "this Chung has a place in central London, so I went after him.

"It took a little time, but eventually I tracked him down, followed him to a hotel in the middle of the city. And the rest of that crowd were there. Again it took a while, but if I stood around long enough—which I was obliged to do—they were in and out of there regular as bees at a hive. Which includes this Jake Cutter, who is supposed to be on all the most-wanted lists right across Europe!

"But this was—I don't know—a very weird scene, Luigi. Weird as shit. They were using the hotel's back entrance, these people, but they were the *only ones* who used it! Like, you know, maybe it belonged to them? And that wasn't all, 'cause while they seemed to have the run of the place, this big, expensive hotel, none of them was *registered* there! I know because I phoned the desk and checked it out. This Cutter, Trask, Chung, and all the others: they don't have rooms in that hotel. Like weird, right? I mean, how do *you* figure it, Luigi?"

Lefranc's pause was deliberate, so that it might even seem he was playing some kind of guessing game with his boss; but in fact he only desired to break the other's silence, to know that he was being heard, to be told that he was doing okay, and just to be able to *converse* with this fucking Sicilian like . . . like another human being and not as if he were a piece of shit!

But while Alfonso Lefranc was human (or perhaps subhuman), Castellano wasn't like any other man he'd ever known, and sometimes he seemed anything *but* human! Like the time on that yacht for instance—which Lefranc still nightmared about—and like right now, as the silence between the two lengthened, extending itself and growing ever more deafening.

So that Lefranc gave a massive start, when at last Castellano's warning growl sounded from the phone: *"Alfonsoooo . . . !"*

"I'm getting to it, I'm getting to it!" Lefranc babbled, as he suddenly realized that in the other's eyes he was indeed just such a piece of shit and nothing more. But his nerves were really jumping now; it was always the same when he had to speak to Castellano; there was no pleasing the guy, who simply didn't appreciate all the hours of hard work that people put in on his behalf. But *Christ,* it had been a mistake to task the bastard's patience like that! And an even bigger one to keep on doing it! So that finally, with a deal of twitching and jerking, Lefranc continued with his report.

"Luigi, this hotel has seven floors. Stand outside and you can count 'em. But the room numbers only go up to six-four-two. As for the rear entrance and the elevator in back of the place: that really *does* belong to them! So it doesn't take a genius to figure out where they are, right? The only place where they can be? They're up there on the top floor, sure!

"Okay, so that's *where* they are, but it still doesn't tell us *who* they are or what they're doing, and obviously I couldn't just phone the place and ask what was going on up there. And I certainly wasn't about to go barging in there myself and, like, make a target of myself for this Jake Cutter. Which meant I had to get a man inside.

"Well, I'll cut a long story short—"

"Thank goodness for that!" said Castellano sneeringly.

"—And get right to it," Lefranc went on. "I paid a guy to go in, spend a couple of nights at my expense, do some cautious snooping and find out what he could. This is how it turns out:

"The top floor isn't a part of the hotel as such; it's the HQ or offices of a bunch of international entrepreneurs—what-the-hell-ever *that's* supposed to mean! Also, my snoop found out that they sometimes eat in the restaurant on the third floor.

"So a couple of days ago, I finally had to move in. I mean I *had* to—you'll see why in a minute—but I was careful and got a room on the first floor. And before I let my snoop go,

I had him plant a bug where these people eat in the restaurant.

"That was why I had to be in the hotel. See, I was obliged to use whatever equipment I could get hold of; I didn't want to buy expensive, quality stuff in case somebody got curious about what I was doing. But like, with the cheap stuff . . . hey, I was just a guy checking out his two-timing wife, right? But because it *was* cheap stuff, it didn't have too much range. So that's me in the hotel . . .

"And talk about after-dinner speakers: Luigi, I heard some weird *shit* coming out of that restaurant!

"This outfit, these, er, international entrepreneurs: they call themselves E-Branch—and are they *connected*! I heard some talk about a 'Minister Responsible'—like, maybe a *government* minister? And the way they speak is really something else; it's almost a foreign language. English, but coded. So okay, foreign languages are a hobby of mine. Italian, Russian, English—you name it—these are things I'm good at. But codes are something else. And these people . . . sometimes it's like they're speaking in some kind of fucking cipher!

"Stuff about precogs, locators, espers, and telepaths—and like that. Weird conversations I could only just go with, about extraps, and GCHQ, gadgets and ghosts, and some kind of ongoing search for a trio of invaders: three guys called Vavara, Malinari, and something that sounds like, er, Schwarz? Kraut, maybe? And Greek and Italian? So if that's not international, tell me what is?

"Sure I know what a telepath is, and this GCHQ's a part of the British security setup, right? But as for this other stuff . . . it's all a mystery to me!

"Anyway, the leader of these people is this Ben Trask, but the others—Chung, Liz Merrick, and two other guys called Ian Goodly and Lardis Lidesci—they all seem to be pretty high up in the rankings. And there are plenty of others. I mean, I must have watched two dozen different types, male and female, in and out of that hotel's rear entrance. But no rolled umbrellas, pinstripes or bowler hats. Just normal, everyday, ordinary-looking people, if you can believe that.

"And that's about it, Luigi. I'm all done. No, wait, there was just one other thing. It's about these three invaders. When these E-Branch types talked about them, they grouped them under one funny-sounding name. It was . . . it was . . ."

"Well?" said Castellano, his voice not so much threatening now as keenly interested, even fascinated.

"Shit! I'll remember it in a minute," said Lefranc. "But I have it on tape, anyway, which I'll be bringing back with me as soon as I can get out of here. Er, Luigi—?"

"Which might not be for quite some time," said Castellano, after a moment's thoughtful silence. "Because what you've told me is . . . very interesting, Alfonso. It's possible you may have stumbled upon something of great importance. As for Jake Cutter . . . at first I thought he was just—how does one say it?—an innocent bystander? Someone who got in my way and had to be put aside? I'd never thought of him as anything more than that, not until you saw him with those people in Australia. But now . . ."

"Yeah?"

"Now I see him as something very different." Castellano's voice was deep and dark now. "I think it's possible—I don't know how, but I *think* it's possible—Jake Cutter knows things that I would dearly love to know. Suddenly he is very important to me, and not alone because he's killed off some of my top men and may even be trying to kill me. No, it's *why* he's done these things—and why he continues to do them, despite that he must know his life is in jeopardy—that interests me."

"Er, because of the girl, right?" Lefranc was baffled. His understanding was that it was a vendetta, pure and simple.

"Wrong," said Castellano, his voice deeper yet. "Cutter is working for someone, some cause: this E-Branch, as it now seems. But I fancy they're no simple policemen, these people who would appear licensed to take the law into their own hands, or ignore it entirely. And Jake Cutter is no simple law officer . . .

Lefranc waited, said nothing, and in another moment it

was back to business as his master continued in a more normal, less intense manner: "Stay on it, Alfonso. You've done well, and I'm not displeased with your efforts so far. But I'm sure there's a lot more to be learned about these people. So you'll stay right where you are. If you need money, it's not a problem; as of now you have full access to the London account. But I want results. Stay in daily contact—any time of the day or night—but use Garzia's number, not this one. Garzia will pass on whatever you tell him to me. And above all else, be careful and remember: if you should ever be caught and questioned, the last thing you'll ever say—the last word you'll speak—is my name. Because it really would be the last thing, ever . . ."

"Sure, Luigi. Don't worry about it," Lefranc answered, the corner of his mouth twitching uncontrollably, where he stood in his domed booth on Victoria station. But Castellano didn't hear him because he had already put his receiver down.

And then Lefranc remembered that group name he'd been searching his memory for. And: "Wamphyri!" he told himself, now that it was too late to tell anyone else. "Shit, yeah, that was it: Wamphyri!"

The intercity diesel had long since departed the platform, and the Gatwick Express had just pulled in, bringing passengers from the airport into the city. Hanging up the phone and exiting from under the dome's privacy, Lefranc scarcely noticed two cowled nuns making their way along the platform toward the taxi rank; he had enough on his mind already.

And as for the nuns: unseen in the shade of their cowls, their eyes shone with a luminosity created of a dedication to something other than their order; indeed, to a new or entirely different order of being, that was anything but holy. And they had more than enough on *their* minds to ever notice someone like Alfonso Lefranc . . .

"Luigi, do you think we can talk . . . ?" In the villa at Bagheria, Garzia Nicosia stood by the desk of his once-friend and now his master—or, as Garzia preferred to consider their relationship, his mentor, the vampire Luigi Castellano—and patiently waited on his reply.

Tall, broad-shouldered, and as straight as a rod, Nicosia was an imposing figure in his own right. Despite his pale features, he was as dark and brooding in his mind as the history of his country. Sicilian in both looks and nature, he was entirely loyal to Castellano and a deadly enemy to his master's enemies. He was, indeed, "in thrall" to Castellano, which meant that his loyalty was based principally on his awe of the other; on that, and on a basic understanding of his powers, and a promise more than fifty years old that one day he would share those powers.

Unlike Lefranc, Nicosia would never dream of playing word games with Castellano; he knew from past experience that in any conversation with this man one listened and learned (and, where applicable, obeyed), asked only the most relevant of questions, and other than that made no attempt to discuss, redirect, or in any way impress oneself upon the flow of Castellano's words and thoughts. Also, while commonsense suggestions might on occasion be sought, accepted, and even appreciated, opinions were out of the question.

As Castellano himself had once remarked: "I've found that personal opinions are generally slanted in the direction of personal advantage. Since I only ever concern myself with opinions which tend to *my* advantage—namely *my* opinions—I'm obliged to view those of others with some suspicion. Often as not, I've discovered them to be the devices of ambitious men. And I can't abide men with ambitions beyond their station . . ."

Which basically was the reason why Castellano—last in an ancient line of men and monsters—rarely actually *conversed* at all. Rather he expressed himself and made known his wishes, and generally shaped his future by directing the actions of others; and to interfere with his thought processes was to distract and anger him. Garzia Nicosia, his companion since boyhood, was one of only a handful of men who had ever been able to speak to his master (his friend, his mentor) on something of a level playing field. Even so, it was a field with many pitfalls, and one must always be careful where one stepped. . .

Castellano remained seated in his armchair; he leaned forwards with his left elbow on the desk, a long-fingered left hand supporting and fingering his chin. His thoughtful gaze lay upon the telephone, silent now in its cradle. But after several long brooding moments—sensing Nicosia's eyes upon him, and finally acknowledging his statement, which had also been a request—he stirred and looked up. Then, fixing the other's feral eyes with his own burning gaze, he nodded and said: "I think perhaps you are right: it's time we talked. Years ago—ah, but how *many* years, eh, Garzia?—I promised you an answer to a certain question, indeed to many questions, despite that I myself didn't know all of the answers. I was vain enough to believe that in the fullness of time I would learn the greatest mysteries of this thing, and eventually come to understand its mechanics. And so I have come to understand . . . some of it, and to know some of the answers. But tell me, Garzia—do you still remember the questions?"

"Of course," said Nicosia. "They were how, and why, and to what end? What of tomorrow? And will it be forever? These were a few of them—which both of us asked, if memory serves—and time would seem to have answered at least one or two."

"Such as?" said Castellano.

"The how, for one," said the other. "How do we go on, down all the years, while others die and crumble to dust? Well quite obviously, 'the blood *is* the life.' In drinking the blood—the lives of so many others—we have prolonged our own. But as for eternity . . ."

"You doubt that what we have is forever?"

"Forever is . . . it's a very long time," Nicosia could only offer a shrug. "It means tomorrows without end. But knowing you the way I do—and having known you all these years—I sense an uncertainty in you that wasn't there before. It's as if even the soonest of those tomorrows, the one following today, is now indefinite. Oh, it will definitely *arrive,* we can be certain of that . . . but can we be sure that we'll be a part of it?"

Castellano stood up, stretched, strode out from behind his desk. "If some other had said what you have said," he answered, "I would take it hard and perhaps consider it wishful thinking. For it would hint of a future in which I had no part. It would at least *hint* of such a possibility. But you are not any other, Garzia. You're my man, whom I caused to be like myself. And I'm sure that life or undeath burns as fiercely in your veins as it does in mine. You might—now don't deny it, Garzia, for I know I'm not the easiest person to live with—you *might* in certain circumstances wish *me* dead, but never yourself! And, of course, if I were to die, then in all likelihood you would be following fast on my heels. Following me to hell, as it were. Well, if we were believers."

Garzia said nothing, but simply watched the other pace the floor to and fro. "But the fact is," Castellano continued, "that you *do* know me well—far better than anyone else—and what you have sensed in me does your perceptions credit. Uncertainty, you said, and you are not mistaken . . ."

And when Nicosia remained silent: "Have I ever told you my story?" Castellano stopped pacing, halting in the middle of the floor. "Well of course I have! A half dozen times or more, over the years. But only to you, Garzia, because you are my one confidant: my 'blood brother,' eh?" And he chuckled in a rumbling, deep-throated fashion. "Ah, but if I can't trust you, then who can I trust? My blood is yours, and yours mine, and if men were ever to discover us for what we are"—he was sober again in a moment—"your fate would surely be the *same* as mine."

"You know you can trust me," said the other. "And not only because of what we are now but what we have always been. Foundlings as infants, we were inseparable friends as boys. When our guardian took us to the USA in 1930, we were innocent children. Then, as we grew to youths the war loomed. Having found our way into the Mafia, we avoided the conflict, returned to Sicily, and brought back something of the American dream with us. Except by then it was our dream, or more properly yours: a dream of great power, wealth, even of empire. What happened between us . . . was an accident, which brought about a change in both of us. But in you that change was . . . it was *profound*, a fathomless thing!"

"A taste of blood, yes," Castellano nodded. "Which was all it took. My only true friend's blood—your blood, Garzia. And indeed my change was profound. But go on, tell it as you remember it."

"We went to a powerful don in Palermo," said Nicosia. "Don Carlo Alcamo; he was to be our patron and ease our way into the Sicilian brotherhood. But Don Carlo refused us! The war was on; we must keep our heads down; the Mafia would pull in its horns, shrink down into itself (for the time being, at least), and Don Carlo wasn't about to enlist any would-be young bloods, untried soldiers such as you and I."

"How very true," Castellano nodded. "Our blood *was* untried, at that time. Yet mine burned like a fire; it leaped in my veins until I could no longer contain it! I was twenty-two years old, already a whole year past manhood—which to others of the time was the age of consent—to me the age of *ascent*; for the fire in my blood demanded that I rise up! Yet this old man, this Don Carlo, he would hold me down. As if I were a child."

And Nicosia took it up again. "After the American invasion, you were a passenger on the back of the first tank into Palermo from the south. You pointed out possible pockets of resistance, which of course included Don Carlo's place. On your advice they blew it to hell, and him with it!"

"I became a hero to our 'liberators,' " Castellano chuckled again. "I was an untouchable, at least as long as the Americans held the island, which would be for quite some time. Of course, the other dons knew who had brought down Don Carlo Alcamo. They knew, but could do nothing about it. I (or perhaps I should say we), *we* were feted at the American bases as fifth-column heroes of the Sicilian Resistance! It gave us a taste of power. We ran the black market and took control of prostitution. With all the American troops that were on the island, both lines proved very profitable. So that despite the gradual resurgence of the dons, we were very much 'in.' And from that time forward they weren't ever able to put us out again. Until finally they accepted us."

"Now all the Old Guard are dead and gone," Nicosia carried it on, "while the new have forgotten or weren't ever aware that we were—that we *are*—those same 'young bloods' from seventy years ago . . ."

"All of which is *our* story," said Castellano. "But mine is still untold. Not from its beginning. Perhaps you would like to hear it again?"

"Refresh my memory, by all means," said Nicosia. "It's a story that has always fascinated me."

"As it should," said Castellano. "For after all, it's your origin, too . . ." And in a while he continued: "Foundlings, you said, which in your case was true enough. Found on a doorstep wrapped in a torn blanket, on a cold winter night in Nicosia, the Sicilian village from which you took your name: *you* were a foundling, Garzia, yes. But as for myself, the story is somewhat different.

"I wasn't a foundling as such—wasn't left to my fate on a doorstep by some peasant woman who littered me out of wedlock under an olive tree or in some goatherd's barn, no—but I will admit that I, too, was a bastard, and I know some would have it that I've been one ever since! Well, however that may be, there was no cold doorstep in my history. My mother was a girl from a family once of high standing, though of diminished means at the time of my birth.

"Later I would meet and even get to know her, and then she would try to explain why I'd been abandoned; or rather, why she had been obliged to give me secretly into the care of relatives in Nicosia, where you and I met and grew up together. But where you took the town's name, I had my own. I was a Castellano from the beginning—even though I wasn't! For if I'd been given my father's name, then it would have been something else entirely.

"The story put about was that I was the orphaned infant

of a Genovese line of Castellanos; my father had died in a hunting accident in Italy, and my mother in childbirth, in giving birth to me. My only living relatives were the Sicilian widow and her simpleminded but harmless son who had taken me in. In fact the widow was my grandmother, and the simpleton my uncle, though he never knew it. The story which my 'aunt'—my grandmother—and my mother had concocted was their way of protecting not only me but my mother, too!

"But from what? What was the true story, eh?

"Well, my mother was a true Castellano, which gave my name some legitimacy at least. Her name was Katerin and she had gone into service as a young girl. A servant girl, yes, in the house of her masters in the Madonie: in fact Le Manse Madonie, in the high mountains forty miles east of here. And I was the child of those masters, those two men, those respected brothers in their high house, perched like an eagle's aerie on the very edge of a chasm. And where better for such as them to dwell, eh? For they were both great birds of prey, those Francezcis.

"But surely I couldn't be the child of both? No, of course not. But such had been the way of it that my mother wasn't able to differentiate! They had both had her, from time to time, and whenever it took their fancy. Anthony and Francesco: I could be the son of either one!

"So then, why hadn't she tried to escape, to run away from Le Manse Madonie long ago? And why didn't she even now, to care for me where I was hidden away?

"Ah, but my mother was in thrall to the Francezcis no less than you are to me, Garzia, and perhaps even more so. For unlike our relationship, the fact that we are, well, 'friends'—or as close as our natures will allow—she *loathed* the brothers, yet at the same time was drawn to them irresistibly, like a moth to the flame! But she hated to leave me alone and motherless, too, at the close of each fleeting visit when the brothers were away on business and she could come to see me. That was in the early years. Later the Francezcis only rarely left Le Manse Madonie together, and my mother's visits became fewer and fewer . . .

"I mentioned relationships. They are all we can ever know, Garzia, such as we are. Relationships, yes. But were we ever in love? Did we ever have girls to make our hearts beat faster, or to break them with their fickle ways? Well, and perhaps we *were* in love, now and then, as young men in America. But never since then. Or rather, never since 'the accident,' as you are wont to call it. But that was no accident, Garzia; it had been bound to happen, sooner or later, to me if not to you. *That* was the only accident: that it was you . . .

"But I've drifted from my story. Let me get back to it:

When I was old enough to understand her whispered words—but not yet old enough to understand their meaning—my mother told me things. Or rather, she would *say* things to me, which at the time made little sense. She spoke of blood: of some frightful thing in my father's blood—in all the Francezci blood—which might also be in mine. She talked about vast treasures at Le Manse Madonie, and of cellars filled with a king's ransom. I should be heir to all such treasures, she said, but at the same time she was concerned that I was heir to something else. And I could often feel her eyes upon me, those wide, hag-ridden eyes, as if she were fearful of finding some strange taint or sprawling cancer in me. Of course, I understand all such things now, but at the time . . . what was I but a child?

"Her masters the Francezcis were ageless, my mother said. They were their own fathers . . . they were even their own grandfathers! Now I ask you, Garzia, what was a child of five or six tender years to make of that? And despite that they had powers, and for all their wealth and servants and great house, Le Manse Madonie, still they were afraid of the sunlight! And so saying, as if to prove or disprove some lunatic theory, she would even drag me into the light!

"Well, not so mad after all, as it turns out. But fifteen years to go before the sun would begin seething on *my* flesh . . .

"And I must watch myself very carefully, she said, and be ever on my guard to ensure my goodness and worthiness, so that I would make a benevolent man, pure in my thoughts and 'humane' in my heart. At least, I *thought* that she said humane, but she may simply have meant human.

"And time and time over she warned me not to look too far ahead, but to leave the future well alone. I remember she said that to me—to a mere child who never in all his waking hours looked beyond tomorrow or the day after that—as if somehow I might think to hatch some kind of plan against the future! Not in my *waking* hours, no. Yet in my dreams . . . ah, but they were something else!

"I dreamed of my own business; I saw myself as the head of a demolition and construction company right here in Sicily. But I was too young as yet to even understand my dreams! This thing of mine—my ability to see into the future, in dreams—it has a name; it's called oneiromancy. My mother mentioned it by name one time, and said, 'That is where they get their power: from a living monster in a pit in Le Manse Madonie, a *Thing* that looks afar, even into the future. It, he, the *Thing,* is oneiromantic, and the Francezcis are of its blood. And you, Luigi . . . you are of their blood . . . and when she said things like that to me, my mother would shudder . . .

"I dreamed of us, Garzia, you and I, and our coming adventures in America. It was no great surprise to me when my 'aunt' died and my babbling uncle was taken into care, and your guardian adopted me and took both of us with him to America to seek a better future. No, for I had already seen what my future was to be. Something of it, anyway. But while my dreams invariably came to pass, I could never say *how* they would come about.

"For example: in recurrent nightmares that used to bring me screaming awake, I dreamed of blood! But I never told anyone what was in those dreams; not my 'aunt' or her babbling son and most *definitely* not my mother, no! For even as a child, as yet only slightly precocious, I was somehow aware that if *she* knew for certain what was in me, and what was making its presence felt even then, it would not have gone well with me. Poor woman, I'm sure that she would have killed me out of hand, in the belief that she was doing me a favour.

"But while I suspected that I was different, I could never in a hundred years have guessed *how* different, eh?

"Dreams of blood, yes. Blood to drown in, like a river in flood. Dreams of myself, awash in blood—red, rich, slippery blood—which covered me head to toe! Obviously I was bleeding to death; I actually *felt* close to death in those dreams! That was why I would come screaming awake in the dead of night. How was I to know that it wasn't my blood, Garzia, and that it wasn't death but life . . . ?

"In America, I dreamed of excavating treasures out of the earth of my homeland. But the earth was bloody, as if my sharp and shining spade was biting through the bodies of people! And there I stood under frowning cliffs, in a vast chasm or quarry, ankle-deep in earth and gore, with the shrill voices of all of these buried people shrieking at me, cursing me for disturbing their unquiet graves. But mainly they cursed my forebears, for putting them down there in the first place.

"And that, too, was prophetic, speaking not alone of what had been but also of what would be. In short, it would come to pass. For if not precisely as I had dreamed it, still the vast treasures that the Francezcis had salted away *would* be brought up again—by me: Luigi Castellano by name, but a Francezci by birth and by blood! And indeed those great treasures *have* been and *are* being brought up even now. If proof should be required, only look about this study . . .

"Also in America, where now we were youths, I dreamed of a great war and saw its waves washing over Sicily. And knowing it was time we came home, I convinced you that our place was here. We returned and the war came; it brought with it our so-called allies the Axis troops, and finally the Seventh Army and our American 'liberators.'

"As for the rest of the story—*our* story, from here on—it becomes far easier to relate. Except, Garzia, we've still not dealt with 'the accident,' as you have always preferred to call it. Perhaps you would like to tell that part?"

Garzia nodded. "The part I remember best, yes. After two-thirds of a century, many events seem to flow together and get distorted by time. But *that* event has always remained clear in my mind. It was like this:

"The war was over, and you had built up your construction company out of our profits from the American occupation forces and from other ventures. Many of our towns and cities had been battered. In Catania, Palermo, Messina, and many other places, ruins sprawled in every direction. Terrible for some, but work for us. Castellano's Construction Company grew rich from demolition work alone, without that we ever 'constructed' a single building!

"But in Palermo a new don was coming into prominence: Don Pietro Alcamo, son of Carlo! And Don Carlo's death three years earlier had been your responsibility. Pietro was well aware of that, and despite that we were now accepted by the rest of the Mafia heads—for whom the construction company was supplying a 'legitimate' money-laundering outlet, converting the profits of more 'orthodox' mob businesses such as extortion, prostitution and the postwar black market into readily available funds—still Pietro vowed to avenge his father's death.

"One night in Palermo, after we'd eaten and as we made our way back to the car, he struck, the upstart Pietro and three of his soldiers. They were waiting in ambush in a dark, bombed-out alleyway. But having learned this part of our business in America, we were scarcely strangers to it; and, moreover, the night was always our friend . . . and more especially yours.

"You *sensed* them there, Luigi! What is more, you had seen it coming; your strange dreams had forecast something of how it would go down. We foiled the attack; their knives, pistols, and garottes stood no chance against the sawn-off shotguns that we carried under our American army great-coats!

"But in fact this was the first time that we had actually killed with our own hands. Oh, we had been involved in our fair share of gangland wars and murders in America, and we'd ordered punishments or corrections here in Sicily which sometimes went wrong and resulted in death; but *we,* ourselves . . . we had kept our hands 'clean' until that night. And you had always managed to contain or hold at bay whatever it was in your ancestry, in that 'tainted' Francezci blood of yours, that your poor mother had so often tried to warn you about . . ."

"Until that night, *yessss*!" Castellano hissed, for he was no longer able to resist taking the story up again. "But you've made it sound so much easier than it was, Garzia. To think that someone or ones who were destined to live as long as you and I, possibly forever, immortal, should have come so close to death! Today . . . why even the idea of such a threat infuriates me. But of course we didn't know—

"—Until that night, when two of Pietro Alcamo's bullets found their way to you. The one shattered your left knee, while its twin passed right through your neck and very nearly severed an artery. It did puncture the arterial wall, however, so that by the time I got you to the car you had lost a lot of blood.

"Indeed, I had your blood all over me; I was scarlet from its drench! Yet while I despaired for you, Garzia, I exulted in the knowledge that Pietro Alcamo and his men were lying in that alleyway, all crumpled and bloodied and dead. For when they had fallen I had gone to them, standing over them where they lay on the hard cobbles, letting them see me while yet they were able. And watching them suck air through the froth and bloody bubbles of their pain, I had reloaded my double-barrelled weapon, fired it, reloaded again, and so blown their fucking heads off!

"But what a release, what a rush, what a joy! Ah, and what a *waste,* eh, Garzia? For if I'd known then what I know now; all of that good blood and fresh red meat . . . but there again, from swine like that it would probably have choked me!

"Instead it freed me, broke the chains of my humanity. For in fact I had been shackled by my facade, by the physical shell that designated me a man. And I was far more than a man. A creature of myth? Well, no longer. I was a reality. I was real and I existed. I had killed. There was blood on my hands, and blood in my eyes; it lit the night for me like a lamp! I could see in the dark! And I could smell my victims a hundred yards away, in that alley where I'd left them to rot.

"As I carried you to the car—bore you on my back with a strength I'd never before known—all of these sensations came to me, reinforcing yet again the knowledge that I was different. As yet I had no name for it, I didn't know what to call myself, but I knew that I was as different from other men as night from day.

"And it was your blood, Garzia—*your* blood was the final catalyst, 'the accident'—that at long last gave me that name.

"At my place in Palermo you were more dead than alive, but I knew what to do. Out of nowhere the knowledge came to me. You were my friend (in those days we still spoke of such things, of friendship and such), and you were in need—but so was I! The events of the night had roused me up. At last I knew what I was missing, the final piece in the puzzle that would make me complete.

"You bled from the bullet hole in your neck. But while the blood was pumping out of you in ugly jets, matching the urgent beating of your heart, I could see that the spurts were faltering, and your pulse was growing weaker second by second. I felt panicked—yet at the same time was filled with an overwhelming urge. I bit my lip watching you as you gradually succumbed, and the taste of my own blood filled my head like roaring laughter, telling me what to do!

"And so you see, it was no accident, Garzia, when my mouth closed on your neck, to take from you and to give of myself. No accident but destiny. I *knew* that you wouldn't die but would be with me for long and long. And at last I knew what to call this thing that was in me, which now was transfused in you."

"You were a vampire!" Garzia sighed, his feral eyes aglow and his mouth falling open to display the gleam of razor teeth.

"I was and am just such a vampire!" Castellano nodded his affirmation. "But I suspect that I am more than *just* a vampire. Your recovery took three days, three short days for your wounds to heal and for you to rise up, but from that day to this—"

"—I have been the same as you!" said Garzia.

"Well, perhaps not quite that," Castellano gloomed at him, "but a vampire, certainly."

At which point footsteps sounded, and in a moment a man in coarse peasant's clothing, with a rifle slung on his back and a bandolier across his chest, appeared in the arched entrance.

"Sir," he said to Castellano, "a Russian gentleman is here to . . . he's here to see . . . to s-see . . ." But seeing the eyes of his masters fade from their feral luminosity to shiny black, he stammered to a halt and stepped back a pace.

Briefly then—as yet not fully recovered from the passion induced by memories of his awakening—Castellano leaned towards the messenger in that weirdly menacing way of his. Then he spun on his heel and told Garzia: "Please see to our visitor, this . . . this 'Russian gentleman,' will you? Frisk him well and see him in. But Garzia, make sure he enters of his own free will."

12

Dead Silence . . . Natasha . . . Death of a Russian Gentleman . . .

TWENTY-FOUR HOURS EARLIER, IN MARSEILLES, Jake Cutter, assisted by the incorporeal wraith, revenant, or evil essence of Korath-once-Mindsthrall, had tried talking to the dead. Or, to be more specific, for the first time in his waking hours he'd attempted to contact *one* of them—the Frenchman called Jean Daniel, who had been the first casualty in Jake's war with the drug-dealing mob boss, Luigi Castellano.

"This is where the skinny bastard died," Jake explained to Korath, "right here in this alley. So if I'm likely to find him anywhere, this place is probably my best bet." And because deadspeak frequently conveys more than is actually said, Korath saw it all as it had happened, in vivid if kaleidoscopic detail, in Jake's mind and memory:

A rainy night two and a half years ago; a tall, pale, thin man with thinning, slicked-back hair, leaving a bar in the wee, small hours and getting into his car; the door slamming . . . and Jake wincing a little where he stood in the shadows just twenty-five yards away. But no, the shock or vibration of the car door being slammed hadn't been sufficient to do the job—which was good, because Jake wanted Jean Daniel to know what had happened and who was responsible for it.

Then Jake coming into view, stepping out into the middle of the shining, rain-slick alley as the car's headlights came blazing alive; standing there with his legs slightly apart, like an invitation—like some gunfighter out of the Old West—as his angular figure was silhouetted in the headlight beams. But Jake was no gunslinger, and the only weapon was the car itself—

—Its wipers sluicing drizzle from the windscreen, and Jean Daniel twitching, jerking, as he leaned forward to peer through his window, down the alley at Jake. To peer at him, and then to recognize him! For Jake was waving at him and beginning to walk casually forward, head-on towards the car.

A moment later:

The Frenchman turning the key in the ignition . . . and Jake knowing exactly *what he was thinking: that he was going to run this fucking idiot English asshole down! He* thought *so, anyway. Then Jake hitting the deck as the explosion ripped the darkness and a few glass fragments flew overhead.*

And Jean Daniel sitting there in the smoking car—pinned to his backrest by the steel core of the steering column, which the blast of three ounces of plastique had driven clean through his guts—probably realizing but not yet fully believing that the terrible pain he felt was death. Death in the shape of Jake Cutter, looking in at him through his blast-shattered window.

And the Frenchman's mouth falling open, slopping blood as Jake reminded him of what had amounted to a challenge, but one which now had been answered in full:

"So now you know who hits the hardest . . ."

"Jesus!" Jake groaned, feeling sick, dizzy, disoriented where he reached out a hand and leaned against the wall of the alley. "Jesus Christ—I did that! No good kidding myself it was just a nightmare. I actually did it—that and worse. And right now I'm planning to do more of it!" But:

Most excellent! said Korath. *And such a fitting punishment. The rapist raped, gutted on the single thrust of a most awesome iron penis. Why, I believe that I myself could not have devised a more—hah!—"ironic" ending for such as him. The only pity: that he didn't live long enough to repent his evil deeds.*

This from a vampire! Jake thought. While out loud: "Oh, I think he's repented them," he answered, steadying up again. "If not then, by now for sure. But that still doesn't absolve me."

Then, frowning, he wondered: So what the hell's wrong with me now? Absolution? I'm not a Catholic . . . I'm not an anything! Should I really be sorry for what I've done? Should I really be asking for forgiveness? Perhaps it isn't me who's asking. Maybe it's this other guy, the one who left all sorts of his personal luggage in my head . . .

Bah! said Korath. *Jake, there is this weakness in you. And its name is conscience. These brutal men raped and drowned your woman, and they would have drowned you. And as for Jean Daniel: he would have run you down, crushed you to pulp under the metal body of his vehicle. So tell me now, how is it you feel ashamed that you struck him down? An eye for an eye, remember?*

"Shame?" said Jake, with a shake of his head. "But I'm not sure it is shame. As for conscience: well, it's that, certainly—but that's not all it is. Korath, I *murdered* that man, these men. Whether they deserved it or not, *I* did it. Okay, so I know I'm not an especially religious type, but until I can *make* life what gives me the right to take it away? And that's it, part of my paradox, my dilemma. On the one hand I know that I had to do it—and that I'd do it again, *will* do it again, with your help—but on the other I feel sick that I have to live with it, the fact that I'll probably be having nightmares about these things for the rest of my life. But the greatest paradox is that I did these things to purge myself, to cleanse my spirit of the utter hatred I felt for these bastards . . . and that now I'm beginning to wonder what good it's done if I only end up hating myself?"

Fortunately, said the other in a little while, *such mixed emotions are beyond me. Indeed,* most *feelings of love, pity, and self-doubt are beyond me. I recognize them in you because I can still vaguely remember something of them in myself: my years as a boy and a youth in Sunside, until Malinari's bite freed me of all such weaknesses.*

"Weaknesses?" Again Jake shook his head. "I think you have it backwards. These are our strengths—human strengths—lacking which we'd be no better than . . ."

. . . Than the Wamphyri? Korath had seen it in his mind. *But if that's true, why do strong men such as Trask fear them so?*

And as Jake searched for an answer to that:

Let me try to explain things to you, Korath continued, *and when I'm done, then by all means deny me if you can:*

Love is a thing that wears men down; it bends them to the will of the object of their affection. But lust *is what drives the greater beast on to satisfy his need! And while compassion and sacrifice make men poor—diminishing their stature in the eyes of ever-watchful enemies—avarice and vengefulness make them powerful, so that lesser men are wary of them. And surely it must be obvious that the man who trusts no one can never be betrayed? For where trust and com-*

panionship frequently lead to betrayal, the very cornerstones of survival are mistrust, envy, jealousy, and territorialism. And always remember, that while a good and tender heart is also tender to the taste, a heart full of poison tastes only of the piss that keeps it pumping! Tolerance is what lets an idle servant sleep late abed, while terror *finds him at his post, guarding his master's—*

"—Enough!" said Jake.

Eh? Enough? I'm barely started!

"And you're done. Enough of your word games."

But my reasoning wasn't intended as any kind of word game, I assure you! Since the very beginning—since Shaitan himself—the Wamphyri have lived by these principles, and—

"And died by them," said Jake. "Don't forget, Korath, that it was a man—a very *human* being—that Malinari, Vavara, and Szwart ran away from in Starside. As for why strong men such as Ben Trask fear them: they don't fear for themselves but for the weak ones of this world, the ones who *do* believe in such 'principles,' such rubbish as you were spouting. And that is the big difference between me and Trask. What I am doing is for myself, while what he does is for all of us."

You do admire him, then?

"How can I do otherwise? How can anyone not admire someone whose life is dedicated to the truth? And his truth has it that you are wrong. So that while for the moment we're obliged to be allies of a sort, don't get carried away and think that you can sway me to your cockeyed 'principles.' I don't want anything to do with them."

And:

Bravo! . . . Bravo! . . . Bravo! It seemed a hundred deadspeak voices whispered in concert in Jake's mind. But they were faint and distant, and some seemed uncertain. Only a hundred of them, out of all those many millions. Because for the time being only a small minority of the Great Majority were on his side.

Hah! said Korath. *Do you hear them, the so-called 'teeming dead?' Well a handful of them, anyway. It seems that your words—spoken against my principles—have convinced a few of them that you are not quite the menace they took you for. So let me, too, congratulate you, Jake: bravo!* Huh! *What a pity it doesn't bring us any closer to speaking to this Jean Daniel.*

Jake had to admit that that was true enough. He and Korath had been here for quite a while now, but as yet nothing had happened; he wasn't too sure how to go about it, this conversing with the dead. In fact the only thing he knew for certain was that he mustn't shout at the dead. That had never been the way of the Necroscope, Harry Keogh, and it wasn't going to be his.

(But . . . had he read about that somewhere—or had he been told about it—or was this knowledge just one more example of the foothold that Harry's revenant had gained on his mind?) But in any case, and that apart:

How *did* one go about introducing or announcing oneself? Or did one simply wait until someone else opened the conversation? All well and good, but what if no one wanted to?

Jake's thoughts were deadspeak, and while his shields were down Korath could read them as clearly as the "spoken" word. He had done so, and now said: *Well then, perhaps we're wasting our time here after all? Since you now speak so highly of Ben Trask and his people, maybe we'd be better off serving* their *purpose, tracking down Malinari and his kind—which, incidentally, has been my argument since the beginning. Let's face it, Jake: this vendetta of yours is a paltry thing compared to what the people of E-Branch are doing.*

"But it's *my* paltry thing!" Jake stood up straighter as he felt his resolve firming up again (or perhaps as the real Jake Cutter came more properly into his own, took control of himself, and shook off the aura of someone else). "Castellano—him and one other murdering dog—they are *my* paltry things! Thanks for reminding me, Korath. How does it go? An eye for an eye, right? And what was that other thing you said? Something about 'a good and tender heart,' how it will also *taste* tender? Hey, who am I to argue something as monstrous as that with a creature as monstrous as you, a vampire? But as for my heart: where Castellano is concerned it only pumps piss. So don't you go worrying about *my* weaknesses, Korath 'once Mindsthrall.' Me, I'm not in thrall to anything, least of all my emotions."

Bullshit! Even as Jake said it he knew it wasn't so—that in fact his emotions were in turmoil—that he was fighting off someone else's emotions, or what was left of them. And to cover his vulnerability, with a snarl of frustration if not an actual shout, he opened every deadspeak channel and said:

"Jean Daniel, you murdering French bastard, where the hell are you?" And:

Right first time, a mournful voice sounded clear in Jake's mind. *I'm in hell, Jake Cutter—where you sent me. A graveyard in Avignon, the town where I was born. At least that's where my bones are. My burial was a quiet ceremony, just a small handful of people to see me off; Luigi Castellano must have hired them, I reckon, for I had no friends above the ground. And none below it, as it now appears! So there you have it, that's my lot: the loneliness, the darkness, and the endless silence of the grave. The "dead silence," until I sensed you here.*

Startled at first, and feeling the small hairs rise on the back of his neck at the weirdness of this thing, Jake recovered and responded: "You're getting used to it, then? The situation, I mean?" Caught off guard, he didn't know what else to say, how to carry it forward.

The what? The situation? (Disbelief, astonishment, in Jean Daniel's dead voice.) *Used to it?*

And Jake quickly went on, "At least you've worked out some kind of mobility for yourself, or you wouldn't be here." It had suddenly dawned on Jake that he and Korath were probably in the wrong place after all. If the Frenchman's grave was in Avignon, that's where his spirit should be, too. Yet Jake's rapidly developing metaphysical powers told him that Jean Daniel was here; he could *sense* the other here, his presence. But:

Used to it? the other moaned again, his voice a shuddering deadspeak sob. *Do I sound used to it? What, to being, dead, you fucking idiot?! No, I'm not* used *to it. I* hate *it—the graveyard in Avignon, this place, the whole fucking bit! But because I died here, in this lousy alley, sometimes I can't help drifting back here. That bar over there, it was a haunt of mine. And now I really* do *haunt it! At least,* I *know when I'm there, even if no one else does. But what's the point of being there if I'm . . . if I'm* not *there? I can't see, hear, smell, touch, or taste anything; I'm not even a ghost as such—just a thing, floating in the everlasting darkness. Or rather, a nothing. And even the dead ignore me. And you ask me if I'm used to it? Some sense of humour you've got there, you dumb English shit! So now fuck off and leave me to my misery, made more miserable by your presence and the knowledge that in the total lousy vacuum of this place, the only one I can ever talk to is the one who put me here, the lousy fucking Necroscope himself, Jake Cutter! Damn it to hell, why couldn't* you *have died—you and that Russian bitch both—when we pushed your car over that bridge into the river?*

But Jean Daniel's insults flew right over Jake's head; the fascination of this thing was such that he scarcely heard them. He *did* hear himself referred to as the Necroscope, however, and said, "Is that what they call me?" For it still hadn't sunk in; as yet he wasn't ready to accept or handle the role even if the teeming dead wished it. Which they didn't, not yet.

What are you deaf? The Frenchman said after a moment. *Are you still here? What the fuck difference does it make what anyone calls you? A piece of shit by any other name, and all that. It's what you* are, *Cutter: a Necroscope!* The *Necroscope: like a maggot in the minds of the dead! In my mind, anyway. So get the hell away from me. Leave me alone.* No longer sobbing, but very much fainter now and more distant, it seemed that Jean Daniel's deadspeak voice floated to Jake on a series of muted, dwindling sighs, from someone who was quickly drifting away from him.

"Wait!" said Jake urgently. "I need to talk to you."

It was like a command, and Jean Daniel came drifting back. *What?* (He sounded puzzled). *Are you magnetic, too? It's as if I felt you turning me, pulling me.* But a moment later: *No, you're not magnetic,* the Frenchman said. *It's just your warmth, that's all. As a fire draws a draft, you draw the dead. Oh, you're the Necroscope all right! But you're not all warmth and light, Jake Cutter, for I can feel your dark side, too. Yeah, and your cold side, for that matter . . .*

That would be Korath. And as suddenly as that, Jake understood that to the Great Majority—who "existed" in the nothingness, the nowhere of death—Jake must seem like a lone candle in the dark, the warm glow of a small, flickering flame. But by the same token Korath would seem like an even greater darkness, as cold as the spaces between the stars.

Korath knew that, too—had known it from the start—and so remained silent. But Jake could sense him there, in the back of his mind, listening intently. Doubtless the dead vampire was monitoring his progress. So best to get on with it; for failure would only set Korath off again, complaining about wasted time.

"Jean Daniel," Jake said, "get this straight: I don't like you any more than you like me. You tried to kill me . . . you *did* kill the woman I loved, and paid for it. In my book, that makes us even. But only *just* even, because while you've moved on now, beyond pain, I'm still hurting."

Oh, really!? said the Frenchman, his deadspeak voice dripping sarcasm. *Well lucky fucking me! So while I am merely dead, it's a whole lot worse for you because you're actually* hurting, *right? And it's my fault, and I should feel bad about it. Sure, I can see that. So let me think it over; give me a minute or so to work out a way to tell you how badly cut up I really do feel about all this, okay? And meanwhile*—GO AND FUCK YOURSELF!

"So then—" Jake gritted his teeth, but carried on regardless "—it seems dying hasn't taught you anything: in death you're the same worthless bastard that you were in life. Maybe I shouldn't be too surprised at that, because that's in the rules according to Hoyle, too: we are what we are, and death doesn't change us. But you've got something I need, Jean Daniel, and I want you to give it up. So here's the deal: talk to me, tell me what I need to know, and then I'll leave you in peace."

Something you want, eh? (Now the Frenchman laughed, however high and shrill.) *So what's this, the Inquisition? I might have been born in Avignon, but in the twentieth not the thirteenth century! Oh, I know what you want, Necroscope! Hey, while I'm definitely not partying with what you'd call "high society" down here, I'm not* entirely *out of touch either . . . know what I mean? Like, you've been quite the busy little bastard lately, right?*

And again, instinctively (if with someone else's instinct), Jake knew what the dead man was talking about.

Yeah, that's right (Jean Daniel's incorporeal nod.) *Wilhelm "Willie" Stuker was next on your list, then Francesco "Frankie" Reggio. Me and both of them, taken out one, two, three, by you. Which makes it kind of obvious what you're doing, and also what you want from me, right?*

"Stuker?" said Jake. "That fat, slimy Kraut queer? Was that his name, Stuker?" He shook his head. "I never knew him by name—only by his ugly looks."

Is that right? the Frenchman said. *Well he sure wasn't any prettier when* you *got through with him! He told me about it . . . how you packed his asshole with plastique, set a fuse, and left him counting down the seconds to the big bang. I mean, I didn't see mine coming, but Willie—Jesus, he* knew *about it! His ass really* was *grass—or gas, whichever . . .*

Poor Willie! We called him that, "Willie," not because his name was Wilhelm but on account of his twig dick. I never saw a thinner dick on a fatter guy! But it wasn't just Willie's willy you vaporised, Necroscope. You blew his mind, too! He never was any too stable, but during the countdown he completely lost it. Likewise Frankie Reggio: not raving mad, no, but pretty "burned up," for sure! How's that *for a sense of humour? Not bad, for a dead man, eh? But you know—just thinking about how those guys went out—it would really make my eyes water, if I had any! It has to be said, you burned both of them pretty good. Especially Frankie.*

"An eye for an eye," Jake answered, trying his best *not* to think about it. "Since they liked it dirty, those two, that was how I gave it to them. You all got what you deserved. So you've been talking to them, have you?"

Willie doesn't talk much, said the other. *He only gibbers. The couple times I bumped into him, I didn't get much sense. He was a queer and a gutless coward in life, but since physical is no longer an option, there's only one of those things he can be in death. He was crazy with fear when your plastique ripped him apart, and that's the way he's stayed.*

"He was your colleague, and you don't give a damn?"

What? My colleague? said Jean Daniel. *I didn't give a shit for the fat slob pervert when I was* alive! *So why should I care now? And the same goes for Frankie. I mean, maybe I could use a little quality company around here—but those two? Castellano kept Frankie around because he scared the competition almost as much as the boss man himself. But as for Willie Stuker: I don't know why* anyone *would keep him around. Unless it was because he was so fucking nasty! Castellano likes nasty.*

And Jake said, "See, you *can* talk once you get going."

Yeah? said the other. *Well I'm really glad you enjoyed it, because as of right now I'm all talked out. Luigi Castellano is one subject I won't* ever *talk about, dead or alive. Not to you, and not to anyone else. And since there* is *no one else—except a load of dead fucks who won't have anything to do with me—I guess I'm safe.*

Jake sensed his fear and said, "You're scared of him? Even in death? And you're the one who called Stuker a coward?"

And after a moment's silence: *I don't know,* said Jean Daniel, *maybe I am still scared of him. And maybe I'm not, not any longer. Maybe I even hate him, if only because he's still alive and I'm dead. But let's face it, Cutter, I couldn't hate anyone as badly as I hate you. So forget it, because I won't be giving you any kind of edge over Castellano. If you go up against him, you're on your own. Against him and his boys: you haven't a cat in hell's chance. Even one on one, no way you can win. So maybe we'll be talking again some day. In the not too distant future, I hope.*

"Worthless bastard!" said Jake.

Maybe you picked the wrong man, said Jean Daniel, his deadspeak very gradually fading. *I'm no nark. Maybe you should have gone after Alfonso Lefranc first. Or is he next? Well whatever, bad luck to you, Necroscope . . .*

"Lefranc?" Jake frowned. He had never come across the name before and didn't know who the other was talking about.

But Jean Daniel "heard" the thought and said: *Sure you do, you dumb English shit!* And his deadspeak automatically conjured a picture of Jake's fourth quarry—the last but one of the men who had been there that terrible night in Marseilles—a man he had tried to trace, so far without luck.

And yet suddenly Jake started as he remembered an incident at the airport in Brisbane, when he had been about to board the UK-bound Skyskip with Trask and his E-Branch espers. For it was then he'd thought to see this selfsame face staring at him through the flexiglass wall that secured the boarding area from the viewing promenade. This sallow, badly pockmarked face on a small, thin, shifty-eyed man. A weaselly man, with an aura that was distinctly rodentlike . . . he'd been there one minute, gone the next.

At the time Jake had thought he'd imagined it. Considering it a symptom of his obsession—when from time to time he would see these hated faces wherever he looked, even though three of them were no more, dead by his hand—he had simply put it out of his mind. For after all, what would one of Castellano's gang be doing out in Australia?

His thoughts were deadspeak, of course, and:

Not very hard to figure, said the Frenchman, his deadspeak growing fainter as he drifted away, doubtless returning to Avignon. *Castellano probably sent Lefranc out there to keep his eye on you, because you were making a nuisance of yourself. Alfonso is Luigi's intelligence agent, a spy, the sneakiest bastard you could never wish to meet. But at the same time he's pure rat: a grass, a nark, an informer. I think Luigi will kill him one day even if you don't. That guy's got more mouth than a porn star's got pussy! He's a liability. It's like he just can't help mouthing off. Maybe you should have taken him out first, Necroscope. It's a sure thing Alfonso would have talked to you.*

"Oh, you've talked your share," said Jake. "I've got a new name to conjure with, and you've proved at least one thing that I'd heard about but hadn't experienced."

Such as? A whisper now, in the deadspeak aether.

"Such as how when people die, they go on doing as they did in life. You're the dead proof of it, Jean Daniel. You were and you still are a worthless scumbag."

Fuck you, Necroscooope! (But all the edge, the poison, the vindictiveness, gone now from the dead Frenchman's voice, while a renewed burst of hushed sobbing replaced it, rapidly tapering away into nothing.)

"Likewise, I'm sure," said Jake, but to himself now.

And then silence . . .

Disappointed, Jake stood alone—yet not alone—in the alley in Marseilles. And eventually Korath said: *Your diplomacy seems somewhat lacking.*

"Oh?" said Jake. "Diplomacy? With scum such as that? Maybe you mean I'm not as good at lies and word games as you are."

I suppose that could be it, said the other, without taking offence. *But all that profanity, vituperation, verbal abuse . . . such language came as a great surprise to me! You're not always so, er, forthright.*

"Me?" Jake protested. "The way I heard it, most of the badmouthing was down to him! Anyway, I was only answering in kind, giving back as good as I got. 'When in Rome,' and all that."

Among the Wamphyri, Korath said, *invective is seldom used. Why warn an enemy by cursing him when swift and decisive action will speak far louder than any words? What purpose is served by swearing at an insubordinate thrall?*

Even the harshest of words will fly right over his head, for they are only *words and he is a vampire! But if on the other hand his* head *should do the flying, when it is shorn from his shoulders—*

"—Too late for him," said Jake, "but the rest of the gang will get the message."

Exactly, said Korath. *Indeed, we have a saying: stakes and stones may break our bones, but calling—*

"—Will not harm us?" Jake nodded. "We have much the same saying on this side of the Gate."

So then, said Korath. *Better to simply kill than to curse, don't you agree?*

"Which sounds about right for Starside," said Jake, "but I don't think it would go down too well here! As for swear-words: they're used mainly for emphasis; often as expletives, or where the user hasn't got much of a 'decent' vocabulary. So Ben Trask says, anyway. But the Wamphyri don't use bad language, eh?"

(Korath's deadspeak shrug.) *In order to goad an enemy into mindless, headlong action and so disadvantage him, perhaps. But as a matter of course, no.*

"That could be worth remembering," said Jake.

As you will (another shrug). And, after a moment: *But all that is for the future, and as for right now: what's next? Will you try to locate this "gibbering" Willie Stuker, or attempt to speak to the "incendiary" Frankie Reggio? Surely not the latter, for his language is almost sure to be* (hah!) *"inflammatory," and his response of no value whatsoever. Your victims owe you nothing, Jake. Which means that there is only one among the teeming dead who* does *owe you, and even that is a dubious supposition.*

"Natasha," said Jake softly. And then, frowning: "But did you say dubious?"

Certainly. For haven't you often thought it, and haven't I seen it in your mind? Are you not in large part responsible for Natasha's . . . for her current situation?

For some few seconds Jake was silent. Conscience, yes. And Korath had hit the nail right on the head: what was burning him up inside was as much down to himself as to anyone else. For if he hadn't met Natasha in the first place . . .

. . . But he'd had this argument with himself a hundred times before, and it always came out the same: while he was partly to blame, others were far more so. Jake's guilt lay in that he had loved Natasha, which caused her to love him; theirs lay in that they had killed her for it.

And if the only way to get back at them was through her—

—*You will go to her, then. But where?*

"The only place I know," Jake answered, his voice breaking just a little, before he could catch it.

Korath saw it in his mind: the bridge near Riez, under the Alps of Provence. The broken wall, where Castellano's thugs had rammed Jake's car—with Jake and Natasha trapped inside—over the edge and into the torrential Verdon River.

"The river was in flood," Jake told him. "I managed to get clear of the car—don't ask me how, for we were both drugged. But I survived while Natasha . . . didn't. I wasn't strong enough to swim, let alone go back under for her! The next thing I knew was when I washed up on a bank downstream. The car wasn't found for weeks, but when it was she was still in it. So I don't know—can't say for sure—but maybe it's possible something of her has lingered on right there where she died."

You don't know where she's buried?

"She was cremated," said Jake. "I . . . I read about it. She went up in smoke, I can't remember where. It seems I've blotted most of that out of my mind."

But the bridge? The river?

"That's a place I'll never forget," said Jake. "Its coordinates will be with me forever."

Just along the alley, a uniformed gendarme in the recessed entrance to a store had been watching Jake for some time. There was something vaguely familiar about Jake's face, and there was *definitely* something strange about his behaviour! He alternated between leaning on the wall and standing up straight, pacing to and fro and standing stock-still, holding his head cocked in an attitude of intent listening, and talking to himself. It wasn't possible that he talked to anyone else, for he was quite alone.

But his face . . . a picture in the wanted gallery, perhaps? The gendarme stepped out of the store doorway, started down the alley towards Jake.

Jake saw him coming and turned a corner out of sight.

Hah! The gendarme broke into a run, arrived at the corner and turned it . . . and skidded to an astonished halt. There were no more street corners in the vicinity, just blank walls for at least a hundred yards. And no open windows or doorways anywhere in sight. Not so strange in itself, except there was no sign of the fugitive, either! In fact there was nothing—

—Just the final swirl of a dust devil collapsing onto the sunbaked pavement. For Jake Cutter, reluctant and as yet unaccepted Necroscope, had doorways of his own . . . or almost of his own.

And until they *were* his own, if ever, his "colleague," the dead but ever-available vampire, Korath-once-Mindsthrall, would be there to play the role of keeper of the keys . . .

Not too many miles inland of Marseilles, under the Alps of Provence, the weather was very different. Black clouds were rolling south off the peaks in what was promising to be the first storm of the season. High up in the foothills, the narrow road over a stone-built, humpbacked bridge was mainly deserted. Far below, on the road's zigzagging asphalt ribbon, one or two cars crawled like bugs along the winding contours, their chrome fenders glinting with chitin facets where occasional beams of sunlight forced their way through the threatening thunderheads.

Jake stood by the low wall of the bridge, looked over and down, and shivered. He wasn't cold but he shivered. The stones under his hands had been recently cemented in place; no lichen or moss had grown on them as yet; it was a very obvious repair to the eight-foot gap that Castellano's thugs had created when they crashed his car through.

And down below, the water was a shallow, calm-seeming lake in the vast bowl that the river's rush had cut in its rocky bed through all the centuries, a lake that narrowed to a bottleneck where the river speeded up toward its next whitewater descent, and the one after that, and so on.

So that Jake wondered, "Did I really live through that? How many falls did I take before I washed up?"

Following the river's course and rocky descent through his host's eyes, Korath answered, *If I did not know better, I would have said your first was surely your last!*

"The river was in flood," Jake answered, "and the lake was full to its brim and spilling over. Otherwise we'd have hit the bottom and solid rock. But as it was, we were no sooner through the wall than we were in the water. It would have been—what? Maybe twenty feet deep?" He shook his head. "Seemed a whole lot more than that at the time . . ."

You were very lucky.

"Yes, I was," said Jake quietly, but with the emphasis on the *I*. And shielding his thoughts, keeping them to himself: *But she wasn't.*

Except . . . which she was he thinking about? Standing there at the wall, suddenly Jake reeled—

—Reeled and sat down with a bump—on the grassy bank of a Scottish river! It felt as real as if he were actually there, and he wasn't any longer Jake but someone else, the only one he could be in this place thinking these thoughts:

"Ma, are you there?"

But she wasn't there. She'd moved on. Gone to join an even Greater Majority in a special place beyond the beyond. And poor little Harry (that was what she'd always called him) was on his own. "Ma?" he said again.

And Korath repeated him: *Ma? Jake, who are it you are talking to? Your mother, here?*

No, of course she wasn't. Wasn't even his mother but Harry Keogh's. It was just another connecting thread—something that both Jake and the original Necroscope had in common—that the situation had conjured into being in

Jake's mind. Just a memory that was all. But not *his* memory . . .

And as quickly as that he was back at the wall again, back in the Jake mind, the Jake reality.

Jake? (Korath's voice again, and actually anxious!)

"It's okay," said Jake, still a little shaken. "It was the river, that's all. It was like, I don't know, a feeling of déjà vu, or something. See, Harry and I, we both lost someone in the same kind of way. Harry lost his Ma in the water, and I—"

—But as his thoughts returned to Natasha, they, too, were like an invocation.

Jake? Her voice, which he'd thought he would never hear again. Natasha's voice, as if she whispered in his ear, causing Jake to gasp and wheel about . . . but in fact she only whispered in his mind.

And paradoxically, because this was Natasha, Jake found it far *less* believable, far less acceptable, than when he'd talked to Harry, Zek, Korath, or even Jean Daniel. For Natasha had been as real to him as life itself—no, she had been real to him *in* life itself! Jake had *known* her—the warm, living, breathing, sadly smiling, oh-so-*real* Natasha, and people who you know just don't talk to you when they're dead.

Well, and hadn't the Frenchman been real, too? But despite Jean Daniel's reality—his three-dimensional status in Jake's mind—still he'd been a stranger, a cardboard figure, a target on a shooting range. Yes, a target, all shot to pieces now. And therein lay the paradox.

Jean Daniel and the others, they simply didn't matter, but Natasha was *still* real in Jake's memory. And hearing her voice, for all that it was a deadspeak voice, brought it all back in a flood of emotion. And:

"God!" he said. "Oh God! I let you down! I let you *drown!*"

Jake, Jake, Jake, she said with a voice like the sea in a seashell. *Stop punishing yourself. You didn't let me drown. No way! You just couldn't stop it, that's all. And Jake, something you should know: I never felt a thing. I didn't wake up, didn't know, didn't suffer.*

"And yet you're suffering now," he said. "Your voice: it's so faint. So weak."

But that's not because I'm suffering, Jake. You see, I was cremated; which is how I'd asked for it to be, in a will I made a long time ago. Cremated and my ashes scattered on the wind. I had always fancied myself a free one—even when I wasn't, even when I was trapped—for it was my way of escaping from things. So now I am free, flying on the wind. I'm in the storm clouds on the mountains there, and I'm falling in rain on the forests and into the seas. I'm thinning out as I go, spreading myself fine, you might say. But that's okay because the less there is of me, the greater my freedom.

"And yet you're here, too?"

Because I had to be. It's all a matter of will, Jake. When I heard about you—

"—About me? But how did you hear about me?" (Jake's voice was beginning to break now.)

The Great Majority talked about you, she answered. *So many of them, Jake: it was like a shout going up! They felt how warm you were, and at first thought you were someone else. Then they saw that you weren't—and how they argued then! They're arguing still, because as yet many of them daren't trust themselves into your care.*

"Daren't trust themselves?" Jake shook his head; he didn't understand. "But who do they think I am, the angel Gabriel?"

Ah, but they might, they just might! Natasha answered. And before he could query her meaning, she went on: *Jake, listen. I can't stay here—it's an effort just* being *here. But I thought you might come back some time, and I was right.*

Now Jake was ashamed, because he hadn't come simply to *see* Natasha—not just to talk to her or commiserate—but to ask her about Castellano. He could see how selfish, how thoughtless that was now. But even so, over and above any feelings of self-reproach, he could sense something else: an irresistible force, driving him on.

And for the first time Jake knew for sure, without knowing how he knew, that this wasn't simply a matter of revenge. There was unfinished business here; something that someone else might have started, but that he must see through to the end. And his thoughts were deadspeak, of course.

Castellano? Natasha said. *You feel guilty because you came here to find out about him, and not just to talk to me? But you don't know how much easier that makes all of this, Jake!*

"Easier?" For a moment Jake thought that she was trying to take some of the weight off his shoulders; but no, for he could actually feel the wave of relief that flowed out from her! "But . . . how does it make things easier?"

Because I have guilty feelings, too! She told him. *Guilty, yes—for all those hoops I put you through . . .*

"Hoops?" Jake shook his head. "But I don't know what—"

But you do *know what! Haven't I told you I'd always wanted to be free? You were that freedom, Jake. In the real world, the world of the living,* you *were that freedom—or you would have been.*

It took a while to sink in, until:

"I was your way out," he said, feeling suddenly empty. "I was your passport out of a terrible situation . . ." But following the emptiness, replacing it, gathering in him until he expelled it in a sigh . . . as much and perhaps more relief than he'd felt in Natasha! Which was also wrong, surely? Or was it?

She heard that last, and answered:

I played at being in love, for my own ends. And you joined in the game: you got caught up in it. But it's all right, Jake, and it's worked out fine. Because now we're both free.

Jake spent a moment thinking it through, then said: "Could it ever have worked for us, do you think? I mean, could it have become more than just a game?"

Both of us had lives before we met, she reminded him, *and we were both carrying too much excess baggage. Some things that I have done . . . I can't say for sure, but I might have found any normal sort of lifestyle tame by comparison! And maybe I'm mistaken, but I sensed that it was the same for you. No use trying to guess what the future* might *have brought, Jake, or even what your own future might yet bring. Best to face it as it comes.*

"I know," he nodded. "The future is like shit: it happens. Or as some people might say, it's a devious thing."

Not for me, she answered. *My future's here, blowing in the wind. But now that we've talked, surely you'll see that there's no longer any need for revenge against Castellano, and—*

"Oh but there is!" Jake cut in, as once again he felt that driving force, that need to finish unfinished business. "Not so much vengeance now, but a need, definitely. Will you help me? I want to know his power base, and what I'll be going up against, and where to look for him."

And it's not just for me? (Her deadspeak voice was anxious again.) *Are you sure of that? I don't want you putting yourself in harm's way, endangering yourself for a lost cause.*

"I can't be sure about the cause," he answered truthfully. "Isn't simple justice enough? But since I'll be going after him anyway, the main danger will lie in being unprepared."

Following which she told him what he wanted to know: Luigi Castellano's power base, his possible whereabouts, the strength of the soldiers with which he surrounded himself.

But it seemed she had barely enough time. Her voice was in the wind and was rapidly blowing away; she finished with a sigh and what might have been a kiss, the touch of a single raindrop against Jake's gaunt, unshaven cheek. And then she was gone.

Or he thought that she was . . .

But as soon as Jake (and Korath, too) had also left that place—as the first real rain came lashing out of the darkening sky, and the wind began gusting with the force of a storm—then:

Thank you, Natasha, said Zek Foener, the merest whisper in the metaphysical deadspeak aether. *Both for giving him peace of mind, and for helping him to find the way ahead.*

That must have been hard for you, clearing his conscience like that.

Not really, said the other, even less of a whisper. *For it was at least half-true: Jake really* was *going to be my passport out of that mess.*

Then I won't ask if you actually loved him, said Zek.

And I won't tell you, said the other. *But Jake's free now, and has his own life to live. My memory is one piece of excess baggage that he no longer has to take with him along the way.*

Then let me thank you for myself, said Zek. *For your selfless attitude. You see, I've had my problems, too, which you've resolved. For you're right, Natasha: freedom is everything. And there's someone I would set free, too, if only I knew how.*

And as the storm gathered force, and lightning lit the sky over that empty bridge under the Alps of Provence, their voices faded and drifted apart; Zek returning to her mission on behalf of the new Necroscope, and Natasha intent on going her own way, the way she had chosen, in search of freedom absolute.

She at least would have her way, for all the world's winds were waiting for her . . .

Twenty-four hours later:

In a dusty room floored with roughly hewn hexagonal stone flags, in the extensive cellars under Luigi Castellano's villa near Bagheria, the master of the house and his second-in-command took a brief respite from grisly labours and talked.

"You did well," said Castellano, the red flaring of flambeaux reflecting in his scarlet gaze, as he gloomed sardonically on the tools that Garzia had used to question a certain "Russian gentleman," their visitor from Moscow. Garzia's tools lay upon a stone table where he had thrown them: hammers with leaden heads coated in rubber; a joined pair of metal cups the size of large hen's eggs, which could be tightened on a man's tenderest parts by turning knurled screws;

a metal headband, with more projecting screws so positioned as to be over the eyes and ears of the wearer, knurled on the outside and filed to sharp points on the inside; thumbscrews, tongs, and spoon-shaped gouges, and so on. A torturer's museum.

"Antiques," Garzia answered, rolling down his sleeves. "My collection. You have your treasures, from Le Manse Madonie, but such as these have more appeal to me. I'm told that truth drugs will do the job as well, but where's the pleasure in that?"

A low moan sounded from an adjacent room, and the vampire Castellano cocked an ear in that direction. "Consciousness," he said. "So soon! An amazingly resilient man, don't you think? He held up well, and was extraordinarily reticent—at first."

"He knew the truth meant death," said Garzia with a shrug. "But when he realized that death would be preferable, and that in any case it couldn't be avoided . . ."

Garzia nodded. "What point then in holding back?"

"And for all the drawn nails and crushed bones, scarcely a drop spilled," said Castellano. And once again: "Extremely well done, and very enlightening once his tongue was loosened. But I could see how you relished the work. I would hate to think that you might one day have me upon your bench!" His coarse laughter echoed for a moment or two in the smoky gloom, then tapered off to a phlegmy gurgling.

"Or me upon yours," said Garzia, watching Castellano clean his hands and forearms on a towel.

"But such a shame that we are reduced to this," Castellano grimaced as he tossed the soiled towel aside and commenced soaping down his arms in a bowl of tepid water. "Surely this Georgi Grusev—this spy for Gustav Turchin—surely he could see when we brought him down here that the game was up? If he had spoken sooner he might have saved himself a great deal of pain."

"And *that* would have been the real shame," said the other. "We so rarely have the opportunity to practice . . ." He picked up and examined a pair of pincers, their jaws stained a rusty red. "If I had been on top form, he would have talked sooner."

"Each to his own means and devices, of course," Castellano answered. "But unlike you, I do not find a man's most sensitive parts to be on the outside. And naturally females are even more susceptible in that respect. As for tools, I have my hands—"

—Which were finally clean. But they could never be clean of their atrocities.

And as another low moan sounded from the adjacent room:

"Perhaps we should see to our needs now," said Garzia, his voice thick with lust. "Grusev must be very close to death, and if his heart were to stop pumping . . . such a waste! Before that, however, won't you tell me how you knew he was a spy? Was it your oneiromancy, or just a clever guess?"

"Well it's true that I've had certain dreams," Castellano answered. "Dreams that go back . . . oh a very long time. But the trouble with dreams lies in their meaning, their interpretation. For years now I've anticipated the advent of a man who will try to destroy me; but whether by infiltrating my organization—as this Russian would have done—or by more direct means . . . who can say? On the other hand, some odd things have been happening recently, and I would be a fool if I had failed to notice their obvious connections.

"Odd things?" Garzia frowned. "Like the problem we've been having with this Jake Cutter?"

"Cutter for one," Castellano nodded. "What, a single man—an apparently 'ordinary' man at that—who has taken out three of my best, and done it so very inventively? Obviously he's not so ordinary! But it's a tangled skein, Garzia, and difficult to unravel. For example, how is it that Cutter is no longer one of Europe's most wanted? Our various connections in the Surete and Interpol seem just as baffled as we are. I'm told that the word has come from above, from the highest offices, which we haven't yet penetrated, that Cutter's apprehension is no longer considered a priority! He is off the hook . . . but who or what *got* him off the hook, eh?"

Castellano had commenced pacing the stone floor; he leaned forward, seeming almost off-balance in that aggressive, loping, praying mantis–like posture, to which his second-in-command had long since grown accustomed.

But in a little while, when Garzia remained silent, he mutteringly continued: "No, Jake Cutter is by no means an 'ordinary' man, and his involvement in this—this whatever it is—goes a lot deeper than any simple vendetta. Indeed, he could even be the one I've been waiting for, who featured in those earliest dreams of mine. And the hell of it is, I once had him right where I wanted him! But I thought he was only interested in the girl, Natasha. If I had suspected otherwise—that she was only a tool, a means he was using to get to me, and that in fact *I* was the focus of his . . . his what? His investigation?—then you can be *sure* I would have got my hands dirty long before now!"

As Castellano loped and talked, his frustration had become increasingly apparent. His voice was a low, rumbling growl; his scarlet eyes bulged in a deathly grey face twisted with hatred, and his lips were drawn back from gleaming, knife-like teeth. A split tongue writhed in his cavern mouth. Garzia had seen these transformations before, but rarely so pronounced.

"Oh, *yesss!*" Castellano went on. "How I would have enjoyed wringing it from him, until all of his secrets were mine! Then, instead of leaving it to those four fools, I would have seen to it *personally* that Jake Cutter bothered me no more!"

"Luigi," said Garzia, as his master came to a halt, trembling with rage in the middle of the floor, "I'm not at all sure I understand what you're saying. Your powers, your reasoning—such things are beyond me."

"No, of course you don't see," said Castellano. "For I am what I am, while you are what I made you. But I *remember* things Garzia! I *connect* things and total them like numbers, until the sum of their parts is clearly visible. And if they don't add up . . . then I worry about them. There are matters here that go far deeper than we see on the surface. They go back in time, as far back as my mother, and as far forward as the present . . . beyond which I can't any longer see. And that is an odd and disturbing thing in its own right: that I no longer dream . . ." He glared at the other, Garzia, who could only shrug.

"Then let me try to explain," said Castellano. And after a moment: "In the last days of Le Manse Madonie, before it fell into the gulf and took the Brothers Francezci with it, my mother had more time for me. That is, I could see her more frequently, but always in secret. For she swore that if ever her masters should find out about me, if ever they discovered that one of them had fathered a son, and there was issue from their use and abuse of their servant, Katerin, then that they would surely kill her—and me, too!

"And so, even as I myself was rising to power, I kept well out of their way. No easy matter, for they were advisers to all the heads of the Mafia. You will remember, Garzia, how in those early days I rarely brought myself into prominence? And now you know the reason. I knew that my mother's warning was genuine. I *knew* that if the Francezcis believed they had spawned me, then that they would kill me.

"Anthony and Francesco, they used her. No longer sexually, no—for she had grown old and they were still young—but as a servant in Le Manse Madonie, as before, and also as a messenger and a spy. When she was out and about on Francezci business, in Bagheria or Palermo, then she would contact me, and I would find a way to see her.

"But the *things* that she told me! That the Francezcis were monsters, and Anthony a changeling creature that waxed in shape and form! That they kept their own father in a dungeon pit, and feared the end of their days—which was coming!

"She reminded me of vast treasures in the caverns under Le Manse Madonie, gave me documents which she had kept hidden away all those years—the records of her brief confinement, and of my birth—and told me of my legacy: that I was the only 'legitimate' heir to the estate of the Francezcis.

"As to why she did these things: because the Thing in the

pit under Le Manse Madonie had forecast the end of the Brothers Francezci; also, because she feared that the madness of Anthony would be the end of her, too. Not that she was afraid of dying, no, not at all—on the contrary. For having seen what she had seen in their service, knowing what she knew of the horrors in and under Le Manse Madonie, death was a prospect she welcomed.

"Now think, Garzia. My own grandfather—a monstrous Thing so gross that they kept it in a pit—had forecast the downfall of his sons, the Brothers Francezci. *Forecast,* yes! And now you must see where my oneiromancy has its origin! These things connect, do you see?

"Let me get on:

"Not long before the end, the fall of Le Manse Madonie, my mother told me that the Francezcis feared a man. I repeat: *they feared a man,* Garzia! One man. He had been into their vaults to rob them; impossible, according to my mother, but he'd done it. A man who came and went like a ghost—who moved through stone walls and steel vault doors like they were water, or as if they had no substance at all—but nevertheless a man who was flesh and blood, just as we are flesh and blood. The Francezcis, they were vampires, Garzia, even as we are vampires, yet they feared this one 'ordinary' man.

"He had a name; he had *two* names! One was Harry Keogh, and the other was Alec Kyle. So, perhaps there were two such, these men who could come and go like ghosts. The brothers traced him, or them, and discovered that he/they were members of an organization—called E-Branch!

"Ah! I saw you start!" Castellano pointed a slender, trembling finger at his second-in-command. "You are beginning to see the emerging pattern. Oh, yes, Garzia: E-Branch—that selfsame organization of which Lefranc spoke only a few short hours ago: the organization which now gives Jake Cutter its protection. So quite obviously, he is an agent of this E-Branch.

"But if there were any doubt, I have yet more proof.

"I have mentioned how my oneiromancy no longer works for me, how I no longer see the future in dreams; not even a hint, not even a glimpse. My last dream of that kind was more than a month ago. Its theme had been repetitive for three years, yet I had never before seen it so clearly.

"In it, I saw two faces and a shadow. A man, a woman, and a shadow. The first was handsome, the second beautiful, and the other . . . was *other*. But like you and me, Garzia, all three were vampires. They were very *great* vampires, and they were here!

"The handsome one: I saw him clearly. He dwelled in a high place called Xanadu, like Kubla Khan, yes. In my walking hours I checked, and Xanadu exists—or rather, it existed!"

"That casino resort in Australia," said Garzia. "Where you sent Alfonso Lefranc."

"My reasons were twofold," Castellano nodded. "Other than myself, Lefranc is the last survivor of Jake Cutter's vendetta. Therefore, one: I was using Lefranc as a lure—in the same way as I used Frankie Reggio—to see if he would attract Cutter's attention away from me. And two: I was eager to know more about the vampire master of Xanadu. But I have to admit that the last thing I suspected at that time was that Cutter, or rather, this E-Branch for which he works, was interested not alone in me *but in others like me!*"

"But they were," said Garzia. "And they destroyed Xanadu!"

"Yes," again Castellano's nod, "and for all I know, a very handsome vampire with it—*just as they had destroyed Le Manse Madonie some thirty years ago!* For that's what they do, Garzia: they *kill* such as you and I, and destroy all our works!"

"And Cutter?"

"Is an agent in a long line of agents with strange skills. It can only be so. Harry Keogh, Alec Kyle, Jake Cutter. Not one and the same after all, for as I've seen with my own eyes, this Cutter is only a very . . . he's only very . . ." Castellano paused, stood frozen like a mantis in the moment before it strikes. But he had nothing to strike at. Not yet.

"Only very—?" said Garzia, frowning.

"Young," said Castellano finally and flatly. "Keogh, Kyle, and Cutter . . ." Then, slamming his fist into his palm: "What? Do you suppose it's possible, Garzia?"

The other flapped his hands, looked bemused.

"Do you know the expression—about using a thief to catch a thief?"

And Garzia gasped. "You think that they're using a vampire . . . to track vampires?"

"It would explain a great many things," Castellano nodded. "Somehow they control one of our kind, and use him as their pet bloodhound. Keogh, Kyle, Cutter—they could indeed be one and the same. Ageless, as we are ageless. Silent and secret, as you and I are silent and secret. *Hah!* But of course Keogh, and Kyle—and now this Jake Cutter—*of course* they come and go like ghosts! Even as we come and go, when we have a mind."

"But you told me Jake Cutter was only a man." Garzia waved his arms aloft. "And you have actually *seen* him!"

"Seen him?" For a moment Castellano frowned, before slowly continuing: "Yes, I saw him—I had him in my power—a man who dared not betray his true nature to another of the *same* nature, who would know how to deal with him! His was the cunning of the vampire, Garzia; he survived that clumsy 'accident' which those four idiots arranged, escaped from the car and returned to kill three of them. What's more, he also escaped from that prison in Turin, when according to very reliable contacts there he should have been weighted down with enough lead to roof over a church! Now tell me, who but an accomplished vampire could do that?

"As for his vendetta: I cannot doubt but that Lefranc will be next . . . and then myself! Except that's not going to happen.

"Forewarned is forearmed, Garzia, and we'll be waiting for him. Jake Cutter first, and then this E-Branch. So they want to know my movements, do they? And this Georgi Grusev, sent by the Russian premier, was their sniffer dog? See how these old enemies have now joined forces and are in league against me. As for my whereabouts: well obviously they now know where I am. And if they plan to use Jake Cutter against me, so be it. Indeed, I'll send him an invitation via Moscow: this Grusev's ears, his eyes and all his fingers. They'll have his prints, of course, and so will know his fate . . ."

In a little while, when Castellano's silence made it clear that he was done, Garzia said, "And so our cover—and likewise our nature—is blown. These people who know where we are, and what we are, they won't suffer us to live, Luigi. The drugs we deal in is one thing, but what we *are* . . . is something else. Is it the beginning of the end, do you think?"

The other unfroze, turned his gaze upon Garzia, and smiled a monstrous smile. "Apart from yourself," he said, "I have kept my poisons trapped within me. But if it's to be war, then we'll need troops of our own. Not these simple thugs, these so-called 'soldiers' with which we've surrounded ourselves, but vampires, whose lust for life is as great as our own."

"Time to start recruiting, then," Garzia nodded.

"How many men," said Castellano, "are in the gardens?"

"A dozen," the other answered.

"Then we shall start with them," said Castellano. "A small nucleus at first, but in the next day or two rapidly expanding. And as for anonymity: 'synonymous with longevity,' is it? I say to hell with it! Anonymity be damned! For I fancy we'll soon be *fighting* for our longevity, Garzia!"

His second-in-command's gaze went to the arched doorway to the adjacent room, from which once more a low moan had sounded. And licking his coarse lips in anticipation, he said "Luigi, it shall be as you say, of course. But first, before that, there's something we really should attend to."

"Yes, we should," Castellano agreed, leaning in that weird way of his in the direction indicated. "For as the blood is the life, for too long we have held ourselves in abeyance. Time now to fortify and make strong. Come . . ."

They entered the other room, one of many in the deep labyrinth of cellars under Castellano's stronghold villa, and stood for a moment by the table bearing Georgi Grusev's body. "A Russian," Castellano commented, "but scarcely a gentleman."

"Or if he was," Garzia gurgled, "you'd never know it now!"

Their naked victim was manacled to the table hand and foot. Heavily built, his pale body showed severe bruising around ribs, knees, ankles, and wrists. His fingers and toes were bloody red blobs where the nails had been drawn, and he was still bleeding from the ears, though not profusely. His rib cage bulged on the right, where broken ribs were pushing outwards.

"His breathing is irregular," said Garzia.

"But his pulse is still strong," Castellano answered. "And that is all that matters."

Quickly they stripped off and loosened the manacles, tied the Russian's feet together and hooked them to a chain that dangled from a pulley in the ceiling. And without pause, hauling on the chain, they hoisted Grusev's body vertically—head down, hands and arms dangling—until his head was some seven feet from the floor. And as Castellano dragged the table to one side, his man Garzia stood on a chair and cut the Russian spy's throat ear to ear with a razor-sharp knife.

Then, as the warm red cascade began, Garzia set the still-living body spinning on its chain, got down from the chair and kicked it away, and joined his awesome, awful master where Castellano stood naked, open-mouthed and crimson-eyed, staring up in hideous ecstasy while his pale flesh was drenched from that as yet living, twirling font of vampiric life.

But now an additional transformation—a metamorphosis of sorts—took place in these monsters; for not only were Castellano's and Garzia's mouths gaping wide, *but also the very pores of their bodies,* making their faces and forms alveolate, honeycombed like sponges!

All the better for soaking up the spurting life-essence of an alleged Russian gentleman . . .

Part Three
Meetings and Confrontations

13
In Enemy Territory

ON SATURDAY MORNING, ABOUT 10:30 LOCAL time, Liz Merrick, Lardis Lidesci, and Ian Goodly boarded the Russian-built ferry, *The Krassos*, at Keramoti.

From the lower of two observation decks, they watched maybe a hundred passengers come aboard on foot, also two German tourist buses and several large Greek flatbed trucks; but this late in the season, neither the freight deck nor the passenger decks were filled to capacity. And despite the cloudless sky (or maybe because of it, in this long El Niño summer), there were only one or two private cars parked centrally between the trucks and buses, none of which carried the foreign plates that would have identified them as tourist vehicles. The renowned Mediterranean sunshine wasn't any longer a blessing but a curse, and with the temperature already in the eighties and climbing, almost everyone had had more than enough of it. The ferry's passengers were looking forward to a breath of fresh ocean air.

Minutes after the last vehicle and persons were aboard, the tailgate was raised, and the vessel powered up and reversed out into midharbour. There, vibrating alarmingly as the rudder was held over, it turned about, picked up speed, and churned for the open sea. In a surprisingly short time Keramoti had dwindled to a toy town against a backdrop of green and yellow foothills and purple mountains, and in as much time again the mainland itself had narrowed down to a thin wedge floating on the Aegean's blue horizon, with a hazy grey crest of mountains that might just as easily be clouds.

As for the bulk of the passengers, they were mainly Greeks; and Liz, who as a child had holidayed frequently in the islands with her Graecophile parents, found them *very* typical—indeed, almost stereotypical—of the island folk that she had known:

The obligatory, toothless old grandmother in a black dress and black headsquare, weighed down with a battered suitcase and a plastic bag of red mullets, complaining endlessly of the heat and the fact that her poor fish would surely have "gone off" by the time she got to Krassos town. And another (who might be the first's sister) with two live chickens squawking exhaustedly in their wicker cage with every lurch of the ship. And yet a third encumbered with her young grandchildren, twin sisters and their disobedient, hyperactive brother, who insisted on climbing onto the bottom bar of the rail and reaching too far out in order to feed crusts of bread to the vessel's shrilling seagull escorts. Soon called to order by a gruff deckhand, the latter banged his chin in his haste to get down, and fled wailing to his granny's lap.

Then there were the tourists: mainly Germans from the buses on the freight-deck, but also a few British and other nationalities. The latter were late holidaymakers, extempore travellers who knew they'd have little or no trouble finding accommodation off-season on a wilting Greek island.

"Mad dogs and Englishmen . . ." said Goodly, watching from the shade as young British couples paraded the open decks in shorts and open-necked shirts, or no shirts at all. "They'll be burned to crisps before they even see a beach!"

Liz nodded. "Whiteys from Blighty," she said, as she remembered what she and the other E-Branch personnel had been called by their friends in the Australian special forces when they had first arrived down under. "Thank goodness for my Aussie tan. At least *I* shouldn't blister!"

"I wouldn't be too sure, if I were you," the precog warned. "Outdoors in heat like this . . . even shaded you're not safe. It bounces off sand, steel, and even stone."

"What does?" Lardis inquired.

"The sunlight," said Goodly. "Mercifully, I seem immune. I don't tan easily, and I've always preferred my skin pale."

"Myself," Lardis shaded his eyes, "I never imagined any sun could rise so high or get so hot. No wonder my ancestors called this world the Hell-lands! On Sunside it gets warm—but never too warm. Then again, it never gets too cold, either."

"I've read about your world in Branch files," Liz told him. "And I think I'd like to see it some time." But:

"No, you wouldn't," Lardis and Goodly told her, almost as a man. And the Old Lidesci followed it up with, "Not just now, at any rate." Then he sighed and turned his face away.

The precog knew what was bothering him and said, "Nathan?"

"Nathan, aye," Lardis answered. "Nathan and everyone I left behind to fight my fight. If all was going well, we should have heard about it—heard from *him,* from Nathan—long before now. That lad, Nana's boy, he could come here just as easily as when he brought my Lissa and me out of Sunside. Why, he can come and go like . . . like Harry Hell-lander himself! Like the Necroscope that Harry was and Jake Cutter might yet become! He could do it aye, and he *would* do it, certainly . . . if all was well." Lardis shrugged, sighed again, and fell moodily silent.

"Three years," the precog nodded his understanding. "It's a very long time, yes. But looking on the bright side—er, given that there is one—while we haven't heard from Nathan, neither have we heard from anyone or any-*thing* else. The Starside Gates stand open now, that's true, but since that terrible night when the Refuge was destroyed nothing has come through them. The Romanian Gate is blocked permanently, by ten thousand tons of rock, and despite that Premier Gustav Turchin doesn't have control of the other Gate at Perchorsk, still he seems to have good intelligence of it. So . . . perhaps you're worrying needlessly."

The three sat together on a bench in the shade of the upper deck, facing the stern and watching the ship's wake. Liz sat in the middle, with Lardis on her left. Behind them, an open hatch led to the "passenger lounge," a large indoor seating area with a bar for soft drinks, tea, coffee, and biscuits. With its shade and so-called air-conditioning (two overhead fans that turned far too slowly) the lounge had lured the bulk of the passengers in out of the sun. Occasionally, however, a Greek or other national would come out through the hatch to light a cigarette.

One such smoker, a mature, smartly dressed man with his arm in a sling, had emerged just a few minutes ago. Standing at the rail nearby with his cigarette, at first he appeared to have no great interest in the three people on the bench. But on hearing snatches of their conversation—which should have been meaningless to any outsider—he had gradually edged closer, until Liz and the precog were suddenly aware of him . . . the way he stared at them as if fascinated.

Liz's reaction was instinctive: to open telepathic channels and see what was on this inquisitive stranger's mind. She was a good "receiver" but her sending was as yet underdeveloped; with the exception of Jake Cutter, she'd had little success with it. Also, heeding Ben Trask's warning, she had been keeping a tight rein on her telepathy. Venturing into enemy territory like this, she didn't wish to alert anyone to her presence—and certainly not Malinari the Mind! But now, looking at this stranger's face and gauging the thoughts behind his penetrating stare:

What? (He was thinking, as his jaw fell open.) *Am I hearing correctly? The Gates, and Perchorsk? Necroscope, and Harry? . . .* The *Harry? Harry Keogh? These people must be E-Branch! . . . They can* only *be E-Branch!*

Liz took a deep breath; her elbow dug sharply into the precog's ribs as her hand dipped into her shoulder bag to find the grip of her modified Baby Browning. "He knows us!" she gasped.

But Manolis Papastamos was fractionally quicker. "Yes, I am knowing you," the compact Greek policeman said, stepping behind them and sticking his left arm in its sling between them before bringing it up under Liz's chin from the side. "We've never met—and I caution you to be very careful what you are doing with your hand in that bag—but I *am* knowing you, most definitely. You are Ben Trask's people, E-Branch!"

They looked—saw the blued-steel muzzle of an ugly,

squat little automatic poking out of the sleeve of Manolis's sling—and Liz froze with her own weapon only half drawn from her bag. Goodly was rising to his feet, beginning to tower threateningly over Papastamos, and the Old Lidesci was looking astonished and struggling to stand up. But the Greek policeman wasn't alone.

Two of the men who had been with him in Kavála were emerging from the lounge intent on enjoying a smoke on the open deck with their chief. Taking in the scene at a glance, they immediately sprang to flank the bench and one of them produced a gun. In that same moment, seeing that the chance meeting was rapidly turning into a confrontation, Manolis held up his right arm and hand and snapped, "Everyone holding your fire!" And to Liz:

"Young lady, I am Papastamos. Ben Trask may have mentioned my name to you? In which case you will know that I am a friend. Please don't shoot me or do anything to cause me to shoot you!" And then, after waiting a moment to let that sink in: "You must be, er, Liz?"

Still uncertain what was going on, Liz nodded. But Papastamos's mind held no threat, and so she relaxed, breathed easier, and took her hand out of her bag. Manolis grinned and drew back his left hand and weapon into the sling and out of sight. "Very well," he said. "This is much better, don't you agree?" Then he signalled to his man to put his weapon away, glanced all around the deck to ensure that no one had witnessed the brief burst of activity, finally turned to the spindly precog and looked up at him.

"You will be . . . er, Ian Goodly?" And, as the other nodded: "Yes, I see it now. Ben's backup team. It is thee coincidence, that we should meet like this." He turned to Lardis. "And you?"

"This is Lardis Lidesci," Goodly introduced them as finally the old man got to his feet.

"Lardis?" Manolis frowned. "Lidesci? A Romanian, perhaps? I don't think Ben mentioned you."

"That's possible," Lardis grunted. "I'm nobody round here."

"Not true," the precog shook his head. "Lardis is very much a somebody. But he's not Romanian."

"Ah!" Manolis looked at Lardis again. "You E-Branch people: all of you mysterious! You have thee powers, eh?"

Lardis shrugged. "Powers? Not me, not really. I've a seer's blood in me, if that's what you mean—not to mention a spot of rheumatism!—but what I do have is knowledge."

And Liz said, "Lardis's presence here is . . . it's something of a secret. If Ben Trask wants to tell you about him, I'm sure he will."

"You don't trust me yet." Manolis nodded his understanding and grinned a tight grin. "I don't blame you. Me, I don't trust anyone! And where we are going, you shouldn't either."

Looking at him—looking straight into his eyes—Liz said, "Oh, I think we can trust *you* at least, Inspector Manolis Papastamos. Currently based in Athens, you head up a squad of drug-busters. An expert on the Greek islands, you've worked with the Branch before. You have a lot of respect for us, and I know Ben Trask and David Chung hold you in the highest esteem—which is all very well, but—" And here Liz paused and frowned. "*But* . . . you aren't supposed to be involved in all this!" Her frown lifted, and she tilted a knowing eyebrow at him and said, "You're gate-crashing this one, aren't you?"

"Ahhh!" Manolis said, this time with more feeling, as again his jaw fell open. "I know what you have done! But this is thee same as thee poor Zek, or Trevor Jordan. They, too, were—"

"Telepaths, yes," Liz cut him short. "But don't go changing the subject. You were asked to stay out of this, Inspector. You aren't supposed to be here. When I called you a gate-crasher it was because I saw it in your mind: you were wondering how you'd explain what you're doing here to Ben Trask."

The other narrowed his eyes and chewed his lip, and after a moment said, "Well, maybe. But this is Greece, and I'm a Greek. And anyway, my men and I, we'll be of use. We have thee special weapons. But please, I would like that you call me Manolis." He turned again to Goodly.

"So then, Lardis has knowledge . . . he understands thee ways of thee enemy, and Liz reads thee minds. But what about you?"

"I read the future—sometimes," said the precog. And then, as Manolis went to reach in his inside pocket: "For instance, I won't accept the drink you're about to offer me. If anything, I take a shot of scotch, not brandy." And when Manolis produced a flask, "But on the other hand," Goodly continued, "Lardis would very *much* appreciate it!" His smile was warm, contrasting oddly with his gaunt frame and undertaker's pallor.

Manolis's face was full of awe. He shook his head in disbelief, looked at the flask in his hand, and said, "Fantastic!"

Liz glanced at the precog and said, "It seems that credentials are all in order, then?"

And he answered, "Long-term, I see only the most beneficial of mutual collaborations coming out of all this."

"Me, too!" said Lardis, wiping his mouth after a long swig from Manolis's flask. "Exactly what you said!" And then to Manolis: "What *is* this stuff?"

"It's Metaxa," said the other. "A very special brandy. But surely you are familiar with it?"

"There are many things in your world—er, your *country,* I mean—that I'm not yet familiar with," Lardis answered. "But as for this stuff, I certainly intend to be!"

"Ah, you E-Branch people!" said Manolis, shaking his head. "You are amazing!" And then he frowned. "But . . . *you* are Ben's backup team? Just thee three of you?"

"For the time being, yes." Goodly answered. "Ben intends to build up his forces slowly."

"Assuming there's time, of course," said Manolis darkly. In answer to which the precog could only shrug his shoulders.

"Very well, then." Manolis nodded his head decisively. "Now there are six of us. As for Ben: he can argue all he likes, but thee fact remains that I am Greek and Greece is me, and I won't have thee *vrykoulakas* in my islands!" He indicated the hatch to the lounge area. "Let's go inside, drink some iced tea and make thee proper introductions. Krassos is only twenty minutes away; we'll soon be in thee territory of thee enemy."

And twenty minutes later, they were . . .

Krassos town was typical of any Greek island seaport: its deep-water harbour where a hundred yards of mooring fronted the ugly concrete landing concourse, its bollards, capstans, and piles of heavy ropes, its tractor tyres hanging from the jetties, taking the crushing weight of ships that lolled on the oily swell. And behind the various landing stages, the wide, dusty service road that was the town's main artery; and behind that the shops and tavernas, with streets and alleys leading into the shaded heart of Krassos town itself.

Disembarking with their luggage, the E-Branch people and Manolis's contingent noticed a pall of smoke over the eastern district of the town, perhaps a quarter-mile away. One antique fire engine was drawing off sea water at the harbour's eastern extreme, while from some unseen location in the same direction—probably the site of the fire—the high-pitched, *dee-daa, dee-daa* wailing of another fire engine was clearly audible.

Just before disembarking, Manolis had adopted "a disguise"; a false moustache that turned down towards his chin had altered his appearance completely, and the blue-black stubble that he'd been allowing to sprout ever since his "accident" was beginning to hide his facial bruises. Very Greek from the onset, his features might now be described as darkly handsome if not swarthy.

Now, ushering "his" group to one side of the concourse away from the bustle of disembarking passengers and the excited honking of traffic, he asked Goodly, "What's our destination? Where are we meeting up with Ben Trask?"

The precog—who every three hours had been in contact with London by phone—answered, "Ben has arranged for us to stay at the place where he and Chung are accommodated in Skala Astris. That's a little fishing village between—"

"I know it," Manolis stopped him short, and spoke to one of his men in rapid-fire Greek. The man went off to speak to a bus driver in charge of one of the German tour buses. "Andreas will try to get us a lift on thee bus to Limari on thee eastern side of thee island," Manolis explained. "They can drop us off along thee way. A lot less conspicuous than taking a taxi. We'll know in a minute or two, but I think it will be okay. Andreas can be . . . persuasive. And meanwhile, do you see that smoke?" He shook his head worriedly. "If it means what I think it means . . ."

"And what do you think it means?" said Liz.

"We will see as we pass through Krassos," Manolis muttered, and from then on remained silently introspective until Andreas returned.

Andreas had managed to get them a ride on the bus, which in any case was only a little more than half full. When the German tourists had taken their seats, then Manolis and his party were allowed to stow their luggage in compartments under the bus and climb aboard. They found seats in the deserted rear end.

As they got under way, Manolis went up front to have a word with the driver. Returning, he said, "It will be something like an hour, with a few stops, before we're in Skala Astris. Meanwhile—*huh!*—we should 'enjoy thee views.' Well, to be truthful there are many beautiful villages, bays, and beaches on Krassos. Where thee mountains come down to thee sea, there are some very high, winding, and dangerous stretches of road, too! If anybody knows that, I do! Later, if you look out from thee right side of thee bus, you'll think you are floating on thee air! That's after we get out of town, of course. But before then, look over there."

To the left of the main road east out of town, a fire engine was mainly silent now where it pumped water on a blackened, steaming, gutted heap of rubble that might be the remains of a small hotel. "Oh?" said Goodly. "And what are we looking at?"

"Someone is destroying important evidence, I think," said

Manolis, scowling. "That place, it was an ice factory for thee island's hotels, its tavernas and fishmongers. Yes, but it was also thee place I used as cold storage for thee mutilated body of a woman washed up from thee sea. Ah!—but she had a leech in her throat, that one!"

"Was it alive?" said Liz, her eyes wide in morbid fascination. "Did you see it?"

"I saw it," Manolis nodded, and shuddered. "But alive? No, it was dead—thank God! And I burned it."

"Now someone has done the same for her," said Goodly. "But I don't think it was Ben Trask. If it had been, then an incinerator would have sufficed."

Manolis agreed. "No, this has nothing to do with Trask. Or at least I *hope* not, because if it has it means that they know he's here!"

"I shouldn't think so," said the precog. "This is Vavara's work, all right, but she wasn't covering her tracks on Trask's account. She's done this because *you* were here, Manolis—and because she knows you're still alive. A precautionary measure, that's all. But it's her work, certainly, or Lord Nephran Malinari's and the Lady Vavara's together."

"Just call her *Vavaaara*," Lardis growled the name out. "She was no Lady, that one. According to Szgany legends five hundred years old, Vavara scorned all such titles because she knew how false they were. She was Wamphyri, and proud of it. And she was *Vavaaara!* On Sunside she was feared as much as any Lord, and as much by the women as by the men."

Manolis looked at him and frowned, glanced curiously at the precog and Liz, then returned his gaze to Lardis. "What is that you are saying? Legends five hundred years old? And Sunside . . . *thee* Sunside in a world of vampires? Is this what you are meaning when you say you have thee knowledge? But if so, then where does a man come by such knowledge? Thee way I understand it—"

"Manolis," Goodly cut in. "E-Branch keeps its secrets. It's how we survive. Everything on a need-to-know basis. It's as

Liz said before: if Ben Trask wants you to know certain things, you may be sure he'll tell you." And before the other could ask any further questions: "And now *I* have a few things to tell him. . . ."

Krassos town had been left behind; the view outside the bus had opened up into one of dramatic coastal countryside and blue expanses of ocean, the sparkling Aegean on the right and wooded slopes, spurs, and rocky foothills rising to the left. The precog took out a miniature phone, extended a tiny earpiece on its cord and plugged it into his ear, and tapped in Trask's number.

Trask answered almost immediately. "Yes?" His anxious voice was distorted by interference, a lot of unusually heavy static, plus feedback from the vehicle's amplifier system, which issued the occasional announcements of a young German tour hostess.

"A lady and her escorts are on their way," the precog said.

"Good," said the other. "When can I expect you?"

"In a little less than an hour."

"Fine. Is all well?"

Then there was a lot more of the hissing and popping of static before Goodly could answer: "Yes, but . . . we made some new friends along the way. And I believe you and your companion know them. You've, er, holidayed out here in the Med with one of them once before . . ."

There was a long pause before Trask growled, "And just how many of these friends have you picked up along the way?"

"Three," Goodly answered. "They seem very attached to us."

Another long pause, and yet more static, before: "Then perhaps I should arrange some extra accommodation. Anything else?"

"We had to take a bit of a detour," Goodly was careful how he phrased it, "because of a blaze in Krassos town. Apparently some kind of refrigeration plant has burned down. But they just about had it under control by the time we passed. Had you heard about that?"

"It was on the local TV," Trask answered, trying to keep

it light. "That and some other interesting stuff. It's all down to this dreadful heat, I suspect."

"Yes," the precog answered. And with typical British phlegmatism: "There seems to be quite a lot of heat coming down. And a lot more to come, I fancy."

Trask thought about that for a moment or two, then said, "I think we'd better wait and bring each other up to date when you get in. And by the way, how are you travelling?"

"Er, on a bratwurst special?"

"I know where it stops," said Trask. "I can try to meet you there. It wouldn't do to leave you standing around for too long getting all hot and bothered in the midday heat. Best if we get you off the street as soon as possible."

"Couldn't agree more," said the precog. And: "Be seeing you soon, then." He switched off. . .

The main traffic circuit through Krassos town was roughly circular. Vehicles from the east swept around the back of the town, swung south and then east onto the port's service road and past the harbour, and so on out of town. Thus as the E-Branch party, including Manolis Papastamos and his men, had left the seafront in the bus for Limari, they had failed to notice the black limo that came gliding along the promenade behind them and parked in a lot west of the concourse. And more importantly, the two nuns in Vavara's limo had failed to notice them.

Had their tracks crossed, however, Manolis would definitely have noticed. For this limo was a car he would remember for the rest of his life.

The nuns were only a few minutes late, but that was enough. A minor traffic accident had blocked the ring road north of the town, and so they'd been held up, which had caused them to miss the arrival of *The Krassos*. There would be, however, three more ferries from the mainland during the afternoon and evening, and the nuns had their instructions: to keep covert surveillance in the town's harbour area, to watch for the arrival of any odd or suspicious-seeming strangers, and to report regularly to Vavara at the monastery east of Skala

Astris. While their "mother superior" had made light of Malinari's warnings to his face, still she wasn't fool enough to ignore them completely.

As for today, however, the nuns where they sat in the shade of a taverna's awnings directly opposite the deep-water harbour—sat there cowled, pale and silent, with their faces muffled, and their hagridden eyes hidden behind dark sunglasses—would have nothing to report . . .

Just before 1:00 P.M. local, Trask was there to meet his reinforcements on the main road through Skala Astris. There was no time for anything other than perfunctory greetings as he helped with their luggage and ushered them down a narrow, shaded alley toward wrought-iron gates that opened into a large and pleasant garden of flowering hibiscus, pomegranate, and fig trees.

A sign on the gates had named the place as Christos Studios, and the studios in question were pantile-roofed chalets, hidden away between the trees in a roughly circular pattern, each with its own pathway and outdoor patio area. The lavish use of varnished Mediterranean pine against recently whitewashed walls and blue painted window shutters and door panels gave these accommodations a very ethnic, welcoming look, and south of the garden a low wall formed a secondary horizon to that of the sea.

Beyond the wall, a hanging sign over the empty doorway of a bamboo- and raffia-roofed bar said, THE SHIPWRECK, which suited the place perfectly since its design gave it the look of having been washed up on the beach. From within, the sandpapered voice of Louis Armstrong sounded on an ancient vinyl rendition of "We Have All the Time in the World," complete with all the jumps and scratches of ten thousand replays.

"This place is perfect," said Liz, as Trask took her to the door of her chalet. And then, on second thought, "Or rather, it would be if we were here simply to enjoy it. The sun, the sand, and the sea. Perfect, yes." And she went inside to unpack.

But as Trask walked Goodly and Lardis to another door, well out of Liz's hearing, the precog glanced at him and said, "What was that she said? The three esses, sun, sand, and sea? But she missed out the most important *S* of all."

"And what would that be?" Trask asked him.

"The screaming," said Goodly, with a curt nod. "For I think there'll be quite a bit of that, too."

"You've seen it?" Trask gripped his elbow.

"Something of it," the precog answered. "In my dreams, last night at the hotel where we stayed in Keramoti. Of course, it's possible they were *just* dreams—which would be natural enough in the circumstances—but I've kept them to myself because of Liz."

"First get yourselves sorted out inside," said Trask. "Then we'll talk about it. Let's meet in say, fifteen minutes? In The Shipwreck there."

"Fine," said Goodly. And he and Lardis entered their chalet with their luggage.

Then it was Manolis Papastamos's turn. He and his men had a slightly larger chalet, accommodation for all three, into which they tossed their bags with scarcely a glance inside. And again Trask said, "Fifteen minutes to unpack your stuff and settle in, and then a get-together and briefing in The Shipwreck."

But his tone of voice had echoed his displeasure, and as he went to turn away, Manolis took his arm. "My friend," the Greek policeman began, then checked himself and added: "I take it you are still my friend?"

Trask looked at him, his moustache and stubble, the genuine anxiety in his eyes, and couldn't help but grin, however wryly. "Always," he said. And then he replaced his smile with a frown. "But still you're a stubborn, pigheaded man. I wanted to keep you out of this—for your own good."

"But why?" Manolis threw up his good right hand in protest. "Because this . . . this *vrykoulakas* bitch knows me? I've thought about that, too. Just exactly *how* does this creature know me? I mean, where could she have seen me? *Has* she actually seen me—or is her dirty work performed by her minions?"

"Minions?" Trask stared at him.

"But don't you remember?" (It was Manolis's turn to frown.) "On Ródhos, Halki, Kárpathos—that Janos Ferenczy business? He had his thralls, his watchers and spies; he even recruited some of your people—thee poor Ken Layard and Trevor Jordan! So why not this Vavara? Ben, if I have to I'll leave both of thee big fishes to you and your people, but whoever it was pushed me off that cliff and killed Eleni Babouris: they're mine! Now believe me, my men and I, we'll do whatever you say. And you'll be glad of our help."

"Actually," Trask answered, "I can probably use you. You're not nearly as badly banged about as I thought you were—or if you are, you're good at hiding it. That Fu Manchu moustache and the facial growth hides just about everything! As for your men: they'll do well enough from what I've seen of them, and they'll benefit from not being known by anyone, not even me! But that's all right, introductions can wait until the briefing in fifteen minutes. Okay?"

"Okay," said Manolis. "But just one thing: Where's Chung?"

"He's in the administration building through the trees over there," Trask pointed. "He's on the phone, exchanging situation reports with our HQ in London. By the way, Chung and I have the chalet next door to Liz's should you need to know anything."

And Manolis nodded. "See you in Thee Shipwreck," he said, as Trask went back the way they had come . . .

The Shipwreck wasn't nearly the wreck it appeared from outside. Within, its spacious floor was crazy-paved with polished marble, and it was level throughout—a rare thing on *any* Greek island, where it's usually impossible to find a table that doesn't tilt at least a little to one side. Under the cleverly arranged raffia and bamboo "camouflage" of the roof, there was a varnished pine ceiling where fishing nets festooned the high corners like vast cobwebs. Mediterranean conchs and fan shells decorated the nets, and some of these were wired to an electrical circuit and fitted internally with small tinted light bulbs. Of an evening, the subdued and intermittent glowing of the shells would add an almost submarine effect to the bar's ambiance.

A row of sturdy bar stools stood empty at the well-stocked, pine-topped bar itself, while comfortable wicker armchairs were evenly spaced around its glass-topped, bamboo tables. The walls were painted with Aegean murals.

Thus the Christos Studios setup in its entirety—with its secluded, shaded accommodations, and The Shipwreck in its beachfront location—made for a very pleasant and satisfactory base of operations. So thought Trask as he and his esper colleagues rearranged the seating, moved three tables closer together, and sat down. The only absentee was Chung, who was still busy on the phone.

It was *very* pleasant, yes, Trask thought—in which respect Liz Merrick's observation that the place was "perfect" had been acceptable and accurate . . .

. . . But then again, so were Ian Goodly's presentient dreams accurate—probably. For Trask had a great deal of faith in the precog's "wild talent," and with every good reason. But however it worked out, there was a lot more to E-Branch being here than the sun, the sand, and the sea. This definitely *wasn't* going to be any kind of beach party.

"Ah, civilisation!" said Manolis, as he and his two entered the bar precisely on time.

As Trask had noted, Manolis's men looked very capable. The one who was built like a battering ram—short in the legs but broad-shouldered, and with a chest like a barrel—was Andreas. He had close-cropped hair on a bullet head, a wicked smile with more than a hint of menace behind it, and eyes blue as the sea. His father was Greek but his mother had been an American; she'd died when Andreas was a child, since when he'd lived in Athens.

Andreas's colleague, Stavros, was a few years his junior at perhaps twenty-seven years of age. He was as Greek as they come and had shining black hair, brown eyes, and an athletic, almost Olympian figure. Liz found that she couldn't help comparing him with Jake Cutter. It wasn't his face (his too-straight nose and very Mediterranean looks put paid to that), so maybe it was the way he fitted his jeans. The silhouette was . . . reminiscent, to say the least. Or perhaps it was simply that Jake was constantly in her thoughts.

Close behind Manolis and his pair as they entered the bar, a man who was a stranger to all but Trask followed them in. He was a handsome, angular young Greek, who introduced himself as the proprietor's son. "I'm Yiannis and I run the bar," he told his guests in perfect English. "When I'm not here my wife will be. Katerina is currently taking her siesta but she'll be here tonight." And then, turning to Manolis, he said, "But what you said about 'civilisation' . . . no." And still smiling, he shook his head. "Not The Shipwreck. Not my place."

"No?" Manolis looked surprised.

Yiannis pointed out through a window in the shape of a porthole—pointed east along the sea wall to where Skala Astris's hotels, shops, and tavernas made an untidy huddle that somehow marred the tranquility of the view—and said again, "No, *that* is civilisation! I remember when I was a boy and there was just a beach. But civilisation? It doesn't come galloping down on us quite so fast these days, now that tourism is dying off, but if it ever starts up again . . . that's when I'll move The Shipwreck a little farther down the beach. I can't say if it's a blessing or a curse. I am making a living off the slow death of my home, my island. But I like to think the disease is not incurable and that it will stabilize eventually."

"I see what you mean," said Manolis. "Then take what I said as a compliment. You have a most, er, agreeable place here."

Yiannis gave a little bow and went behind the bar. "And you may take this as a compliment," he said. "The compliments of my bar, customary when new guests come to Christos Studios. Please allow me to take your orders and serve drinks on the house."

"Bravo!" said Lardis at once, beaming his pleasure. "Metaxa for me, if you please." His promise to familiarize himself with that drink was now well on course to being kept.

The rest of the E-Branch people took cooling fruit drinks; Manolis and his men ordered ouzo on the rocks in tall, frosted glasses. After serving the drinks, Yiannis excused himself and left his guests to their own devices. People were due to check out and he had duties to perform; he would return shortly.

Then Trask got down to it. "The place is just about empty," he said. "Which suits our purpose ideally. There's a handful of Germans staying in the other studios. Most of them have hired a car or cars, and Yiannis tells me they're usually out from dawn till dusk; there are better resorts and beaches on Krassos than this one, and that's where they'll be. Which means we're fairly private here.

"As for Yiannis: from what I can gather, he's a bit down in the mouth because business has been very bad this year. You can blame this weird El Niño weather for that. Other than that he's a pronounced Anglophile and will see to all our needs.

"Chung and I have been here since last night, and we've had time to do some thinking and planning. We've picked up a couple of maps—enough for everyone—that are far more detailed than the one you gave us, Manolis. They're not quite Ordnance Survey standard, but they're pretty good." He handed out folded maps.

"Manolis, you'll need to guide your men through this. It's probably better that you do it later, for I don't know how long Yiannis will leave us on our own.

"Okay, we all know what this initial phase of the operation must be: to find Malinari and Vavara in their dens without them finding us, and to discover how far their vampire contamination has spread. Once we know that it might be possible to call down some firepower on them. I say 'might' because we don't have the same degree of cooperation here as we had in Australia. Indeed, if the Greek authorities knew what we're doing here they'd most likely kick us out! The last thing they need to hear—and the last thing we dare *let* them or anyone else hear—is that there are vampires on the loose in the Greek islands! That is, not if we want to retain some kind of sanity in the world.

"Very well, now open up your maps. This is Krassos. Densely wooded mountains built of the world's finest marbles, farms and fishing villages, sparse foothills that climb to rearing cliffs and ledges fit only for goats, rocky bays, shallow harbors, and sandy beaches. Idyllic in its prime and an island paradise, now it poses a threat far worse than tourism and Yiannis's 'civilisation,' creatures who would take it over—and the rest of the world with it—just as insidiously, but far more terribly and totally.

"So where, when, and how are we to look for our enemies?

"Well, the rules aren't as simple as they may seem. Nor is the territory. We have here some three hundred square miles of island, composed as previously described, and Vavara and Malinari could be quite literally anywhere within its borders.

"Here's what I want done with immediate effect." He turned again to Manolis. "Get in contact with the island's authorities and see if you can find out if anyone has been reported missing and where from. I think that—"

"Wait!" Manolis stopped him. "I checked this out when I was here dealing with thee woman with thee leech. There are no missing locals, tourists, nothing. And thee island is far too small a place for thee peoples to go absent without being noticed."

For a moment Trask was silent, but then he nodded and said, "And so you've proved your point: that your presence isn't only of use to us but probably indispensable. For that's one line of inquiry closed, saving time that we would certainly have wasted . . . for which my thanks. But it does leave a major question unanswered. If Vavara has been here for the better part of three years, then what—or who—has she been living on?"

And Ian Goodly put in, "We know that these creatures aren't *required* to take blood—it isn't an absolute necessity—but it is an inescapable fact that they do enjoy taking it. As they are wont to say: 'The blood is the life.' It keeps them strong, and over a long period of time they would surely weaken without it. Also, I simply can't imagine them denying their leeches. So perhaps what we're looking for—"

And again Manolis jumped in, "Is a small village or community of say one hundred or less peoples, all of whom have fallen under thee bitch-vampire's spell. And my friends, let me assure you that there are several such villages on this island! For I, too, have given thee problem some thought, and now *I* ask you to look at your maps."

His finger stabbed at his map, which lay unfolded on one of the tables. "Here in thee Ypsarion Oros mountains, thee village Panagia, whose men quarry thee local marble. Population, a mere seventy, according to thee legend. And here at Theologos, fifty diggers at an archaeological site predating thee Roman occupation. Also thee mountain resort at Kastro, where people bathe in thee hot spring to cure their aches and pains. Permanent staff: seventeen. Vavara could be in any of these places, and in twice as many others just like them."

"Chung and I had come to more or less the same conclusion," Trask nodded. "Even in the more densely populated towns, still the numbers only run to a few thousand. Not only does everyone know everyone else, but also his business! If Vavara was there—what, this strange, beautiful, foreign woman who is only ever seen at night?—she'd be taking a big chance. So we're agreed on that point: it would seem most likely that she has inveigled her way into a closed or remote, probably mountainous community and gradually taken it over. That way she's had no need to kill any of her recently recruited thralls, who are simply there to, er, *supply* her loathsome needs. *Ughhh!*"

"Then we're decided on how to start," said Goodly. "We must visit these places—in full daylight, of course—and see if we can detect anything out of the ordinary."

"We have to visit *all* such places," Trask nodded. "Not

only the ones Manolis has pointed out, but every other location that might fit Vavara's requirements. And we have to be very careful how we go about it. Until our backup forces arrive from London we're only eight strong, and I'm not going to be calling anyone else in on this until we have definite targets. So I suggest we split up into three teams."

"What about vehicles?" said Liz.

"Chung and I have already hired a car," Trask told her. "We need two more. And Manolis, you and your men need some suitable clothing—touristy stuff, you know?—to put a finishing touch to your disguise. Can your men handle that?"

"No problem," said Manolis. "They can even do it now, while we talk. I noticed a sign where we got off thee bus, a car hire firm in Skala Astris." Giving Andreas and Stavros instructions, he sent them off into the village. It took but a moment.

"Teams, then," said Trask. "But I want to keep our talented members split up as much as possible."

"Talented?" Manolis raised a querying eyebrow, then snapped his fingers and said, "Ah, yes—of course! Thee locator, thee telepath, and thee, er—?"

"Precog," said Goodly.

"*And* the one who knows things," Lardis tapped his nose.

"No," Trask told him. "It's not you I'm concerned about. If these bastard things weren't able to track you down at night, I fail to see how they'll detect you here in broad daylight!"

He turned to the others. "But out there on the road when we go looking for them, I don't want you clustering your minds too close together. Liz, you have to keep a tight rein on your telepathy. Malinari has been into your mind once and I've no doubt he could do it again. Chung's talent is similar: it reaches out from him to locate things, and might itself be located." And to Goodly: "Ian, I'm not too concerned about you; your thing comes and goes, true, but as far as we can tell it has never betrayed you. While the future is a devious thing which will try to hide itself even from you, it's yet more elusive where others are concerned. In short, your talent isn't detectable—thank goodness for small mercies! The same goes for me. But we *are* espers all, and for all we know Malinari, or Vavara, for that matter, could be spotters: creatures who may recognize the psychic signatures of people like us. If that's true, then Liz and David Chung are especially at risk, and we must keep them apart. So here's what I suggest:

"The teams will be made up as follows. Manolis, Lardis, and Liz; David Chung and Stavros; Ian Goodly, Andreas, and myself." He waited for comments and there were none. "One team, still to be decided, will concentrate on local information-gathering and act as odd-jobbers . . . there are bound to be some odd jobs that have to be done. The other teams will split up, one going east, and the other west around Krassos. The roads are mainly coastal with lesser tracks and trails leading off into the mountains. Manolis, I hope your men choose four-wheel-drive vehicles, as I did!"

"I'm sure they will," said Manolis.

"But all this is for tomorrow," Trask continued, "and we'll use the remainder of today to settle in, rest up, acquaint ourselves with these maps, the topography, the local who's-who and know-how—including any relevant items of gossip, of course—and so on and so forth . . ."

As he finished speaking, the locator, David Chung, appeared in The Shipwreck's shady doorway.

"As for local knowledge," he said, "—or gossip if you like—I've just this minute overheard Yiannis chatting with a pair of departing Germans in the lobby of the admin building. "Seems there was a fatal accident the night before last, and the circumstances are just a bit suspicious. As for news from London—well, that's suspicious, too." He entered, flopped into a chair, wiped his forehead and said, "Phew, this heat!"

"What kept you?" said Trask.

"Would you believe sunspots?" the locator answered, shaking his head in disgust. "It would appear that communications worldwide are going haywire. Pocket telephones are out of the question. They've always had their problems, as we know, but now . . . anything more than twenty miles, all you get is static. It's all come on very sudden, apparently. It took a while to get through on the regular telephone in the lobby, and then I had to decode John Grieve's double-talk. What he told me isn't reassuring."

"Go on," said Trask worriedly.

"Jimmy Harvey found a device in the restaurant downstairs," Chung said. "A bug—low-powered and short-range—it couldn't possibly transmit outside the four walls of the hotel. So Jimmy checked with reception to see if it was an inside job. The only likely candidate was some French bloke who'd checked in shortly after we got back from down under. The register has him down as one Alfonso Lefranc, and HQ's first thought was that it must be an alias. So, they checked it out with Interpol and . . . what do you know! Lo and behold, the guy's a nark for Luigi Castellano! Then our lot did a check with the airlines, and as far as they can tell Lefranc is still is town. They're out looking for him now. And that's only that one . . ."

Trask's head whirled. Castellano? Jake's hang-up? What the hell was going on here? But he logged the information and said, "What else?"

"A scrambled message has come in from Gustav Turchin," the locator answered. "He thinks that by now his man must have infiltrated Castellano's organization. He says he's got a lot of faith in this person, and fully anticipates that he'll soon be able to tell us just precisely where this Sicilian scumbag is. After that it's up to us. But he's anxious that we begin looking into his personal problem back home . . . presumably meaning Russia, or more specifically Perchorsk."

"Yes, it does," said Trask. "And is that it?"

"No," said Chung, squirming a little in his chair. "There's one more item, and you're not going to like it."

"I haven't liked anything yet!" said Trask.

"You'll like this even less," Chung said, "but it may teach us a lesson. If only we'd learned to stick with our ghosts; but no, we mess with our gadgets, too. The trouble with them is the more we use them the more we rely upon them; we let them do our figuring for us—even when common sense is shoving the answers right up our silly noses! Okay, someone at HQ was playing about with the extraps, and it seems they punched in the right question . . . or, depending how you view it, the wrong one."

"Go on. What was the question?"

"Well, not really a question," Chung said, "but a scenario, or a simultaneous equation, certainly. You know how it works."

"Pretend I don't," Trask answered, "and get on with it!"

"I . . . I just want you to stay calm," said Chung. And then, without further pause, "Very well, the equation was this: Bruce Trennier equals Australia equals Malinari the Mind. Denise Karalambos equals Greece equals Vavara. And therefore Andre Corner equals England . . . equals . . . ?"

Trask gave a start and sat bolt upright in his chair. *"Good God almighty!"* he said. And then, hoarsely: "How could we be so blind? Malinari took Bruce Trennier for his lieutenant because Trennier knew Australia."

And Goodly came in with, "Vavara took Denise Karalambos for her knowledge of Greece or the Greek islands, namely this Greek island."

Which left Liz to finish it with, "Szwart took Andre Corner—a psychiatrist, formerly of Harley Street—for his knowledge of . . . *of London*!"

Only Manolis, who wasn't in possession of all the minutiae, failed to appreciate the situation. But he knew it was serious when Trask bounded from his chair and almost upset the tables.

"Millie!" he croaked, his face more gaunt than ever. "God, I have to get onto London right now! I have to talk to Millie!"

Chung was on his feet, too, and quickly said, "I knew you would. So I made arrangements that they'd call us back in just fifteen minutes. If you'll just slow down and take it easy, by the time you get over to the lobby—"

But Trask was already on his way.

Liz followed after him; Lardis, too, because his Lissa was

at E-Branch HQ, but Chung and Goodly stayed behind to explain the situation as best they could to Manolis. It didn't take too long, and when they were through Manolis nodded and said, "Ben, he still has thee poor Zek on his mind. And now this. Thee new lady in his life could be in danger."

"Exactly," said Chung. "Someone's tried to bug the HQ and we don't know how much they got, and it's possible that Szwart, who or whatever he is, is in London. And one of the last things Ben did before we left was to warn everyone of the possibility that the Wamphyri—"

"That they might try to make thee preemptive strike, yes," said Manolis.

Then, toying with drinks diluted by melted ice water, the three sat silently, lost in their own thoughts, and waited for Trask and the others to return . . .

In the mazelike cellars of Luigi Castellano's Bagheria villa, Castellano and his man—or his familiar creature, his thrall, Garzia Nicosia—stood in a musty, cobwebbed room with a low, vaulted ceiling, and spoke in voices that reverberated eerily from wall to wall, echoed out into the labyrinth of subterranean rooms and corridors, and returned as sighing whispers.

The room was carved from the bedrock, and regularly spaced columns supported the claustrophobic ceiling. In nitre-streaked walls, two-foot-square niches had been cut three feet deep around an oblong circumference of about 180 feet, each of which—more than two hundred of them—contained ancient, crumbling remains. In addition, however, many niches contained remnants that weren't nearly so old, which had been stuffed in among the collapsed wood of coffins and the mouldering rags and skeletons of the rightful occupants.

"The burial chamber of the Argucci family," said Castellano, his face ruddily lit by a flaring faggot held aloft in Garzia's hand. "They were a large family, and for two hundred years when they owned the ground above and all the many acres around, they incarcerated their dead in this vault.

A great family, yes, who planned to *remain* a family, and keep themselves together as one unit even in death. These vaults—or cellars as they are now—were hewn accordingly.

"But various disasters followed, feuds, many trials and few tribulations. Their fortunes waned; the Arguccis were split up; they travelled abroad into Italy and farther afield. The estate was sold off and became an olive grove, and when that failed I, Luigi Francezci, called Castellano, bought it up.

"As for a detailed history of the Arguccis—a progressive family tree—it's written on bronze plates over each of those niches there, under all of that powdered coffin wood, grime and spider debris . . .

"Ah, but prior to selling the old place off, and determined that his forebears should never be moved or disturbed, the last of the Arguccis fashioned the ingenious doorway to this burial chamber. And back in a time when the estate was the centre of a small but flourishing olive-oil empire—long before you and I came here, Garzia—the enterprising proprietor discovered it, probably by accident.

"Well, good for him, and good for us. For since he is long gone now, we're the only ones who know of it."

Castellano glanced at a wooden table where piles of ancient ledgers, notebooks, and manuscripts were long fallen into decay. And sitting on a rickety chair, he went on. "Enterprising, yes, this old olive-oil baron. He kept his 'regular' accounts in the house upstairs, but the true measure of his profits was stashed away down here!

"Well, give him his due—he may have been less than honest when it came to fiddling the books and declaring his taxes, but he never once disturbed these dead and mummied Arguccis."

Garzia swept his torch lower, until the niches in the walls came alive with dancing shadows, jumbled old bones, and yawning skulls; skulls that seemed to protest, albeit silently, through jaws fused in rictal shrieks. And:

"Indeed," Garzia agreed. "It appears he desecrated nothing, that olive-oily old man, but left all such to us!"

"The perfect retreat," said Castellano. "Spacious overhead,

and secret places underground. It's almost a fortress—walled and well-protected—with our men in the grounds and, as a last resort, ourselves: stronger than other men and less inclined to injury and pain. I've often wondered just exactly what it would take to kill one such as you or me . . . but I'm not ready to find out just yet."

"Perhaps later," Garzia said, "when the men we've infected have had time to stabilize? For then they'll be vampires, too."

"Well, perhaps," Castellano considered it. "For I would be interested to find out, certainly. To know how much punishment creatures such as ourselves can take before giving up our ghosts. But for now . . . let's get done with this." He stood up.

On the dusty floor between them lay the naked, drained, and mutilated body of the Russian double agent, Georgi Grusev, with his jaws wide open in much the same fashion as many of the mummified figures in the walls. Having hung by his heels in Garzia's torture chamber overnight and all through the day, rigor mortis had locked Grusev's jaws in that position; likewise the unholy, inverted cross of his outspread arms. Garzia had taken care of that—by breaking the arms at the shoulders and folding them down.

Now the vampires took up the body, Castellano at the head, and Garzia at the feet, and without pause fed it headfirst into the nearest niche. As it went the crumbling bones of some elder Argucci, entombed two hundred years before, fell into dust and gave it passage. And the silent screams seemed louder yet, but Castellano and Garzia didn't hear them.

Then, as the nightmare pair dusted themselves down and left the burial chamber, Garzia looked back in satisfaction. Several dozen pairs of feet—none of them Arguccis, but all with their flesh in various stages of decay or completely sloughed away—protruded from their niches like Georgi Grusev's . . . except his were firm as yet, however cold, and their toes pointed upwards.

And as that secret door swung shut on its hoard of violated

dead, becoming a solid stone wall once more, the monster Garzia paused to scuff out certain telltale marks on the floor—twin tracks where Grusev's heels had dragged in the dust—and then extinguished his torch and followed the darkly flowing shape of his master as Castellano led on . . .

14
The Sun, The Sand, The Sea—and The Screaming?

BEN TRASK WAS MOMENTARILY ABSENT, BUSY on the phone talking to London. But after he had been gone for only a few minutes, his second-in-command, the precog Ian Goodly, had begun to fill in for him. Always aware of the future's relentless encroachment, Goodly had rarely been known to waste time.

"Manolis, I recall your saying something about weapons," he began. "It was while we were on the ferry. You told Liz you had special weapons. Now what was all that about?"

"Ah!" said Manolis. "But Ian, you weren't in on thee Janos Ferenczy affair, were you? We learned a few things that time."

"I know," said the other. "Those files are required reading for everyone in E-Branch. But all of that was twenty-five or so years ago. What does it have to do with the here and now? Apart from the fact that we're back in the Greek islands, that is."

"What weapons have you brought with you?" Manolis answered the precog's question with one of his own.

"Standard E-Branch stuff," Goodly shrugged. "Basically nine-millimeter Brownings with a few special adaptations. We've had three years to develop them. Silver-tipped bullets, mainly. And now there's a new one that shatters and releases a quantity of concentrated oil of garlic into the target."

"They let you through customs with this stuff?" Manolis was surprised, but only momentarily.

"We're E-Branch," said the precog. "The weapons were inside a diplomatic bag. No problem at our end, in London. And at this end—"

"You're tourists," Manolis nodded. "No one checks tourists. Not when they're coming *into* Greece. Tourists are money. These days, we only check for terrorism and drugs."

"That's right," said Goodly. "And Liz tells me that ten or more years ago she was a frequent visitor. She would come over with her parents, as tourists. They were never once checked."

Manolis could only shrug, perhaps apologetically. "Er, thee Greek peoples are too trusting," he said. "Maybe. Or let's just say that we have fewer red-tape restrictions, eh?"

"Anyway, that's our weapons dealt with," said Goodly. "Now tell me about yours."

Manolis turned to David Chung. "You, my friend—my very good, my very old friend—you were there, and you understand, I'm sure."

The locator reached into a pocket of his lightweight jacket and slid a pair of single-headed spearheads of the type used in spearfishing onto the table. Hinged inch-long barbs flew open as they slithered to a halt, and the spearheads gleamed a dull silver where they lay. The metal was very slightly tarnished—or more properly tinted—with the bluish bloom of old coins.

"Silver plated," said Chung. "I've had them all this time. The first chance I get, I'll be buying the very best speargun I can find."

"Exactly!" Manolis exclaimed, picking up one of the spearheads. "Thee other policeman who was with me in Kavála, I sent him back to Athens. He will go to my house—a certain drawer in my study—and mail me a parcel containing just such items. Meanwhile I, too, shall buy a speargun, and others for my men. We are in thee Krassos, a Greek island, and even thee children do thee spearfishing. Except with our guns, we will be looking for thee bigger fish, eh?" He looked at Goodly.

"I see," said the precog. "Not only silver but also stakes, of a sort . . . the sort that can't easily be pulled out!"

"I have three spearheads," said Manolis. "With David's two, that makes five. We will need five guns. And I know thee best, thee most powerful kind, to buy."

"We also have concentrated oil of garlic," Goodly told him. "Not so much a weapon as a protection. It does sicken them, of course, and when injected can seriously incapacitate and kill. But in order to do that without a gun . . . you have to get much too close."

"And that's our arsenal," Chung shook his head. "Not a hell of a lot. As for doing any *serious* damage, any kind of scorched-earth, or rather ground-clearing policy that might be required; well, Ben Trask has already explained why we can't expect much help."

"Not from thee authorities, no," said Manolis, "but *I* might have a few ideas. We'll talk about it later—here comes Ben and thee others now."

Trask was calmer now, also Lardis, but Liz was looking very concerned, as she had been ever since leaving E-Branch HQ. She had managed to get a minute or two on the phone after Trask was through, and had enquired after Jake Cutter. But HQ had heard nothing from him, and they had more to do right now than worry about Jake.

All three sat down, and Trask said, "I've given HQ their orders. They're to tighten their security wherever possible and remain on station. That is, they're all to move into the hotel, into HQ accommodation. They're pulling in staff from the various foreign embassies, cutting back on police work, keeping on their toes. But despite all that, still we're over-stretched. We have a team down under, making sure we didn't overlook anything during our 'visit' down there. We have other people out looking for Luigi Castellano's spy, this Alfonso Lefranc. And of course we have our terrorist squad on full alert, as always. The techs are having huge problems with all of this sunspot activity, and their gadgets aren't worth shit right now. And the temperature isn't letting up a damn, which means everyone's feeling drained. So much for my calling for backup! If we strike lucky out here, then obviously I'll have to find some extra help from somewhere. But until then—" Trask shrugged, looked from face to face, and finished off with, "We'll just have to manage as best we can."

"Well," said Goodly, "you did say you'd build us up slowly. Nothing's changed, really—except that we now know we may have some problems back home. So, since there's nothing else for it, I say we leave it at that and get on with what we came out here to do."

"That's the commonsense solution, yes," Trask agreed. "And it's the *only* solution. Except—"

"Except now we'll not only be worried for each other," said Lardis, "but for our loved ones, too. In my case those at home, my real home, and also the one . . . in my new home.

Trask looked at him and offered a grim nod. "Ironic the way things work out, isn't it? Nathan brought you out of Sunside to keep you out of danger, and in the last month or so you've been up to your neck in it!"

"And don't you try to keep me *out* of it!" Lardis scowled.

But Manolis sat up straight in his chair and said, "Ah! And *now* I am sure! Piece by piece I have put it together, and now I see it all. Thee only possible explanation—how any man could live so long without having discovered Metaxa!"

It lightened the atmosphere at once, and Liz was unable to resist reaching out to touch Manolis's mind. His wink confirmed what she'd suspected, that his seemingly untimely joke had been intended to do just that—to lighten the atmosphere, which had been far too serious. Likewise Trask and the others; they'd all needed to ease up, smile, relax a little. And Manolis had shown them the way.

"*Huh!*" the Old Lidesci grunted, then grinned a wicked grin. "But talking about Metaxa, where's that Yiannis got to?"

And Liz, determined now to throw off all of her anxieties, said, "Manolis, I hold you personally responsible, in that you may have created a monster!"

And Trask said, "Lardis, promise me you'll go easy on that stuff? We still have a job to do."

For precisely on cue Yiannis had come back, and Trask let his people order a second round of drinks to take to Manolis's accommodation, where he would begin to detail their individual tasks in private. Then, as they left The Shipwreck, he smiled however wryly, shrugged, and said, "What the heck . . . why not? Let's eat, drink, and be merry, for tomorrow . . . ?"

Pausing, he held back a little, took Ian Goodly's arm and steered him out of earshot of the rest, and quietly asked him, "So how about it? How about tomorrow?"

But the precog could only sigh in his funereal fashion and answer, "For the moment, it's as much a mystery to me as it is to you, Ben. Eat, drink, and be merry, for tomorrow we die? Is that what you're saying—or asking?" Then, when Trask made no answer, he sighed again, shook his head and said, "No, I don't think so. Not tomorrow, anyway."

A little over an hour later, Andreas and Stavros returned with two four-wheel-drive cars. They were no sooner in than Manolis sent them out again, this time to buy some "suitable" clothing and to find—if such existed in the huddle of Skala Astris—a hardware store that stocked spearguns. Meanwhile, he'd been on the phone to a local police office about the rumoured fatal accident, and also to his office in Athens, checking to see if there had been any breakthrough in tracking down Jethro Manchester's Greek "charity." About the latter:

"No," he told Trask, after sending his subordinates off on their latest mission. "This is real *money* we are talking about. Thee only man with thee authority to release such informations is thee Governor of the Bank of Greece. He's away and won't be back till Monday, and his deputy is a coward who cannot accept thee responsibility! Anyway, today is Saturday and thee banks are officially closed now."

Trask nodded. "Stalled again," he said. "The answer has to be right there in some bloody bank's computer, and I can't get at it because someone is away and it's the weekend. Also, what with this weather and all, I couldn't even have my chief tech, a man called Jimmy Harvey, hack into it if I wanted to, and *if* he knew which computer it was, because the gadgets at HQ are all acting up. It's a hellish frustrating business, Manolis."

Trask was sitting inside the shade provided by the raffia awning over The Shipwreck's entrance, watching David Chung and Liz fooling about in the warm, shallow water at the rim of the sea. Close by, keeping an eye on the pair, the Old Lidesci was seated on a slab of rock with his jeans rolled up and his feet dangling in the water. As for Ian Goodly: he was taking a nap, perhaps hoping to do a little precognitive dreaming.

"They are having thee good time, eh?" said Manolis, indicating the people on the beach.

"Yes, but don't be mistaken," Trask told him. "When there's work to be done, they'll do it. As for what's left of today . . . it's too late to do very much else. This late in the season, an hour or two more, and the sun will be setting. Then we'll split up into two or three parties, have our evening meal at a decent taverna, get a good night's sleep, and an early start tomorrow." He looked down across the beach. "From then on we're likely to be pretty busy, so my lot may as well get some enjoyment out of all this while they can."

"I am agreeing," Manolis answered. "But personally, I have one more thing to do before tonight."

"Oh?" Trask looked up at him.

Manolis nodded. "When my men return with thee colourful T-shirts and thee shorts, I shall have one of them drive me up to a village in thee foothills. This unfortunate, 'suspicious accident' that David mentioned? Well, thee burned body of a young man is lying in a coffin on a table in his poor mother's house up there in thee hills, and I want to see it."

Trask stood up and said, "You think that maybe—?"

Manolis gave a noncommittal shrug. "I don't know. But after what happened to me on this Krassos, I have a problem with thee word 'accident.' I was in a car and barely survived. This other one was riding a motorcycle . . . and didn't."

"Take Lardis with you," Trask nodded. "If there's anything to be known about the victims of vampirism, he knows it. And if this wasn't just an accident, he might well know that, too."

"His special knowledge?"

"Manolis," said Trask, "one way or the other, that old man has killed more bloody vampires than you and I and E-Branch put together! Just take my word for it."

"Oh, I do," said the other. "I have seen his machete, and I have counted thee notches in its grip."

"Exactly," said Trask. "And one other thing before you go. By all means let this man's mother know that you're a policeman—I suppose you will have to do that—but don't give her your real name, and don't let her think that your investigations are in any way extraordinary. I don't want any rumours getting back to our enemies."

"Ah, Ben, Ben!" said the other. "But you're forgetting that I *am* thee policeman, and that when necessary I can be thee fox, too. Have a little faith in me, yes?"

And waving to attract Lardis's attention, he set off across the narrow strip of beach to speak to him. . .

Manolis and Lardis were late getting back. The sun had set and a dusky evening was coming down when Stavros drove them back in through the gates of the Christos Studios.

Then the party of eight split into three smaller groups and headed for the lights of the nearest taverna along a dirt track that paralleled the seafront. Since as yet there was little or no letup in the temperature, and no reason to hurry, they took it easy, assumed a casual "holiday" attitude, talked in lowered tones, and kept well within view of each other.

A handful of holidaymakers were out and about, on their way to or returning from their evening meals; young Germans walking hand in hand in the smoky evening air, along with a few English couples, their heads were paired off in silhouettes against the darkening amethyst horizon, merging when they paused to whisper their lovers' secrets. For a Greek island is a Greek island.

That at least was as it should be . . .

Feeling the heat—and only now beginning to feel the sunlight she'd absorbed radiating from her—Liz had changed into a light summer dress and sandals. Trask and his men had dressed in short-sleeved shirts and shorts, but Manolis and his two had chosen to wear lightweight trousers. As Manolis had explained: "On a night, we would be too conspicuous in shorts. Thee Greeks are more conservative, and since we are obviously Greeks . . ."

He, Trask and Lardis formed the rearmost group, and as they walked Trask queried him about the motorcycle accident.

"Myself," said Manolis, "I can't be absolutely sure—but please understand, I speak as a trained policeman. I mean I *am* sure, but without thee firm evidence—" He could only shrug.

"Explain," said Trask.

"Well," said Manolis, "this youth had apparently consumed a lot of ouzo. This is according to thee statements of friends he had been drinking with earlier—right here in Skala Astris, actually. When they left him he was drunk and his bike wouldn't start. He was pushing it. Thee next morning, he and his machine were discovered in a dry riverbed. Maybe he'd tried to get his bike going on a downhill stretch of road—or it could be that he was freewheeling—I don't know. But apparently he crashed."

"So what's suspicious about that?" Trask queried.

"Thee driving mirror on his handlebars was broken," Manolis went on, "presumably in thee crash. It seems he must have flown from thee bike, broke thee mirror in his flight . . . and cut his own throat. It *seems* so, anyway."

"Cut his throat?" Now Trask's eyes had narrowed. He sensed the strangeness here—detected the quiet but as yet unproven conviction in Manolis's voice—and suddenly the evening felt that much cooler.

"Indeed," Manolis continued. "Thee glass was still stuck in thee wound. Unconscious, he died where he had fallen."

"Ah!" Lardis came in. "But he didn't 'just' die, did he? I mean, there was more to it than that, now wasn't there?"

"Burned," Trask said, nodding his understanding. And then, to Manolis, "Didn't you originally say that he was burned?"

"Yes," the other answered. "After it crashed, thee machine caught fire from thee petrol in thee tank. And since thee youth and thee machine landed in thee selfsame spot—"

And again Lardis came in. "He *flew* from the bike, yet both lad and machine ended up in the same place? *Hah!*"

"I see," said Trask. And to Manolis, "Is that it?"

"That's it," Manolis replied. "From me, at least. Anything else, you should ask Lardis here. For what remains lies more in his 'province,' yes?"

"What remains?" Frowning, Trask turned to Lardis. "So what *do* you make of it?"

Lardis's normally rough voice was more grim and gravelly yet as he answered, "I understand that Manolis needs proof—that on this world 'evidence' is everything—but I can assure you it's perfectly clear to me, here as it would be on Sunside. Except there these monsters have no need to cover up their evil deeds. But I tell you I could *smell* this thing, as I've smelled it fifty times before! There was a taint in the air—my flesh was clammy from it—and I knew what it meant. Someone or thing had *caused* this so-called accident. And the selfsame someone or thing had cut this poor lad's throat with the broken mirror and set fire to him and his machine in order to conceal a foul murder. It's as simple as that."

"But no positive proof," said Manolis and Trask, almost in unison.

"Oh, but there is!" said Lardis. "We saw the lad's slashed throat, and then we visited the scene of the crash and saw the burned-out bike. Fortunately there'd been no dry brush in that riverbed, or the blaze might have spread. Instead it had *only* burned the bike—and the lad, of course. But he wasn't burned up entirely, and what Manolis has so far failed to mention—"

"Is thee blood," said Manolis then, his voice quieter yet. "Yes, Lardis is right. Thee big problem is thee blood."

"The blood?" Trask looked at each of them in turn.

"The blood that is the life," Lardis growled. "But you see, there *wasn't* any blood, Ben! This lad had spilled his life out, yes, but not into the dust of that dry riverbed."

"Now you have it all," said Manolis. "And to hell with thee lack of evidence! Frankly, until someone can explain to me thee absence of that young man's blood, I have to agree with Lardis. Deep inside, I can only believe that this was thee work of thee *vrykoulakas*!"

After that, it would have been very difficult for the three to present or maintain any sort of carefree holiday facade. There again, since they were older, more mature men, no one would be expecting them to act like kids out of school. And as for this most recent symptom of the island's vampiric infestation: they agreed that for the moment they would say nothing to the other members of the team.

They, at least, should be allowed to enjoy the pleasures of dining out in the Greek island atmosphere, and also of sleeping well in their beds tonight.

Tomorrow would be soon enough to bring all of this to their attention and shatter any illusions of an idyllic Greek island. Not that a great many of those remained, anyway . . .

At the Sunset Taverna, a clean but unremarkable little place at the western extreme of Skala Astris's sea wall—a place nestling under a huge canvas canopy, with sky-blue plastic stacking chairs, and square white tables that refused to balance without three beermats under the offending or "short" legs—the eight disparate colleagues took seats, remaining in their subgroups but positioning themselves to stay within earshot of each others' tables. David Chung, Stavros, and Liz were at one table, Andreas and Goodly at a second, while Trask, Manolis, and Lardis occupied a third.

A gentle breeze off the sea stirred the warm night air a very little but was nevertheless welcome; the conversation was mainly light and cheerful, and Andreas and Stavros both proved to have more than a fair smattering of English. Following Trask's earlier warnings, his three espers reined back on their special talents and refrained from exercising their metaphysical minds. Thus the meal passed without incident, until towards the end.

Other than the eight, the taverna was quite empty. This was scarcely the fault of the proprietor—his cooking couldn't be faulted, and the atmosphere was very pleasant—but the fact of the matter was that there were almost as many tavernas in Skala Astris as holidaymakers.

As they were finishing up, however, two young Greeks riding motorcycles pulled up on the road behind the taverna, put their bikes on their stands, entered, and took a table in a far corner. Manolis saw them, stared hard at one of them for a moment, then quickly averted his gaze. And:

"Don't look now," he told Trask and Lardis under his breath, "but I believe I have seen that one before—thee one with thee screaming skull on his jacket, yes."

The pair ordered ouzo with water, and finally the one whom Manolis had mentioned looked their way—and gave a start. "Ah, see!" said Manolis then. "And it appears that he recognizes me, too!"

It was a fact—the youth's eyes seemed riveted on Manolis, and his face had paled in a moment. He was so distracted—so alarmed, apparently, to find Manolis here—that as he reached for the drink that had been placed within arm's reach, he almost toppled it from the table. And Manolis said:

"*Aha!* I know him now. He was skulking about in thee village in thee hills, when Lardis and I were about our investigations. So then, what does he know that I should know but don't, eh? I have seen that look, and been in thee similar situations, many times before. So then, and now we employ thee method of silent intimidation."

He looked at his men at the other tables and gave a jerk of his head. Totally in tune with their boss—with a rapport that came from many years of service together—Stavros and Andreas stood up and moved carefully but purposefully towards the young men. The policemen didn't look like the kind that any young man should argue with, and as they went Manolis sat at his ease, with his feet stretched out, staring indolently at the victims of his "silent intimidation."

Then Andreas spoke in Greek to the one with the screaming skull jacket, and whatever it was he said, it brought that one babbling to his feet in a moment. Prodding him in the shoulder, Andreas snapped one short word at him, and the youth collapsed back down again into his chair. Meanwhile, Stavros was cautioning the other youth—who looked scared to death and about to flee—to stay right where he was.

And finally Manolis said, "I think that now, perhaps, these big hard biker boys are ready to tell me something. But it will be best if I speak to them on my own, without involving you."

With which he slowly stood up, made a show of brushing himself down, and walked casually, almost swaggeringly, across the floor to the corner table. There he sat down, and while Andreas and Stavros looked on, spoke to the youths for several minutes.

Finally he was done with them and let them go, and returned to Trask and Lardis. "Time we left," he said then, as the biker pair started up their machines and rode off into the night.

"So, what's going on?" Trask enquired.

"It would best suit our purposes," the other answered, "to talk about this back at thee Christos Studios."

But there was something new in Manolis's voice. The knowing front that he had presented to the youths was entirely absent, and there was little or nothing of the hardened, arrogant Greek policeman about him now. . .

* * *

Back at Christos Studios in The Shipwreck, where a pretty young Swiss woman, Yiannis's wife Katerina, served last drinks before retiring, Trask held his "O" Group for tomorrow, Sunday. Before that, however, he wanted Manolis to explain the business in the taverna.

Manolis had already spoken to his men; back on the mainland he had asked them to trust him, and without going into too much detail had told them there was a "problem" on Krassos. For even with their background of total loyalty to him, he'd feared that to tell them too much in the early stages of this game would be to damage his credibility. As things developed, however, it was and always had been his intention to put them more fully in the picture. Now that things were definitely developing, he'd spent time talking to them as they walked back from the taverna.

Thus all eight of the party were seated in a huddle in The Shipwreck to hear what he had to say, and then to accept orders from Trask.

"Those two in thee taverna," Manolis began. "They saw me up in Astris, thee foothills twin of Skala Astris. They suspected then that I was a policeman—perhaps even a special policeman, a detective, in my civilian clothes—and it worried them. Why? Because they were thee drinking companions of thee man who died in that motorcycle 'accident!'

"You see, they had not been good boys that night. All thee barrels have their bad apples, right? And Krassos, too, has its little criminals—er, as well as thee big ones we're seeking, of course. So, those two and their dead, roasted, *empty* friend, they were three of Krassos's bad boys, with thee criminal records as long as your arm. But all petty little thefts, rowdyism, and like that. They style themselves after thee American and European biker gangs. *Hah!* What a joke!

"So, they're not very eager to meet up with thee policemen, these two, and they knew I had spoken to thee dead man's mother. Who could say: perhaps she had mentioned her son's friends, eh? And perhaps I would come looking for them. Why, it was possible they might even find themselves blamed for what had happened!

"Tonight, and by pure coincidence, they went to thee Sunset Taverna. And they went there for thee same reason we went there—to keep out of sight in that quiet little place. But, ah! Who should happen to be there but myself, which is giving them thee shock. When Andreas spoke to thee one with thee screaming skull jacket, he at once began to explain about his dead friend, said that he and thee other one had nothing to do with it—but that they might know someone who did.

"There had been some troubles that night. These three, they had been out looking for thee girls—English or German girls, thee tourists—to have a little fun. And thee dead man especially, he had a bad reputation like that. But this time, he had picked on thee wrong girl, or woman, and he'd definitely picked on thee wrong pair.

"A pair of them, yes—a man and a woman—right here in Skala Astris, eating and drinking wine, in a taverna closer to thee middle of town. Then, when these three bad boy bikers had approached their would-be victims, to have their fun, thee man had reacted violently. So say these two cretins, anyway. Their friend—now their dead friend—was thrown over thee sea wall into thee harbour, him and his bike both! But these motorcycles . . . they are not thee toys! As you have seen, they can be heavy machines. So this was a strong man, a *very* strong man indeed.

"After that, they used thee anchor of a small boat to help their friend rescue his bike from thee sea, then left him to go off into Krassos town. And that's it . . ."

"And a description?" Trask said. "Of this man and woman?"

"Ah, yes!" said Manolis. "Thee descriptions. And so to thee point, eh? But there's no doubt in my mind, Ben, but that these creatures were thee ones we seek. It was them, Vavara and Malinari. Thee man was tall, well over six feet. He was strange and foreign . . . but also handsome, exotic. And when he clasped thee dead man's head between his hands, that one froze and went weak at thee knees. That was how he handled him so easily."

"Just like he must have clasped Zek!" Trask said, breathing the words out and almost choking on them. "Malinari the Mind!" Then he cleared his throat and said, "What about the woman?"

"That is thee strangest of all," Manolis replied. "She was . . . magnetic! She had this aura about her. She was so beautiful that she seemed to shine . . . yet they could remember nothing of her actual looks." And:

"*Vavaaara!*" said Lardis then. "Five hundred and more years old, that one, and born in another world, another time. Yet now she is here. Ben, we've found them. Definitely!"

"No," Trask shook his head, his voice a husky whisper again. "We know they're here, but we haven't found them yet. Tomorrow, maybe—but not yet, not tonight. The nighttime is their time. They're too strong at night. But I'll find them tomorrow, or if not tomorrow the day after that, or the one after that. If it's the last thing I do, I'll find them . . ."

He looked at Liz and David Chung. "You two—and especially you, Liz—now more than ever you must watch yourselves, keep a tight rein on your talents. Tomorrow morning, when these filthy things are down and sleeping and we go to seek them out, that's when you'll come into your own." Again he cleared his throat.

As they nodded their understanding, Trask relaxed a little. "Very well, now let's talk tomorrow through, go a little deeper into the details. These are the things I want done . . ."

After that: it took perhaps an hour of instructions, questions, and clarifications, and when it was done they all retired to their rooms and tried to sleep.

For Liz that proved difficult. A developing telepath, whose range was ever improving, she occasionally read her colleagues' minds unintentionally, without even trying. But tonight, in Ben Trask's case Liz had sensed that she knew his thoughts anyway. It was the look on his face whenever he spoke a certain name.

The name of a man or creature whom Trask despised and hated above all others. Malinari: Lord Nephran Malinari, of the Wamphyri! And Liz couldn't help wondering just how tight the mission would be with the Head of E-Branch leading it. For personal was one thing, but this time, with Trask—

—This time it was *very* personal!

And then, of course, there was Jake. Always in the back of her mind, Jake. She supposed she loved him—she knew she did—but Jake was involved with his own vendetta, and she wasn't a part of it. No room just yet for a new love in his life, for it was a *lost* love that he was trying to avenge. Liz knew that she shouldn't feel jealous about a dead woman, but she did, and she worried about Jake. She didn't know where he was, or how he was . . . or even *who* he was, not really.

But then again neither did Jake. Not really . . .

As Liz tossed and turned awhile, Ian Goodly left Lardis to get his rest and went to Trask's chalet.

He found Trask and Chung talking, drinking coffee, not yet quite ready to sleep. Trask welcomed him in, sat him down, and asked, "What's on your mind?" But unlike most people when they ask that question, Trask meant it not only literally, but also metaphysically.

And the precog answered in kind. "Exactly," he said. "It's been on my mind awhile now, and it's time we talked about it."

"Those dreams you mentioned earlier?" Trask sighed by way of an apology. "I hadn't forgotten, but we've been pretty busy. This afternoon when you were sleeping, I didn't want to disturb you. Also, since we'll be working together tomorrow, I thought that would be soon enough. But on the other hand, right now is fine if it's bothering you."

"Bothering and puzzling both," said Goodly. "For as usual, the future is being an utter bastard—er, if you'll excuse my French. I'm shown things, but I'm not given to understand them. So I was thinking maybe two heads would be better than one."

"Let's have it then," said Trask. "What have you seen—or foreseen, if that turns out to be the case."

"I think it probably is the case," Goodly nodded. "Because this afternoon when I was sleeping, I was revisited by the same repetitive dream. Before . . . well it *might* have been a dream—I mean, I dream just like anyone else—but when these things start repeating, ganging up on me . . ." And he shrugged.

"A warning, or warnings," said Trask.

"Well, that's how they have frequently worked out," Goodly answered. "But the future isn't biased that way. I've seen good things as well as bad—occasionally, anyway."

"And you've never been wrong," said Chung admiringly.

Goodly looked at him. "Only in my interpretation," he said, and added, "—until recently. For as you may recall, I also saw Jake Cutter as being with us—with E-Branch—for some time to come. That was when we were in Australia, since when I've been proved wrong. In the short term, anyway. For where's Jake now? And as for the long term, the future . . . as always, it remains to be seen."

"I know where I would *like* Jake to be," Trask growled. "We could certainly use his talents—the bloody hothead—if he were here! But as you say: it remains to be seen. So then, tell us about your dreams."

"They go back a few days," said the precog. "Back to London and the HQ, after we got back from down under, just as all of this was beginning to break."

"I remember," said Trask. "Something about black-robed figures, tunnels, and hooded eyes?"

Goodly nodded. "And a shape, or shadow, coming ever closer. But as for that last, I haven't seen him since flying out here with Liz and Lardis."

"Him?" said Trask. "This shadow is a he, then?"

Again the precog nodded. "But don't ask me to describe him. He is literally a shadow, a dark blot, a flowing . . . *something*. If I were to hazard a guess, however, I would say he could only be—"

"Lord Szwart!" said Trask. "And he's in London. That's why you haven't seen him since you came out here. You've distanced yourself from him."

"And that's what I meant about two heads being better than one," said Goodly. "For I had come to the same conclusion, but I needed someone else to corroborate it. If what you just said is 'the truth of it'—and who could possibly know the truth better than you?—then indeed it has to be Szwart, and probably in London, yes."

"My worst nightmare," said Trask. "A thing as loathsome as that coming ever closer. But not to us, not while we're here."

"Not to you but to the ones you love," said Chung. "Millie in your case, and Lissa in Lardis Lidesci's."

Trask looked at him sharply and frowned. "Millie? Whatever makes you think that I—?"

But both the locator and precog were looking away from him, as if not wishing to hear it. Trask thought he knew why, and in Chung's case he was right. But on hearing Millie's name spoken, Goodly had averted his eyes for a different reason entirely.

"There's no more use in my lying than in someone trying to lie to me, right?" Trask said. "But Millie and I—it's only a very recent thing. So how come everyone—?"

"Oh, you've let it slip, given yourself away now and then," Chung cut him short. "But even if you hadn't, good news travels fast!" He grinned, however briefly.

"Yes," Trask nodded. "Especially in E-Branch!" And then to Goodly: "Okay, but we already know about Szwart. And I've done what I can to safeguard the HQ and everyone in it. So go on, what about the rest of it?"

"The rest of it is as it was," the precog answered. "Black-robed figures, drifting or floating . . . and something sinking, a blob of light receding into watery deeps . . . and a warren of burrows or tunnels, all filled with something horrid . . ."

"I remember all that," said Trask. "So, what's new? Didn't you say something about screaming?"

Goodly took his time moistening his lips before answering. "Yes, the new stuff is about screaming. But it's something you aren't going to like too much, Ben, and—"

"I don't like *any* of it!" the other cut him short. "So out with it."

"—And it's sort of contradictory," the precog continued, as if he hadn't been interrupted. "I mean, just because I have seen it, that doesn't mean it will be the *way* I've seen it."

"Contradictory?" Trask frowned. "And it doesn't have to be the way you've seen it?"

"That's right," Goodly answered, "yes. For if my being here on Krassos has distanced me from Szwart, and if he's in London, then why hasn't being here distanced me from . . . from everyone else in London? Or is it just because I know them so well that their futures are clearer to me?"

Now Trask felt his throat go dry. "So then, this really is about our people back home," he said. And steeling himself, "Go on, tell me about it."

And the precog's voice was shaky as he said, "I saw women—but I saw them *burning*, Ben! They were clad in black rags, and the flames were leaping up from them, consuming them. They held up their arms to the sky, and their eyes were luminous with joy and . . . and . . . I don't know? Relief, maybe?"

David Chung's jaw had fallen open. "Joy? They were burning, and screaming, and yet they were joyous, relieved?"

"This isn't . . . it isn't easy," Goodly shook his head. "And I don't understand it any more than you will. But no, it wasn't these burning women who were doing the screaming. The screaming was coming from someone else, the odd woman out. *She* was screaming, in absolute horror of something that she could see which I couldn't. And instead of looking up, she was looking down—at a gaping chasm that had opened under her feet—a yawning black hole that seemed to go down forever . . ."

As Goodly paused, his face ashen, so Trask rose and went to him. And Trask's face was as pale as the precog's as he grabbed his shoulders and shook him. "I've ignored it up until now," he snarled. "But I've been seeing it in your face ever since I let you in here. I've probably been ignoring it all evening—since you woke up from your nap—but I've known there was something wrong. And now I know what it is."

The precog could only sit there, rocked by Trask's terrible anger, shaking his head in dumb consternation and looking as if he wanted to die, yet knowing it wasn't his fault.

"It was Millie you saw, wasn't it?" Trask said huskily, his voice breaking now. "It was Millie doing the screaming—*and you know that it's going to fucking happen!*"

And finally, as Trask released him and turned away: "But we *don't* know that, Ben!" Goodly spoke up. "We only know *something* will happen. We *don't* know how or when or why—or what the end result will be."

Trask had collapsed on his bed, his elbows on his knees and his face in his hands. "God *damn* you!" he raved, his whole body shaking. "You and your fucking talent! God damn us all!"

Chung went to him but didn't touch him. "Boss," he said quietly after a moment. "This isn't Ian's fault. It's like you said, a warning. It gives us extra time to speak to HQ again, tell them something's coming down and they've got to look after the women. It's a warning, that's all."

Trask took a deep breath, looked up, said, "David, you know it doesn't work like that. How many times have we seen it? When Ian says it's going to happen, it's going to happen. And that's it. There's no escaping it."

"But we don't know *how* it will happen," Goodly repeated himself, "or what the end result will be."

"Jesus! *Jesus!*" said Trask, jumping to his feet. "I have to speak to London again. But . . ." He looked at his friends, shook his head, and said, "You two, I don't know how to say I'm sorry for the way I acted a moment ago. I don't even know if I should just yet. I hate this. I hate our talents. Why can't we be like other men? Why do we have to suffer all this shit? What in hell did our forebears do that we had to be born fucking freaks? Ian, I didn't mean to go off at you like that. But Millie—my God—Millie!"

"It's all right," said the precog. "I hate it, too, Ben. We all do. People say we're talented, but I say we're cursed. Just don't . . . don't be concerned with anything else right now. Just go and speak to HQ."

And without another word Trask took his jacket and went out into the Mediterranean night . . .

Morning, the sun just clearing the horizon, and it was probably the coolest it would be all day and well into the next night.

"Now we really are tourists," said Liz, a passenger in the lead car as all three vehicles headed out from Christos Studios and went their various ways. "To all intents and purposes, that is . . . except the real one."

"I used to 'tour' Sunside," Lardis chuckled gruffly. "But I called it 'beating the bounds,' and I rode in a caravan or went on foot. That was how the old Szgany chieftains protected their territories. The farthest I ever went was into Starside, to the last great aerie of the Wamphyri. But that was before Trask and Chung and Goodly and Zek and Nathan, before they all brought it crashing down, of course."

This was news to Manolis, who was driving. "What?" he said. "Ben Trask and thee others, they were all with you in a vampire world?"

"In *my* vampire world, aye," said Lardis. "And without them, I don't suppose I'd be here talking about it. For they're brave lads all, these E-Branch people. And me and my kind, the Szgany as a race, we'd have been goners without them."

"E-Branch," Manolis nodded. "Brave ones, yes—and so many of *them* are thee goners now, gone away for ever. I knew one of them, a man called Darcy Clarke, quite well, but I don't think either of you will have known him. He was before your time with thee Branch. We did some work with thee *vrykoulakas* bastards on thee island of Halki, he and I. That was like—it was like a nightmare!—but we lived through it. Did I say lived through it? *Hah!* Darcy had this thing inside him, his talent, which so protected him he should have lived to be a hundred! Yet now he is no more. No more Darcy Clarke, Ken Layard, or Trevor Jordan, and no more Jazz or Zek."

"Did you know Jazz? Jazz Simmons?" Now it was Lardis's turn to be surprised. "Ah!—but he was a fighter, that one! I named my boy after Jazz. My only son, Jason Lidesci, who by now would have been a chief in his own right."

"Would have been?" Manolis glanced at him.

"The Wamphyri got him," Lardis growled, and turned his face away. Following which they fell silent.

And as these men from different spheres dwelled awhile with their own private memories—memories that, however disparate, were linked by common factors—Liz relaxed as best she could and thought about what they were all doing here . . .

The three recce or initial-search teams consisted of Lardis, Manolis, and Liz in their four-wheel-drive vehicle; Stavros and Chung in a second; and Trask, Goodly, and Andreas in the third. This first phase of the operation was simply to look the island over, and if possible to pinpoint the location of the infestation. Namely, to find Vavara and Malinari, and to do it in broad daylight when the Great Vampires were least active and probably wouldn't realize that they'd been discovered.

Manolis and his party went west, back towards the capital. Bypassing Krassos town on its ring road, they would swing north on the coastal route, then east along the "back" of the island, and eventually meet up with Ben Trask and his party at a place called Skala Rachoniou. By then they would have covered no more than thirty miles or so on the actual coast roads, but twice as many again in their forays inland on secondary roads and tracks to the various foothill and mountain villages.

Along the way and apart from Krassos itself, they would pay visits to every village, community, and archaeological site, of which there weren't too many, and acting as tourists assess the viability of each place as a possible aerie or vampire hideout. That was their brief: to carry out a reconnaissance of half of Krassos, while Trask and his party covered the eastern half of the island. Also, since Manolis's men hadn't been able to find spearguns in Skala Astris, he intended to stop at the various fishing villages en route until he'd found what he wanted.

As for Stavros and Chung, they were "staying local," in the countryside around Skala Astris because it seemed the most likely hunting ground. The unidentified woman with the leech had been washed up only six or seven miles away; Vladi Ferengi, the Gypsy chief, had camped there with his people; Manolis had been forced off the road close by; and Vavara and Lord Nephran Malinari had actually been sighted there on the night that a would-be Hell's Angel made his fatal error. Also, and most logical of all, David Chung was E-Branch's chief locator. If the vampires were in this vicinity, Chung should be able to find them . . .

That being the case, Liz suspected that she and Lardis had been sent on a wild-goose chase west *away* from Skala Astris for a similar reason, or more properly, the opposite reason: it was simply Trask's way of keeping them out of the line of fire. And if by chance they should get into trouble anyway, then the very capable Manolis Papastamos would be on hand to get them out. As for Manolis: he seemed one hundred percent fit again. He drove confidently—*too* confidently on roads like this, Liz thought—and if he was hurting at all he didn't show it.

But there again, he *did* have injuries, and it might well be that Trask was taking care of Manolis, too, if only by ensuring that he was well out of it.

Thus Liz felt she could afford to relax a little. And maybe because she had been keeping her telepathy on a tight rein, she also decided that now would be a good time to get some practice in. The sun was in the sky; the temperature was already rising; the Wamphyri would be in their beds or skulking in the darkness of their as yet undiscovered aerie, and so she'd have little or nothing to fear from them just yet. So she thought.

Certainly her heart felt lighter now that she was speeding west, as though she was leaving something dark and terrible far behind. If only she could leave her dark and terrible fears for Jake behind her, too, then her world would be a brighter place; and that despite all the horrors she had known in her time with E-Branch, and others that she supposed must surely be waiting for her around some future bend.

But hopefully, not around the *next* bend . . .

It was noon of a baking hot, very frustrating day when finally Liz brought the car to a halt where the road cut through a high spur overlooking a long white beach fronting the small village-cum-resort of Skala Rachoniou. She had taken over driving when Manolis's shoulder had started to play up, and now he was resting up beside her, "easing the pain," by pulling on a bottle of Ouzo 12 purchased at a liquor store in one of the villages en route. Lardis—thank goodness—had remembered Trask's request that he keep his drinking to a minimum, and he'd refrained from buying Metaxa, though Liz guessed he'd been sorely tempted. Now he was sitting in the back of the car, sipping from a bottle of mineral water that he was sharing with her, doubtless feeling envious of Manolis.

"That's it," said the latter, glancing at a map where he'd folded it onto the dashboard. "Thee Skala Rachoniou. According to thee legend on my map, which has two umbrellas to signify a beach resort, thee place is very popular for thee swimming and snorkelling. *Huh!* But thee map has almost as many umbrellas as thee beach! Just look down there!"

"Deserted," said Liz. "Well, almost. All of that wonderful ocean, and I can't see more than two or three swimmers."

"It is thee white sand," Manolis nodded. "You can't walk on it, it's so hot."

"Don't you believe it," said Liz. "I'll walk on it, just as soon as we can get down there. I've never sweated so much in my life."

And Lardis, with a pair of binoculars to his eyes, growled, "At least we'll have no trouble finding Ben and the others. In fact I think I can see their vehicle from here." He handed the binoculars to Liz. "That taverna in the middle of the straight stretch of road, the one with the blue canopy."

"I see them," she said, and passed the glasses to Manolis.

"By now they'll be wondering where we've got to. We'd best get on down there." Letting out the clutch, she drove the car back out onto the last mile of winding road to the beachfront . . .

"So what kept you?" a worried-looking Trask wanted to know when the three joined him, Goodly, and Andreas in the stirless shade of the open-sided taverna. "I was just beginning to feel uneasy about you. We've been here for something like an hour now." And waving for the waiter, he called for sandwiches and iced drinks for the latecomers.

"We had a tyre blow out on us west of Krassos town," Liz told him, "and Manolis did some damage to his shoulder trying to fix it. Lardis and I finished the job. Also, we had to try almost a dozen hardware and fishing stores before Manolis could find the right kind of spearguns. He needed spears with the right gauge of thread to take the silvered spearheads. Then he had to chase up someone who was willing to open up his store for him—it is a Sunday, after all, and late in the season. And finally . . . finally there seemed to be lots more road up into and down from the mountains than we'd reckoned on."

And before Trask could say anything else, she went on, "How long do you plan on us being here?"

"Maybe another hour," Trask shrugged. "Give you time to get your breath, have a bite to eat, soak up a little liquid. Why?"

"Because I for one intend to soak *in* a little liquid!" she told him. "In fact, a lot of it. Manolis can supply the details of our recce, not that there's much to tell." And shrugging out of her dress to reveal the bikini underneath—but leaving her sandals on her feet against the heat of the sand—she set off out of the taverna and down across the narrow strip of beach to the sea.

Watching her go, Lardis said, "That Jake Cutter's one lucky lad. Or he would be if he'd see sense. She has the hips for it, that one."

"You should be past that stuff," Trask told him, but Lardis only grinned.

"When I'm past *that* stuff," he answered, "then by all means shoot me!"

But Trask was frowning. "She was short with me," he finally worked it out. "And she also seemed a little evasive. So what's bothering her now, I wonder?" While he didn't mention it, he'd also noticed faint purple shadows under Liz's eyes, a sure sign that she'd been concentrating her mind, using her telepathy.

Manolis stroked his chin, looked at Trask shrewdly, and said "Maybe she feels thee same way I feel: that you sent us west to keep us out of danger."

"But I—" Trask began to protest, then saw how pointless it would be to lie. "But I'm trying to keep us *all* out of danger!" he said. "We're not expendable, none of us, and I'll need every one of you if we're to see this thing through. Okay, so maybe I seem a little overprotective of Liz. But Nephran Malinari knows her mind, and I don't want to use her talent until I absolutely have to. Not anywhere near someone as powerful as he is, anyway. Then there's Lardis. He's my responsibility, too, and—"

"As you were mine, on Sunside that time," said Lardis. "But I didn't try to keep you from doing your bit."

"—*And* his wife is waiting for him back in London," Trask continued. "So how am I supposed to explain it to Lissa if I go back without him?"

"And me?" said Manolis. "What about me? Are you responsible for me, too? Am I not thee big boy in my own right? Ah, but you didn't want me in on this in thee first place, did you?"

Trask threw up his hands. "We had to recce this island!" he protested. "I chose you three to do the western half. So you've done it. And now . . . now if you're ready, I think I'd like your report," he finished lamely.

"Our report?" Lardis repeated him. "But it's like Liz told you. There isn't anything to report. We didn't find anything."

"And you, Ben?" said Manolis. "What did you find?"

Trask shook his head. "The same as you," he said. "Nothing. Wherever these creatures are, they're keeping their heads down. And so we're left with Chung—and I can't get through to him."

"Let me try him again," said Goodly, taking out his phone. But it was no use; the locator's phone had been activated, they knew that much, but his words were lost in the hiss and sputter of static caused by sunspot activity.

"So what now?" said Manolis.

"Now we go back to Skala Astris," said Trask, straightening up in his chair. "What the hell? It's early days, and we're not nearly beaten yet. Out in Australia, we had thousands of square miles to cover. But we did it in the end. And what's this place but a huge chunk of marble in the middle of the sea? We'll find the bastards, if not today then tonight or tomorrow night. Like I said yesterday: the nighttime is their time. And so it is—but it could well prove to be our time, too."

"Of course, we didn't cover *all* of our half of the island," said the precog.

"Oh?" Manolis looked at him, then at Trask.

"We stuck to the coast road," said the latter, "but there's a major route right through the mountains—the highest part of the island—that we'll look at on the way back. We may as well go back together, in convoy."

"Whatever you say," said Manolis.

But leaning towards the Greek policeman, Trask was suddenly frowning again when he asked: "Is that ouzo I can smell on your breath?"

"Er, that was for my shoulder," said Manolis. "To ease thee pain." And then, recognizing a certain look in Trask's narrowed eyes, he sighed and added, "Well, not *entirely* for my shoulder, perhaps—but it did help a lot, I promise you that!" And when the look didn't go away, "However, since you insist—" Catching the waiter's eye, he called for coffee, black . . .

By the time Manolis was down to the dregs, Liz had finished bathing and was coming back up the beach. And by the time she'd reached the taverna, her gleaming, sun-bronzed skin was already dry.

15
The Searching—The Finding—The Seething

HAVING JUGGLED THE CREWS A LITTLE, TRASK had taken over driving the lead vehicle. Manolis was his front-seat passenger, reading the map, and Andreas sprawled in the back. Behind them, as they climbed into the densely wooded mountains along contour-hugging roads, Goodly drove the other car. Lardis had moved up front as the precog's navigator, but map-reading skills were scarcely a necessity—Goodly was simply following where Trask led. Liz was taking it easy in the back, and all the windows of both vehicles were wound all the way down.

"At least we're out of the sunlight," said Trask, beginning to feel more comfortable in the shade of ramrod-straight pines. "Why, it's like being in a regular forest! Apart from this terrible heat, we could be in Canada or even Norway."

"Thee Krassos peoples are especially proud of their wooded mountains," Manolis told him. "And of their marble, of course. Some of thee world's finest marbles are quarried here in these mountains. This is thee Ypsaria 'massif.' Well, not so massive to thee great world traveller, perhaps—I mean, it isn't thee Rockies—but very impressive on a small Greek island, yes?"

"It's green, it's shady, and I can breathe without setting fire to my lungs," Trask answered. "So it's good enough for me. Not too good for driving, though. Quite apart from the winding road—which is bad enough and demands a lot of concentration—this dappled light is very confusing. It's almost as bad as driving at dusk. But in contrast to all the heat and the glare of the coast roads, it's very refreshing indeed."

He glanced sideways at the Greek, who sat studying his map, and went on. "What's so interesting with the map? There's only this one major road, if you can call it that, so it's not likely we'll get lost."

But Manolis was frowning now and stabbing with his finger at a point on the folded chart. "Here is thee *very* interesting item," he said, musingly. "An hotel, close to a trig point. At twelve hundred metres, it is perhaps thee second highest place on Krassos. From up there we can scan thee entire island coast to coast."

"Good," said Trask. "We'll take a short break there." Then he saw that Manolis was still intent on the map. "So what else are you looking at? What's bothering you now?"

"Just thee name of thee place," said Manolis. "It's called . . . it's called Thee Aerie!"

Trask gave a small start—then thought about it, shrugged, and said, "And so it should be, if it's the vantage point that you say it is. Let's face it, it's hardly likely that Malinari and Vavara would be advertising their presence, now is it?"

Grinning sheepishly, Manolis offered an apologetic twitch of his shoulders. "No, of course not," he said. "What? A place like that . . . it would be much too obvious. My mind is working overtime, I think. But I received thee funny sensation to find such a name on thee map. Or perhaps 'funny' is thee wrong word. In any case, now I'm feeling very stupid . . ."

"Oh, I don't know," Trask told him—for the fact was that it had given him a 'funny' sensation, too. "Let's face it, this is a nervy business. We're all going to be a little jumpy until we've got something solid to go on." Then, changing the subject to detract from the other's embarrassment: "And is that it—no other places of interest? No little hamlets tucked away off the road?"

"There are two other places of interest," Manolis answered. "Or at least, they are of interest to me."

"Oh?"

"Let me explain," said the other. "This morning I had thee opportunity to speak to Liz about your work in Australia. That was while we were driving to Skala Rachoniou. What she told me sounded like World War Three! What? Flamethrowers, napalm, and helicopter gunships? Amazing! And that was when you were going against only one of these creatures."

"Good liaison," Trask explained. "Our Minister Responsible was able to convince the Australian authorities to give us all the help we needed. This time around, however . . ."

"I know," Manolis nodded. "A different country, different authorities, and a different situation. Still, our weapons are pitiful by comparison, and in pitifully short supply."

"I feel mainly responsible for that," Trask told him. "If I hadn't been so quick off the mark to get out here . . . but on the other hand, what difference would it have made? We have to deal with these monsters, and must do so with whatever weapons are to hand."

"Precisely," said Manolis. "But as Liz explained it to me, thee Australian infestation was so deep-rooted that you had to burn and blast it out of existence. Well, good—but we won't be doing much blasting and burning with a few spearguns and a handful of nine-millimeter automatics!"

"I know," Trask answered. "And if things get really bad, I might yet have to get my government to tell yours what's going on and try to enlist their aid. But that isn't going to happen if it means creating a panic situation right across the world! However, I do have the power—if only as a last resort—to call in air strikes from British warships in the Med. In which case, there'd be hell to pay later explaining it away. It would go something like this: 'Today in the Mediterranean, a British military exercise went disastrously wrong when planes from the aircraft carrier . . .' Et cetera, et cetera."

"Right," said Manolis. "And that is why I find these other places on thee map interesting. One is a marble quarry on thee far side of this mountain; thee other is a deserted airport in thee foothills just before we are reaching Limari on thee east coast."

"An airport?" Trask was surprised. "But I was told Krassos doesn't have an airport."

"Work was started four years ago," Manolis explained, "and came to a halt a few months ago with thee failure of the euro, the devaluation of thee deutschmark, and a big decline in tourism. An independent German airline with its own small fleet of VTOLs went broke, and since they were footing thee bill . . ." He let it taper off.

"I hadn't heard about that," said Trask.

"Nor I, until I was over here that first time," said Manolis. "But when one chats with thee locals, then one hears such things. All very interesting . . ."

"But I still don't know *why* you're interested," said Trask. "I mean, what has a quarry and an abandoned airport to do with our lack of weapons?"

In answer to which Manolis smiled slyly, winked, and said, "Perhaps nothing—and I don't want to get your hopes up—so it's best that you just wait and see."

Then he turned in his seat and began talking in Greek, and very rapidly, to Andreas; and that one nodding his understanding, even though Trask couldn't follow a word. Indeed if anyone had asked him, Trask would have remarked that it was all Greek to him . . .

The tree line had fallen away behind and the road was that much steeper by the time The Aerie came into view amidst a jumble of fanglike rocks that formed the uppermost crest of the Ypsarias. It wasn't so much that trees wouldn't grow up here as that they couldn't; there was no soil to speak of where vast marble outcrops thrust for the sky and only a handful of tortured, wind-blasted shrubs and herbs found root among the boulder clumps.

And there was the "hotel," The Aerie, looking like a scaled-down version of an ancient Crusader castle, its walls white in the brilliant sunlight, silhouetted against the aching blue of a cloudless sky.

There was a parking area at the foot of that final jumble, and Trask swung right off the road onto a bone-dry surface that threw up a cloud of dust, which momentarily obscured the vehicle behind. Then the hood of Goodly's car appeared, and as the dust settled, the precog slowed to a halt alongside the lead vehicle. Blinking owlishly, he switched off his engine, leaned from his window, looked at Trask in the other car, and raised a querying eyebrow.

"We're taking a short break," Trask called across to him. "This place is called The Aerie, and apparently it will afford us quite a view. That is if you feel like making the climb, of course."

The Aerie was impressive in a gaunt, and antique sort of way. It reeked of ages past, like fossilised bones or the crumbling pages of an old, illuminated manuscript. Trask's reference had been to the access route: a steep climb up steps hewn from the near-vertical rock face, along a series of dizzy, zigzagging causeways. Mercifully the way was at least partly covered over; canvas canopies, torn in places by forgotten winds, flapped in the rising thermals but somehow managed to cast a little shade onto the time-hollowed steps.

There was or had been another means of ascension, evidence of which was still visible. A broken gondola lay rusting in one corner of the parking lot beside a derelict boarding stage, and a steel hawser was dangling loose from a gantry and pulley, its end lying coiled in the dust. Another length of cable was hanging halfway down the escarpment from the arms of a projecting crane, where winding gear stood idle above a wide landing bay.

"That must be . . . how high?" said Liz, craning her neck and squinting up at the landing bay under the square flat roof with its tessellated wall. "Ninety or maybe a hundred feet vertical? Well, personally I'm glad that thing isn't working, and I'll be only too pleased to do this the hard way!"

"Oh?" the Old Lidesci growled. "Then maybe I'll remind you of what you said when we get to the top. *If* we get to the top!"

And as the party of six set out to climb, Manolis recounted

what he'd read of the place in the legend on the reverse of his map. "Thee Romans quarried white marble in these mountains, and thee original place was probably built by them. Later thee Crusaders took it over as a lookout. You will see why when we get up there. Most of thee Crusader lookouts and castles were built in thee high places; self-explanatory, of course. In thee later times there were earthquakes, and thee place collapsed inwards. Later still there were invaders, who pulled thee ruins down for whatever reasons. When Thee Aerie was built here, thee selfsame stones were used, and it has been standing as we see it now for some two hundred years or more. Recently, it was refurbished as an hotel—er, if not quite thee five-star. I mean, take a look at thee place. It is thee veritable 'ancient ruin,' eh?"

At the top of the stairway, an old, partially crippled Greek gentleman and his two sons were waiting to greet them. They had seen the vehicles arrive and had hoped that their visitors were prospective guests. Gesturing the party inside a cavernous room where massive pine beams supported a vaulted ceiling, the proprietor recognized Manolis and Andreas as fellow countrymen, and began to speak with them at some length. While these three were thus engaged, the younger men of the household showed Trask and his people to a panoramic window and invited them to look out.

The view was breathtaking; all of the southern coast of the island was visible, from Krassos town fifteen miles to the southwest, to Limari only seven miles away to the southeast. Lardis was staggered. "There's nothing quite like this in all Sunside/Starside!" he wheezed, still catching his breath from the climb. "So much sea, sun, and sky! All of that colour! From the top of the Barrier Mountains of home, I've gazed on forests on the one hand and a boulder-strewn wilderness on the other, but nothing like this."

One of the young men of the house had understood something of what the Old Lidesci said, if not his references to the vampire world, and commented, "But from thee roof, you are seeing even more. Thee whole island—all of thee Krassos!"

Andreas and Manolis had joined them at the window, and the latter was looking a little downcast. "Thee old man has told me a sad story," he said. "For twenty years he and his family have made a living up here, but barely. Recently, however, some five years now, thee tourism has been bad. Now in this El Niño year, finally they are broke. They had four guests for just two weeks in May . . . and nothing else but occasional travellers, like us. Thee old man, he says he must close down now; his sons will go to Krassos town to find thee work. I feel sorry for him."

Trask nodded. "Not the best place to open an hotel."

Manolis disagreed. "It is an *excellent* place for thee fresh air, thee swimming, thee hiking through thee mountains! He says thee cooking is superb, and thee rooms big and airy. And as for thee views—"

"The views are wonderful," said Liz, "and we've just got to go up to the roof. But did you say swimming?"

"You'll see," Manolis nodded, and he spoke to the young men in Greek. "There. And now they'll take us up to thee roof. Ben, I couldn't leave without doing something for these poor people. So I've ordered drinks and a little food on thee roof. It is my pleasure to pay, and I shall leave thee large tip. So shall we all. Come."

The interior stairways rose steeply from level to level of all four high-ceilinged floors. Along the way, the Old Lidesci took the hindmost position with Liz at his elbow. Noticing the way he would pause every now and then to sniff at the air, she asked him: "Is something wrong?"

"Eh?" Lardis looked at her, blinked, then shook his grizzled head. "No, nothing. This place may be called The Aerie, but it smells only of life and humanity and time. Especially of the latter. I have seen *real* aeries, Liz—the great aeries of the Wamphyri—which stank of death and undeath. The walls of this place have windows where the sun gets in, and they're hung with pictures and tapestries. The ones I knew were clad in the bones of men and beasts, furbished with the fats of women, and draped at the windows so heavily that *no* sunlight got in! So don't you concern yourself that perhaps I've noticed something odd, for I haven't. It's just that old habits die hard, and I entered this place of my own free will."

She nodded and said, "Good," and thought to herself, *I wish I'd never asked!*

By then they were up onto the roof, surrounded on all four sides by massively thick, five-foot-high walls with the merlons and embrasures of a regular castle. Manolis called to Liz, drew her attention to the west-facing wall—one of the two sides of The Aerie that had not been visible from the parking lot—and indicated that she should look out and down.

Perhaps a mile away to the west, the ultimate fangs of the Ypsaria range climbed some six or seven hundred feet higher yet with twin spurs that advanced in parallel, like the spined back of some impossibly huge, petrified Jurassic stegosaurus, almost to the foot of The Aerie itself. There, finally, they crumbled down into boulder clumps and sheer-sided outcrops, of which the last one formed The Aerie's foundations.

But only a hundred yards from The Aerie's base, between the spurs where they were less pronounced, a natural rock basin had been fashioned into a swimming pool, with a paved sundeck and a ceramic surround in a classically Greek pattern that traced the basin's oysterlike contours. A flagged path led from The Aerie through sculpted boulder jumbles to the side of the pool, where a three-metre diving board projected over the deep end. Several small stacks of sun-bleached loungers were also positioned poolside, along with a bundle of parasols, and the setup as a whole would have looked very appealing if not for the fact that—

"There's no water!" said Liz.

And Manolis held up his hands in dismay. "Those peaks over there. They are thee natural water trap. In thee winter months, thee rain flows down between thee spurs like a river. It passes through cracks in thee rocks into a natural reservoir and feeds a well at thee foot of Thee Aerie. Thee water has always kept a certain level. No matter how much water is taken out, thee well refills itself to that same level. It had never once run dry in living memory . . . not until three years ago. Thee swimming pool used water from thee well—crystal-clear, pure drinking water. But three years ago, suddenly thee level is dropping. When they take out thee water, it doesn't refill." He paused and shrugged "Obviously thee greatest need is water for living, not for swimming. So thee pool—"

"Goes empty," Liz finished it for him. "No pool, no guests. No guests, no money. A vicious circle."

"And thee circle keeps on turning," Manolis nodded. "Now we have thee *El Niño*, and no end in sight. And so I feel sorry for these people . . ."

The rest of the party had spread out around the walls; they were gazing out through the embrasures—following the curve of the world, the island of Krassos in its entirety—from horizon to horizon. But in the southern wall, Liz spied a canvas-draped pedestal . . . the base of a telescope.

She removed the canvas, polished the glass on the sleeve of her dress, looked for small change in her pockets. Manolis gave her some silver coins; she thanked him and slipped one into the slot. As the instrument whirred into life, Liz put her eyes to the binocular scanners, then turned the metal barrel on its swivel until it pointed south and some thirty degrees west.

"What are you looking for?" Manolis asked her.

"Skala Astris," she answered. "The Christos Studios. I just wondered if I might be able to see them from here." But in fact that wasn't all she was wondering.

Ben Trask saw what she was doing and came striding. Having overheard their conversation, he'd detected something in Liz's voice and knew that what she'd said wasn't the whole truth. He came quickly, with a worried expression on his face. "Liz?"

But Manolis was still talking to her. "You'll be fortunate, I think, to see thee studios from here. It must be six or seven miles. Still, if thee telescope reduces thee distance to—"

"Liz!" Trask said again, more urgently.

As he took her elbow she let go of the telescope and turned to face him. Standing close by, Manolis thought the look on her face was oddly defiant. But by now, like Trask himself, Manolis had noticed the darkening purple under Liz's eyes. And suddenly he, too, understood.

Straightening up and holding her head high, Liz said, "So, then—am I going to be mollycoddled for the rest of my life by you and E-Branch? You weren't taking such loving care of me out in Australia, when you threw us in at the deep end, Jake and I. So what's changed now?"

"Liz!" Trask growled warningly. "What, are you crazy? You know what's changed. Australia changed everything. And I didn't throw you in at the deep end, not really. Ian had forecast—"

"That we'd be okay, I know," Liz cut him short. "So if you can put so much faith in the precog's talent, why not in mine?"

Trask took her shoulders. "Because Malinari can't hit back at Ian, that's why! Because he can't follow his talent home to its source! And also because that filthy, bloodsucking bastard . . . because he's already taken too much of what I've loved, of what I've lived for. Too much life, Liz—the lives of others, and too much of *my* life, which I'll be paying for forever—so I'm not about to let him have yours, too."

Liz knew what he meant. He was only now getting over Zek—getting over it, but he'd never be able to forget it, not until Malinari was dead—and now Millicent Cleary was or might be in some kind of trouble, too. Liz could read it in Trask's mind as clearly as if he was speaking it out loud. Not the whole story, just his obvious concern. Similarly his concern for her—for Liz herself—was also crystal clear.

Just looking into Trask's eyes she could read the truth of it, as if his talent was working in both directions: *He had lost Zek . . . Millicent Cleary was trying desperately hard to step into the breach and help Trask pick up the pieces, and she was close to succeeding . . . Liz had now replaced Millie as Trask's kid-sister figure. Of course he worried for her.*

Still feeling a little hurt, but knowing now how much

Trask was hurting, too, gradually Liz's shoulders relaxed and she let the tension drain away. A moment or two more and she was sorry, if not apologetic. But at least she was willing to explain.

"It's just so bloody frustrating!" She blurted it out. "And yes, I know you've seen the purple under my eyes. I always have it, but even more so now. That's because I've spent the morning scanning every little town and village we've been into since we left the Christos Studios. Not in defiance of your orders, Ben, not really, but because I guessed you'd sent us out on—well, not a wild-goose chase as such, but you didn't think we'd have too much to worry about in the west of the island. And you were right—there's absolutely nothing there. It had to be done, I know, so it wasn't a total waste of time, but—"

"You feel that I haven't made the best use of your talent," Trask cut in, releasing her shoulders.

By now the others had come to see what the fuss was about. Ian Goodly, who was first to arrive and had heard something of what was going on, said, "She could be right at that."

Trask looked at him. "Oh?"

The precog nodded. "Ben, I don't know what's coming—let's face it, I rarely know what's coming, not precisely—but whatever it is, it has to come soon. I can feel it in my bones just like that time on Sunside/Starside."

"The Big One?"

"Just like that, yes," said Goodly. "And as for Liz's frustration, I can feel that, too—my own, that is—*and* everyone else's. There's trouble brewing at home, and yet we're out here on Krassos doing nothing. At least, that's how it feels."

"We've covered the island," Trask answered. "Okay, so it's been frustrating. Do you think I don't know that? Well, I know it as well as the next man—or woman." He glanced at Liz. "But we *have* narrowed it down. We're fairly sure now that what we're looking for is closer to home." Again he looked at Liz. "Closer to Skala Astris, I mean. That *is* what you were doing, right?"

"You know it is," she answered, lowering her head a little.

"Without even a by-your-leave?"

"I'm feeling what Ian is feeling," she said. "Time slipping by, and the future coming down on us. I might actually be picking it up from him, or from you, from Manolis, from Lardis. And since we had no luck this morning—I don't know—I just felt the need to speed things up, that's all."

Trask looked at Goodly. "How about it?"

"I can't see that it can do any harm," the precog answered. "Broad daylight, and the sun like a blob of molten gold high in the sky. Wherever they are, they have to be down and sleeping."

"In which case, what's the point?" Trask licked his suddenly dry lips. "I mean, how can Liz hope to pick them up?" But:

"No," Liz shook her head. "You can't back away from it like that. Lies—even half-lies and white lies—don't come easy to you, Ben. This worked well enough down under, didn't it? And how about Jake? You had me monitoring him when he was sleeping, didn't you?"

"If any harm should come your way," Trask's voice was husky now, "I'd never be able to forgive myself." Then his gaunt face hardened up again, and he said, "However, since it was bound to come to this sooner or later, and if you're set on doing it . . . let's get to it."

On impulse, Liz stepped closer and kissed his cheek. "Don't worry about me," she said. "I'll be careful, I promise you."

"Very well," he answered. "But you'd better let us hear it. Tell us what you're seeing, and for God's sake be on your guard for anything . . . for whatever you might find."

Meanwhile the telescope's internal mechanism had whirred to a standstill, and Manolis fed a new coin into its slot while Liz again prepared herself. Then, brushing back her hair, applying her eyes to the binocular viewers, she began her commentary.

"Actually, the coast looks to be only a few miles away. Not even that. The beaches are beautiful . . . gold merging into turquoise where the sand meets the sea, then into blue, and deeper blue. I'm following the coast road from east to west. That must be Limari, close to where that woman's body was found washed up . . . then the road moves away from us, travelling south. I can't trace it all the way because of embankments, cliffs, and places where it's been cut through spurs. Now, I can just make out . . . make out the towers of a place just off the road, a place like a fortress or castle, built right at the rim of the sea cliffs. It has these high square towers . . ."

"That's the monastery," said Trask, his voice hushed so as not to disturb Liz's concentration. "We passed it this morning, on our way out here."

"I remember," said Goodly, keeping his normally high-pitched voice as low as possible. "It had a sort of portcullis gate and picket door in the front. The gate was closed, the picket door, too. There were notice boards on the hard standing that fronted the place; we passed so quickly I didn't get the chance to read them. I don't recall seeing any monks, though, but this being a Sunday they'd probably be at their devotions."

"Monks?" said Manolis. "Nor should you expect to see monks. That one is more properly thee convent, or nunnery. It has thee nuns of a special order, yes, but no monks, only thee women . . ."

The precog gave a small start. "Women," he said, and swayed just a little, which no one noticed. "Nuns . . ."

Liz had paused. Intent on her viewing—and her telepathy—she seemed to have stopped breathing while gazing at the monastery. But now she moved on: "The road has gone, disappeared now behind mountain spurs where they fall to the sea—"

"Where I was pushed from thee road," said Manolis.

"—And now I'm approaching the outskirts of Skala Astris. I can see the seafront and a thin white horizontal line that must be the sea wall. But . . ." She paused again, and edged the telescope back just a fraction, towards the east.

"What is it?" said Trask.

"Something I nearly missed," she answered. "There's a knoll in the way that partly obscures it."

"Obscures what?" Trask was insistent.

"A building," she said. "East of Skala Astris, some kind of building on a promontory. I can see its cupola—or maybe that should be cupolas—where they're lined up in my line of sight. But the place must be quite large. It can only be an hotel, yet I don't recall seeing it on . . ."

"Yes?" said Trask.

And now her voice was a whisper as she continued ". . . on any map."

"Liz?" said Trask, frowning as he moved closer.

"There's something . . . something there," she continued, so softly that the words were difficult to make out, no more than a sigh. "Ben, I think . . . I think there's something there!"

"That's enough!" He took her round the waist, almost lifted her away from the telescope, which obligingly turned itself off.

Liz seemed a little unsteady on her feet; the shadows under her eyes were purple blooms now, and despite her suntan she had a drawn, wan look. Trask held her up and asked, "Are you okay?"

"A bit dizzy," she answered. "But that's okay. I've had the same thing happen when I've used ordinary binoculars. It's when the perspective changes: something to do with knowing that what I'm looking at is a great deal farther away than it appears."

"But you did read something?"

And now Liz's eyes went big and round, and for a moment she clung to him for support. So that when she said, "Oh, yes!" her small shudder transferred to him. "Yes, I'm sure I did."

"In that hotel place close to Skala Astris?"

"In *both* places," she answered. "In the hotel—if that's what it is—and in the monastery."

"The monastery?" Trask's jaw fell open. "For God's

sake—the monastery? But, that's the *last* place I would have thought to . . . I would have thought to—"

"To look?" Goodly finished it for him, as the significance of what Trask had said struck both of them simultaneously. And then, turning to Manolis, the precog queried: "These nuns you mentioned—the women of this order—how is it they live in a monastery? I thought monasteries were for monks, and that nuns dwell in abbeys? And there's one other, perhaps more important thing: What do they wear, these women? Do they have their own special attire? I mean habits or cassocks?"

"Here in Greece," Manolis answered, "a monastery is just a place inhabited by thee holy peoples, thee worshipful peoples, which may be men or women—but not thee two together. And it is thee same with abbeys. Have you never heard of an abbot?"

"Of course I have!" said Goodly, annoyed with himself that he'd made such a simple if understandable mistake. "And their robes?"

"With thee hoods, yes," Manolis answered. "They hide their faces with thee hooded robes, to avoid making thee temptations. I saw several of them when I was here with poor Eleni. Come to think of it, there were two of them in thee alley outside thee police post in Limari where Eleni and I . . . where she examined thee body of that woman . . . *that woman with thee leech!*"

Trask had gone cold. In the blazing midafternoon sunlight, he'd gone as cold as death itself. And he could feel the short hairs at the back of his neck prickling as if electrified. "Is it possible?" he husked. "I mean, is it even thinkable?"

And Lardis said, "Oh, yes. It's thinkable. To defile these holy women—but what a splendid jest—to such as Vavara! For to the Wamphyri there's no such thing as a higher power. Might is the only right. And so to find a people who believe in such a power, and to such an extent that they worship as these nuns do . . . she would *delight* in defiling them, proving them wrong."

"But *I* could be wrong," Liz said, which caused everyone

to look at her. Apart from the shadows under her eyes, which were fading moment by moment, she seemed to be herself again.

"How do you mean?" said Trask. "What exactly *did* you feel, or sense, or whatever?"

"At the monastery, very little," she answered.

"But enough that you paused there," said Goodly.

"I felt—I don't know—a *shiver*," she said. "As my view passed over that place, a chill. Similar to the sensation I get when I look at someone who knows what I can do and doesn't want me reading him or her . . . like Millie Cleary, for instance, when her shields go up. Then it's just a coolness, a mental warning sign saying 'keep off.' But this time . . ." She shook her head.

"Go on," said Trask.

"This time, it was like a single drop of ice-cold water on my spine," she told him. "It landed on the back of my neck, and ran all the way down. A shiver, like I said."

"And that was why you paused there?" Trask pressed her.

"Yes," she answered. "But the more I concentrated, the less I got. If someone was there—if someone or ones were sleeping there, in those towers—they must have thought they were very safe. And when they felt my probe . . ."

"Then their shields went up," said Trask. "They sensed your intrusion."

"Perhaps," Liz answered. "But only on a subconscious level. I mean, I was shut out, yes, but I wasn't investigated. That's one way of looking at it. But on the other hand—I don't know, maybe we're putting too much emphasis on this. What if I wasn't shut out at all? What if there's nothing there and I was simply trying too hard? I shivered, yes, and felt strange, but what if I wanted so hard to find something—" she shrugged undecidedly, "—that I found it anyway? Maybe I was mistaken. I'm hardly an expert at this sort of thing, and—"

But Trask shook his head. "What?" he said. "And you're the one who was questioning me about *my* faith in your talent? Liz, you sensed something all right. When I was holding you, I felt you shuddering. It went right through me. You might be able to fool yourself that way but you can't fool me. I know the truth when I see it, and I saw it in you." He nodded curtly. "So now tell me about the other place on the outskirts of Skala Astris. You said it might be an hotel. What about that?"

"That was different again," Liz said, grateful now for his support. "It was faint, so very faint. And it was . . . misty? I mean, it was like looking through a fog. I felt something, saw something, but it was so vague that I can't describe it."

"Try," said Trask. "For as I recall, you couldn't describe it out in Australia either, not at first."

"That's right," she said. "When I first probed Jethro Manchester's island, I had this same kind of problem and couldn't translate my feelings. It was the weird aura of the place."

"You have to remember," said Trask, "that we aren't talking about human beings. In your day-to-day work, you're coming into contact with *human* minds. The thoughts you read—the pictures you receive—are from *human* beings. But the Wamphyri have gone beyond that. They aren't human, not any longer. Perhaps we need to translate their thoughts differently."

"May I speak?" said Lardis.

Trask glanced at him—at the Old Lidesci, with an entire lifetime's worth of experience—and said, "Of course you can. What is it?"

"It's something you were saying just a moment ago," Lardis answered. "And it's what you did this morning."

"What we did?"

"What you, Ian Goodly, and Andreas did—all three of you, aye." Lardis nodded. "For it seems you drove right past both of those places without so much as a glance at them. Well, perhaps you glanced at them, but that's all . . ."

By now the young men of the house had brought food, drinks, and pitchers of water up onto the roof, and they were also busy arranging parasols to throw shade on a nest of chairs and small tables. Seeing them beckoning, Liz said, "Let's get out of this sunlight."

As they sat down under the parasols and Andreas poured iced drinks, Trask turned again to Lardis. "You were telling us what we did," he said.

"Or more properly what you didn't do," said Lardis.

"We were remiss, is that what you mean?" Trask frowned. "We should have been more alert, should have looked closer?"

"Should have," said Lardis, "and if it were anyone else you were looking for, you *would* have, aye!"

Trask shook his head. "I'm not with you."

"No, and you weren't with it this morning, either!" Lardis growled. "But don't you see—this is Vavara and Lord Malinari we're dealing with! *Vavaaara,* who is all things to all men, and to most women. And Nephran Malinari—also called Malinari the Mind!"

The precog began to see what he was getting at. "Not quite your average Lord and Lady," he said.

"Anything but!" snapped Lardis. "Vavara, she isn't what you see. She's what she *wants* you to see! And when she's asleep—d'you really think she would leave herself unguarded? When you drove past that monastery, you saw what she *wanted* you to see: a monastery! But it isn't, no. Nor has it been, not for two or maybe three years by my reckoning. Not as long as that vampire bitch has been in residence there!"

"*What?*" The idea struck Trask like a hammer blow, he found it that hard to believe. "Are you telling me they can actually do that?"

"Just as surely as the Szgany of Sunside are able to hide from the Wamphyri," Lardis answered, "closing down their minds so that the vampires can't sniff them out, so the Wamphyri can hide from us. Don't your telepaths have their shields, so that others can't read *their* minds? Can't your locator, David Chung, control his scanning so that others can't locate him?"

"But . . . why haven't you mentioned this before?" Trask was almost lost for words.

"Because I thought you knew!" Lardis answered. "Because it has to be obvious. For after all, most of these Great Vampires were once Szgany, and just as we have some of their skills, so they have ours. But Vavara and Malinari together . . . of course they could do it. And Liz: why, she was lucky to read anything at all! Or maybe she's not just lucky, maybe she's good! And I mean *very* good!"

"Lardis is right," said the precog. "We really *should* have been expecting something like this. We E-Branch people, anyway. And you especially, Ben."

"Me?" said Trask.

"Yes," said Goodly. "We've all of us read the Keogh files, but reading about something and experiencing it are completely different things. You were there, that time down in Devon, the Yulian Bodescu affair."

"What about it?" Trask was completely at a loss.

"When you flushed out the Bodescu household, didn't Harvey Newton see something that he thought was a dog—or at least a loping shape—running for cover? But it wasn't a dog. It was Bodescu himself."

"But they're shape-changers, for Christ's sake!" Trask protested. "We all know that much."

"*And* mind-changers," said Liz. "I would have bet my life on it that it was you, Ben, who was speaking to me in the Pleasure Dome in Xanadu. I *did* bet my life on it, and almost lost."

"Something else we should remember," said Goodly. "When we tracked Malinari down in Australia, it wasn't him who gave the show away. Trennier led us to Manchester, who in turn led us to Malinari. It was his thralls who gave Malinari away. So perhaps the same thing is happening here. Maybe Liz has found . . . maybe she has found what Vavara has made here, what she's made of the *people* who were here . . ."

"Your hooded figures?" said Trask. "Your burning women, all dressed in their black, hooded robes?"

"That's what it's beginning to look like," said the precog.

And Lardis put in: "And don't forget those sweet Sisters of Mercy that Vladi Ferengi told us about.

"Or thee nuns outside the police post," said Manolis.

"It's all fitting together," said Trask.

"It wasn't fear," Liz murmured, almost to herself.

"What's that?" Again Trask turned to face her.

"In Australia," she answered, "when I sensed the thoughts, or more properly the feelings, of those people on Manchester's island, *that* was fear. They were afraid of the future, of what it would bring. They were scared to death of Malinari and what he'd done to them through Bruce Trennier. In other words, it was just like you said, Ben." She met Trask's gaze, looked straight into his eyes. "They were *human* thoughts, *human* emotions . . . or at least they were at that time, when they'd only recently been vampirized. But what I got from the building near Skala Astris, that wasn't fear. It was like looking into a very young baby's mind. I'm not talking about innocence, but rather emptiness. A kind of wandering, wondering vacancy."

"You're describing idiocy," said Trask. "Childishness without innocence."

"You're right," Liz nodded, and once more shivered, despite that she wasn't cold. "For now and then, I've looked into *their* little minds—babies, that is. What telepath could resist it? Haven't we all wondered what's going on in there? Well, I found that they're constantly searching—for knowledge of the world, I suppose. But the feeling I got when I probed that place near Skala Astris, it was . . ." She paused and gave a small twitch of her shoulders, a baffled shrug.

And still looking directly into her eyes, Trask said, "The opposite? Is that what you sensed? Instead of seeking to know, to learn, to understand, what you felt had lost the ability to know. Babies evolve. But what you sensed—"

"Had *de*volved, yes!" said Liz. "Well, maybe . . ."

Trask took a deep breath and said, "Let's finish up here. I want to get back to base, see what Chung's come up with, if anything. And if nothing, at least we know where to point him now. So let's go."

Manolis fished a wad of notes out of his pocket, tossed it on the table. Andreas wrapped skewered meats in paper napkins, and grabbed up a bottle of mineral water.

On the way down from the roof, Manolis told Trask: "Myself and Andreas, we'll take one car. You and your people return to Skala Astris in thee other."

"You're going to take a look at that quarry, right?" said Trask.

"And thee deserted airport," Manolis nodded. "But please—Ben, my friend—before you do anything back at base, wait for me, yes? I'll get finished as quickly as possible. I shouldn't be more than an hour at most. And since Andreas has thee food, we can eat on thee way . . ."

A little after three-thirty, Trask and his party arrived back at the Christos Studios. They had used secondary roads through the foothills to avoid passing the monastery and Liz's unknown building on the eastern approach to the village.

Chung and Stavros weren't back yet, so the four waited for them in The Shipwreck, where Yiannis played some antique music for them. The scratched and battered favourites of forty years ago sounded again in the Greek afternoon.

Perhaps signalling the end of a seemingly interminable summer, a breeze off the sea had cooled the sands; a pair of young German couples had taken the opportunity to come wandering barefoot along the beach, exploring this western extreme; they were just leaving as Trask and his people settled in.

While Yiannis served drinks, Trask spoke to him. "Yiannis, is there some kind of large hotel to the east of here, maybe a mile beyond Skala Astris? It stands on a promontory, I think."

"Palataki?" Yiannis nodded. "It means 'the little palace.' It's a strange old place, all fallen into ruins. But it isn't a hotel. You can see it from the beach. Something of it, anyway."

"Really?" said Trask. "Look, let me get my binoculars, and then perhaps you'd show me."

There were binoculars in the car; Trask got them and walked down the beach with Yiannis, until small waves called up by the breeze sent ripples up the sand to their feet. The shadows were already beginning to lengthen when Yiannis pointed to the east and said: "There. You can see the twin cupolas, and the roof of the building beneath them behind the tall pines. Not very Greek looking, is it?"

With the glasses to his eyes, Trask replied, "No, it isn't. I would say it was German."

"And you'd be right," said the other. "I can tell you about it, if you're interested."

It took him a few minutes to tell Trask the history of the place, and he finished up by saying: "When I was a youth—er, a long time before I met my wife, you understand—I would take my girlfriends walking up there for some privacy in the grounds of the little palace. It was—how do you say it?—ah, yes: 'a favourite haunt' of young lovers. More recently, however . . ."

"Yes?" said Trask.

"Now it's just a haunt," said Yiannis. "Strange stories, of a ghost with yellow eyes who stands guard over the old ruin. If I believed in ghosts, I might suspect it was the lady herself."

"The Lady?" Trask's flesh prickled at the back of his neck.

"The sainted lady, yes," said Yiannis, turning and stepping out, back up the beach towards The Shipwreck. "Agia Varvara, the saint whose small shrine stands in the grounds of Palataki." He said it just as easily, just as casually as that, without ever knowing that Trask had gone cold through and through . . .

After a moment, Trask started after him. "Did you say, er, Vavara?" He tried to keep his voice even.

"Varvara," Yiannis called back to him. "The way you say it, it sounds as if you're missing out the first *r*. In fact it's *Var*vara, which in English translates as Barbara."

"A Greek saint, you say?" Trask's mind raced.

"Yes. The shrine has been there as long as I can remember."

And Trask wondered, *Has she seen it? Vavara herself? But of course she has! And would she be able to resist it, the supreme irony of it? Not according to Ladis, she wouldn't.*

Now, for Trask, the mass of evidence seemed overwhelmingly conclusive; but as yet his overall knowledge, his tactical intelligence, was insufficient to set a covert war in motion. This evening, however, working as a team with their esoteric skills, and sure now of their targets, he and his espers should at last be able to probe deep into the dark heart of vampire territory. And once they knew the total of the forces facing them—and as soon as their own forces were strong enough—then no amount of mental camouflage or alien evil would keep Trask and his people from their goal: the total destruction of Vavara and Malinari, and of everything they stood for.

And walking up the beach in Yiannis's footsteps, Trask was glad now that he wasn't himself a telepath. For if he had been . . . then he couldn't for a moment doubt but that he would turn to the east, shake his fists at Palataki's cupolas, and beyond them the towers of a once-monastery, and hurl his threats, his curses, his vengeful rage and determination, at both.

"Look out, you lousy bastard Things!" (He would shout with his enhanced mind.) *"You, Vavara, you fucking hag—and especially you, Malinari! Your very presence here defiles earth, air, and sea—the entire world! But I've found you, and I'm going to make you wish you'd stayed in Starside. I'm coming for you, you grotesque bastard monsters. Make no mistake, Ben Trask and E-Branch, we're* coming *for you!"*

But since he wasn't a telepath, he was unable to offer any such threat, any such challenge. And that was just as well . . .

David Chung and Stavros, and Manolis and Andreas, arrived back at the Christos Studios almost in tandem, with only a minute or so separating them. Liz met them, took them straight to Trask's accommodation.

Trask hadn't been wasting his time. Despite the continuing—indeed worsening—sunspot activity, which had effectively destroyed ninety-five percent of all electrical communications worldwide, he'd managed to get through to the HQ in London, warning them to be wary of nuns. Weird as it must have sounded, that in essence had been his message: the D.O. was to get onto the major airports and tell them to check all incoming flights from Greece for nuns. If any such were discovered, ways should be found to detain them just long enough for Special Branch to put tails on them. And then they should be "kept the hell away from E-Branch," but at the same time the Branch would take over covert surveillance from the police. All of this to be arranged through the Minister Responsible. "Give the bugger something to do . . ."

Mercifully the D.O. was John Grieve, whose *tele*-telepaphic talents weren't in the least affected by the weather; his less than cryptic reply had been: "A new guise on an old *geist,* eh? It's amazing the kind of people who pick up bad habits, right?"

"Or who get infected with them," Trask had told him, before asking after Millie.

"She's gone home to get her stuff together; says that since she's to be locked up here for the duration, there are bits and pieces she needs," Grieve had told him. "She takes over from me at eight o'clock tonight my time."

Trask had been alarmed. "She's out on her own?" But:

"No," Grieve had reassured him. "I arranged a plainclothes police escort for her. When she's got her stuff together, then she can call for another detective to bring her back."

And Trask's final question, before the incredibly bad line broke up completely: "Any news on that Lefranc freak?"

"We have . . . locator . . . Special Branch . . . we . . . gadgets . . . nothing . . . useless . . ." And then nothing more, except the hiss and sputter of static.

Trask had a portable fax machine that hadn't worked since leaving England. But he had tried it anyway, to no avail. When he'd fed his message into the slot—PUT HALF A DOZEN PEOPLE ON STANDBY FOR THE MED. WE MAY NEED HELP.—and after requesting a printout confirmation copy, all he'd got was an A4 sheet of something that looked like a Japanese cryptogram, which endlessly repeated itself down the page. And he'd believed he knew what Grieve had meant by "gadgets . . . nothing . . . useless."

The Head of E-Branch, while he wasn't a prude, wasn't much known for cursing either, but: "Hell and damnation! Fuck every-fucking-thing!" he'd complained, slamming the machine back into a bulky briefcase. "And especially El-fucking-Niño!"

Which had taken place just a moment before Liz knocked on the door and brought the others in with her. They sat on beds, chairs, a small table, whatever was available.

And Trask said: "David, you first. Shoot."

The locator stood in the middle of the chalet's tiny floor space and said, "I got something, and I got nothing." He tossed a plastic bag onto his bed beside Manolis. The sleeve end of an ugly, armoured, insectlike piece of metallic machinery—like some kind of hollow tool—projected from the bag where it lay. Manolis took it out, frowned suspiciously, went to put his hand into what was obviously some kind of gauntlet. But:

"Don't," said Trask. "It's nasty enough as it is. Just flex your hand inside that thing . . . you could do someone, including yourself, an injury. It's what's known in the trade as a Wamphyri battle gauntlet." Then he turned to Chung again. "Nothing?"

"Right, and yet wrong," said the locator, looking harassed. "I can't pinpoint it because we're in the middle of it."

"Go on," said Trask.

"Nothing more to say," Chung shrugged. "If I look forward, backward, left, right, up, and down, I get nothing. But if I go outside the area and look inwards—this entire place seethes! I don't mean *this* place, but this area. It's contaminated. If I had been using my talent from the first moment we got here, I'd have known right away. But as you're aware, and as you ordered, I was keeping it on a tight leash."

"So, then," said Trask. "The whole place 'seethes,' but you

can't be more specific. So tell me, where does it seethe most?"

Chung thought about it for a few moments, then said, "Along the coast road between here and Limari. But that's only a guess. I mean, it came and went. I seemed to sense something there . . . and then I didn't."

"Are you sure we can't narrow it down?" said Trask. "Should I give you a clue? How about a mile east of here, for example?"

Chung stared at him and narrowed his slanted eyes a little. "Funny you should say that," he answered. "But since I couldn't say for sure . . . I just wasn't about to send you off on a wild-goose chase."

Liz nodded understandingly and said, "It left you in doubt of your own talent—the same as it did to me."

"It?" said the locator, looking from face to face.

"Something that Vavara does," said Trask, and quickly went on: "How about the monastery? Did you get that far?"

Now Chung's jaw fell open. "How did you know—?"

"Okay," said Trask, cutting him off. "Here's what we're going to do. Another hour and it'll be cooler and darker. The sun will still be visible in the west, and it will still be shining on the places where these bastards sleep easiest in their beds: the high places in their aeries, that is. Well, we've found two places that just could be their aerie or aeries. And now I want to know what's in them." He opened a map and stabbed at it with his forefinger. "Earlier today Liz found us this knoll—it got in the way when she was looking through a telescope. It happens to be the highest place in this vicinity, and if I haven't forgotten my map-reading skills these contours allow for an almost clear line of sight on both locations. That's where we're going next."

He stood up, said: "Boys—and girl—you have fifteen minutes to get tidied up, changed, and to do what you've got to do. Then we're on our way. We've got to get this next phase over and done with before sundown, for obvious reasons. So let's go."

And fifteen minutes later, they went . . .

* * *

Using two of the four-wheel-drive vehicles, they drove along a farm track skirting an olive grove, then about a mile inland to the foot of the knoll. The knoll's base was formed of a scree skirt that extended all the way round what was in fact a marble outcrop. On the south-facing skirt, the slope was about one-in-three and it was marked with crisscrossing goat tracks through hardy herbage to the foot of the outcrop. The vehicles made the climb without too much difficulty, but from there on the eight had to go on foot.

Trask was concerned for Lardis and said it might be better if he took it easy and waited there, but the Old Lidesci insisted that this was his kind of climbing. "What is it but a small hill?" he said. "In my time I climbed the Barrier Mountains!"

"This isn't your time," said Trask, making hard work of it up the boulder-studded slope.

But climbing past him, Lardis answered, "Nor yours, by the look of it!"

With one hundred feet to go they climbed into sunlight that came streaming from the west, and as the high dome of the knoll levelled out so the going became that much easier. From the top the view was all Trask could have wished for: almost due south, the cupolas of Palataki reflected the sunlight where they stood up from the grimly gothic building below, and to the southeast the monastery's towers were lit with gold where the cliffs fell sheer to the sea. In that same direction, the Aegean itself was already shaded, its deep blue surface flecked with small white wave crests.

With very little time to spare, David Chung and Liz chose a flat-topped boulder to use as a table, and set themselves up to gaze through their glasses first on Palataki's gilded cupolas.

"Now remember," Trask reminded them, as they settled to the task, "this place stands on top of a mine. We may not find what we're looking for in those cupolas or even in the main building. According to what Yiannis says, the promontory was mined extensively—almost hollowed out—during a prewar German mining operation. So for all we know Vavara might have quite literally gone to ground. On the other hand, we suspect she's in the monastery, in which case there must be something else in Palataki. Malinari? We don't know . . . but we do *want* to know."

"We'll go in hand-in-hand," said Liz quietly, "riding each other's probes."

"But carefully," Trask told her. "Oh so very carefully. And be ready to get out if anything—if anything—"

"If anything probes back," the precog, Ian Goodly, finished it for him.

The locator had Malinari's gauntlet close to hand, its dull metal casing softly agleam in the gradually fading sunlight. In the west, the sun's lower rim had already touched the blue-grey crest of a distant range of hills.

The two espers stood shoulder to shoulder with their elbows resting on the boulder, their heads hunched forward, the binoculars to their eyes . . .

After a minute or so of almost complete silence, disturbed only by the shuffle of nervous feet on chalky ground, suddenly Liz said, "Seething, yes—that's the way I would describe it, too, David—but what's it seething with?"

"It isn't Malinari." The other offered a negative twitch of his head and placed his trembling right hand on the gauntlet's scaled surface. "This weapon of his is stone cold dead. If Malinari were there, I'm certain I'd have some kind of reaction by now. But something's there, for sure."

"Go down," said Liz. "Cut through the trees to the building itself, the lower floors, the cellars, and even—"

"Stop!" said the locator, his voice cracking like a whip.

"What is it?" Trask said hoarsely.

"Mindsmog!" Chung whispered now. "There's someone—there's some*thing*—there."

"I've got him!" Liz answered with a whisper of her own.

"Vampire!" Chung breathed.

"How many?" Trask snapped. "I want numbers."

And after a moment: "Just the one," said Liz. "A caretaker, I think."

"Caretaker?" Trask very carefully put his hand on her shoulder. But:

"Ah!" Liz gasped in that same moment, withdrawing her probe and snatching the binoculars away from her eyes so quickly that they almost slipped from her grip. "I think he must have sensed me. I felt him stiffen."

"Leave it be!" said Trask at once. "Don't go back in there. You've done enough. David?" Now he touched Chung.

"It's okay," the locator told him. "I've moved on past him. He might have picked up on Liz, but not me. He definitely isn't Malinari. I'm going down—down into the mine, now—into the earth. For it's the earth that's doing the seething. It's . . . I don't know . . . but it's poisoned, down there."

"What is it?" said Trask. "What have you found?"

But once again the locator could only reply with a negative twitch of his head.

"Let me read *his* mind," said Liz. "David's mind. That way I won't be in direct contact, and whatever it is won't sense me."

"Do it," said Trask.

And in a moment, "This is it," Liz said. "An imbecile mind, or minds. The devolved thing that I sensed from the roof of The Aerie. That is what's doing the seething. It's . . . it's *growing* down there!"

And finally—recognizing it for what it really was—she shuddered herself into Trask's arms and said, "I think it must be the same as that awful garden under the Pleasure Dome, where Peter Miller had rotted down into that hideous—"

"Deadspawn!" said Trask. "Or *un*-deadspawn, if you like."

The locator was finished for the moment. "I can get nothing else," he said, glad to be out of it and resting his metaphysical mind and his eyes both.

"You've done fine," said Trask, "both of you. But we're not finished yet. Now, while there's still time, I want you to look at the monastery. . . "

16
Malinari Dreams of Blood—Vavara of Treachery—Their Dreams Coalesce

THE SUNLIGHT WAS ALMOST GONE, REDUCED TO a pale yellow stain on the walls and bastion-like towers of the monastery as once more Liz and the locator took up their binoculars, focussed them for greater range, and commenced scanning. And this time Trask said nothing at all—made no comment with regard to safety measures—for there was now a tangible tension in the evening air which would make any such warnings redundant.

"The towers?" Liz queried.

"The towers, yes," Chung's almost imperceptible nod, as he sent his probe spearing down his line of sight. "The one that's closest to the road. I have its highest windows focussed now."

"Check," said Liz, her voice a breath of air.

Then the locator's shoulders shook in an involuntary shudder. And: "God!" he gasped. "Mindsmog—but mindsmog like I've never felt it before—so thick you could cut it with a knife!"

"Me, too," Liz whispered. "A blanket of mental fog, an impenetrable mind-shield. And behind it, someone sleeping. Except it isn't just a shield but a warning that says: 'This close and no closer.' And now . . . and now . . . what on earth?"

"What?" said Trask, urgently. "What?"

"It's gone!" Liz answered. "I mean, it was there for a moment, and now . . . no mindsmog, nothing."

"No," said Chung. "Not nothing, but something . . . something different. It's like . . . like a warm, scented wind blowing outwards from the monastery. A soothing, balming breeze, carrying the message that this place is . . . that it's—"

"Benign!" Liz finished it for him. "Fresh and clean. Wholesome. There's nothing there but goodness and even saintliness." And she actually shrugged her shoulders before continuing, "But of course. For after all, the place is a monastery."

"A lie!" Trask reminded her, while from nearby, the Old Lidesci said:

"*Vavaaara!* You're seeing what she wants you to see! All but Ben, who sees only the truth."

"The other tower," Trask snapped. "Focus on the tower standing at the rim of the cliffs. But quickly now, while the sun is still on it." Even as he spoke, twin shadows commenced creeping up from the high fortress walls, covering the towers with their gloom. And all that was left of the sun was a yellow blister on the hills of the western range.

Working in unison—locator and telepath together—Liz and Chung followed his instructions. "I've got it," said Chung, and Liz said:

"There, there!"

Their probes were linked, each magnified by the other. They saw the shadows creeping—no, sweeping—up the high walls of the tower, transmuting it from gold to the faded yellow of ancient stone. Then:

"It's . . . dim," said Chung. "And it's dark, empty."

"No, there's something there," Liz answered him. "Some kind of light . . ."

"Careful!" said Trask, as his espers continued to gaze down the barrels of their glasses . . .

. . . Where at first the lenses framed grey light, then feral yellow light, *and finally a gush of crimson!*

And as if the binoculars were suddenly filled with blood—which was exactly how it had felt—they dropped them and went staggering away from the boulder. Choking back their horror and cowering down, it seemed they were hiding from something; and a single word or query—a single hollow grunt like that of some great pig—continued to reverberate in their minds.

W-W-WHAT? . . . W-WHAT? . . . WHAT!?

Then it was gone, finished—cut off as they withdrew their probes—and a wind sprang up out of the twilight, to cool the dome of the knoll.

Trask grabbed Liz and held her tightly, and Manolis went to steady David Chung where his feet skidded on loose pebbles. For all of them had felt something of what the espers had felt.

"What was it?" Trask spoke to Liz, shuddering in his arms.

"It was him," said Liz. "I'm pretty sure of it. I mean, who else would dream of . . . of blood? We may have woken him up, but I don't think he had time to get a fix on our probes. He'd most likely think the intrusion was some kind of nightmare, or maybe a part of the normal waking process. God, at least I hope so!"

Chung nodded his agreement. "I think she's right. Myself, I often start awake. That's what it felt like: some kind of weird awakening, like an ice-cold wavefront washing outwards from him. But a *red* wavefront, of frozen blood. Certainly it froze mine!"

At which precise moment:

Malinari's gauntlet on the boulder made a metallic sound—then gave a *clang!*—and sprang like some terrible insect seven or eight inches into the air. A moment later and it fell inert, but with all of its murderous blades and hooks fully extended, to the marble-chip gravel of the knoll's stony dome.

Shaken, the eight looked at each other and began to breathe again. "It's metallic," Ian Goodly piped. "As the sun went down and that wind sprang up, it got cooler and contracted, and some mechanism inside was activated."

"I agree," said Trask, his rasping voice more than a little shaken. "But while you're the precog, still it's an omen. And I don't think there's any doubt now but that Malinari is there in that tower, in what used to be a monastery."

Chung was steadier now. Since he was in charge of the

alien weapon he knew it better than any of them. "I think you're both right," he said, taking up the gauntlet and putting a slim hand inside it. A moment more to search with his fingertips, and its lethal arsenal of punches, hooks, and gleaming blades *ch*-chinged from sight one after the other, as they slipped back into their housings.

"Now let's get out of here," said Trask. "The light's going and it'll soon be dusk. The last thing I want is to be out here in the dusk. And certainly not in the dark."

As they went scrambling their way back down the side of the knoll, no one disagreed with him . . .

Dreams of blood, yesss! *Dreams of a life of lust and greed, and of ascending to a Lord . . . followed by banishment and suspended animation in the frozen northern wastes. Of the great melt, and of the return to Starside and the toppled stumps of once-mighty aeries. Then of a man of the Szgany, called Nathan, whose weird powers were such that they made life—and undeath—unbearable in what was once a paradise; where beyond the Barrier Mountains, in Sunside, the Szgany fatted in the forest like so many cattle. A land of milk and honey,* yesss!*—and blood, of course—the very font of perpetual youth.*

Dreams of youth, and of ages flown . . . and youth flown with them. But a man need not look *old, not while there is blood for the taking. Nor need a woman look old, for that matter.*

Dreams of Vavara, and of her aerie—this fine monastery—and of the sibling horde she fostered in Palataki, keeping them to herself and denying him their use.

Oh, Vavara . . . you ungrateful, greedy, withered bitch! Just how many ages have you depended upon your counterfeit "beauty," your lying, mass-hypnotic talent, to extend your existence? The years are countless. And all of that time you've let your metamorphism lapse. Unused, it has wasted like an atrophied muscle, become useless to you. And now like a fool you've trapped yourself here in a castle on the edge of an alien ocean!

But I, *Nephran Malinari, shall not be trapped when they—*
—trapped when they—
—when they come?

"W-w-*what!?*" Malinari snapped awake. *"What!?"*

He jerked bolt upright on his pallet, so suddenly that his companion through the long hours of daylight was dashed to the bare boards of the floor.

"What? What's that?" She, too, came quickly awake, looking up from where she sprawled naked beside the pallet, and seeing, almost as if for the first time, Malinari's face.

But where last night he had seemed strangely handsome when he "rescued" the ex-New Yorker, Sister Anna, from her would-be tormentors, the former sisterhood, now in his moment of truth, Malinari was more surely Wamphyri!

His hair shone black where it was brushed back behind conchlike ears, falling like a small cloak around his shoulders. His brow was high and slate grey, as was all the flesh of his naked body and alien features. His eyes were crimson—the colour of blood itself—and his convoluted snout flared when he sniffed at the air like a nightmare hound, or more properly a great bat. But worse than the rest of these anomalies together, Malinari's jaws were incredible, monstrous where they gaped at some unseen presence. And:

"Too soon!" he snarled, and the words rumbled from him like an avalanche. "They're here—they've found me—too soon!"

"What? Oh, what?" Sister Anna's hand flew to her mouth. "Is it Vavara . . . I mean, our Mother Superior? Has she heard us? Am I to be punished for my sins?" And she gasped as she gazed upon her nakedness, the great bruises on her breasts and thighs, the rusty brown web of his sperm where it matted her pubic bush and glued it to her belly. For she had thought it was a dream, only a terrible dream!

Malinari heard her, and it was as if he'd just this moment noticed her. "Eh?" he grunted, wrinkling his nose at her. "Vavara? No, it isn't Vavara, you shivering sow! It's worse—it's much worse—than Vavara."

"What have I done?" Anna whispered, her hands like crippled moths as they fluttered over her bruises. "I . . . I remember how the sisters held me trapped in my room. I didn't want to let them in but they promised they'd do me no harm. All they wanted was to talk, to tell me of their plan. I was the last . . . I had lasted the longest, and my innocence was important to their . . . to their plan—?"

"They 'planned' to use you," Malinari scowled, his features gradually returning to normal as he recovered from the shock of his awakening, "to break and abuse you." He stood up in an easy flowing motion, caught her under the arm, and hauled her upright. "I saved you from being wasted, that's all. When I took you the first time, you were as tight as the hole that's left where the stalk is pulled from a ripe plum—and that was good. But to be honest, I don't know which of your openings I enjoyed the most. You used your mouth to very good effect—well, for a novice." And then he grinned a rabid wolf's grin, so that Anna could see the split, devil's tongue wriggling in the cave of his mouth.

But what was he saying? Something about *her* mouth?

She licked her saltily scaled lips, and . . . that taste!

Caught up by Malinari, Sister Anna stood aghast, shivering. She tried to cover her nakedness, her irreparably defiled body, her very soul . . . if she still had one. But she was weak in all of her limbs. And there was pain—such pain—in those several parts of her body that . . . that she had always . . .

She opened her mouth to scream her denial—and Malinari's hands flew to her head—one to grasp her throat, the other to cover her mouth.

"Be quiet!" he hissed. "Or she really will hear you. I want her to sleep on, if she *is* still asleep. Get dressed—throw on that hooded sack that you wear to cover your 'sinful' body. Ah, but how pleasurable this sinning, eh? Consider yourself fortunate, little Anna, that a master broke you open with real flesh, and not those sluts with their lifeless wooden pricks!" Releasing her suddenly, he thrust her away.

Anna trembled so much she could scarcely pull on her habit, but finally it was in place and she said, "I must go to her, to Vavara, and repent what I've done. I—"

"You'll do no such thing," said Malinari, more nearly a man now. And as she turned her face away in shame: "*Look* at me!" he commanded her. "Look at me now!" She couldn't refuse as he held her head between his hands, but more gently than before.

"Do you know why you thought it was a dream?" he said.

She could only answer with the smallest shake of her head.

"Because I took it away from you. When I was in you, I told you to forget. And now I'm telling you again. Forget that we've been joined, and that you've felt my flesh expanding within you and my cold seed flooding your openings. Nothing so . . . so *vile* has ever happened to you! What, you? A virgin nun?"

"But . . . my bruises," Anna whispered, as her eyes rolled up and her mind felt the ice of his hands, his awful power sucking at her memories, erasing them.

"You fell," he told her. "You fell on the steep steps, when you ran from those filthy, lustful women. That's all you remember. And if Vavara or anyone else asks about me, you'll say you don't know me, except as the good Father Maralini. There, now—*there*! And as for that which you thought was a dream—why, it *was* a dream!"

Again he released her, and as Anna's eyes rolled down, they gradually focussed. Then she blinked, gasped, and said "W-why am I here?"

"I picked you up, my dear," he answered, "when you fell."

"Yes," she whispered. "I . . . I fell on the steps."

"Indeed," Malinari told her. "But you are only bruised, and nothing broken. Now you must go, for it's evening and the monastery will soon be awake. Tongues would wag, I fear, if you were to be found here, and Vavara would doubtless hear them."

"The other sisters . . ." She shuddered violently.

"Avoid them, yes," he nodded. "Lest they chase you, and you are made to fall again. Now leave me." And abruptly opening his door, he thrust her out . . .

* * *

Malinari dressed quickly, then stood in the centre of his cell-like room and sent out his probes. It was still very quiet. The nuns were asleep, or barely waking, in their cells. And Vavara, in the other tower . . . her spell held true. The lying stench of goodness, mercy, and virtue—all of these things, of which in fact she knew so very little—enticed and enwrapped Malinari's cautious probe until he almost believed them himself . . . except he knew better. *Hah!* But so much for the bitch: she slept on.

Vavara slept, yes—but what of those others, whose spying had brought him snarling awake? The roof of the tower, its parapet, would make for a perfect vantage point.

Standing to one side, where no stray ray of lethal sunlight would strike, if such remained, he drew back the heavy drapes—layer upon layer of them—from one of his narrow windows. But the sun was down and twilight gathering. Good.

He left his tiny room, swept up the stairs to the trapdoor, and let himself out onto the tower's roof. It made an excellent vantage point, yes, and would make for an even better launching platform, when the time came. For as Malinari assumed his vampire form, lifting his face to sniff the night air, he was sure that the time *would* come, and soon.

The air was alive with the chittering of bats. Inaudible to others, it was as though they spoke to Malinari. A pity that he didn't understand them, or rather that their tongue was foreign to him. Ah, but if only this were Starside, and these creatures his familiars. Ten thousand eyes, and all of them searching the night at his behest!

But sight is only one of the senses, and a mundane sense at that. Malinari knew the signatures of certain minds—his memory was such that he could never forget them—and he knew the psychic pattern of a certain group-mind, the one he believed had wrenched him from his sleep. But on the other hand, he also knew that he was as prone to nightmares as ordinary men; except his were more nightmarish yet. Which meant that it was possible, barely, that he'd been nightmaring; that in reality his shields had *not* been brushed by the probes of would-be intruders, would-be assassins. But he had to be absolutely certain, for his very existence depended upon it—

—Likewise the cessation of Vavara's, the ungrateful hag.

Westward, the gradually fading rays of a vanished sun stuck up like spokes over the distant hills. That was the first place Malinari looked. Drawn by the menace that had been, he narrowed his eyes to scowl at the last shred of gold on the western horizon. But the sun was truly down and night fast approaching.

Nighttime—his time—when Malinari's powers were potent beyond the most exaggerated expectations of merely human espers. And there in the west . . . trace elements in the psychic aether, like a taint in the balming dusk of evening. His lips drew back in a silent snarl; his concentration was such that the cloak of hair rose up from his shoulders as if electrified; he separated out the various "scents" making up the telltale group-signature of a body of people known as—

—Known as E-Branch! They *were* here! They really *had* found him! And, of course, they had found Vavara, too. Even adversity can have its compensations. In this case he knew what he was up against, and she didn't. She didn't even know they were here—and wouldn't, not if Malinari had any say in it.

But there was no denying his vampire-enhanced senses, those warning "odours" adrift and dispersing on the aether, which yet permeated his innermost mind:

The female, Liz (an emerging Power, that one, who should be dead in the ruins of Xanadu, and yet was here, albeit inexplicably). And that cursed locator, with his mind like a lodestone, or a Starside wolf sniffing at the heels of its prey; he'd come very close to costing Malinari his life, that one!

These were the principal elements discovered by his probes, but they weren't by any means the only ones. No, for the group-signature was reinforced by others whose talents were harder to define or understand.

Trask, for instance. The one "scent" he had left behind was one of utter loathing—of Malinari! And Malinari knew why. It was because of Zek, the telepath he'd encountered and killed in Romania when first he entered this world. She had known all the secrets of these people, this E-Branch, and if he had been able to drain more of them from her before killing her—

But too late now to cry over spilled blood and a beautiful, wasted female body. Zek had been Trask's, yes, and Trask wanted revenge—which by Malinari's lights was perfectly natural. But as for Trask's talent (for all of these people were talented), as yet it remained a mystery. Malinari had read something of it in Zek's mind, as his cold hands drained her knowledge away: it had something to do with truth. But what good was such a talent against the centuried disciplines of a Lord of the Wamphyri? If one can only tell the truth, or recognize the truth, how can he hope to prevail against the very Father of Deceit? There can be no common ground, no interface, where *everything* is an untruth! And the Great Vampire was never born, or made, who couldn't lie his heart out.

Such reasoning, or *un*reasoning, was a word game that Malinari played with himself, perhaps to reassure himself . . .

Then there was this other, the one like a spindle, tall and thin, whose mind seemed singularly weird. Malinari had touched upon it that time in Xanadu, but only in passing; a tentative, cursory probe at best. Indeed, he had scanned the entire group, but since at the time he had been intent upon making an escape, there had been scant opportunity for any kind of in-depth probing. And as for the tall one—the "precog," yes—his mind had seemed as open as a book, yet at the same time blank as a page as yet unwritten!

For it appeared that his mind held few memories for Malinari to steal—only his *present* thoughts, as fleeting as the moment—as if he made room for the future by obliterating the past, or as if for him time worked in reverse! Patently he *remembered* the past, but the focus of his mind was on the future. Definitely a very peculiar mind, and a talent that was stranger yet.

And again Malinari was prompted to ask himself: What

use is a skill which is so unreliable? And if the future is so devious as to defy interpretation, how then may one use it to any great advantage . . . ?

They were all members of this E-Branch, these people, these esoteric defenders of their world, their Earth. Liz, a telepath like Zek before her. And Chung, with his batlike radar. Trask, who knew "the truth"—but who yet might be led astray, if one possessed the skill for it—and the precog, who had little or no faith in *his* talent at all!

These four, and how many others? For there were others, Malinari knew that for a certainty. So much at least he'd had from Zek's mind before killing her: the fact that there *were* others. At least one more had been here with the group this very night, not long ago and not too far away. His signature was very faint and previously unknown—or at least Malinari had not separated it out before tonight—yet was vaguely familiar. If this were Sunside he would hazard a guess, indeed he would wager upon it, that this one was Szgany! That much he would know, if not where he was hiding. But this wasn't Sunside . . .

And finally there was one other, absent now from the group, whose signature Malinari remembered from Xanadu. He remembered it . . . but wasn't able to detect it, not tonight. Which was as well. For whereas Liz was a burgeoning mentalist Power of some potential, that one, Jake—the one she'd called out to in her terror of the mushroom garden under the Pleasure Dome—*he* was already a Power, a very real PRESENCE in the psychic aether!

Malinari remembered how, when Liz was trapped in subterranean Xanadu, she had cried out into the psychic aether for help; a pitiful cry from an impossible situation.

Moreover, he remembered how he'd gloated, while using his own superior mentalism to send her this message: *Ah, no, little thought-thief. No one can help you now. You thought to use your mentalism against me, but Malinari has used it against you! I have lied to Ben Trask—impossible! But I've done it—and I have located and lost your locator. As for your marvelous precog: he scans the future but senses only confusion, for the death and destruction that he foresaw was not mine but his own, and yours, and Xanadu's. Now you cry out to this Jake—your lover, perhaps?—but where is he? Oh, ha ha haaaaa!*

That had been his final message to her, yes, before he had been obliged to concentrate on the job in hand: to destroy this E-Branch utterly. But at the time he had professed or pretended to know much more than he'd actually known of these people. And for all Malinari's telepathic skill and experience, he had only once before come across a mind with a signature like Jake's—a veritable whirlwind of esoteric numbers, symbols, and formulae—and that, too, had been in Sunside/Starside.

Aye, and Malinari remembered that one only *too* well. His name—his *hated* name—had been Nathan, and he'd been a scourge on all of Malinari's works. On his, and Vavara's, and even Lord Szwart's. If the likes of Nathan were here, and if E-Branch numbered such as *him* within their ranks . . . what then?

And again Malinari found himself wondering about the escape of these oh-so-tenacious people from incendiary Xanadu and from all the traps he'd laid for them there. How had it happened? It should have been impossible. Liz should *never* have escaped from the guardian of his garden, and as for the bomb he'd planted in the elevator, which wrecked his blister aerie: that should have taken care of at least two of them, including their leader, Ben Trask. Yet all had lived through it with barely a scratch. Malinari knew that for a fact. Soaring overhead as he made his own escape, he'd seen them alive in Xanadu's gardens. But even then they had been in direst peril from the inferno that was Xanadu; which yet again they'd escaped, as witness their presence here.

Nathan and Jake . . . one and the same? No, never. The first had been a Sunsider born, his psychic aura unmistakably Szgany. While just as undeniably, Jake was of Earth, of this world; for his aura—however briefly touched upon—had spoken of cities, science, and sophistication as opposed to forests and foraging, and the artless "innocence" or "naïvety" of Sunside's nomads.

Not one and the same, then. But two of a kind? It began to seem likely. Able to come and go in the wink of an eye, and so effect these apparently miraculous escapes. And that signature of constantly mutating, meaningless numbers. Perhaps they were more than just a signature; it could even be they were a Power in their own right. Meaningless for the moment, yes—meaningless to Malinari—but who could say what the future might or might not bring? If ever this Jake should fall into Malinari's hands (or if he could be lured into them), what then? And what hope for mankind, on this or any other world, if Nephran Malinari were to gain control of a talent such as that?

"Malinari?"

He lurched against the parapet wall, starting at the sound of her voice and instinctively reinforcing his shields to guard his thoughts. Not that Vavara's mentalism was any match for his own, but Malinari knew how treacherous certain of his thoughts had been, and how they might have betrayed him. And:

"What's this?" she said sweetly, as he turned to face her. "A guilty conscience?"

Vavara's guise was radiant, no less than on the night they had dined out together. And though Malinari knew it was *only* a guise—and despite his earlier excesses with Anna, when he had gone at her endlessly through the long night hours, but yet carefully, so as not to damage her—still he felt the need to possess Vavara . . . and at once put it aside. She could wear a man to a frazzle, this one, and afterwards, when he lay exhausted . . .

. . . In the stumps of old Starside stacks, the gross females of a certain species of spider had similar mating habits. Their tiny mates were never seen except as empty sacks, their thorny parts as dry as dust, forming little piles of debris under the silken webs of their terrible lovers.

Vavara's question had been barbed; gathering his wits, Malinari smiled wryly as he answered it. "Guilty? But of course I am, always, and I won't deny it. How can I, for I am Wamphyri! And so are you. But a guilty *conscience*? Surely not. After all, one must first have a conscience!"

"And yet you started," she said, moving closer.

He shrugged and answered, "Because I didn't expect anyone up and about so close to sunset. That glow in the west there? The sun is barely down."

"That much is obvious," she answered, "and I know it. Else I were not here—nor you. But you're an early riser, Nephran Malinari." (Was there something in her voice? An edge of suspicion, perhaps?)

He shrugged again—sensed her weak, exploratory probe—and redoubled his shields. "My dreams were uneasy."

"Mine, too," she told him. "It seems some of these stories you told me—of your failure in Australia, and of the people who chased you from your bubble aerie—have affected me badly. Would you believe, I even dreamed that they were here?"

"Really?" Malinari feigned surprise.

"Indeed! And such was the nature of my dreams that despite the watchers I have on the seaports, tonight I shall send out some of my women to scour the land around."

Vavara's probes were less exploratory, more aggressive now, and Malinari had had enough. "Let's hope they find nothing," he snapped, and made as if to move towards the open hatch.

Quickly putting herself in his way, Vavara said, "But don't you see anything peculiar in all this? And don't you agree that it's a very strange thing, Nephran—even a singular thing, in the light of my dreams—to find you out here in the twilight, all nervous and out of sorts, scanning afar?"

"Out of sorts?" He raised an eyebrow. "Scanning? Why, Lady, I—"

"Ah, no!" Vavara grated, suddenly leaning forward to sniff at him, her guise crumbling. She let it go deliberately—for effect, he supposed—and in a moment her beautiful eyes were melting into fire, bubbling like cauldrons full of blood, while her leathery black-bat nostrils wrinkled back, gaping

as they fed on his odours. "I'm no *Lady,* Lord Malinari, and never call me that again. I know only too well what I am, and I know what *you* are! When I dream of treachery, betrayal, and wake up seeking an answer, only to find you up here on the roof, sending your probes out into the night . . . isn't it understandable that I should ask myself: to what end?"

"Treachery?" He loomed over her, fighting to stave off his own fury, which had been galvanized by hers, and met her fiery gaze with a crimson look of his own. "Against you, Vavara? Neither by word nor deed! How can you even think it? And as for betrayal: Of what am I accused now? Without me, how would you have fared on this island, in this monastery? Where would you have seeded your deadspawn crop? No, if anyone has been betrayed, surely I am that one: Nephran Malinari, whose hard won monies purchased dark and dank Palataki, wherein to breed your horde—to which you deny *me* access!"

Vavara scarcely appeared to hear a word he said, but moved closer still, sniffing at him all the harder with her wrinkled, convolute snout.

"You *smell!*" she grunted, her guise almost entirely dissolved away now, revealing the wrinkled hag underneath; but a hag as strong as three strong men, with a leathery hide, and claws and teeth like knives. "You smell of sex—with one of mine no doubt—and especially of lies. Also of . . . what, fear? Apprehension? Are you afraid of me, then, Malinari? No, I think not—but you should be! Of what, then? Of something out there in the night, perhaps, which you've sensed with your much-vaunted mentalism?"

He might have answered with a blow to flatten her snout, or one to shatter her scythe teeth, but Vavara's shawl had slipped from her right arm, and he saw that she wore a gauntlet. It was a Lady's gauntlet—more "delicate" than a Lord's, and designed for flensing rather than braining or dismembering—but just as deadly against an unarmed man.

Malinari was no coward, but neither was he a fool. And backing away from her, he lied: "I sensed *nothing* in the night! But is it any wonder that I'm up here scanning abroad? Wouldn't you do the same if it were you who was being thrown out, obliged to take your leave of this place? I have a ways to go, and so must plan my route."

She was taken aback. "Plan your route? Take your leave—?"

"But isn't that what you wanted?" he said. "To see the back of me? Haven't you told me as much to my face? Ah, but it's all too visible in *your* face, and in your attitude, Vavara, without that I employ my 'much-vaunted' mentalism to read your mind."

She stood back a pace, withdrew her weak probes, and rapidly adjusted her own shields. "But—"

"And so you *shall* see the back of me," he cut her short. "I leave tonight."

"Tonight?" Vavara's features flowed; she was a woman again; she gathered up her shawl and hid her gauntlet in its folds. "I . . . I had no idea. You said nothing."

"There was nothing to say. You want me gone, and so I shall go. My only regret, that our past 'friendship' means so little; that for all I've done to help you, you have offered nothing in return."

"Meaning my holdings in Palataki?" She narrowed her eyes.

"Exactly. Your holdings . . . *and* your women."

"Hah!" she gave a snort, but by now her features—albeit difficult to ascertain—were those of a beautiful woman again; it was her guise, of course. "You're nothing more than a thief, Malinari. You take, and only then think to ask my leave!"

"But I *did* ask," he answered. "Er, before I took."

"You asked, and I told you no. Once was enough, with Sara."

"And so it comes to this," Malinari sighed. "The parting of the ways."

"Yes, and we'll be all the better for it," Vavara answered. "You and I—and that thing called Szwart—the farther we're apart, the better we appreciate each other. For as you yourself said but a moment ago, we're Wamphyri, after all." Then, changing the subject: "What will you take with you?"

"I brought nothing," he shrugged, "and I shall take nothing away. I have monies in many currencies . . . I'll find a place in Bulgaria, or even Romania. Properties are cheap in Romania, and the tongue is close to our own. Also, I've heard tell of crumbling old aeries in the mountains that go wanting for a master."

"And so you'll start again?"

"Nothing else for it," he answered.

"And how will you make away?"

"There are plenty of boats for hire in Krassos town," Malinari continued to lie, making it up as he went. "I can pay for my crossing . . . or not, depending on my mood. But don't concern yourself, I won't leave any evidence behind. You've had trouble enough. I'll travel by night, rest by day. It's the only way."

"And it won't concern you that I'm so far ahead of you, and presumably Szwart also?" Vavara was frowning now; she was puzzled, plainly unsettled by this sudden turn of events.

"It's a wide world," he answered, "peopled with kind hearts and gullible fools. With luck, I'll even find me another Jethro Manchester."

"But even so, deadspawn takes time to mature," she quickly, maliciously reminded him. "And you haven't the makings. No lieutenant of long-standing, with spores in his blood or a leech in his body, to use in the seeding of a garden. Why, before you've so much as started, this island and all the Mediterranean lands around shall be mine, and England and France Lord Szwart's. Our original plans are in disarray, and I now must plan for myself. Surely you've realized as much, that you are now on your own?"

"All true," said Malinari, "and I do realize it, of course. But while the rest of this world is fighting *your* plagues, mine will be brewing all unsuspected. So that in the end it shall be as it has always been, survival of the fittest."

"The fittest?" Vavara lifted her chin and smiled luminously at him. "Myself, obviously!"

"That remains to be seen," said Malinari. "But now you must excuse me. I shall be gone within the hour." And as she grudgingly stood aside, he left her there on the roof . . .

From his tower room, Malinari reached out with his mentalism to find Sister Anna. He seized upon her signature and told her:

If you would be out of this place—away from this sinister creature and her sisterhood of evil—come to me now. I, Father Maralini, shall leave this place tonight. And of all the sinful women within these walls, you are the only one worth saving. Do you hear me, Anna? If so, then come to me.

Of course she heard him, and came at once. He knew when she was at his door; quickly drawing her inside, he said, "Anna, my dear, do you know the way to Palataki?"

She nodded, then gasped as his cold hands went to her head. "Meet me on the side road where it rises to the Little Palace," he commanded her then. "Meet me there in the midnight hour. But keep to the shadows and don't stray too close. The woman Vavara has a man there who would harm you."

"Yes," Anna answered, with her eyes rolled up so that only the whites showed . . . the whites, and also a little yellow that Malinari had put there during her seduction and defilement, and even a few flecks of crimson other than that of normally bloodshot eyes. Seeing it, he knew that she was his thrall, and that his power was not diminished. A little of his essence was worth a pint of any other's. So he was wont to tell himself.

"Can you do it?" He gave her a little shake, half-stirring her from the stupor induced by the numbing action of his hands. "Can you get out of here and make your way unseen to Palataki? It's a distance of some five or six miles."

"I can do it," she sighed. "It will be easy. Vavara has me on watch tonight, and so I can slip away."

"Good!"

And as her eyes rolled down again and blinked at him: "But Father," she said. "I thought perhaps you'd called me here for . . . for something else? Something . . . other?" Leaning closer, she brushed against him until Malinari felt the thrust of her stiffening nipples even through the coarse weave of her habit. And oh, that sly, suggestive smile on her face! It was wicked, that smile, so that indeed he knew his power was undiminished, and that Anna was or would be a vampire! But:

"Ah, no," he told her, directing her to the door. "Not now, for I must away. Later, perhaps, in Palataki. And Anna—do not call me Father. From now on call me master. Do you understand?"

"Yes, master," she sighed, as she left him and floated off into the darkness of the monastery . . .

At about 8:30, as he made his way westward along the coast road to Skala Astris, Malinari heard a motor's growl and stepped out of the way onto the tinder-dry vegetation beside the road. Vavara's limo pulled up, its window wound down, and its nun driver leaned her hooded face out into the night.

"What is it?" Malinari recognized the faintly feral glow of her eyes and knew she was Vavara's true thrall.

"The mistress saw you leave," that one said, "and since she was sending us out and about tonight, she thought we might take you into Krassos town."

"I want no favours of your mistress," said Malinari.

"But she insists," said the other. "She said that we should . . . that we should see you safely on your way, and—"

"And safely off her territory, aye!" Malinari snarled.

"—And that you would appreciate . . . that you'd appreciate her concern for you," the nun continued, albeit gaspingly.

Malinari showed her his teeth and half-turned away . . . and then, on second thought, turned back. Since it was obvious that Vavara wouldn't rest until she knew he was gone for good—and since it suited his purpose to give the bitch just such a false sense of security—accepting this ride into town could well work to his advantage.

"Your mistress . . . is very gracious," he said. "The road is a long one into Skala Astris, and I can't be certain of finding a taxi there. Also, since I wouldn't want to draw attention to myself by walking these night roads . . ."

The back door of the vehicle sprang open. Malinari got in, and without further pause was carried into Krassos town. As for the cowled women seated in front—brides of a holy order, upon a time, now "wedded" to the *un*holy hag Vavara—they never once looked back. It could be that they feared him; indeed, Malinari was sure of it—

—But he fancied they feared Vavara a great deal more . . .

They dropped him in a dark, deserted alley on the outskirts of the seaport town, then continued with their "duties." Malinari had scanned their minds on the way into Krassos; he knew where they were going: to relieve their sisters keeping watch on the incoming ferries, the last of which had recently docked.

Wanting to give them time to get out of the way, he walked along the seafront toward the harbour, until he found a taverna with upstairs seating that looked down on the main road. Ordering red wine, he sat listening to soothing bouzouki music while watching the gyrations of a belly dancer on a television screen over the bar. Reception was very poor, making the figure on the screen fade in and out like a stroboscopic special effect. Malinari couldn't watch for too long because it made his head ache, and anyway he was keeping an eye on the road, or trying to. But this close to the centre of a major town—this close to people—he was at his usual disadvantage. Namely, he could *hear* them.

He could hear them *thinking*. And recognizing only too well the dangers inherent in that, he tried *not* to hear them. Which worked for a little while, at least . . .

Affecting his best manlike appearance, Malinari didn't seem out of place in this setting; he might well be Italian, French, or even cosmopolitan Greek. The taverna's subdued blue lighting hid his paleness, and his hair was fashionably long, loose, and flowing, except at his temples and upper sideburns where it was lacquered back to disguise the upper extremities of his fleshy, conchlike ears. These might otherwise have betrayed him—but betrayed him as what? As a foreigner with malformed ears?

Other than that Malinari was, to all intents and purposes, just another lone, late-season tourist on a night out, enjoying the cool of evening after another incredibly hot day. Oh, there might also be something a little odd about his nose—a certain flattish look, as if nature had pushed it too far back—but in any case the taverna was three-quarters empty, and none of its patrons was paying him more than casual attention . . .

. . . Which might have been because of his eyes.

Let anyone look at him curiously or for too long, and Malinari would fix him with a certain look, with those eyes of his under their high-arcing eyebrows—those oh-so-penetrating eyes, which were black as night yet oddly luminous and, at a certain angle, even feral. And then, for all his sharply creased black slacks, polished shoes, silk shirt, and fashionable lightweight jacket—for all such trappings of mundane civilization—then there would be something primal, something of the great predatory animal about him. And whoever was watching would sense the danger and quickly look away.

This made it easy to maintain his integrity—his physical isolation, that is—but as for his *mental* isolation . . .

Lord Nephran Malinari, of the Wamphyri! Malinari the Mind, aye. They hadn't called him that for nothing, in old Starside. It had been both his blessing and his curse; it still was, but now, more often than not, it was his curse. His talent working in reverse, working against him. And tonight, here, and now . . .

. . . He could hear them.

Their voices in his mind. Their teeming thoughts—lustful, greedy, malicious, dirty, bloody, hateful, scheming—it was as bad as being back on old Starside in the time of the blood-

wars, before he'd suffered his great defeat and was banished north!

Indeed, it seemed to Malinari that the only real difference between the Wamphyri and humankind—other than their physical strength—was that the Great Vampires admitted of their tremendous passions, giving vent to them and revelling in their excesses, but human beings sought to bury theirs out of sight, pretending they didn't exist. But they did, they did!

That was what made men the perfect hosts. Surely it must be so, else there were no Wamphyri!

And all of their secret voices, gabble-gobbling away in *his* head, invading *his* mind! Those three fat-gutted, greasy-looking men, where they sat close to the bar and gazed up at the belly dancer.

One of them was thinking: *How I would love to be into that. All that loose flesh. I'd fuck her arse, her tits, her armpit . . . anything but her sweaty cunt!*

And another was climbing unsteadily to his feet, making for the toilets where he would masturbate the grease out of his fat dick. All he *could think of was the throbbing in his pants!*

While the third was simply sitting there with a limp penis, wishing, wishing, desperately *wishing! But since wishing wasn't doing him any good, in the* back *of his mind he was going at the belly dancer with an imaginary knife, slicing at the parts that no longer worked for him, gutting her like a fish. And not just the dancer but* any *woman—the poor, impotent bastard . . .*

Their thoughts—*theirs,* and not Malinari's at all—but all of them and a hundred more exactly like them infesting *his* mind from near and far. A roaring on the one hand, and a whispering on the other, but all of it intermingling into a mental uproar. It was maddening! It was so . . . so *maddening!!!*

Hearing a small, splintering report, he saw that he'd been clenching his glass so tightly that it had cracked. That was a very bad sign—even an ominous sign—which warned him that his old trouble was surfacing again. But he couldn't afford to let it, not tonight.

Pushing the cracked glass to the far side of his table, he sat there trembling, watching it dribble red awhile, and drinking from the bottle. But the spilled wine only reminded him of blood, the rich red blood of the fat bastards in this bar, and in the street below, and in the town, and in all the cities of all the world!

So that when the bartender suddenly appeared from nowhere, plumping a new glass down on the table, Malinari came close to starting to his feet, grabbing him, and . . . and he wasn't sure *what* else might have happened then! But seeing his eyes, their luminosity, the bartender backed away from him and didn't come back. Nor would he return later when Malinari left—not even to collect payment—such was the shock, and the impression of pent violence he'd seen mirrored in Malinari's eyes . . .

Malinari got a grip on himself.

Stifling his trembling and stabilizing his mental shields to deflect all outside influences, he slowly became his own man again. The screen was blank now, the belly dancer gone, and the night air was cool where it came in across the balcony. It blew on Malinari and his hot mind both, gradually cooling them down.

And barely in time.

For down below, Vavara's black limo was cruising east along the seafront, heading back towards the monastery, and Malinari's mental condition had been such that he might easily have missed it. But no, he was fine now, and it was time he was on his way.

The bartender was nowhere to be seen. Since Malinari didn't care whether he paid for his wine or not, he simply rose and left, went downstairs to the side of the road, and flagged down the first available taxi.

By the vehicle's dashboard timepiece it was a minute or so before ten o'clock, and with time to spare, Malinari was being driven back along the coast road toward Skala Astris.

Or more precisely, toward Palataki . . .

A little more than an hour later, Vavara's lieutenant, Zarakis Mocksthrall, stood in the shadow of the crumbling Little Palace and looked down from the promontory on the scattered handful of lights and ribbon of road that was Skala Astris. The tavernas, what few had been open, were all closed now, and the last fishing vessel had bobbed home and was safely at mooring.

In the west, the twinkling jewel lights of Portos, Peskari, and Sotira were strung out along the coast, gradually dwindling into the distance, and a brilliant half-moon laid a path across the sea. Except for the occasional clatter of transports along the road, all was quiet.

Time now to take a turn about Palataki's overgrown gardens, checking for intruders and ensuring that Vavara's candle still burned in its small, central shrine.

It was his mistress's vanity, Zarakis knew—and her idea of a joke—to keep that candle burning there; her mockery of all such symbols of faith, even as the images that she assumed mocked true beauty and femininity. For no such candle was ever before lit for Vavara, not in Starside or anywhere else, until now . . . unless it was a candle of corpse grease, whose special "incense" she enjoyed to inhale.

And Zarakis (vampire that he was, more than a mere thrall, and indeed a lieutenant), even he shuddered. "Mocksthrall," she had named him, as she named all of her thralls, and he accepted without question his station as the first lieutenant, currently the only lieutenant, of that very heart of mockery, the eidolon Vavara. For Zarakis's life, or rather his undeath, was *itself* a mockery in her service. But be that as it may, it was far better than the true death and no life at all . . .

It was a strange night, Zarakis thought, where he followed familiar paths through the gardens, causing the sweating ground mist to swirl about his ankles. There was an unaccustomed stillness in the air, as if it were full of some weird expectancy or charged with the static energies of a gathering storm . . . which might well be the case. For the very gentlest of gentle breezes off the sea was cool at last, and it seemed that this freakish summer was finally at an end.

But as he drew near to the little shrine, where the night's first candle had already guttered out—*what was that?* A presence, here at Palataki!? Zarakis paused suddenly between paces, stood stock-still, and sniffed at the air. And letting his vampire senses flow out from him, he held his breath and waited to see what they would detect.

Somewhere nearby, a tiny Greek owl hooted its forlorn, solitary note, like a single drop of molten gold on the motionless air. Motionless now, aye, for even that gentlest of breezes had ceased to blow. But . . .

. . . No one was there—else he were stealthier far than Zarakis! And as he lit a new candle and placed it in the window of the marble shrine, to glimmer its deceit there in the darkness, he remembered what Vavara had told him just an hour or so ago: that he should be especially careful this night, and attend his duties as never before. She had not been specific, but then again her mood had been a bad one, and Zarakis had known better than to ask questions. She could flay you with her tongue, that one; and if that didn't suffice, she had other tools with which to finish the job!

But best not to think such thoughts, for one could never be sure that she wasn't—

Zarakis! Vavara's voice, sounding in his mind, cutting into his thoughts like a razor-sharp knife! Ahhh! He went cold as death—the true death—and wondered if she'd been listening. Mentalism wasn't her forte, no, but if she were near, and concentrating . . . and the night so still!

Zarakis, where are you? Her sweetly lying voice calling out to him, and behind it her sour signature, like a discord in the psychic aether.

She must be here to spy on him, to ensure that he was about his duties as instructed. What? All these years of service, and still she didn't trust him? But no, no—he *hadn't* thought that last—he *mustn't* think such things, but pull himself together and answer her call.

"Mistress, I am here!" Zarakis spoke out loud, yet quietly, breathlessly, and knew that she would hear him anyway. "I am in the gardens, near the marble shrine. Your candle burns, and all else is well. But where . . . where are you?"

I am waiting for you, Vavara answered, *near the entrance to the Little Palace. Hurry now.*

"Of course," he babbled. "I'm on my way. But mistress, what is the matter? I mean, when you were here earlier, you seemed—dare I say it?—out of sorts with yourself? What is it that so concerns you?"

For a moment there was silence, and Zarakis thought perhaps he'd said too much. But then:

But I was *out of sorts,* she answered to his relief, *And I was more than a little short with you, Zarakis—which is why I now bring you a small token of my esteem. Or should we say, a special tidbit?*

A tidbit? But how very rare! How very strange! And her mental voice . . . was there something different about it? Or was it just an effect of this weird night, the peculiar atmosphere?

Zarakis was now at the dark entrance, but where was Vavara? "Where are you, mistress?" he enquired. "I can't see you."

Oh, you great laggard! She chided him, but without discernible malice. *I grew weary of waiting for you and have proceeded to the spawning chamber. Follow me down. There is something you must see.*

"And my tidbit?" Her mood seemed such that he was prompted to be forward with her.

She is with me! said Vavara. At which Zarakis made yet more haste . . .

The way down into the nitre-streaked cellars—and then through the alveolate bedrock to the old mine workings—was treacherous with pitfalls, but Zarakis was familiar with it as with the back of his own hand. From the day his mistress first purchased Palataki, it had been his lot to patrol its grounds, the ruined building itself, and its underground labyrinth of tunnels, mine-workings, and natural caverns. The latter had been hollowed out by the sea ages before the Mediterranean's seismic activity had folded the rock and thrust it up to form Palataki's promontory, and it was in just such a cavern that Vavara's misted spawning chamber was situated.

Zarakis, as he emerged from an access tunnel into the main chamber, fully expected to see his mistress there—also to see the "tidbit" she'd brought with her, presumably one of the nuns from the monastery, one of the younger nuns, Zarakis hoped. But what he did *not* expect to see was a chamber empty of life other than the creeping loathsomeness covering the floor, and the now tumescent fungi with their gills distended, ready at a moment's notice to release their lethal spores.

But in fact the cavern wasn't entirely empty of life, which became apparent just a moment later when Lord Nephran Malinari, Malinari the Mind, stepped from the deep shadows behind Zarakis and grasped his head between his hands.

It took but a moment.

Zarakis opened his mouth to cry out—and then was unable to do so. He made as if to wrench himself free—and found himself immobilized. And as he went to his knees, Malinari released him, but just long enough to move round in front of him before once more clasping his head. And:

"Ah! Agh! *Arghhh!* Tidbit?" Zarakis grunted then. For apart from his shock, that had been his last coherent thought before Malinari's hands took him, and so was the first item of memory to be deleted. "M-m-my tidbit?"

Then all of his limbs jerked spastically, as if galvanized by a powerful electrical current, and his head shook violently: entirely involuntary reactions to the other's preliminary examination. But:

"No, no!" said Malinari. "Hold still, lest I hurt you even more." And extending his semiliquid forefingers deep into Zarakis's ears—dislodging the ossicles, the malleus, incus, and stapes, each in its turn, and passing through the inner chamber to the cochlea, and from there tearing channels along the nerve connections to the brain—he said: "As for your tidbit: alas, that was a lie. No tidbits here, Zarakis. At least, not from me to you. But from you to me? Well, we shall see."

And then he laughed and went on, "Except, it was not me who lied to you but your mistress—or so you imagined. For just as Vavara's hypnotic powers allow her to create a near-perfect imitation of beauty, so I have imitated Vavara herself! No, not physically, but in your mind! Or rather, that which *was* your mind, which is now mine."

Malinari's hands, transformed by metamorphosis, covered Zarakis's head like twin purple-veined webs—like the leaves of some huge carnivorous plant—as the terrible extrusions that were his forefingers continued exploring his silently shrieking victim's brain. And blood from Zarakis's violated ears trickled down his neck to soak his collar, while the awful pressure from within caused his eyes to stand out in his face . . .

. . . Until Malinari used his thumbs—as long and slender as pencils now—to dislodge those eyes, push them aside and enter their bleeding orbits the better to absorb Zarakis's memories.

"What you have heard, what you have seen, and what you have known," Malinari murmured. "These are the things I seek."

"Urk! . . . Uk! . . . *Argh!*" Zarakis gurgled, as his body began jerking again.

But the ice of Malinari's hands soon brought him back under control, as that Great Vampire told him: "Ah, no! Don't try to answer. I don't require you to answer *physically*, Zarakis. The answers are all here in your head. All of the secret places you've discovered down here in this buried maze, where a man might hide if he had need. The bolt-holes that lead out of this place, which you kept secret even from Vavara. The location of her boat, and how to get there. The whereabouts of its fuel cache, and knowledge of its operation. *Ahhh!*"

And all of it flowing out, drawn out of Zarakis, into

Malinari's mind. But not all of his memories, not all of his learning, and certainly not enough to kill him. For he was a vampire after all; a lieutenant who aspired—or who had once aspired—to be Wamphyri, and would prove very hard to kill by this means alone. Even with his mind three-quarters incapacitated, emptied of knowledge, his vampire essence would fight on, those strands of mutant DNA that one day might even have metamorphosed into a leech. And:

"There now, there," Malinari murmured, withdrawing his red wet hands and reshaping them. "Rest now, and live, Zarakis. For if or when that mistress of mirages reaches out from her monastery aerie with a piddling probe, I want her to be able to read your signature here and to know that all is well . . . even if it isn't."

With which he dragged the drooling lieutenant far back into the access tunnel, then into a cobwebbed niche where he propped his limp body against the wall before setting off with all the authority of a man born to this labyrinth (or one who had lived here for a long time) to examine Vavara's boat for himself.

As he strode across the spawning chamber, the protoplasmic devolved filth of the cavern reached out and groped upwards as if to grasp him.

And though there was no mind there to mention, still Malinari lashed out: *Begone! I am not for you!*

Recognizing his authority, like a hand scorched by a flame, the filthy mulch at once snatched itself back and withdrew from him; and sneering as he went on, Malinari was uncaring where he stepped or how many toadstools he crushed . . .

17
Jake Cutter—Reconnaissance

THREE DAYS EARLIER, THURSDAY EVENING:

Why Marseilles? Korath was curious. *What will you do here?*

"I need time to think," Jake murmured low under his breath, apparently muttering to himself like a disturbed person—which in a way he was—as he walked the city's boulevards. "Time to rest up, think things out. Things have changed, and yet they haven't. I need to get it sorted." His words were deadspeak, of course; thoughts would have sufficed, but he found it easier to actually speak, as if to a real, three-dimensional person walking beside him.

Real, yes, said the other, *however incorporeal. But walking beside you? No, except in the sense that our route is the same. Alas that our destinies aren't.*

"Our destinies?" Jake was only half-listening.

My destiny, said Korath bitterly, *when all of this is done, is to return to my dank and dreary sump. While yours . . . can be whatever you make it. Unfair, wouldn't you say?*

"That's life," said Jake, shrugging, and wishing that the vampire would shut up so that he could think—think about *how* things had changed, and yet hadn't.

No, said the other, *I'm obliged to disagree. It isn't life but death. And you can take it from me, Jake, that the two have nothing in common!*

"Much like you and I," said Jake.

Except your mind, Korath reminded him. *From which you have the power to exclude me in a moment. Your mind Jake: the one sentient place in all my empty universe. The* only *place where I can touch, taste, hear, see, and even feel—but only what* you *feel, or sense, and oh-so-temporarily.*

"So instead of constantly moaning about it," Jake replied, "why not make the best of what you've got while you're able?"

Because it isn't the best that I could *have . . . or of what you could have, that's why.*

"That again!" said Jake, crossing the road to a bank where a cash outlet stood gleaming in a windowed recess. "I'm to open my mind, let down all my shields, and bid you enter of your own free will, right?" He was getting wise to the other's aims now, and also to his motives. Long-term residence.

Yes! Korath replied at once, a little too eagerly. *From which time forward—or at least until our dual objectives were met—we would act and react almost as one. We would be as twin wheels, their cogs meshing precisely, working in perfect unison. You would no longer need to call out for me in times of danger, for I would* know *the danger! I would already* be *here, advising, assisting, even protecting you. Why, I would know your needs at once, and all of* my *instincts would be yours! So that in time—and given that I'd be here to encourage you in your efforts, of course—it's even possible that you could learn Harry Keogh's formula for yourself. Then, in every respect, at last you could be the Necroscope that he was!*

"That's if I wanted to be the Necroscope," said Jake. "And I'm not at all sure I do. There's a lot more to this than meets the eye, more than Trask and his people have told me. Even when they did tell me something, I got the impression that what they *weren't* telling me was a lot worse! So when this is all over—and by the time I know everything, if ever—it's possible I'll feel even less inclined than I do now. Right now it looks like I've swapped Harry Keogh for you, and if that's really the case . . . then I was robbed! As for your 'instincts' being mine: what instincts are we talking about here? Your vampire instincts? In which case, I don't think so."

Ah! said Korath. *A poor choice of words on my part. Let us say instead my heightened senses. For with our minds inextricably linked, so tightly meshed, you would be heir to my superior perceptions. Your sense of smell would be that of the wolf; you would have the hearing of a bat, and the night-seeing eyes of a cat. What price then the lives of this Luigi Castellano and his so-called "soldiers"?* Hah! *Small chance they'd have against one such as you . . . and I . . . or us.*

"But there are a couple of senses you seem to have skipped over," said Jake. "Your sense of taste, for example. And I like my meat well done. Then there's your tactile senses. But when I touch a woman I like to know she's thrilled, not chilled. And I want to sense her quivering, not shuddering." He shook his head "No deal, Korath. And there's something else . . . two somethings in fact. I don't much like the idea of being 'heir' to anything of yours. Let's face it, I've already been 'willed' something I didn't ask for. As for being 'inextricably linked'—it's that word inextricable I don't much care for. Which means we're back to square one, and you can forget it."

Bah! said the other. *But you'll come to your senses yet, I think. Or to mine.*

It was 4:30 and the bank was closing. On seeing the automated teller, Jake had reached for his wallet, his plastic. But he didn't have any plastic, and the cash machine was useless to him. Nor did he have any real cash money. For the last three or four weeks E-Branch had been seeing to his needs. By now they'd have fixed him up with an identity, too, and anything else he'd required, *if* he had stayed on with them. And if he'd known that what he and Natasha had had—or what he'd thought they had—wasn't real . . .

But he was out now and it didn't seem likely he'd be going back. He couldn't if he wanted to, not until this was over. For it was as he'd told Natasha: it wasn't just her—wasn't *just* revenge for what they'd done to her, and to him—but something else inside him that was driving him on. Something someone else had started, that he had to finish. That was what was bothering him: things had changed, and yet they were the same . . .

He wondered how Liz was doing, wondered if she missed him.

Probably, said Korath. *Didn't I advise you to stay with E-Branch and deal with their problems—and with mine—first?*

"See what I mean?" Jake muttered. "It's bad enough having you on the edge of my mind where I can keep an eye on you, let alone inside it where I can't! As for Liz . . . don't talk about her. Don't even think about her."

But they were your thoughts, Jake, not mine! said Korath. *What? Do you think I would take that sort of advantage? Not at all. Why, the very idea is abhorrent to me! For even a vampire—a gross and monstrous creature such as I was—has a measure of honour . . .*

"Oh, really?" said Jake. "Well, honour among thieves I've heard about. But I have to tell you, your kind have a very bad rep."

In life, or undeath, I have to agree, said Korath. *But in the true death—? Even a vampire has time to recant.*

"Not according to Harry Keogh."

Bah! And there's more to that *one than meets the eye, too!*

"Such as?"

I can't say, Korath answered. *The Great Majority know, but they won't speak to me. And then there's what you've said about E-Branch: how they, too, are evasive on that subject . . .*

He let it taper off, but something he'd said had stuck in Jake's mind, and:

"How are your shields?" he said.

Eh? Korath seemed surprised by the change of subject. *My shields? They are in good order, of course. Vampires were ever adept at shielding their minds.*

"Good," said Jake. "Then from now on shield your thoughts from the Great Majority, and direct them only at me. Since the teeming dead won't have anything to do with you, it strikes me you could queer my pitch, too."

You are ashamed of me!

"If you say so," said Jake.

Hah! A snort of "righteous" indignation.

But Jake's thoughts had moved on. "Cash," he muttered. "I need a place to stay, and hotels don't come cheap."

Don't you have any friends either, then? Korath's comment was deliberately snide.

"I have, or had, some," Jake answered. "A few. Which probably answers your earlier question, too—it's why I came back here—because I have friends in Marseilles. Here, and in Nice, and even in England . . . but on second thoughts, I wouldn't want to involve them in this. Anyway, the bank's about to close and people are looking at me. So let's move on."

But not too far, said Korath.

"Eh?"

You need money, don't you? And where better to get it than from a bank?

Jake thought about it for a moment, then blinked and said, "You mean, I should use this Möbius Continuum thing to—?"

Indeed, Korath sighed impatiently, cutting him short. *It's an incredibly useful tool, Jake. Far more so than a key. But it seems to me you've a lot to learn—er, for a vicious murderer, that is. In fact, you're rather innocent! So why don't you just walk back across the road, and sit awhile under those umbrellas outside that cafe? You can watch the last of these people leaving the bank, while I engage myself in other small diversions.*

"Diversions?"

Well, Korath explained, *since you shouldn't be seen paying too much attention to the bank, I wondered if between times . . . perhaps I might persuade you to direct your gaze elsewhere? For example, just look at all those pretty little French girls. The way they sit—cross-legged like that—all* moist *and* warm *in their skimpy little dresses. Aren't they just fascinating? Why, there's nothing quite like* that *in all Staaaarside!*

If anyone else had said such a thing, Jake might well have chuckled. But Korath's lascivious deadspeak voice was a gurgle, a grunt, the sound of snot in a rooting pig's snout, a bubbling pit of depravity. And the mind behind it just didn't bear delving into.

Thus, when Jake sat down under one of the umbrellas at the cafe across the road from the bank, he made a determined effort *not* to look at the pretty little French girls, and for the time being at least, Korath remained moodily silent . . .

The bank vaults were not what Jake had expected. They were like Russian dolls, within dolls, within dolls: "impenetrable" doors behind doors, behind doors. But doors whose designers hadn't in any way anticipated the Möbius Continuum, and never would learn what had happened here. On the other hand, they *had* anticipated thieves, and alarms had been going off from the moment Jake materialized within the secure area and tripped the sensors. After that he moved fast, passing through or "around" the doors in a matter of seconds.

In the innermost vault Jake found what he wanted: the day's take bagged up in its various denominations, all neatly pigeonholed in a rack of metal shelving. This wasn't Fort Knox—not even remotely—and there was only a handful of small bags for the taking. But there again, Jake wasn't a thief, and he wasn't out to make a big killing here. He would be more than satisfied with just a few thousand francs to see him through until—

Until the next time? Korath cut into Jake's thoughts, and quickly went on to explain himself: *For who knows? perhaps this sort of venture could easily develop into something of a habit?*

"And that would suit you right down to the ground, right?" Jake spoke through the handkerchief mask that hid his face from the security cameras, as he took up a bag with the legend FIFTY THOUSAND FRANCS, IN HUNDREDS. "Your 'instincts' sort of rubbing off on me, is that how you see it?" He replaced the bag, taking up another that said TEN THOUSAND FRANCS, IN FIVES.

Er, something like that, said Korath. *But why is it you've chosen the lesser amount?*

"When all of this is straightened out, if ever," Jake told

him, "I may even give this money back . . . or maybe not. Because I don't have to. This was my bank, Korath! No, not this branch, but my bank. And as it happens there's a lot more in my account than I intend to take. So in fact it's like I'm simply making a small withdrawal here."

Bah! said Korath disappointedly.

"And that's it," Jake told him, as he ripped the bag open and stuffed his pockets. "I've got what I came for, and now we can go."

But Korath was silent now, and the alarms were still sounding . . .

"Korath?" Jake said, aware of a sullen silence in his head and beginning to sweat in the breathless confines of the place. "It's time we weren't here."

And after a little while: *What would happen to you,* said the other, *in the event that I forgot Harry Keogh's remarkable formula and left you here for them to find? For the fact is, Jake, it's no easy trick to keep conjuring those figures and symbols. In my world, we had little use for numbers—mathematics was literally an unknown science. A Lord or Lady of the Wamphyri would keep a tally of his or her thralls, and that was about it. But as for decimals, fractions, and algebra . . . I mean, algebra? All such would be algibberish, to the Wamphyri! And the Szgany weren't that much smarter.*

"This isn't funny," said Jake, sweating harder. "You got me in and you can get me out. So get to it. Roll those numbers and I'll do the rest."

Ah, but where's the incentive in that? said Korath. *What, I should do all the work while you reap all the benefits? Perhaps our arrangement—this so called "partnership"—wasn't such a good idea after all. I feel that I am being used, and all those constantly mutating equations make me dizzy. Wherefore, I think we should . . . renegotiate?*

"I don't follow you," said Jake, despite that he did.

Indeed you do not, said the other, *not any longer. Nor need I follow you. We go together, as equals, or not at all.*

"That again?"

That again, said Korath, *but for the last time. So make up your mind, Jake, what's it to be?*

Jake listened to the alarms, sweated some more, then tossed several bags of money onto the floor . . . and sat down on them.

What? Korath seemed astonished. *What are you doing?*

"What's it look like?" Jake answered. "I'm waiting for them to get here and throw me back into a different kind of cage. Or they might simply shoot me on sight. Let's face it, I'm trapped here, caught red-handed. For me, it's the end of the line. And for you—I don't know—a return to that sump you're so fond of? The one I rescued you from?"

Ah, no! said Korath, and Jake sensed a sly deadspeak smile, albeit one that wavered. *You'll break before they come.*

"No way," said Jake, putting his hands behind his head and leaning back against the shelving, making himself comfortable.

Then let this be the end of it! Korath blustered, but very nervously now. *For in any case, I can see no future in it.*

"The police will be into the bank by now," said Jake, "and the guy with the keys will be on his way. Ten more minutes and they'll be opening up this vault. If they don't shoot me first, E-Branch will probably lay claim to me. Then I'll be forced to tell Trask about you, and he . . . will have various options."

Such as? Positive alarm now, in Korath's query.

"He has telepaths, access to all kinds of shrinks. They'll probably try to get into my mind and force you out. That'll be the first thing they'll try. But whatever they do, it will have to be better than you. After that—I don't know—prefrontal lobotomy, maybe? Even the word is unpleasant, right? The way it sort of slithers off the tongue: lob-ot-omy . . . *Ugh!* You'll be a part of the part they lob."

You're bluffing!

"No," Jake shook his head, "I'm serious. You're testing my strength, and I'm not giving in."

What if E-Branch doesn't claim you?

"Then I'll languish in jail," said Jake, "and you'll be up against the same problem. Except by then they'll know who I am; which will mean that in future it will be harder to move around undetected, and I'll be easier to find and kill. And if or when I die, you die. Ben Trask took a little of the heat off me, but this is bound to put it on again, and . . ." He broke off, put a finger to his lips, and whispered, "What was that?"

Eh? What? Jake "felt" Korath's start. *I heard nothing.*

"The sound of the outer lock clanging open," Jake told him. "You didn't hear it because I'm slowly raising my shields—*and* the stakes. I bet you've never played poker, have you, Korath?"

Wait! Korath cried. *If you do that—if you shut me out—we'll lose contact, and I won't be able to . . . to . . .*

"To save my neck?" said Jake. "That's right, you won't. And yours is in the same noose. So now who's bluffing?"

Why are you so . . . so obstinate? Korath whined.

"They're at the second lock," said Jake. "So we'd better be saying our farewells. By the time I've shut you out, they'll be in."

No! Don't do it! STOP! the dead vampire "shouted" in Jake's mind.

And a moment later, when Jake said nothing: *Damn . . . damn . . .* DAMN*—but you're good!* Korath grated the words out as if they were choking him, and gave a furious shake of his incorporeal head before continuing, *And of course you're right: I* was *only testing you.*

Jake relaxed his shields a little, stood up, and said, "Did you say something? Or was it someone out there, opening up this last door?"

Here, Korath growled. *The formula. Use it now, and let's be gone from here.*

And before the vault door could be opened, as those weirdly flowing equations commenced scrolling down the screen of Jake's mind, so he made a door of his own and stepped through it . . .

* * *

As yet, Jake was by no means expert at judging the coordinates. He emerged rather clumsily from the Continuum on a popular seafront esplanade east of the city, but directly in the path of a young couple who walked arm in arm on the broad pavement. Before he could open his mouth to excuse himself, the young man apologized for *his* clumsiness—he obviously hadn't been watching where he was going—and Jake escaped into a store that he knew sold quality optical instruments: the place that had been his original target destination.

He bought a pair of binoculars, found a shaded doorway, and moved on to Paris.

We really must begin to master this thing, Korath told him. *We must be more discreet how and where we emerge. Incidentally, where are we now? The way you keep your mind half-closed, I can never tell for sure.*

"What good would it do you to know?" said Jake. "You're not familiar with this world."

And never will be at this rate! Korath answered. *Very well, I accept that I was out of order in that vault—but you can't blame me for trying. Even so, I wasn't trying to take advantage of you, but simply attempting to ease the way for both of us. I can't help you if I don't know what you're about, and certainly not while you insist on keeping your mind half-closed to me.*

"Which I do."

Indeed, Korath sighed. *Which prompts me again to ask: Where are we?*

"We're in the Saint-Germain Depres district of the French capital," Jake told him. "Paris, the Latin Quarter. I used to come here with my mother from time to time, and we stayed at several pleasant little hotels."

But why here?

"Why not? The food's good, and I'm not much known here. And anyway, what's the difference? We can go anywhere we want to."

And after a moment's pause: *I like that,* said Korath.

"Oh?"

You said "we." You're beginning to think of us as a team.

"And so we are, according to our original agreement," Jake answered. "Why, I might even let my shields down a little, if I thought I could trust you not to pull any more stupid stunts."

You have my word, said Korath, making it sound just sincere enough. *For that was a pointless exercise at best.*

"Very well," said Jake, "my perimeter shields are down. But I'll know in a moment if you try to intrude a step further than that. Unlike the bank, *my* inner vaults are out of bounds!"

Now we're getting somewhere, said Korath. *I can tell you're becoming accustomed to this. And that is good! But don't try to run before you can walk.*

"Meaning?"

We've both a way to go before we master this thing. While I can now read your thoughts clearly, see what you see, and so on and so forth, still I can't guide your physical actions. If you were attacked, you would have to rely on your own battle skills to get you out of trouble.

"Exactly the way I like it," Jake nodded. "Having you *in* my mind, and having you *control* it are two different things. Since I need access to the Möbius Continuum, the first is something I have to live with. But that's as far as it goes."

And in a little while: *Obstinate, yesss,* Korath hissed, before falling silent . . .

Jake found a small hotel, booked in under an assumed name, and paid cash for three nights. He didn't know if he would need as much time as that, but best to be prepared.

In his rooms he showered, lay on the bed with hands behind his head, locked Korath out of his mind for the time being, and tried to think things through in private. Which wasn't too easy because pictures of two women kept intruding. Natasha was one—but rapidly fading now, even as she dispersed herself and faded in death—and Liz was the other, taking on sharper definition.

Liz, sweet Liz . . . but not so sweet once she'd set her mind on doing something, on getting somewhere. Gutsy Liz. Gritty and even earthy Liz, in a certain kind of way. Long-legged and sexy Liz, yes . . .

Then Jake realized that this wasn't so much an intrusion as a part of the overall problem; whether it would work or not, he now saw Liz as a major part of his future. Assuming he had one.

And of course he *could* have one—he might *still* have one, with E-Branch—if by now he hadn't entirely ruined his chances by running away, and at a crucial moment at that. He remembered what Trask had told him: that when E-Branch could trust him, it would be his home, his family, his everything; and also that it would protect him with every fibre of its being. He also remembered Trask's warning: that if he were to cheat, try to put his own agenda first and run off, how that would be the end of it.

Except Jake felt that he hadn't so much run off as been . . . what? Called away? Sidetracked? Lured by something—or someone—inside him? Unfinished business, yes, which someone else had started.

Someone like the Necroscope Harry Keogh, perhaps?

But if that were the case, why hadn't Harry explained it or tried to tell him about it? Granted the Necroscope had admitted that he "wasn't entirely there"—that his elevator didn't stop on every floor, and his revenant had been watered down in order to operate on different, far-flung levels—but shouldn't he at least have known his own purpose here?

Well, whatever the Necroscope's purpose in choosing him as his instrument, and in burdening him with all the problems that went with it, Jake Cutter had a cause of his own to pursue. And lying here on this bed wasn't going to get it done. Or was this urgency—this tightening of his guts, this compelling need for action against Castellano—was it simply *another facet* of the unknown force that was driving him? *Damn!* It was like some kind of maddening, ever-decreasing circle that must sooner or later drive him headfirst up his own backside!

To hell with it!

He jumped up, went down to the lobby, and obtained a map of the locality: Paris and all the roads and countryside around to a radius of fifty miles. And back in his room he studied it. He remembered a factory on the way to the Côte-d'Or and Dijon, the route his mother had used to drive when they visited Paris, and the map brought several landmarks back to memory. Jake had been there, and so knew their coordinates.

Back in his room he let down his shields, invited Korath in and told him, "We've work to do."

Then, after buying a sturdy sausage bag in the hotel's gift shop, and using a stall in the gentlemen's toilets as a private launching site to the Möbius Continuum, they were on their way. Jake couldn't know it but the original Necroscope had used just such jumping-off places in his time.

Or on the other hand, maybe he did know it. Maybe something deep inside him was remembering . .

They were in the French countryside between Nemours and Courtenay, not far from the southbound motorway. Jake was leaning on a three-bar fence in the last of the day's light, staring along an access road at a modern-looking factory complex set in three or four acres, all enclosed behind a fifteen-foot-high security fence. And of course Korath looked with him.

So, then, said the vampire in a little while. *Perhaps breaking into places is catching after all. But what is this place?*

In all the surrounding countryside there was no other building to be seen. A river, woods, and several small lakes, but no buildings—and Jake knew why. "They make industrial explosives here," he said. "Including one called plastique, with which I'm fairly familiar. I used it in the SAS. Demolition was something I was good at. It seems I had something of a flare for it." And changing the subject, but not really: "Notice how quiet it is?"

I was wondering about that, said the other.

"The closest place is about a mile away," Jake told him. "A hospital built on rollers on the Saint-Valerien road."

On rollers?

"So that if this place goes up, the hospital will shift but it won't get blown away," Jake answered.

Ah! said Korath. *Now I know what you're talking about. This plastique: you used it when you were a soldier, you say? But it seems to me you've used it once or twice since then, too.*

His words evoked brief but violent memories, sending a pair of scenes flashing across Jake's mind one after the other: *Jean Daniel, almost cutting himself in half when he started his car, and a fat German faggot being torn apart in the blast that blew him screaming into hell.*

"That's right," said Jake, "but my source of supply on both of those previous occasion was very limited and cost me a great deal of money. This time I need a whole lot of the stuff, and I don't have time to fool around trying to buy it from people who crack safes for a living."

Why should you? said Korath, *when you could be the greatest thief of all time?*

Jake ignored that last and said, "A place as big as this, a couple of acres, with contents like that . . . there are bound to be guards, night watchmen."

Indeed, said Korath. *And plainly my vampire senses would be invaluable. That is, if we were as one.*

"You never give in, do you?" said Jake. And then, cursorily, "Forget it. All we need is a diversion, and I have the makings. Anyway I'm not too concerned. In a place like this, the guards won't be armed with anything more dangerous than nightsticks."

They took the Möbius route into the grounds of the factory, an area well away from the main building, where wooden pallets, empty crates, and other containers were stacked ready for collection. Having checked that the coast was clear, Jake took wads of toilet paper from his sausage bag, poured a brandy miniature onto the paper, quickly set fire to it, and tossed broken pieces of a tinder-dry crate into the flames.

Another Möbius jump took him into the shadows of the

main building—the one with all the NO ENTRY, and skull-and-crossbones warning signs—from where he could watch the action. In a little while alarms began to sound, then shouting voices and running footsteps, while floodlights snapped on all around the perimeter wire.

"Now," said Jake. "While they're coming out, we go in."

Inside the factory, the incidence of NO SMOKING signs, and of skulls and crossbones and other pictorial warnings of fires and explosions, was like a signposted path to Jake's objective; the more signs he passed, the closer he was to what he sought. So that in just a few seconds and two or three Möbius jumps he was filling his sausage bag with top-quality plastique in containers like giant toothpaste tubes.

Then it was time to go. And when Korath conjured Möbius's equations again, Jake still hadn't seen a single guard.

When Jake tossed down the heavy sausage bag on the floor of his hotel room, he felt Korath wince. For the dead vampire had seen in his mind the devastating properties of this stuff, which was as much as he knew about it.

But Jake grinned humourlessly and said, "So what's worrying you now? *You* are already dead."

But—

"But don't concern yourself," Jake told him. "I could jump up and down on this stuff wearing hobnailed boots. It will only work with microwave radiation, a detonator, or excessive heat—which is why I started that fire back at the factory. I knew it would attract a lot of attention—and fast! As for detonators: I have a small cache hidden away in Marseilles. We can pick them up later. But the night is young, and I'm getting hungry, so I'm going to eat first in the restaurant downstairs. After all, I'm only flesh and blood."

As I was, upon a time, said Korath. *Ah, well, at least I'll be able to taste it, if only secondhand.*

"Who said I was taking you with me?" said Jake. But he took him anyway . . .

* * *

Jake ate well—too well—and along with the good food and a bottle of excellent wine, everything else caught up with him all at once. Suddenly realizing how tiring it could be to share his mind with someone else, and a mind that was full of problems of its own at that, he decided to make an early night of it.

But Jake's weariness wasn't only down to Korath and a full stomach. The metaphysical Möbius Continuum had sapped him, too; the very weirdness of the thing was totally draining, with side- or after-effects not unlike the glorious hangovers he'd used to suffer after his drinking sprees when his mother died. And then to top it all off there was what Natasha had told him: the fact that their affair hadn't been real was a downer despite that it had freed him—

—Which in turn led to the biggest paradox of all: that it *hadn't* freed him in every respect, and that he couldn't *ever* be free until his vendetta with Castellano was resolved one way or the other . . .

He had taken a second bottle back to his room with him, and he'd started to open it before having second thoughts. The idea had been that a couple of extra slugs would settle him down for a good night's sleep . . . but wouldn't it also dull his mind? He couldn't afford that, not with Korath waiting on the threshold. Probably best to stay sober, he thought, or not to get any more drunk than he was now.

But to be doubly sure he issued the usual warnings, and banished the dead vampire back to his sump. Following which he was asleep almost as soon as his head hit the pillows . . .

Jake didn't dream, and he *did* get a good night's sleep, without any intrusions from Korath.

Something you probably didn't know, that one told him, when Jake called out for him. *But even the dead grow weary. We do as we did in life, Jake, and for a third of our lives we slept! So is it so strange that we occasionally shut down in death? Well, let me tell you: it makes for a very pleasant escape. Myself, I would spend* all *of my time sleeping if not for you . . . for what else was there to do, before you and Harry Keogh came along? So you see, no less than you, I, too, have been wearied by the weirdness of all this.*

"Breakfast," said Jake, finishing shaving. "And then I need to buy some new clothes. Black pants, pullover, shirt, shoes—the whole bit."

All in black?

"Yes," Jake nodded. "It has to be my training coming out in me. Since we'll be doing most of our work at night, that has to be my colour."

Your colour?

"The colour of night."

Ahhh! said Korath. *And after you've purchased your clothes?*

"Then we'll visit that list of places Natasha gave me, that bastard Castellano's properties, the bases he works from. First we'll find him, and then—"

You'll kill him.

"An eye for an eye," Jake answered—then staggered just a little, as a feeling of déjà vu took him unawares.

Oh? said Korath, for he had felt it, too.

"It's nothing," Jake lied, aware that he'd suffered several of these spells just lately: paramnesia, as they called it. But whatever they called it, the feeling was real and lingered on a while . . .

I thought we were going to do most of our work at night? Korath queried grumblingly. For he could "feel" the sun warm on Jake's back where he lay propped on his elbows, on a hillside of bone-dry stubble, looking down on Castellano's villa near Marseilles. While the hot weather was beginning to break inland, it hadn't yet reached the Mediterranean coast.

"Your eyes might be up to that, but mine aren't," Jake told him, as he adjusted the focus of his binoculars. "And don't tell me how much easier it would be if I had your eyesight, et cetera, and all of that stuff. My eyes are just fine—better than most. And anyway, this has to be done in daylight. I need these coordinates for later. I only have to see a place, and lock on; then its coordinates go straight into my head and get filed away for later. I don't 'remember' them as such, I just know them."

How do you know that?

"Didn't I know how to find that swimming pool in Malinari's Xanadu? And the garden of our safe house in Brisbane? The Latin Quarter in Paris, the plastique factory, and this place?"

I accept that you know, said Korath. *But I don't understand* how *you know. Do you?*

Jake shrugged and said "It just . . . came to me." Like maybe he'd inherited it. Along with a lot of other stuff, apparently.

But if you already know these *coordinates, why are we here?*

"The coordinates of this hillside, yes," said Jake. "But of the insides of that villa, no. I only remember one room in that place, and I almost wish I didn't. But it's all too vague in my memory . . . I wasn't in the best possible condition at the time. Anyway, right now I'm looking into a large downstairs room that might be a study. And I've got its coordinates."

And that's all we're here for?

"No. For as you're well aware I'm also looking for Castellano himself. But at this visit, yes, it will have to suffice. I needed an exact reference and I've got it. A room in that house which I know I can find unerringly from now on any time I want to."

But when precisely?

"When I'm ready . . ." He held up a mental hand, said, "Please be quiet, now. I just saw some movement in there, and I want to know who it is."

It was a bent old man, who had just this moment entered the study. There was nothing especially sinister about him; he went about dusting furniture, some items on a desk, and moved to the windows to check their locks. A caretaker, by his looks.

"Castellano's not at home," said Jake. "It seems to me this place is empty. Time to move on."

To Genoa, San Remo, Bagheria—all the places that Natasha told you about?

"One at a time, yes," said Jake. "You have a good memory."

A legacy of Malinari, Korath answered sourly. *The only good thing he ever gave me—and only then by virtue of what he took* from *me! But—do you have the coordinates to those places?*

"No," Jake answered, "so we'll do it by trial and error. It was dumb of me, really. I should have taken them from Natasha's mind. But my own mind . . . was elsewhere at the time."

So where do we start?

"San Remo, because I've been there," said Jake. And so they went to San Remo . . .

San Remo, gateway to the Riviera di Ponente.

Jake knew the bars, the city, and the lifestyle. That of the rich, anyway. But right now he was slumming. He went to a small bar he knew—a dingy little place that served great pizza and toasted sandwiches, and his favourite beer, imported Dortmunder Actien on tap—had brunch and a beer at the bar, and while he ate talked to the bartender.

The bartender spoke good English, and Jake spoke some Italian; they got on well enough. The bartender remembered him from previous visits; he kept his voice low as he asked: "Where have you been hiding, Jake? Your face was in the papers awhile, but not recently. They let you off the hook or something?"

The place was almost empty, only two other people seated by the door and locked in conversation, so Jake considered it safe to talk. "Or something," he grinned humourlessly, then got down to business. "I'm looking for . . . for an old friend of mine. A bit of a dark horse called Castellano. A Sicilian, I think. But he owns property close to San Remo, and I wondered if you—"

"—If I might know of him?" The barman, small and balding, wiped his hands on his apron, then cocked his head on one side enquiringly. "Do you have a problem with this person, Jake? If so, you should know he is a bad one. I don't know him, I never saw him, but some of his people—or the people he deals with—come in here from time to time. These are *not* nice people."

Jake nodded. "I know. But you don't need to worry. I don't know your name, and I've never been in your bar in my life."

"But if they hurt you enough, you'd tell them otherwise."

"They're not looking to hurt me," Jake answered. "They're looking to kill me. That's why I want to get there first."

"Ah!" said the other, blinking rapidly.

"So you needn't worry," said Jake. "If I'm alive when this is over, they won't be. And if I'm dead, I won't be doing much talking, right?"

Except perhaps to me! said Korath.

Jake told him, *Be quiet,* then glanced around the room. The place was still empty, so he took the opportunity to pass a wad of francs over the bar. A bank teller's paper wrapper was still intact, with a stark black legend 1000 FR. standing out as if illuminated. And: "Can you do me an exchange?" said Jake.

"For lire?" The bartender raised an eyebrow, began to shake his head.

"No, for another beer," said Jake. "Pull yourself one, too—and keep the change."

Then, without pause: "Two kilometres east of San Remo," the bartender muttered, as he snatched up the money and put it away under the bar, "where the mountains come down to the sea on the coastal road to Imperia. We call it Millionaire's Row, and this Castellano has a place there. I gather he's not often home, but there are usually one or two of his drug-dealing friends there, local hoods who look after the place when he's away. And like I said, sometimes they come in here. Which is why it would please me if you were to leave now."

"I'm on my way," said Jake, getting off his bar stool. "And thanks. But just one more thing. Does the place have a name?"

"Castellano's place? Er, yeah, I think so," said the other, his brow wrinkling in concentration. "It's called, er, Le Manse—let me think—Le Manse . . ."

"Madonie?" The word sprang into Jake's mind out of nowhere.

"Right," the bartender nodded. "Le Manse Madonie."

As Jake left the bar, Korath said, *I don't recall that Natasha named the place?*

"Neither do I," said Jake. "But I suppose she must have."

Jake found a *cambista* and changed francs to lire, then hired a cab to take him to Imperia some twenty-five kilometres east of San Remo. Barely out of the city, he asked the driver: "Do you know the names of these places?" He meant the fabulously rich dwellings built into the mountainside at the left-hand side of the road. On the other side, the cliffs fell sheer to the sea.

As good as gold the driver reeled the names off, and waved out of his widow at the houses as he sped past. Driving as only an Italian would on a road such as this, he seemed oblivious of the danger immediately to his right.

And shortly: "Le Manse Madonie!" he cried, and Jake told him to pull off the road for a moment while he "got his bearings"; true enough, though "coordinates" might have been a better term for it.

It was as Jake had feared. The house, a flat-roofed, chalet-style building, whose broad front was propped on stanchions and projected from the cliff overhead, could only be accessed via a steep private road. And there was no obvious vantage point from which he might view the property through his binoculars. As for the actual location of the place: that had already fixed itself firmly in his mind, which would have to suffice for now.

And so on to Imperia, where Jake found a cafe with panoramic sea views, drank several cappuccinos, but mainly sat lost in his own thoughts. It wasn't yet noon, but already he could feel the pressure building to go places and get things done. He knew what he wanted to do, but wasn't too sure about the places. Not sure at all about one of them.

What's on your mind? Korath felt obliged to ask him after a while, because Jake was keeping it to himself.

"Le Manse Madonie," said Jake, opening up a little.

We've just been there, said Korath.

"But not the one I know," Jake answered. "Not *the* Le Manse Madonie."

There's more than one?

"Unless I'm going mad, yes. Because I know the coordinates of another Le Manse Madonie—I think."

You think? said Korath. *So maybe you got something from Natasha after all. Where do you* think *this place is?*

"That's just the problem," said Jake, as he sat gazing into the southeast, frowning five hundred miles out across the Ligurian Sea. "I can't say where it is for sure—but I *think* it's somewhere out there. And I know we do have to go there."

By all means, said Korath, conjuring the Möbius equations.

As Jake had remarked to his incorporeal "friend," he wasn't too sure where he was going—but he did know that he had to go there, if only to find out. And perhaps to find himself, too . . .

He was getting used to the Möbius Continuum now.

At first he had had to keep his eyes closed. It wasn't that Jake was afraid of the dark, but there's dark and there's dark. This was the primal darkness before there was light, and before there was matter, and weight, and time. A place "between" space and time, yet parallel to both of them. A universe between universes. And an absence of "everything"—which must include even the vacuums that Nature so abhors—is darker far than simply an absence of light.

After he had got over the eyes-closed stage, then he'd kept them shuttered, which somehow served to make the blackness grey and was more acceptable. But now he accepted the blackness, the utter emptiness, itself. And despite that the Möbius Continuum was nothing, he could *feel* it all around him. And through Jake, Korath could feel it, too.

It's like death, the vampire said, *and yet it's alive. Not warm like you, but not cold either. You can feel it—*

"—And therefore, according to the laws of physics, it must be feeling me," said Jake, his voice the merest whisper. For in the Möbius Continuum even thoughts have weight, and a normally spoken word can be like a thunderclap.

I know nothing of physics, said Korath.

"That's what worries me," Jake told him. "Neither do I. Or I didn't use to. So I'm not sure whose physics these are . . . or even if they're physics. Metaphysics, maybe. Möbius physics."

I only know what your mind shows me. And you're not showing me everything.

"But there's something I would certainly like to show you," said Jake. "If only because I want to see it myself—again."

Er, shouldn't we be there by now? said Korath uneasily.

"Where?" Jake whispered.

Where we're going.

"But aren't you interested? There's something I want you to see en route."

But in a place such as this, what's to see? More darkness?

Jake shook his head and said, "Light! The birthlight of the human race." And there was that in his voice—an unaccustomed humility—that made Korath want to see it, too. And:

By all means, said the vampire. *Show me this light.*

"Harry Keogh showed me this in a dream," said Jake, "which was of course more than a mere dream. It must have been, for I remember the coordinates. And they're here!"

The past-time door opened, and Jake stood at the threshold. Korath looked out through his eyes, seeming to hear with Jake's ears, the incredible one-note *Ahhhhhhhh!* sound of myriad angelic voices, like a vast unearthly choir in the sounding chambers of some cosmic cathedral. But in fact there was no sound; time and the Möbius Continuum *have* no sound, else it would be the unbearable cacophony of everything that has ever been and is still to be. It was all in the mind—in Jake's mind—as it had been in only a small handful of other minds before his. A phantom sound that *should* have been there, as the only possible accompaniment to the awesome scene beyond the door.

It was like looking into three-dimensional space, the heart of some incredible blue nebula. For at its source, indeed there was a hazy nebulosity.

The beginning, Jake said, reverting to pure thought now, as if in a place like this, speech were more than unnecessary, even irreverent. *The source of all human life.*

And out of the nebulosity, uncountable blue threads—like living neon filaments—seemed to thicken as they came speeding away from the clustered centre towards the observers. *The life-threads of humanity,* said Jake, knowing it for a fact, without remembering if he had been told it or if this were his natural instinct speaking. *Every single one of those threads is or was the life of a man, a woman, a child. In the heart of the cloud there, that was the time of the emergence*—but *how many millions of years ago?*

Korath found his "voice" at last and said, *Some of them . . . they don't reach the door but falter and blink out. And some of them* snap *out of existence, while others gradually fade.*

The difference between a sudden termination, said Jake, *and a gentler, more gradual death. The difference between an accident or fatal disease, and the creep into old age. But just look at them. When you look into deep space you're looking back into time, Korath. And the same here, except here we're looking back into Man.*

All of those twisting, twining, outwards-rushing blue life-threads, all sentient, thrusting, seeking. Moving from the past to the present. *This is Mankind,* said Jake simply. *Everyone who ever was, and those who still are.*

That one there, said Korath, *that blue thread, is you! Your past. Just see how it crosses the threshold—into you! But as for me—I don't have one.*

That's because you're dead, Jake told him. *And when you did have one it was red, not blue, the scarlet thread of a vampire. Back there along my life-thread, there are more red threads. Do you see them?*

Yes, Korath answered, *but they're far away and falling farther behind with each passing moment. And most of them . . . have stopped. Snapped out of existence. Permanently.*

Terminated, said Jake. *Malinari's people, who Ben Trask and E-Branch and I stopped out in Australia. Because we daren't let the red contaminate the blue.*

And Korath's deadspeak voice was very small now as he said, *We seem to be moving. This past-time door, and you and I, we're being pushed away.*

But: *No,* Jake answered, *not pushed* away. *We're being pushed forward. By time itself. Pushed into the now.*

Don't you mean into the future?

Into the now, said Jake again. *The future is another place, and maybe I'll show you it another time.* It seemed a contradiction in terms, but it would have to suffice.

They moved away from the past-time door, and a moment later Jake said, "We're here." Wherever here would turn out to be . . .

It turned out to be the surface of a road up the steep contours of a mountainside, with the rim of a high plateau up front, and the broad expanse of the sea below and behind.

"The Madonie," said Jake, knowing it for a certainty, without knowing how. "A mountain range in northern Sicily. And down there, Luigi Castellano's quarry—the quarry in the gorge that Natasha told me about—where ostensibly he mines stone for his 'building projects,' while in fact he's mining buried treasures that were stolen by the Nazis in World War Two. Natasha told me about it, yes—and it was one of the places I had scheduled to visit—but I know I didn't get these coordinates from her."

From where then? said Korath.

Jake shook his head. "I just knew them. It seems that I . . . that I remembered them?"

From the original Necroscope? Harry Keogh?

"It's not the first time," said Jake. "There are times when I speak—or when I've spoken—to Lardis Lidesci, when I got the same feeling. He evokes a weird sort of pseudomemory in me, when I seem to remember the places he talks about, places where I can't possibly have been, because they're in another world."

Jake's binoculars hung from his shoulder on a strap. Now he opened the case, took them out, and looked through them into the quarry under frowning cliffs.

"I feel that I've stood here before," he said. "But I don't remember that quarry . . . where those men and machines aren't so much quarrying as turning over rubble fallen from . . . *huh?*"

He paused abruptly, and swung the binoculars up, up, up the face of the sheer gorge to the rim of the plateau—craning his neck to focus on that which he knew should be there but wasn't—only a rim that was fresh and deeply scarred, as from a fall of thousands of tons of rock. He saw the great scar in the face of the high plateau—

—and in the next moment watched it blur out of existence, until it became what he had *expected* to see in the first place: Le Manse Madonie, as it once was!

A squat, white-walled castle, mansion, or château, perched on the edge of oblivion, where a moment ago there had been only a mighty bight in the raw cliff face! An unassailable fortress, standing at the rim of a precipice that towered at least twelve hundred metres over the gorge and the sloping scree wall of the rubble-strewn quarry.

The place was there in the eye of Jake's mind—real, if only for a moment—and then was gone!

What is it? said Korath, alarmed as Jake staggered and very nearly fell. *What's wrong?*

"You didn't see it?"

What, in your inner mind? Your secret *mind? You know better than that!*

"It was Le Manse Madonie," said Jake. "It *was* Le Manse Madonie—but now it's only that heap of rubble there, which Luigi Castellano excavates for the treasures it once contained."

But how do you know these things?

"Partly from what Natasha told me—that Castellano wasn't mining rocks here—and partly from memory."

But not your memory.

"No," Jake shook his head. "Not mine . . ."

Harry? Another deadspeak voice in Jake's mind. But definitely not Korath's, for this one was entirely human. The voice of someone who had died here, who had mistaken Jake for the Necroscope, Harry Keogh!

Jake had given a small start; now he got his wits together, and said, "I'm not Harry. I'm just a friend of his. At least, I hope so."

Not Harry? said that new voice in his head. *Well, you could have fooled me! I felt your warmth*—exactly *the same as his—and I just knew it was him! But what the hell . . . any friend of Harry's is a friend of mine. Especially around these parts.*

"These parts?" said Jake.

Sicily, said the other, with a deadspeak nod. *And more especially this part of Sicily. It's been quiet as the tomb around here!* And Jake "heard" a slightly hysterical deadspeak chuckle. *I mean, man, I was beginning to think I'd never get to speak to anyone again! It's these Sicilians, you know? Like never a peep out of any of 'em. See, they had their own code in life, and—*

"—And what they did in life they continue to do in death," Jake finished it for him. "A code of silence."

That's right. But listen, if you're not Harry, then you can only be this other fellow, this, er—?

"Jake," said Jake. "Jake Cutter."

Yeah, right, said the other, far less excited now. *And the Great Majority haven't made up their minds about you yet. See, even out here in the deadspeak wilderness, still I get to hear the occasional whisper.*

"The teeming dead do seem to have some kind of problem with me," Jake answered. "While I don't quite understand it, I can't deny it. But either way, I wouldn't want to get you in any kind of trouble. It seems to me you've enough of that already."

Absolutely, said the other. *You can't be in any deeper shit than being dead, man. But on the other hand, I really* can't *get in any deeper shit! So what's the difference? Anyway, it's like I said: any friend of Harry's is a friend of mine.*

"You're an American, right?" said Jake. "So who are you?"

Who was *I, do you mean?* said the other. *Hey, you know, you're a lot more like Harry than you know? I remember he asked me that selfsame question, and I answered it the same way, too. But damn it, it looks like I'm a lot rustier than I thought; my manners are all shot to hell! Excuse me, will you? I* used *to be J. Humphrey Jackson Jr.—and I* used *to build safes. I built a safe in the cellars of Le Manse Madonie, which* used *to stand up there on the rim of the gorge. The brothers who owned the place must have thought I'd seen too much, so they fixed it for me to have a little "accident." End of story . . . until the Necroscope came by and squared things for me.*

"He squared things for you?" Jake sensed the importance of all this. "How did he manage that?"

He brought Le Manse Madonie down, said Humph. *Right down to its foundations. Blew it to hell, right into the gorge, and one of those Francezci brothers—madmen that they were—with it. He said he'd square it for me, and he surely did. But of course he had his own motives, too.*

Jake *knew* all of this, or not quite all of it. But the more Humph talked about it, the more it filled in the blanks in his head. "Do you reckon you could tell me the whole story?" he said. "You see, quite apart from any trouble with the Great Majority, I have problems of my own that need sorting out."

Anything you want to know, just ask away, said Humph.

Which was as far as they got, for just then there came an angry shout from the direction of the quarry.

Jake had his binoculars in his hand, and the sun was glinting off the lenses. Someone in the quarry had seen those bright flashes of light and was looking back at him through binoculars of his own. The workers down there were some four hundred yards away, and there was rough ground in between, rising to the spot where Jake stood. All of which gave him a safety margin.

So he thought, until he looked through his glasses again.

Among the people down there, there were more than just hard-hat types. Along with the many coveralled workers in and around the diggers and mechanical shovels (all of them marked with the legend CASTELLANO & CO) several men were equipped with metal detectors and other electrical ground-sweeping gear—

—While others were simply "equipped."

"Guns!" said Jake, as a bullet spanged, sending sparks flying from the road's metal safety barrier a few inches away from his hand. And as the *crack!* of the shot echoed off the walls of the gorge: "That was just a warning shot!"

You're not safe here! cried Korath, bringing into being the Möbius equations.

And Jake told him, "I couldn't agree more. So let's not *be* here." And to Humph: "I'll be back."

Drop in any time, Jake, said that one. *It'll be a pleasure. Let's face it, it's not as if I'll be busy or anything.*

There was a cutting just a few yards up the road. Jake ran for it, and as he passed out of sight of the men in the quarry, froze the dizzily mutating equations in exactly the right place and ran straight in through the invisible door that sprang into being.

Where to? said Korath "breathlessly," in the ultimate darkness of the Möbius Continuum.

"Back where we came from," said Jake. "Imperia."

He knew the coordinates, and together they went there. . .

18
Jake—Déjà Viewer?

IMPERIA TO GENOA WAS A LITTLE OVER FIFTY miles, and since Jake didn't know the route and had no co-ordinates, there was nothing for it but to take a cab.

He asked to be dropped in the docklands area, and then went looking for a drug dealer—any drug dealer—in the warren of bars, sleazy clubs, and markets in the narrow alleys and smelly side streets adjacent to the wharves.

Why here? Korath wanted to know.

"Where there's low-life, there's drugs," Jake told him. "In London, Marseilles, Miami, Hong Kong, you name it, it's the same story. Here in Genoa, it's a safe bet the drugs arrive in boats and before the big dealers get to see them, the little people—the couriers, bent customs officials, and others on the take—they all get their cut, enough to satisfy their own needs. Just as long as they're not too greedy, that's okay. In Italy, which is still the home of the Mafia, being greedy doesn't pay except in six-foot plots of dirt. Anyway, people on the waterfront—any waterfront, anywhere in the world—they know about things like this. So that's why we're here."

You seem to know a lot about it yourself, said Korath. *From Natasha no doubt, when you were lovers?*

But Jake's private life was his own, and there were memories of Natasha—despite that she'd been a courier herself, among other things—that he knew he'd hold dear to the last. For which reasons he answered: "I only know that if I wanted to roll some of my own, this kind of place is where I'd find the makings." And because deadspeak, like telepathy, frequently conveys more than is actually said, Korath knew what he meant.

It's a dangerous place, then?

"It has its moments, I imagine," said Jake. "But smoking is just a beginning. Then there's injecting, and now there's a new line in designers: micros you can lick off the back of a stamp. If you think blood's an addiction, I've got news for you. These dealers are bloodsuckers no less than the ones you knew on Starside, Korath. But at least when a man dies from drugs, he *stays* dead! And that's about the best I can say for them."

In a small bar where you could cut the air with a knife—a place that stank of marijuana—Jake cornered the barkeep in a booth that he was slopping out and spoke to him. This time, the man being a complete stranger, Jake made no immediate reference to Castellano. But still he came straight to the point: drugs.

"You wanna buy?" said the barkeep, an unkempt skeleton of a man with shifty, deep-sunken eyes.

"No," said Jake, "I'm making a delivery. You know what they say about nice things, how they always come in small packages?"

"Micros? Designers?" The barkeep shook his head. "Smokes, I can help you with. These days they're almost legal, legitimate. Nobody even cares anymore. But that kind of stuff—I'm not in that league. That's big business you're talking—and if you're such a high roller, how come you're sniffing around in a little joint like this? Uh-uh," he shook his head. "I'm not buying it. Cops and their narks aren't too welcome here, friend."

From which Jake gathered it was time to call on this one's basic instincts, and what had worked in San Remo might just as easily work here.

Jake still had francs; he slapped a wad on the table in the booth and said: "I'm just in from Marseilles, a courier. I came in with a friend who's selling his, er, 'business interests' to me. He had to get out because he's too well known. But it seems he left it too late. Just an hour ago he was recognized and the police arrested him. They want to speak to him about—oh, this and that, you know? But me being new to this, my friend was the one with all the contacts.

Now I need to deliver the goods, and the sooner the better. We were supposed to off-load to a dealer with property—a legitimate front—here in Genoa. And since this is a guy who doesn't like to be kept waiting, I'm ready to pay for directions."

Some people had just come in and were standing at the bar. The barkeep looked at the money, licked his lips, and said, "So who is it you're looking to meet? I mean, you do know his name, right? I can't help if I don't know where your stuff's supposed to be going."

And now it was make or break time.

"Castellano," said Jake. "Luigi Castellano. I think he's a Sicilian." He saw the barkeep give a nervous start, and quickly went on: "But hey, don't worry about it—if you can't help me, I'll find somebody who will." He reached for the money, but the barkeep beat him to it.

"Try Frankie's," he said, stuffing the wad in a wide pocket in front of his greasy apron. "Frankie's Franchise. It's a dive in a cobbled alley off the next street east of here. Anyone can direct you. But friend, if anyone asks who sent you—it wasn't me."

"Don't worry," said Jake again. "They're expecting me."

And just one minute after he'd left, the barkeep picked up his telephone and made absolutely sure they *would* be expecting him . . .

Am I to understand, said Korath, when Jake was back out in the street and on the move again, *that you intend to walk straight into a bastion of your greatest foe, a man who has twice tried to kill you? Surely that is madness! The Möbius Continuum must be rotting your mind! And as for the wretched . . .* creature *you just spoke to—who in Starside would be meat for the provisioning—why, I would offer up my naked throat to a rabid wolf before placing any trust in that one! Yet the way you spoke to him, I felt certain he must be your long-lost brother! So tell me: why are you so determined to die, Jake?*

"You don't know Castellano like I know him," Jake answered. "And I'm not too dumb where other people are concerned, either. In the event our friend in the bar back there talks to someone in Frankie's Franchise—that's *if* Frankie's really is Castellano's place—so much the better. Except I don't want to give them too much time to figure out what they're going to do with me, so we have to be getting a move on. And look, I think that must be the place down there, that doorway with the red double 'F' sign overhead." He pointed down a long, narrow alley.

But—

"But the thing is," Jake explained, "we do have the Möbius Continuum—and you'll just have to take my word for it that it isn't rotting my brain. Any trouble I can get into, you can get me out of in double-quick time. But I do have to satisfy myself that this is Castellano's place before . . . before I—"

Yes?

"Before I blow it all the way to hell!" Jake growled. "I'm going to take out *all* of this bastard's places, to let him know there's nowhere he can hide. What do you think I've been doing, Korath? I haven't simply been looking for Castellano, I've also been checking out his rat-holes. And if this is one of them, it has to go."

And if he's here, inside Frankie's Franchise right now, at this very moment?

"He won't try to kill me," Jake answered, "not right away. He'll probably want to talk to me first—not to mention a lot of other, much more unpleasant things he'll want to do to me—*before* he kills me. But we aren't going to let that happen."

I see. (Korath was very thoughtful now.) *So then, this is how you'll take your revenge, by destroying Castellano's every bolt-hole before you strike at the man himself—and by letting him know that you, personally, are responsible.*

"Something like that, yes." said Jake. "An eye for an eye. This bastard has lived on fear for so long—not only the fear of his enemies but also of the people in his own organization—that it's time someone taught him the real meaning of the word. Castellano has *fed* on fear, he has *battened* on it. But now I'm going to make him choke and maybe throw up on it, too."

You want him to know you are coming. And all along, you've been taunting him . . . even when you killed his men!

"Especially when I killed his men." Jake nodded. "But that wasn't just to get back at him. Those bastards deserved to die at least as much as he does."

Hah! Korath grunted then, but with such emphasis that Jake could almost see the gape of his once-jaws, the snarl of rough lips drawn back from fang-like teeth. *But I was so* right *about you, Jake Cutter! You are indeed my kind of man.*

"I'll take that as a compliment," said Jake.

As it was intended, said Korath. *So then, what next? What's the plan? How do you intend to do this thing?*

"If I find out that Frankie's is what we think it is," Jake answered darkly, "I could be out of there as quick as you could roll those numbers, and back in again with one of those bombs I made up: three pounds of plastique on a ten-second fuse. But of course I need to go inside and get the coordinates first."

Ahhh! Korath sighed his "appreciation." *You'll kill him and anyone who is with him, and destroy half of the street into the bargain. Oh, such mayhem! Bravo!*

Which gave Jake pause. He had been rushing headlong, but he wasn't in fact a murderer in the usual meaning of the word. And he didn't want to be. "Half the street?" he said, and shook his head. "No, for innocent people would die. After that there'd be no going back. The Great Majority would never forgive me, and I don't suppose I'd ever forgive myself."

Ah! (Korath was disappointed.) *Then you had better think of something else. And quickly, for we're there.*

"We'll have to play it by ear," said Jake, as he pushed his way through batswing doors, under the unlit neons of the double F sign . . .

* * *

Frankie's Franchise was a dive of the worst kind, a place where all the social debris of Genoa could convene and feel perfectly at home. Nighttimes would find it full of wharf-rats, prostitutes and their pimps, pushers, perverts, and almost every other variety of sleazy low-life. Dirt was ingrained into the floors; the poor lighting and filthy, flyspecked windows did little to conceal the presence of small cockroaches on the walls, and the stench of narcotic cigarettes and stale booze was almost strong enough to qualify as a taste. Also, it was very noisy, at least at first.

When Jake entered, an antique American jukebox was playing 1950s rock-and-roll music (Chuck Berry, judging by the uniquely clangorous quality of the guitar) and the volume was turned all the way up. But as the batswing doors creaked to and fro behind him and Jake paced forward into the place, the plug was yanked, the music groaned to an abrupt halt, and the handful of greasy-looking types at the bar turned as a man to stare at him.

He was a stranger here, true enough, but Jake knew that his presence scarcely warranted so much attention. It could only be that he had been informed upon, and he knew by whom.

All unseen, however, the dead vampire Korath went with him, and as yet Jake didn't feel too uncomfortable; he didn't go in fear of his life. The Möbius Continuum—or rather his ability to use it—was a very comforting concept.

When Jake sensed movement behind him and the batswing doors stopped swinging, he knew that someone had stopped them and was now guarding the entrance. These people wouldn't want to be disturbed in the pursuit of their "business" with him. And that in itself—the fact that they were very intent upon him—tended to reinforce Jake's opinion: that Frankie's was indeed a front, one of Castellano's outlets or bases of operation.

So then, this was the scenario: Behind Jake, some heavy; to his right, the bar; on his left and five or six paces ahead, a corner wall with a sign pointing to the toilets. And ambling "casually" toward him from the bar, four thugs, while one other stayed right where he was, looking on. Other than that, Frankie's seemed empty—had *been* emptied, Jake suspected—in anticipation of this moment.

But not in anticipation of the next.

"I want to talk to the boss," Jake said. "That's Luigi Castellano I'm talking about." And he kept walking toward the sign that said toilets. Three of the thugs, as ugly brutes as anyone would want to imagine, came to a halt. The fourth kept right on coming, and he was the ugliest of all. He was a street fighter, a bruiser, a torpedo. Jake believed he could break a chair over this one's bullet head and it wouldn't stop him.

"Georgy," said the one at the bar in broken English. "Bring the jerk over here and sit him down where we can watch him. And *don't* you be hurting him. Not too much, anyway."

"Uh!" said the torpedo, and kept coming.

"And Vince," the one at the bar continued. "See if the telephone's working again, and if it is call Bagheria. Let The Man know what's going down. See if he can guess what just walked in here like it owns the joint."

And in a shadowy corner there was movement, and the musical beeping of a telephone as someone tapped in the numbers.

But Jake's apparently suicidal approach had got him almost everything he wanted to know: Bagheria, Sicily! Sod's law, when the last key on the ring is the one that fits the lock. And the last location on his list, which he hadn't yet visited, was the one he was looking for. Just an hour or so ago he'd been within a few kilometres of his main target—Luigi Castellano himself.

Jake didn't want anyone to see him using the Möbius Continuum. If the toilets had no windows or back way out, well tough. Let these people figure out how he'd made his escape. But first he would at least try to make it appear that he had simply made a run for it.

His pace picked up, and Georgy angled after him. But Jake was at the corner, turning it, and pushing open a frosted-glass door that hid the urinals and toilet booths from view. Stepping through, he heard Georgy grunting close behind—too close. And quickly turning, he used all his strength to slam the door shut on the bustling torpedo.

Georgy came right through it in shards of shattering glass, grunting his surprise and then his pain, as his face and reaching hands were cut to ribbons. Hearing all the noise, the other thugs came charging after him—only to see him sprawled there in his own slippery blood, skidding in it as he tried to get to his feet.

As for Jake . . . there was no rear exit, no windows, nowhere to hide. But "the jerk" was already gone . . .

Why back here? Korath wanted to know when Jake emerged from the Continuum in his hotel room in Paris.

"Things to do," said Jake. "I now know everything I need to know with regard to locations—"

Except the one in Bagheria.

"—Which I'm leaving till last. Castellano is there, and if I take out all of his other places, that's probably where he'll stay. Going by what Natasha told me, he's well protected there; he's 'safe' there . . . or so he thinks. As for its location, its coordinates: well, since he runs his bogus construction company out of Bagheria—"

The place shouldn't be too hard to find.

"Correct," said Jake. "So for tonight—if only for tonight—Castellano is safe. But as for his rat-holes . . . at least one of them is going out with a bang. Frankie's, I think."

Really? With all the loss of innocent life which that might entail?

And again Jake pondered that before answering, "Well if not a bang, a big ball of fire, definitely—but in the early hours of tomorrow morning, when we can be fairly certain the place is empty."

And if you're mistaken and someone is there?

"Then he'll be one of Castellano's—the one at the bar who was giving all the orders, maybe—which in my book makes him a drug-pushing scumbag and worthy of the heat."

Good! said Korath. *But that leaves us with a lot of time on our hands.*

"No, not really," said Jake. "Frankie's taught me a lesson, that even with the Möbius Continuum as back-up, it isn't a good idea to go into places like that unarmed. So obviously I need a gun, and I know where I can get one."

Oh?

Jake nodded. "The armoury at E-Branch HQ. I know the coordinates. The door's secured and alarmed, of course, but we won't be using the door. I don't want them to know I'm there—don't want any confrontations, scenes, or problems—or anything else that might interfere with what I'm doing now."

Confrontations and problems with Liz, you mean?

"Don't get to know me *too* well!" Jake warned then, and went on: "Also, while these binoculars of mine are just fine in daylight, they're useless at night. But as I recall there are also nite-lites in the armoury. Since the place in Bagheria is Castellano's stronghold and he's likely to have people on watch, we won't be going there in daylight hours, so—"

We'll steal a pair of these night-seeing glasses?

"I'll borrow a pair," said Jake, "yes. Then I want to check my equipment—" he nodded toward the sausage bag where it stuck out from under his bed, "—and have a good meal, and after dark I'm going back to the gorge under the Madonie mountains to talk to Humph. Then an early night, so I can be up and mobile in the wee small hours to deal with Frankie's Franchise."

And the other places?

"Tomorrow is another day," Jake gave a grim nod. "Didn't I explain how I want Castellano to know the real meaning of fear? That's why we'll do it bit by bit, so he can see it creeping up on him."

There followed a moment's silence, and then: *You will never know,* Korath gurgled in his deepest, darkest, and most guttural deadspeak voice, *the pleasure it gives me to work with one such as you on a mission such as this.* And Jake sensed that the dead vampire was genuinely appreciative. But still:

"How I wish that I could say the same," he answered, with a shudder that he couldn't quite repress . . .

E-Branch wasn't as easy as he thought. When he emerged from the Continuum inside the armoury he must have stepped in front of a sensor. It made no great difference; by the time the alarm went off he had already picked up a 9 mm Browning (modified for its special ammunition), three spare magazines, and a long flat box containing one gross of rounds. And since the nite-lite binoculars were in plain view there on a shelf, he took them, too, and was gone from the place as quickly as that.

"And that's it," he said, flopping onto his bed in his room in the hotel in Paris. "I'm all equipped."

But are you prepared? said Korath.

"That, too," Jake answered. "Oh, I have to clean up this gun and fill the clips, and maybe change the fuses on those bombs I put together—for even using the Möbius Continuum, five-second fuses don't allow that much time—but that's about it for now. So, since we'll be out and about tonight and in the early hours of the morning, right now I'm going to rest up."

Sleep, you mean? said Korath.

"Yes. I don't know about you, but I find regular use of the Möbius Continuum to be draining. It must be the exhilaration—the rush, and the weirdness of it—that's getting to me."

Which is your polite way of asking me to leave?

"Correct," said Jake. "And remember, the usual warnings are still in force."

But of course! Korath snapped, his tone suddenly bitter. *As your "partner" what else could I expect?* Huh! *The fact of it is you see me as nothing more than a beast of burden!* And feigning his frustration—or perhaps not, it would have been difficult to tell with any of his lying kind—he went his way, retreating from the fringes of Jake's mind . . .

And when Jake was sure that his unwelcome part-time tenant was gone: "Just like a genie trapped in his lamp," he murmured, but to himself this time. "The only difference being, with Korath I'm getting more than the normal quota of three wishes—as many shots at the Möbius Continuum as I want."

But as for what Jake had told Korath, that was true enough, he did feel drained of energy. And as gradually he fell into an uneasy sleep: "An evil genie trapped in his lamp," he continued to murmur to himself, "who hopes that by 'befriending' me he'll be able to talk me into giving that lamp a rub. Which will suit me just fine, as long as I remember not to rub him up the wrong way."

The last thing he did before actually falling asleep was to glance at his wristwatch. The time was a little after 5:00 P.M. and the light coming in through his windows was just beginning to fade a little. . .

As ever, Jake's dreams were overshadowed by a twisting, twining, figure-of-eight Möbius Strip symbol, accompanied by myriad formulae whose numbers and symbols—familiar yet baffling—were both guardians and gateway to the metaphysical Möbius Continuum. Endlessly those equations went scrolling down the screen of his mind, and he knew exactly, instinctively, where to stop them in order to form one of those enigmatic doors that were only ever visible to him, a door that would take him out of this universe into some place other than our plane of existence.

He knew how to *stop* the equations, yes, but he still didn't have a clue how to conjure them into being out of nowhere—how to start them mutating and flowing—and he still couldn't remember their composition or sequence. In his dreams it was easy: they were simply there, adrift in his mind, ready at a moment's notice to flow with his tide, spring into being at his calling. But in his waking hours the idea was too fantastic, too "otherworldly," too *un*real to be believable. Which was the problem in a nutshell, but Jake didn't know it yet: that to believe was to be enabled—that he had been *endowed* with the knowledge—and that it was simply there.

And behind those shining figure-of-eight symbols—behind all the numbers and formulae—the whispering of the Great Majority was ever present, like a skittering of dried-up leaves in the deadspeak aether.

They argued about Jake and about Harry Keogh, almost as if the two were one and the same. They argued about what Harry had become, he and two of his sons, before they were no more—but without actually *saying* what they had become—and then went on to argue the merits, the pros and cons, of even having commerce with such a thing as a Necroscope, a man who speaks to the dead. It was as if a great court were in session in the graveyards of the world, and Jake was the one being tried.

In his defence, Jake recognized Zek's voice, and he *thought* he knew the voices of several others. No, he *did* know them: the voice of Sir Keenan Gormley, from his tiny plot in a Kensington garden of repose; and that of "Sergeant" Graham Lane, an *ex*-ex-Army physical-training instructor, from the cemetery in Harden, County Durham, England. But *how* did he know these things, these people? Even in his dreams such knowledge was puzzling.

As for the "prosecution": these seemed to Jake to be bitter people mainly—people who had failed to make their mark on the world—who had left no one behind to remember them, and nothing to be remembered by; which meant of course that they had no reason to desire any kind of contact with or knowledge of the living world. For such as them, that world was gone forever; they were resigned to contemplating the dark eternity of death without a backwards glance. No-hopers in their lives, they were that way in death, too.

But in Jake's (or Harry's) defence:

We loved the Necroscope. (Like a hiss of spray on a distant shore.) *He never let us down, not even at the end; never caused us pain, except we brought it upon ourselves in his defence. He was vulnerable, yet risked everything. He was our light, he was our warmth, he was all we had. And before him we had nothing—not even deadspeak, not even each other.*

And against Jake:

But that was Harry Keogh . . . and at the end we didn't trust him either! As for this one: he simply isn't the same. Where is his humility? He's neither Harry nor Nathan. He's Jake, and the company he keeps doesn't bear mentioning!

And on Jake's behalf:

But he could *be the new Necroscope!* (This was Zek Foener's sweet voice, surely.) *With the help of the Great Majority, Jake* could *be! He doesn't know, doesn't understand, and yet he seems to* remember! *He remembers some of it, anyway—including things that the original Necroscope may well have forgotten—and for all we know he could be trying to complete something that Harry left unfinished. In fact I'm sure he is. But as for Harry: he's gone now, gone beyond recall, except perhaps by Jake, who is as close to the original as we're ever going to get. That's why we have to give him his chance.*

And against:

His light and warmth are suspect; a shadow follows him, and it is cold in its heart. We know what it is, and we should turn away from Jake, leaving him to whatever fate awaits. He doesn't *know, doesn't understand, it's true. But let's face it: what he doesn't know . . . can't harm us!*

And for:

Well, good for you! (Sergeant Graham Lane's rough, military deadspeak voice; Jake "recognized" it without knowing how.) *But say what you like, there are plenty of us who are determined to speak to Jake anyway—just as we were to speak to Nathan that time. Ah, but as I recall you were against that, too! Who would have been the losers if we'd listened to you then, eh? So don't fool yourselves you can keep us quiet forever, because we won't let you. And meanwhile, if any harm should come to Jake because of your cowardice, remember this—it will be held against you. It will be on* your *heads!*

And against:

Then perhaps we should turn away from you, too. Do not defy us in this matter, not unless you actually desire to be shunned by all the teeming dead!

And Sergeant again: *Better wait and see who turns away from whom! Death is unforgiving, as will the Great Majority be unforgiving, if you're proved wrong and you've denied them their one last chance of renewed contact with decent human life.*

And against:

Ah, but isn't that just the problem? I say again: the company this Jake keeps simply doesn't bear mentioning! So if you really are concerned for decent "human" life . . . well, perhaps you'll first consider that. . . .

And so the argument raged, to and fro—a background babble of distantly whispering voices, the hiss of static in the metaphysical deadspeak aether—with Jake understanding none of it, or so very little that it made no difference . . .

He started awake, and the dream—but oh-so-much more than any ordinary dream—at once faded from memory.

It was 9:00 P.M., dark outside, and very dark in his room.

"Korath?"

A cold breeze blew on Jake's mind as he switched the lights on. *I am here,* said the dead vampire, oozing out of nowhere.

And yawning, Jake told him, "It's time we were on our way—almost." He rubbed sleep out of his eyes, tried again to remember his dream. But it was no good, it was gone.

Our destination?

"First let me wake up." In the bathroom Jake splashed water on his face, towelled himself dry, then walked into the living area and changed into his black clothing. Picking up his Browning, a spare clip, and his nite-lites, he said, "I want to go back to the Madonie. I need to talk to Humph."

You aren't taking your explosive devices with you?

"Later, maybe, but right now I won't lumber myself."

Without another word, Korath conjured the Möbius equations. Fascinated as ever, Jake watched those constantly mutating numbers and symbols scrolling down the screen of his mind, stopped them where he knew they would form a door, then stepped through it, out of his room and into the Möbius Continuum—

—And just a moment's thought later, back out of the Continuum into Sicily's Madonie mountains.

The wall of the gorge was a pale, dusty yellow in moon and starlight. Jake stood on the road as before, looking down into the quarry in the guts of the gorge. Down there, a night watchman's brazier glowed orange, but there was no movement. An owl offered its faraway hoot, and crickets chirred like frying bacon, doing their thing in the scrubby roadside herbage. Other than that the night was silent, and far too warm, of course.

Turning round, Jake looked out over the Tyrrhenian Sea from his high vantage point. The lights of Capo d'Orlando were visible in the east, and those of Bagheria and Palermo in the west. The path cast by the moon on the sea was incredibly lovely, and Jake found himself thinking of Liz Merrick—but Liz in another world, another time—in a world where there would *be* time, for them to be together . . .

Well, maybe. But not yet.

Realizing that he was silhouetted against the eastern skyline, Jake moved to the mouth of the cutting and sat down on a large flat boulder. Using the nite-lites to scan the quarry, he found the night watchmen (two of them) where they took it easy in the cab of a mechanical digger and smoked cigarettes. Their smokes made tiny points of bright white light in the grey-blob masks of their thermally-imaged faces. They didn't pose any kind of threat.

"Now to find Humph," Jake murmured quietly. His words were deadspeak, and an invitation.

Look no further, said Humph. *Nice that you've come back so soon . . . I think.* There was something in his voice that hadn't been there before: he seemed reluctant. Jake wondered about it, but thought it best not to ask.

"This isn't a social call, Humph." He got straight down to

business. "I've come to ask what you know about Harry Keogh."

The other was silent for a moment, then said: *He was a good friend of mine, you know? Did for me what I couldn't do for myself. He was the same with all the teeming dead: the Necroscope fixed what they were no longer capable of fixing.*

"Fixed?" said Jake.

He righted wrongs, took care of unfinished business. In my case, he blew that fucking *place—Le Manse Madonie—right off the mountain! He had his own reasons, I guess, but it served my purpose, too. So I suppose what I'm trying to say, I don't tell tales out of school, Jake. If the Great Majority aren't talking to you, well, they probably have their reasons. Out here in the Sicilian sticks, for all that I'm left mainly in the dark, I do get to hear the occasional piece of gossip. And—*

"And you're right," Jake cut in, "they don't trust me. They won't let me prove myself. But it was Harry himself who gave me this thing, landed me in this mess. Believe me, Humph, I didn't want to be the new Necroscope. But I'm stuck with it anyway."

I've heard as much, said Humph. *The truth is I've had more visitors just recently—*

"Since I was here?" Jake cut in.

—than in the last seventy or so years. (Humph's deadspeak nod.) *In fact, as long as I've been here!*

"The Great Majority," said Jake, a little sourly. "They've warned you off."

Something like that, said Humph. *But hey, there are people on your side, too! Anyway, it seems there's been a lot of talk, and they've taken some kind of vote—like, politics, you know? Yeah, even in the hereafter. It was kind of one-sided from what I can make out, but the result is your friends are forbidden to talk to you—for the time being, anyway. And that goes for me, too. But as I said, any friend of Harry's, et cetera. Er, within limits.*

That brought something back to mind, and Jake said, "Do

you know who Sir Keenan Gormley is, or was? Zek Foener, or Sergeant Graham Lane? Well, they'll vouch for me, I know that for a fact . . . *shit*!" For suddenly he remembered the details of his dream, and knew that they definitely *would* vouch for him! But just the three of them, out of all the Great Majority? If Jake wanted to get on the right side of the dead, it seemed he'd have his work cut out.

Humph didn't know any of the names Jake had mentioned; he'd never so much as heard of them, hadn't been allowed to speak to anyone who was in favour of Jake, not yet.

See, said Humph, *I know what's wrong. It's something you're carrying around with you—emphasis on "thing." Oh, I can feel your warmth all right, but you also have a shadow. It's cold in that shadow, Jake. Cold and scary. It's clinging much too close to you; and even to someone incorporeal as I am—someone with no physical senses at all—still that shadow smells something awful. That's because it* is *something awful!*

Jake sensed a great stirring of rage deep inside—not his own but Korath's—and knew that despite his request that the vampire keep his deadspeak thoughts shielded and converse only with him, still his "companion" was on the verge of breaking silence and speaking in his own defence.

Furthermore, he sensed, he somehow knew, that this was what the Great Majority most feared: intercourse with the unknown, a creature like Korath—a creature neither living nor truly dead (not even now, in the normal sense of the word), yet possessing knowledge to endanger both the living and the dead alike—and that he must intervene before the situation deteriorated out of control. Wherefore:

"Let me explain something," said Jake. "You know how Harry went places as easily as snapping his fingers? From A to B, but without crossing the distance between? He did it by using something called the Möbius Continuum. He made invisible doors that only he could see or use. But to do it he needed a mathematical formula. I don't have that formula, Humph. My 'shadow'—as you call him—he has the formula. And without him I'm stuck, only half the Necroscope you knew. Not even half, because for a long time now I've been learning that this Harry was something else, a hard act to follow. No way I can match up to him," Jake shook his head. "And no way I can carry on his work, either—even if I was willing to—not without the help of the Great Majority. So you see, I'm sort of caught in the middle, between the devil and the deep blue sea."

The devil, yes, said Humph. *That's pretty much how the dead think of your "shadow," the* Thing *that travels with you.*

"But he only *travels* with me," said Jake. "He's not part of me. And without him I couldn't travel at all. His mind contains the formula that lets me make my doors, but it's useless to him without me. For my part, I have the physical means to do it, to travel from A to B without crossing the distance between."

Else you, too, would be useless to him, said Humph thoughtfully. *So what does he get out of it, this dead—or undead—travelling companion of yours?*

"Only my promise that when my work is done, then we'll deal with his problem. Bottom line: revenge. You see, Humph, my case is much the same as yours was before you met up with the Necroscope. I want to rid the world of a cancer that caused me grief and that's destined to cause more grief if it isn't rooted out. As for my so-called 'shadow': well, it could be argued that his case is far more important than mine—in fact I'm sure it is. But something inside me insists I do my own thing first."

These are personal vendettas, then? said Humph.

"In a way they are," Jake admitted it. "Mine is, for sure—except I can't be absolutely sure even of that! But anyway, and as I said, if I don't correct it, it will cause a lot of others grief, too. My world is full of people, Humph—the children of the Great Majority—and drugs are terrible things. So you tell me: Are the dead really so eager to have their own kith and kin join them, addicted in life, and addicts forever in death, dead before their time, because of this man I'm chasing down? He's a monster, Humph, and I've sworn to put him down with or without the help of the teeming dead."

You know, said Humph, *the more you talk, the more you sound like Harry Keogh? So tell me more—convince me, Jake. I mean, I really do want to be on your side.*

"There has to be some kind of connection," Jake said then, "between this place, Harry Keogh, and me. The first time I came here, I was *drawn* here without knowing where I was going. All I knew was I had to come—as if I was trying to recall something that someone else had forgotten. I just *knew* to come here, like a different kind of déjà vu, but far more real than that. And I looked up there and 'saw' Le Manse Madonie; I *expected* it to be there, *remembered* something someone else had seen. Harry Keogh? It seems the only logical explanation to me."

To me, too, said Humph.

"He was doing something here," said Jake. "Not just for you but for himself, and maybe for the world. But while I know what he actually did—that he took out Le Manse Madonie—I still don't know why. Because you wanted it done?" He shook his head. "That doesn't add up; it doesn't seem a strong enough reason to me. So what *was* his motive, Humph? You've already admitted that he had one."

And after a moment Humph said, *Maybe you should try asking yourself what it was that* always *motivated the Necroscope. What it was that he did, and did so very well, so very thoroughly.*

"But that's easy," Jake shrugged. "He killed vampires."

Humph said nothing, but his silence spoke volumes . . .

Jake's jaw fell open. "He killed vampires!" he said again, almost in a whisper. "So these brothers—what was their name, the Francezcis?—they were vampires?" And when his informant remained silent: "Humph?"

I'm out of here now, said that one. *We're onto a forbidden subject, Jake.*

"But—"

But I can't say any more, Humph backed off. *Except to wish you luck, and hope it all works out for you.*

Jake felt him fading away, back into the silence of death,

and called out after him, "Just one more thing . . . . Humph?"

Better make it quick, then. (Like the footfalls of a mouse in Jake's metaphyical mind.)

"The Francezci treasure," Jake said, his thoughts swiftly, chaotically flowing, telling a lot more than he actually said, "the reason the brothers needed a vault: Harry blew it off the mountain along with Le Manse Madonie and it lies buried in the gorge. But how does Castellano—this drug-running bastard I'm trying to bring down—how does he know about it? How does he know it even existed? What's the fucking connection!?"

Got to go, Necroscope, said Humph. And his deadspeak voice was so faint now that Jake wasn't sure he even heard it. *But I can tell you something: vampires don't give in easily. They're incredibly tenacious things, Jake. The Francezci line, it went back a hell of a long way—back into history, back into time. So who can say? Maybe the same line goes forward, too.*

"Goes forward?"

Talk to you soon, Jake, said J. Humphrey Jackson Jr. *Or at least . . . I . . . hope . . . soooooo.* His deadspeak voice dwindled away to nothing.

And somewhere up in the mountains the owl hooted again . . .

Things were starting to come together, but not fast enough for Jake. Driven by those unreasoning, inexplicable urges from deep within—with the pressure constantly building—he could feel his frustration mounting with each passing moment. He knew he'd have to take it out on something, and soon, or else explode!

And explode was the executive word.

Sensing Jake's mood, Korath kept the peace and did what was required of him without question.

In Paris, Jake fully equipped himself before going back to the gorge. Back on the road—standing in the open, silhouetted against the night sky where he would be seen—he fired three rapid shots into the air to attract the attention of the night-watchmen. As they came at the run, he watched them through his nite-lites. As far as he could tell they were ordinary working men, and he had nothing against them. But all of the machinery down in the quarry, that belonged to Castellano. Anything that happened here—to this machinery and this close to home—was certain to enrage and unnerve the bastard.

Well fuck him!

As the night-watchmen drew closer, scrambling up towards his position, Jake moved into the shadows, took the Möbius route to their brazier's glow, and from there into the cab of the digger where he'd seen them smoking. A few seconds to plant his charge and he moved on to the next vehicle.

He planted five charges in all, all with twenty-five-second delay fuses, then returned to the shadows under the wall of the gorge. Using the Möbius Continuum, it had been as simple and as quick as that.

The night-watchmen were less than fifty feet away from him; they peered this way and that into the night and saw absolutely nothing, not for the next few seconds. After that . . . but they just wouldn't believe what they would see after that.

Jake glanced at his luminous watch and counted it down: "Five, four, three, two, one—*bang*!"

Five bangs in fact, coming just a few seconds apart.

The big digger was first, of course. The explosion drove it down on its huge shocks—which at once tossed it back into the air in two main parts and lots of lesser, blazing debris. For a big, heavy vehicle it rose up quite a way—until its ruptured fuel tanks tore it asunder in midair. By which time a massive, eight-wheeled dumper truck was teetering about on its nose, and three of its great wheels were leaping this way and that across the floor of the quarry, blazing as they went.

On the road, the night-watchmen cowered down; Jake, too, as the fireworks show continued. A second digger, but smaller than the first, was performing aerial cartwheels, its severed caterpillar tracks lashing the air like a pair of gigantic, crippled snakes. As for the site shack—a not inconsiderable structure that *used* to stand on the far side of the quarry—that was in the process of dispersing itself far and wide, reduced to fifty thousand fragments of splintered timber, buckled aluminum cladding, shards of glass and plastic, and nuts and bolts that flew everywhere, spanging like bullets.

Last to go was a conveyor belt and sieve equipment, used to filter coins, precious metals, and other items out of the rubble. In a spectacular explosion, the various components of the setup disintegrated, and for several long seconds the sky rained fire and scraps of unidentifiable junk.

Then the roaring of the flames, black smoke roiling for the sky, drifting sparks and smaller, secondary explosions as drums of fuel oil got hot and blew themselves to hell, and the quarry seeming to slump into itself, almost as if the rubble and everything else was melting down into one big lake of fire.

Jake had moved back behind a jut of rock when the first of the fires lit the night. Now, using what little Italian he knew to the best of his ability, he called out from that position to the night-watchmen where they stood gawping down into the ruins of what had been a work-site:

"You men, do you know why you're alive? You're alive so you can tell your boss, Castellano, just exactly what happened here. Be sure to tell him who did it—me, Jake Cutter—and that I won't rest until I've destroyed all that he owns, everything he ever touched. And you can also tell him that when I've finished with all that, then that I'll be coming for him."

They looked—saw only the fires reflected off the face of the cliff—and shrank back. They were out in the open, on the road, sitting ducks, and Jake was nowhere to be seen. They both had weapons, sawn-off shotguns by their looks, which now, amazingly, they threw down.

Then, as they backed off and turned to head down the road toward the distant coast, one of them called back: "We won't be around from now on. So tell him your f-f-fucking self!"

Jake knew what he meant. After what had happened here, any attempt to explain things to Luigi Castellano would be more than their lives were worth . . .

Do you feel better now? Korath asked him as they sped along the Möbius route to Paris.

No, Jake answered in like mode. *But I will when the rest of tonight's work is done.*

Marseilles? Korath queried.

Haven't I warned you about that? said Jake. *Haven't I told you not to try to get to know me too well?*

But it was in your mind clear as crystal, said Korath, *and your thoughts are deadspeak. You no longer shield them from me like you used to, and I had even begun to hope that perhaps we—how shall I say it? That perhaps you and I—that maybe we were drawing closer together?*

"Think again," said Jake. *"I must be getting careless, that's all."*

Before Korath could utter his usual "disgusted" snort, they were back in the Paris hotel room, where Jake quickly re-equipped himself . . .

On the hillside overlooking Castellano's Marseilles villa, Jake used his nite-lites to scan the place. His binoculars' thermal-imaging system showed that there was no heating in the house—but then, who would be using central heating in weather such as this?—except a small white patch in a lesser building to one side, probably the boiler room. The nite-lites couldn't pick up concealed human movements, however, not unless there was a lot of heat attendant.

Still empty? said Korath.

"Probably," Jake answered. "But in any case we'll keep our eyes open." It was becoming easy now to forget that Korath was incorporeal.

Or you will, the other reminded him, *while what I see will always be secondhand—pictures relayed by your thoughts, and likewise clouded by them—and not by direct vision. Just one more example of how much easier it would be if we were one. No requirement for these night-seeing devices then; we would know at a glance if the house was occupied, and if it was we'd soon sniff out the occupant.*

"It sounds irresistible," said Jake drily. "Thanks, but no thanks." And having turned down Korath's "offer" yet again, he fell silent and studied the villa.

What is it? said Korath after a while. *Why aren't you moving? What gives you pause? Are you afraid?*

"I was afraid," said Jake. "I've only been in that bloody awful place twice, and both times I *was* afraid. Afraid of what they were doing to Natasha—and of what they might do to me. And they did it both times. The first time, one of them raped her, and then kicked several shades of shit out of me. And the next time . . . they *all* raped Natasha, killed her, and tried to kill me. And Luigi Castellano sitting in the shadows watching, enjoying, directing everything."

Which is why we're here, said Korath. *Tonight you get your own back, against the house at least.*

"Both times," Jake went on as if Korath hadn't spoken, "it happened in a bedroom. For a long time now I've shut that room out of my mind, the room where I was forced to watch what they did. It's at the back of the villa, I think, but on the ground floor like the study. I shut it out because I couldn't bear to remember. But now, in the dark of night . . . I can *feel* it down there. I can almost *taste* that fucking room . . . and I know its coordinates."

And that's where you'll plant your bomb.

"Exactly," said Jake, as Korath conjured the Möbius equations. "If that's my ground zero, maybe I'll be able to forget it. Some of it, anyway. But that's only the villa. The rest of it will stay right with me until I catch up with Castellano."

The bedroom was as Jake remembered it. He swept it once with a tiny torch, planted his bomb on the floor in the centre of the room where he'd been bound to a chair, and prepared to leave.

But then, as he shaped the constantly mutating Möbius equations into a door:

"Uh? What? Is someone there?" A voice—old, sleepy, speaking French—coming from somewhere else in the house, probably the study at the front. What, the old caretaker?

Jesus! thought Jake, as he stepped into the Continnum, and out again into the study. The bomb had only a ten-second fuse, and time was ticking away.

The old man had thrown a blanket onto the floor as he rose from the couch where he'd been sleeping. As Jake rushed toward him, he almost tripped on the blanket, felt it wrap around his feet. But stumbling forward he managed to gather the caretaker up, and swept him through another hastily conjured door—

—And out again on the hillside.

"Eh? W-what?" the caretaker gasped, losing his balance and sitting down heavily in the stubble. Which was all he had time to say or do before Castellano's villa went up in a thunderous uproar of light and sound and fire that set the hills echoing and dogs barking all the way into Marseilles. The distance between the villa and Jake's hillside vantage point was maybe five hundred feet, but that wasn't going to be distant enough.

The blanket from the study was still wrapped around Jake's feet; he kicked free, threw himself down alongside the old man and yanked on the blanket to cover them both. Chunks of debris struck against the blanket, bounced off and fell to the ground. There was a pattering of lesser fragments, and then a smell of burning. The blanket was smouldering.

Jake threw it aside, stood up, and drew the old man to his feet. Patches of stubble were burning, and in the sky, fluttering like fiery kites, scraps of curtains, bedclothes, and other soft materials were drifting on thermals from the blazing ruins of the villa. Around a small central crater, lesser fires were springing into being as burning floorboards, rafters, and fragments of shattered furnishings continued to fall. The place had been totally gutted, and it was perhaps a good thing that Luigi Castellano had enjoyed his privacy; there were no other private homes or buildings within a quarter mile.

You spared no effort with that one! said Korath quietly, in awe of Jake's perceptions of the destruction.

But Jake wasn't listening. "Are you all right?" he held the old man up with one hand and unobtrusively frisked him with the other.

The caretaker looked at him and asked, "What happened?" And looking down at his stockinged feet: "My shoes! I left them . . . in there?" And his eyes were huge where they gazed on the ruins of the villa.

Apart from his feet, he was fully clad in a shirt, trousers, and a crumpled lightweight jacket. He'd obviously been taking a nap. Cool and still in the darkness of the house, keeping a low profile, he hadn't showed up in Jake's nite-lites.

"I saw you running from the house," Jake lied. "It was burning. I helped you to get up here. Maybe you got hit on the head or something?"

The old man felt his head, said, "I . . . I don't know. I had a nightmare, I think. Something ran at me, and then I was here. But I shouldn't have been sleeping in the first place! And I'll lose my job! They'll sack me!"

"They?"

"The agency." The caretaker flapped his hands. He had been in shock but was coming out of it.

"What agency?" Jake asked him.

"The agency that employs me," said the other. "I look after rich houses when the owners aren't there."

"But what about Mr. Castellano?" Jake's voice had hardened "Isn't he your employer?"

"Eh?" said the other. "Mr. Castellano? I don't know him. I only have his card, in case something happens. And now . . . now something *has* happened! *Mon dieu!*"

"Show me his card," said Jake. And the old man, still very uncertain of what had happened, rummaged in his jacket pockets until he found Castellano's card.

Jake glanced at it, said.

Remember this. The numbers and the addresses both.

Done, said Korath in a moment.

Odd, said Jake, *that for a creature whose world had little use for written words and numbers, you happen to be so good at remembering them.*

The words and numbers, Korath replied, *mean nothing to me. I remember their patterns, that's all. My legacy from Malinari the Mind, remember?*

Sirens were sounding in the distance; a convoy of vehicles came speeding from Marseilles, their lights and coloured, revolving strobes strung out along a winding road.

Jake spoke again to the old man: "Here's your card back. But do me a favour. When you speak to the police, don't mention me."

"But you saved my life!" the other protested.

"Do I have your word?"

"Of course, if you insist. It's the least that I—"

"But when you call Castellano," Jake cut in, "by all means tell him about me."

"I don't even know who you are," said the old man.

"Just tell him an Englishman was here, okay?"

The old man looked mystified, shrugged, and finally nodded his acquiescence.

"So until the fire engines and police get here, you may as well stay where you are and watch the show," said Jake. "As for me, I have to be going."

The old caretaker was indeed watching the show—the fires dying out, others starting up, and what was left of the villa's walls crumbling in the furnace heat under a gradually drifting, mushroom-shaped pall of black smoke—but as what Jake had said connected, he turned to him, or to where he had been, and said, "Going?"

Better, perhaps, if he had used the past tense, since Jake was no longer there . . .

Part Four
Pseudo Memories and Mayhem

19
Jake—Remembering

AS HE SHOWERED, FIRST IN HOT WATER, BUT gradually increasing the cold until he could take no more, Jake gasped, "You know, I'm starving?"

The Möbius Continuum, said Korath. *It obviously depletes you. But as for me: I am beyond all such, and my situation is different entirely—I am starved of life itself! Perched on the rim of your mind, I cannot even appreciate the true taste of your food, only an echo of the pleasure which* you *derive.*

"But better than sitting in your sump, right?"

Anything is better than that! said Korath. *As for starving you don't know the meaning of the word. When your one option is to take the bone plug from the knuckled backbone of a flyer and sip on his grisly spinal fluids,* then *you know the meaning of the word!*

"What? Would you try to turn me off eating?" Jake grimaced. And when Korath declined to answer: "The hotel restaurant will have closed by now, but I know an excellent Chinese restaurant in Soho. I ate there with Lardis Lidesci. He's from your world—one side of your world, anyway—and he thought the food was great."

I am at your service, said Korath.

Jake dried off, swept his hair back. Normally he preferred it done professionaly, braided into a pigtail by a barber, but tonight he made do with a simple band of black elastic. And he dressed simply, too, in the clothes he'd brought with him when he left E-Branch, which he'd had cleaned and pressed up by the hotel . . .

In Soho it was 10:20. The place was alive with young Londoners out in the unseasonably warm night. The Chinese food was good, likewise the Chinese beer with which Jake washed it down.

Afterwards, walking in Oxford Circus—breathing the city smells, and taking in the sights and sounds—he said, "Well?"

Well? Korath answered.

"The food?"

Was good, said the other. *You thought so, anyway.*

"Better than spinal fluids?"

Better than those of a flyer, yes, Korath answered darkly.

And Jake chose not to question him further.

So what now?

Jake shrugged. "I could head for Leicester Square, but it's too late to take in a movie," he answered. "Pity, for they were showing *Predator 2020* just a few days ago. On the other hand, all that gratuitous violence—the blood and guts and what have you—would probably get you all worked up, so I suppose it's just as well. Which leaves us stymied; too late to do anything worthwhile, and too early to visit Frankie's. I want to ensure that place is empty, shut down for the night, before I shut it down permanently. Of course, I could always ask you to give me a break, return to your sump, leave me to enjoy my own company a while?"

Go back to Radujevac? Korath protested. *That dreary place? But why?*

"Well," said Jake, "you'd be surprised how close we are to E-Branch HQ right now. Even without the Möbius Continuum, it's no great distance."

Ah! said Korath. *Liz again. She's on your mind. That's why you came to London.*

Jake shrugged undecidedly. But then, however reluctantly, he said, "No, that's definitely out. It was just a thought, that's all. Or rather, she *is* on my mind—how can I deny it when you know she is?—but I can do without the complications. And anyway, I have things to think about, other things to do."

Such as?

"For one, there's a number I want to call," said Jake. "And

for two, there's a surprise package I have to make up for Frankie's Franchise."

Oh? said Korath. *But weren't you the one who was concerned about* my *craving for gratuitous violence? Perhaps I'll yet convince you that we're very much alike, you and I.*

But Jake only shook his head and said, "No way. Everything I'm doing has been—it *feels* like it's been—arranged for me. My course has been set for me. I have no choice. It's like I'm driven to do what I'm doing."

Precisely, said Korath. *And what of myself? I did not want to become a vampire, Jake. But when I became one, do you think that I was not driven? Why, I could no more deny my blood than you can deny your mysterious urges!*

"Well, maybe," said Jake. "But we're different anyway. And now we're going back to Paris."

But first he "dropped in" at a garage he knew in Marseilles, explained how his car had run out of gas, bought a three-gallon container and had the attendant fill it from a pump.

Your surprise package for Frankie's? said Korath.

"Part of my package," Jake told him. "And all it lacks now is a thimbleful of plastique to wrap it up very nicely, thank you . . ."

From the Paris hotel Jake tried an international connection to Bagheria, Sicily: Castellano's number from the old caretaker's card, but all he got was static. Communications were bad worldwide and getting worse. Which left only one thing to do.

It was 11:30 when Jake undressed and stretched himself out full-length on his bed. He felt wide awake and didn't think he would actually get any sleep, but it was worth a try. Maybe he could glean something useful from the ever-present whispers of the teeming dead; perhaps the Necroscope Harry Keogh himself—if anything was left of him—would put in an appearance, and Jake could ask him one or two leading questions.

And so he tossed and turned, and was genuinely suprised

in a little while when a customary numbness, the prelude to sleep, began to invade his mind and limbs.

At which he lay still and let himself drift . . .

. . . At 3:30 A.M. a sleepy switchboard operator gave Jake the early call he'd booked. The phone rang a good half-dozen times before he picked it up and mumbled his thanks, and it took him another ten minutes to get himself together and work out where he was and what he was doing here.

Then, splashing cold water on his face, Jake complained to Korath, "It's like—I don't know—like my brain is fogged up? You must be right: using the Continuum is draining me." He spoke in all innocence, never for a moment suspecting that his dead "partner" already knew what was affecting him, and that in fact he alone was the source of the problem.

But indeed Korath was "tired," too—or more properly frustrated—and the cause was the same; the only difference being that he knew why, that it was because he'd spent the last four hours trying to penetrate Jake's shields and bury himself even deeper in his unwilling host's mind. The frustration came from having failed, and utterly. For now, even when Jake's mind was only partially shielded, as in sleep, still it was impregnable.

Whatever powers had been willed to him—literally "willed" to him, by the will of the Necroscope Harry Keogh—it seemed they'd taken root and were growing exponentially, and Korath's earlier opportunities had passed him by. Cajoling didn't work; neither promises, threats, nor stealth. He had tried them all, and now he would have to find a different key to the innermost rooms of Jake's mind.

But all of the probing Jake had suffered as Korath searched for a breach in his defences had taken its toll of him. Even in sleep, unaware of Korath's assault, he'd fought back; his metaphysical mind had resisted, held, and repelled. Which accounted for his weariness and for Korath's mounting frustration.

On the other hand, the dead vampire considered himself fortunate indeed that in the last few seconds before Jake woke up, he'd succeeded in inserting a hurried posthypnotic suggestion that the sleeper forget his attempted intrusion . . .

"Are you there?" said Jake, calling Korath back to earth—as it were—startling him and causing him to gather his wits. "You're very quiet. What's on *your* mind for a change?" (Almost as if he'd guessed what had been going on here, though in fact he hadn't.)

I'm here, Korath answered. *I was silent because you didn't require me to speak. Did you want something?*

"No," Jake replied. "It's just that when you're quiet like that, I can't help wondering what you're thinking. See, Korath, this barrier between us works both ways. Just as my inner mind is forbidden to you, yours is forbidden to me." And then, perhaps a little suspiciously, "Maybe we should *both* be grateful, eh?"

Whatever you say, said Korath, as he carefully strengthened his own shields . . .

Dressed all in black, Jake returned to the cobbled alleyway in Genoa, where the double F neon sign was still unlit and the way was almost blocked by the day's garbage, reeking and steaming in piled plastic bags and rusty refuse skips. Frankie's Franchise was flanked by a dingy, flyspecked pizzeria on one side, and a tiny hardware store selling fishing gear on the other. Jake could only hope they were insured. But what the hell: whoever owned them, they'd be better off anyway.

Looking at the upper storeys, Jake saw that the windows of Frankie's upstairs rooms were boarded up. But since the neighbouring windows had been hung with dirty curtains, he supposed he'd better check inside.

He could see inside both the hardware and pizzeria, and so had the coordinates. There were no alarms, and quick checks of both places showed him that they were unoccupied. Good. Now he could get on with it.

Back to Paris for his "gear," and from there directly into Frankie's barroom. And: "Goodbye, Frankie's," Jake growled, as he pressed the button on his five-second delay firebomb. Just enough time to fashion a door and get out of there.

At the end of the alley he looked back, wincing and automatically shielding his eyes from what he knew was coming.

Gratuitous violence indeed! commented Korath, as Frankie's Franchise went into its death throes.

First a flash of brilliant yellow light—like daylight in the gloomy night street, as if someone had switched on the sun—and then the sound of a double explosion, but the two blasts coming so close together that they were literally inseparable. A sharp *crack* as the plastique went off like a mortar bomb, the sound stretching itself out and changing in timbre into a long-drawn-out protracted howling, like a jet engine on test, as the petrol ignited and was propelled by the plastique in pressured sheets of fire along every avenue of expansion.

The effect was almost nuclear. The roof came off Frankie's Franchise, hurled aloft on a pillar of fire, while at the front the door and windows bowed outwards—almost as if the building had taken a deep breath—before exploding into the street in a frenzy of fire and bricks and glass. And as the lower structure disintegrated, so the gutted upper storey remained in place for a brief moment, apparently suspended on the heat alone, before crumpling down into the inferno below.

Then, as the initial dazzle faded—as the flames roared up and a great ring of smoke shot with fire rose skywards—so the adjacent buildings followed suit, settled on their foundations, groaningly tilted inwards, and finally spilled their substance into the sprawling cauldron of yellow fire. And:

"Done," said Jake with some satisfaction.

But the fire is bound to spread, said Korath.

"It can take the whole waterfront area out for all I care," Jake answered, "so long as there are no human casualties. There shouldn't be, for with the weather the way it is and everything bone-dry, the fire services are bound to be on standby."

They were, and as Jake stood there awhile longer surveying his work—as astonished people in their nightclothes gathered and sirens began to sound—so Korath made ready to conjure the Möbius equations.

Then, as the first of a fleet of howling fire engines began to arrive, Jake moved apart from the crowd into the shadows and made his exit . . .

Back in Paris, he phoned the Bagheria number again and actually got through. In a crackle of static he heard the phone taken up, and then a gravelly voice inquiring, "Who is it?" But it wasn't Luigi Castellano's voice.

"I want to speak to the man who *runs* the hounds," Jake said then, "not to one of his dogs. So go and get him—and make it quick, while we still have a line."

There was a moment's pause—more fizzing and popping—and finally a voice that Jake recognized instantly, a deep-rumbling, powerful purr that he'd never forget till the day he died, and knowing what he knew now, not even then. "Who are you, and what do you want?" that voice said.

"I want you, Castellano," Jake answered. "And as for who I am, you already know that. I'm the one who took out your place in Marseilles, and your little gold mine under the Madonie, and just a few minutes ago Frankie's Franchise in Genoa."

"Jake Cutter," said the other, but his voice was no longer purring. Now it was a snarl, a low growl, a threat in itself—which made any verbal abuse redundant. It was a dark, primal voice, that *said* "Jake Cutter," but which *meant* "You're a dead man!"

"Cutter, right," Jake replied, "and I've been cutting into your organization, your lousy rat-holes. Next, I'll be cutting into you."

"What?" said Castellano. "All of this for that little *cunt* Natasha? A drug-running slut who had been fucked by every boss in Moscow? Was she really worth dying for, Jake Cutter?"

"You tell me, you bastard!" Jake spat. "For you're the one who'll be doing the dying."

Then the static flared up worse than ever, indeed so badly that Jake was barely able to make out the other's reply: "When you come I'll be ready, Jake. Just you and I, winner take all. And be sure I *will* take you! I'll keep your balls in a jar until they rot, to remind me of you, and your screams in my head forever, so that I can listen to them before sleeping. Your screams and Natasha's sobbing . . . a duet, like a lullaby, you know? So do please promise me that you won't keep me waiting too long, won't you?"

"It'll be sooner than you fucking think," said Jake—

—And then there was only the static, and perhaps a clattering sound as the phone was hurled down in Bagheria . . .

Korath had been in Jake's head and he had heard everything. *Do you know,* he said, *this Luigi Castellano might easily have been Wamphyri? The way he taunted you . . . I've heard just such talk in Starside. Haven't I told you about that? The way great enemies would taunt each other before fighting, to enrage each other beyond wisdom's reach? I fancy that Castellano has tried to do the same. And it seems to me he succeeded!*

Jake scarcely heard him. Furiously he paced the floor, his face grimly determined, his fists clenched. "The black-hearted bastard!" he muttered. "You're right, he's taunting me. But if he knew what I've got he wouldn't be so damned cocky."

Nor do we know what he has, said Korath wisely. *That place in Bagheria: Isn't it his stronghold, guarded by his best men? Perhaps you are the one who shouldn't be so damned cocky.*

"They don't have the Möbius Continuum," said Jake.

But they will *have bullets,* Korath answered. *It only takes one bullet in the right place, Jake, and that's you finished—not to mention myself . . .*

"If I knew where the place was," Jake grated it out through clenched teeth, "I'd do it tonight, right now!"

Exactly what Luigi Castellano wants you to do, said Korath. *He wants you to go rushing in, all unprepared. But no, let your head be your guide, Jake, and not your heart. And certainly not your hatred. Revenge is a dish—*

"Best served cold, I know," Jake cut in. Then, frowning, he said, "But where did you hear that one?"

In Starside, said Korath. *Where else?*

"It seems we share a good many sayings," said Jake.

It's hardly surprising (the other's deadspeak shrug). *Men are men in whichever world, and their darkest passions are the same—except in the Wamphyri, of course, in whom man's vices are multiplied tenfold, and likewise his lusts and rages.*

"So how is it you don't get all fired up?" Jake asked him. "You're Wamphyri, or would have been. You say I'm infuriating, obstinate, always giving you a hard time. So why don't you get mad at me? How is it that you're always the coolheaded one?"

But I do *get mad at you!* said Korath. *Very. And you should consider yourself fortunate that you'll never know how angry I get! But—*

"But?"

It is simply a matter of continuity, said the other. *Where you go, I go, and what you suffer, I suffer. What of me without Jake Cutter? What becomes of me if you should die? I am nothing without you. And so, when you play the hotheaded fool, I shall remain cool. For as I've said, it's a matter of continuity, and I simply can't afford to let you commit suicide.*

"Thanks a bunch!" Jake growled. "But the way you tell it, I keep getting this feeling not so much of continuity but of permanency. So I think maybe I should remind you, when we're done, we're done."

I hadn't forgotten, said Korath. *But we've a way to go yet. First Luigi Castellano, then Lord Nephran Malinari, Vavara, and Szwart. That was our deal, and I shall stick by it.*

"Good," said Jake. "Let's leave it at that, then." But deep down inside he was still very uneasy about this so-called "partnership," and knew he always would be until it was over . . .

* * *

Jake woke up at 9:00 A.M. Saturday morning, washed and dressed, pushed his sausage bag of plastique deep under his bed, and had a late breakfast in his room before calling for Korath.

And how do you feel this morning? asked the vampire.

"In a hurry," Jake answered. "As always I feel driven, but *not* to suicide!"

So I see, said the other. *You're much calmer than you were last night.*

"That's because I've taken your advice," Jake answered. "I was a bit hot under the collar last night, that's all, but now I've cooled down. It's probably a good thing that I don't know where Castellano's place in Bagheria is, otherwise I believe I really would have gone there."

Which would have been both dangerous and contrary to your original scheme, said Korath. *For if memory serves—which it does, and extremely efficiently—you want Castellano to feel the noose tightening slowly, slowly, and bit by bit.*

Jake nodded. "Until the knot is pressing up tight against the back of his neck, yes," he said.

So then, how do we proceed? What is today's agenda?

"Today we find Castellano's place in Bagheria and check it out," said Jake. "And tonight we *take* it out, and him with it! But between times, this evening, we go back to San Remo, Millionaire's Row."

The last of his rat-holes?

"Exactly. Let him feel the noose tighten that extra inch."

But by now he knows what you've done; indeed, you told him as much yourself! The total destruction of his villa in Marseilles, and likewise the fire at Frankie's Franchise in Genoa. As for the wreckage of his machinery in the Madonie mountains: he will have seen that for himself.

"So?"

In San Remo . . . he may be waiting for you. Or if not Luigi Castellano in person, his paid men certainly.

"That's a risk I have to take," said Jake. "I have to, for

it's part of the plan. I *want* to be seen in San Remo."

But why?

"Because he'll know that if I'm there I can't be in Sicily at the same time."

Ah! I see! said Korath. *Believing that you can't strike at him on the same night, in the space of just a few hours, he'll feel secure. You'll take him by surprise!*

"That's the plan," Jake nodded. "But I can't take him if I don't know where he is or how well he's defended. So that's my next task. Do you remember the address on that card?"

The address? said Korath. *But of course I remember it. Oh, yesss! For thanks to Lord Malinari—called Malinari the Mind—I remember almost everything...*

Just a few kilometres out of Bagheria toward Trabia—a little west of the Milicia where it ran to the sea, and frowning down from rough, gradually rising ground across the motorway toward the Tyrhennian coast—Castellano's headquarters looked sombre even in broad daylight. But more important, the villa looked deserted.

"I don't get it," said Jake, from where he lay on a patch of stony ground behind a clump of small rocks, staring down on the place through his binoculars. "We've been here for over an hour and nothing has so much as twitched down there. But there are cars—what, six of them?—out front, and there's smoke rising from two of the chimneys. So where is everybody?"

Inside, obviously, said Korath.

"And they never come out?"

But surely that's their prerogative. (Korath's incorporeal shrug.) *Would you come out, if you knew someone was waiting to pick you off?*

"They don't know I'm here."

But they do know you're somewhere.

"You think they're simply lying low?"

I think they are doing as I would do in the current situation, said Korath. *They're taking no chances.*

Jake shook his head concernedly and said, "This is a waste

of time. I don't like this place; I feel exposed and I'd gladly move on, except I'm not satisfied with the coordinates. I mean, I can return here, to this location, any time I like—and I'm pretty sure I can put down in the middle of those olives within the grounds, too—but I know nothing at all about the interior layout of the house. So how am I to get inside?"

Must you get inside? said Korath. *Can't you simply bomb the place from outside, against its walls?*

Again Jake shook his head, and growled, "No. I'm not going to blow it inwards, I'm going to blow it up and out and off the face of the map! Wrecking it isn't sufficient. I want to remove it, permanently, as if it was never there."

As if it were never there? I can't see how that's possible, said Korath. *Surely there will be rubble?*

"Not necessarily," said Jake. "Not if I use thermite."

Thermite? (This time Korath was at a loss; he had little or no knowledge of science, and all he had seen in Jake's mind was fire, as used at Frankie's Franchise.)

"A different kind of fire," Jake told him. "And a different kind of heat. Thermite: it's a mixture of oxidized metal—iron will do nicely—and powdered aluminium."

Brown rust and white rust? (It was all beyond Korath.)

"Something like that," said Jake. "We call it chemistry."

I call it magic! said the other. *Also, I saw some of Nathan Keogh's handiwork on Starside, and that was just as devastating as yours! Malinari thought so, too, else I wouldn't be here. So obviously Nathan has or had access to just such powders. Explosive powders, burning powders, and liquids that ignite into fireballs out of hell!* Hah! *Is it any wonder the Szgany called this world the Hell-lands?*

"But from what I've heard and read of Starside," said Jake, "you've got it backwards. Anyway, let's get out of here. We can figure out later how to get better coordinates."

As you wish, said Korath, conjuring the Möbius equations . . .

* * *

Jake had the addresses of friends in Australia, members of the elite Australian SAS, with whom he'd worked in the first phase of E-Branch's assault on Malinari. And he also had the coordinates of a government safe house in Brisbane.

He "went" there and was surprised (but shouldn't have been) to find the place dark. The safe house was dark both inside and out, and silent. The silence meant nothing (the house was quiet because it wasn't in use), but the darkness was weird . . . until it dawned on Jake that while it had been midmorning in France, in the Australian tropics it was 8:30 P.M.! Something he would have to get used to: the fact that with the Möbius Continuum as his means of transport, the world was now a very small place.

Jake put the lights on in the central operations room, and checked one of the telephones. It was working, and he tapped in the home number of W. O. II "Red" Bygraves. Jake's hopes weren't too high that he would be able to contact him, but for once the static wasn't too bad, and amazingly Red was at home.

"What yer doing over here, mate?" said Red, after Jake told him who he was.

"I've come to ask a favour," said Jake. "Er, a big one."

"Well, it can't be too big, not after what you did for us," said the other. "Where are yer?"

"I'm in the safe house in Brisbane," Jake told him. "I only just got here. I have your telephone number but no address, and I realize we may be thousands of miles apart. But I was wondering if we could maybe get together and talk? Then I'll tell you what I need."

"Well, it's true that we *could* have been thousands of miles apart," said Red, "but the fact is I'm at home in Gympie, a few miles up the road."

"Gympie?" Jake couldn't suppress a chuckle. "What in hell's a Gympie?"

"It's a town some ninety miles north of you," Red answered. "And don't you go taking the piss out of my home town!" But he was chuckling, too. "Hey, stay where yer are and I'll be there in an hour and a bit."

"You're on," said Jake. "And pick up some beers and a bite to eat on the way."

"Done," said the other. "But hey—yer wouldn't be in any kind of trouble, would yer?"

"Always," said Jake. "But don't sweat it, what I'm trying to do needs doing, even if it isn't exactly on the right side of the law."

"No sweat, Jake," Red assured him. "With me and the other blokes who worked with yer, yer couldn't ever be on the wrong side. I'll be there in a tick." And the phone went down . . .

Thinking to get a breath of fresh night air, Jake took the Möbius route out into the high-walled gardens. But if anything it was warmer than the last time he'd been here some few weeks ago. The stars were glorious, and the smell of eucalyptus came wafting from trees on the other side of the wall.

But up against his side of the wall, a pair of articulated, open-sided monorail cars lay keeled over where they had come to rest when he brought them through the Möbius Continuum from the mountain resort of Xanadu. He'd brought the cars, the SAS team, and a handful of E-Branch personnel, too. And in doing so he'd saved their lives.

Er, we *saved their lives,* said Korath. *Credit where credit is due, Jake. My numbers, your door.*

"It feels like years ago," said Jake.

Live fast, die young, and leave a handsome corpse, Korath answered.

"A Szgany saying?"

Indeed.

"We have it, too," said Jake. "Also one that goes: doesn't time fly when you're having fun?"

Are you having fun, Jake?

Jake shook his head. "Not a bit of it. Life's too short for all this shit. But I know I won't be able to live it right till all of this is behind me."

Ah, life! said Korath. *How wonderful it was to be alive*

and young, and to walk in the woods of Sunside with a young girl on my arm. Then his thoughts turned sour, as he continued, *But all that was when I was a Szgany youth, and my feelings are different now. It's being here with you that brings these memories to mind. You walked in this garden with Liz.*

"I've told you not to talk about Liz!" Jake snapped.

And you held her in your arms in your room at E-Branch HQ when you were both near-naked. Ahhh! And Jake could almost feel the slow drip of his drool.

"Where but for you I might even have made love to her—you creepy, Peeping Tom bastard!"

But—

"—But I'm glad now that I didn't," Jake cut him short, his voice a snarl of loathing. "What, with a nightmarish *thing* like you in my mind? No way! But if she'll still have me, it'll keep until all this is over and you're well and truly out of here!"

Korath's patience was exhausted, too—and his own frustrations steadily mounting—so that he wasn't quite in control of himself when he gurgled: *Ungrateful dog! Did you say, "when I'm out of here?" Ah, but that might not be for a long, long time!*

"What?" said Jake at once. "What's that?"

I meant nothing! Korath was immediately on guard—guarding his own tongue, his thoughts, lest they should betray him again. *But your constant carping . . . I have difficulty coping with it. When you need me, I answer your call—I have never* once *put a foot wrong—and what do I get in return?*

"What do you get?" Jake railed at him then, bringing up his shields in full force to drive Korath from the rim of his mind. "You get sent the hell away from me, that's what you get! Go on back to your sump in Romania, Korath. And if you choose to stay there, that's up to you. I was doing just fine on my own, and I can do it again. So the *hell* with you!"

Don't do it, Jake! Korath cried, but his cry rapidly fading.

You'll need me. I spoke in anger and meant nothing by it. Jake? Jaaaake! And then he was gone, and Jake stood alone in the garden.

But not for long. Korath was right and he did need him, and would in the near future for a certainty. So in a little while, when he'd cooled down, he relaxed his shields and said: "Very well, come on back. But let's concentrate on the job, right? No more talk about Liz and no more veiled threats."

And in a moment: *As you will,* said Korath, subdued now. *I took our friendship a little too far, that's all. But remember: I, too, am under duress. I do what you ask of my own free will, it's true, but only to achieve my own agenda. Which is the destruction of Malinari and the others. And what is to stop you—when you've got what* you *want—reneging on our deal and going off without me?*

"If only I could!" said Jake. "But I would know that you're always there. I'd know that the moment I relaxed you'd be back, pestering as usual."

And so it's stalemate, said Korath. *It seems we are obliged to trust each other.*

"With me, that isn't a problem," Jake told him. "I've never broken a trust." But:

You did with E-Branch, Korath reminded him.

And again he was right. "Because I had to," said Jake. "You know me as well as anyone now, and you *know* I had to. The thing that's driving me on isn't letting up. I can feel the time ticking by second by second, the minutes, the hours. And Castellano is still alive. It's not just him and me, and it's more than an obsession. It's necessary. It's . . . it's what I do." (Now where had *that* idea come from? It wasn't what Jake did at all . . . but maybe it was what Harry Keogh had *used* to do!)

However, before he could investigate that line of thought more closely: *I understand,* said Korath. *I feel exactly the same about my enemies. And it is* very *necessary, yessss . . .*

* * *

When W. O. II Red Bygraves, a slim, well-muscled, crewcut redhead in his early- to mid-thirties, arrived at the safe house in his open-topped, military-looking four-wheel-drive, Jake opened the gates manually to let him in.

Then, after they had greeted each other: "What?" said Red. "No one else here? How did yer get inside to use the phone?" A simple slip of the tongue, for even having seen what Jake could do at firsthand, teleportation was hardly a common or easily acceptable concept.

Jake didn't waste time but showed him—took Red's arm and swung him through a Möbius door, and out again into the control room—then held him steady as his jaw fell open and his eyes stood out. *"Jesus H. Christ!"* the SAS man gasped, as he came close to dropping the six-pack and container of food that he'd brought with him.

"Don't," said Jake then. "I mean, try not to use terms like that." For once again he felt guided by principles that weren't necessarily his own.

Red didn't understand the sudden change in Jake's tone, but he didn't argue either. He was too startled for that. "Like . . . I knew yer could do that," he said, "but I wasn't *expecting* yer to do it. Good grief, mate! Is that how yer arrived here? Like, all the way from Blighty? Good grief!"

"From Sicily, actually," said Jake. And then, as they began to relax and to eat, he told Red what he wanted.

"Thermite?" The other shook his head. "That's a tough one. I can't get it for yer, but I know a man who can. Well, maybe." And tapping a number into the telephone, he went on to explain, "This'll get the barracks. They'll check me out and put me onto the boss."

"The boss?" Jake repeated him.

"You know him," Red nodded. "You saved his neck—and mine—and quite a few others, too."

"Major Tom?" said Jake. "Well, that's what Ben Trask calls him, anyway."

"The same," said Red. Then he spoke into the phone, reeled off a number, gave a codeword, finally nodded his satisfaction, and passed the phone to Jake, saying, "Better yer should speak to him yerself. That way I won't be telling any lies for yer."

A number was ringing; when it was answered Jake recognized the authoritative voice at once.

"Major, this is Jake Cutter," he said. "You might remember me. I'm in Australia to ask a favour of you."

"Jake?" said the other. "You're damn right I remember you! A favour, you say? On behalf of E-Branch? Any time, Jake. What can I do for you?"

Jake waited for a sudden burst of hissing, popping sunspot static to fade away, and then told him. "But," he finished off quietly, "this isn't for E-Branch. It's for me."

That gave the major a moment's pause. "And you know how to use this stuff?"

"Yes," Jake told him. "As you may recall, your men used it at the Old Mine petrol station in the Gibson Desert. And I'm what you could call a quick study."

"You're a quick something, for sure!" said the major. "But no guarantees what you'll use it for, right?"

"For good," said Jake. "Only for good. Or put it this way: the world won't be the worse for it. In fact, it will be a lot better off."

"And when do you want it?"

"Just as soon as possible," said Jake.

A moment's pause, and then, "You've called at an opportune time," said Major Tom. "A couple of your boys, E-Branch people, I mean, are with some of my people at the Old Mine place right now. They're blasting it open again, going inside, making sure that nothing was overlooked in there. When that's done they'll roast the place and seal it shut permanently, with thermite."

"Trask said that would be happening, yes," said Jake.

"How's your, er, mobility?" said the major then. "I mean—"

"I know what you mean," said Jake. "That's how I got here."

And there was another moment's pause. "Jake, I owe you. A lot of people owe you more than they can ever repay. So here's what I propose. Our people will be finishing their work at the Old Mine any time now, probably tonight. So while there can't be any 'official' handover of this stuff, I think we can, er, 'lose' a small cache somewhere in that location. Should we say, buried eighteen inches deep at the foot of the first warning signpost you come to as you climb the ramp from the road?"

"That would be just fine," said Jake gratefully.

"But as for this conversation," the major hurriedly continued, "well, obviously it never happened."

"Roger that," Jake answered. And indeed it was obvious that their conversation had never happened, for already he was talking to himself . . .

Jake and Red finished eating, then sat around for a while drinking Red's beer.

"Most of us were given a couple of weeks off," said Red. "I mean, we were told to forget everything that had happened. Just like the boss told you, it had *never* happened—if yer get the picture—and we should go home and get it out of our systems. Which is why I was home when yer called. And yer know, it's not at all hard to forget? There was some weird shit going down. It was like a bad dream."

"That's right," Jake nodded, "and there's plenty more weird shit going down right now. I'll be in on it eventually, but not until I've sorted out this other thing."

"Which is personal, right?"

"I thought it was," said Jake, "but now I'm not so sure. It *was* personal, but now it's a lot more than that. Anyway, that's where I'm at, and I'd better be on my way."

"But not before yer get me back out into the garden, okay?"

Jake did it, and this time Red's knees buckled as Jake took his arm and led him out into the night beside his vehicle. Then, leaning on the car to steady himself, he said, "Well, I've seen some stuff in my time, but this . . . I still don't believe it!"

"Me neither," said Jake, and then added, "I mean, I'm still

getting used to it. But will you be okay driving home?"

"I'll be okay, yeah," said Red, still unsteady on his feet. "But in any case a damn sight safer than with you, I reckon! So you can take the high road, Jake, and I'll take the low road—every fucking time!"

"But I'll be in Scotland—or wherever—before ye!" Jake grinned.

"And yer welcome," said the other. "But just you be careful that's all. Be sure not to get lost in . . . in *that* place, where or when or whatever it is."

He got into his car, turned her round, and drove out through the gates. Jake closed them after him. Outside, Red applied his brakes, turned in his seat to look back and wave. He was barely in time to see a swirl of leaves and dry debris spinning like a miniature dust devil, drawn up from the garden by the vacuum of Jake's door and already beginning to settle.

But as for Jake himself, it was as if he'd never been there at all . . .

Jake went back to his Paris hotel, booked his room for an extra night, then threw himself on his bed. It was a little after one in the afternoon in France, yet still he felt tired.

"Jet-lagged," he mumbled to himself, as he fell asleep. "Or Möbius-lagged. Or something."

And for once Korath left him alone. Jake's shields were now stronger than ever, and his mind completely impenetrable. There was no longer any possibility of taking up permanent habitation in either his conscious or subconscious psyches—not without he first invite such an invasion and deliberately open his mind to it—and Korath's only remaining hope was that some situation would arise where Jake simply couldn't refuse him.

He knew that Jake wouldn't grant him total and irrevocable access in order to get *himself* out of trouble (that had become obvious during the abortive episode in the bank vault), but he might be persuaded if a loved one was in difficulty. There was only one such loved one that Korath knew of and chances seemed slim . . . but who could say?

The future was ever a devious thing—a difficult thing to gauge—and with E-Branch still in pursuit of Malinari, Szwart, and Vavara, Liz might yet find herself in dire straits.

After all, it wouldn't be the first time . . .

Jake woke up at 3:30, shaved and showered, ate a light, early evening meal, and went out to find a barber.

All sweet-smelling and dandied up, said Korath later, when Jake was getting a little exercise by returning on foot to the hotel through the evening streets. *Live fast, die young—*

"And leave a handsome corpse," said Jake. "Yes, I know. No need to be so morbid."

In my position it is difficult to be anything else! Korath answered. *Tonight will certainly be our most dangerous mission so far—yet you make preparation by prettying yourself up!*

"The pigtail keeps my hair out of my eyes," Jake answered. "And the wash and shave leaves me smooth, so that when I apply my makeup it will take more easily."

Your makeup?

"Camouflage," said Jake. "To help me merge with the night. I was once a soldier. As a career it didn't last too long, but I did learn a few things."

That's as may be, said Korath, *but all these cosmetic preparations, they serve to remind me of the way a certain Starside Lady would decorate her thralls—with garlands of flowers, and honey rubbed into their skins—before serving them up screaming to some favoured warrior creature!*

"With friends like you," said Jake—then paused as he felt a warm splash on his neck. Rain! That was why it was dark early tonight: the sky was overcast, and he had been so busy with his own (and Korath's) thoughts that he hadn't noticed. The weather was breaking at last, storm clouds rolling down from the north.

And as the fat, heavy drops came faster, Jake took the Möbius route the rest of the way to the hotel . . .

* * *

It's barely dark, said Korath, as they set out for San Remo.

"Barely dark here," Jake told him, "but it's an hour later in Italy. And if their weather is anything like ours, it'll be even darker."

It was, and as Jake stepped from the Continuum at the precise coordinates where yesterday he had stopped the taxi—on the Imperia road where it had been blasted from the sea cliffs—he stepped straight into the teeth of a thunderstorm!

Clouds boiled on high and jagged veins of lightning pulsed, patterning the sky out over the Ligurian Sea. Overhead, jutting from the cliffs on stanchion supports, the modern reincarnation of an ancient house of evil—Le Manse Madonie—loomed like an updated aerie, brought into sharp relief and made prominent not only by the lightning but also by illumination from within. The high, ocean-facing balcony was flooded with light, and just for a moment Jake thought to see someone up there on that wind- and rain-swept platform.

But the rain was slanting against the cliffs, making everything a blur, and he couldn't be sure. Already soaked, stepping soggily into the shadows, Jake looked up again at a sharp angle and saw nothing; but inside the house itself vague figures were on the move, their rain-blurred outlines appearing on the patio windows, their faces peering out, then drawing back and disappearing. These were Castellano's people—drug-running bastards just like him—using and looking after the place in the boss's absence, and on this occasion perhaps defending it. But tonight, in weather like this, surely they would be a little lax? Surely they wouldn't be expecting trouble on a night such as this?

Well, whether it was expected or not, trouble was coming.

Jake had three charges, one for each of the stanchion supports. Take those out and the entire house would be a write-off, and most likely the people inside it, too.

It wasn't his intention to cut through the stanchions themselves—massive steel I-sectioned girders, that would take acetylene cutting gear and lots of time—but simply to blast them loose from their seatings in the cliffs. To which end his charges were each half as powerful as the one he'd used on the place in Marseilles: enough to fracture and dislodge the entire face of the cliff, let alone the support girders.

Now he had to get onto the narrow maintenance ledge at the base of the stanchions, but in the downpour and the darkness he could barely see the ledge; his angle of observation was acute, and the coordinates were very uncertain. The access road had to be safer, so Jake made a Möbius jump a hundred yards back along the main road to a lay-by where the narrow one-lane access road branched off and climbed steeply toward the house. From there a second jump carried him up level with Le Manse Madonie itself, enabling him to see the ledge from above.

Now the coordinates were lodged firmly in Jake's mind, but in the moment before he jumped he thought he saw, yet again, a furtive movement in a shaded area of the balcony; someone moving there, and the glint of dull metal as lightning flashed to throw back the shadows. Whoever it was—if anyone at all—he must be sheltering under the tasselled canopy of a porch swing in one corner of the balcony.

Which was why, as Jake emerged from the Continuum onto the rainwashed service ledge directly beneath the suspect area, he did so with extreme caution, crouching down as his eyes scanned the boards of the balcony just fifteen feet overhead. He could see very little, only bars of light slanting through the inch-wide spacing in the boards, but was fully aware how those bars must be lighting on him, picking out his movements and banding him like a zebra. If there really was someone up there, and if he took a pace forward, leaned on the rail, and looked over . . .

Jake worked as fast as he could, cursing under his breath as every bright flash of lightning silhouetted him against the slippery rock face, and managed to plant the first two charges in the Vs where the stanchions had been concreted into sockets which had been drilled deep into the cliff face. But then, as he put down his sausage bag beside the final stanchion and yanked out the third and last charge, his haste let him down.

A pocket torch lying loose in the sausage bag was dragged free along with the charge. Before Jake could stop it, it fell . . . bounced . . . switched itself on . . . went twirling down into the darkness, flashing like a beacon as it spun!

The clatter had been heard, the light seen, and from overhead the lookout barked, "What the *fuck* . . . !?"

Holding his breath, Jake rammed the last charge into place and set the timer button. The task had taken no more than sixty seconds; the timers were set respectively at eighty, sixty, and just twenty seconds for the last one. This way Jake had allowed himself a comfortable twenty-second window of escape before the first blast, which would be followed in short order by the second and the third.

No problem at all, if he hadn't been seen.

But he had been seen!

And as Jake straightened up from his task in too much of a hurry, so his feet skidded on the wet rock surface and he only just managed to keep his balance. It was time he was gone from here, and Korath was already rolling the numbers.

Feet clattered on the boards overhead; there came the well-known ch-*ching!* of a small-arms weapon being armed, followed by a blast of deafening sound—not thunder but the obscene clamour of an Uzi firing down *through* the overhead boardwalk—and Jake heard the splintering of wood and the angry-insect buzzing of bullets passing too close by.

Caught off balance, Jake's old-fashioned, outmoded survival instinct found him reaching for his own weapon, stupidly ignoring the numbers that were even now scrolling down the screen of his mind; and all the while Korath shouting, *Jake, make a door! Make it now! Jake! Jaaake!*

But Jake was skidding about on the slimy rock surface again, and a hatch had opened in the balcony's boardwalk. Ladders were released, swung on oiled hinges, and slammed down; and legs came into view, followed by a body, and finally an arm and hand with an Uzi that jerked and shuddered as it hosed spurts of fire and a stream of bullets blindly in Jake's direction.

He fired back, the *crack! crack!* of his 9 mm Browning automatic almost drowned out by the stutter of the Uzi. But the man on the ladders gave a cry, let go his grip and was thrown backwards, and at the same time a white-hot something—a brilliant light—hit Jake in the head, dissolving everything around him and turning the night to a whirlpool of blinding pain.

I'm hit! Jake thought, as everything slipped away from him, until all that was left was the Möbius formula, constantly mutating in his dimming mind's eye.

Make a door! Korath screamed again, and finally got through to Jake in his last few moments of consciousness.

Jake had slipped from the ledge; falling, he felt the night air rushing past him and knew there was something he must do. A door, that was it. He must stop the numbers and conjure a door.

And he did . . . he brought a door into being directly in his path . . . the path of his descent.

From above and behind Jake as the first charge detonated, a huge hot hand reached out to fling him headlong into the primal darkness of the Möbius Continuum . . .

Jake was a long time surfacing, and it seemed an even longer time before he realized he wasn't just dreaming but floating, adrift in some unknown medium, and that someone was shivering, gibbering, and cursing where he hid in the smallest possible niche of Jake's mind. But wherever Jake was it was dark—oh so dark—and as quiet as the tomb. Or quieter.

It must be night, Jake thought, the very thought bringing a fresh burst of pain, like bright lances of agony splintering in his head. And:

Jake? said the whimpering thing that clung to him like grim death, the thing that *was* grim death, the dead vampire, Korath-once-Mindsthrall, where he trembled at the rim of Jake's gradually awakening consciousness. *Jake? Is that you? Is it really you?*

Oddly enough, Jake had to think about that. He wasn't sure it was worth it (thought itself was painful, and he would much rather simply float here) but he *had* to think about it. Was it him, really him, or was it someone else? Before, on that ledge under Le Manse Madonie, he'd felt afraid. But now he only felt sick. Sick with the pain in his head, and the stickiness where he put up a hand in the dark to gentle the place where he hurt. But he wasn't any longer afraid.

Afraid? No, not here in the Möbius Continuum. For the Continuum was his place, where he hadn't felt afraid for—oh, for as long as he could remember! Not since August Ferdinand Möbius himself had shown him how . . . how to gain access? That had been in Leipzig, Möbius's tomb there . . . hadn't it?

Tomb again. What the hell was it with tombs? "Quiet as the tomb" . . . and "Möbius's tomb" . . . and the teeming dead in their "tombs," all arguing the merits, the pros and cons, the differences between Jake and Harry. As if there was a difference. And as for Leipzig: Jake had never fucking been there . . . had he?

Jake, wake up! You're delirious! said Korath, with a catch, almost a sob of relief in his deadspeak voice. *You're not Harry Keogh; you* are *Jake Cutter! And you've been hurt. But there was nothing in there—in your head—and I thought you were dead. Take my word for it, Jake: being hurt is far better than being dead! So pull yourself together and get us out of here.*

Not Harry Keogh? But then why did Jake remember so much of what Harry had been, what he'd done and what he'd left undone?

It's only a germ *of Harry!* said Korath. *The smallest* spark *of him. He gave you*—hah!—*a piece of his mind!*

But no peace of mind, said Jake, as he came out of it more quickly now. *Just a jigsaw puzzle with too many missing pieces. And piece by piece, I'm putting it all together. I'm gradually . . . remembering?*

Which is good! said Korath. *For knowing what Harry*

knew can only make us stronger. (But his voice carried no conviction.)

It can make me stronger, said Jake, the pain gradually subsiding, *but I'm not so sure about you.* And there was something in his tone that warned Korath to tread very carefully here.

I don't know what you mean.

I mean, said Jake, *that there once was a time when the Necroscope had an unwelcome tenant, just as I have you. Harry was plagued by a dead vampire whose name . . . was Faethor Ferenczy!*

The memory came home to him out of nowhere, just like that. Wrenched loose from the ceiling of some inner vault where contact with the original Necroscope had lodged it—shaken free as the result of violent action, concussion, and pain—it drifted like a fall of dust, writhing into a recognizable pattern where it settled on the whorls of Jake's brain. Paramnesia, yes. Not one of his memories, but a memory nonetheless.

Of Faethor Ferenczy!

Faethor, clinging to him (or to Harry?) like a leech where he sped down a future-time stream; their conversation as fresh in Jake's mind as if it had taken place yesterday, or as if it were occurring right here and now:

"You see this blue thread unwinding out of me," Jake heard himself (or Harry) saying to Faethor. "It's my future."

And mine, Faethor answered doggedly.

"But see, it's tinged with red. Do you see that, Faethor?"

I see it, fool. The red is me—proof that I'm part of you always.

"Wrong," Jake/Harry told him coldly. "I can go back because my thread is unbroken. Because I have a past, I can reel myself in. But your past was finished where you died back in Ploiesti, Romania. You have no thread, no lifeline, Faethor."

What? The other's nightmare voice was a croak. Then—

—The master of the Möbius Continuum brought himself to an abrupt halt, but the spirit of Faethor Ferenczy hurtled on into the future. *Don't do this!* he cried out in his terror. *Don't do it!*

"But it's done," the Necroscope called after him. "You have no life, no flesh, no past, nothing, Faethor. All you have left is the future. The longest, loneliest, emptiest future any creature ever suffered. And now, goodbye!"

H-H-Harry? . . . Haaarry! . . . Haaaarrry! . . . HAAAAA—! as the Necroscope closed the future-time door, to shut Faethor out forever.

But before that door slammed shut, Jake/Harry looked again at the blue thread unwinding out of him/them, and saw—

Jake! . . . Jaaake! . . . JAAAAAAKE! Korath shouted. *Get a grip of yourself!*

Reluctantly, Jake relaxed his hold on this pseudomemory—this fragment from the original Necroscope's past—which disappeared as quickly and mysteriously as it had come. And as for what Harry had seen before the future-time door closed . . .

. . . *Let it go!* cried Korath. For he, too, had witnessed the pseudomemory, and his dearest wish was that the entire episode should disappear forever from Jake's mind. *Be glad that you are yourself and forget Harry Keogh. He is no more!*

But the episode wasn't disappearing, not entirely. Jake continued to cling to at least one part of the pseudomemory as strongly as Faethor had clung to Harry.

He *knew* what he'd seen, and: *I know how to be rid of you,* he said . . .

What? said Korath, thoroughly alarmed. *You would do that to me? Send me screaming into a never-ending void?*

I didn't say I would do it, Jake said. *I said I know how to do it. As a last resort, of course. Until which time—*

"You can be absolutely certain that I will honour our contract to the full, said Korath.

I know that you'll have to, said Jake. *For while you're outside my mind—in contact with me, but outside me—I can ditch you any time I want to in exactly the same way as*

Harry ditched Faethor. Which means from now on you d-aren't put a foot wrong.

For several long moments there was a total, sullen silence in the Möbius Continuum while Korath thought about it, until he answered, *But since it isn't and has never been my intention to put a foot wrong, I'm not in the least concerned! Only that you persist in thinking of me in such terms. And now perhaps you'll stop worrying about it?*

And his deadspeak voice was so sincere that Jake was almost convinced.

Almost . . .

20
Zante—San Remo—Australia—Krassos—London

JAKE SEARCHED FOR THE COORDINATES FOR THE Paris hotel . . . and found nothing!

Didn't I tell you there was nothing in there? Korath said nervously.

Jake didn't answer him but searched for other coordinates. But Korath was right; it seemed his mind was empty of them. It was as if a file had been downloaded from his brain, or worse, deleted entirely.

What's going on? Jake wondered, as Korath's obvious alarm gradually infected him, too. *No coordinates? What's happening here?*

Perhaps it is simply a part of the healing process and we have to be patient, Korath answered. *But I repeat: before you regained consciousness, there was nothing in there. Your mind was as empty as the Möbius Continuum itself!*

But it appeared that the Continuum wasn't entirely empty, for even as Korath spoke, so something bumped into Jake's face. He automatically groped for it, and found his gun, free-floating in the dark weightlessness. He'd obviously dropped it when he was hit at Le Manse Madonie, and it had fallen through his door with him. Now he held on to it, like a drowning man to a straw.

A drowning man? said Korath. *And something about a straw? Jake, you're not making sense!*

Disorientation, said Jake. *A bang on the head, which still hurts like hell.* Even as he said it, another bout of sick dizziness swept over him.

I entered your mind, Korath told him, *deep into your mind. Er, in a purely exploratory mode, you understand? Your shields were down, and I was trying to revive you. But—*

Amnesia, said Jake. *Not paramnesia this time, but just . . . just amnesia? I can't remember the coordinates. None of them!"*

Memory loss, yet specific to this, said Korath, his alarm increasing by leaps and bounds. *As one part of Harry's memory was revitalized in you, so it dislodged another: your instinctive knowledge and use of Möbius coordination!*

Okay, said Jake, trying not to panic. *But surely* you *remember the coordinates? You must, for you've remembered everything else! The Continuum's equations, for instance.*

I remember the sequence *of the formulae,* Korath moaned now, *and the shape of the thing, but the numbers themselves are as meaningless to me as they are to you! As for your coordinates: they are not numbers but locations, places and things which only you know, buried deep in a part of your mind that I can't reach . . . which is the reason I entered you, Jake: to see if I could find a safe coordinate. But all I found was emptiness.*

Which must have scared the shit out of you, said Jake, *else you'd probably still be in there! Even at a time like this, you never give up trying, do you?*

I dared hope, Korath tried hard to change the subject, *that given time time we would transfer automatically to Harry's Room at E-Branch HQ. But it appears that thread is now broken, leaving us adrift in this place!*

Jake felt a spinning motion. He was no longer in control of the situation. And the more the vastness—the utterly unknown size, structure, nature, and purpose—of the Möbius Continuum impressed itself upon him, the faster he spun.

In the total darkness and weightlessness, he put up a hand and traced a shallow scabbed-over burn from just above his left eyebrow, along his temple and into his sideburns. There was dry blood on his hollow cheek, and the tip of his ear felt crusted. *I was creased,* he said. *An inch lower and a little to the right, it would have gone in through my eye and ripped out the back of my skull!*

It has ripped out something, certainly! said Korath.

The coordinates, said Jake.

What, are they back? Sudden hope, elation in Korath's deadspeak voice.

No, said Jake, as another wave of nausea threatened to roll him under. *I meant the coordinates were ripped out of me. Maybe permanently. Now there's only the spinning . . . the sickness . . . and . . . oh, God!*

And the darkness, suddenly exploding like a bomb inside his head; the whirling darkness inside, which was almost as dark as that outside, and Jake sensing he was about to pass out again.

But in the midst of all the darkness, a distant pinpoint of light; and Jake knew that if it was the last thing he ever did, somehow he must get to it. He willed himself in that direction, and the pinpoint immediately expanded. But in the moment before he reached it—even as Korath cried, *It's a door! It's a door!*—the effort overcame him. And he wasn't even aware that he was falling *through* the door, and didn't even feel the sting of the gravel on the path where he sprawled facedown, or the cool night breeze wafting over his prone body . . .

He woke up to the light—but a natural light—and to a painful throbbing in his head that caused him to screw up his eyes against both.

He was lying on a bed, under a white sheet in a white room, and a strange man and woman were looking worriedly down at him, concern plainly written on their faces.

"Eh?" Jake said. "What? Where am I?"

The woman, young and pretty, took his hand and spoke to him in what Jake suspected was Greek. His knowledge of the language was only very limited, so he shook his head. A mistake, because that only made the throbbing worse.

"English?" the young man said. "Are you English?"

"Yeah," Jake told him, his voice a dry croak. "And you have to be Greek." A safe bet, and not only because of the language. The whitewashed room, varnished pine bed, fixtures, and ceiling beams all spoke of Greece; likewise the light coming in through an open window, that special Mediterranean light. "May I have a drink of water? And would you mind telling me where I am?"

The young woman went out of the room, and the man said, "We are Greek, yes. And this is our house."

"On a Greek island," said Jake.

The young man's eyes opened in surprise, bewilderment. "But of course!" he answered. "Thee island of—"

"Zante," said Jake. "Zakynthos, in the Ionian." He was sure of it. It had come to him out of nowhere, but still he was absolutely certain of it. And since he'd never been here in his life, that was a mystery in itself! But one thing for sure, he felt good and safe here. Now why should that be? Could it be the feel of the place? Its clean, familiar smell?

"You are thee tourist, yes?"

"No," said Jake, then immediately changed his mind and took the easy way out. "Yes, you're right, I'm a tourist. I had, er, an accident . . . I think."

He struggled to sit up; the young Greek helped him, telling him, "You are lucky that we found you. You were outside. We had been to a friend's house, a party, last night. We got home late—between one and two in thee morning—and found you collapsed on thee path near thee front door."

Dim memories were stirring, but pseudomemories, Jake knew. It was the only possible answer. "This is . . . Zek's place," he said. "Zek Föener's place, near Porto Zoro, in Zante."

"Ah!" said the other. "You are knowing Zekintha? My

father, he bought this house from Zekintha. For me and Denise, my wife. But that was, oh, some four or five years ago! In thee English, my name is Dennis."

"Dennis and Denise?" Jake blinked, looked puzzled. He still felt woozy.

"This is Zante," the other shrugged. "Thee island's patron saint is Saint Dionysios. Many peoples here are called Dennis for this reason. Dennis or Denise."

But Jake was thinking about what Dennis had said about Zek. Yes, of course she would have sold the place four or five years ago—when she married Ben Trask. Zek and Harry Keogh had been friends for years and the original Necroscope had probably felt safe here, too. But safe from what? What had his problems been? Whatever, this place had stuck in his mind, as it was now stuck in Jake's; the only coordinates he/they had remembered, and the only place Jake had been able to flee to.

Flee? Now where had *that* thought come from? For Jake hadn't actually fled here but had been drawn here, hadn't he? Maybe it was Harry who had "fled" here upon a time. And again Jake asked himself, fled here from what . . . ?

"Help me up," he said. Pulling back the sheet, he found himself naked down to his underpants; his clothes lay neatly piled on a chair nearby. Dennis was concerned and told him to take it easy, but Jake struggled into his trousers and staggered toward the window. Even before he got there, however, he knew what he would see.

"We had a doctor to you this morning, at first light," said Dennis, following him. "He is thinking you were shot. A hunting accident, perhaps? Sometimes there are hunters in thee woods."

"Could be," said Jake. "I'm something of a hunter myself—now and then."

Outside the window, a balcony, and below the balcony steep, densely wooded slopes falling to the sea. The Mediterranean, or more properly the Ionian. Jake knew it—knew this place, even this room—and felt that if he turned round quickly, he might even see a lovely girl asleep in that selfsame bed. At least he would *remember* seeing Penny there. But not his memory, no, for Jake had never known a Penny. It was totally maddening!

"Where were you staying?" Dennis asked. Jake scarcely heard him. He was lost in his own thoughts and the fleeting memories of another. They came and went. Happy memories, sad memories, a changing sea of memories: calm, angry, storm-tossed. A farewell to all this. A departure. This had been Harry Keogh's stepping-off place, to somewhere else . . .

"Eh? Where am I staying?" Jake said. "Don't worry about it. I'll be okay now." For while everything else was swirling—all of these pseudomemories drifting in and out of whichever crevice of esoteric knowledge housed them—Jake's coordinates had returned and firmed up. And not only those coordinates he knew, but quite a few that someone else had known before him.

And Dennis said, "You should get that wound seen to, er—?"

"Jake," Jake told him. But damn it, he'd almost said *Harry*!

"The doctor said it should be stitched, but since thee scab was healing . . ."

"It's fine," said Jake, putting on the rest of his clothes, looking for his Browning, and failing to find it. "It'll be just fine."

By the time he was fully dressed, Denise had returned with a pitcher of water and a glass. Jake drank deeply, gratefully, then said, "Thanks—for everything. And now I'll be going."

"And your face?" said Denise. "We didn't wash you."

"My face?" Jake crossed to a mirror. She meant his charcoal camouflage from last night, gone streaky now on his face. Which reminded him to double-check: "What day is it?"

The young couple glanced at each other, shrugged off their bewilderment, and Dennis said, "It's Sunday."

Jake looked at his watch and made a quick calculation. Two in the Ionian afternoon, which meant that some seventeen hours had passed since he'd bombed Le Manse Madonie outside San Remo. He should go back there (would go back there, after he'd called Korath) to take a look at the damage.

"Do you need a taxi?" Denise asked him. And more anxiously, "Are you sure you'll be okay?"

"I'm sure," said Jake, making his unsteady way through this well-known house to the front door.

They stood and watched him walk out into the brilliant sunlight, and up the gravel path through the pines toward the road into Argasi. After just a few paces, Jake saw the scuffed patch of gravel where he'd landed after making his exit from the Continuum, and just off the path a glint of dull metal in the undergrowth. It was his gun. He picked it up, pocketed it, and knowing the way, continued up the path.

Jake pictured a big motorcycle—it could only be a Harley-Davidson—throbbing up this track to the road, and knew it was much more than just a picture in his head. And he wondered what it would feel like to ride a big bike through the Möbius Continuum? Well, and maybe *he* would try it some time. If he, the real Jake, was still around when all of this was over.

Reaching the road, he looked back. But Zek's place was lost from view, hidden in the pines. It was a terrific view out over the Ionian, and Jake knew he'd always liked it. And as for Zek: she meant a whole lot more to him now, and he knew how much she must have meant to Jazz Simmons and later to Trask . . . and even to the Necroscope Harry Keogh.

Just thinking of her was like an invocation. She was there, in his mind, at once. Or her sweet deadspeak voice was, anyway.

Why did you come here, Jake?

"Zek?" He quickly recovered from the suddenness of her presence. "What, you're still speaking to me? Still risking getting yourself in trouble with the Great Majority?"

Where there's a prosecution, there has to be a defence, she answered. *And I'm it,* advocatus diaboli, *but I didn't come here simply to speak to you. This time it's coincidental.*

"Ah!" said Jake. "I see. This was your special place—your genius loci?—and you were drawn back here, even as I was."

He sensed Zek's deadspeak nod. *I often find myself drifting back this way. But you? You say you were drawn here?*

"I had a problem, an accident, trouble in the Möbius Continuum," Jake explained. "For a little while the only place I knew was this place. Which just goes to show how very close you must have been to Harry Keogh. Or him to you."

Zek was at once anxious. *An accident? Yes, I can sense your pain. But you're okay now?*

"I've felt better," Jake answered, "but I'll get by."

And you're on your own for once.

"Korath?" said Jake. "I haven't shaken him, if that's what you mean. But for a while there my mind must have seemed a very dangerous place, and he went AWOL. In fact, I was just about to call him. I need him, Zek. Without the Möbius Continuum I can't follow things through, can't finish what Harry started."

Ah! (The very smallest deadspeak gasp, which scarcely disturbed the aether at all.) *You think that's what it's all about? That Harry has chosen you to complete some specific task?*

"Harry discovered, fought, and killed vampires, didn't he?" said Jake. "If nothing else, wouldn't he want to avenge you?"

But with Jake's shields down, Zek read a lot more into his answer than just that. *This isn't about me,* she said. *Harry was gone from the living long before me. It's true that he couldn't abide vampires—and if he were here now he'd still be working alongside E-Branch—but that's not what you meant. It's only a part of what you meant. So what's the rest of it, Jake?*

"I don't know the rest of it," said Jake. "You're right and there's something more to all this than what E-Branch is doing, but I've been left in the dark. Ben Trask and the rest of them, they know things they haven't told me, things they *daren't* tell me! They want me to work blind, to be their new Necroscope without telling me what went wrong for the first

Necroscope. I know he had powers they haven't told me about, and also that for all of his skills and knowledge he's no longer here. He's *dead,* Zek—dead and gone—and it wasn't old age that got him! You knew him probably as well as anyone, and since coming here I've discovered that he came to see you before he quit this world. What was it made him leave us, Zek? Him and that girl, Penny? Lardis Lidesci has as good as told me they went to his place, Sunside/Starside—but why? To fight vampires there in their own spawning ground? But was that the only reason? The puzzle is too big for me, Zek. I can't find all the pieces and the picture eludes me. In fact, you're the only one who gives a damn and is trying to help me!"

They all give a damn, Jake! she answered at once. *You don't have to worry that you're on your own. You're not, and when the teeming dead get to know you the way I'm coming to know you . . . you'll have a lot more friends, believe me. But the Great Majority, and E-Branch, too, they're playing this game by the rules. The dead won't give their loyalty to just anyone; they need you to prove yourself. Likewise E-Branch, but for reasons you don't yet understand; perhaps it's about those missing pieces that you mentioned. And remember, Jake, you haven't helped your case too much by running out on Ben like this.*

"You know I've run out on him?"

But isn't it obvious? she answered. *You're here on your own, aren't you?*

"For now I'm on my own, yes."

Well, then . . . ?

"Listen," said Jake. "E-Branch thinks I have my own agenda. Well, I thought so, too, at first. But it isn't any longer *my* agenda! I thought that I was avenging the death of . . . of someone I cared for. But I've since spoken to her and she's let me off the hook. By that I mean she's taken a lot of pressure off me. Fine, but it hasn't made any difference, hasn't changed my course one iota! I *know* that I've got to see this through, get it over and done with, and finish . . . and finish—"

—Something that Harry started?

"I think so, yes."

And for a little while there was silence in the deadspeak aether. Then Zek said, *Jake, there was a very painful time in Harry Keogh's life. Of all the painful times, this was one of the worst. It was a time of lies, incredible deceit, enormous danger, for Harry and for the whole world. At the end of that period even the dead deceived Harry; they had to, in order to keep faith with him. And E-Branch were the worst deceivers of all, even though they thought they were doing the right thing. A paradox? Not if you knew the whole story. But the point is, Harry* himself *didn't know the whole story, and wherever he is now, he still doesn't. That period—those years—were like lost years that never happened. And even if we could speak to him now, to an entirely whole Harry, still the Great Majority wouldn't tell him. There was pain enough in his life, without that we add to it in his afterlife.*

As for that girl you mentioned, Penny:

Penny came later, when Harry was just about done here. He brought her to me here on Zante; they paid me a visit, shortly before leaving this world for good. She loved him and believed she could have a life with him. Maybe she could have, but that wasn't to be. There was an accident and . . . Penny didn't survive it. But do you know, I've since "spoken" to her, and Penny has no regrets? It seems that living a few days with Harry had been like living a fantastic lifetime—or even two lifetimes. But don't ask me to explain that last, for I can't.

When she fell silent, Jake prompted her, "These lost years you mentioned. You're thinking maybe they have something to do with me, with what's happening to me now? But how, and why?"

You said it best yourself, she told him. *Maybe you're the one he's chosen to finish something he started.*

"But I've spent time with Harry," Jake answered. "You know I have. So if there really is something he wants me to do, why didn't he tell me about it when he had the chance?"

The only reason I can think of, said Zek, *is that perhaps he himself doesn't know what it is.*

Jake's head spun, and not alone from the constant nagging pain of his wound. "You mean, some part of him remembers something he should have done, but not enough to know what it is? And I've got to do it for him?"

From what you've told me, that seems the likely answer.

"So what *did* he do during those lost years?"

Those of the Great Majority who know—and there's only a small handful—won't talk about it, Zek answered. *They certainly won't tell me, for they long since made a pact never to speak of it. For Harry's sake.*

"Even though he's dead now?"

We've already been into that, she sighed.

Jake shook his head in frustration. "The dead aren't talking about it, not even to you, one of their own? *Huh!* But how about the living? Why hasn't Trask said something about it?"

Because he's like me, said Zek. *He doesn't know.*

"Then for Pete's sake tell me something you *do* know!" Jake felt like tearing out his hair. "What the hell was it with the Necroscope that Trask and E-Branch are afraid to talk about!?"

There was a brief silence, and he could feel how torn Zek was when finally she said, *I'm sorry, Jake. Sorry I can't tell you more. But I will tell you this much: being a Necroscope—being* the *Necroscope—will be no easy thing. Not for you, and not for the teeming dead. 'What the hell,' you asked. And yes, it can get pretty much like that. Pretty much like hell.* Talking *to the living, or rather to you, is one thing, and if that was all there was to it . . . but it isn't. And the dead learned long ago, in Harry's time, that one thing can lead to another. That's why they're so quiet, lying still, keeping their peace. At least for the time being.*

"They don't care to talk to the living?" Jake was baffled. "They really believe in this RIP hokum? They don't give a damn for their former lives in the world they've left behind; don't want to know how their kids are doing, how the world itself is getting on and everything they created is being used and built upon by their survivors?" He shook his head. "I don't get it."

But they do *care!* said Zek. *More than you can know. And if and when they come round to our way of thinking you'll see how very* much *they care. And that's the answer to both your questions: why for now the Great Majority aren't communicative, and why E-Branch can't tell you all about Harry. The world needs a Necroscope, Jake. But it has to be the right one. He has to be brave and careful, and he has to care about what he's doing. He has to care for the dead, because they may have to pay a very high price for caring for him . . .*

"I'm wasting my time," said Jake. "And I'm getting nowhere. But I do trust you, Zek. So if this is how you say it has to be . . . then I suppose this is how it has to be."

One thing more before we part, said Zek. *Don't be too despondent, Jake. However slowly, we* are *winning the battle; more and more of the Great Majority are coming over onto your side, seeing things your way. However slowly, the tide is turning in your favour. For despite every obstacle in your path—all the difficulties and uncertainties—you haven't given in. What's more, your light burns in our darkness more like Harry Keogh's with every passing hour. And the Thing that you carry with you—which the dead fear more than anything else—hasn't gained ground but lost it. You're ahead of the game, Jake, and all we have to do now is make sure you stay there.*

"But I have sent a few less than worthy people your way," said Jake, remembering the outlines he'd seen through the wet patio windows of Le Manse Madonie. "Knowing how much the dead respect life, that can't have improved my image too much . . ."

Actually, said Zek, *you also cleared an awful lot of debts along the way. For you're right: not a one of them was worthy. They were murderers all, and they're all excluded. They aren't to be counted among the Great Majority.*

"They're excommunicated?"

Always, said Zek. *Committed to the darkness where they'll do no more harm. And now I have to go.*

Jake felt her drift away, but it was only after she'd gone that he realized Zek hadn't answered the one question that she could have answered, to which he was sure she knew the answer:

Why had Harry Keogh, the original Necroscope, deserted our world for Sunside/Starside . . . ?

A car honked as it went by, and Jake suddenly realized that he was on the road to Argasi, walking in the brilliant Ionian sunlight. He had walked as he talked, as if to a corporeal person. Once you were used to it, that was what deadspeak was like. But now he was alone again, walking nowhere and to no purpose.

Korath came as soon as Jake called out for him. "Where were you?" said Jake.

Where else? said the other gloomily.

"Sleeping?"

Sleeping, resting, being alone. You're not the only one who can suffer from exhaustion, you know. That business in the Möbius Continuum was . . . it was fatiguing, to say the least.

"Sleep and weep," said Jake. "Are you telling me you missed yet another opportunity to get inside my head?"

I missed nothing! Korath snorted. *Nor have I forgotten that we have a deal.* What he didn't say was that with Jake's mind in shock, or at best in something of a turmoil, he had felt better off out of there. *Anyway, why did you call me? What's next? Now that you've become aware of the attendant dangers, is it at all possible that you've finally given up on your vendetta? But no, I can see that was too much to hope for.* And he fell silent.

"All done?" said Jake. "Well good! Thanks for asking after my health. I'm fine, thank you. I nearly got my head blown off, but I'll live. Now I need to get back to Paris, clean up, eat a decent meal, and get some healing sleep. Because tonight—"

—*We'll be busy again.* Korath groaned.

"That's right," said Jake.

And do you trust yourself to use the Möbius Continuum? Are you sure that what happened won't happen again?

"The coordinates are all back in place," said Jake. "Better than before. And there are a couple of new ones, too. But don't worry, I won't be checking them out. Not yet a while, anyway."

Huh! Korath grunted, as he set the Möbius equations rolling down the screen of Jake's mind. This time the esoteric math was more familiar; Jake could even see patterns emerging; the weird symbols and numbers no longer had power to awe him. They were a key, that was all, to the metaphysical Möbius Continuum, and he felt he would soon be able to grasp that key for himself.

Until then—but only until then—Korath would remain the gatekeeper. These were secret thoughts, which Jake kept guarded in those innermost vaults of mind to which as yet Korath wasn't privy. Thus both men—or one man and a creature—had secrets known only to themselves. And Zek had been quite right: as yet, Korath hadn't taken the upper hand.

Not as yet . . .

It was 12:40 P.M. in Paris by the time Jake had cleaned himself up, taken some aspirins, put a plaster on his head, and his head gently on the pillows.

Feeling ill and fearing a relapse, he had no sooner arrived in his room than he'd banished Korath back to the ruined Romanian Refuge. Then his nausea had returned with a vengeance. He'd felt too sick to eat; the pain of his wound was sending regular stabs of lightning deep into his brain; it was as well that his plans for the night ahead were vague, since he might now have to abandon them entirely. But that as a last resort.

For still he hoped his condition would improve with healing sleep. And who could say? Maybe his plans would work themselves out, too.

Then a strange thing, as if "things" in Jake's life weren't strange enough already. But as he closed his eyes to sleep, Liz was on his mind again—

—And in the next moment she was *really* on his mind!

He came bolt upright in his bed, his attitude one of intent listening. It came from far away—some kind of contact, brief, filtered by distance, the merest telepathic touch—as if for a moment Liz's scent was in his nostrils, her sweet breath on his face. No more than that, but it was more than enough. Jake felt a chill in his soul; it made the short hairs at the back of his neck prickle and stand up straight.

Now what the *hell* was that? But it was gone before he could question or examine it, or lock on to its location. And after a while he lay back down again, but wonderingly.

She'd felt . . . disturbed? Not fearful but deeply disturbed. She'd been searching for something telepathically. Not for Jake but for someone—or something or *things*—other. But as always Jake had been on her mind, and the effort that Liz had put into whatever it was she was doing had been such that her probe had reached out to touch upon his thoughts, too.

It was the rapport they had between them. Despite that Jake might be considered undeserving of Liz's affection—and regardless of the distance between—the connection was still there.

It, the *connection,* was or had been there . . . but where was Liz? He reached out for her—sought a direction, a co-ordinate—and found nothing. The moment had passed.

And Jake had no way of knowing that on Krassos, in a place in the mountains called The Aerie, Liz had been looking through a telescope, searching for Vavara and Malinari; no way of knowing that shortly she'd be on her way with Trask and the others back to Skala Astris.

No way of knowing—not yet—that E-Branch was hot on the trail of mankind's greatest enemies, and that much like himself, Liz was only a few short hours away from unthinkable horror.

Which was as well. For if he had known, then he never would have slept . . .

It was dark when Jake woke up, and he was hungry. But the pain in his head had reduced to a dull throbbing with no more lightning flashes, and he found he could think quite clearly.

He dressed, called for sandwiches in his room, then called for Korath. And Korath came:

"Like a genie in a bottle," said Jake. His words were deadspeak, of course, and conveyed his meaning.

A bottle, or a lamp, said Korath, with a mental shrug. *What odds? Either one would make a pleasurable grave . . . compared to a cramped metal pipe in a drowned, subterranean sump!* And then, changing the subject, *I see that you're feeling better.*

"Not as good as new," said Jake, "but a little better, yes. And that's good, because we have things to do. First some bombs, big ones, that I have to put together—"

Bombs that blast, said Korath.

"—And then there's something I'm to collect from the other side of the world."

And bombs that burn.

"Precisely." Jake nodded.

Explosions, and chemical fires, said Korath.

"That's right."

You realize, of course, that this time Castellano will most certainly be waiting for you?

"That seems likely," said Jake, as he finished eating. "But I still hope to surprise him. The Möbius Continuum gives me all the edge I need."

But it wasn't enough of an edge at Le Manse Madonie, Korath reminded him.

Jake sighed and said, "I see you're your cheerful self, as usual. Anyway, what happened was my mistake and I won't let it happen again. But talking about Le Manse Madonie, it's time we took a look at that place to see what damage I did."

Jake took nothing with him but his 9mm Browning automatic and a spare clip, and he and Korath went to Italy, to the coordinates of the slip-road where it left the highway and climbed to Le Manse Madonie—or what was left of it.

The sky was clear and the place bright in starlight. Where Le Manse Madonie had looked out over the Ligurian Sea, a vivid white scar showed in the face of the cliff, like the new flesh under a scab that has been torn away. There was simply nothing there; the slip-road ended at a sheer drop down to the highway, where the entire cliff face had been blasted loose. And it had taken Le Manse Madonie with it. Down below, bulldozers were at work clearing the last of the rubble from the road to Imperia.

You can be sure that no one lived through that! Korath was obviously awed. *Whoever it was who shot at you, he is no more.*

"Actually," said Jake, "I had hoped that someone had lived through it. That way he might have reported *my* death, too."

But he sensed the "shake" of Korath's head. *No, Castellano must know by now that you aren't the one to die so easily. And I'm sure he* will *be expecting you.*

"You're probably right," said Jake. But he wasn't about to let that stop him. Or rather *something*—the force that drove him on—wasn't about to let it stop him. No, for the original Necroscope, Harry Keogh, had gone up against far worse dangers than these—

—Hadn't he?

In the sprawling Gibson Desert of western Australia, somewhere on the three-hundred-mile trail between Wiluna and Lake Disappointment, Jake exited from the Möbius Continuum at coordinates remembered from his brief time with E-Branch and the grim work they had done there.

It was early morning and relatively cool. Jake stood at the edge of the road—more nearly a track—and looked north and a little east at the rugged country ahead. The last time he was here it had been with Liz, and he'd been looking through binoculars. There was no requirement for those now;

he knew the way well enough, and perhaps even too well.

His vantage point was the crest of a rise in the road where it began to dip down into a riverbed that had dried up in prehistoric times, and he gazed at the base of a knoll that bulged at the foot of a massive outcrop or butte. The road (or ancient riverbed) wound around the ridgy, shelving base of the outcrop and disappeared north.

On the shelf above the road, at the base of the knoll, that was where the Old Mine petrol station—a front for Nephran Malinari's vampiric activities—had been situated not so long ago. Then E-Branch had discovered it, and now . . .

. . . Now the face of the knoll was fire-blackened, the ground around had been scorched clean of vegetation, and the entrances to the old mine's workings had been blocked by hundreds of tons of rock blasted from above. They'd made a good job of it, even as good as Jake had made of Le Manse Madonie.

Jake knew that if he moved closer to the actual site of the petrol station he'd find evidence of recent activity; as recent as last night, when E-Branch and Major Tom's men had been checking the place over, opening it up, searching it minutely, and closing it down again, this time sealing it for good. But he didn't need to go that close.

Where a ramp of hard-packed earth rose from the road to the elevated shelf in front of the knoll, he found what he was looking for, a hardwood stake with a warning sign that read:

HEALTH HAZARD!
TOXIC WASTE! KEEP OUT!

Just twelve inches away from the foot of the signpost, the ground had recently been turned. Jake glanced at the sign again and thought: *Health hazard? Well, what's buried here is definitely going to become a health hazard for someone!*

He didn't have a spade but the ground was still very loose. Down on his knees, scooping up earth and pebbles with his bare hands, he soon dug down to the canvas shoulder-straps of three thermite charges in their haversack containers. After that the rest was easy; he simply hauled on the straps, gradually dragging the haversacks up out of the loose soil.

And now you're all set, said Korath.

"Right," said Jake. "But we've time to go before it's one o'clock in the morning in Bagheria, Sicily. And that's when I intend to hit him: in the wee small hours of the morning, when all good men and true should rightfully be in their beds."

Good men and true, maybe, said Korath. *But what about monsters? From what you've said of him, this Castellano is one of the worst. Well, for an entirely* human *being, that is.*

Jake could only agree. For neither he nor his dead vampire companion had any way of knowing just how close the latter had come to revealing the truth of it.

Which was how things stood when they took the Möbius route back to Jake's hotel in Paris . . .

Some hours earlier, on the island of Krassos, events had moved on apace.

With the sun down and the dusky Greek twilight settling in, Trask and his people had left the knoll where Liz and Chung had made their observations on Palataki and the monastery, returned to the Christos Studios, and commenced contingency planning for the night ahead.

"We now know more or less what we're up against," Trask told the others where they gathered in his and Chung's accommodation. "The monastery is Vavara's and so are its nun occupants. And you can feel sorry for them all you like, but it won't help them. That's the way things are, and there's no hope for any of them. Ian will confirm that he's already seen them burning—or rather, that he's already *fore*seen them burning. But that could well be a symbolic thing, as some of his forecasts have been in the past, because God knows *we* don't have anything to burn them with! However brutal it might sound, I only wish we had!"

"Er, excuse me," Manolis quickly cut in. "But it's possible there *are* other options on that front which might still be open to us. But please go on. I can explain when you're finished."

Trask nodded and continued. "So, then: the monastery has to go, and especially since Vavara has a houseguest, Lord Nephran Malinari. Now, that's a fact: we know that both Vavara and Malinari are in residence, and that the monastery must have become some kind of hell for its rightful dwellers . . . they're *already* burning, if you see what I mean. Perhaps that's what our precog has seen." He paused to glance at Goodly. But Goodly's face was gaunt, even paler than usual, and devoid of any message.

"Then there's Palataki," Trask went on, "or the 'Little Palace,' as the locals refer to it. We can't be absolutely certain what's there, but whatever it is it has to be of Vavara's doing. She's been here long enough to have created some sort of garden like that nightmarish cavern under the Pleasure Dome in Xanadu. It's mainly guesswork, I admit, but going on what Liz and David seem to have detected there it's our best bet. Malinari, Vavara, and presumably Szwart, too . . . it looks like they've been lying low while they created these bloody vampire mushroom farms. And I won't insult your intelligence by attempting to explain their purpose. But when I think of Szwart, somewhere under London . . . my *God!*" Trask lurched upright, clenched his fists in a mixture of fury and frustration, and commenced pacing the floor in what little space there was.

And when he'd got himself under control again: "So then, what have we got going for us, and what are we up against? Or I'll put it another way. Since we seem to have very *little* going for us, what's against us?

"Well, the answer to that is just about every-bloody-thing! If I thought we had time to spare, it might be possible to call for air strikes from a British warship in the Med. But for that they'd need pinpoint accuracy—grid references off an Ordnance Survey map simply wouldn't do it—and we don't have our techs out here as yet. And of course this weather, all of the sunspot activity and what have you, is playing merry hell with our gadgets back home, so that even if we could talk to our people we couldn't use satellite surveillance.

"So that's about it. It's highly unlikely we'll be able to call for naval support, time definitely isn't on our side, and the longer we sit twiddling our thumbs, the greater the chance we'll be discovered.

"In which event there are two possibilities. One, that Malinari and Vavara will try to take us out, which seems unlikely; he's met up with us before and knows we aren't a pushover. Two, that they'll turn those nuns loose to cover their escape. I for one have had enough of Malinari escaping. I feel like—I don't know—like Nayland Smith, I suppose, on the trail of Fu Manchu: I want the bastard dead!"

Trask stopped pacing, flopped down on his bed, and finally finished off with, "Well, that's where we're at. Right now I'm waiting to talk to London HQ, let them know how things are, and find out what's happening with them. But it's not all bad news. Yiannis stopped me as we came in; he was all excited about the weather, going on about how it's breaking over northern Europe, and how the sunspot activity is easing off. Fine, but even if I get a clear line later tonight, still we can't expect any reinforcements before midday tomorrow. Until then we're on our own. So that's me done, people, and now it's your turn. I could use some clever ideas, because frankly I'm fresh out . . ."

He looked at Manolis, said, "You had something to say?"

Manolis nodded. "Today, on our way back from Skala Rachoniou, myself and Andreas, we went to take a look at thee marble quarry and thee airport. It's a Sunday, nobody doing thee work . . . just security guards at both places. *Huh!* Security guards! But this is Greece—or more especially a Greek island—and security isn't what it used to be. No one tries too hard on an island where you can't make a getaway. And what is there worth stealing in a marble quarry anyway, eh? Or a deserted, disused airport, for that matter?"

"You tell me," said Trask, frowning.

"Dynamite!" said Manolis. "In thee quarry, a shack with a rusty padlock, watched over by an ouzo-soaked, sleepy old man who looks more like a shepherd than a watchman. It will be—how do you say it—like taking thee lollipop from thee baby?"

"Candy," said Liz.

"Ah, yes, thee candy!" Manolis nodded. "Thee big sticks of very powerful candy. And at thee airport, an underground reservoir of high-octane aviation gasoline. Avgas, Ben, with access through a hangar. And standing in thee hangar, a loaded tanker waiting for tomorrow morning, to be driven to Krassos town and ferried across to thee mainland. At least, that's where it was destined for. But now . . . ?"

Trask thought about it, smiled grimly, and asked, "Can you do it? You and your men?"

"Can thee fishes swim?" said Manolis. "So then, here is my suggestion. Since my men aren't thee mindspies and can't be of use in that kind of surveillance, we'll send them to make thee necessary, er, acquisitions, which they'll later deliver to us at a prearranged time and location somewhere on thee coast road between Palataki and thee monastery. What do you say?"

As Manolis's plan had unfolded, Trask's eyes had lost something of their dullness. Now they gleamed where they looked for the approval of the rest of the team, his gaze moving from face to face. "Well?" he said.

"It's a very horrible thought," Ian Goodly couldn't manage to suppress a shudder, "but it would explain the burning. . . ."

And David Chung said, "A big tanker like that, it could go right in through the monastery's gates, tearing them open like tissue paper. And a stick of dynamite in the right place . . ."

And Liz asked Manolis, "Isn't it a lot to ask of your men? I mean, are you absolutely sure they can do it?"

But Manolis shook his head. "Liz, there are no absolutes, no certainties here," he said. "So what can I tell you? But if you're asking are they qualified . . . believe me, they are *more* than equal to thee task."

"So how will they go about it?" Trask asked. "I don't want

the nitty-gritty, just the big picture. You've obviously given it some thought."

Manolis nodded. "Stavros here was for three years a driver in thee Greek military. Anything with wheels, he can drive it. But he goes with Andreas only as a passenger on thee first leg of their short trip."

Trask said, "I see. Andreas drops him off close to the airport, where he'll, er, appropriate the tanker."

"He will rescue it, yes," said Manolis. "And while he does that, Andreas will be driving on to thee quarry—"

"—To rescue the dynamite," Trask nodded. "But dynamite is dangerous stuff."

Manolis beamed. "Precisely! And before he joined me in thee drugs squad, Andreas was with antiterrorism. He is thee expert with thee explosives."

Andreas offered a slightly intimidating grin, puffed up his massive chest, sighed, and gave a self-deprecating shrug.

"But it has to be tonight," Manolis reminded everyone, "for tomorrow thee tanker won't be there. And a thing as big as that—thee biggest weapon in our arsenal—we can't simply take it and hide it away until it is needed. If we're going to take it, we're going to have to use it."

Again Trask nodded. "That's understood." He stood up. "And the beauty of it is we still have some time—several hours at least—to make up our minds. Now I suggest we take a break in The Shipwreck. This place is much too confining and I feel shut in. We'll be a lot more comfortable in the bar, and we can have Yiannis or Katerina fix sandwiches. If we stay apart from other guests and keep the volume down, we should be able to talk just as well there as here."

"Good!" Lardis Lidesci grunted. "I'm hungry—not to mention thirsty. Listening to you lot prattle on . . . well it's very dry work."

"But if you're thinking of Metaxa," Trask told him, "you're allowed just one. It's looking more and more like tonight could be *the* night. If so, then later we'll be needing our wits about us."

"One last drink to success, then," said Manolis. "It sounds good to me . . ."

The Shipwreck was empty. But the small television set above the bar was working. The evening news was showing, and at long last it was watchable. As Yiannis had reported, the sunspot activity seemed to be waning; all the hissing and crackling, the bilious flashes of static, and the fading in and out no longer entirely obliterated either the sound from the speakers or the screen's images. It was still a far cry from being good, but it was the best it had been for quite some time.

Yiannis must have seen Trask and the others walking towards the bar, for they had no sooner settled in their chairs than he entered and served drinks. They ordered toasted sandwiches, and Yiannis made to go off into the small kitchen annex at the rear of the bar. But before doing so he paused and spoke to Trask.

"The news with Turkey is very bad," he said. "Another territorial dispute. The Turks are claiming Lesbos and Samos again. These islands are very close to the Turkish mainland, and both governments are sabre-rattling. It's all very worrying."

"It must be," said Trask.

"On the other hand," said Yiannis, "a sort of uneasy status quo has prevailed ever since the invasion of Cyprus in the sixties. So let's hope it's just another bout of bad-tempered bluster."

"Perhaps it's this godawful, interminable El Niño weather!" said Trask. While his face showed his understanding of Yiannis's concerns, still he made light of them if only to ease the young Greek's mind and improve his mood.

"Ah, but you could be right!" Yiannis grinned at last. "So by all means let's blame El Niño. But as I believe I mentioned earlier, the weather is finally breaking. A cloud belt is heading south, and rain is expected as early as tomorrow afternoon. What a relief that will be!"

"And the sunspot activity—?"

"—Is definitely dying down," said Yiannis. "It's all been reported on the news. International lines and satellite communications are going to be fully operational again in just a few hours. In fact if you still want to contact London, there's no reason why you shouldn't try now."

"Perhaps I'll do just that," said Trask, smiling and again making light of it—despite that he felt like running for the phone! "Thanks for the tip."

"You're welcome." And Yiannis went off to make sandwiches.

Trask waited until the young Greek was out of sight, then stood up and told his people, "Save a bite for me." And as he sauntered from the bar: "Right now I want to check my gadgets, see if they're back on line. Or maybe I'll just try the phone in the admin building."

"Do you want company?" Goodly enquired.

Trask shook his head. "Stay here and eat. I'll be speaking to London, and there's nothing you can say that I can't."

"Ask after Lissa," Lardis called after him.

"Of course," Trask answered, looking back. And glancing at Liz, before she could embarrass herself: "I'll be asking after everyone. That's if I can get through."

And then he was gone, out of the door . . .

An hour earlier, in a London where the evening's dusk was just turning to a night that threatened storms:

No one uses the tubes anymore, Millicent Cleary thought to herself when some unspecified trouble on the line ahead caused Millie and the plainclothes Special Branch man escorting her to leave the train at King's Cross with maybe a dozen other stranded passengers. *But then again, can anyone blame them?*

The Victoria Line was one of the few underground transport systems that still functioned, at least in part, and even that small handful was subject to frequent disruption. This was how it had been ever since the great flood of 2007. Rising sea levels and water tables, higher tides and a Thames that regularly overflowed its banks; the water came in faster than they could pump it out! Many of the older tunnels had collapsed and been washed away; some of the deeper systems were dry, depending on the strata, but had been made inaccessible or dangerous by the collapse of older, shallower levels up above. Today's disruption was just one of many such that Millie had suffered when she travelled into the city from Finsbury Park.

But this evening had been one of *those* evenings. First her escort's car had refused to start again when he picked her up; then it had been impossible to find a taxi; the train had come in late—probably as a result of whatever problem it was that had now shut the line down—and had then stood throbbing and vibrating in the station for so long that most of the passengers had got off and left. And now . . .

. . . Now she gave a little cry as the high heel of her left shoe got jammed in a grating right there on the platform, tearing the shoe right off her foot.

Her escort—a tall, well-built man in a light summer suit—tut-tutted as Millie hopped around on one foot, commenting, "Just isn't your night, is it, luv?" Taking her arm and steadying her, he went down on one knee and reported, "It seems this heel of yours is—*uh!*—well and truly stuck, I'm afraid."

"Damn it!" Millie replied hotly. "What else can go wrong, I wonder?" Looking along the platform, she felt deserted, experienced a kind of panic, on seeing the last few disgruntled passengers hurrying into the various tunnels to the stairways and elevators. The train was already backing out of the station.

But along there, a grubby little man—a *very* small man, a dwarf, even—was climbing up onto a bench and reaching up with what looked like pipe-cutters to the power cables running along the tiled, arched curve of the tunnel. Now what on earth . . . ?

"There," said Millie's escort. "That's got it. Didn't want to break the heel off, that's all." But coming upright with her shoe, he saw the puzzled look on his charge's face changing to a frown, and heard her gasp as Millie's telepathic probes collided with other thoughts in the psychic aether.

My Lord, a sinister mental voice was whispering in Millie's head. *Your sabotage plan worked. She is here! And we are fortunate. With the exception of one man, she is alone!*

Millie's eyes opened wide as her head jerked around to look the other way down the platform. A pair of nuns in black hooded robes were standing there; just standing there, watching her—but their eyes were like yellow points of light in the shade of their cowls, and the dark, ugly thoughts or message had issued from one of them!

Then, even as Millie's hand flew to her mouth, it came again: *My Lord, do you hear me?* One of the nuns cocked her head on one side, enquiringly.

But the next thought that Millie heard came from someone—or something—entirely different:

Yes, I heard you, said that gurgling, glutinous, telepathic voice in Millie's head. *And so did she, I fancy! But tell me—is it dark?*

Too late, Millie's escort had seen the dwarf and the shower of sparks that met the little man's efforts with the pipe-cutters. "What in the name of . . . ?"

In the next moment it went dark—dark as night, as all the lights went out—but not before Millie had jerked her head and eyes in the direction of the new, completely alien thought, and stared *down* at the grating under her feet! Down there, she knew she'd seen something moving . . . a flowing motion, like sentient sludge, in the unknown gloom of the station's service levels.

Then the grating tilted under her feet, sending her sprawling, and she heard her escort's cry of alarm and outrage as he was sent flying away from her. And in a moment, floating out of the darkness, the feral-eyed nuns were upon her, hauling Millie upright, and fastening on her with hands like iron claws.

And something black—even blacker than the darkness—was rising before her, oozing up endlessly from the underworld, and its voice was in her head, saying:

Be sure not to harm her. She is my prize, my hostage, and I don't want her damaged.

Finally, seeing its eyes and its jet-black shapeless shape, Millie knew what it was for certain. And as her worst nightmare reached out for her, so she fainted.

Following which . . . nothing.

It had been Ben Trask's intention to go to the Christos Studios administrative building and try the telephone there, but hurrying along the path between the chalets, as he was about to pass the door to his and Chung's accommodation, he heard a telltale beeping from within.

His gadgets might indeed be "back on line," but it remained to be seen if they were working or just acting up.

He swerved toward the door, let himself in, listened to the beeping. It was a portable fax, in his briefcase under his bed. Someone was wanting to send him a message, and only one someone sprang to mind: the duty officer at E-Branch HQ.

Trask yanked the briefcase out, plumped it down on the bed, took out the fax machine—a flat, half-inch-thick device just big enough to take A4 paper, with a slot at one end, a keyboard, send and receive keys, and a little red light that was blinking on and off apace with the beeping—and shoved a sheet of paper into the slot before pressing the receive key.

The machine purred, and in a count of five the A4 sheet was propelled out again. Trask snatched it out of the slot and read it:

> BT: if you're getting gggx this please respond. xtoup 1g
> I have news. DO.

There was some interference, but at least Trask had got the message. He fed another sheet of paper into the slot and typed:

> I have a decoder. So send your stuff scrambled.

Then, after hitting the send key, he drummed his fingers on the machine's casing and waited for the printed sheet to appear. When it did, it read:

> I have a decrntpggoder. So send yourxtpgg stuff scrambled.

As if it wasn't scrambled enough already! But a lot better than nothing. And in went a third sheet of paper.

This time he had to wait a minute—then two, three, three and a half—until he was just about to rave at the damn thing for going on the blink again, but eventually the machine burped and ejected its coded message.

Meanwhile Trask had taken the decoder—a machine much like the first in shape and style but less complicated—out of his suitcase. It had no keyboard and just one switch, and contained its own printout paper.

Now Trask pressed the switch and fumbled the sheet of gibberish into the decoder's slot. The machine scanned the message, whirred, and the decoded printout began jerking and stammering its way out of the slot.

Trask couldn't wait so ripped it out and read:

> Aussie job finished. All clear. Shttpx n%ggh!? I'mrddgb redirecting the party to you. You can expect them by Tues first dhhggx light. Do you read? If so, more to follow . . .

And Trask spent several frantic minutes coding and sending:

> I read you good! I have a request for tonight. Is HMS Invincible in range of Krassos? Plan B refers.

The fax lit up again; Trask fed it a blank sheet; out came the message, asking him to wait while the duty officer got hold of a tech. He fed in another sheet, and waited . . . eventually a coded message . . . the usual rigmarole, and:

> No go on Plan B. Don't send coordinates. Two reasons. The Min Res [meaning the Minister Responsible] is here. Grttpxxgggeek radar and early warning systems are op-

> erational but functioning badly. They might blame Turkey. War in the Med. Two: Invincigtttx ble has satellite coordinated targeting. No good in darkgggttoh ggness unless previously programmed or guided in by satellite. Do you read? If so, more to follow . . .

And: "Yes, God *damn* you, I read!" Trask rasped, as he used the fax. He was so busy that he barely noticed that the precog Ian Goodly had come in and was sitting at the foot of the bed, reading the messages where he'd thrown them down.

After that it was five everlasting minutes before the last, short, enciphered text was delivered and decoded:

> Bad news. Sorry to report. Half anxxgj hour ago. Special Branch man down. He was hkkygg Millicent Cleary's escort. Not serious. He was able to call it in from King's Cross underground. But Millie is missing. Every available agent on it. We'll find her, but you had to know. JG/DO.

And Trask just sat there reading the thing, over and over and over. But Ian Goodly, precog that he was, had seen it coming and was already out of the door. To hell with caution now. Plan B was a goner and they must revert to Plan A—which had always been that they would deal with things themselves if they had to, working it out as they went along.

So thank God for Manolis Papastamos and his men!

That was how things stood, and when Trask woke up from his current daze, his disbelief—and when his rage was on him in full—that's how things would be . . .

21
Convergence—Hell on Earth, and Under It

JAKE WORE A THIN STRIP OF ADHESIVE PLASTER under a black headband that served a dual purpose in keeping both the plaster and his braid in place. With charcoal stripes on his face and hands, and dressed in black from head to toe, he was almost as dark as the night itself.

He carried a black sausage bag containing three bombs, each made from three pounds of plastique, plus Major Tom's haversack devices, the thermite bombs that he'd picked up in the Gibson Desert in Australia. In addition, he'd fashioned a lanyard for his Browning, which he carried tucked snugly into his trousers; this was a lesson he'd learned from his temporary loss of the weapon following the firefight at Le Manse Madonie. The nite-lite binoculars completed his equipment; he wore them with their strap around his neck.

At 12:30 A.M. local time he emerged from the Möbius Continuum at previously noted coordinates between Trabia and Bagheria less than a quarter-mile south of Castellano's headquarters. It was the same vantage point from which he'd studied the place on his earlier visit, and the same problems waited to be resolved: he still had no notion of the internal layout of the house, and no way of knowing how many of Castellano's people were in situ. The one thing in Jake's favour (other than the Möbius Continuum itself): the night was dark under a slow-moving cloudy sky, and all good men and true should be in their beds. He hoped so, anyway.

Which I've heard before, said Korath, *and which I answered. This is no ordinary man, Jake. Nor is he good and true. I can't help but worry that this is your most dangerous venture yet.*

"Mine and yours both," Jake answered under his breath. "For without me there's no you."

You don't have to remind me, said Korath. *And of course I'm worried for both our skins, despite that mine is an empty one.*

Kneeling in the cloud-cast shadows behind a clump of rocks, Jake frowned at the scene presented by his binoculars. Downhill and downwind from his location, Castellano's stronghold looked even more forbidding than it had in full daylight. In the dense olive groves surrounding the house, four evenly spaced blobs of ghostly grey light floated along narrow paths winding under the trees. Made visible by Jake's nite-lites' thermal-imaging, they were Castellano's men keeping watch on the perimeter.

Following the heat trail of one of them, Jake saw him go to the outer wall, watched as he climbed stone steps, saw him look out into the darkness in Jake's general direction.

Jake wasn't too concerned, for unless the man was equipped as he was equipped he wouldn't be able to see much of anything. And yet—

—The short hairs at the back of Jake's neck prickled. He took a sharp breath, ducked down, took cover. It was a feeling, that was all. No, it was more than that: it was the very *deliberate* way the guard had looked out across the wall, turning his head as if to slowly scan the rough, gradually rising ground in the direction of Jake's position. That was what had caused Jake to take cover: the fear that he might be seen! But *how* seen, in this darkest of nights? Maybe this one had nite-lites after all, but Jake didn't think so. And the hairs at the back of his neck were still prickling.

Having seen what Jake had seen, through his eyes—and having felt his apprehension—now Korath said, *There's something wrong here. Something strangely familiar about the* feel *of this place. And it isn't simply that we've been here before. Frankly I don't like it at all.*

"You and me both," said Jake under his breath. "This isn't a good place to be. I sensed that the last time we were here.

But it's where I *have* to be if I want to get the job done. And I do want to get it done."

Yes, I know that now, said Korath. *And since I can't dissuade you I'll give you my fullest assistance. But still I say to you, this place has dangers more than we perceive.*

Jake nodded, eased himself into a more comfortable position from where he could look out again between the rocks, and eventually answered, "An old—or perhaps that should be new—adage continues to apply. Just as you were a cautious one in life . . ."

Had to be, Korath cut in, *in order to survive in Malinari's service. Well* (a deadspeak shrug), *for as long as I survived.*

". . . So you go on in death," Jake finished.

But this time it isn't like that, Korath tried to explain. *This time it's very different. This place is . . . too quiet. No, it's* un*quiet! Why, even the teeming dead are silent here!*

Jake remembered what Humph had told him at the site of the original Manse Madonie. "This is Sicily," he said. "And as I've just reminded you, what the dead did in life, they continue—"

—And I *continue to tell you,* said Korath hotly, *that this is different! Why don't you listen to me, Jake? Surely you can feel it for yourself? The silence here is . . . absolute! Haven't I told you how I eavesdrop on the dead in their graves? But not here. Oh, they may well be* listening *to us, but they're not saying anything. They're not saying anything at all—not even to each other!*

And now, as Jake saw the grey anthropomorphic blob get down from the wall and continue on its patrol through the olives, he felt it, too: the utter silence in the deadspeak aether. And he suddenly realized that he had become used to the whispers of the dead, so much so that unless he concentrated they were less than a hiss of background static in the receptors of his metaphysical mind. But in this place even that hiss was absent, as if the teeming dead held their breath . . .

Exactly, said Korath. *As if they are waiting for something. For you to join them, perhaps? I hate to sound morbid, but your future isn't looking too bright, Jake.*

"My future?" said Jake, slowly lowering the nite-lites. And again, but more thoughtfully, frowningly, "My future . . ."

Eh? said Korath, unable to read Jake's mind, because as yet his thoughts weren't fully formed.

"Past and future!" Jake breathed the words out, as his dead familiar began to get the idea.

You intend to look through a future-time door, said Korath. *You'll trace your blue life-thread and so witness your survival . . . or whatever. Which in turn will determine your next step.*

But Jake shook his head. "The future's a devious thing that can quickly lead a man astray," he said. "Harry Keogh rarely if ever risked looking at the future, not in any great detail. But the past is there and there it will stay, utterly immutable. No need to fear what's already happened, for it can't be changed."

Neither can the future, said Korath. *The thought is crystal clear in your mind.*

"For which reason I daren't *look* at the future," said Jake. "For if I did I might try to change it, and the future—"

Would resent and resist it? said Korath.

"Something like that, yes," Jake nodded. "But what is past is past, and it just might help us to know what we're going up against. So roll those numbers, and we'll go down to the gates of that house."

The house? But you'll be seen!

"No, for we won't be there long enough. But I want to know who—how many people—have passed through those gates in the immediate past. And the only place I can find the answer is *in* the past! Proximity, Korath. Having passed through those gates, that's where their life-threads will show up in Möbius time."

While explaining, Jake had used his nite-lites and chosen a spot under the wall close to the gates. And he'd made sure that the fuzzy grey blobs were nowhere near.

It took but a moment, or no time at all, to go to the coordinates that Jake had chosen, and one more moment for Korath to roll the numbers a second time.

Entering the Möbius Continuum, Jake relocated to the coordinates of a past-time door. On the threshold it was NOW, but in the far distance the blue nebula of mankind's birth was brilliantly lit and its myriad neon streamers or threads writhed outwards to the past-time door itself. And one of the threads had a manlike cross section—Jake's shape—where it merged with him on the threshold, seeming to push him ahead of it.

My past, Jake said then, mindful that speech wasn't needed, that even thoughts have weight in the Möbius Continuum. *Only go back far enough, and everything that I've been, that I've done, will be found somewhere along this thread.*

I too had a thread upon a time, said Korath, his deadspeak voice very small.

Which came to an end when Malinari and Company broke your bones and crushed you into that pipe under the Romanian Refuge, said Jake. *If you were to fall through this door, that's where you'd end up, back in the sump, to "relive" everything that has happened to you since you died there, over and over again, forever. But my thread is a lifeline—literally—that we can follow into the past, returning along it to the NOW when I've learned what we're up against.*

Korath was nervous. *Are you sure about that, Jake? I mean, that we can get back safely? You wouldn't be thinking of forcing me out back there . . . would you?*

Yes, I'm sure, Jake answered, speaking with all the authority of the original Necroscope. *And no, I won't force you out. You're not thinking straight, Korath. I need you, tonight more than ever.* And:

Of course, the other sighed his relief. *Of course you do.*

Without giving it a second thought (for if he had he might well have abandoned the idea) Jake launched himself through the past-time door, willing himself backwards down the time stream. The blue threads, the time-trails of mankind, appeared to accelerate towards him, and the single-note *Ahhhhhhhhh* sound of a celestial choir rose in pitch—like a temporal Doppler effect—as he sped into the recent past.

And it was then that the truth became known . . . but such a truth!

Some of the blue threads racing towards him, apparently on a collision course, were rapidly changing colour. A good dozen of them, merely tinged with pink at first, were quickly losing their blue neon tints, fading to azure with carmine cores, and then—

—And then turning a very distinctive, a very uniform red. Bloodred!

At first Jake was stunned, but then he reversed his plunge into the past, turned and sped for the NOW. There, leaving the past-time door behind him, he went directly to the coordinates of his vantage point and emerged, shaken, with Korath clinging to the rim of his mind.

The dead vampire's voice was full of anxiety as he "breathlessly" inquired, *Did you see? But of course you did, for I saw through you.*

"Oh yes, I saw," Jake answered, his throat dry as dust and his own voice harsh and croaking. "We go up against your kind, Korath. Vampires!"

Then for your life's sake—and also for what I have come to know as life, in you—don't do it.

"But I have to," Jake told him, believing that he now knew what this was all about—or some of it, anyway. "I can see it now. This is what Harry left undone. He told me that he'd seen scarlet vampire threads crossing mine in future time. The same thing we've just seen in the recent past. They haven't crossed mine yet, because that's still to come. Tonight."

You can avoid it if you want to.

"But I'm not going to," said Jake. "What will be has been, and in this case vice versa. Without that Harry understood it, he knew he was responsible, that something had survived—that something lived on—from the time of his lost years. This is it. It's what he was doing at the original Manse Madonie: destroying vampires. But one of them escaped his notice—"

And came here?

"—And put himself about, certainly! He *survived,* Korath. Anonymity is synonymous with longevity. He hid himself away in his own evil underworld, a monster taking the shape of a drug-running murderer. But isn't that one and the same thing?"

Castellano?

"The very beast," Jake nodded grimly. "Castellano, and now his men."

Yes, I see, said Korath. *Recently, in these last few days, He has vampirized them as his undead bodyguard!*

"Exactly. We've seen them changing, from human to inhuman. But as yet we haven't seen the reddest thread of all. The boss himself is hiding in that place down there . . . which in itself speaks volumes, tells me that he's afraid of me."

Of course he is, for he has felt your wrath. But Jake, you can't go up against them all. Not on your own. A dozen that we know of, and their master Castellano, and at least one lieutenant . . .

"A lieutenant, such as yourself?" It gave Jake pause. "You think that Luigi Castellano is Wamphyri?"

He's no common vampire, be sure, Korath answered. *Yes, and now I know what it is that has been troubling me so ever since we arrived here. Looking at that house . . . why, it was as if I looked at an aerie on Starside!*

"Then that's all the more reason why we must stop him now," said Jake. "We've forced his hand. He's made vampires. And now, if he survives, he'll put them to use. We can't allow that."

Then let's say our farewells now, said Korath. *For this is surely the end of you—and of me! What? You'll attempt to go into that house, knowing nothing of its mazy ways, prowling to and fro, planting your bombs, and hope to go undiscovered? And a house full of vampires at that, all of them on the alert, as witness these guards in the olive groves? But this is madness, Jake, and you—we—cannot possibly succeed on our own!*

But then:

Jake, said a different voice—a once resolute voice, but now sad, tired, disillusioned—in the otherwise empty deadspeak aether. Zek's voice, which Jake recognized at once. And:

I tried, Jake, said Zek despondently. *I, or we—for there are plenty of others on this side, on your side, who believe in you—we've tried. Indeed the argument is still raging on, but the Great Majority have come to no firm decision.*

"How did you find me?" he asked her.

I know your mind now, she answered. *I was a telepath, remember? And despite that you carry* him *with you, your presence lights the dark like a softly glowing beacon. I'm only sorry I couldn't bring you any better news; sorry that the Great Majority—no longer so great in my eyes—seem intent on letting this thing play itself out to the end.*

Jake could only shrug. "Don't worry about it. In my current situation, I don't see that it matters too much anyway. I mean, what could they do for me except mess me about? My mind's cluttered enough already—with Korath and with you, and with the shattered memories of another, Harry Keogh—without that the Great Majority should get involved. I don't need their advice, Zek, and since that's all they can offer . . ."

But it isn't all that we can offer, said another voice. *And you* do *need our advice, our help, Jake. Yes, even as much as we need you, Necroscope.*

As if he had been tapped on the shoulder, unexpectedly and in a strange, dark place, Jake had started violently on hearing this new, previously unknown, unannounced voice; but in another moment he was more concerned than startled. For it was so brimming with pain, this voice, that it spilled over, and he winced at the unthinkable sufferings it evinced. But physical pain? In a voice from the grave, from one who should be beyond all such mundane miseries?

And now Zek's gloom lifted, and her voice was like a light shining in his mind when she said: *Ahhh! Thank goodness! Someone speaks up at last! And see, you're not alone, Jake. Didn't I tell you it would be so? Here is at least one who is willing to help you, and he is not the only one. Indeed, he's only the first of many. They'll rally to your call, I know they will.*

"Who are you?" Jake spoke to the stranger.

Ask who I was, said that one. *My name is Georgi Grusev, and I was a Russian criminal who tried to redeem himself by working as a spy for Gustav Turchin. Alas that Turchin didn't know what kind of danger he was sending me into, though he would probably have sent me anyway, and I couldn't possibly know the nature of the creatures I came to spy upon.*

"Castellano?" said Jake.

The same, the shade of Georgi Grusev answered, with a deadspeak shudder. *A vampire—him and his man both.*

"His man?"

You may call him a man for now, said the other. *His name is Garzia Nicosia, his master's right-hand "man," yes, but in fact they are both monsters. I saw their faces as they worked on me. At first they* looked *like men, but later . . . they didn't.*

"Worked on you?" (Jake grimaced, for from the tone of Grusev's voice he knew what kind of work that had been, and that it was the source of the Russian's agony even now, so intense that Grusev continued to "feel" it even in death.) "To what end?"

To discover Turchin's reasons for sending me to spy on them. And Castellano also asked about you. But what could I tell him? Nothing, for I didn't even know your name. He asked about someone called Harry Keogh, too, and Alec Kyle, and an organization called E-Branch. And if I had known anything at all, believe me I would have told him! But none of what he asked meant anything to me, so I told him nothing. Which only served to make him and Garzia Nicosia work with that much more . . . enthusiasm.

"So in fact you died for me," said Jake, with something of a catch in his throat. For it wasn't too hard to guess what had happened. Ben Trask must have asked the Russian premier to find Castellano, and Turchin had sent Grusev here to verify the drug-runner's whereabouts.

Died for you? said Grusev. *For you and those others I spoke of? Not really. I died because I didn't know anything* about *you! I was only here to confirm Castellano's whereabouts. But in any case, I'm fairly sure now that they would have tortured, mutilated, and murdered me anyway! It is their nature, after all. So let's get on, for what's done is done and can't be changed. But it can and* must *be avenged! Since it can only be avenged by you, and since you seem to think you're in my debt, I shall hold you to it.*

Grusev paused for a moment, and then continued: *Through all my pain—which will abate, I think, as eventually I erase it from my memory—I have sensed you near, felt your warmth, and listened to your thoughts. And I know you seek vengeance for others as well as for yourself. Ah, but you can't ever know how* many *others, or how very close they are! Oh, they are silent; what else would you expect in a place such as this? But they* remember *only too well, Necroscope, and their loathing of Castellano is no less for all their silence. I tell you this so that you'll know you're not alone in this thing. Not at all. Take my word for it, Jake: once you start on this, you won't be alone.*

Jake believed he understood. Grusev could only mean that he wouldn't be alone in spirit—that all of Castellano's previous victims would be willing him on to win—but he also knew that willpower wouldn't be enough on its own.

"Any solid information you can give me," he said, "you know I'll be glad to accept it."

And Georgi Grusev told him (told him some of it, at least): something of the layout of the house, its sprawling cellars and secrets, and gave him several coordinates he could use to good advantage. But he didn't tell him all of it. For if he had—

—Then Jake might never have gone to work at all . . .

In Krassos it was 1:45 A.M. local time—the small hours of the morning—and Ben Trask was cold now; rather, his mind was *icy* cold following hours of feverish and incapacitating horror. The horror of knowledge, recognition, and acceptance, and of the contemplation of the unthinkable. But finally the fever was off him; Manolis's plan of action was in place, and all Trask could do was wait and think. Think back on it all (but carefully) and try not to go out of his mind again.

The trouble with Millie had been bad enough—no, much more than that, it had been hell on earth for Trask—but then, the rest of it . . . it had all been too much.

The precog Ian Goodly had stepped in and taken over command when that message from E-Branch HQ had sunk into Trask's brain: the fact that Millie Cleary's escort had been attacked, knocked unconscious in the London underground, and the fact that Millie herself was missing. Missing? But that was only the half of it, for Trask had known in his heart of hearts that Millie was now with Lord Szwart!

Yes, he'd gone a little mad, when his only thought had been to be out of there—to get the hell off Krassos and back to London, England, as quickly as possible, and join the search for Millie—but at last the other members of the team had managed to convince him that there was nothing he could do. Then, after he'd realized that he wasn't any longer in any fit shape to run the show, he'd handed things over to the precog.

And just as well, for the worst hadn't yet been. But it had been coming, and in short order. And now Ben Trask thought back on it all . . .

Just after midnight, they had gone out in all three vehicles to carry out a final reconnaissance of Palataki and the monastery. To all intents and purposes the island had seemed dead; most of the late-break tourists had gone home, back to England and Germany or wherever, and the street and house lights in Skala Astris had been almost outnumbered by those of a small handful of fishing vessels on the wine-dark sea. Like the abandoned ghost town in some old Western movie, the last twenty-four hours had seen Krassos turn into a ghost island.

In one way that was a good thing: with all the action that had been planned for tonight, they wouldn't want too many observers—to many "innocent bystanders"—getting involved, which was why timings were so important. For it was all set to happen in the small hours of the morning, when Krassos was fast asleep and the undead were wide awake. It was important that they were all up and about, that none remained hidden away in some secret crypt or other where they might go undiscovered.

The way Goodly saw it—and Trask, too, when he was better able to focus his mind between bouts of red rage—Malinari and Vavara had done a superb job of trapping themselves. The monastery stood on a jutting promontory, and likewise Palataki, with only one access route to each location and no other easily identified exits or escape routes. Both places faced outwards to the sea, looking down from sheer cliffs, and in fact the former had been built on the very edge and was surrounded by deep water on three of its four sides.

The monastery, yes—when the tanker of avgas ripped out its guts, any survivors of the blast would have to come out through the wrecked gates to escape the inferno. There they'd come under fire from Trask (if at that time he felt up to it), along with Manolis, his man Stavros, and Lardis Lidesci.

Meanwhile Andreas would have joined up with the second task force—consisting of Goodly, Chung, and Liz, who waited near the entrance to Palataki's approach road—and would have shared with them his stolen dynamite and instructed them in its use. Then, when Manolis contacted them by mobile phone to order them to action, they would commence their assault on the Little Palace.

This last had been calculated to take a lot longer than the grisly work at the monastery; Palataki had its vast underground system of mine tunnels, after all, and the wooded slopes of the elevated feature where it stood would offer cover to any man or thing trying to escape from the explosions and subsequent small-arms fire. But with any luck Manolis and his team would soon be finished with their business at the monastery, and able to join up with the second group to finish the job at Palataki.

That had been their basic, almost rudimentary plan. But all of it still to come, still some two hours in the future, as the three groups had driven out with lowered lights from the Christos Studios a little after midnight, two of them to carry out a final recce of the target locations, and the third on a thieves' mission to the airport and marble quarry. All of which had been one hour and forty-five minutes ago.

But between then and now, disaster!

And while Trask continued to think back on it, principally he thought of the one thing that no one had taken into account: that while their task *seemed* to have been made less complicated by virtue of the island's rapidly dwindling number of tourists, so had their own eventual discovery. For if Vavara and/or Malinari suspected that E-Branch was here, it had now become a very easy thing to track them down using a simple system of elimination. Out of the few dozen remaining foreigners, Trask and his people were a collective that would have been hard to miss.

Therein had lain the seeds of his near collapse . . .

Because Liz was a telepath, and this was a night reconnaissance when the mentalist Malinari might be expected to be active, she had been left behind at the Christos Studios. At any other time the precog Ian Goodly would have left someone with her, just to be on the safe side. This time, however, he couldn't afford it. Every member of the two recce teams was vital to their success, and not a man of them could be spared. Trask was better off in the company of his closest colleagues; despite that he had been badly shaken, his lie-detector intelligence in such matters was invaluable. Lardis Lidesci was needed if only for his "sense of smell," the fact that he could sniff out one of these creatures almost on sight. The locator's talent was completely indispensable; Chung would know it at once if anything had changed since he'd last scanned the two areas of vampiric infestation . . . and so on. Manolis considered it important that he have a last look at the monastery, just to be sure in his own mind that his plan would work, and of course the precog Ian Goodly himself must be present on the off chance that his unpredictable temporal abilities would allow him a glimpse of whatever was to come.

A shame that the precog's talent wasn't working at the time we set out, Trask thought. But there again, who could blame Ian Goodly? The future was like that, and there was no getting round it. And surely if anyone was to blame it was Trask himself. But at the time his mind hadn't been focussed; his thoughts had been somewhere else; his lie-detecting talent had been knocked right out of sync by the devastating news from HQ. And so what he'd seen—the truth that he'd failed to recognize—hadn't impressed itself upon him until it was much too late . . .

He had been in the back of Manolis's four-wheel-drive as it left the Christos Studios and drove down the side street to the main road through Skala Astris. As the last vehicle in the convoy of three, its dipped headlight beams had smoked where they cut through a fine haze of dust thrown up by the lead vehicles. And as Manolis had turned right onto the main road, then Trask had looked back through the rear window.

His own window was wound down—as were they all, for the night had turned warm and airless again—and a cloud of dust and exhaust fumes had found its way inside. That was why Trask had turned his face away, to avoid the dust cloud. But as he had looked back through stinging watery eyes, so he had thought to see something: two of Skala Astris's elder citizens (as he had then believed them to be), standing with their heads close together in a shop dooway. Two females, yes, in what looked like the standard black garb of Greek peasant women; they'd quickly turned their faces away and drawn back into the shadows of the doorway . . . possibly to avoid the same cloud of dust thrown up by the cars.

And that had been that . . .

Then the lead vehicle (containing Andreas and Stavros) had accelerated and pulled away, leaving the other two contingents to get on with their recce.

In Trask's vehicle, Lardis had sat up front beside Manolis; in the car in front, David Chung was the passenger with Goodly at the wheel (the idea being that the pair would probably work better in tandem, "hitching rides," as it were, on each others' incredible talents).

And so they'd allowed a quarter-mile of distance to develop between the cars, driving first past the Little Palace standing almost unseen behind the pines on its gloomy knoll-like feature, then three miles farther along the coast road to the spot where Manolis had been forced into his precipitous dive into the sea, and finally on to the gauntly looming, shadow-shrouded monastery on its promontory jut, standing sentinel over its terrible secret and the deep dark ocean both.

A mile beyond that Goodly had turned his vehicle around in a lay-by, stopped to get out and wave Manolis down, and the five men (or at least four of them) had put their heads together and spent a few minutes of precious time in voicing their opinions. The fifth man—Trask himself, lost in his own thoughts—had simply gone to the sheer side of the road, to stand looking out over the sea. As for the other four: David Chung, who was probably the most important of them all this time out, had led off:

"Things have changed. Not drastically, but they've changed. Previously, when Liz and I looked at Palataki, we saw—I don't know—a mindless, seething something; life of a sort, I suppose, but what kind of life I just can't say. Maybe it's one of those mushroom gardens, like the one under the Pleasure Dome in Xanadu. But the place did have a vampire caretaker, most likely Vavara's lieutenant. Well, that was then and this is now. As we passed by Palataki tonight I was giving it everything I've got, my full concentration, and while that seething something hasn't much changed, the lieutenant has. That is, he's no longer there—but something else is. I detected a much stronger force, but only very briefly. It was there and it was gone—as if perhaps it had sensed my probe, withdrawn, shut itself down. Vavara? Or Malinari? It could have been either one. But I'm pretty certain that it was Wamphyri! As to whether or not there were thralls in attendance: I don't know, can't say. For this one's aura was so strong it overshadowed everything else."

But as the locator had finished speaking, so Trask had come to his senses and rejoined the group. "Probably Vavara," he had husked then. "Tending her garden. But that's simply an educated guess and by no means a certainty. I'm not sure of the truth of anything anymore."

"But it's a cleverly reasoned guess," Goodly had joined in, "for what would Malinari be doing at Palataki? I can't see that the territoriality of the Wamphyri would allow for that. But in any case there's only one of them there, so it's academic."

And Manolis had added, "Being separated may even have weakened them. I would rather take them on one at a time than both together."

Then Lardis Lidesci had turned to Chung. "David, what else did you sense? I mean, at the monastery. Maybe that'll give us a clue as to who's at Palataki. Myself, I could smell vampires in both places."

And he'd been right, for Chung had answered, "I sensed that same lying outer shield, the facade that we saw before. Perhaps it's there as a permanent stamp of Vavara. But this time I knew what to expect and looked much deeper, and so saw that this so-called monastery is the pits of some weird sort of hell!"

"And its women, once-nuns, are *burning* in hell!" the precog had nodded. "Just the way I saw them."

"Maybe they were," Chung had continued. "Maybe some of them still are, but that's not how it felt. It *felt* colder than deep space, and made my flesh creep. It was as if I'd located an ice-cold cesspit, and they were all wallowing in it. Think about it, if you dare. Everything those dedicated women have kept bottled up inside them all their lives—everything they've denied themselves—it's all out now, and they're revelling in it!"

"Which is about what you'd expect," Trask had nodded. "They are Vavara's now, and there's not one of them who we can save."

At which Chung had nodded his reluctant corroboration. "I'm sorry to have to say it, but I couldn't detect a spark of human decency in the entire place."

Then Goodly had turned to Manolis. "How's your plan looking now?"

"It looks good, and it's thee only plan we've got," Manolis had answered. "That parking area in front of thee monastery, it allows plenty of manoeuvering space for thee big tanker. Anyway, it's far too late to try to change anything now. By now Stavros is halfway to thee airport. Thee tanker is as good as his. When he meets up with Andreas before they return to us, then he will have thee fuse—a stick of dynamite—with which to light thee greater bomb!"

"So that's it," the ever-gaunt Goodly had nodded his cadaverous head curtly. "Now we go back to the Christos Studios for Liz, deploy to our locations, and wait for Stavros and Andreas to meet up with us . . ." (A glance at his watch.) "Which they're all set to do in just a little over an hour from now."

"And on the way back I'll try scanning those places again," Chung had told them. "See if I can get a better reading."

So much for that final recce. Almost everything had seemed to be working as scheduled—at least until they'd returned to the Christos Studios. . .

Trask shivered where he sat in the back of the car, back at the lay-by a mile east of the vampire-ridden monastery, and felt the shivers travel right through his body from head to toe. So maybe the cold wasn't simply in his mind (and soul?) after all but also in his bones, a more natural, physical location. *Which has to be good,* he thought, *for we'll need to be cold—all of us, and in all our parts—if we're to do what has to be done. But me especially. Burning myself up won't do any good, but an ice-cold finger on the trigger may yet shoot a silver bullet or two through the hearts of these alien bastards!*

And thinking back on the rest of it—on the reason why he felt so cold in his body, his mind, and his soul—Trask knew he was right and that he must stay this way until this ugly business was brought to a close . . .

They had returned to Skala Astris in reverse order: which is to say, Manolis had been first away, with Goodly following on half a mile behind. And this time Trask had sat in front beside Manolis, while Lardis occupied the backseat.

But as Manolis had approached the monastery, so he'd slowed down on being met by a blaze of headlights that came from a car heading towards him. And it was only when the other vehicle had swung right off the road, after its headlights turned away from them, that they'd seen what sort of car it was and where it was going. Then, as it turned into the parking area in front of the monastery and kept going, Manolis had gasped:

"Vavara's limo! Thee car that rammed me into thee sea!"

"It's gone in through those great gates," Lardis had cried, from where he gazed through the rear window. "Through the gates and into the monastery. But the windows in front were down, and I saw the driver and front-seat passenger. They were black-clad nuns, of course. Two of Vavara's women . . ."

(And even now, in the lay-by, those words came back to haunt Trask: *Black-clad nuns, of course . . . two of Vavara's women.*)

For it was only then that he had realized how totally he'd come to rely upon his lifelong talent, and how miserably insecure he'd become without it; how badly he'd let the side down by losing his grip on things and letting it slip away. But finally, as the Old Lidesci's words had sunk in, so Trask's weird talent had returned to him at least in part, and he'd known the truth:

Black-clad nuns . . . two of Vavara's women! For despite that he had been dazzled, he'd seen them, too, as the big black limo turned off the road towards the monastery. And in that selfsame moment he had known where he'd seen them before! Then:

"Turn around!" Trask had cried out to Manolis. "We have to go back, right now, and in through those gates!"

"Eh? Are you mad?" But Manolis had slowed down more yet.

"We can't do that!" Lardis had gasped his protest from the backseat. "What, and drive headlong into a hornet's nest? Anyway, the gates are closing even now."

"Then drive on!" Trask had howled, grasping Manolis's arm.

"Drive like hell for Skala Astris, and pray that I'm wrong!"

But he hadn't been.

At the Christos Studios, even as Manolis brought the four-wheel-drive skidding to a dusty halt, Trask had been out of his seat and striding for the chalets. But Katerina, Yiannis's wife had been there almost as if to meet him. Carrying a tray with a glass of milk and a plate of sandwiches, she'd looked more than a little bemused.

"Twenty, maybe twenty-five minutes ago," she'd told Trask, "Liz asked me for sandwiches. I having to work late anyway, so I make some sandwiches for her. Now she is not here. Maybe she takes thee night swim, eh?"

By which time Manolis had come from behind to take Trask's arm. He'd also taken the tray from Katerina, telling her, "You are probably right. But don't worry, I will make sure she gets thee sandwiches. Thank you."

But as Katerina excused herself and headed for the administration building, Trask had suddenly gone weak at the knees. Staring at Liz's chalet, trembling violently in all his limbs, and shaking his head in disbelief, he'd stammered, "The lights are on, and the door . . . the door's open!"

"Try not to think thee worst, my friend," Manolis had tried to calm him.

But Trask had wrenched himself free, saying: "What? Don't think the worst! You bloody idiot! I *know* the worst!

Surely you can see it? They saw her lights burning, and she answered the door thinking it was Katerina! Liz! Oh my God, *Liz*!"

That was when Manolis had grabbed Trask more fiercely yet, and as Lardis came on the scene he, too, had helped. But that look on Manolis's face had been sufficient, warning Trask that if he didn't quiet down and get a grip on himself immediately, the somewhat younger, rock-hard Greek policeman wouldn't hesitate to do something about it!

By then the other car had arrived; it had taken just a few seconds to explain what was happening; they'd all gone in different directions, searching for Liz—

—And not finding her . . .

Half an hour earlier:

It was a little after 11:15 P.M. local time—which is to say Greenwich mean time—when Millie Cleary regained consciousness in a dry, musty-smelling darkness. She checked the time by risking the oh-so-slight motion involved in opening her eyes to slits and glancing at the luminous dial of her wristwatch. This was an habitual, instinctive thing, almost a reflex reaction to dawning consciousness; Millie always checked the time on waking up. But while 11:15 was *when* she came to, and easily ascertainable, the *where* of it was something else entirely.

That she was underground seemed undeniable (Millie vaguely remembered something of her nightmarish descent to this place), but where and how deep underground . . . who could say?

And then, remembering how she'd been taken, and by whom—and on feeling a certain stiffness in her neck—Millie's first truly coherent thought was: *Oh my good God! Don't let it be! Please don't say it's happened!*

But then, as her left hand flew to the slender column of her neck, massaging both sides under the ears and searching for telltale punctures, so a voice came to her out of distance and darkness, saying: *You need not concern yourself, little thought-thief. For it has* not *happened . . . not yet. First I require you to see what I have done, to know what I will do, and of your own free will to acknowledge me your lord and master. Also I will require you to explain certain problematic matters of the outer world, so that in good time I may give them my attention. And finally, when we better understand each other, when I know what you know of this E-Branch and its slayers—who are even renowned to have killed such beings as myself—then I shall make you more truly mine, immortal within certain strictures, and send you into the world to do my bidding. My emissary and plague-bearer both, aaaaye!*

"Szwart!" Millie gasped his awful name into the almost tangible darkness, which to her five cringing mundane senses felt like so much black velvet.

And: *Indeed!* that gasping, rasping, gurgling voice answered in her head. *I am the Lord of Darkness and the Master of Night. But Szwart? Simply Szwart? Ah, no! For I am* Lord *Szwart to such as you, little thought-thief.*

"Where am I?" Millie found herself whispering. And far more to the fearful point: "Where . . . where are you!?"

I am about my business and may not be disturbed. I spoke to you because I sensed that the fear in your mind might kill you. Such a strong mind in such a frail, entirely human body. An odd paradox, is it not, that one such as you—with mentalist powers almost the equal of my own, which I admit are only middling for a Great Vampire—should be so utterly at the mercy of your own darkling fears? Hah! *I suppose that it's "all in the mind," eh? Oh, ha-ha-haaa!* (His mental "laughter" was numbing, and the silence that followed it terrifying, until eventually he continued. *Ah, but your sweet human body* is *frail, and I do not want you rushing blindly to and fro in the darkness, perhaps dashing yourself down from a high place, and so becoming . . . useless to me. As to where you are: you are in just such a high place, and I counsel you not to move too suddenly or too far.*

While Szwart had spent time "talking" to her, Millie's eyes had gradually grown accustomed to the no-longer-utter darkness. Now as he fell silent, she thought to detect movement:

a dimly flickering light source that periodically disappeared, only to come on again but closer. And something else: she began to hear soft footfalls, and a faint, wheezy breathing.

Millie was lying on her right side on what felt like an old mattress. Stretching out her left arm and hand in front of her, she felt soft dirt where the mattress lay on the ground. Straining her eyes to look beyond the mattress's rim, she saw an edge of hard darkness, like a solid beneath the liquid velvet of the upper air, and beyond that sensed a great emptiness. She lay on the edge of some subterranean chasm; hence Szwart's warning not to "rush to and fro" or even "move too suddenly."

But what is this place? Millie wondered, this time guarding her thoughts. The last thing she needed was a conversation with Lord Szwart. And now she unfroze her mundane senses, and called them into play despite their unwillingness.

It wasn't cold, but it wasn't too warm; the temperature was adequate. Behind her, against what felt like a vertical wall of rock, a blanket lay rumpled where it had been thrown aside. For a single moment Millie allowed herself to touch and identify it before snatching back her hand. She didn't know who or what had lain in it.

A cliff in front and a solid wall of rock behind; she must be lying on a ledge. But how high above the floor of the chasm? The flickering light source was closer and steadier now (a candle? It must surely be), and likewise the slow shuffle of feet, the sound of almost asthmatic breathing. The candle was perhaps eight feet below Millie's position on the ledge (she must therefore be some twelve feet above the actual floor), and it seemed to be advancing over a fairly even surface. For the time being, so much for touch and sight.

As for hearing: the place was an echo chamber. It had acoustic qualities. She only discovered that fact now, when for the first time she let herself breathe more easily, without holding it to a whisper, and was at once conscious of the air whistling in her lungs and out through her mouth, its sound amplified by this cavern of darkness. The beat of her heart, too: its thudding was like the steady pounding of some distant trip-hammer.

Moving to the edge of the mattress, she reached out again, her hand creeping to where the floor suddenly fell away. But in doing so she dislodged a pebble from the rim; in a split second it landed with a small clatter, which was followed by a multitude of fading, hollowly clattering echoes. And:

"Ah! So you've come to 'ave you?" A human voice that seemed short of breath, coming from the direction of the candle's tiny flame; a wheezy whisper that yet carried easily in the dark, so that even the whisper had its echoes.

The motion of the candle had stopped; now it came on faster and the footfalls a little heavier. And behind the candle, holding it up, a tortured shape that Millie at once recognized from earlier. Small and humpbacked, this could only be the dwarfish man she had seen on the underground railway platform before the lights went out. The little man who had *put* the lights out. One of Lord Szwart's creatures, obviously.

My only one now, said Szwart in her mind, causing Millie to start, because for a moment she'd let her guard down. *Or rather, he was the only one. But now I have you, too. He's not the most handsome of men, to be sure. But then again, who am I to criticize? In any case, don't be afraid. Wally will not harm you. He knows of your importance to me.*

Your only one? (Millie couldn't help but think it). *What of those women, and Andre Corner?*

Ah yes, those women, Szwart repeated her (mockingly, Millie thought). *And Andre Corner. Hmmm!* (He paused, as if to consider it.) *Well, Vavara's women have served their purpose. And as for Mr. Corner—an "expert" in the minds of men, who couldn't have fathomed mine not even in a hundred years—he is a long time gone. But he was useful, in his way. He guided me to London and told me of older, gloomier places in lightless burrows beneath. But then I discovered this forgotten realm, the most ancient of all Londons, since when I have made it my own.*

Millie shuddered, and Lord Szwart felt it. *You find me ugly, don't you?* he growled then, very menacingly. *My per-*

son and even my thoughts. Ugly, aye. Very well then, so be it! And enough *of this for now! Until I return in person, better for you that you guard your thoughts well, little thought-thief, and be sure not to distract me further. Lord Szwart is about his businessss . . .*

Szwart was gone instantly from Millie's mind. But the hunchback Wallace Fovargue was closer now, and for the time being he was a more physical reality if not an actual threat. Millie had seen the candle's glow vanish somewhere to the left of her dark horizon, some distance beyond her feet, but from the same direction she could still hear Wally's heavy breathing as he climbed some sort of stairway to her level. Now the "candle" came swaying up into view, and Millie saw that in fact it was an ancient oil lamp with the wick turned low. And behind that dim glimmer, Wally himself, like a lumpish monochrome menace from an antique horror film.

With Wally approaching her along the wide ledge, Millie got to her knees facing him. In doing so she felt her frilly blouse fall open, unbuttoned where it had been pulled from her trouser band, and felt the cups of her bra cutting her flesh where they had been lifted up over her breasts to expose them. She quickly adjusted her clothing, tucked the blouse in again, then held up her hands before her defensively, with her fingers crooked into raking claws.

"I warn you," she said, gaspingly. "Don't try anything."

Wally had seen her fumbling with her blouse and had come to a halt. "Er, about your clothin'," he whispered then, his voice surprisingly timid, panting like a dog. "It 'appened when I . . . when I dragged you up 'ere. But you shouldn't be thinkin' I did it delib'rately, 'cos I wouldn't do somethin' like that without . . . without permission. I don't need to, see, 'cos I 'ave . . . I 'ave my pictures."

The senses of sight, hearing, touch, and now smell. And Millie couldn't help thinking: *God forbid taste!* But smell was the most recent sense activated, and it was one that she could well have done without. For the stomach-wrenching stench that wafted from the ex-flusher Wally was one of ordure, London's sewers in full flood. It was even on his breath, carrying to her across a distance of six or seven feet, so that she must literally turn her face away.

As if reading her mind, Wally drew back a pace and said, "I don't look much, I s'pose, and I prob'ly smell a bit rank—but that's the place. It's the gettin' 'ere what does it. The mucky ways you 'as to go an' all the manoeuv'rin' in tight spots. But hey, you don't smell so good yourself, now. You're still pretty though. And nice to . . . to touch."

Touch: the fifth sense, and Wally had crept forward an inch or two on the ledge, his free hand half raised. Millie's vision was improving moment by moment, helped by the lamp no doubt but also of necessity. Now in relative close-up she saw the dwarf's patchy, flaky face, his raw, ravaged scalp, where tufts of hair had fallen from the scabby pink surface under his slipped halo. And:

"You . . . you're sick," she said, without intending a *double entendre* but recognizing it immediately. "I mean, you look ill. And I wish you wouldn't stare at me like that."

"Sick?" he repeated her, letting his hand fall to his side again. "Ill? That'll be the 'epatitis, I s'pose. They told me I might become a carrier. Or p'raps it's the Weil's disease, what you gets from rat's piss. The 'azards of livin' in a place like this. Anyway, 'e said as 'ow I should show you the place—show you 'is 'andiwork—while 'e's testin' the flue. Are you up to it? Can you walk? Oh, an' by the way, I'm Wally."

Millie ignored the hand that Wally again held out to her, stood up, and said, "He? Do you mean Lord Szwart? And if you do, do you know what Szwart is? Do you know he's a vampire who will drink your blood—if he hasn't already?"

"Eh? *Eh?*" Wally started, glanced all about, licked suddenly dry lips, and turned up the wick of his lamp. "A vampire? A monster? Oh, I knows all that! I know 'e can come in the dark, too, an' you won't never see or hear 'im. An' I know that if I think too 'ard 'e knows what I'm thinkin'! Eh? Why, 'e can even speak to me from miles away, 'cept I'm not too smart at such as that, an' can't make 'ead or tail of it. But I knows what 'e wants me to do, okay, an' does it quick like. So will you, if you've any sense."

Millie nodded. "And do you know what he *doesn't* want you to do? That he doesn't want any harm to befall me?"

Wally looked at her slyly, handed her the lamp, and began to turn away . . . then paused and over his malformed shoulder said, "I knows that, too. But there's 'arm an' there's 'arm. I mean, it's 'uman comp'ny what's important, right? An' it's not like a bit of touchin' can do any 'arm, now is it? Touchin', an' a bit of a cuddle, p'raps? I mean, we're a very long way down, lady, an' for you there haint no goin' up again, 'less 'e sends you. By which time you'll be 'is, an' you'll always come back to 'im . . . an' to me. Arter all, it's 'uman comp'ny what's important, right?"

Millie shuddered uncontrollably and said, "Turn up the lamp a little more and let's see the place. I might easily fall."

"Turn up the lamp?" Wally said. "Well, since 'e's not 'ere I s'pose I might. But 'e don't care for too much light, so if you should 'ear 'im comin' you must tell me."

"If I hear him coming?" Millie answered, following after the dwarfish figure where he led on, and looking about for something to hit him on the head with. "I should have thought you'd recognize his approach sooner than I."

"Two 'eads work better than one," Wally answered. "And mine haint workin' too good at all these days." Again his sly glance back at her. "The rest of me's in fair workin' order, though."

They were down the stone stairway and onto the floor of the place, which Millie saw was a vast cave. "Just how did you find this place?" she asked her guide. "How deep under London are we anyway?"

"Me? I didn't find it," Wally answered. "Lord Szwart found it. Don't arsk me 'ow. But men was 'ere before 'im. Romans, I reckon, two tharsand years ago! As for 'ow deep: well, four or five Saint Pauls's Cathedrals, easy."

"Romans?" Millie gazed on a floor fashioned from hexagonal stone flags that were inches deep in dust in places, and close to hand a sunken area tiled in decorative if grimy mosaics; it could only be a Roman bath.

"Look there," Wally directed her, "against the wall. Them statues, to Mithra, Summanus, an' the others."

She held up the lamp and looked. Crudely hewn from stone, a row of ten-feet-tall statues leered down at her from raised pedestals. A sun-crowned Mithra, with a hammer in one hand and the head of a bull in the other, appeared especially sinister. The radiating rays of his sun-crown looked more like serpents. And next to him a figure Millie didn't recognize; it was naked and manlike but didn't appear to haye a mouth. Where its navel should have been, a tapering tentacle stuck out from its belly.

"Summanus," Wally wheezed. " 'E was a rare one. We've never known much abart 'im. But from the looks of it, 'e wasn't much shaped like us."

"Metamorphic," said Millie. "He might even have been Wamphyri!" She turned to her loathsome escort. "You seem to know a lot about these things . . ."

"British Museum," Wally chuckled. "I've read up on 'em, I 'as. As for all the others, they's been defaced. See?"

Millie held out her lamp again, and saw that he was right: the other statues had been hacked about. Their faces were gone along with various limbs, and one of them lay over on its side.

"Some secret society must 'ave 'ad this place," said Wally. "Them Romans—sect members—would come darn 'ere to worship. But they 'ad their fads; their gods came an' went; an' event'ally them Romans went with 'em. This is all that's left."

"And no one else knows this place even exists?" Despite her circumstances, Millie found it fascinating. "And you . . . you've been to the British Museum, to research all of this?" It seemed incredible.

"Plenty of times," Wally answered. "But not durin' hopenin' 'ours, you understand. See, I knows other ways of gettin' in."

"And you know the way up from this place, too," said Millie. "You could show me the way out."

"Could," said Wally. "Won't. 'E wants you 'ere. An' come to think of it, so does I." That sly look was on his face again as he took a step closer. Millie backed off until the backs of her knees struck against something and she sat down . . . on a raised slab of cold stone.

"That's a sacrificial dais, that is," Wally grunted, and he was speaking low, no longer wheezing. "Them Romans did a bit o' that, now an' then. 'Specially in a secret place like this."

"Yes," she gasped, quickly standing and putting the massive slab between them. "I can see how they might have. But tell me, why doesn't anyone know this place is here?"

Wally shrugged. "What good is a secret place that everyone knows abart? An' it was a long time ago. Since then, all kinds of landslides, small quakes, collapses. I was a flusher—been all through the underworld, I 'ave, every sewer an' tunnel an' waterway—an' I never found it. But Szwart, er, *Lord* Szwart, 'e 'as a thing for deep, dark places. An' they don't come much deeper or darker than this."

He had begun edging round the sacrificial slab towards her when Millie noticed something: a strange, flickering glow from a place where the cave bottlenecked under a natural rock arch. And as Wally reached for her—as for the first time she noticed the great width of his shoulders, and his hugely muscled upper arms—she said, "Perhaps that's Szwart coming now."

"Eh? What?" Wally literally danced in sudden fright, twirling like a grotesque ballet dancer, his head and eyes jerking this way and that.

"That light," said Millie. "From beyond the arch there."

"Eh?" Wally panted, his breath coming in foul wheezy gasps again. And then, with a sigh, "Oh, that!" But the sly look was gone now as he said, "Come on, then, an' I'll show you. Arter all, 'e said I was to show you what 'e'd 'fashioned' darn 'ere. Me, I'd 'ave said 'grown,' but 'e said 'fashioned.' "

Following the little man to where the hexagonal flags gave way to dry, crumbly earth, and passing under the natural arch, Millie saw what Lord Szwart had "fashioned."

She no longer needed the oil lamp (but held on to it anyway if only as a weapon) for Szwart's garden had its own illumination: a blue bioluminescence covering an area some twenty feet in diameter in the even greater cavern beyond the archway. The light was given off by what was growing there, in that sunless loam half a mile under London: a subterranean garden of black, vampiric fungi. Black mushrooms clustering there, their domes glistening with what looked like sweat; their distended gills heavy with spores. Deadspawn, as E-Branch had come to term it!

But while the mushrooms were rooted in that lifeless soil, it couldn't possibly be the source of their nourishment. Then, when Millie saw what was: that pair of black, hooded garments, nun's robes, habits, lying crumpled to one side where they had been strewn with a small pile of undergarments . . .

. . . For a moment her mind went blank, so that she scarcely heard what Wally was saying to her, or to himself, in a small, awed voice. " 'E reckons as 'ow they don't really need to feed," murmured the little hunchback, "but that this lot will be just like mother's milk to her babies, an' their issue will be that much stronger. As for meself, what would I know? I says as 'ow 'e's probably right. But Gawd, haint it a mess?"

And Wally was right, it was a very terrible mess indeed . . .

22
Jake—His Call is Answered. E-Branch—The Assault on the Monastery.

SCARCELY ABLE TO ACCEPT THE EVIDENCE OF her own senses—not *daring* to believe her eyes—Millie's hand flew to her mouth. Stifling a scream and suppressing the rising of her gorge, she stared in horror first at the pile of discarded clothing, then at the fungi, but especially at that bloating mushroom garden, and prayed that she wasn't going to pass out again.

Only an hour or two had passed since Millie had seen these terrible women in a London tube station. It could only be Lord Szwart's incredible metamorphic power, something in his monstrously alien nature, that accounted for such as this in so short a time.

For now, in the middle of the cluster, Millie saw a mound or tangle of pale, throbbing, pinkish blue flesh! *Human* flesh! A rounded thigh was clearly discernible, and a slack face with one eye closed while the other stared vacantly; also a lolling breast, with its large nipple standing weirdly erect!

And in and around those slumped not-quite-corpses, a writhing nest of protoplasmic conduits—bloodily pulsing, external arteries of monstrously mutated flesh—was siphoning nutrients from this fresh human compost, and feeding them in a thin spray to the dead soil and so to the deadspawn mushrooms. The living, beating hearts of these once-nuns were pumping out the liquids of their own bodies!

"God!" Millie gasped then, as she felt her senses begin to slip away. But Wally caught her, held her up, led her stumbling to a boulder and leaned her against it.

And as he took the lamp from her and lifted it high: "Listen!" he said, cocking his head on one side. *"Listen!"*

"What?" said Millie sickly. "What?"

"The flue," said Wally. "E's finally got it open. A passage to the overworld, for the wind to blow, an' carry 'is plague to mankind. That's 'ow 'e says it'll work, anyway."

And now she could hear it—a wind coming up, as if out of nowhere—and see it, too, in her mind's eye: a flue, a shaft, an ancient chimney to the overworld, now unblocked by Szwart to create a draft and carry his deadspawn up into the world of men . . . into the heart of London!

Resilient lady that she was, finally Millie's legs couldn't any longer support her. She remained conscious, but only barely so. She felt the hunchback half-dragging and half-carrying her, back into the lesser cave. But massively built as he was, still it took time. Time to get her up onto the slab, not as a sacrifice, no, but as a sex toy; time to fumble her blouse open, and wrench her bra loose, and time to lift her lower body, yanking her trousers and panties down to her ankles, thus exposing her to the lamplight and his own bloodshot eyes.

And there he stood in all his triumph, masturbating wildly, and mumbling, "Better than pictures! Much better than any dirty fuckin' pictures!" But why play with himself when, for the very first time in his life, he could be into a real woman? Szwart's orders were entirely forgotten now, as Wally dragged Millie to the end of the slab, opened her thighs and got between them.

Millie knew what was happening; looking into Wally's warped mind, she *knew* he would do it!

But as he leaned over her and as one hand slid under her: *Ah, no, my son!* came that voice in Millie's head—and also in Wally's. She knew it from the way he suddenly stiffened, his hands jerking back from her. And as finally she forced her eyes to focus, she saw what Szwart did to him.

That great head with its crimson, burning eyes! That night-black shape standing there, silhouetted in faltering lamplight! That outstretched arm and hand—or was it a hand?—reaching for Millie's tormentor, hovering over his misshapen back.

For a single brief moment it *looked* like a hand, and then didn't. For incredibly its digits had reshaped themselves and melted into a two-pronged claw! And while it was fluid one moment, that crablike claw, in the next it was plated with blue-gleaming chitin, with one sharp stabber and one serrated cutting edge. And finally:

My son, Szwart gurgled, *I treated you fairly and have been good to you. I, Szwart, who am not much known for my goodness, have been good to* you *as none before me. But* you . . . *have been bad. My orders are for obeying, my son, and he who cannot obey them cannot live with me. For the miserable thing that you are you have served me well, but your service is now at an end . . . in one respect, at least. Ah, but the garden which I have made also has its needs, especially now that the way is opened . . .*

"No!" said Wally, just once, as the claw descended. Millie heard a rending *schluck!* sound, and, as Wally was dragged away from her, the crunch of his malformed backbone being severed.

The last thing she saw before fainting was the great black shadow moving away, dragging Wallace Fovargue after it towards the blue-flickering archway . . .

As fate would have it, Jake Cutter's assault on Luigi Castellano's principal residence and headquarters in Sicily commenced only a few minutes before E-Branch's two-pronged attack on the Krassos monastery and the Little Palace east of Skala Astris.

"I want to do the cellars first," Jake told the dead Russian, Georgi Grusev. "The way I see it, what with these vampire bodyguards patrolling the grounds of the place, the last thing Castellano will expect is an attack from within, and certainly not from below. And anyway I want to level the house, bring it right down to the ground. You've told me the cellars are extensive? That's good, for when the walls start melting the entire house should go down—what's left of it."

Ah! said Korath, seeing what was in Jake's mind. *Then you intend to follow my advice after all. You'll plant your plastique bombs* outside *the walls of the house.*

"Now that I know what we're up against, that has to be the safest way," Jake answered, nodding absently as he trained his nite-lites on the house in the olives and took one last, calculating look at it. "But the thermite must come first, to make sure it gets good and hot in those cellars before the bombs go off all at the same time. That way, when the house implodes, I can be sure of reducing it—and everything in it—to so much smoke."

And Grusev came in with: *But will your thermite charges—just three of them, as I understand it—be sufficient? Those cellars* are *fairly extensive. I was given a guided tour of the place before they got to work on me, and I can assure you it's a warren down there, easily as spacious below as it is above.*

"There's heat and then there's heat," Jake answered. "I've seen this stuff in action, as used by the Australian military, and this is *real* heat! Just an ounce of this stuff in the nose of an armour-piercing shell will scour out a tank, set off its ammo, and weld its turret shut. And when it's cooled down, you won't even be able to find the crew. Twenty-first century warfare—*ugh!* Which reminds me I'd better leave the other stuff, the plastique, right here for now, in case of accidents." And he took his prepared bombs from the bag and placed them carefully on the ground.

You've convinced me, said Grusev.

But not me, said Korath. *What if Castellano has positioned some of his men down there? I mean, what if he's there himself—for whatever reason?*

"I can't see it," said Jake. "He may well have lookouts at the windows, but surely he won't be looking inwards? And if he or some of his creatures *are* down there . . . so what? We can be out just as quickly as we're in."

Now see how heavily you rely on me, said Korath.

"But not nearly as heavily as you rely on me," said Jake. "Or rather, on my continued existence."

Korath offered a deadspeak shrug. *So, since there's little to gain in arguing the point, I suggest we get on with it.*

Jake spoke to Grusev. "You told me there's a big storeroom down there for all kinds of designer- and micro-drugs?"

Yes, the Russian answered. *Three billion dollars' worth, as Castellano boasted when he showed it to me. Of course he could afford to, because he knew—or thought he knew—I wouldn't ever be talking to anyone about it.*

"Right," said Jake. "So we'll start there. And then, if for some reason we're not a hundred percent successful, still we'll know we've hit this bastard in the second-best place—his wallet!"

There was nothing left to be said, so Korath set the Möbius equations scrolling down the screen of Jake's mind again, and a moment later Jake conjured a door and stepped through it. Then, homing in on Grusev's coordinates, he (or they) went there—

—Into the darkness of Castellano's cellars.

Feel for the wall on your left, Grusev advised. *You'll find a shoulder-high light switch.*

"Got it," Jake whispered, switching on the lights. But what he didn't know was that as well as making an electrical connection, he'd also broken one.

And in the house overhead:

"Luigi," said Garzia Nicosia, as a red light began flashing on a security display panel in Castellano's study. "Something's wrong downstairs, in the cellars . . ."

"Oh?" Castellano glanced up from a pile of paperwork on his desk. "So some clumsy fool has managed to trip a switch. Who do we have down there?"

"That's just it," Garzia answered, checking the panel again. "Nobody's down there. Not in the storeroom, and not anywhere in the cellars. No one that *I* have sent down there, anyway!"

Castellano took a sharp breath, stood up, and leaned forward in that mantislike way of his, with his knuckles turning white on the desktop where they took his weight. For a second or two he remained in that position, glaring at nothing in particular, apparently listening for something beyond Garzia's range. Until at last his eyes focussed and turned blood-red. And:

"Ahhh!" he hissed. "As I have sensed him before, so I sense him now but closer than ever. It's our ghost, Garzia. Or rather E-Branch's ghost, Jake Cutter, who comes and goes as sly as . . . yes, even as sly as a vampire, without leaving a trace. Ah, but this time he's been caught out by a simple gadget. Come—come quickly now—and bring grenades!"

"Grenades?" Garzia's jaw fell open. "But what of the damage they'll cause? And why would you need them anyway? If he's here he's trapped, and he's only one man!"

"You'll never learn, will you, Garzia?" Castellano growled, loping out from behind his desk. "He's one very dangerous, very *deadly* man! As for damage: he's done enough of that already. If it means we get him, we can afford the loss. And now we'll find out who is the deadliest, this Jake Cutter or Luigi Castellano. So bring two of our men, Garzia, and grenades—stun grenades, for I want this man alive—and meet me in the cellars. But be quick, oh-so-quick, before this crafty Jake Cutter fashions his own brand of hell and slips away again . . ."

In the cellars, Jake was almost finished. The thermite charges were fitted with six-minute-delay fuses, and with ample time to move from room to room without invoking the Möbius Continuum, he had let Grusev show him the secret doors to several hidden chambers. All of these had low, vaulted ceilings supported by once-sturdy walls or columns, but the stone was old and nitrous, the mortar rotten, and Jake was satisfied that his thermite charges would completely incinerate the place and bring down the entire house—or its debris—into the resultant inferno.

Jake had left his first device in the drugs storeroom, his second in a virtual Aladdin's cave of treasures from the quarry under the Madonie, which Castellano hadn't yet released onto the antiquities or precious-metals markets, and was in the process of planting the third in a room that Grusev had identified as a torture chamber. He might well have chosen a different location for this third charge, but as he had passed quickly through the cellars Grusev had insisted that another vault, adjacent to the one in which he'd been brutalized, should be left alone.

It is a burial chamber, the dead Russian had explained himself, *a mausoleum—the catacomb of the Arguccis, a once-great family—whose occupants have suffered enough of interference. I share it with them, and when Castellano's house comes down we shall be buried properly and forever. However, the Arguccis and I would prefer that our bones were* not *calcined in thermite. If it must be, then it must, but we think there are better choices. This torture chamber, for instance. It is a terrible place, and one that richly deservers to burn!*

Jake had agreed at once, at which Korath had commented:

Previously, you haven't seemed especially respectful of the teeming dead—certainly not of Castellano's henchmen, of whom you so ruthlessly, ingeniously disposed—yet now I sense your reverence increasing by leaps and bounds. Is this an additional effect of Harry Keogh, do you think? Is it possible that you're succumbing to his greater influence, his, er, implant? Just how long do you suppose you'll remain your own man, Jake?

"I don't know," Jake had answered in a hoarse whisper. "But as long as it's Harry's influence and not yours, I don't especially give a damn! So stop distracting me."

All of which were deadspeak thoughts that went out into the metaphysical aether. And despite that as yet the Great Majority remained silent, still they were privy to them . . .

Stealthy as cats, and as silent, Castellano and his lieutenant, Garzia, accompanied by two vampire thralls, had descended a central staircase into the cellars. Now, as Jake Cutter yanked the ring-pull activator on the third thermite charge and backed off from it, they heard the echoes of his movements coming from the torture chamber.

What they *didn't* hear was Jake's deadspeak, as he told

Korath and Grusev: *That's it, the last charge is set, and the others have been fermenting for maybe two and a half minutes now. Three more and this place will start cooking—and there'll be no stopping it.*

But while Jake's deadspeak went unheard, his movements were more than enough to advise Luigi Castellano of his whereabouts. And with a finger to his lips, cautioning his creatures to silence, the Sicilian master vampire accepted a stun grenade from Garzia, armed it, and without pause lobbed it through the open door into the torture chamber.

On the point of asking Korath to display the Möbius equations, Jake had heard the ch-*ching* as Castellano armed his stun grenade. Momentarily frozen, paralysed, he saw shadowy figures at the doorway, how they snatched themselves back out of sight . . . *and* out of danger!

"Korath!" Jake cried out loud—

—Just a split-second before the grenade went off!

By then the numbers were rolling down the screen of Jake's mind again, but too late to do anything about it. Indeed, even the *thought* of doing something caused the equations to disintegrate, flying apart on the rim of Jake's temporarily blasted mind.

He had heard the clatter as the grenade landed and bounced, and he'd actually managed to dive for cover behind a benchlike device that looked menacingly like a rack. But that was as much as he'd achieved before the blast.

Not designed to kill, the stun grenade hadn't produced much heat except in the immediate vicinity of the explosion. But of blinding light and deafening sound there'd been plenty—enough to disassociate, disorganize, and deaden the mind of any normal man of flesh and blood. And Jake Cutter was no exception. With fresh blood in his ears and nose, curled in the foetal position, he cradled himself in the smoke-filled chamber, listened to the gonging in his head, tried to stop the starbursts from blooming behind his eyeballs, and simultaneously attempted to make sense of Korath's hastily reconstituted equations; all to no avail.

And following fast in the wake of the explosion, Castellano and his creatures were into the room, falling on Jake and dragging him to his feet.

Holding a handkerchief to his mouth, Castellano glared redeyed at Jake where he sagged between a pair of vampire thralls, his head lolling stupidly. "So then, Mr. Jake Cutter, we've met before, you and I. But this time I know what you are, and there are questions you must answer; not least how you managed to get in here. Garzia, it seems to me this is your area of expertise. You will supply the incentives, and I'll ask the questions."

"The lights are shot," Garzia coughed and waved a cloud of smoke away from his face. "The blast. I'll light a torch."

Light flared as he thumbed a cigarette lighter and lifted its steady flame to an oil-drenched torch in its wall bracket. But as the smoke began to clear and the torch came sputtering alive, Garzia gasped and pointed at the thermite charge where Jake had planted it beside the wall. A thin curl of smoke was drifting up from its haversack container.

"What?" Castellano snarled then. "What?"

"Bomb!" Garzia shouted. "That's its fuse burning!"

"You English *bastard*!" Castellano brought Jake a stinging, backhand blow to the face, which did nothing to help clear his head. And turning to his lieutenant, "Get rid of it," the Sicilian said. "It must have a long fuse else this saboteur would have been out of here by now. So into the old well with it. It can't do much harm down there. The blast will be contained."

But the ancient well, a walled shaft almost a hundred feet deep, was in another room, and the "bomb" was smoking. Looking at it, Garzia blinked. Then he went for it, reached towards it . . . and shrank back. He reached for it again, and again shrank back. "Luigi, I . . . I can't do this!" he gasped, his eyes bulging and his face twisting in the flaring torchlight. "I can't . . . I mean I can't . . . *I just can't do it!*"

"You fucking idiot!" Castellano howled. "Do you want it to explode!" But of course that's exactly what Garzia didn't want it to do, not while he was standing beside it.

"You two," Castellano yelled at the men holding Jake.

"One of you do it. There's big money in it for the man who does it." They scarcely moved, except to shuffle their feet and glance at each other. For a moment Castellano looked as if he, too, might panic. But then he took a vicious-looking gun out of his pocket and pointed it at his men saying, "And there's a bullet for you—for both of you—if you *don't* fucking do it!"

At which point Jake moaned aloud, "Two . . . two minutes."

"Eh?" said Garzia. "Two minutes? You hear that, Luigi? This thing goes off in just two minutes!" He couldn't know that Jake was mumbling about the other charges, and that this one still had three, three and a half minutes to go. But in any case:

"Two minutes?" Castellano snarled. "That's like a lifetime! So *fuck* all three of you worthless, spineless dogs, and I'll do it myself! Just look after this one until I'm back." And snatching up the haversack by its strap, he loped from the room.

Jake's head was clearing, the gonging oh-so-slowly receding "Korath," he whispered. "Where are you?"

"Eh?" said Garzia. "Korath?" He grabbed Jake's hair, yanked his head back, and spat, "What's that? You have help down here? You fucking—!" He lashed out, rocked Jake's head back further yet.

Again the Möbius equations disintegrated, collapsing into a whirlpool of jumbled numerals and esoteric algebra, replaced by pain and a million bilious flashes and pinwheels of light. Held up, pinioned between Castellano's thugs, even if Jake had somehow managed to conjure a door, still he wouldn't have been able to use it except perhaps to fall through it.

But in the back of his mind: *Enough of this!* Grusev's disgusted bark. *What? And you dare call yourselves a "Great" Majority? He fights evil—the worst possible evil—and you would let him fight alone? Well, that's your business, you* cowards, *but never mine. The Necroscope does this for us—he suffers it for* me—*and also for you Arguccis, all lying still there. But Jake has the power and can't use it, because you haven't told him* how *to use it. I can feel it in my bones: my dead flesh cries out to me for action, animation, and life in death. And I for one must answer the call of my flesh!*

Other voices came up out of nowhere. *We Arguccis were never cowards! Nor are we now. All we wanted was peace, and we had it . . . until this dog Castellano came along, defiling us and using our tomb as a charnel house. As for the Necroscope: we feel his magnet lure, too, even as we have felt his living warmth in our endless night. Only let him ask for our help, and he shall have it.*

Jake heard all of this without understanding its real meaning. But as a drowning man clings to a straw, so he knew he had nothing to lose. And:

"Help me," he whispered then. "I don't see how, but if it's at all possible then please, please *help* me!"

At which a massed sigh went up throughout all the deadspeak aether . . .

Luigi Castellano never made it back from the old well. For even before Jake had thought to ask for help from the teeming dead, someone had anticipated his needs, stirred himself up, and was waiting in the shadows. And when Castellano heard the dragging footsteps behind him, and after he had turned in his tracks to see who made them—

—He couldn't believe what he saw!

Some short distance away, the lights were still burning in the drugs storeroom, and white smoke as dense as a ground mist was only now beginning to roll out ankle-deep through the open door as the first of the thermite charges began to cook. Similarly, the device that Castellano carried was suddenly issuing a lot more smoke and starting to feel hot. But still he hugged it to his chest, gurgling and gagging as he took one stumbling step after another, backwards away from the dead man.

A dead, disfigured man, yes! A man who Castellano couldn't help but recognize! Georgi Grusev, lurching from the direction of the Argucci mausoleum! His eyes . . . but there *were* no eyes, just black sockets, with blood dried black on his hollow face; the flattened silhouette of his head, where Garzia Nicosia had taken his ears to send to Gustav Turchin; and his arms—which should have been dangling loose from the shoulders because Garzia had broken them there—now reaching with fingerless hands, reaching for Castellano and with vengeful intent!

Grusev came on, and a wave of heat came with him, detracting from the heat that Castellano felt welling from the device against his chest, which he held between himself and the apparition.

But an apparition? Of course! Surely that was all it could be: a nightmarish hallucination conjured of his own dark imagination. For tortured, butchered, murdered men don't walk—do they? Yet this one did, and behind the Russian came others who weren't nearly so complete or functional, clumping and reeling and even crawling through the thickening smoke!

The hip-high wall of the well was behind Castellano where he stumbled backwards to avoid the stumps of Grusev's terrible fingers. He felt his chest burning and saw that his jacket and waistcoat were smouldering, issuing smoke. The thermite charge was beginning to melt in his agonized hands! He tried to throw the device from him—throw it at Grusev—but it was sticking to his chest, fusing with him.

Finally, as Castellano began to scream, Grusev's mutilated hands reached him, pushing him backwards to where his backside struck the wall. The Sicilian's legs stopped, but his top half kept on going. And as he lost his balance, turned upside down, and fell shrieking into the well, Grusev's blackened, protruding tongue came unglued from the roof of his mouth to issue a gurgled farewell:

"Burn, you filthy, loathsome thing!" he said.

And then, slowly and deliberately—as Castellano's screams rose to the pitch of a whistling steam kettle, and quickly died away—the dead man turned and went stumbling back towards the mausoleum. And behind him the obscene mouth of the well belched smoke and heat, and the rancid steam of a boiling vampire . . .

Back in the torture chamber, Garzia and the two vampire thralls had heard Castellano's scream. Jake heard it, too, where he was fighting desperately hard to pull himself together, in the sure knowledge that at any time now the temperature would suddenly rise by a hundred, a thousand, and then ten thousand degrees.

"That sounded like Luigi!" said Garzia, his face a pallid skull-mask where he held Jake's head up by his braid, sniffing at him like a rabid dog. "Your friends got Luigi!" Taking out a knife, he showed it to Jake. "If Luigi's gone, then I'm the new boss, the next in line. But unlike him, I won't be wasting time fooling about with you."

"Garzia," said one of the thralls, "if you're the boss it's time we were out of here. This place is getting hot, filling up with smoke. We'll be lucky to find our way out . . . that's if we don't get blown apart trying!"

"You're right," said Garzia. "We daren't wait any longer." And to Jake: "What kind of bomb was it anyway?"

"Thermite," said Jake, able to see and hear at last. "They were incendiary bombs—all *three* of them. And I think you've left it too late!"

"Too late for *you,* for sure," said Garzia, making ready to draw his knife across Jake's throat.

But: "Garzia!" The thralls shrank back, let go of Jake, and one of them pointed a trembling hand at the smoke-wreathed doorway.

Garzia looked and saw something—saw a stream of rotting, crumbling somethings—that came walking, crawling, and flopping through the smoke that was now spilling into the chamber. Their cerecloth garb was falling from them in wormy shreds and tatters, and pieces of *them* were falling, too, crumbling apart under the stress and strain of unaccustomed movement. But like the mummified figures that shed them, even these fretted limbs didn't lie still but kept right on coming!

"Agh!—aghh:—*agghhhh!*" said Garzia, the knife falling from his numb fingers, as the long-dead Arguccis closed on him and his vampire thralls.

And Jake, as he backed away, couldn't believe what he was seeing—or what he was hearing—as the dead men told him: *Go now, Necroscope. There's no more work for you here. Your vendetta, and ours, is over. But remember this night, and never let it be said that the Arguccis were cowards.*

Jake's flesh crept on his arms and back; his hair stood up as if electrified; his jaw fell open and his eyes bugged. This impossible thing that was happening here . . . *he* was its author! He knew now what a Necroscope was—knew what it was that Trask and E-Branch hadn't been able to tell him—knew *precisely* what those esoteric skills were that they had been hinting at.

Necroscope: not *just* a man with the power to look into the minds of the dead and talk to them, but one who can raise them up from their very graves. And he was it, and he had done it!

A wall of heat came blasting in through the doorway. Those Arguccis closest to the door burst into flames, and still Jake stood there, backed up against the far wall as if pinned there, stunned by the knowledge of what he was and what he had done.

He saw the leading Arguccis converge on Garzia and his men—saw the shrieking three dragged under and buried in ancient, desiccated flesh and nitre-clad bones—and despite the heat he felt his own blood freezing in his veins.

Until suddenly: *Jake!* Korath was shouting in his metaphysical mind. *Get out of there! Here are the numbers, the Möbius equations. Can't you hear me? Can't you see the numbers? Use them, Jake, and make a door! Your time is up!*

And as a mass of liquid stone and jumbled bones came seething through the doorway like so much lava—which it was, of a sort—Jake accepted the equations and conjured a Möbius door. And not a moment too soon. For even as he half-staggered, half-fell through it, so the temperature throughout the cellars shot up as if someone had opened a different door entirely, a portal to hell!

Then he was out of there, and through the Möbius Continuum, and back to his vantage point on the rising ground south of the doomed house . . . where he emerged in the cool of the night, and promptly sat down with a thump.

But we're not finished yet, Korath told him, almost as much in awe and horror of Jake as Jake was of himself. *There's still the plastique, the house itself.* And:

Don't leave the job half finished, Jake, said Georgi Grusev. *Don't we deserve a proper grave, the Arguccis and I?*

Jake looked through his nite-lites. A half-dozen grey-blob figures were fleeing from the house, which itself had become a shimmering grey mass in the crosshairs of the thermal-imaging lenses. Castellano's vampire thugs were getting away, escaping into the cover of the densely grown olives. And Jake knew that Korath and Grusev were right, he had to finish the job. But:

"I . . . I can't see how I can deal with the ones who've got out of there," he said. "But as for the house, that has to go, yes."

Jake's plastique bombs were already rigged with detonators. Setting two minutes on each device, he activated the timers and took the Möbius route back down to the house.

Streamers of white smoke were belching from the open doors and geysering from the chimneys now, and the windows all splintering from the pressured heat within. In very short order Jake planted his bombs at the bases of the front and back walls, and at one major end wall. The remaining end wall was of recent and far weaker construction, part of a modern extension that probably housed the boiler room and generator. Jake was sure that it would be destroyed along with the more fortresslike building.

All done he stood off, and saw that he needn't have worried about the escapees. For Castellano's remaining vampire soldiers hadn't gone any further than the ancient olive groves . . . *where for more than fifty years their master had been burying many of his victims under the grotesquely twisted roots and branches of those hideously nurtured trees!*

All blackened leather and gleaming white bone, these nightmarish, lurching, long-dead cadavers, too, had answered Jake's call, levering themselves up from their shallow graves to herd the terrified vampire mobsters back toward the burning house.

And their timing was perfect, for the two minutes were up.

Jake was near the gates, sheltering in the lee of the high stone wall, when the house went up or inwards. But even before that final, colossal, triple ex- or implosion, the place had been ablaze and beginning to slump down into itself, its buckling walls slowly settling into the cauldron of the cellars.

Caught within a few yards of the simultaneous detonations, the last members of Castellano's vampire mob were ripped apart, literally disintegrating in a blast that threw the material of the house inwards and upwards, creating a mighty mushroom stem that rose into the sky, and a furious wind that rushed outward to flatten the closest of the olives. The ground shuddered and the flash of light was blinding, the explosion senses-shattering, as the house ceased to exist. And when the echoes stopped coming back from the hills, then Jake looked again.

Not that there was much to see: just a vast flattened area where the place had been, and tons of hot dirt and rubble spattering down out of the sky, and geysers of steaming, lavalike stuff spouting up volcanically from the surface of the quaking slag . . .

"Done," said Jake then. "But how well done? Did anyone get away into those olive trees?"

There's a way to find out, Korath answered "breathlessly" in Jake's mind.

In the Continuum they looked forward through a future-time door at Jake's blue life-thread winding its way into a life as yet unlived. But in the immediate future there were no scarlet threads.

It seems we got them all, said Korath with a grateful deadspeak sigh. *In all that blue, I can't see a trace of red.*

"Not in this location, anyway," said Jake. "It appears the Arguccis were correct: my vendetta is over now. But as for your problem—and E-Branch's, and the world's at large—well, that remains to be dealt with."

His comment might well have been an invocation. For as Jake emerged from the Continuum back at his vantage point to collect his sausage bag:

Jake! Liz Merrick's telepathic cry of terror—a whisper in the psychic aether—coming to him from six hundred miles away.

"Liz!" He gasped out loud, starting and glancing all about, straining his eyes in the darkness to see where she was, before realizing that she wasn't. "Liz?"

Jake! it came again, but much clearer, louder now, as Liz's probe fastened on his. And with it came pictures—as vivid as the reality from which they were plucked—on the screen of his mind; such a whirling kaleidoscope of surreal scenes and sensations that Jake could scarcely accommodate them. And all of this from Liz, a good "receiver" but an alleged amateur when it came to "sending," except that with Jake she had this rapport. *Thank God,* he thought, *for this rapport!*

Or perhaps not, for the scenes and sensations were at least as terrifying as what he'd just been through, because Jake knew they were part of Liz's reality:

Fire and thunder, and the ground shaking underfoot as in an earthquake . . . a wild flight from searing liquid fire, followed by a dark confining space . . . and in the midst of all of this a terrible female face, as shrivelled and wrinkled as a prune and hideous as hell, glaring, glaring, glaring *through crimson eyes in a demoniac mask of hatred which even the devil himself would be proud to wear if he were a woman!*

It came and it went, that telepathic cry for help, lost its coherency and dissolved away, as the threat that Liz faced overwhelmed her. But locked in Jake's mind as if branded there, the coordinates remained. Then:

Ahhh! said Korath, who in those brief moments had been

more "in sync" with his host than ever before. *Jake!* he cried. *Jake! But surely I know this creature? Indeed, for in all the world—in* two *worlds—there could never be another such as this. Oh, I know her now. It is, it can only be . . . Vavaaara!*

Fifteen minutes earlier, outside the monastery on Krassos:

The night was very still. From somewhere in the dark pines, a Greek owl declared his authority by hooting a single drop-of-silver note, and after some seconds was answered from more than a mile away by a neighbour who was likewise intent on defending his territory.

Nothing else moved or made a sound . . .

Then a low rumble, gradually growing louder, and in another moment the quiet and velvet darkness of the Mediterranean night was shattered by the revving of engines, as Manolis Papastamos hurled his four-wheel-drive off the road and onto the gravel of the parking area, aiming it at the forbidding monastery gates.

With full headlights blazing, the vehicle roared in a ruler-straight line across the open space, until at the last possible moment Manolis yanked the steering wheel hard over to the right, stood on the brakes, and almost turned the car over before skidding to a sideways halt in a cloud of dust some ten feet to the right of the gates. By no means a pointless display or exercise, the swath cut by the car's headlight beams, along with the twin beacons of its red rear lights, had played the part of a laser beam guiding a bomb to its target.

The target was the monastery itself—in whose high windows a scattered handful of lights were now flickering into being—and the bomb was a tanker full of avgas, driven by Stavros!

Some fifty feet behind the lead vehicle, Stavros had driven off the road onto the parking lot's hardstanding, straightened up his tanker on the correct "trajectory" as designated by Manolis in the smaller vehicle, and applied his air-brakes. And as the tanker hissed to a halt, so Manolis went running towards it. Lardis Lidesci and Ben Trask had also left the car and taken up positions on both sides of the gates. Anyone or thing who tried to come out through those gates now would have to fight its way past them. And they weren't in any mood to let that happen.

Back at the tanker Manolis yelled up to Stavros leaning out of the cab window, "Ready?" And with a grim nod, Stavros revved the big engine to a coughing snarl. Yes, he was ready. Six feet from the rear of the powerfully throbbing vehicle, Manolis took out his cigarette lighter and touched fire to the short fuze of a stick of dynamite that was secured to the tanker's fat belly. And then, to be doubly sure, he went to the back of the vehicle and spun the stopcock on the release valve.

Seeing the flare of the burning fuse in his rearview, Stavros rammed the tanker into first gear, drove it lurching towards the monastery's huge gates. Rapidly accelerating and leaving a trail of highly volatile avgas in his wake, he waited until the last moment before throwing the gears into neutral, opening the cab's door and jumping out. Rolling as he hit the dirt, he came to his feet and ran towards Trask, who had stationed himself at a safe distance from the inevitable impact.

As for Manolis: he was running as fast as he could, to join up with Lardis Lidesci in the lee of the massive wall, when the tanker smashed into the gates—

Smashed into them and through them in a deluge of shattered timbers, and roared on across the courtyard, gardens, and cloisters to a head-on collision with the monastery's main structure midway between its rearing towers. The clamour was nerve-shredding as steel met stone, when for several long seconds all that was heard was the screech of rending metal, the howl of a motor gone mad, and the landslide rumble of dislodged masonry falling from on high; so that for a moment it seemed the mission was a failure.

But as the four cringing, crouching men outside the monastery's walls began to straighten up, then the dynamite exploded. And the dynamite was only the detonator for the real thing . . .

* * *

Liz remembered answering the door back at the Christos Studios, then nothing else until she'd woken up in the back of the black limo, to find them dragging her out of the car into the monastery's courtyard; "them" being a pair of incredibly strong women in the garb of nuns. Indeed they were, or had been nuns, and as Liz had shuttered her eyes and feigned unconsciousness, putting out a brief telepathic probe to confirm her suspicions, finally she'd known where she was.

Those terrible thoughts—of lust and bloodlust—coming at her from every direction, and in the heart of it all a brightly flaring candle of innocence, purity . . . but one whose cold calculating glow she'd seen before and knew for a lie!

And so Liz had lain still—which wasn't easy because her neck was stiff and aching where she'd been rabbit-punched—and let them carry her into darkness, into the now unholy monastery, up two flights of winding stairs where their heels clattered on cold stone, and finally into the presence of the awful luminosity, the lying light of Vavara.

There she had been put down on a low bed or pallet, where she'd groaned, turned on her side, and made sure she faced the wall. And when she'd felt a seemingly gentle hand on her shoulder, shaking her, then she'd groaned again—but oh-so-softly—and continued to feign unconsciousness. Until:

"Smelling salts," a sweet but authoritative voice had said, the voice of the lying luminosity speaking to her thralls. "Go, fetch smelling salts—no, wait! One of you stay, tell me about her: who she was with, how many, and where they are now."

And when Vavara had heard the details—or as much of them as her informant knew—then: "So. It must be this E-Branch of which Malinari spoke. Malinari the Mind, aye—the treacherous, lying dog! No wonder he up and ran! And I was right: he *knew* they were here, and so ran off, leaving me to fend for myself. But they are only seven now and I have this one. Will they dare attack me, knowing that she is mine? I think so, for Malinari warned me that even as we are ruthless, so is this E-Branch . . . in which case I must prepare. So go now, and gather the women down to the cloisters, where I shall speak to all of you together."

Then, as Vavara's thrall had hurried out and her footsteps came echoing back from the stairwell, that hand again on Liz's shoulder, but no longer gentle—whose touch had been as much a lie as Vavara's bell-like tones—and the vampire's coarsely whispered, "And as for you, my pretty, my oh-so-pretty: when I return we'll talk. For pain is such a wonderful stimulant, and I know that it will loosen your tongue . . . but only *loosen* it, mind you, letting you keep it awhile longer at least. Ah, but while a tongue is requisite to coherent conversation, lips are not. What midnight lover will want you then, I wonder, when in the dark his lips meet nothing but gums and teeth and hardened scar tissue?"

Then she'd moved away; Liz had heard the door closing and a key grating in the lock, and for the first time since regaining consciousness she'd been able to relax the mental shields that, in close proximity with Vavara, she'd kept firmly in place.

After that, she had been up and about in a moment. From the barred window she had looked down on the courtyard, where after what seemed an age she'd seen flitting shapes emerging from the central and tower structures, gathering in the cloistered areas under laden fig trees and flowering bougainvillaes. A beautiful setting for a hideous congregation. And Vavara's voice—like a chime of small bells—floating up on the night air.

She had told them what to expect: no mercy, and had gone on to describe their duties if they desired to survive—how they must kill, slake their thirst, take no prisoners, destroy their enemies to a man. "Which is what they're intent on doing to you—*and* to me!" she had finished. "I for one don't intend to let it happen. But you . . . must make your own decisions and fend for yourselves. As for when it will be: soon, I fancy. For that dog Malinari has stolen one of mine and fled. Aye, and he was eager to be away."

Then Vavara had lifted her chin, angling her head until her hypnotic gaze locked on the high barred window where Liz stood looking down. And as that flock of once-holy women, now vampire thralls, had begun to disperse, so their mistress had turned in a swirl of black cloak and vanished back into the building . . .

Terrified, then galvanized by the look that Vavara had cast at the high window of her prison, Liz had determined to fight, defend herself when that "Lady" returned. But whatever Vavara's business was below it had taken her some little time, until Liz had begun to hope that she'd been forgotten. Not so, for that was when she'd sensed Vavara's presence and heard once more the key grating in the lock. Then:

The door thrown open! . . . Liz standing there, with a wooden stool in her hands, raised high . . . she had struck with all her strength—at nothing!

Seeming to melt aside, Vavara had reached out, snatched the stool from midair, hurled it away. And: "Would you hurt me, my pretty?" She'd said, making Liz feel *so* ashamed that she had even tried! What—to brain so lovely a thing, so gorgeous a creature? Even to think it had been a sin! And Vavara standing there, all aglow with a beauty that hurt, a hypnotic simulation of purity and irresistible warmth.

Irresistible?

No, I am deceived! Liz had drawn back, sending a telepathic probe to corroborate the truth of it—

—And at once recoiling from the horror at the heart of all that false beauty, the shrivelled, bloodsucking *Thing* that was Vavara!

Vavara had known she was discovered; relaxing her guise and turning to a hag, she'd advanced on Liz, showing her a gleaming sickle-shaped knife.

"For you," that twisted, pitted, leathery-black monstrosity had croaked then. "For your face and beautiful body. But before that—or during—you'll tell me all."

At which there had sounded an angry growling of motors, the shriek of tortured brakes, and a startled flutter and squawking from the nuns down in the courtyard and cloisters. And how Vavara had thrown herself at the high barred window then, croaking her fury and stamping her feet at what she saw.

But her rage had lasted only a moment or so before the survival instinct of the Wamphyri took over. Then, turning from the window—silent now but more deadly than ever—she had fallen upon Liz and aimed a stunning blow at the side of her head! And as Liz had blacked out, so she had thought to hear the sound of more, heavier revving, and a great crashing . . . and whatever it was that was happening down there, it was for now the saving of her natural beauty, probably her soul, and almost certainly her sanity . . .

Ben Trask straightened, stepped away from the four-wheel-drive, which had been partly sheltering him, was aiming his 9 mm Browning forward and edging toward the ruined gates, when the tanker went up and threw him back against the car again. Not the blast, for the wall protected him, but the sheer ferocity of the *sound,* the rush of light and heat spilling out from the gates, expanding across the parking area, and the ground lurching under his feet.

And falling backwards like that he saw a weird thing: behind the wall, like the blooming of some cosmic orchid, a boiling dome of brilliant orange that rose higher than the wall itself, sending volcanic firebomb streamers spiralling upwards and outwards in every direction, in the grandest, most terrible fireworks display that Trask had ever seen. And the weird thing was this: silhouetted against that searing fireball, a flock of great black tattered birds was rising on the thermals, tumbling where they flew, with their blazing pinions outspread, like so many phoenixes reborn in that great inferno! And who could say, perhaps they were born again—or at least renewed, their souls if nothing else—for they were nuns in their habits, and their aerial acrobatics were not sustained . . .

Stavros had been quicker off the mark than Trask. Shouting at the older man to run like hell, he was already in their car, spinning its wheels and kicking up gravel as he made a run from what was happening—

—a wave of molten fire, spilling through the gates and up over the wall!

Trask ran, made a headlong dive, and with his legs sticking out from the passenger's door was carried to safety.

On the other side of the gates the wall was higher. Manolis Papastamos and Lardis had backed off with their hands up before their eyes to shield them from the crisping heat, but they were safe where at last they turned and ran for it, Manolis dragging the Old Lidesci after him. And as Stavros brought the car skidding to a halt, Trask got out and looked back.

To think he'd thought it possible that something might have tried to escape from that! Yet even now, as the fireball shrank back and the monastery blazed, a handful of staggering, burning figures emerged from the gates like human candles in the night. And Trask might have fallen to his knees and prayed for his own soul—forgiveness for what he'd been a party to—if he hadn't first seen them praying for theirs!

Standing there in a semicircle, with their arms held up and open, looking to God in their final moments and hoping He would see them, the nuns prayed—or simply acknowledged, whichever—crumpled, and fell. But in the moment of their going down, even as the feral light went out of their eyes, Trask could swear he saw their smoke shimmering into haloes where it rose up, before a second tongue of fire roared out through the gates to devour them.

The monastery lit the coastal road for half a mile in both directions; a twin-towered torch, it stood tall on its promontory and burned with a vengeance. Within its walls the place was surely a seething cauldron by now. But Trask saw only the nuns where they lay crumpled, their smoke rising up. The precog had foreseen it and as always he'd been right: the future will out, no matter what. Yet, as it now seemed, not quite always. And:

"*Damn* you, Ian Goodly!" Trask sobbed like a child where he leaned against the car to avoid collapsing. "Damn you and your talent and the lying, bitching future to hell!" The last thing he had asked the precog to do, before they'd split up and gone their separate ways tonight, was to look into the future seeking evidence of Liz. Was she alive in time yet to come, or was she gone?

And the gaunt and grey-faced Goodly had answered him, "Ben, I can't be sure. But I think—and I hope and pray—that maybe she'll survive. But where Liz is now, surely the most important question is will you *want* her to survive? And worse still, will you *allow* her to?"

Trask had heard, understood, and shuddered to his soul. But hope springs eternal, and echoing in his mind the key words had been, "I think maybe she'll survive." Those were the words that had kept him going.

Until now . . .

Manolis and Lardis had arrived; as the latter got into the back of the car, Manolis saw Trask's face. "There's no time for that now, Ben," he said. "We've got to move on. This isn't over yet. Thee Little Palace, Palataki, is still waiting for us."

Trask looked one more time at the monastery . . . and Manolis saw him give a massive start as his bottom jaw gaped open. Then the Greek policeman followed Trask's gaze and understood why. A big black limo—Vavara's limo—had come crashing out through the blazing wreckage of the gates and was careening towards the four-wheel-drive!

Three of the limo's wheels were burning. Its roof and hood were badly dented, shedding rubble and large chunks of masonry. Its nearside windows had been blasted out, and a front door was hanging from a single hinge, striking sparks from flints in the gravel where it jounced and clattered. The rear doors were both open, flapping like a bat's wings. And looking something like a monster in its own right—seeming hell-bent on a head-on collision with the stationary car—the vehicle came fishtailing across the parking area.

But no, throwing up a stinging spray of gravel as Trask and Manolis hurled themselves aside, passing so close that its near-side rear door was torn off on the back of the four-wheel-drive, the limo raced on, heading for the road.

"She got out!" Trask gasped. "God damn her, Vavara got out! That can only be the witch herself . . . I *know* it's her!"

And as the big black car went slewing onto the road and the front door tore loose, they all saw that indeed it was her: that nightmare hag crouched over the wheel, her great jaws gaping and her crimson eyes glaring at them. Vavara, alone in that blasted, shell-shocked wreck of a car. She alone had escaped.

"Get after her!" Trask yelled, his hatred buoying him up as he piled into the car. And as Manolis got into the front passenger seat alongside Stavros, Trask grabbed his shoulder and told him: "Now its your turn. This is the selfsame vampire bitch who drove you off the road and killed your pathologist friend. Very well, now let's give her a taste of her own bloody medicine!"

What Trask hadn't seen and couldn't know because no one had suggested it might be so, was that Liz was in the limo's trunk, and that yet again Ian Goodly had been right: if only by virtue of Wamphyri tenacity—the fact that Liz had been indoors with Vavara, who like most vampires maintained a bolt-hole or escape route—she *had* survived.

This far at least . . .

Having heard and understood Trask's harsh, vengeful comment to Manolis, Stavros needed no further urging. Screaming their protest, the gears meshed and the vehicle's tyres churned dust and gravel as he fishtailed it out onto the road, straightened up, and went hurtling after Vavara's black limo.

She had maybe ten seconds' start but wasn't much of a driver, and despite her more powerful vehicle Stavros was soon catching up with her. "Her car is bigger and heavier," Lardis said from where he sat beside Trask in the back. "Do we really intend to ram it from the road? Who will be ramming whom, I wonder? It's a very long way down to the sea, and quite a few sharp rocks to bounce off before you get there."

"The sharper the better," Trask growled. And to Manolis in the front passenger seat: "Can Stavros handle it?"

"If anyone can, Stavros can," Manolis answered, hanging on for dear life as his man wrestled with the steering and took a sharp right-hand bend. Stavros was trying to hug the cliff wall on their right, but centrifugal force slid the car out into the oncoming lane. Fortunately in the dead of the Krassos night the road was empty, and for a mile ahead it was straight before the next series of bends.

A hundred or so yards in front, Vavara was doing no better; she hadn't regained control after taking the bend, and the limo was all over the road. A stream of sparks trailed the big black car where a dangling muffler skittered like a crippled snake.

"Now's your chance!" Trask gripped Stavros's shoulder.

Stavros accelerated, slowly closing the gap between himself and the battered vehicle in front. Vavara saw him coming in her rear view and moved in closer to the cliffs rising on her right. Determined to keep her pursuers from the inner lane, she would let them overtake her, then do to them what they planned to do to her. But she hadn't reckoned on Manolis, three-times champion marksman of the Athenian police force.

"Hold her steady now, Stavros, my friend!" Manolis barked, as he leaned out of his window and took aim with his automatic. Now Vavara saw him, and began weaving this way and that across the road. Then, brilliantly inventive—acting before Manolis could find his target—suddenly she slammed on the brakes!

Stavros recognized the mechanics of the thing: her limo was by far the more massive machine; he would bounce off it, and if he bounced in the wrong direction—

He stood on his brakes, and the four-wheel went into a long slewing skid, coming very close to running out of tarmac on the wrong side of the road—the sea-cliffs side—before stalling and jerking to a standstill. Vavara's limo, however, had slowed but not stopped. Now, stepping on the accelerator, she put distance between. The chase was on again, and minute by minute the time and the miles were steadily ticking away.

In a little while Palataki became visible as a dark silhouette on its knoll perhaps half a mile ahead. "We don't know who or what's in that place," Trask yelled over the snarling of the car's motor. "We don't know what she might activate if she gets there. But we do know she's desperate—and that the other team isn't expecting her!"

"Got you," Manolis shouted back. And to Stavros, "Get right up behind her again, but this time be ready for thee tricks."

Stavros obliged, was assisted by the fact that the road had started winding once more and Vavara couldn't handle it.

And as Manolis again leaned out of his window: "Aim at her tank," Trask yelled.

They were almost through the winding stretch; the last bend was a right-hander; the side road to Palataki was less than 250 yards ahead, when Manolis took a deep breath, held it, and squeezed off three quick shots.

The limo was swinging into the bend, sliding out across the road to the left, when one of Manolis's shots missed the petrol tank but took out the left-hand rear tyre. The rubber tore like paper, the wheel rim sparked where it chewed into the road, and almost in slow motion the limo turned over onto its side, sliding across the road and through a flimsy wooden fence. A moment more and it had nosed down out of view.

"We *got* the bitch!" Trask shouted, thumping Manolis's back as Stavros brought their vehicle to a halt. And even before the car had stopped moving, the Head of Branch was out of his door, running to look over the edge of the road.

Down there, the descent to the rim of the actual sea cliffs was steep but not sheer. Somehow the limo had rolled over again and righted itself, and it was plunging headlong down the rocky slope in a fall that all the small, stunted pines, kindling-dry undergrowth, and the best brakes in the world couldn't hope to halt. Gravity simply wouldn't be denied.

Manolis joined Trask in time to see the end of it. And: "I know exactly how thee *vrykoulakas* bitch is feeling right now," he said. "And I'm glad!"

At the very edge of the high sea cliffs there were several upthrusting outcrops—future sea-stacks, like the ones standing out to sea—where tortured strata had buckled and broken in the Mediterranean's frequent geological upheavals. The limo clipped one of these, spun off, and came to rest with its front wheels over the rim. The *limo* came to rest, but Vavara didn't. Hurled out by the impact, she formed a tattered, spinning kite-shape as she vanished beyond the horizon of the cliffs, and her croaking shriek echoed up to Trask and Manolis for long seconds where they stood watching . . . until finally it was cut off by a far, faint splash. Then:

"Good," Manolis grunted. "Thee water is very deep here. And I do know what I'm talking about!"

"But you survived," said Trask. "And God damn her—she's Wamphyri! She might survive the fall and the water, too!"

"Possibly," Manolis answered. "But nothing we can do about it. There's no way down. And even if there was, one wrong step in thee dark . . ." He let it trail off and shrugged.

"I hope she sinks and sloughs away!" Trask snarled then.

"But meanwhile there's Palataki," Manolis took his elbow. "Come, my friend. Thee time is wasting . . ."

Looking east from Palataki, Ian Goodly, David Chung, and Manolis's Number Two, Andreas, had seen the sudden flare-up on the horizon, and moments later they'd heard the rumble of man-made thunder. In combination, these things were the signal they had been waiting for. And now it was their turn.

Shored up in the knowledge that Trask and the others would soon be joining them, and each of them armed with half-a-dozen sticks of Andreas's dynamite in addition to their more conventional weapons, they had driven their vehicles up the crumbling, overgrown ramp and climbed to the knoll's plateau. There in the grounds of the Little Palace, well back from the gothic-looking building itself, now they prepared for the work of demolition.

Before that, however, the two espers wanted to know exactly what it was they were destroying. In close proximity like this—closer to this place of dread than ever before, and knowing that their presence on Krassos had been discovered and they no longer required to remain secretive or anonymous—now was the ideal opportunity.

"Ah, but what if it's Malinari?" said Goodly. "David, your talent is probably more accessible to him and makes you vulnerable. Mine isn't—at least, I don't think so—so let me use it first, now, before you take any unnecessary risks. Let's for once try to fathom exactly what the future has in store for us, without galloping headlong into it."

"Be my guest," said the locator, with a small shudder. "But to tell you the truth I've already tried, and all I got was the creeps! This place is wall to wall mindsmog. It's in the Little Palace, it's under us, and all around us. But it isn't specific to any one spot, and its source must be heavily shielded. Which can mean only one thing: it's definitely Wamphyri, and probably Malinari. So be my guest—only for God's sake be careful!"

While they talked, the third member of their team, Andreas, could only look on; perhaps he wondered what the two were going on about, but he remained silent. Manolis had told him to do exactly as they said, and that was good enough for him. But the sooner they got some action going the better; this place had to be the last place on earth where anyone in his right mind would want to be, especially doing nothing.

And Andreas, as down-to-earth a man as might be found—but a man who trusted his own natural instincts—was exactly right in his feelings and apprehensions.

The gloom under the tall, spindly pines seemed full of some alien sentience; the three men *felt* watched, sensed unseen eyes upon them. And a sickly ground mist swirled about their ankles, barely drifting aside when they moved but clinging to them, for all the world as if wanting to know them. In a place like this, however, and the espers as preoccupied as they were, the writhing of the mist so suited the scene that neither man recognized its significance.

Then there was Palataki itself, standing tall, gaunt, mist-wreathed, and rotten to its heart and subterranean burrows;

its hollow windows like rows of soulless eye sockets, as if it were the unseen watcher. And the silence like a suffocating shroud—a silence that hurt the ears, because they strained in vain to catch a sound—beneath which nothing moved except the ground mist and the three men themselves . . .

Looking more cadaverous than ever in this fraught setting, in the dappled shade of the pines and the almost luminous glow of the ground mist, Ian Goodly closed his eyes and lowered his head to his chest. And leaning against one of the cars for support, he pressed slender, sensitive fingers to his temples and forced himself to think . . . of absolutely nothing!

Deliberately voiding his mind, albeit temporarily—wiping it clean of everything he had ever known or now knew, emptying it of all knowledge of times past and present—Goodly sought contact only with the ever-devious and unforgiving future . . .

. . . And touched upon something else entirely.

Down in the maze of mine shafts deep under Palataki, Nephran Malinari felt the tremors in the mist that issued from his vampire pores and uttered a long-drawn-out sigh. "*Ahhhhh!* They are here, and much sooner than I thought. Which means that you and I must stop this pleasuring now, for there's work for us."

He spoke to Sister Anna, as naked as a newborn babe—but no longer as innocent—where she sat astride him with her nipples brushing his chest and her backside wriggling deliciously, working at him with her womanhood and moaning her pleasure.

"What's that?" she answered almost absentmindedly, and continued to jerk herself up and down on him, tossing her head to and fro more frantically yet. "There's someone here?"

"Enough now!" said Malinari, lifting her from him. "We have other things to do. There are men up there who would kill me if they could. Indeed, it's possible they have already killed your ex-mistress. But I know a way out, and we shall flee to safety, you and I." It was a lie; it had never been his intention that Anna should "flee" anywhere, but that she'd remain here as his rear guard. And standing he told her, "Now dress yourself while I listen and discover what they are about."

Pouting, Anna obeyed him, and Malinari turned from her and stood still, "listening."

His probes went out, traced a path through his mist to the disturbance, and there found Ian Goodly, the precog, his weird mind empty of all thoughts except of the future. And:

So, Malinari thought. *He seeks to learn the outcome of the venture in advance. A coward, this precog? No, a wise man. But by no means wiser than Malinari. He has emptied his mind until it is blank. Well, then, now let me see if I can put something back into it. Something for Vavara, I think, that greedy bitch vampire who in my hour of need offered me nothing! This way, I take my revenge while E-Branch takes the blame. Then, when the score is even, the scales balanced, and Vavara disadvantaged—*if *she yet survives—I shall find myself a new place in which to start over. But not, I think, in this world . . .*

In short order, as quickly as he could, Malinari transmitted a series of telepathic scenes along his probe, and couldn't help but laugh at the result of their impact.

Up above, Goodly straightened from his half-slumped position and his eyes shot open—but they were vacant, glazed, as if filmed over. Gasping for breath and shaking like a leaf, he threw his hands wide, slamming them up against the side of the car to steady himself.

The locator stepped closer, grabbed him and gasped, "Ian, what is it? What did you see?"

The glazed look drained from the precog's eyes, and blinking rapidly—shaking his head as if to clear it—finally he answered, "It . . . it wasn't the future, David. It was the NOW, and it's waiting for us below!"

"The now?" Chung frowned. "But what is it?"

"It's much as we suspected," the other stood up straighter, subconsciously brushing himself down, as if he'd been lying in something unpleasant. "It was some kind of plot or garden—a spawning site, like the one Jake Cutter destroyed in Xanadu—and there were human remains in it. *God*, it was loathsome!"

"Show it to me," said Chung at once. "Since E-Branch will have to deal with it eventually—even after we've buried it, *if* we can bury it—they'll need to know its precise location. So show it to me now, and when we've brought the place down on top of it, still I'll know where they have to drill to put the thermite right into the heart of that filthy stuff!"

The precog shook his head. "You don't understand," he said. "I'm not the locator, David, you are. Yet I saw the now *and* the where of it! Someone showed it to me, as clear and much clearer than any picture from the future. And looking through his eyes, I saw that thing bloating down there under Palataki. As for who showed it to me—" Goodly's voice shivered to match the tremors in his spindly frame, "—I can still hear his crazy laughter!"

"Malinari?" Chung's eyes went wide. "Are you saying he got into your mind?"

Goodly nodded. "It had to be him—and I must consider myself fortunate there was nothing in there for him to steal! But how to explain it? Why would he want us to see what's festering away down there? It's almost as if he were urging us to destroy it!"

"Perhaps he was," said Chung. "For after all, it's not Malinari's garden but Vavara's."

"Then put it this way," said the precog. "Since *he* is down there, too, why would he want us to destroy *him?*"

"He wouldn't," Chung shook his head. "It's impossible. The tenacity of the vampire doesn't allow for it."

"Precisely," said Goodly. "He *wants* us to destroy Vavara's garden, but he himself . . . he must have an escape route!"

"You've *got* to let me see," said Chung again, urgently now. "Lead me to him, and right now! We have dynamite. If he's still down there, we might even be able to cut him off!"

The precog nodded, and without another word he emptied his mind of all thoughts . . . and the link was immediately reestablished. Now Malinari's vampire mist worked against its author; he was taken aback to feel this deliberate, impertinent, even insolent contact! Goodly's mind, when he emptied it like that, was a mental magnet to Malinari's probes; they couldn't resist it. Malinari saw it as a challenge to his superior skills, and sharpening his wits he waited to see what would develop.

Nor did he have long to wait.

Zeroing in on Goodly's link, following it to Malinari, the locator's very different probe lanced home. He didn't actually see Malinari, or Vavara's deadspawn garden, but he did "locate" them, and knew exactly where they were.

Then, as he felt Malinari's awesome mentalist mind sucking at him like a telepathic black hole, colder than outer space: "There!" he gasped, quickly withdrawing. "I got it. Better still, I got him—*and* his escape routes! But it's possible he got something from me, too, though I'm not sure what."

"You know where he is?" Goodly had pulled himself together now. "Can we reach him?"

"He's there," Chung pointed at Palataki, dead centre. "And . . . and he's down *there!*" Straightening his arm, he lowered his finger to an angle of maybe forty-five degrees. "A hundred feet or so straight down."

"In an underworld of his own," the precog said. "All those tunnels, crumbling mine shafts and caverns. I saw that much at least, when he showed me the garden. The place is as hollow as wormy cheese! But you mentioned his escape routes. Where?"

"At both ends of the place, directly under those cupolas," Chung answered. "Way down below, the stairwells are hewn from the rotten bedrock, with old wooden staircases coming up from the mine shafts and caves to the crumbling basement. Malinari can effect his escape from either end of the building."

"So if we blast those basements and stairwells," said the

precog, "fill them with tons of rubble, he'll be trapped down there." He turned to Andreas, showed him a stick of dynamite. "After you've heard our explosions—coming from both ends of Palataki—then you can take out the midsection. Meanwhile, you wait here for the others, tell them where we are."

Andreas understood well enough. "Is okay," he nodded. "I ready. I waiting." And he held up a stick of dynamite in a tightly clenched fist.

Goodly and Chung set off at once, went loping through the mist—Malinari's mist, entwined with the crawling "sweat" of Vavara's deadspawn—toward the old building, the locator making for one end of Palataki and the precog for the other.

And for the moment neither man found anything odd in what he was doing (not beyond the accepted weirdness of the situation) nor in the way he'd been inveigled into doing it.

While down below Malinari bayed like a moon-crazed hound—but kept it to himself, shielded in his mad mind—as he gave Anna her instructions before setting out along his *real* escape route: the one that would first intercept Ian Goodly's descent, before taking Malinari to Vavara's boat in a cave over the rim of the slumbering sea . . .

23
The Upper Hand—The Nether Regions

IN THE SICILIAN NIGHT, LOOKING DOWN AT THE seething, quaglike remains of Luigi Castellano's razed headquarters—unaware that Ben Trask and E-Branch had carried out a similar, almost simultaneous attack on an alleged monastery on Krassos—Jake Cutter reeled from the sudden knowledge that Liz was in danger.

And from Vavara! Korath reminded him, seeming to relish the thought.

"I have the coordinates," Jake gasped. "I have to go there, now!"

What, and put yourself in jeopardy yet again? And not only yourself but me, my entire future?

"You don't have a future, Korath," Jake answered. "You're a dead thing. But Liz is very much alive. So show me those equations, and I do mean now. She's in bad trouble."

Oh, I agree! said Korath. *She is in the very worst possible trouble, for Vavara has her. And Vavara is Wamphyri!*

"So what's your problem?" Jake had no time for this. "Luigi Castellano was Wamphyri, too, wasn't he?"

Indeed he was, but he didn't know it. He had no one to show him the way. He followed the ways of gangland fools, instead of his true nature. As a result of which he is dead, when he might have been the ultimate master of your world. Vavaaara, *however, is a different being entirely, and moreover she has your Liz—which makes this a very different situation.*

"You've been thinking it out." Jake was becoming desperate now. He sensed something coming to fruition in Korath's incorporeal mind, felt the ex-vampire lieutenant's sudden presence as a real entity and not just as an undead cypher. "All very well and good, but this isn't the time for thinking. We've got to go to Liz, and right now."

Ah! So now it's "we," is it? Korath answered. *Moreover it's the "we" as in you and I, close colleagues in this venture. The "we" as in if and when it suits you, and no longer the "I" that I've been obliged to suffer when it doesn't.*

"What the hell are you talking about?" (Jake didn't believe it. Some kind of contrary argument or word game, at a time like this? Just what did this dead creature think he was up to—or shouldn't he ask?)

Oh, you know very well what I am up to, said the other, his deadspeak voice darker than ever, like the glutinous gurgle of the subterranean sump where by all rights he should have lain trapped forever, and not just his polished bones but his loathsome intelligence, too.

That last thought was Jake's—unshielded and irrepressible as the anger he felt rising within himself—and Korath read it without even trying. Wherefore:

You would have me trapped there still, wouldn't you, Jake? he gurgled. *But too late now for that. For when you needed me, I answered your call. You the master, and poor dead Korath the slave, the obedient genie in a bottle . . . until* you *let me out. Ah! Finally the truth strikes home. Oh* yessss! *You've had your last wish, Jake, and now the genie has the upper hand!*

"You crazy bastard!" Jake raged. "I need those numbers now. What does it matter who has the upper hand? Liz in is trouble!"

And how do you plan to save her? the other sneered. *You, a mere man, against Vavara? Why, you don't even know what kind of trouble Liz is in! Also, you have no weapons: your gun is lost, and your bombs used up. And the most important question of all: How will you get there, those many miles away across the sea?*

"I'll send you back to your sump!" Jake clenched his teeth.

By all means, said Korath. *And let Liz die—or worse!*

"You bastard!" Jake panted, but much more quietly. "Why did you wait until now? You could have done this before."

But not so surely, Korath chuckled. *And never so enjoyably.* And as his chuckling slithered off into the deadspeak darkness: *Make up your mind, Jake.* His voice hardened. *What's it to be?*

"Damn you to hell!" Jake growled. "I'll conjure the Möbius equations myself."

He tried. The numbers came; they swirled, began to form a maddeningly familiar pattern, commenced their mutating, dizzying scrolling down the screen of his mind. But just when Jake thought he had it . . . the formula abruptly fell apart, collapsing to a pile of shattered symbols and crumbling cyphers.

Not so easy, is it, Jake? said Korath.

"You've bluffed me before!" Jake cried.

Indeed I have, but not this time. Korath was very sure of himself. *Before, it was your life that was in jeopardy. And in order to save myself I must save you. Since when I've seen how much you love this Liz; why, she's in your every thought, your dreams, your very heart! So now the boot is on the other foot: in order to save her, you must give me what I want—innermost access to your mind, so fused with you that you may never more return me to my sump!*

Jake found it unthinkable. "You, part of me, forever?"

Korath sensed the refusal on the tip of his host's tongue, and knew that Jake was just stubborn enough to issue it. Before that could happen, however: *Not forever,* the vampire said. *I am not without honour, and I shall hold to our original compact. I said that I did not want* you *to have the power to reject me and send me back to my sump. I did* not *say that I wouldn't go of my own free will.*

"But you also said that we'd be fused." Despite that Jake was shaking with anxiety for Liz, still he was hesitant.

A mere mode of expression, Korath brushed it aside. *Fused only in the sense that we would act as one against our mutual enemies, in perfect and seamless collaboration. But come now, Jake. Time is wasting. Hurry, before it's all used up!*

"And when this is over, you promise you'll get out?"

My word on it, yes. When Lord Mălinari, Vavara, and Szwart are no more—when I am avenged—then I'll return of my own free will to that watery sump and you can lock me out forever.

There was no way round it; even knowing the danger Jake had to accept it, for something told him that Liz was in worse danger still. And so he gritted his teeth, nodded his consent, and groaned, "How do we go about it?"

Simply invite me in, Korath breathed in his mind, like the gasses rising from a swamp. *Simply let down your shields, open your mind, and of your own free will accept meeee!*

Jake could no longer resist. Without further pause, lowering his shields, he opened his mind to its very core, inviting the dead yet undead Thing that was Korath-once-Mindsthrall in. And finally, as he felt that swift cold flow, that nightmarish oozing in the innermost conduits of his being:

Ahhhhh! said Korath . . .

In the trunk of the big limo, Liz had somehow managed to brace herself against the worst of the buffeting that she'd suffered. But when the limo had struck the outcrop at the edge of the sea cliffs and spun sideways, then her skull had made sudden, sharp contact with something hard and metallic, and for a few minutes she'd lost consciousness.

On coming to, and feeling the teetering or gentle seesawing motion of the car—not knowing her situation but sensing that there was no longer any forward motion—she had searched about in the darkness and found a heavy car jack strapped in position in one corner of the large trunk. It had taken a little time to loosen the straps, but after that—aware by then that her movements somehow governed the inexplicable motion of the car—she had set to work. And she was still banging on the curved lid of the trunk near the lock when Jake arrived.

His coordinates hadn't let him down; it was as if he'd been listening to an echo of Liz's cry for help as he'd zeroed in on her. And as he emerged from the Continuum at the rim of the sea cliffs, the first thing he heard was the clamour from the trunk of the black limo, while the first thing he saw was how dangerously the vehicle was perched on the edge of oblivion.

For the space of a single heartbeat he froze. For it was as if he'd been here before, with Natasha. But no, he wasn't about to let it happen again.

It took just a moment to release the catch—and there she was: bruised and awry, wild-eyed and shivering, but Liz for all that. "His Liz," as Korath had had it. She held the car jack to her chest, clutched in her white-knuckled hands, and for a second Jake thought she would try to throw it at him. But then she let it fall as her eyes went wider still.

"Jake?" she gasped. "Jake?"

"Yes, it's me," he said, not knowing what else to say.

"Jake?" she repeated herself, louder now as she reached up her arms to him.

"That's right," he stepped closer, reaching for her. "But Liz, for God's sake stop moving about!"

If he could have seen himself as she saw him, silhouetted in starlight against the dusk of the Aegean night, he wouldn't have been in the least surprised at her expression. He was hot, grimy, dishevelled. He stank of thermite and man-made thunder. And blazing in his charcoal-streaked face, his eyes were just as wild as her own.

She tried to stand up, fell into his arms, and as the car tilted he took her weight and lifted her out of the trunk. The rim of the trunk scraped her knees as the limo groaned a final protest, lifted its rear end and went sliding out of view. But they heard its grinding metallic death cries as it crashed its way down the face of the cliff, and the splash when it hit the sea before sinking at once to a salty termination.

"Jake," she sighed again, as he held her.

"Are you okay?" He held her tightly, looked all about, saw their predicament: the precipitous slope above and the edge of the cliffs in front.

"Yes. No. I don't know!" she answered. "I don't think anything's broken, but I'm aching in every joint, dog-tired, and bruised to bits." And with a small hysterical laugh, "In fact, you could say I'm totally knackered! How about you? I mean, I barely recognized you."

"I'm good," he nodded. "At least I think so—physically, anyway." He cranked his neck at a steep angle, and asked, "But is that a road up there? I have to get us out of here." And to Korath:

I need the Möbius equations.

And answering him with a small, dark, deadspeak chuckle, *Be my guest,* said the other.

Eh? Jake didn't understand. *More word games? Something else you want from me?*

No, Korath answered, *for I now have everything—as do you. So by all means go ahead. Try to conjure the formula, Jake, and see what happens.*

Jake did it; set the numbers rolling in perfect order down the screen of his mind. They reached the point of collapse . . . and *didn't* collapse! He stopped them, watched them form a door, walked Liz through it and took her up to the road.

And as they emerged on high: "You lousy bastard thing!" he snarled out loud.

"What's that?" said Liz, dizzier than ever and unsteady on her feet. "What did you say?"

"Nothing," said Jake. *Everything! This bloody creature has cheated me all the way down the line. I had the Möbius formula all along, but every time I tried to use it he fucked with my equations! I thought it was me—thought I wasn't up to it—but it was him!*

His thoughts weren't shielded, and this close she couldn't mistake his meaning. Moreover, she knew he would explain everything to her now, because he would have no choice. Before that, however, there were more important matters.

On the eastern horizon, that glow lighting the sky: it had to be the monastery. Liz's head cleared; she reoriented, remembered what she and the others had been about here. And:

"Palataki!" she said, looking west, where twin cupolas rose menacingly over the trees on a night-dark promontory. "E-Branch is at the Little Palace, and we have to join them there."

Now it was Jake's turn to frown and ask, "Come again?"

"Trask and the others," she answered. "They're at Palataki, that place on the promontory there. We did it, Jake—tracked down Malinari and Vavara. And that bonfire in the east: that's Vavara's place burning."

"And Palataki?"

"We think that's where she kept her deadspawn garden," Liz told him, "and God-only-knows what else. We've got to go there, help them get done with it, finish whatever they're doing."

"I don't think I'm up to this," he shook his head. "I mean, I don't know what's going on here!"

"Then try this," she said. "Link with me, Jake, but make it good, like never before."

She pressed herself to him—looked straight into his eyes—showed him a kaleidoscopic history of events. And Jake reeled as he took it all in.

"We . . . we seem to be getting better at this," he gasped.

And Liz nodded. "Both of us, when we're working as a team. We *must* be getting better else you wouldn't have heard me. You wouldn't be here, and neither would I. If I had managed to get that trunk open and tried to climb out . . . I could easily have gone down with the limo."

"This rapport thing," he said, but Liz made no answer. She was clinging to him still, and gazing into his eyes.

Jake was aware of Liz as never before, this most desirable woman. Her mouth was very close; God, how he wanted to kiss it, and be much more than just the other half of a team!

Then do it, said Korath. *Kiss her and be done with it. And I promise I won't look, or feel, or let myself get too . . . er, excited? Oh, ha-ha-ha-haaaa!*

"Lousy bastard thing!" Jake snarled yet again, drawing back from Liz and putting her at arm's length.

But her expression didn't change as she said quite simply, "It's okay, Jake. I know now. And I think I understand what was wrong with our relationship . . . before." And with a curt nod of her pretty head, "But now we have to go."

Perfect timing, for even as she spoke there came the rumble of a powerful explosion from the direction of Palataki . . .

Five minutes earlier:

David Chung had taken the landward descent into the Little Palace's underground labyrinth, and Ian Goodly had entered via the stairwell under the ocean- or south-facing cupola. Both men were equipped with pocket torches, and the dangerous conditions of their work—the fact that Palataki was rapidly falling into decay—had been immediately apparent. The place was literally a death-trap where rotten floorboards threatened to give way at every turn, and wormy and crumbling staircases teetered beneath their feet. In addition to which they knew that a Great Vampire—indeed Lord Nephran Malinari of the Wamphyri—was down here somewhere, and that even with their dynamite, their weapons, and silvered ammunition, still they were taking the direst of dire risks.

But there was no way round it; they must block these exits off and destroy Malinari's escape routes, and once they had him sealed in down below, then they would be able to relax a little. Meanwhile, it was a very nervy time.

The precog had determined to descend to as great a depth as he dared, light a stick of dynamite with a long fuse and let it fall into the stairwell—hopefully all the way to the bottom—then get out of there with all speed. Surfacing, he would light a second, shorter fuse, and once again let gravity complete the task while he put distance between. Of course, he had the dubious benefit of being prescient; he had not "foreseen" any harm coming his way as a result of this action. But as Goodly above all other men was aware, the future is a devious thing, and he had never been given to see everything. Indeed just recently he had considered himself fortunate to see anything! It was almost as if his talent had given up on him—which might in itself be a warning, and was in any case a very ominous circumstance . . .

Pausing every half-dozen treads or so to listen for sounds of movement from below, and hearing nothing, Goodly had descended to Palataki's basement down groaning wooden staircases. In that cobwebbed sublevel he'd found stone stairs hewn from the crumbling bedrock, whose spiral he'd pursued into the darkness. The good, strong white beam from his torch had shown him fresh footprints in dust lying inches thick on the steps, proof that this route had been frequently patrolled; which in turn served to remind him of Chung's earlier warning that maybe Vavara had left a caretaker down here to manage her loathsome garden.

At a depth that the precog calculated to be some fifty feet below Palataki's basement, he thought he heard or sensed a slight movement—the merest waft of air, as if something had stirred in the gloom just beyond his torch's range—and came to a halt on a level floor in a low-ceilinged man-made chamber. The place was shored up with mouldy timbers, and as he turned in a circle Goodly saw that he was at a junction of four tunnels uniformly cut through the rock, each of them descending at some thirty degrees into the sentient-seeming darkness.

Since these tunnels must surely reach down to the old mine workings, it was more than likely they had been hewn as escape routes for German miners and geologists searching for valuable mineral deposits in the shallow labyrinth which presumably lay fifty or more feet below; that last according to the locator's calculations. In the event of tremors or cave-ins, the trapped workers would have have been able to flee from most quarters of the mine to this chamber, and from here on up into Palataki. A similar system would have been in use at David Chung's end of the building. In which case Nephran Malinari was simply using bolt-holes that had been in use all of seventy-odd years ago—

—Which in turn meant that were probably other entrances or exits . . .

Other escape routes? For Malinari?

But no time to dwell on these things, for suddenly the precog found himself shivering and very much afraid.

At his feet a second stone stairwell yawned; it wound down into the nitre-streaked rock, and had a vertical central shaft that was ideal to Goodly's purpose. Wherefore, this far and no further. Clipping his torch to the right-hand epaulette of his safari jacket and taking a cheap cigarette lighter and a stick of dynamite from a deep side pocket, his hand was beginning to shake as he thumbed the wheel to strike a spark—

—And it shook even harder when nothing happened. It must be a misfire and nothing more. He was about to try again, when for a second time he felt that waft of disturbed air. Scarcely daring to breathe, clammy with dread, he turned his body, aimed the beam of his torch down each of the four tunnels in turn . . . and in the last one saw a writhing, knee-deep wall of mist expanding in his direction!

Above, in the grounds of Palataki, this mist had seemed in keeping. But down here it was something else again. And so was the dark shadow that reared up and swept toward him out of the heart of it!

Malinari! he thought, freezing. *It's Malinari!*

Yessss! a voice hissed in his head. *Lord Nephran Malinari, Mr. Goodly, so-called precog. Ah, but you did not foresee this, did you? Oh, ha-ha-haaaa!*

The wall of mist collapsed like a wave, flattening itself to a ground mist that drifted forward to lap at Goodly's feet. Seeming to cling to him, it strengthened Malinari's mentalist contact; and stepping toward the precog—seeming to flow no less than the mist he issued—the Great Vampire drew closer, his arms and hands *lengthening* where they reached for his paralyzed victim.

But paralyzed, frozen? At close quarters like this, it had to be Malinari's telepathic influence that kept Goodly immobilized, anchored. And if that were so, then the precog knew what to do about it.

Malinari was battening on Goodly's knowledge, his thoughts—thoughts of the past, and certainly of his fearful present—battening on them in preparation to siphoning them off. But the precog was a man with a special skill, who on occasion saw more than the present and remembered more than the past. Sometimes, in order to boost his talent, he emptied his mind of all knowledge—which he did now—leaving nothing for the vampire to leech from him. Or rather, nothing but blood!

But while the blood remained, the telepathic "ice" at once melted away out of Goodly's veins and mind, and he was his own man again. As for Malinari:

Snarling his frustration, scarlet-eyed and gape-jawed, the Great Vampire was almost upon his intended victim. And forcing a twisted smile he hissed, "Well then, Mr. Goodly, if you won't let me do this the easy way, there's always the hard way!" And his fingers elongated into writhing, blue-veined worms as they extended themselves towards Goodly's face.

While the precog had a gun in his inside pocket, he knew he wasn't the best shot in the world and was fairly certain that a flesh wound just wouldn't suffice. So since this time it had to be final, he dropped his stick of dynamite and snatched another with a shorter fuse from his pocket. And striking fire from his cigarette lighter—which finally worked—and applying it to the fuse, he deliberately featured his actions in his thoughts, showing and even telling Malinari exactly what he was doing.

"Clever, ah *clever!*" said the monster, falling back a pace, then another, and shrinking a little as Goodly stole backwards up the stone staircase, holding the dynamite with its sputtering fuse out towards him. "But tell me—isn't it obvious that you'll destroy yourself as well?"

"Perhaps, perhaps not," the precog croaked from his tinder-dry throat. "But if the blast brings this entire place down on you, then I'll be satisfied either way."

Malinari's furious burning gaze went this way and that; all about him he saw shrivelled timbers and rotten rock, everything in a state of decay. It wasn't going to take much of a blast to bring about a complete collapse. And so:

"In the unlikely event that you survive your own incredibly daring but stupid act, Mr. Goodly," he snarled, turning from the precog and flowing back into his mist, "remember this—"

—That I shall certainly *remember you!*

"But only if you survive it, too," said Goodly. And climbing faster, scrambling for his life, he let the dynamite fall.

Then upwards, ever upwards he fled, climbing like a madman; and mirrored in his flinching mind's eye, the spitting and sputtering of the short fuse as he counted the even shorter-seeming seconds to the most doubtful future that he'd ever imagined . . .

At the other end of the Little Palace, the locator, David Chung hadn't descended nearly so deep into the earth; for his way had been more difficult and dangerous yet, where the timbers of the upper staircases were eaten away and every other tread prone to instant collapse the moment he planted a foot on it. Yet slowly but surely he had managed to make his way down to the basement, and despite that he was hampered by his talent—the fact that the atmosphere was so permeated by mindsmog that he felt he was suffocating—still he had searched about until he'd discovered the dark mouth of a stone stairwell so choked with fallen rocks and cobwebbed debris that he hadn't dared to proceed farther.

At which point he'd heard the sobbing . . .

Palataki's basements were extensive, and at first the locator hadn't been able to determine the source of the sound—an odd circumstance in itself, for he *was* a locator! Obviously the mindsmog was so thick here that it was deflecting his probes in the same way that powerful magnetic currents deflect compasses. Indeed, it was warping them all to hell! But he didn't need his talent to tell him that someone (some female? Liz Merrick, perhaps?) was distraught down here. And as the sobbing grew louder his principal purpose in this place was temporarily forgotten.

After all, Liz had been taken by Vavara, and by Chung's own reckoning Palataki's underground was Vavara's domain, where she nurtured her loathsome garden. That being the case . . . mightn't Liz be imprisoned down here?

For several breathless minutes Chung had remained absolutely motionless listening to the sobbing—as pitiful and heartrending a series of sounds as any he had ever heard—until he couldn't stand it any longer. By then, too, he'd discovered its origin: the choked stairwell. But moving closer to the mouth of the shaft and aiming the beam of his torch down into the tight, seemingly impassable space below, so he'd inadvertently stepped on a piece of rotten timber, causing it to snap underfoot—

—At which the sobbing had ceased on the instant, and he'd known that someone was holding her breath!

"Who is it?" he had whispered into the darkness down there. "Is it you, Liz? Is that you, crying?"

No answer, but Chung believed he'd heard a gasp.

"Liz, it's me, David," he raised his voice a little. "Can't

you move? Has Vavara got you trapped down there? Give me a signal if you can. Some kind of movement, maybe?"

And at last a voice answered his, but it wasn't Liz's. "Go away!" (Almost a little girl's voice, on the edge of hysteria.) "I know who you are, and what you'll do to me if I should come out. You're Vavara's man, or that false Father Maralini."

Chung saw movement deep down in the hole, a white feminine face, and a hand that covered her eyes from the bright beam of his torch.

"I'm neither one," he said then. "I'm here to destroy Vavara and . . . and that false father. But who are you?"

"I'm Sister Anna," she answered, and he heard the sound of rubble shifting, hands clawing. "I am—I was—a nun at the monastery. But then Vavara came, and later that wicked father. Since when I've been hiding out where they can't find me. This place is Vavara's, yes, but she doesn't come this way."

"But . . . how long have you been here?" Narrowing his eyes, Chung took out his gun and cocked it.

"Too long. But now I can't live like this any longer—in dark holes in the earth, only coming out when it's daylight—so even if you're not who you say you are, I give in." And the sobbing and scrabbling came louder yet.

Hands that once were white came up over the rim; now grimy, with broken nails, they were streaked red where sharp rocks had cut them. Chung turned his torch a little to one side as an oh-so-pretty face, similarly streaked, came into view.

"I . . . I'm stuck," she husked between sobs. "Please help me up out of here."

"Show me your face," he said then, as the mindsmog suddenly thickened.

"But the light from your torch . . . it's blinding," she answered, emerging a little farther, dragging herself up until she sat on the rim of the steps.

"Your face," Chung insisted. "I need to see your eyes."

At which there sounded muffled footsteps from behind,

and a rending of rotten wood as a stair tread collapsed. And starting massively, the locator glanced back over his shoulder.

That was all the diversion that Sister Anna needed. Batting Chung's gun and torch aside, she came to her feet . . . her feral eyes like lamps in the dark. And, "This is from my master!" she hissed, lifting a long curved knife on high.

But her triangular eyes made for a perfect target, too, and Manolis Papastamos's torch beam found them just a single moment after his bullet, which made a very small hole between them and a fist-size hole where it blew out the back of her skull.

"Jesus! Jesus!" Chung gasped, rearing up and away from her, as Anna's mouth yawned open and her feet left the floor and she flew backwards into the stairwell. Flopping from view, she went thundering into darkness, taking half a ton of rocks and rubble with her.

"Are you all right, my friend." Manolis grabbed Chung's arm to steady him. "I couldn't see too well, but well enough, thank God! But tell me, did that *vrykoulakas* bitch touch you? Did she perhaps . . . claw you?"

"Yes, no—I mean I'm okay," the locator babbled. "And no, she didn't touch me. But she would have. Oh, Jesus—she *would* have!"

"Very well," said Manolis. "And now for thee dynamite. Give it to me, for I see that you are shaken. Three sticks, I think, right down that hole. And whatever else is down there with thee dead bitch, we send it to hell, too, yes?"

And the locator was only too glad to agree and comply . . .

Up above: while Manolis had gone after Chung, Ben Trask had run to the southern end of the Little Palace, entered the ruins, and commenced a descent along the same route taken by Goodly. Stavros, Andreas, and Lardis Lidesci had remained on the surface to keep watch for anyone trying to escape from the doomed building.

But as Trask had reached the basement, so he'd heard Goodly coming up from below. Now, as the precog appeared in the stairwell, panting and gasping for air, Trask armed his Browning and prepared for the worst. No one or fearful Thing pursued Goodly, however—unless it was his own terror—and he finally managed to draw air and yell, "Get out, Ben! For Christ's sake get out! Any second now, this place is going sky high!"

The precog couldn't know it, but by all rights he should have been dead. He *would* be dead, if the short fuse on that stick of dynamite hadn't been damp and decayed; and he would most *definitely* have been dead, if Lord Malinari had so much as suspected it! But even now, deep down below, that faulty fuse was fitfully sputtering, gradually eating its way to the sweating explosive charge.

And in a nightmarish ascent up swaying staircases—where handrails gave way at a touch, rotten steps splintered or fell into dust beneath their feet, and all thoughts of caution were abandoned as disaster loomed ever closer—the two men fought against time and gravity to make it back to the surface.

But as pale blue starlight gleamed above where it entered through Palataki's empty windows and doorways, and the espers emerged onto the ground floor—Trask first, pausing to reach down, grab the precog, and drag him up the last of the steps—so the first stick of dynamite went off, which at once set off the second. The floor shook as the double blast front raced up through the stairwells and basement to the ground floor, while down below there commenced a rapid chain-reactive disintegration as everything collapsed in upon itself.

A moment more and dust and debris came jetting up through every crack and crevice, billowing into the ground floor rooms and spilling out into the night. And as Palataki shook, vibrating on its weakened foundations, window and door frames popped and groaned, and loosened tiles came sliding from the roof.

But staggering out of the wreathing dust clouds, Trask and Goodly coughed and choked their way into the open, backed away from the stricken Little Palace to a place of safety, and only then paused to witness the rest of the drama.

First: Manolis Papastamos and David Chung at the other end of the building, ducking out through a teetering door frame as more blasts thundered up from the bowels of the earth. Second: Andreas and Stavros, hurling sticks of dynamite in through the windows at Palataki's midsection, then running off to shelter under the pines. And the trees themselves shaking as the earth underfoot commenced a jittery dancing.

And finally the explosions: one, two, three, four—but no longer muffled by earth and rock—and the ground-floor walls blown outwards, and the flames blossoming in Palataki's heart, into which the old building subsided in a seeming slow-motion, while the trees shook more yet and deep cracks appeared in the earth.

Then: "Time we were gone from here," said Ben Trask, when he and his six colleagues gathered at their vehicles.

"I couldn't agree more," Goodly wheezed, still getting his second wind. "We've done all that we can for now, and it feels like this place is coming apart at the seams."

"Yet we still don't know how successful we were," Manolis said.

And Trask nodded, answering: "And we've still to count the cost. Poor Liz . . ."

"Oh? And what about me?" said a familiar, sweet but shaken voice from the shadows under the trees. And a moment later Liz stumbled into view. Right on her heels came Jake like a smoke-ghost, all dark and grimy.

"Liz!" Trask said. "Liz!" His knees were trembling so hard that he almost fell. His "little sister" was safe!

It all took a few moments to sink in, but any celebrations would have to bide their time. For the ground was shaking more violently yet as the chain-reaction of imploding mine workings caused subsidence in the upper terrain.

Then, as a handful of house lights flickered into life in Skala Astris along the coast and the group's vehicles departed Palataki in convoy down the knoll's quivering ramp, all unseen in the grounds of the shattered ruin, the last thing to go was Vavara's—or more properly *Var*vara's—shrine. Its customary candle had not been lit since the death or devolution of Zarakis at the hands of Malinari, and now the earth yawned open to swallow it in a single gulp.

Thus the holy place that Vavara had made *un*holy by claiming it for her own was no more.

The *shrine* was no more, at least.

But as for Vavara herself . . .

Exerting all the great strength of a Lord of the Wamphyri, and yet grunting from the effort, Malinari single-handedly dragged Vavara's boat—an eleven-foot caïque, with a typically Greek sun-shade canopy—down from the mouth of its cave and across a narrow, inaccessible strip of shingle beach to the sea. Vavara would have experienced no such difficulty; assisted by her man, Zarakis, launching this thing would have been the easiest of tasks.

But Zarakis was no more; along with his vampire mistress's deadspawn garden (and for all that Malinari knew or cared, the hag Vavara herself) that long-lived lieutenant out of Starside was by now dead and gone, and for a little while at least Lord Nephran Malinari would be obliged to perform such menial tasks himself.

Straining to get the boat into the water, he thought back on the rush of events since he'd left the precog Ian Goodly to his presumed fate under Palataki . . .

Fearing to be trapped down there by the imminent explosion, he'd made for the safety of the boat cave. But the greater the distance he'd put between himself and that sputtering stick of dynamite, the more it had dawned on him that something must be wrong—or right! The fuse must have burned itself out, or the dynamite was faulty, or something. But by then it had been too late, and far too dangerous, to turn back. A pity, for despite that his survival was as ever uppermost in his mind, the Great Vampire had determined not only to destroy Vavara's garden but also to cause E-Branch and its members as much damage as possible. He could only hope that Sister Anna had had more luck.

At the secret sea cave, Malinari had waited until he heard the first of the explosions before getting to work on the boat. He had reasoned that the confusion overhead, almost 150 yards farther inland at Palataki, would help camouflage his own activity. Believing him to be trapped below them, the E-Branch agents would surely be too busy to probe for him; and with all the noise and disturbance, their talents would in any case be disadvantaged. Also, he would keep a tight rein on his presence, shielding his thoughts and deadening his aura as only Malinari the Mind knew how. The puttering of his outboard engine as he fled across the calm, night-dark sea would not be heard . . . or if it was they'd think it was one of a handful of small fishing vessels whose lights dotted the darkness between the shore and the horizon. But of course *his* vessel would show no lights at all.

And now, as more devastating explosions sounded, this time from on high, beyond the rim of the sea cliffs, finally Malinari floated the boat out upon the ocean and clambered on board. Using a short-armed paddle to straighten the craft up with its prow aimed at the open sea, he stepped to the stern and seated himself, took the tiller, and made to start the engine.

Which was when *she* came!

She came from the east, hand over hand and clinging to the cliff face, not letting herself fall to the damp shingle until she was well clear of the sullen sea. And as Vavara's feet hit the beach, then Malinari heard her. So intent on shielding his own thoughts from others, he had failed to detect hers. And in another moment she came flopping across the shingle, floundering through the water, and up into the prow of the caïque, her eyes blazing with all the fires of hell and a gnarled, barbed, accusing finger trembling with rage where she aimed it at him.

Her tongue was barbed, too, as she hissed: "Oh, you treacherous *dog!* What, a dog that bites the hand that feeds it? No, for Lord Nephran Malinari is more treacherous far! A *wild* dog, then—a great grey wolf—like the grey brothers on the Starside flanks of the Barrier Mountains. But no, for even they have honour while Malinari has none! *Hah!* I have done all canines a great disservice by linking them with such as you!"

Externally calm but boiling inside, Malinari started the engine, opened the throttle, jerked the boat into motion. And as Vavara sat down with a bump, he told her. "If you continue grinding your teeth like that, you'll wear them to stumps."

Shoulders hunched, with her eyes seeming to drip sulphur, Vavara came creeping along the floor towards him. Plainly she intended to attack him! "Madame," he told her, "I've acted only in your service—and in my own, of course. Didn't I wait for you until the last possible moment, even until they commenced blowing Palataki apart?"

"Liar!" Vavara answered, continuing to creep toward him.

Malinari saw how ravaged she was. "What happened to you?"

He seemed so genuinely concerned that Vavara blinked her surprise, holding back for a moment and explaining: "My vehicle was forced from the cliffs; I flew out, into the sea; I swam, climbed, crawled, swam and climbed again. My clothes are ripped to shreds, my flesh, too, and my not inconsiderable patience entirely used up. And it's all down to you, Malinari the Warped and Treacherous Mind! Now the reckoning. I hope you are prepared." Licking her leathery lips, great jaws chomping, again she came on.

"Then I really do think I should point out," Malinari told her, "that while you are a very worthy woman, I am a man, with all the advantage of the greater strength of a Lord of the Wamphyri. However angry you may be now—and however unjustified your anger—rage alone will not sustain you."

"Then perhaps this will!" She pulled a gun from her ragged clothes, but even as she moved Malinari snatched up a jerry can of fuel and hurled it. Vavara was thrown backwards; her weapon flew from her claw hand, and the jerry can glanced off her into the sea. Then they were at each other's throats as the caïque throbbed out across the ocean.

Eventually it was stalemate. In the bottom of the boat, he clutched her windpipe in a massively strong hand, and Vavara's left hand was on his face, its long barbed fingers hooked into the orbits of his eyes.

"I could tear your throat out!" he told her.

And unable to talk, she nevertheless answered: *And I would blind you on the instant!*

They pushed apart and lay gasping, glaring their hatred at each other. And! "Are we done, then?" he enquired. "If not for good, at least for now?"

"A truce," she answered, rubbing her throat. "At least for now."

Malinari regained the tiller. "I'm sure you had a plan. So where are we going?"

"My first plan is in ruins," she croaked, seating herself in the prow. "For thanks to you yet *again,* a third of our fuel is now lost in the sea. It was my intention to head for Istanbul via the Dardanelles, which is now out of the question. And so I'm forced to adopt my second plan."

"Which is?"

"Which isn't so pleasant or so easy, and involves a degree of suffering."

"Tell me about it," said Malinari.

"No," she answered. "For I see that you are right. You are the stronger and the more devious. If I were to tell you what I've planned, what use would I be to you then?"

"As you will," Malinari shrugged. "So where shall I direct the boat?"

"Get out of the way and let me take the tiller," she answered. "I shall direct it, for I know where we're going. And on the way my vampire will replenish me."

"So be it," Malinari grunted.

And as they changed places: "Wrap yourself well," she told him, "if your intention is to sleep."

"Sleep? I think not!" he answered. And raising an eyebrow, "Do you find the nights cold, then?"

"No." Vavara smiled a grim smile. "But when the sun

comes up it will be hot and deadly. It will find us adrift and possibly becalmed."

"Oh, really?" said Malinari. "And only a *degree* of suffering!"

"Perhaps something more than a degree," she shrugged. "But all part of my plan."

"Then let's hope your plan is a good one," said Malinari . . .

En route to the Christos Studios in one of the cars, Jake told Liz and Ian Goodly what he had been up to—gave them the bare bones of his story, at least—and the precog in turn told him about Millie in London: the fact that she'd been taken by Lord Szwart.

And in the second car Ben Trask sat alone—sat there with David Chung, Manolis, and Lardis, yet still alone, or at best with his thoughts—on the one hand thrilling to the fact of Liz's survival, while on the other . . . he knew it would take a long time, if not forever, to recover from Millie Cleary's . . . to recover from her whatever.

But as the three cars returned to base, and the weary band parked them, got out, and stood together for a while, with lots to say but unwilling to break the unaccustomed silence—

—Suddenly Goodly went limp at the knees, uttered a soft, sharp cry and might well have fallen, but Jake and Liz propped him up and leaned him against one of the cars. Ben Trask, when he saw the precog's pale face, knew exactly what had happened; he saw "the truth" of it at once. But it had little enough to do with his weird talent this time, for he'd seen Goodly looking like this before. And:

"What is it, Ian?" he said at once. "What have you seen?"

"Damn this thing!" Goodly straightened up and took a deep breath. "When I want it I get nothing. But the moment I relax, right out of the blue—" He stared directly into Trask's eyes. "She was in your thoughts, right? And in mine. And that's what prompted it."

"She?" said Trask, not daring to hope. "She?"

"It was Millie, Ben," Goodly told him. "I saw Millie!"

"Millie?" Trask's jaw fell open. "How? Where? *When?*"

"It was close," the precog answered. "The immediate future, I think. But she's alive, Ben—she *is* alive!"

"Where alive, for God's sake?" The Head of Branch looked as if he was about to start dancing now, shifting from one foot to the other and back again in his nervous anxiety.

"I don't know," Goodly answered. "A dark place, and Ben—there was a darker shadow, a shape, a *thing,* close behind her. Millie was very frightened. She was reaching out . . . for Liz?" He turned to look at Liz, and nodded. "Yes, for Liz. And Jake was there, too."

"What?" Trask's eyes opened wider yet. "Jake was there? My God! But *of course* he was!" He grabbed hold of Jake's arm.

But before he could say another word: "It's okay," Jake told him. "It's okay. If it can be done, we'll do it. And I'm ready when you are."

And speaking as one Liz and Chung said, "That goes for me, too . . ."

Jake made two Möbius trips to London and transported Trask and the E-Branch crew back to their HQ. Once there, it took just a few minutes to kit him out with the equipment he required, and the rest was up to Liz and the locator.

By 12:35 A.M. local time, the giant screen in the Ops Room was displaying a detailed map of London's subterranean systems, and Chung was standing before it with various items of Millie's personal belongings—a ballpoint Paper-Mate pen, a small hand mirror she used when applying her makeup, a lipstick in a silver-plated holder—close to hand on a desk. Liz stood beside him, bruised but undefeated, ready at a moment's notice to add her own special skills to his.

And with Trask and Jake looking on, the locator placed his left hand on Millie's things and the widespread fingers of his right hand on the map. Then:

It was as if his hand was drawn to a certain spot: central London between Waterloo and the Embankment. And, "This is it!" he whispered, as his index finger began vibrating like a water diviner's hazel twig. "Millie's there but deep, deep down. Too deep for me to gauge, and far deeper than anything we've known about before, that's for sure. It's beyond me to explain it. I can tell you this, though: she's reaching for us, else I don't think I could have found her so quickly. But there's a hell of a lot of interference—mindsmog! She's not alone down there, or something's so close it makes no difference—and it's not too hard to guess what or who it is! I don't think that he has detected my probe, but his mere presence is fogging everything up, making it hard to maintain contact."

"Keep trying," Liz told him, placing her left hand on top of his on Millie's things. "Just stay with it and guide me to her, and if she's trying to reach us I should be able to tell. Telepathically speaking, we've 'rubbed shoulders' fairly frequently, Millie and I. I'd know her signature anywhere. And if there's one thing I'm good at, it's receiving."

"God almighty!" Trask kept groaning, whispering to himself over and over again where he stood a few paces apart with Jake. "Good God almighty!"

And: "Take it easy," Jake whispered back, but to no avail. "Just try to relax and take it easy."

"But that's Millie they're talking about," Trask answered, a little louder now. "It's Millie . . ."

"Yes—yes it is!" said Liz. "It's Millie, reaching out to us. And I think . . . I think I've got her! I can't read her . . . only her fear, making my—*ugh!*—making my flesh creep! And the mindsmog is . . . it's overwhelming! But I've got her."

"The coordinates?" said Jake, moving to her side and placing his hand on top of hers and the locator's. And immediately he was into her mind, reading what she read, and *knowing* where Millie was.

Liz knew what he would do—what he was here to do—and said, "I'll go with you."

But Jake shook his head. "Haven't you had enough of danger tonight? You've done your bit, Liz. Now it's my turn."

He looked at Trask—as haggard a sight as ever he'd seen—who simply nodded and said, "Bring her back to me, Jake, and I'll ask nothing more of you ever again."

"Whatever," Jake answered. "But if it all works out, there may well be something I'll ask of you."

"Anything," said Trask. And then, frowning: "But I thought you'd solved your problem?"

"One of them, yes," Jake answered. "Maybe we'll be able to talk about it later—I hope."

A moment later, a final glance at Liz where she stood biting her lip, and Jake turned to his right, took a pace forward, and was gone . . .

In the Möbius Continuum, Jake asked Korath, *Will you help me?*

Against Szwart? Korath answered. *No one can help you! Trust to luck and your weapons. Szwart saw such used on Starside, and they worried him considerably. My best advice: get in, find the woman, and get out!* Don't *go up against Szwart—not on his own ground. Avoid him if at all possible, and if not—run!*

But if I needed your help, Jake pressed him, *you'd give it to me?*

Of course, said Korath sourly. *What happens to you happens to me, remember? If you die, I die, and return to my sump. I've tried that once and didn't much like it! So the answer is yes—of my own free will I'll help you—if needs be. But don't play me for a fool Jake, and don't for a moment think I didn't understand what you were saying to Trask about your "other" problem.* Hah! *So despite that we are now one, still I'm obliged to be on my guard. Well, so be it.*

Following which, only one thing remained to be said. And as the coordinates firmed up in Jake's mind and he made a door, he said it: *Be on your guard now then, Korath, for we're there . . .*

Jake's torch was strapped to his forehead like a miner's lamp; pausing before stepping out through the invisible frame of his door, he switched it on. And with the strong, broad white beam penetrating an otherwise stygian darkness, he emerged onto the hexagonal stone flags of that place of long-forgotten esoteric worship, abandoned more than eighteen hundred years ago by its Roman sect members.

Millicent Cleary was there but Jake didn't at once see her; she was huddled behind the raised sacrificial dais, making herself as small as possible. But while Jake didn't see Millie, he couldn't help but see the giant, roughly hewn statues of Mithra and Summanus were they stood in a row with others of their pantheon. And as the beam of his torch threw the carven gods into monstrous, almost living relief and their shadows moved on the wall of the cave, he fell into a defensive crouch.

Jake's heart quickened; his finger went to the trigger of his flamethrower; he applied a half-pressure and saw the pilot light flare up a little, and only at the last moment recognized the true nature of what he was seeing. But taking a deep, grateful breath as he straightened up, he was suddenly aware of what seemed to be furtive movement. And now he wheeled in the direction of the sacrificial slab.

And there *was* furtive movement, but in no way hostile.

Having seen the glare of Jake's torch as he swept the cave, Millie had got to her knees behind the dais, drawing herself up until her white face edged up over the rim. In the split second before she ducked down again, Jake saw her eyes—the perfectly normal eyes of a very frightened woman—blinking in the harsh glare of his torch. And as she disappeared he said, "Millie? Is that you?"

"What?" Her small whisper reached him. "Who? I mean, yes—yes, it's me." Trembling in every limb she managed to stand up, and Jake saw that she was exhausted, staggering. "But who—I mean, who are you? Not that it matters much, as long as you're really here."

"It's Jake," he answered, as it dawned on him how he must look to her in his combat suit, still streaked and dirty, with a lamp glaring on his forehead, the flamethrower's cylinder on his back, and half-a-dozen grenades attached to his belt.

"Jake Cutter—from E-Branch." Finally he had accepted it: he really was one of the team now.

"Jake?" she said, emerging from behind the dais. "Oh, thank God!"

They moved together and she clung to him for a moment. Then he said, "Where is he? Where's Szwart?"

"Enlarging his flue, I think," she answered, her body shuddering against his. "He didn't think the wind was strong enough for the job." And she quickly explained her meaning.

Wally Fovargue's lamp was still flickering under the arched entrance to the cave of the garden. With Millie cowering behind him, Jake went to it, took it up, and handed it to her. "Turn it up full," he told her. "The brighter the better." Then, passing beneath the arch, he saw the garden's *ignis fatuus* bioluminescence—and in the next moment saw the garden itself.

And clinging to his combat jacket, almost holding him back, Millie said, "Is that what you saw under the casino in Xanadu?"

"It's much the same," Jake nodded grimly. "And this is what I did to it!"

His intentions—his thoughts—were crystal clear in his metaphysical mind, and of course they were deadspeak. And even as he applied first pressure to the trigger of his flamethrower, so they were heard and answered:

Don't! said an unknown deadspeak voice. *Don't you use that weapon! There's methane darn 'ere—marsh gas, firedamp, call it what yer will; the gas given off by rotten vegetation, shit, an' all the dead dogs an' cats what's been washed darn 'ere since forever—an' you could blow yerself to 'ell just as easy as that!*

Jake eased his finger off the trigger, and speaking out loud said, "What? Who are you?"

"Eh?" said Millie from behind him.

"Nothing," Jake told her, and switched to deadspeak. *Who is it? And if what you say is true, why hasn't the oil lamp set it off, or the pilot light of my flamethrower?*

It's in pockets, streams, said the other. *When yer see that there pilot light flare up an' sputter, that's 'cause it's in the air—an' the same goes for my old lamp. But if yer fires that flamethrower thingy, chances are yer'd get a kind o' chain, er, a chain—*

A chain-reaction? Jake prompted him.

Right, said the other. *As for who I am: Wallace Fovargue is who I* was. *Then Szwart killed me 'cause I was . . . well I was* hinterested *in the woman.*

Jake looked at Liz. "Wallace Fovergue?"

"An ugly, diseased little dwarf," she told him, picking the reason for Jake's question right out of his mind. "He was a flusher; he worked in London's sewers. Szwart killed him, and I think he ended up there," she pointed a trembling hand, "in the heart of that dreadful garden. But Jake, there's something else you should know. Something more important."

"Oh?"

"I've been keeping tabs on Szwart—telepathically, I mean. I could sense him up there somewhere, working on enlarging this flue thing. You'll have noticed that the current of air flowing over these fungi is stronger now?"

"I noticed," said Jake.

"When these mushrooms spawn the wind will lift their spores up to the surface through the tubes and into London. But just a moment ago, I lost contact with him. I think Szwart's shielding himself, which probably means he's 'heard' me talking to you. I don't think we have much time left down here."

"He's on his way back?"

"That's my best guess," she answered.

'Ere, whoever you are! said Wally. *Are yer still listenin'?*

Yes, Jake told him, *but make it quick.*

'Ow'd yer get darn 'ere? Wally was curious. *I mean, I knows every bloody tunnel an' pipe an' sewer from 'ere to the surface, an' I could never 'ave done it so quick!*

It's a trick I do, said Jake. And in a matter of seconds—using a kaleidoscopic series of scenes straight out of his mind—he showed Wally something that words couldn't have explained in the same number of hours.

An' you talk ter dead folks, too, said Wally, wonderingly.

Er, dead folks . . . well, they're my friends, said Jake.

Does that include me? said Wally. *I mean, for all that I've been . . . yer know, a bit of a lad?*

Millie hadn't told Jake how much a bit of a lad, but in any case the Necroscope would feel sorry for anyone who ended up in this kind of mess. And so he shrugged and answered, *No point in being your enemy, Wally. Not now that . . . well, not any longer.*

See, said Wally, *I can feel myself gettin' all used up. The garden is suckin' on me, an' soon I'll be gone. But I reckon 'e was wrong to do this to me. I never did 'im no 'arm.*

You'd like to help me, said Jake. *Is that it? You know something that can help me?*

'Elp you? said Wally. *I can more than 'elp you. I knows 'ow yer can blow that bastard Thing and 'is fuckin' garden away for good, that's all!* (There was a sob in his deadspeak voice now.) *I mean, Szwart's fuckin' toadstools are leechin' on me, suckin' me away to nothin' at all! But you can stop 'im, Jake—you can stop 'im. It's the gas, yer see—it's the gas!*

"Jake," said Millie, tugging at his jacket. "A moment ago I felt Szwart's probe. He's coming, Jake! And any time now, he'll be here!"

"Okay," he answered. "I'll get you out of here, then return and finish up."

"You won't have time!" Millie shrilled. "Look at the garden, Jake. Look at the mushrooms!"

He looked, saw what she meant. One by one, the black-capped domes of the mushrooms were flattening out, their gills opening, and the first red-coloured spores beginning to drift free. "Dim the lamp," Jake told Millie then. "Put it out, then wait for me back at the dais." And to Wally: *What do I have to do?*

I 'ave a nose for such things, Wally answered. *'Ad to 'ave a nose for 'em, else I couldn't have been a flusher. Yer put a foot wrong darn 'ere, yer a goner! So when Szwart first showed me this place, I sensed the gas and told 'im where it was.*

Where? said Jake.

Be'ind the wall o' the cave there, said Wally. *I s'pose 'e thought it would stunt the growth o' 'is mushrooms, so 'e used rocks an' mud an' . . . an' other stuff to block it up— 'cause it kept leakin' in 'ere, see? There's a whole chain o' caves darn 'ere—a bleedin' labyrinth—an' the one next door is full o' gas.*

Other stuff? said Jake.

Eh?

You said he used other stuff, to block the hole?

Mud an' crap an' . . . oh, all sorts o' stuff. (Wally seemed reticent.) *But you can pull 'is wall darn again, Jake. Pull it darn an' let the methane flow through into 'ere. Excep' by now there'll be a 'uge body o' gas—a whole bloody cave full! An' when it mixes with the air in 'ere—an' arter you applies a flame to it . . .*

Boom! said Jake.

Yers, said Wally. *But a damn sight louder than that!*

Putting out his flamethrower's pilot light, Jake let Wally direct him to the wall in question. And sure enough there was a walled-up area beneath what had been a natural archway like the mouth of a cave. *It is a cave,* Wally insisted, *but all blocked up now, as yer can see.*

Jake's torch picked out the rocks where they'd been piled, and the black mud mortar that Szwart had used to seal the gaps between them. He was pretty sure he could pull the whole thing down again, and letting the nozzle of his flamethrower dangle, he set about to do just that.

He started at the top of the arch, got his fingers into the mud and gave a yank on something soft in there—

Then went flailing backwards, tripping and almost falling, as a human hand and arm lolled into view! The limb was followed by the rest of the body, which came slipping and sliding, stiff as a mummy where it slithered sideways and came to a halt half-in, half-out of the wall.

For a moment startled, finally Jake's Adam's apple

stopped bobbing, and he gathered spit to gulp, "G-God almighty!" Then:

You can say that again! a new yet oddly familiar voice sobbed in the deadspeak aether. *Bad enough being dead, in a place like this, without having you come to gloat over me!*

Gloat? What in hell (*who* in hell, for that's where he was, most certainly) was this person? And what was he talking about?

Jake's thoughts, his questions, were deadspeak, of course, and they were answered at once: *Oh, we've met before,* said Alfonso Lefranc. *Like maybe, at Luigi Castellano's place, in Marseilles?*

Jake stepped in close again and wiped dried black mud from a face he would recognize anywhere: the shifty-eyed, weaselly, pockmarked death-mask of the last of Castellano's men. And now he knew for certain that his vendetta was at an end, for there was no one left to track down.

But still he wanted to know, *What happened to you?*

As in life, so in death, and Lefranc spilled his guts for the very last time. *I saw you out in Australia,* he said. *Luigi told me to follow you and those E-Branch people back to London, find out what I could about all of you. I couldn't know it, but while I was watching E-Branch, someone was watching me! Shit! I should have figured there couldn't be* that *many fucking nuns in London! They seemed to be all over the place! So, I don't know, maybe they thought I was some kind of minder for E-Branch. Anyway, they took me and when I woke up I was down here—wherever "here" is! I was questioned by . . . Jesus, by something I can't even describe, and when he, it, whatever, was done with me—*

"He bricked you up in his wall," said Jake out loud.

Yes, after he'd pushed his hand into my chest and squeezed my heart until it stopped! So that's it, no nice carved marble tombstone for me. But what the fuck? What good is a stone with a legend that says "Here Lies Alfonso Lefranc—a Truly Great Nark?" Anyway, Luigi Castellano would have taken me out in the end, I'm sure.

"Alfonso," said Jake, very quietly now, "consider yourself lucky that I didn't get to you first."

And knowing what Jake had done to the others, Lefranc felt obliged to admit, *Oh, I do, Jake Cutter. I do!*

And as a matter of fact, so did Jake . . .

"Jake!" came Millie's warning cry from the arched entrance to the abandoned Roman temple. "Jake, he's here!"

He turned to look where she was pointing, into the unknown darkness at the far, unexplored end of the cavern, well beyond the reach of his torch. A stream of red spores was beginning to waft in that direction, carried on a draft of foul air from the abyss. Also from the abyss (but a different abyss, called Starside), a black shapeless something was flowing like a sentient, mobile carpet across the floor of the cavern towards him!

With no time left to spare, Jake gasped, "Sorry about this, Alfonso," and yanked the corpse bodily from the wall. And tearing frantically at the crumbling black mortar and ill-balanced rocks, he quickly brought the whole thing tumbling down.

Instantly a wave of stinking gas enveloped him, shimmering in the light of his torch. And as Jake turned away, choking and gasping, Lord Szwart was there, rising up in the rough shape—the *very* rough shape—of a man. A huge, black blob of a man. But a man with far more eyes than nature had ever intended, and all of them as red as the fires of hell!

Szwart was a scene out of madness and nightmare, a sight to freeze the blood of most men—to immobilize them and root them to the floor—but Jake wasn't most men. Having conquered his own nightmares, he wasn't about to succumb to this one.

Korath was in Jake's mind—gibbering as he proffered the Mobius equations—but Jake used his own numbers, his own door, and even as Szwart flattened to a blanket and flowed forward to envelop him, he was no longer there!

Under the archway to the old Roman temple, Jake put Millie behind him, took a grenade from his belt and called out, "Lord Szwart, do you know what this is?"

Szwart was already on the move, rushing at breakneck speed over the floor of the cavern, and even cutting a swathe through his deadspawn garden in his crazed, murderous eagerness. But as Jake armed the grenade and its deadly ch-*ching!* sounded, so the monster came to an abrupt halt. For on Starside he'd known just such a man—one who appeared and disappeared like smoke—and he had seen just such weapons as the one that now came bouncing and clattering across the cavern's dusty floor towards him!

"Count five, Szwart," Jake called out then. "And wave whatever you have that functions as an asshole goodbye!"

Szwart reshaped himself, seethed into a stain on the floor, became a shadow that fled at unbelievable speed in the opposite direction. And conjuring a door, Jake started the countdown himself. But on the count of four he and Millie had already departed that place.

As the door closed behind them, they were given a hot heavy push into the now friendly primal darkness of the Mobius Continuum. And the seismographs at Greenwich registered a mild tremor with its epicenter deep under London, as the entire cavern system and its forgotten Roman temple ceased to exist . . .

Epilogue

THREE MORNINGS LATER, IN TRASK'S OFFICE AT E-Branch HQ, Goodly and Chung finished off briefing their boss on the current state of affairs. As for why Trask needed bringing up to date: according to John Grieve, the Officer on Duty, the Head of Branch had been AWOL for the past twenty-four hours. And by some odd coincidence, so had Millicent Cleary. This tidbit of information was of course all very tongue-in-cheek; for discretionary reasons—however unnecessary—Grieve had reserved it for senior agents only. But in fact there wasn't a single E-Branch member, man or woman, who would have begrudged the pair their time together.

Now Trask was back, however, and the updating session was coming to a close.

"That's about it," Goodly finished off. "Our ex-Australian team is on Krassos now with Papastamos, doing a cleanup job on the monastery and Palataki. Especially Palataki."

Trask nodded. "And the Greek authorities? You say they're buying Manolis's story?"

"Hook, line, and sinker!" Chung came in. "In fact Manolis is a hero—er, not to mention a very convincing liar! He laid the foundations of the thing, and after we'd got Jake's side of it we were able to build on it. You have to admit, it's a wonderful story! Manolis is highly respected, and Krassos is remote enough that no one in mainland Greece is much interested anyway—and Interpol is absolutely knocked out that Luigi Castellano and his organization have been taken out of the picture by Jake Cutter. As they're now aware, Jake was, er, working as an agent of E-Branch throughout. Lord, but that must have been some kind of mayhem! And it all fits in beautifully."

And Goodly came back in with, "The story in brief: Castellano was trying to expand his empire in the Med. After playing the philanthropist and infiltrating the monastery, he was able to purchase Palataki as a way station for his drug-trafficking activities. But the nuns got wind of what was going on, and to complicate matters a joint British and Greek drugs operation—a crackdown on drugs entering Europe from the Med—was putting pressure on Castellano on his regular turf. Seeing their opportunity, rival gangs began picking off his properties and people in Marseilles, Genoa, San Remo, and finally Sicily. So just when the Greeks—namely Manolis and Company—were about to close down his operation in Krassos, Castellano decided to cut his losses, cover his tracks, and get out."

Chung took over. "While Castellano had his own problems in Sicily, his people in Krassos stole a load of avgas, bombed the monastery, then dynamited Palataki, destroying every last trace of his hand in things. But Manolis is still out there with our ex-Aussie squad, trying to 'dig up' further evidence—in fact putting a load of thermite down into Palataki, making sure that nothing survived down there . . ."

And again Trask nodded. "So Jake's role in all of this—?"

"—Was as an undercover agent provocateur, obviously," said Chung. "Which is enough to clear him with all the European agencies. He's a free man."

"And I no longer have a hold on him," said Trask, frowning.

"But you didn't anyway," said Goodly. "You promised, remember?"

"Right," said Trask, albeit noncommittally. And before they could say anything: "Which leaves just one question unanswered, and it's the big one. While we're all here patting ourselves on the back, just how effective were we out there in the Med? Oh, I know we did damage, both home and abroad, but did we get what we were after? I doubt it."

"Malinari, Vavara, and Szwart?" said Chung. "Jake Cutter is fifty-fifty on Szwart. But if he had a flue or a chimney to the surface . . ." He shrugged.

"And I can't believe we got Vavara," said Trask. "I saw her fall into the sea, true—but she's Wamphyri! And the Wamphyri are tenacious. They're survivors. As for Malinari . . ."

"Well, *I* escaped from that place," said the precog. "And if I could do it—"

"—So could he," said Trask. "Which means we're not by any means finished yet."

A knock sounded at the door, and Trask said, "Come in."

Liz and Jake entered, and despite Liz's bruises, she looked a lot better than the last time Trask had seen her. Then again, so did Trask look better. As for Jake:

Trask looked at him . . . and wondered, couldn't *help* wondering yet again what it was about him. Sometimes—if you looked at him quickly, a quick glance—you'd swear it was Harry Keogh standing there. Yet Jake and Harry, they were chalk and cheese, they couldn't be more different. Maybe it was the sudden shocks of grey at Jake's temples, and grey turning white, at that! But it might also be his eyes. Those eyes that looked on things outside common knowledge, those windows on a mind that knew magic!

Trask caught himself staring and sat up straighter. "Hello, you two," he growled. "What, are you a delegation or something? Or simply a team? And whichever, what can I do for you?"

Jake looked back at him, also at Goodly and Chung, and said "The Big Three. Well, I suppose you might as well all hear it."

"And we're all ears," said Trask ingenuously. "But tell me, what's Liz here for? I thought we were going to talk about *your* problem."

"No," said Liz looking directly at Trask, "it's *our* problem—E-Branch's problem, all of us—because Jake's one of us now and we look after our own. And the last time a similar question came up, you said—you said—"

"You said that if you'd got the wrong answer," Jake finished it for her, "then you would have shot me." And with a shrug: "So she insisted on coming in here with me."

Trask's frown was genuine now as he sat up even straighter.

"I think I remember the question," he said. "Wasn't it, 'What's on your mind, Jake Cutter?' "

"Exactly," said Jake, nodding. "And when you'd asked it, we discovered it was the Necroscope, Harry Keogh, who was on—or in—my mind. He was there because he'd left a job undone, and I was perfectly placed to finish it for him. But since then . . . well, now there's something else on my mind, and I don't really think you're going to like it so much this time around."

Trask glanced at Goodly and Chung, and said, "Gentlemen, I think this is between me and Jake—and Liz."

But as his oldest friends headed for the door, Trask's intercom beeped, and John Grieve's voice said, "Sir, the Minister Responsible has a message on the screen. For your eyes only."

"I'll get to it in a minute," Trask told him.

"Get to it now—sir," said the duty officer.

Trask pressed a button and a monitor screen rotated up into view on his desk. He read the message, read it again, and suddenly his face was grey as slate.

The door was starting to close behind Chung and Goodly when the latter staggered, quickly recovered, grabbed the locator's arm and wheeled him back into Trask's office again.

"What?" said Chung, looking mystified. But then he saw that well-known look on the precog's face—and another on Trask's—and said no more.

"People," said the Head of Branch, standing up and reaching for his jacket, his eyes beginning to burn again in that leaden mask of a face, that oh-so-vengeful mask. "Hold everything . . . !"

NEXT:

Necroscope

AVENGERS

Take a luxury cruise into carnage. Follow a trail of terror to the Carpathians. Revisit Starside. Take part in the battle for Perchorsk. Get a precog's-eye-view of tomorrow's Vampire Earth!

And more . . .